THE SERPENT RING
(A Story of Cleopatra)

Christopher G. S. Overton

Published in 2009 by New Generation Publishing

Copyright © Christopher G. S. Overton

First Edition

The author asserts the moral right under the Copyright, Designs and Patents Act 1988 to be identified as the author of this work.

All Rights reserved. No part of this publication may be reproduced, stored in a retrieval system or transmitted, in any form or by any means without the prior consent of the author, nor be otherwise circulated in any form of binding or cover other than that which it is published and without a similar condition being imposed on the subsequent purchaser.

Published by New Generation Publishing

The Serpent Ring

'The Going up of Sothis'

Prologue

In the twilight zone that exists between life and death, sometimes called the 'Astral Plain', time and space collide in a maelstrom of dreams and nightmares. Here all the secrets of men and gods are to be found, but beware; these secrets are not given without a price. In my dreams I see the remains of a small boat, under the silt at the bottom of a lake. What chieftain and his lady are here interred and what is their story? Come with me, then, to this place of dreams and nightmares. Come cautiously to a place called Alexandria where a beautiful lady once lived, her island palace in a bay by this ancient city. This lady's name was Cleopatra and her story was told by her enemies, wicked and jealous men who destroyed her, not by her friends who shared her tears of sorrow and laughter, those whom she truly loved.

A chance meeting on a yacht delivery gave me the opportunity to tell my story. Did the elements conspired to bring us together or were other forces at work? The River Thames had for centuries been a commercial highway from London to Europe and the World, but by the tail end of the twentieth century had declined to an economic muddy trickle. The current still flows as vigorously as ever. An area known as the "Broad Reach" can be one of the most uncomfortable waterways to be on with the wind blowing in the opposite direction to the tide and it was with considerable relief when we changed course into the River Medway.

Our departure from the Orsett Yacht Club in a small Fairy Fisherman Sailing Cruiser to be delivered to the Solent by sea had been in ideal conditions but as the river Thames widened the weather deteriorated. For Patrick, my marine engineer, it was his first experience of life on a small sailboat and he was not enjoying it. But when you are cold, wet and tired, even the Isle of Sheppey looks inviting.

There is a small anchorage at Queenborough used by yachts waiting for the tide, to go up the Thames or for suitable weather to go round the North Forelands. With winds gusting to Force 6 round headlands and an inexperienced crew, I was not alone in thinking better of proceeding. The anchorage was packed. We rafted up alongside a fishing boat and two very smart German yachts on a swinging mooring. I put the kettle on for my inevitable cup of Assam tea, Patrick lit a cigarette and we sat back in the cockpit to take in the scene.

There was a typical assortment of pleasure craft and small commercials. The water was deep enough for small coasters up to ten thousand tons but it was not the place you would expect to see the large custom built motor yacht anchored there. This cruiser, arguably a 'Super Yacht', would have been more at home in Monaco. The kettle boiled so I thought no more of it.

Later, we rowed ashore. The local candidate for the "Monster Raving Loony Party", resplendent in a bright yellow tail suit and matching top hat, did not warrant a second glance. This was, after all, Queenborough and the pub we had just entered was the political party headquarters for the late peer of the realm. The person who caught my eye was a young woman sitting in the corner sipping white wine and eating popcorn. I recognised her immediately; her picture was frequently in the papers and I quite liked her music. Like most successful singers she desperately wanted to be a serious actress and I had seen one of her films which, I felt, relied on her good looks and failed to do justice to her talents.

Being English, naturally, I ignored her. Celebrities generally prefer not to be recognised which is why a number of famous Americans have made their homes in this country. Ignoring her proved to be impossible, she had the sort of stunning presence that demanded attention. Her green eyes momentarily transfixed me, I felt as though I was the only person of any consequence in the bar. We exchanged witty pleasantries and I was soon captivated. Consequently Patrick and I were invited aboard the very large custom-built motor yacht we had noticed earlier. In my opinion one high performance Diesel engine is much like another in a darkened room so Patrick left me with the actress while he had a conducted tour of the engine space.

"So what is a nice looking yachtie like you doing in a shit hole like this?" she asked. This was not the chat up line you expect when you are overweight and over the hill.

"I am a Naval Architect and Marine Surveyor who sometimes gets asked to deliver, by sea, the yachts I have surveyed."

"That's a great way to test if you mean all the nice things you say in your report."

"Yes, if I get it right I get a paid holiday and if I have missed anything on the survey I rectify the defects and it saves the client suing me. So what are you doing here, resting?"

"After Eva Peron and Saint Joan, what domineering women are there left to play."

"How about Cleopatra?"

The actress chuckled in a manner that was reminiscent of someone I had loved and lost a long time ago. "It has already been done by Liz Taylor, the most expensive film ever made and it nearly bankrupted Twentieth Century Fox" she replied.

"I know, the production was intended as two films three hour but was cut together to capitalise on the love affair between Taylor and Burton. The script was written as the film was made so the director Joseph Mankiewicz was writing all night and filming all day. The poor man lived on stimulants and making the film almost killed him, his impractical instructions from the studio were to use the script from the original silent film staring Theda Baral. The resulting film took five years to make and had a run time of over four hours. It was further cut so the British cinemas could present two showings per day; consequently the plot was difficult to follow. What was lacking in historical accuracy was compensated by visual impact; on a large screen you could certainly see what the studio had spent the money on! Liz Taylor played Cleopatra as Liz Taylor, Shakespeare character was Elizabeth I, Amanda Barrie's hilarious portrayal was sultry and ditzy in 'Cary on Cleo'. Vivien Liegh's portrayal was of an insecure girl developing into competent monarch in the Bernard Shaw play 'Caesar and Cleopatra', to my mind, was much closer to the truth. But like his predecessors, Shakespeare and Plutarch, Shaw was mistakenly obsessed with the relationship between Cleopatra and Mark Antony. Cleopatra's time with either Roman was minimal compared to the two decades of her reign, yet paradoxically for a woman who is reputedly the most beautiful and passionate of all time, there are no records of her taking any other lovers. It is inconceivable that a devoted mother and popular monarch like Cleopatra would have taken her own life. The method, the bite of an asp, is unlikely as it would have been both painful and disfiguring. The question is, not was Cleopatra murdered? But who killed her and more to the point, who was she really in love with? The famed writers have portrayed aspects of her but she was so much more. No one has played her as Thea Philopater, seventh Cleopatra, Goddess, Scholar and Warrior, sometimes described as the Last Pharaoh. The writer of one of your hit records described you as a goddess; you are a successful business woman, and a scholar. Who better to play the greatest woman who ever lived?"

"Thanks for the vote of confidence but she was an Egyptian and had black hair, I am blond."

"She was a Macedonian Greek so probably looked more like a modern day Yugoslavian but there are no surviving pictures. The public's perception of Cleopatra is as Ms Taylor but no one really knows what she looked like, the only possible likeness being the marble head in the Capitoline Museum of Rome dating from her two year presence there. Statues were generally sculpted to make the subject to look like a deity; the reverse was true in this incident. In one crucial moment her life literally depended on her making one hell of an impression on Julius Caesar."

"So she was either stunningly good looking or the ultimate fast talker."

"Unusual looking certainly and a fast talker considering she bewitched the most powerful man on the planet so quickly, she was undoubtedly charismatic. Some girls can look stunning in couturier or old sailing shorts and a T shirt." The actress was wearing cut down frayed jeans and a flimsy top, both were about two sizes too small and she clearly had nothing on under them. I was fighting a loosing battle not to look too obviously at her nipples. She looked down at her breasts then into my eyes and smiled.

"A girl either has gotten it or she hasn't" she drawled.

"The Greek word Kharis from which we derive charisma meaning grace and charm" I continued, with difficulty. This young woman clearly had the gift, was not reticent in using it, and was fully aware of her blessing, the effect was devastating. "Originally this word had more sexual connotations; Kharis was a gift from Aphrodite, the goddess of sexual love. When Cleopatra was described as the most beautiful woman in the world, what the ancients meant was that like her predecessor Helen of Troy she was the most erotic."

The actress held up her hands in submission revealing a fine gold chain attached to her navel. On this chain were seven amethyst stones, four large representing Betelgeuse, Bellatrix, Saiph and Regal, the shoulders and legs of Orion and the three smaller stones Alnitak, Alnitam and Mintaka his belt. These stars form the constellation that dominates the southern sky of the northern hemisphere from autumn through to spring. Orion was of such significance to the ancient Egyptians and amethyst highly prised by the Greek royals due to its mythological properties. The jewellery was in stark contrast to her casual clothing the effect, highly erotic. All this was uniquely significant to me. Had I stumbled upon the person that I had been unaware *that I had been in search of for a considerable length of time? My train of thought was interrupted by the actress.*

"O.K," she said "tell me your story!"

'Akhet'

A story of Cleopatra

Book 1

Some two thousand years earlier Dawn shot the bolts and flung wide the purple gates of the celestial palaces bathing the forecourt in glorious roseate light. Four fire breathing, winged, stallions Fiery, Dawn-steed, Scorcher and Blaze emerged drawing a golden chariot. Helios, the sun god, dressed in royal robes of purple, gripped the reins; it would take all his mighty strength to curb the impatient horses, fully refreshed with ambrosia, there was no need for the goad. Gold rimmed wheels with silver spokes turning slowly gradually accelerated as they cut through the mist. Darkness fled and the stars were routed. Lucifer, the morning star some called her Venus others knew her as Aphrodite, inclined earthwards she was the last to abandon her watch. The sky glowed pink and the moon disappeared as the fire breathing stallions rose on their mighty wings. The start of their daily journey was steep, straight into the horns of the charging bull, steering clear of the archer, the jaws of the lion and the menacing arms of the scorpion. The stallions straining at their jewel encrusted yokes.

Helios guided his team along the ruts scored by countless previous journeys, avoiding the biting polar winds, giving earth and heaven equal warmth. Behind him was his eastern palace an imposing building with its towering columns of gold, blazing bronze and ivory. At the entrance were double doors of shimmering silver. This was home for the spirits of time and the seasons, near Colchis between the Black and Caspian seas. To the right of the sun god were the serpent's coils and to his left, near the horizon, was the celestial alter. From the highest point Helios could see all that happened on earth, fearfully he looked down. He was not particularly observant and had, in the past, failed to notice the theft of his sacred cattle by the companions of Odysseus. In the distance Helios saw the Palestinian coastline and the ancient Canaanite city of Askalon where the young Cleopatra Thea Philopater strode the catwalk of her royal barge attended by anxious courteous.

"Askalon is located in the Gaza strip and the date would have been about 48BCE. One can be precise about the location; however the date is rather more difficult."

"Why is that?" asked the actress.

"The Roman's did not measure time in the same way as the Egyptians. The Romans took a year as being three hundred and sixty days whereas the Egyptians were closer to the truth; their year was three hundred and sixty five days. Consequently the Roman calendar was massively out of phase with the seasons. The royal barge, incidentally, would more accurately be described as a Thalamegos."

Cleopatra's blond hair flowed in the easterly breeze, her eyes sparkled like emeralds. She was in a bad mood and everyone on board knew it.

"What do you mean he is too busy? Does he know whose Thalamegos this is? Take me to this insolent man. Am I surrounded by idiots?"

Her physician and close friend Olympos muttered under his breath ruefully; "Rage goddess, sing the rage of Cleopatra daughter of Isis." She was following in the footsteps of her great grandmother Cleopatra II but time alone would tell if her actions would be 'murderous and doomed, that would cost the Egyptians countless losses, so many sturdy souls hurling down to the 'House of Death', great fighter's souls, their carrion, feasts for dogs and birds'. The doctor had been one of Cleopatra VII's closest friends since childhood, he knew her well. This beautiful young woman was undoubtedly a Ptolemy.

The Canaanite city of Askalon was one of the most important cities on the Palestinian coastline. People had lived there since the Bronze Age, this was a true sea port built on a low sandstone hill over an underground spring. Massive walls up to fifty feet high and a hundred and fifty feet thick enclosed the city to prevent an enemy undermining it. These walls were further protected from siege engines by a dry moat and nature in the form of drifting sands from the west and south was a constant threat that eventually consumed the ancient city.

The Mediterranean's had always considered that Askalon was on the 'Way to the Sea' although this major highway was a couple of miles east along the hills. On these rolling hills were fields of wheat and barley and further away orchards and vineyards. There was a wide roadway leading directly to the harbour near the western gate. Here there were many warehouses for goods in transit as this was a thriving metropolis populated by small people dressed in bright coloured clothing.

The diminutive Cleopatra marched into the boatyard office and demanded to see the proprietor.

"You are looking at him," said Apollodorus, without looking up from the papyrus document he was studying.

"I am *Bassilisa* of the Upper and Lower Nile and I demand you show me respect" shouted the first lady of the two lands.

"If I may be so bold, you are the former first lady of Egypt as unfortunately your young brother has just deposed you" replied Apollodorus "and I don't do anything for anyone unless they ask me nicely!"

"I have never been spoken to like that before" yelled the first lady.

"Well this is your lucky day. There has to be a first time for everything" replied the shipwright with a smile. Their eyes met and Cleopatra was momentarily transfixed. In a land of dark haired, brown eyed people the man in front of her had features more like her own. His hair was slightly darker than hers but with a reddish tinge and his bright blue eyes was like sapphires, mocking her. For a moment Cleopatra thought she was looking at a messenger of the gods. Then she noticed a sign on the wall in Greek and Latin.

Ego gleuti hao aduvatos ameoos
Alla daumotos ligos kroch.
Ego facere non potest statim
Autem miraculum tempus exiguous.

"It says here that the impossible you do right away but miracles take a little time."

"Yes that's right" he replied in a tone that was almost patronising. "Patching up your Thalamegos is a great deal easier for me to do than for you to say 'please', which is all that was necessary. As for getting your realm, I mean your *basileio* back I will have to give that one a little thought."

The first lady tapped her foot impatiently. She was an intelligent woman and realised that bullying would get her nowhere. Also, she was intrigued by a man who appeared to fear no one, a quality that could be useful to her. Apollodorus was right, it was the first time she had been spoken to like this. In common with most domineering people she admired those who had the strength and courage to stand up to her. In short she was beginning to enjoy the experience. It is said that in a tense situation whoever speaks first loses. She looked at the shipwright unblinking, then noticed a twinkle in his blue eyes and she began to chuckle like the sound of a mountain stream as it flows over its bed of pebbles. Her mirth developed into a deep low musical laughter that was infectious. When they became serious again Cleopatra tried another approach. She took a deep breath and smiling sweetly, asked.

"Please have a look at my boat and after perhaps you would like to join me for dinner?"

The way to any man's heart is via his stomach so the *Bassilisa* got her way and learned a valuable lesson in the process. Conversely, humour can melt the bonds that encase the coldest woman's heart.

"You refer to her as 'first lady' not 'Queen'. Was she an historic Hilary Clinton?" asked the actress.

"That is a very apt description. There is no Egyptian word for Queen. The word used is Bassilisa, a Greek word. Its meaning is vague being either principal wife or mother of Pharaoh associated with Isis the mother goddess. Not all Pharaoh's were male as Cleopatra VII is sometimes described as the last Pharaoh. The best known female Pharaoh was Hatshepsut, she dressed in the regalia of the Pharaoh's, nemes head gear and kilt, whereas Cleopatra never did.

Later that evening on the Royal Thalamegos Apollodorus was explaining to Cleopatra how the repairs would be carried out.

"So how long will all this take?"

"About one cycle of the moon, at least."

"That long? I need to get back to Alexandria as soon as possible!"

"Look, I know Askalon is not the most inspiring part of the Mediterranean, but what is the hurry? It will take more than a month to recruit and train your army."

"Yes, I know. However, the Romans are on the way and I could end up fighting two enemies." Their conversation was interrupted by her eunuch, Mardian, advising them that dinner was about to be served.

Three quarters of the length of the Thalamegos was taken up by open rowing benches. Aft of these benches was a small sumptuously appointed raised cabin. Inside were three couches around a small table with the fourth side of the table left open for access and serving. The oil lamps had been lit giving the cabin a warm inviting glow. An incense thurible swayed gently in harmony with the boat, the sweet smelling smoke was to ward off the insects that were attracted to the lamp light. Cleopatra invited Apollodorus to recline on the central couch to the rear of the cabin; this was the place of honour. She then reclined on the couch on the right hand of the vessel, the host's position. The third couch, opposite, was vacant as there were no other guests. As was the custom of the time they reclined on the left shoulder. The two handmaids removed the dinner's sandals, washed their feet and made them comfortable with intricately embroidered silk cushions. Reclined in this manner meant that the left hand could be used for little more than holding a bowl while they helped themselves to food from table in front of them with their right hand.

Over dinner the conversation became more convivial and Apollodorus was able to take in the young woman's features. The bridge of her nose was a little higher than what would be considered to be ideal and her ears slightly larger than average, the latter signifying great intelligence. These minor imperfections did not detract from her beauty, if anything they enhanced it. It is said that the eyes are the window to the soul and Cleopatra's were large, green and almost hypnotic. In time she would learn that one look from her would root a man to the spot as though he was the only person of any consequence in a crowded room.

"You are not from this area" observed the first lady.

"No, I come from the Tin Island"

"You don't look like a Sicilian, you look more like an *Angelos*."

"The Tin Island I come from is off the west coast of Gaul."

"I have heard of such a place in the great ocean beyond the Pillars of Heracles" replied Cleopatra incredulously. "I thought it was a myth!"

"I can assure you my Tin Island is a real place and the great ocean is no story told to frighten small children who want to be tax collectors when they grow up. Where I come from it rains all the time and the island is covered with bogs and forests. Julius Caesar had the right idea. He took one look and came back home, muttering something like 'Veni, vidi, vici'. I left as a child, Caesar didn't really conquer Britannia, he little more than explored the place, probably too busy fighting the Gaul. You are not really Egyptian but Achaean, aren't you?"

"Macedonian to be precise, Apollodorus."

"Achaea is the ancient name for Greece, Macedonia was one of the Achaean provinces" I explained.

"What are the Pillars of Heracles?" asked the actress.

"The Pillars of Heracles are the Straits of Gibraltar."

"Angelos?"

"Angelos" I translated. "Literally angel or messenger of the gods, England means land of the angels."

"My friends call me 'Pollo, what do your friends call you?"

"Your Highness or *Bassilisa* Cleopatra, but generally, Madam."

"That's not very friendly. I thought Cleopatra was the family name; you are the seventh, aren't you? I am a republican and have this mad idea that all people are equal. So what did your family call you? Or put it another way, what name uniquely identifies you?"

"I see what you mean. I am Cleopatra Thea Philopater. *Pater* always called me his '*Mikro Thea*' but it would not be proper for you to call me Thea in public. I should like it us to be friends, though. I had a very lonely childhood because we Ptolemy's look on our siblings as rivals for the crown. I have always lived in fear of assassination and the only real friend I had was Pater." She turned her face away from Apollodorus, her golden hair in tight ringlets tumbled round her shoulder, covering her naked breasts. Her sheath-like dress was of the traditional Grecian style.

Apollodorus smiled inwardly and thought "Papa's little goddess" and aloud replied "Cleopatra means 'glory to her father'; *Thea*, 'goddess' and *Philopater* 'father loving'. So you are a goddess who is a glory to her father and who returns his love."

"You make it sound lovely." she replied. Her green eyes were slightly moist as she looked back at him." I know the priests consider me a goddess but right now I feel rather vulnerable with enemies on all sides and a broken boat. I suppose as a republican you are also an atheist and don't believe in gods or goddesses. However, I feel you do not offer your friendship lightly, true *agape* is rare and right now that is the most precious gift anyone could offer me."

"*What is agape?*"

"*In Greek there are four words for love. Eros – sexual love, passion and desire. Philos – love of friends and family, hence Philopater, pater being the Greek word for father. Storge means the appreciation of the world or objects. Lastly Agape is unconditional, without desire, the opposite of Eros. The early Christians used the word 'agape' to describe the love of God. Most scholars today would use that translation, divine love, incorrectly to my way of thinking. I use 'Agape' to sign my text messages to close friends. The Latin word for love, incidentally, is amor which also means charity. This translation anomaly in the context of faith, hope and charity/love has been a major cause of conflict between Catholics and Protestants for centuries to the extent it is said to be what sets us apart.*"

"I find the concept of religion fascinating but I have yet to find a god that I can truly worship." replied the shipwright. "Religion is a convenient means of controlling the masses but to my mind causes more problems than it solves. The idea that some immortal created something as large as the universe purely to satisfy a need to be worshiped is a concept I have a problem with. Or rather the immortal has a problem, one hell of a deep rooted psychological problem!"

Cleopatra laughed. "That is the most preposterous theological argument I have ever heard. The frightening thing is, it is totally logical. You say with some authority that the universe is a big place. Are you interested in astronomy?"

They had finished eating and were slowly making their way forward along the catwalk to the forecastle at the front of the Thalamegos while the servants cleared away the dishes.

"As a sailor, naturally I use the stars to navigate by, but the stars are more than mere signposts. They could be suns like our own sun, warming worlds like the Earth."

"Now you are being silly" laughed Cleopatra, but as she looked into Apollodorus eyes she sensed a feeling of loneliness that made her shiver.

"I am sorry" said Apollodorus "it gets cold here at night. I am from a colder climate so don't notice it. Shall we go back into the cabin?"

"No, that's OK". Then turning to her handmaiden said "Charmian, get me a wrap". Looking back towards the shipwright, she continued "I love looking at the stars. It's a fascinating thought that there could be other worlds out there and I thought Alexandria was the centre of the universe."

"Well you can't believe everything your tutors taught you." said Apollodorus with a smile.

"That's true 'Pollo. Unfortunately, that's exactly what my young brother does, hence my present predicament."

"His teacher told him was that he was indestructible, so to put it to the test he punched a hole in the Royal Thalamegos in a fit of temper?"

"No, the bull did that! Ptolemy's eunuch, Pothinus, manipulated my brother causing the rebellion that resulted in my fleeing for my life." Cleopatra sniffed back her tears and hoped Apollodorus would not notice in the dark. Like all sailors he had excellent night vision and pretended not to see, instead continued to jest, this being the kindest thing to do. There would be plenty of time to gather all the background information on the rebellion and form a plan to regain the *basileio* for his new found friend. Like all men, he found her captivating and utterly irresistible.

"The bull did it?"

"Yes, the bull."

"You mean large, horns, interesting taste in body piercing, causes havoc in a china market by announcing his presence with a moo?"

"I don't think his aspirations were for the purchase of a new dinner service but yes, large, horns, said moo quite often but we hadn't got round to the nose ring, hence the loss of control."

"I have always had my doubts about ship's pets in general but a bull would not be my first choice. Parrots are quite good, or maybe a monkey. Cats are very adaptable. You can't teach a bull to talk, they are no good at acrobatics in the rigging and they wouldn't sit still on your lap and wash themselves. Added to which they are very short tempered and have a bit of a thing about the colour red."

Cleopatra laughed in her low musical way; she had a keen eye for the absurd. "You idiot, 'Pollo. It wasn't a pet, it was sacred." Her previous tears of sorrow were replaced by those of laughter.

"I should think you did call it blessed as in 'the blessed bull's had a fit and charged through the side of the boat so now we are sinking.' Remind me to build the next Royal barge out of metal when we get your *basileio* back."

"So you think you can get my *basileio* back then?" she tried to sound casual but her heart was racing.

"I can't as I am no warrior. However I have the beginnings of an idea. I need a lot more background information and you an extraordinary general.

The following day, Cleopatra, dressed in everyday clothing, was walking along the water side observing the repairs to the Royal Thalamegos with Apollodorus.

"What can you tell me about Ptolemy's camp?" asked the shipwright.

"Quite a lot. He has twenty thousand infantry, mostly the Roman forces known as 'Gabinians' troops left by Aulus Gabinius following the restoration of my *Pater*. The rest are Brigands and Pirates from Syria, condemned criminals, exiles and runaway slaves. He also has two thousand cavalry, veterans of the numerous wars."

"If you know all about his camp it is reasonable to assume that he, or at least his advisors, knows what you had for dinner last night and when you last took a bath. Any plan you make he will know about. You have no more idea who his spy is than he knows who is informing you. No doubt your spy is one of his most trusted servants. No, don't tell me! I don't want to make you paranoid but who can you really trust?"

"Well I trust Olympos my physician as I have been friends with him since we were children, also Charmain and Iras, my handmaids, and naturally Mardian."

"So your brother has a motley army of mercenaries loyal to the highest bidder. What have you got?"

"The Egyptian treasury" replied Cleopatra with an evil grin.

The shipwright laughed then continued "Life is a bit like the Egyptian board game of strategy that involves moving pieces over an alternate square coloured pattern board. All people play these games but the rules vary from country to country as does the name. I know it as draughts but the principle is the same. Your situation is like that."

"Not really. I have two opponents, not one."

"I was coming to that. Tell me the events from *Auletes's* return from Rome to the present time. How and why did you end up in this impregnable fortress in the middle of nowhere?" They walked along the coastline and Cleopatra explained how her father had always been insecure as Pharaoh, having been born to an unknown concubine, resulting in the nickname Nothos or bastard. Ptolemy Neos Dionysus, Cleopatra's father, known as *Auletes* or Fluter was a great temple builder but unpopular with the masses. He wasn't much of a musician and mainly played the flute when drunk, dancing with actors and commoners, much to the embarrassment of his Roman guests. *Auletes* had travelled to Rome to persuade the Senate to pass a law proclaiming him Pharaoh.

"All things are possible in Rome if you have the money. *Pater* nearly bankrupted Egypt, bribing officials to get his law."

"So this obliges Rome to enforce the succession of the Ptolemy's and Cleopatra's?"

"Trouble is, they are busy with their own civil war."

The actress looked bemused so I explained. "Gaius Julius Caesar had spent nine years fighting the Gaul. He was a brilliant general and very popular with his troops. The Gaul wars resulted in the conquest of eight hundred cities, three hundred subjugated tribes and one million men sold into slavery. Three million lay dead in the battlefields across Northern Europe. On his victorious return, a fearful Senate lead by Pompey ordered him to disarm. Caesar was forbidden to stand for a second term as Pro

Consulate so under Roman law was not permitted to maintain an army. You know how it is with boys and their toys; Caesar answered 'testis virtus' which translates to 'witness virility' from which we derive testicles."

The actress laughed "So Caesar said bollocks."

"Caesar did indeed respond with the Latin equivalent of bollocks, he was a consummate gambler and marched on Rome with the war cry 'a desperate man knows no danger' which resulted in civil war with Gnaeus Pompius Magnus leading the opposition. Caesar and Pompey had been part of The First Triumvirate (rule by three men) and Pompey married Caesar's daughter, Julia, from his first marriage. Both men were devastated by Julia's death in childbirth and their alliance crumbled. Caesar drove Pompey out of Rome and he fled to Greece. Meanwhile the Parthians seized the opportunity to invaded Syria."

"Who were the Parthians?"

"The Parthians were the inhabitants of Babylonia and the Persian Empire, today's Iran and Iraq."

"Gaius Julius Caesar?"

"Gaius was his 'praenomen' or familiar name, Julius his 'nomen' or family name and Caesar the 'cognomen' or clan name. Not everyone had a clan name, Mark Antony being a case in point."

"I thought Syria was one of your provinces?"

"It used to be" said Cleopatra coldly, "so when the Roman governor, Marcus Calprius, sent his two sons to ask for reinforcements I thought I could kill two birds with one stone."

"How so?"

"*Pater's* mercenaries, the Gabinians, were living a life of Dionysus, making a nuisance of themselves in Alexandria."

"Who or what was Dionysus?" asked the actress.

"Dionysus was the son of the god Zeus to a mortal mother, Semele."

"Like Jesus is son of God to mortal Mary."

"Yes, in a manner of speaking" I replied, doubtfully "but their teachings were very different. Dionysus gave mankind grapes. He is similar to the Roman god, Baccas, but not the god of drunkenness; he was the patron of ecstatic transcendence, the shedding of inhibitions. Statues generally depicted him with a huge erection; Dionysus was also connected with fertility as the counterpart of Isis and considered a threat to good order."

"Sounds like the strength through joy and producing the master race ideas of Hitler in the third Reich."

"Nothing much changes only the names over the door."

"So you thought if you sent the Gabinians to Calprius and they won you may have got back Syria. If they lost you would have disposed of an unruly element. Either way you would score plus points with Rome. So what went wrong?"

"The Gabinians murdered the Calprius brothers, the messengers."

"O Zeus! So what did you do?"

"Rounded up the perpetrators and packed them off to Syria and the tender mercies of Marcus Calprius."

"Who promptly cut their heads off or fed them to the crocodiles, thus enraging the boys back in Alexandria."

"Meanwhile, the Nile didn't flood so the crops failed, resulting in famine in the country. Ptolemy and his advisors spread the rumour that it was entirely my fault. Had I not been fore-warned I would have sailed back from Memphis along the western Canopic branch of the Nile strait into a civil war. I barely escaped with my life."

"Tell me about this sacred bull?" asked Apollodorus realising that Cleopatra was becoming tearful again.

"The Apis Bull, we believe is the living embodiment of the god Ptah, the patron of craftsman. Your ideal patron should you decide to become religious. This bull lives in luxury in Egypt's second city Memphis. When the bull dies, the successor is selected not from its offspring but by a nationwide search for an individual animal with particular markings."

"Where was Memphis located?"

"*Near present day Assyut and Cairo, at the apex of the Nile delta. From here the Nile divides into the two primary waterways as it flows north to the sea. The western Canoptic branch lead to Alexandria whereas the eastern Pelusic branch lead to Pelusium. A wedge of land between these two waterways was referred to as 'the island' not to be confused with Pharos, an island off Alexandria. The island was covered by an intricate network of waterways with a further five openings to the sea.*"

"You use the past tense?"

"*Global warming is not a recent phenomenon; the polar ice caps have been melting for millennium causing the sea level of the Mediterranean to rise. This and other geological activities have resulted in the course of the*

Nile changing and the delta has moved. Incidentally the spectacle of Cleopatra bringing the Apis Bull into the temple at Memphis made a lasting impression on the people. It was written about affectionately nearly half a century after her death."

"I felt so proud leading the young bull through the narrow streets with the crowds cheering. I was the first modern day monarch to take part in the ceremony. I thought that way I would heal the rift between the indigenous Egyptians and their Macedonian rulers by embracing all the religions".

"I take it that the bull did not kill itself trying to jump ship the hard way, through the side."

"No, the damage did not appear too bad at the time; we didn't have time to check before leaving Memphis."

"The trouble is, the Royal Thalamegos is long and thin. In the river it is supported evenly along its length but at sea it is supported at the wave crests and is unsupported at the troughs. The area of maximum stress at sea is where the bull damaged the planking; consequently the vessel was perfectly sound in the river but started to break up at sea. You were lucky to make it here. The damaged planks will all have to be replaced, that's why the repair will take time. If you were popular in Memphis why not stay there for sanctuary and to raise an army?"

"Memphis is a religious city, I need troops not priests. My grandfather helped the Palestinians when they were invaded by the Judeans so I thought now was a good time to call in the favour."

"So presumably you sailed down the eastern Pelusic branch of the Nile to Pelusium found that the fortress there had already been occupied by your brother. You then continued east to along the Palestinian coastline against the prevailing trade wind in a structurally compromised river boat with the Egyptian treasury as ballast to one of the best fortified cities in the area."

Cleopatra nodded and Apollodorus thought "You may be small and pretty but you lack neither courage nor ingenuity, you are an outstanding lady, one I could so easily lose my heart too." They had walked some way from the port area to open countryside. Suddenly a large yellow and black reptile reared up hissing fiercely. Apollodorus raised the Adze, a large boat builder's axe he was carrying, in defence.

"No, don't kill it!" cried Cleopatra "the Uraeus is the protector of the Pharaoh's. Step to the side where she cannot see you. She is only protecting her young."

Cleopatra had taken Apollodorus by the arm and pulled him out of the serpent's direct line of vision. The look of utter hatred in the shipwrights eyes, which had changed from a friendly blue to grey, un-nerved her. She pulled him away with both hands. When they were a safe distance away, still holding him, she looked into his eyes and saw tears.

"What is it? Why do you hate the snake so much?"

Apollodorus controlled himself with an obvious effort. After a while, he stopped shaking and said in a quiet voice, almost a whisper. "The only woman I ever truly loved was killed by the venom of the Cobra."

"I am so sorry" said the first lady with real feeling. "I suppose it is no help saying that we believe that death by Cobra venom gives direct access to immortality and bypasses the judgement we must all face."

"Actually it does. As long as I remember her in my heart she will never be truly lost."

They walked slowly back to the boat in silence. Cleopatra had a rare gift in that she knew when to leave a man to his silence. No Egyptian would kill a Cobra, to do so would invite ill fortune!

Book 2

On board Cleopatra's Royal Thalamegos later that same day. "So tell me about Pothinus" asked Apollodorus.

"That pompous tart" exploded Cleopatra "is Ptolemy's nurse. He is tall, thin with oiled ringlets and exaggerated makeup that would embarrass a prostitute."

"I take it you don't like him."

"He is a lying, manipulating son of a camel driver's whore, who told me to send reinforcements to Pompeius, which I did believing Caesar to be vanquished. I was trying to stay out of that conflict. If Caesar was defeated the reinforcements would have been of no consequence. However, Caesar was the victor. Now I have antagonised the most powerful man in the world."

"That's a pity; he is the extraordinary General I had ear marked for the recovery of your *basileio*. We shall just have to wait till kid brother and his moronic advisors annoy Jules, which should not take long. Two things I am not clear about; firstly you were able to send reinforcements to Pompeius in Achaea but could not reinforce Marcus Calprius in Syria."

"The troops, and sailors I sent to Gnaeus Pompeius are in my pay roll where as the Gabinians are Roman Centurions, in the pay of the republic. They had not received any wages for some time and had absorbed themselves into Alexandrian society, married local girls, begat children and forgotten their homeland."

"So Rome had forgotten the Gabinians in which case it is not surprising that their response to Marcus Calprius call to arms elicited the response 'go fornicate in your *mater's* dung.' Second question; what happened to the ships and troops you sent to Pompeius?"

"The ships returned to their base at Alexandria however the bulk of the army is making its way back over land along the 'Way to the Sea'. I have sent messengers to intercept them and they will arrive here any day."

"Could Ptolemy transfer the Egyptian fleet to Pelusium?"

"It would be more trouble than it is worth. There are treacherous sand banks off Pelusium and the wind will not be in their favour this time of the year. It is possible but highly unlikely."

"That's good, with the Navy hold up in Alexandria and loyal troops on their way who will form the core of your army. Are there sufficient troops to capture Pelusium?" Cleopatra shook her head and the shipwright continued "Are there sufficient to make a nuisance of themselves and keep Ptolemy's army busy?"

"Most definitely, what is your plan?"

"If I were Pompeius I would make for Egypt and try to raise another army. Jules will realise that is his most likely course of action so will be in hot pursuit."

Cleopatra smiled broadly as understanding dawned. "So we make life easy for them. Pompeius will arrive in Alexandria to find all available armed forces conspicuous by their absence so there will be no one to protect him from Caesars wroth. Thank you Cleopatra! What if he makes for Pelusium?"

"Your brother will probably welcome him with open arms in which case Caesar will form an alliance with you. Ptolemy will be caught in a classic pincer. If Pompeius makes for Askalon you take him prisoner and hand him over to Jules. Either way Gaius Julius Caesar is going to find himself in your debt and will be obliged to uphold your *Pater's* will, slanted somewhat in your favour. The only problem will be how to explain all this to the Pontifex Maximus."

"Pontifex Maximus? Inquired the actress.
"High Priest, one of Caesars many titles."

Over the next few days Cleopatra's army arrived and were dispatched to Pelusium, Apollodorus found his office and shipyard taken over by his new friend as a recruiting station and military headquarters. One evening about two weeks later as they dined on board the Royal Thalamegos, some distance away off the coast of Pelusium a drama was unfolding.

Pompey arrived off the Egyptian coast with ships, money and about two thousand troops. Also with him were his wife and youngest son Sextus. The defeated general had fled to Egypt, as Apollodorus had predicted, to raise a new army. Alexandria was a natural fortress, possessing a harbour second to none and the city was believed to be impregnable. He sent envoys to Ptolemy and from these men the Regents learned of the Roman's ill fortune. It is said that loose talk costs lives and this was to prove to be the case.

Lucius Septimius and Ptolemy's commander-in-chief, Achillas embarked in a small boats and sailed out to the Roman ships. After many friendly greetings they begged Pompey to come over to their boat, declaring that by virtue of the shallow water a ship of that size could not come close to land and that Paraoh Ptolemy was very eager to see him. Accordingly, against the advise of all his fellow-voyagers, he boarded their boat, trusting in his hosts and remarked:

"Where ever an Imperiator wends his way, his is his own slave, even though his steps are free."

As they drew near the land, fearing that if Pompey met Ptolemy he might be saved, either by the Pharaoh himself, his own countrymen or Egyptian sympathisers, Lucius Septimus, who had previously served the defeated general, drew his sword. In silence Pompey understood their plot and recognized that he would not be able to defend himself or escape, he veiled his face and was slain.

Meanwhile Gaius Julius Caesar arrived off Alexandria with ten warships, three thousand two hundred infantry and eight hundred cavalry, relying more on his reputation than actual military strength. The city was in turmoil so he anchored offshore until Ptolemy and his Regents arrived back from Pelusium. It is said that Caesar shed crocodile tears at the sight of Pompey's severed head and finger ring. He must have secretly been relieved that the threat posed by Pompey was removed and only then felt confident to make landfall. The Pontifex Maximus was greeted by angry shouts from the crowds, his symbol of magistrate authority, the Fasces long handled axes, were carried by attending officers known as Lictors. Such a show of Roman authority incensed the Alexandrians. Caesar promptly made himself at home in the Royal Palace.

Three days later an ecstatic Cleopatra burst into the office of Apollodorus, threw her arms round a surprised shipwright's neck and kissed him, saying, "Has anyone ever told you that you are a genius?"

"I do all the time but the rest of the world is a little slow in acknowledgement. Why?"

"You are a genius 'Pollo! Your plan has worked out better than either of us imagined. Gnaeus Pompeius Magneus tried to escape to Alexandria and on hearing that Ptolemy was at Pelusium changed course and sailed there instead."

"So has he joined forces with your brother?"

"Not exactly, they cut off his head!"

"Poor old Gnaeus, in Britannia we have a saying; 'at never rains it pours'. I fail to see why Pompeius beheading is good news."

"Caesar has arrived in Alexandria and has taken up residence in my palace, of all the cheek! As a gift my brother presented Caesar with the severed head of Pompeius."

"Surely Jules was delighted?" replied Apollodorus looking increasingly worried.

"Far from it, Caesar was furious and wept with rage! Apparently he looked on Pompeius as a worthy rival, not an enemy."

The shipwright smiled broadly. "That is a classic example of the philosophy which states that the best ideas are the ones you don't plan but trip over on the way to the latrine and you are probably in Dionysus at the time. So our Jules must now see you in a far better light."

Cleopatra nodded enthusiastically. "He has sent for me and has promised to restore peace in Egypt but how can I get past Ptolemy's troops at Mount Cusino in one piece?"

Apollodorus said nothing but looked at the sign on the wall and back to Cleopatra and winked.

"What's for dinner tonight?" he asked.

The *Bassilisa* hit Apollodorus over the head with a papyrus scroll.

"You are infuriating! Don't you think of anything other than your stomach?"

"Yes I do. We now have just the opportunity I have been waiting for and I will tell you about it at dinner tonight! I have an idea and we will only get one chance. Now go away I have work to do, on my boat!" He put his arm round Cleopatra's shoulder, kissed her lightly and whispered "Do as you are told, Thea, just this once. And one last thing, I want to see you in the most seductive dress you have in your wardrobe and your best jewellery. If you are good, I may take you for a romantic moonlit sail, one way ticket!"

"I can tell you know how to show a girl a good time." Cleopatra said with a conspiratorial grin and returned the shipwright's kiss.

"One last thing, invite Olympos to dinner also, but he isn't coming sailing with us."

Later that afternoon Cleopatra was getting ready for dinner, her handmaids Charmain and Iras in attendance. Charmain was Egyptian, with luxurious thick dark curly hair and hazel eyes whereas Iras was from Nubia or modern day Sudan, her skin was as black as ebony and her braided black hair was decorated with beads.

"He said dress sexy and best jewellery and he would take me for a romantic moonlit sail. I haven't sailed my Felucca for ages and then only in sheltered water. I think he sailed all the way from Britannia in his own boat.

It must be an exceptional boat and he must be an extra ordinary sailor!" said Cleopatra with a dreamy look in her eye.

"But, Madam, he is a commoner, a shipwright. You are a royal!" The handmaid hesitated "Are you sure he is ….."

"Don't be old fashioned, Charmain, *Pater* dated whoever he fancied. Why shouldn't I? You must admit 'Pollo is a real man, so strong, so fearless, except with snakes and so funny, I have never laughed so much as I have this last week. I love the familiar way he refers to Julius Caesar as Jules."

"What does he call you, Madam?" asked Iras doubtfully.

"Thea. No one else would dare to call me that, but he says it so sincerely. I feel like a real goddess and he says he doesn't believe in gods or royalty and yet he makes me feel so special." The three girls giggled.

"How old were they?" asked the actress.
"Cleopatra was only twenty and the handmaidens slightly younger."

At that moment Olympos entered. "Your Highness I am, with respect, concerned about the amount of time you are spending with that Sicilian shipwright" he said.

"Why, Olympos, I think you are jealous." She replied with mocking seriousness.

"I really think that you should be working out a plan to get back to Alexandra, not flirting with some common seaman."

"You are jealous!" said Cleopatra with glee.

"I suppose you have invited him to dinner again?"

"Yes I have. I enjoy his company. Incidentally there are two Tin Islands he comes from the mythical one that actually exists beyond Gaul. He has a plan which he is going to tell me about at tonight. Then he is going to take me for a moonlight sail. Isn't that so romantic? You never took me for a moonlight sail, did you, Olympos?"

"You know I hate the water and get sea sick. Well, if he has a plan I think I should know what it."

"You are invited to dinner; he wants to see you to discuss his ideas tonight."

Olympos raised an eyebrow and departed with a nod.

Dinner was served on the Royal Thalamegos. Cleopatra looked devastating. Her golden hair was in ringlets and a broad gold necklace round her neck. The clinging sheath-like diaphanous dress was nearly transparent, her breasts were bare and her nipples coloured with henna. Both men wondered why she had bothered with clothing, as nothing was left to the imagination. She had a mischievous look on her face as she looked at the men trying not to stare at her obvious charms.

Olympos was the first to speak.

"Well, Apollodorus, what is your plan?" he asked when the servants had left.

"As soon as I tell you, Ptolemy's spies will be on their way to him with the details, so if you both agree with my proposal we will have to implement it immediately. Time will be of the essence. Your friend and mine, Gaius Julius Caesar, otherwise known as Jules, has promised to restore peace in Egypt. To this end he has summoned Her Royal Highness and her kid brother to his democratic eminence. The afore-mentioned royal brat has annoyed our Jules by giving him a present of the head of Pompeius on a plate, literally! This means the *Bassilisa's* previous royal '*faux pax*' with respect to the reinforcements sent to Pompeius, the late headless rival of Caesar, has now paled into insignificance."

"*Faux pax*, what does that mean?" asked Cleopatra.

"It is a Gallic expression" replied Apollodorus thoughtfully. "I think you would say *parapathra* or psudo gradus in Latin. Literally false step or stepped into dung."

"Your language is colourful but I get the sense of what you are saying" said Olympos.

"Your Highness, how do you view Rome and the Romans?" asked Apollodorus.

"With contempt" was the reply with feeling "they have spread round the Mediterranean like a vermin."

"To an extent I agree" said Apollodorus "but I am a Roman realist. They are taking over the whole world. Their language is guttural, their games barbaric and their precious democracy is only available to those who can afford it. Your late *Pater* can make testimony to the latter. Unfortunately they are here for the foreseeable future interfering in all our lives. All dictatorships collapse and fall in time, Rome will be no different."

"Rome is a Republic." interrupted Olympus.

"For the present, but give it time. Caesar is on record for saying that Sulla resigned as dictator far too soon. It is all to clear where Jules ambitions lie, if he is ever made dictator he will dictate in no uncertain terms! What I am suggesting, your Highness is if Rome is going to interfere anyway, let's make them do it on your terms. The choice is yours, either be a client realm or an equal partner with a Super Power, and establish a 'special relationship'. Rome, in general, and Jules, in particular, needs you far more than you need them."

"I know they want our gold to pay their troops and our corn to feed them."

"Special relationship? It sounds like your Margaret Thatcher and my Ronald Regan or more recently Dubya Bush and Tony Blair" said the actress.
"I doubt if Caesar ever greeted the Bassilisa with the salutation 'Yo Cleo' but as previously stated nothing changes, only the name over the door."

"Julius Caesar has a weakness; you know what his troops sing about him;
> 'Home we bring our bald whoremonger.
> Rome lock your wives away.
> All those bags of gold you sent him.
> Went his Gallic tarts to pay.'

Your highness; there is no delicate way to ask you this. I don't know if you have known a man intimately, but the way to recover your basileio is by giving away the most precious gift a woman can give. Would you be prepared to seduce a bald whoremonger, old enough to be your *pater*, who just happens to be the most powerful man on Earth?"

The *Bassilisa* coloured then looked sad. She was on the point of tears. Apollodorus hurried over to Cleopatra and put his arm round her.

"I am sorry" he said "it is too precious a gift to give. We will think of another idea."

"No, it's O.K; I had been thinking the same thing. I am a bit of a romantic and had always dreamed of giving myself for true love, not to further a political objective like most royal women have to. I am a realist, too, 'Pollo. I know the price I must pay to recover my *basileio* and I am willing to pay it. The problem is how I seduce Gaius Julius Caesar." She coloured deep red "I am little more than a girl. I have never done it before. How do I get Jules interested in me?"

"I don't believe I am hearing this" replied the exasperated shipwright. Cleopatra looked puzzled. "You lie there in that devastating dress that leaves nothing to the imagination. You are articulate; you have the most seductive voice I have ever heard and an irresistible presence. Your conversation and action lays all men under your spell and you have the audacity to say all wide eyed, 'I don't know how to allure'."

Olympos recovered from a fit of coughing and laughter, there were tears running down his cheeks. "Apollodorus is right, Madam."

Cleopatra looked from one man to the other in bewilderment.

"All you have to do is slink up to him and touch him lightly on the shoulder, like this. Then look him straight in the eye with those gorgeous green eyes of yours and say. 'Hello big boy, is anything worn beneath the toga?' He will go bright red and stammer something like. 'No it's all in perfect working order. That's if he has a sense of humour" said Apollodorus with a smile.

"What if he has no sense of humour?" asked the Doctor

"We revert to plan *beta*."

"Which is?" asked the *Bassilisa*.

"I kick him in the toga and we race back to my boat before he has time to shout 'guards' and cuts our heads off or feeds us to the crocodiles."

"Lions" corrected Olympos "Romans feed their prisoners to the lions."

They all laughed.

When they recovered Olympos said "So you are going to take Her Royal Highness to Caesar in your boat?"

"Yes, my boat unlike any of the local vessels so we will be taken for foreign traders raising little suspicion with either the Romans or Ptolemy's troops. She is light and fast, we don't need an army of slaves to row her and no big whips to motivate them. Just you, me and the wind."

"How romantic" said Cleopatra, dreamily. "Incidentally we don't use slaves to row our ships, they are too expensive. We use free men and pay them quite well. Money is a better motivator then a whip, Egypt is a civilised country."

"It is two and a half thousand furlongs from here to Alexandria, about three hundred Roman miles. There is a favourable wind so if we sail through the night and all tomorrow and the day after. We must time our arrival just as our Jules is getting ready for bed so with luck he will be alone, which is what we want."

Cleopatra looked doubtful. "A furlong is the same as an Egyptian stades, that's about forty schoenus! Two days to get to Alexandria, no boat can travel that fast."

"I am relying on your enemies believing exactly that!" exclaimed Apollodorus. "At this time of year there is an easterly trade wind which has trapped the Roman fleet in Alexandria. We will have to take turns in steering so I can get some sleep but provided the wind holds my boat can make it easily in that time."

"So you are going to sneak in after dark" interrupted the doctor. "How will you get past the palace guards?"

"You are both familiar with the story 'the Wooden Horse of Troy'. I shall use that basic idea with a rather unusual ability I have. Before I show you I want you both to give me your word to tell no one what I am about to show you and never ask me to do it again." They agreed looking very puzzled.

"Your Highness; can I borrow one of your handmaidens?" The Nubian girl was summoned "Iras, look me in the eyes." The girl did as she was told, Apollodorus held her gaze and said softly "The Doctor has made you a very improper suggestion, slap him round the face." She walked over to Olympos and hit him, the noise broke the spell and Iras apologised profusely.

"I don't know what came over me. I could not help myself" she stammered.

"It's all right, Iras. Now please leave us again" said the first lady.

"No, not yet" said the shipwright "there is something else you can help me with. Don't worry I shall not play any more tricks on you. I want to wrap you in this bed roll and carry you over my shoulder for a step or two." He gently rolled the servant in the bedding and picked her up and laid her over his shoulder, holding her by the legs. "Olympos, you can be Caesar. I bring you a gift from The Great Cleopatra." He carefully laid down the bedding and unrolled it, then helped the puzzled Iras to her feet. "Noble Caesar, may I present the *Bassilisa* of the Upper and Lower Lands, Iras do a little curtsey."

Cleopatra clapped her hands in delight; the doctor raised an eyebrow and smiled.

"Congratulations, Apollodorus. Your plan is ingenious! You smuggle Her Highness by sea in a small boat, past the army at Mount Cusino sail into the royal harbour, then wrap the *Bassilisa* in a bed roll and walk into the palace under cover of darkness. If any of the guards challenge you, you use that rather unusual gift of yours to convince them that everything is in order."

"Precisely."

"I can see some incredible uses in surgery for that gift of yours; you could put the patient in a deep sleep and convince them they were feeling no discomfort. The physician could get on with the amputation, or whatever, without the usual screams of agony that accompany such operations" said the Doctor excitedly.

"Unfortunately, the people where I came from had other ideas. They thought it gave me the ability to talk with the spirits and wanted to make me a high priest."

"That wouldn't be so bad" interrupted Cleopatra.

"You wouldn't say that if you saw the initiation rights! These involve being hit over the back of the head with a large blunt instrument and being laid face down in a swamp. This senseless action with it's unparalleled lack of logic precludes any communications with the spirits being passed on to the living by the recently appointed late high priest!"

"That makes our priests having to shave their heads before making offerings to the gods rather tame. I can see why you are anti religion. You have my word I will never ask you to use your gift again."

The Doctor added regretfully "Your secret is safe with me also." They had all forgotten that Iras was still with them.

"I agree" said the first lady. "I will tell Charmain and Iras to get ready."

"We cannot take your handmaids; we must travel as lightly as possible."

"But I never go anywhere without them!" protested Cleopatra.

"A fact that your enemies are fully aware of!" replied the exasperated shipwright.

"Who will do my hair and make up?"

"When we are near Alexandria we will hove too and I will have to be your stand in handmaid. If I can paint and decorate a boat I should be able to manage your make up as for curling your hair that must be much the same as steam bending a wooden frame."

"If we had more time Charmain and Iras could have given you lessons!"

Apollodorus grinned broadly "They already have! They were a little reticent and questioned my motives. Fortunately they are used to doing as they are told."

Cleopatra smiled and thought "That's why they were questioning our friendship." Aloud she said "So you hatched this plan some time ago and have been preparing ever since."

Apollodorus had launched his small ship earlier that day into the sunlit breakers, stepped the mast and set the sail.

"What was Apollodorus' boat like?" asked the actress
"The planking overlapped at the seams, in the manner known in a later era as clinker built, unlike the local craft. There was a small cabin amidships; otherwise she was open with a single mast and sail, the ends were swept up giving a graceful but pronounced shear line. The design would cause terror in the future as it was the basis of the design used by the Vikings. Unlike its successors, the sail was the more efficient triangular lateen sail used in Egypt, not rectangular."

"This is a rather odd design, why do the planks overlap?" asked Cleopatra as the shipwright helped her aboard.
"Overlapping the planks saves internal framework thus saving weight without losing strength. Your local shipwrights could not build a boat like this, there are no suitable trees. They build them like this in the land of the midnight sun, a strange land where the sun hardly sets in the summer."
"Never gets dark in the summer? You will tell me next it stays dark all winter," jested the first lady.
"Yes, it is pretty gloomy in winter and the rain falls as solid white fluff called snow. The locals dress in animal skins to keep warm."
"It sounds ghastly."
"It is; why do you think I left? They do build some good boats as you shall soon see. Make yourself comfortable and hold that rope while I cast off."
The sail filled and the boat accelerated effortlessly and almost silently into the sunset. Cleopatra felt a tingle of excitement and shivered involuntarily. Apollodorus wrapped a blanket around her and she used the opportunity to snuggle up to him. He steered the boat with one hand, his other was round the young woman's shoulder.
"Does your boat have a name?" she asked.
"Mintaka, after the third star of Orion's belt."

"Don't the Great Pyramids at Gaza mimic Orion's belt?"
"Some say so, but geological studies indicate they were positioned where the topography dictated. The Egyptians believed that the constellation

of Orion was where the Pharaohs spent the afterlife, or was the gateway to the hereafter."

Sailing at night time can, in adverse weather, be a frightening experience but under ideal conditions when the boat is making good progress, without being pressed, the opposite is true. When they were in deep water, just in sight of land, Apollodorus turned Mintaka to follow the coastline to Alexandria.

"Circe, the awesome nymph with lovely braids and a human voice has sent us hardy shipmates a fresh following wind to ruffle our wake, bellying out our sail to drive our blue prow on" quoted Cleopatra.

The sun sank and the roads of the world grew dark. In the short time between dusk and the stars becoming visible the sky and sea merged into one. A peaceful tranquillity enveloped the Mintaka and her two occupants. Cleopatra felt the tensions she had experienced all her life melt away like wax in the face of fire. She had lived in constant fear; this was the first time she had truly relaxed.

"It looks like we are flying through the Beautiful West" she observed.

"What is the Beautiful West?" asked Apollodorus softly.

"It's the large subterranean cavern where the sun sets and begins its night time journey back to the East. This place we call Dat, you would call it Heaven. The Beautiful West is where the dead must first go to have sins not committed during their lifetime read from the 'Book of the Dead'. These sins not committed are tested on divine scales by Glutton, the demon with a crocodile head."

"I thought Sobek was the crocodile god."

"He is. Glutton is a demon, similar to the Hebrew anti god Satan."

"That must be where the expression 'glutton for punishment' comes from" said the actress.

"So does it mean that to die from the Uraeus venom avoids Glutton's judgement?"

Cleopatra could see that her friend's eyes had become moist and quietly answered. "Yes." She desperately wanted to change the subject in the way that Apollodorus did so skilfully when she became upset. Fortunately she had started to feel hungry, a sensation as un-familiar as being able to relax. "Is there anything to eat and drink on board?" she asked.

"Now who is the only one who thinks of their stomach?" laughed Apollodorus. "There is plenty of dried or salted food in the cabin but I don't suppose you would like that. However, there is a basket of fresh figs and bread, if you would like to get them. Also some flagons of wine that is almost drinkable, if not it doubles as wood preserver."

Cleopatra reluctantly moved forward into the cabin, she had enjoyed the security of the shipwright's strong arm round her shoulder. In the cabin were two beds. She soon found the fruit, bread and wine then her eyes fixed onto something that filled her with horror. Cleopatra's scream brought the shipwright into the cabin. He expected to find a rat or at very least a spider but the cause of her disquiet was neither rodent nor arachnid; Cleopatra pointed at a bowl and shook uncontrollably.

"Take them away!" she wailed.

"That is a bowl of beans" replied Apollodorus incredulously.

"They are un-clean! No Egyptian can bear to look at them! Get rid of them Apollodorus – please!"

The shipwright took the bowl and emptied the beans over the side in disbelief.

"They are gone, you can come out now" he assured the frightened girl so she returned to her former comfortable position. "We are even now you have saved me from a snake and I have rescued you from a deadly bowl of beans."

"It wasn't funny 'Pollo!"

"I am not making fun of you Thea. Your fear is just as real as mine, I am sorry I didn't know. I have a lot to learn about your culture, it is a good thing we don't share the same fears because that way we gain strength from each other."

For some reason food always tastes much better at sea than on dry land, the most unappetising fare can be like a gourmet banquet.

"This wine isn't bad" she said "and figs are my favourite fruit. Did you put them on board specially?" The wine was pale straw coloured, slightly sweet and spicy. "What wine is this? It's like nothing I have previously tasted?"

"I like to be prepared for all eventualities" he replied with a smile "it isn't every day a common seaman entertains royalty on his humble boat. We are drinking an un-diluted heady mixture of two wines; one is fermented honey the other flavoured with resin. Mead is mankind's original alcohol; I thought all nations made it in one form or another. The quality varies from that comparable with the finest Falernian wine served at your royal feasts to something looking and tasting like Mules urine, mixing it with Retsena stops the wine turning into vinegar on a long voyage."

"They sat down to a meal and filed their goblets from an overflowing flagon, they poured them forth honeyed mellow wine to the great goddess Athena" quoted Cleopatra. "I do envy the way you have been able to travel as you please, you must have been to many strange and exotic places."

"After life itself, freedom is the most precious gift we can be given. Freedom is not being able to do what ever we want that affects others and their freedom. No, freedom is being able to say 'no' to the things we don't want to do."

"What do you mean?" asked the *Bassilisa*. Apollodorus looked her straight in the eyes.

"Thea you don't have to do this" he said.

"What do you mean?"

"You don't have to seduce old baldy. You could turn your back on the whole thing. We have plenty of food and water on board also half the Egyptian treasury." Cleopatra had wanted to bring all her money back with her but both Apollodorus and Olympos had insisted on her not 'putting all her eggs in one basket.' "Just give the word and I will turn 'Mintaka' out to sea and show you some of those exotic and strange places."

Cleopatra was silent for some time. "It would mean giving up my *basileio*, my birthright and my people. I would cease to be a goddess and become an ordinary girl. I have a duty and a destiny" she was silent again, Apollodorus said nothing. "I can't turn my back on my dynasty and my people, but where would you take me?" she asked. There are times in all of our lives when we can see clearly that we are at an important cross road of our destiny. Both Cleopatra and Apollodorus knew they were at such a cross road, it would be nearly two decades before they would realise just how important and how wrong they both were.

"A strange land where time does not exist, all the women are beautiful and the men virtuous, no one grows old." Apollodorus joked for he knew the first lady had made her mind up to follow her destiny and he thought he knew what he must now do. "Trouble is there is an evil pirate. He has a metal hook for a hand; his real hand was bitten off by a crocodile. The crocodile follows him everywhere; it liked the taste of the hand so much it wants to eat the rest of him."

"The pirate must be your nemesis; you are always going on about being thrown to the crocodiles. How do we get to this land?"

"That's easy" he pointed to Orion "third star on the right."

"That's Mintaka."

"Yes and straight on till morning."

"Your boat is fast but she can't fly?"

"You said a short while ago it was as though we were flying through the 'Beautiful West' of course Mintaka can fly, all we have to do is sprinkle her with fairy dust and hitch up on a moon beam."

"Have you got any fairy dust?"

"No, I used the last of it getting to meet you; perhaps we had better go to Alexandria after all."

Cleopatra kissed him lightly on the lips and said "You are so sweet and so silly. I don't think I have ever laughed so much as I have since I met you. Promise me you will stay in Alexandria, it would not be the same without you."

They finished eating and then Cleopatra produced her seven stringed lyre. She sang in a low husky voice using the instrument to accompany her haunting melody. The words were written by one of her ancestors about the lighthouse that guided mariners into Alexandria.

"A lofty platform guides the voyager by night,

guides him with its light when darkness of evening falls.

Thither have I bourn a garment of perfect pleasure among my friends,

a garment adorned with the memory of beloved companions.

On its height a dome enshadowed me,

and thence I saw my friends like stars.

I thought that the sea below me was a cloud,

and that I had set up my tent in the midst of the heavens."

Apollodorus sat spellbound and began to understand why Cleopatra could not turn away from her realm, no matter how hostile its people were to her. Two evenings later the bright light of the lighthouse on the island of Pharos appeared over the horizon. They had arrived at Alexandria the city described as 'the great wine press of love; those who emerged from it were the sick men, the solitaries, the prophets – I mean all who have been deeply wounded in eros.' Would Cleopatra and Apollodorus be any different?

The wind dropped the following morning so we were able to cut round the back of the Island of Sheppey and out into Whitstable Bay. The actress made me promise to go to her London flat after delivering the yacht and continue the story.

Book 3

Alexandria; Laurence Durrell described the city as 'a thousand dust-tormented streets. Flies and beggars own it today – and those who enjoy an intermediate existence between either. Five races, five languages, a dozen creeds: five fleets turning through their greasy reflections behind the harbour bar.'

We were sat on the balcony of the actress's flat overlooking Saint Katherine's Yacht Haven by the Tower of London. The sound of halyards tapping against masts in the evening summer sunshine was in sharp contrast to the hustle and bustle of the City of London beyond. We were drinking honey mellowed wine (mead with retsina) and eating figs with flaky Egyptian bread.

Cleopatra and Apollodorus rounded the peninsular Cape Lochias; it looked like a giant lobster claw projecting into the sea. To their right was the Island of Pharos three quarters of a mile offshore and connected to the mainland by the Heptastadium causeway. This divided the port in two. They had entered the eastern 'Great Harbour' and to the west of the Heptastadium lay the 'Harbour of Good Return'.

The island of Pharos, three miles in length, was oblong and parallel to the mainland so it gave protection from the open sea and north winds. On this island was a giant granite and marble building, the lighthouse, Apollodorus estimated its height at some 260 cubits as it was visible for thirty miles offshore.

"That is about 130 metres or 423 feet. The Pharos lighthouse was not as tall as Telecom House in London but about the height of the London Eye."

"Over to the left in the lee of Cape Lochias is the private Royal Harbour, but there are submerged reefs. Also, Ptolemy's servants will be there so we had better head for Antirhodos Island to the right of Poseidium" advised Cleopatra.

"I take it that the peninsular is Poseidium. There is an opening between it and the island, why not go through there?"

"There is a reef between us and it, so it will be safer to sail round Antirhodos and come into the inner Royal Harbour to the south of the island.

Antirhodos is shaped like the letter *tau*; we are running in line with the top of the letter, due south" explained Cleopatra.

"What is the letter tau?" asked the actress.
"The Greek letter T."

"The *tau* upright runs east to west" carried on the first lady, "and the base of the letter points towards Poseidium. My principal palace is located on Antirhodos; Caesar has taken up residence there, according to my spies."

The sea was becoming very confused, like boiling water, due to the proximity of the reefs, Cleopatra and Apollodorus were having a bumpy ride.

"Presumably most captains arriving after dark stay offshore and come in at daybreak?" commented Apollodorus.

"Yes, this is the first time I have known anyone attempt the entrance at night time under these conditions."

"Now you tell me. Well at least no one will be looking out for us."

"You do boast to do the impossible right away" replied Cleopatra with a mischievous grin.

"Yes. Now here comes the miracle, smuggling you into old baldy without getting caught. I should like to have moored in the outer harbour so we could make a quick getaway if things go wrong but the water is too rough, Mintaka would be smashed to pieces against the jetty. If we pull this off it will certainly be a story to tell your children. I just hope whichever god you worship is a royalist and a feminist."

"Isis, the Mother Goddess, is my patron she will protect us" was the confident reply.

They rounded the top of the letter *tau* which formed the island of Antirhodos and found the narrow entrance to the Inner Royal Harbour.

"Keep close to the island" warned Cleopatra "there is a wreck to our right." The wind dropped and the water was calm in the harbour. Apollodorus dropped the sail and jumped ashore then made fast the boat, expertly, under Cleopatra's critical eye. "You handle this boat like it is an extension of yourself" she complemented him when he was back on board.

"Thank you. Let's get you gift wrapped and on our way to meet Jules before anyone sees us" he replied. "You will have to direct me as I explain what I see. If old baldy isn't pleased to see you after all this, I shall kick him in the toga and throw him to the crocodiles myself."

"Lions" corrected Cleopatra with a smile "Romans use lions to administer capital punishment. The Ptolemys' cut their prisoner's heads off, by the way."

"Thanks for sharing that with me" replied Apollodorus as he lifted Cleopatra on his shoulder and made his way towards the palace entrance. "So if we incur Caesar's displeasure we become a new line in cat food and if that brat of a brother of yours catches us, we get our heads cut off. It's at times like this I really wish I had listened to what my tutor said."

"Why, what did he say?" was the muffled reply from under the bed roll.

"How should I know, I wasn't listening? It was probably something frightfully useful like 'don't walk through an island palace full of enemies with a royal lady wrapped in a bed roll over your shoulder in the dead of night unless you want to be beheaded and fed to the crocodiles having first been gratuitously tortured'."

"Lions, how many more times, Romans feed prisoners to the fornicating lions" hissed the *Bassilisa*.

"Well what ever we end up being fed to I just hope we give it chronic indigestion."

Apollodorus walked confidently up to the palace guard and fixed him with a hypnotic stare. "I have a present for Caesar from Her Royal Highness Cleopatra, you need not concern yourself" he said. The guard stepped aside without argument and Apollodorus walked on. He gradually became aware of a shaking inside the bed roll, Cleopatra was giggling. She was doing her best to laugh silently but the effect was contagious. Apollodorus bit his lip and screwed up his face but to no avail. Soon the tears were running down his cheeks, his shaking only acted to reinforce Cleopatra's laughter.

"There is a cleaning cupboard at the end of the corridor on the left, lets hide in there for a moment" she whispered. "I need some air."

Gratefully, Apollodorus put Cleopatra down inside the cupboard, shut the door and moved the bedding from her face. Looking at each other made them laugh all the more till their sides ached. He tried to look stern.

"Look, if you're not going to take this seriously I am going back to the boat" he scolded. It had the reverse effect, Cleopatra laughed all the more.

"Stop it; you will smudge my eye make up."

"Typical of a woman! Here we are up to our eyes in crocodiles, lions and beheadings to say nothing of violent Romans, homicidal Ptolemy's and Gabinians, all screaming for vengeance, and all you are worried about is your mascara."

"Well a girl's got to look her best if she is going to seduce the most powerful man in the world even if he is old and bald" replied Cleopatra coyly. "I just hope he isn't fat, I can't abide fat men."

"Wasn't *Auletes* fat?"

"Yes, but he was a Ptolemy. They are supposed to be fat. It is a sign of good living and shows their devotion to Dionysus. Euergetes II was the fattest, he was hugely overweight, and this showed a proud devotion to hedonistic not practical pursuits. They nicknamed him *Physon*, pot belly or fatty, for a good and obvious reason; he could hardly move he was so large."

"So if our Jules has become rotund in the springtime of his senility, it really will be plan *beta*. 'Sorry *Physon*, stuff your special relationship. Cleopatra only goes for the athletic look.' Don't you think it would have saved a lot of trouble if your spy had found out details like his toga size?"

"Togas only come in one size" quipped Cleopatra.

When at last they became serious she gave him directions to where she believed Caesar to be staying. Apollodorus opened the door slightly and having seen it was safe lifted Cleopatra back onto his shoulder. They continued on their way to the historic meeting with the most powerful man in the world.

Gaius Julius Caesar sat alone in his commandeered bed chamber, a large ornate room overlooking the Great Harbour. The view from the windows was dominated by the lighthouse. Like many great political leaders before and since, he ate and drank in moderation. This meant he needed little sleep, so habitually worked late into the night. The advantage of this was that he could work without interruption; it caused him some annoyance, therefore, when there was a discreet tap on the door.

"Come!" he snapped sharply.

The door opened and an anxious guard informed him that a messenger had brought him a gift from Cleopatra. Apollodorus marched in confidently with the bed roll on his shoulder, turned to the guard and said.

"That is all, you may leave us now." The confused guard left. Apollodorus carefully laid the roll on the floor, cut the cords that secured it and unrolled the young woman inside.

"Noble Caesar, may I present Cleopatra Thea Philopater, *Bassilisa* of the Upper and Lower Realms." He attempted to help Cleopatra to her feet; unfortunately, she was barely conscious and breathing with difficulty.

"Thea" he hissed "are you all right? Now is your big moment, say something."

All she could manage was a gasp. Apollodorus looked alarmed and turning to an astonished Caesar said "Don't just stand there get her a drink of water or something!" He fanned the first lady with part of the bed roll.

The look on Caesar's face changed from one of astonishment to one of thunder, his eyes were black and piercing. "What is the meaning of this? Who is this woman?" he shouted.

"I just told you, she is the first lady, Cleopatra VII."

"I don't believe you; Cleopatra is at Askalon, not here in Alexandria."

"Thea, for the sake of all you hold to be holy, say something." To Caesar he shouted. "Look, you pompous Roman, she is definitely Cleopatra. We haven't braved storms and pestilence, to say nothing of the 'Gabinians', in a small boat all the way from Askalon, only to be thrown to the crocodiles because you can't remember what the *Bassilisa* looks like!"

"Lions" croaked Cleopatra. At that moment a young man with curly black hair and a full beard burst in. Like the shipwright he was well above average height and very muscular. Apollodorus was not alone in thinking that this giant of a man bore a striking resemblance to the statues of Hercules.

"What's going, on Dominus?" he exclaimed. "The guards said a strange man had bewitched them and was making his way to you with a package. We think he may be an assassin."

"Your timing is impeccable, Antonius" replied Caesar, gesturing towards Apollodorus and Cleopatra on the floor.

"How nice to see you again, your Highness" said the centurion with a boyish grin. Caesar's expression changed to one of amazement.

"So you really are Cleopatra! Quick, Antonius, help Her Highness to a kline." Antony and Apollodorus carried Cleopatra to the couch; Caesar poured a goblet of peach coloured rose' wine and offered it to her. "I am sorry I only have Falernum." She accepted it gratefully and the colour started to return to her cheeks.

"Thank you, it is much better than the mule's urine that Apollodorus serves on his boat. I am sorry I could hardly breathe in that bed roll and nearly passed out."

"Next time I take you sailing you can bring your own wine, you ungrateful Lady of Two Lands."

"Yes, and you can be wrapped in the bed roll! No, I am only kidding, I enjoyed your wine really 'Pollo" she turned to Caesar and continued. "Noble Caesar, you wanted to see me. It was Apollodorus who devised the subterfuge that enabled me to get safely past my brothers army at Mount Cusino."

"So you really have sailed all the way from Askalon. Was that you in the unusual boat I saw coming in a short while ago? I thought the people mad or very brave coming in after dark in these conditions."

"That was us" said Apollodorus with pride "no one was supposed to see. I think we must be insane coming all this way in a small boat and no guards. You know how it is Jules; a desperate situation demands desperate measures. Its O.K if I call you Jules, isn't it?" The shipwright placed an affectionate arm around the Roman's shoulder and guided him across the room. "Now I hope you are pleased to see us, Jules, what with us leaving the royal guards behind. Her Royal Highness here was hoping to form an alliance, a special relationship, with you and Rome."

"Silence!" roared Caesar "no one calls me Jules."

"Why not?" replied Apollodorus making an exaggerated jump away from Caesar. "It's a nice name, I was thinking, with the Roman calendar being all wrong and seasons not being where they should be due to the calculations for the length of time it takes for the Earth to go round the sun or the sun to go round the Earth, whichever astronomical viewpoint you subscribe to, are wrong. You could commission a study and whack in an extra month to bring everything in line and call that month Jules."

"Shut up, 'Pollo! Do you want to get us thrown to the crocodiles?" hissed Cleopatra, who was recovering her composure.

"Lions" replied the nervous shipwright.

Caesar turned to Cleopatra "Does he always babble on like this?"

"Not always, generally his discourse makes considerable sense; I think he is suffering from stress and lack of sleep. The familiarity you get used to, he puts it down to being a republican, a political view point which you respect" replied Cleopatra with a smile. Caesar noticed Cleopatra's eyes and was transfixed by their colour; he then looked down at her breasts. Roman women did not display their bodies proudly like Greek and Egyptian women did. He dragged his eyes back to Apollodorus.

"You babble like a mad man, and then you come out with a simple solution to a problem that has vexed the best minds of Rome for years. You are familiar in your speech and you perform a feat of seamanship that would make Neptune proud. Your loyalty to the *Bassilisa* is self evident and you show great courage. You annoy me intensely yet I find myself liking you! What is your name?"

"Apollodorus, my friends call me 'Pollo."

"That is an Achaean name. You are not from there you are from the north, Gaul? No, you are from Al'bion." Caesar looked uncomfortable but carried on. "From the way you banter, if you play the pipes I would wager you were Pan incarnate. Do you call him the Jester by any chance, your Highness? I know Alexandrians love nicknames."

"No, but I will from now on" replied Cleopatra with a wicked smile. She was recovering her humour along with her composure then turning to Mark Antony exclaimed. "I remember you; it was you who was so sweet when *Pater* got so horribly drunk at the banquet in honour of his restoration. You were understanding and said that you also had Dionysus as patron. You helped me get Pater to bed."

"That creed is only an excuse for some very un-seasonal quaffing and feasting" muttered Caesar. Antony looked hurt but said nothing.

Cleopatra had now fully recovered and got up from the couch. "Noble Caesar, Apollodorus speaks the truth when he says we have placed our lives in great danger to come to you. He may jest but I am fearful for both our lives." She touched Caesar gently on the shoulder then sank to her knees dramatically, bowing her head. "I place myself in your protection, apart from 'Pollo there is no one to take care of me."

Caesar could only splutter. Mark Antony rushed forward and helped Cleopatra to her feet. "Of course we will protect you, your Highness. I would lay down my life for you."

Apollodorus smiled to himself and thought "Brilliant Thea! You will soon have them both eating out of your hand."

Caesar stepped forward and took Cleopatra's hand "I must apologise for not recognising you, your Highness; you were only a girl when we last met." His eyes were involuntarily drawn to her naked breasts causing her nipples to harden.

Caesar looked down with an effort but this only made matters worse as he found himself looking at her mount of Venus which was clearly visible through the translucent fabric of her dress. Alexandrian women considered the only appropriate place for hair was on their heads and took great trouble to remove all other traces; Cleopatra was no exception to this fashion, she looked down at her breasts then into Caesar's eyes and smiled.

At that moment other centurions entered but Mark Antony dismissed them abruptly. "Everything is in order men, but stay on guard outside, we do not wish to be disturbed" he ordered. Cleopatra was grateful, she was enjoying the attention but a girl can have too much of a good thing.

"Sit beside me Noble Caesar and tell me if you are enjoying Alexandria. You are not seeing my metropolis at her at her best with all the fighting and civil war. May I pour you a goblet of this fine wine?" turning to the other two men "I am sure Apollodorus and Marcus Antonius would like a drink?"

Antony nodded and Apollodorus muttered by way of reply "is Dionysus a hedonist." The first lady served then all with the wine and returned to Caesar's side. Apollodorus resisted the temptation to drain the goblet in one gulp.

"What is your relationship with Apollodorus, your Highness?" asked Caesar.

"You must call me Cleopatra. You are a republican and don't believe in royalty, also its so much more friendly. It is 'Pollo, or rather his boatyard, that is repairing my royal Thalamegos. He made me ask him nicely and invite him to dinner before he would agree to the commission; however, we have become good friends. He is an excellent shipwright and an outstanding seaman; in the short time I have known him I have to come to value his council. I hope to persuade him to stay here in Alexandria."

"I have no ties with the boatyard in Askalon. I only won it in a game of chance."

"I had better not dice against you!" replied Caesar with a smile.

"It was not dice but a drinking match" he replied. Mark Antony was all ears. "When the repairs to the Royal Thalamegos are complete I shall give the yard back to the owner, he should have regained consciousness by then. I should love to stay in Alexandria if you can find me gainful employment; *Bassilisa's Gelotopoios* has a certain ring." He smiled at Cleopatra and added. "This is no place for a humble seaman. You and Caesar have to discuss matters of state. If you will excuse me I should like to return to my boat and make certain her moorings are secure."

Mark Antony took the hint and added "I should like to join you 'Pollo and hear more of your drinking games."

"I should appreciate your company." when they were outside in the corridor he added "Can we borrow some of your guards? I shall explain why when we get aboard."

When the two men were on board 'Mintaka' and they had a goblet of honey mellowed wine in front of them Apollodorus explained about the treasury that Cleopatra had insisted on bringing with them, only to completely forget on arrival in Alexandria.

"So that's why you were so anxious to leave. Her Highness chooses her friends wisely" commented Antony as he took a deep draught from his goblet and nearly choked. "I see you are a fellow bibber, Apollodorus and don't mix water with your wine."

"I know that in Roman society it is considered vulgar but my view point water is for washing and cooking, wine is for making glad the hearts of man."

"So to play the part of Cleopatra I will have to show off an awful lot of myself?"

"Theda Bara's costumes were reputedly skimpy to a 'T' and the film, which opened on 14th October 1917, being so successfully that Theda was cheered and pelted with flowers at the end of the premier. Sadly there are no surviving copies; we can only imagine how good the film was. Our attitudes are shaped by our Christian culture. Much of Christianity has its roots in Egyptian culture, not Judaism. Some are a reaction to Greco Egyptian theology, our attitudes on nudity being a case in point. You will see how Christianity copied the Egyptian bits it liked and reacted to those it didn't."

"So this story has parallels in the politics of today as well as giving insight into our religion and culture. I had better put the kettle on. I bought some Assam tea specially; no doubt you need a cuppa?"

"Is the Pope a Catholic?"

"Or Dionysus a hedonist?" replied the actress as she plugged in the kettle.

"Cleopatra didn't always dress in that manner, certainly not in Rome where she followed the local customs and fashion."

"Bassilisa's Gelotopoios what is that?"

"Jester to the first lady, Apollodorus' official title for himself. The Egyptians were fastidiously clean, they bathed four times a day, both men and women removed all body hair to prevent lice and they were the first people to practice circumcision."

"I thought circumcision was a Jewish custom."

"Moses was brought up as an Egyptian prince, other nations learned the practice from the Egyptians who performed the operation for reasons of cleanliness not religion."

"Al'bion, is that the Latin name for England?"

"The name is derived from albus being Latin for white as in the 'White Cliffs of Dover' these cliffs are visible from the west coast of France on a clear day."

Dawn flung out her golden mantle across Alexandria and the wind that had hastened passage from Askalon and endangered their arrival veered from the north east. There was now a gentle breeze from the west and the Great Harbour was deep blue and as smooth as glass. The cloudless sky was also a deep Mediterranean blue so the early morning sunshine glistened on marble buildings of the metropolis, dazzling Apollodorus as he took in the scene. He was as captivated by the city's charm and found its presence as irresistible as that of its principal citizen.

Mark Antony had left earlier but there were a small detachment of guards nearby. Cleopatra arrived dressed in a clinging sheath like dress which lacked the diaphanous quality of the one worn the previous day. The tight ringlets had been combed out leaving her golden hair with a natural wave which glistened in the sunshine.

"Where did you get to last night?" she scolded him as she came aboard.

"I was looking at your marvellous metropolis thinking I must have died and I am in paradise then the goddess of Alexandria arrived, so I must be in heaven."

"Well I feel sore and used like a prostitute so we must still be alive" she replied with venom.

"I am sorry, it must have been awful for you, but I suddenly remembered all your money on board 'Mintaka' so came back to stand guard."

"Oh Zeus!" exclaimed the young woman "I had completely forgotten about the treasury. I am sorry 'Pollo, I was feeling cross and dirty, Charmain and Iras are schoenus away so there was no one to do my hair or makeup. Then you make me feel much better with the nice things you say."

"What, guarding your money?"

"No, you idiot, about Alexandria being heaven and I its goddess."

"You hair looks like spun gold and your eyes like emeralds so you look lovely to me. How did it go with old baldy? Do you want to tell me about it, Thea?"

"Yes, but there isn't time now. We must get the treasury into a safe place. Caesar has ordered a cessation of all hostilities; Ptolemy and I are to present out cases to him personally so we must hurry. Are those centurions to be trusted?"

"Marcus Antonius thinks so but I have my doubts however as my old tutor always used to say; if you get fussy you go without!"

"It's comforting to know that you did occasionally listen to the poor man" replied the Bassilisa with a smile.

Later that morning in the palace throne room, Cleopatra sat on one throne, Caesar on the other, there being no other seats available. The thirteen year old Ptolemy entered with his entourage, Pothinus the eunuch nurse, Theodotus his tutor and Achilles commander of the household guard. The boy first looked at his sister in horror then saw Caesar on the other throne.

From his vantage point next to Cleopatra it was hard for Apollodorus to decide which caused the greater annoyance to the young Pharaoh, the lack of an available throne or the amiable way his sister was talking to the Roman. The description of Pothinus by Cleopatra as a pompous tart was accurate.

"It looks like your brother would like to throw all of us to the crocodiles" whispered Apollodorus to Cleopatra. "I think we are in for an entertaining morning."

"Ah, Ptolemy, how nice to see you" said Caesar "as you know, I and the people of Rome have made a solemn promise to your late Pater to uphold the terms of his will. It was his wish that Egypt should be jointly ruled by his oldest surviving children, one male one female. That is, unless I am very much mistaken, you and your sister Cleopatra here."

At this point the boy screamed that he would not share the realm with Cleopatra and ran out of the palace. He could not go far as they were on the Antirhodos Island and the bridge to the mainland was raised. Caesar gave Cleopatra a long suffering look; she smiled sweetly to the Roman.

"Crocodiles are too good for him" whispered Apollodorus "haven't you a younger brother? An heir and a spare is the usual royal philosophy."

After a short while Caesar ordered a detachment of Centurions to bring the young Pharaoh back. Cleopatra turned to Caesar and said.

"Pothinus will have spread rumours around Alexandria that you want me as sole ruler because I am pro Rome. Unless you do something to quash these stories there will be rioting."

"I know. When we have your brother under control I intend to address the crowd on the mainland. I have an announcement that will soften them, don't worry."

A large crowd had collected at the end of the Street of the Soma and were spreading along the harbour front overlooking the Antirhodos Island. Word of Cleopatra's return spread rapidly and more people joined the crowd by the Royal Harbour. Caesar's ten warships were anchored in the Inner Royal Harbour and most of his three thousand two hundred infantry were billeted on the mainland. These had been ordered to the harbour to maintain order.

Caesar strolled between the granite columns and down the palace steps onto a limestone paved area bathed in summer sunshine. The Roman walked along the southern top arm of the letter tau that formed Antirodos towards the eastern Royal Harbour entrance. He came alongside the marble statue of Hermes at the end of the southern leg and from this vantage point he could address the people on the mainland. All eyes of Alexandria were on him. A retinue of centurions formed an impromptu guard of honour. The infantry on the mainland came to attention and silence descended on the expectant crowd.

"People of Alexandria" Caesar began "the Senate and People of Rome are your friends; we come as upholders of the law not as an army of occupation. Ptolemy Neos Dionysus, known affectionately as *Aulutes*, charged the people of Rome with the solemn task of trustee to his last will. It was his wish that Egypt should be governed jointly by his eldest surviving son and daughter; Ptolemy and Cleopatra are reconciled to each other and to their Pater's wishes. To celebrate this there will be feasting and a public holiday. In addition Cyprus will return to Egyptian rule." He paused for the thunderous applause encouraged by his infantry.

"Cyprus will be governed jointly by Ptolemy's younger brother Ptolemy X1V and his sister Arsinoe."

"They were not dispatched to their new realm straight away as Caesar, very wisely, wanted to keep an eye on them. Cleopatra's eighteen year old sister Arsinoe was a competent adult but her eleven year old brother Ptolemy XIV was only a child and easily manipulated."

Later, back in the palace Caesar, Cleopatra and Apollodorus were talking informally.

"I hope you don't mind my saying so Domini, but it's not surprising your hair is thinning. You must tear it out over the Ptolemy's and their squabbling siblings, present company excluded, of course."

Caesar looked cross. He was rather sensitive about his receding hair line but he found Cleopatra's laughter infectious. She chuckled in low and musical way so it was hard for him not to join in. With a reluctant smile he replied.

"If you can't curb your 'Jester' unruly tongue, your highness, I will be forced to make use him in the Roman Circus as lion food!"

"I am better at making jokes than saying serious things but I did want to express my heartfelt regrets as to the treatment of Pompeius. He was a worthy rival to you and deserved a more heroic death."

Caesar looked surprised and was genuinely moved. "Thank you Apollodorus. Ptolemy was either swayed by fear that Pompeius might seize Alexandria and Egypt, or from contempt of him in his misfortune as it is usually the case that friends become enemies in adversity."

"Have you been able to recover his body and give him an honourable funeral?" inquired Cleopatra softly.

Caesar nodded "And his murderers will be punished" he whispered.

Apollodorus was up at daybreak the next day; he crossed over to the mainland and strolled along the water front towards the Heptastadium causeway. This artificial causeway was about 2600 cubits long (1300 metres) connected the Pharos Island to the mainland and divided the bay into two harbours. To the east was the principle 'Great Harbour' and to the west 'Eunostos' or 'Harbour of Good Return'. There was a lifting bridge at each end of the causeway enabling ships to pass from one harbour to the other. On the eastern tip of the island Apollodorus could see lighthouse.

"Wasn't the Pharos lighthouse one of the seven wonders of the ancient world?" asked the actress.

"Yes, the lighthouse on Pharos had been built in the reign of Ptolemy Philadelphas but commissioned by his father Ptolemy 1 it was a marvel of both science and beauty."

The shipwright marvelled at the design of the lighthouse which, unknown to him, followed the principal of Euclidian Geometry. The base was square with many windows; Apollodorus estimated that there were about three hundred rooms to accommodate the mechanics and technicians who operated the light. The shipwright later learned that there was a double spiral accent through the centre of the building and a hydraulic mechanism to lift fuel to the fire at the top. A cornice was decorated with tritons and there were inscriptions in Greek dedicating the Pharos to the saviour gods of mariners, Castor and Pollux. The octagonal mid section and circular top supported the mechanism of mirrors made from polished metal that reflected the sun by day and a fire by night. There was a lens to identify ships at a distance too far to be visible to the naked eye. The Alexandrian scientists understood the principle of optics. On the top was a huge statue of the god Zeus.

A canal entered the sea from Eunostos by the dockyard in the Cibolus Harbour near the south western end of the Heptastadium causeway. The harbour, home for the Egyptian navy, and adjacent warehouses were of special interest to Apollodorus. The shipwright followed the waterway south past the western entrance to the metropolis known as the Gate of the Moon. To his right had side was a curved city wall. A system of canals effectively surrounded the city providing water, sanitation and transportation. This was also a secondary line of defence inside the city wall. One waterway joined the Nile due east of the metropolis. Another canal branched off north to emerge in the palace area known as the Basillea between the Poseidium and Cape Lochias, the lobster claw peninsular rounded by Apollodorus and Cleopatra the previous evening on the way into the Great Harbour. Apollodorus retraced his steps to the Gate of the Moon then made his way along the wide, principal thoroughfare. This roadway was sixty cubits wide *(thirty meters or one hundred feet)* and lined with colonnades. Half way along Canopic street at the cross road with the street of the Soma was the tomb of the city founder, Alexander the Great. Beyond this crossroad was the second of three entrances to the metropolis, the Gate of the Sun. The third entrance was at the southern end of the street of the Soma and gave access to the lake Mareotis harbour.

"So Canopic street mimicked the subterranean passage taken by the sun each night from the Beautiful West"

"Yes, the Alexandrian theology was all around them. The eastern canal which ran outside the eastern city wall came inside that boundary near the Gate of the Sun. The Street of Soma ran south from the Royal Harbour to the Lake Harbour on Lake Mareotis. The grid system of streets was laid out so the prevailing winds which came in one of two main directions cooled the city in summer."

"Very ingenious."

"The southern city wall ran along the banks of the lake except where the western canal emerged and round the Lake Harbour. At the crossing of

Canopic Street and the Street of Soma to the south east was Alexander the Great's tomb, The Soms. The priests at Memphis had refused to inter him in Egypt's religious capital so he was buried in the city that bore his name. Alexandria was beautiful, practical and nearly impregnable."

Apollodorus made his way north along The Street of Soma towards the palace on Antirhodos in deep and troubled contemplation. The fleet of seventy two warships were unguarded and could easily be taken by the invading Gabinians if they gained access to that side of the metropolis. But more importantly were the scrolls he had seen in the warehouse. These documents were awaiting translation and would challenge the Egyptian scholars for some time as the script was unknown to them. The language was known to the shipwright and it came from a strange land he had lived in far to the east of Alexandria.

In his mind Apollodorus travelled back to that land and a room he had known so well in another lifetime. The soft sunlight was streaming through the gaps in the bamboo blinds. On the walls were exquisite hangings depicting ferocious dragons and beautiful flowers. Through the open door Apollodorus could see small maple bushes with elegant leaves of red, green and silver. There was a cool gentle breeze and in the background the chuckle of running water. An ancient man with skin like parchment knelt opposite him. This was one tutor he had in-fact listened to intently.

"Knowledge is power my young apprentice, but there is some knowledge that is far too dangerous to share with anyone."

"Is there something you have not told me master?" replied the shipwright.

"All that I know I have freely given you and the elders considered me insane but I trust you. Do not disappoint me my White Ghost!"

As Apollodorus crossed over the water to the island palace on Antirhodos numbing chill invaded his body as he realised the implications of his discoveries but he knew what must be done. Betrayal was betrayal no matter how honourable the motive.

.

Book 4

As the sun set over Eunostos and a party atmosphere descended on Alexandria. It was at the eastern tip of Antirhodos, the base of the letter *tau*, that Cleopatra found Apollodorus studying one of the twin Sphinx that guarded the palace temple.

"You are looking very serious, 'Pollo, what troubles you?" she asked lightly touching his arm.

"I was thinking this Sphinx looks remarkably like your *Pater*. Was that intended?" he replied.

"I know you better than that! In fact I don't think I have ever seen you look so serious. What is the matter, please tell me?" she pleaded.

"Look at that sunset!"

"It's beautiful" replied Cleopatra.

"In my culture a red sky is a bad omen which means blood will be spilt; there will be battle" he replied softly "we may yet be fed to the crocodiles."

"Lions" corrected Cleopatra with a smile.

"I am being serious for a change. I have been exploring the docks over in Eunostos by the Gate of the Moon. There are seventy two war ships there. Did you know you had so many?"

"I can't say I have ever counted them" replied Cleopatra lightly "I was hoping you would take charge of their operation and maintenance. Would you like that, 'Pollo?"

"I should be honoured to take charge of your Navy, but even I can't sail seventy two ships."

"Well, we will have no problem obtaining suitable manpower Egyptians spend much of their lives on the water."

"The problem is, Thea, your brother has twenty thousand infantry and some two thousand cavalry, mostly Gabinians at his disposal. Caesar has just over three thousand infantry, eight hundred cavalry and ten warships. If Ptolemy were to invade and take control of the Egyptian ships, Caesar will be hopelessly outnumbered."

"Caesar says only the Romans are true warriors, no one else can fight."

"I know what he thinks, but unfortunately it isn't true. From his experiences in northern Europe he should have learned that whoever rules the waves rules the world. His first attempt to invade my country almost resulted in his annihilation. He tried again a year later and got as far as the principal river and marshes then had to turn back. My people are far better seaman than the Romans, it's not the sort of thing he likes to be reminded about and I have no wish to become lion food. As you have already stated, Egyptians, like the people Britannia, spend a great deal of their time on the water. Gabinians are Roman veterans, Jules is facing an enemy fully conversant with his military tactics I just hope he has reinforcements on the way. Also, we are going to have to do something about your Thalamegos, the rest of the treasury, not to mention Olympos, Charmain and Iras. I was thinking that I could sneak across the Nile delta by land and bring them back. Caesar wouldn't be able to spare any troops to help, plus it's better if he remains ignorant about your money."

"I don't like the idea of you risking your life going across country to Askalon; remember the twenty thousand infantry and two thousand cavalry at Mount Cusino. With hordes of Gabinians all armed to the teeth and screaming for vengeance because of the way you humiliated them by smuggled me back to Alexandria, why not enlist Caesar's help in recovering the rest of the treasury? Your reputation for heroics is assured with me; please don't take any more risks."

"Protection costs money, generally a percentage. Our Jules' middle name is percentage, he calls it taxation. I would rather give him a percentage of half your money, not all of it. A decade ago following his organising the games at Circus Maximus he owed 700 gold talents; bankruptcy would have ended his political career. He was bailed out by being appointed Pontifex Maximus, high priest, a surprising career move for someone even more theologically challenged than you're recently appointed Sea Lord. Necessity makes for strange bed fellows; Caesar has always been motivated by a massive need for money as well as power."

"It is funny that you should say that, but Caesar lent money to Rabirius, who in turn financed *Alutus*, my *Pater* in Rome. He now wants me to me to repay this debt as he needs the money to prosecute his war in Africa."

Apollodorus thought bitterly; "You have had to pay for your basileio with your money as well as your maidenhead." Out loud he commented; "So you have had to finance for your Pater's law proclaiming him Rex by the Roman Senate? More importantly when the dust settles and Jules leaves Alexandria, you have got to restore Egypt's prosperity."

"I could raise taxes."

"That would be the worst thing to do. The higher the taxes, the harder people try to avoid paying them. Lowering the taxes means the people are more likely to pay, they don't feel cheated so they are less inclined to cheat. Lower taxation means more money in circulation, which in turn is re-invested resulting in greater prosperity and a boost to your popularity. In the long term this means more revenue for you."

"I think I will appoint you Chancellor of the Exchequer not Sea Lord with that kind of logic. I was planning taking Jules on a grand tour of the country. Perhaps it's not such a good idea after all."

"I think it's an excellent idea, just don't show him everything! We may have to fight a war first so don't make too many plans. The best way to see Egypt is from the river, so you will need a boat to take him up the Nile. There is much more to getting your *basileio* back than sailing round the coast from Askalon and military conquest is Caesar's forte; when the fighting stops the difficult part starts. That is going to be the battle for the hearts and minds of the people, only you can win that one with a little help and a lot of money. Your *Pater* nearly bankrupted Egypt buying Rome's approval and was profoundly unpopular with the masses as a result. I am sorry, I know you loved him. That legacy we have to reverse so you can live in peace not constant fear of assignation. Hungry people don't love their rulers."

The announcement that dinner was served stopped any further conspiratorial conversation. During the meal Cleopatra took the opportunity when Caesar was otherwise occupied to whisper to Apollodorus.

"Please don't chance crossing the Nile delta by land just to get my boat, money and friends back. They will come to no harm where they are. When things settle down in Alexandria I will send a message for them to return. The captain is quite capable of bringing them home when it can be done safely also Caesar is sending for reinforcements"

Apollodorus spent the next few days exploring Alexandria, but he remained uneasy about Cleopatra's Royal Thalamegos and the treasury on board. He was also concerned about Olympos and the two handmaidens Charmian and Iras. With a forthcoming war a physician would be invaluable. The *Bassilisa* was becoming unbearable having no one to attend to her cosmetic needs. In the end he resolved to make the journey but tell no one. By now, he reasoned, the repairs on the Thalamegos should be near completion and the Gabinians otherwise occupied with preparations for the invasion of Alexandria. As an honoured guest he could move freely about the Palaces so had no difficulty finding the royal mews and securing a suitable mount.

Apollodorus started out in the early morning. He left the city by the eastern 'Gate of the Sun' following Canopic Street through the Jewish

Quarter. His horse was an unremarkable animal, sturdy but anonymous. There was a thin low mist over the Nile delta signifying that summer was coming to an end. The trail left by the Gabinians hoards did not challenge his tracking skills which as a seaman were non existent, his equestrian skills were little better. Apollodorus reasoned that the troops would know far better than he the best cross country route but he would have to give their camp a wide berth. The countryside was low and flat, the only raised landmarks being the lighthouse and Mount Cusino. Apollodorus was not the only person making that journey; General Achillas was also making his way to the fortress at Pelusium with orders from Pothinus to bring the army back to Alexandria.

Cleopatra was torn between her initial disgust at having to sleep with a man old enough to be her father and the excitement of his power. Peace in Alexandria was fragile and with four royals who despised each other living in close proximity, the atmosphere in the palace became tense. The first lady did not miss Apollodorus for a day or two then on the second night she woke suddenly from a deep sleep and sat bolt upright in bed. When Caesar awoke shortly after, as a soldier he was a light sleeper, he found the young woman crying.

"What is it, amica?" he asked putting his arm around the distraught Cleopatra "did you have a bad dream?"

Apollodorus made good progress on the first day; the countryside was lush and fertile. He encountered agricultural workers dressed in brightly coloured clothing with grey water buffalo, their beasts of burden. Feathery date palms bowed under the weight of fruit provided some shade from the burning sun. The Delta had been the battleground of countless bitter conflicts so there were remains of numerous camps and abandoned settlements. To his left was a marshy transition from dry land into a chain of salt lakes running parallel to the coastline. Half way through the following day luck ran out for the shipwright. He had been on his guard for scouts from the army in front but it had not occurred to him that he was being followed by General Achillas, the one Alexandrian that would recognise him instantly! He had just forded one of the many minor rivers that made up the Nile delta when the General and his escort caught up. Realising the danger, Apollodorus quickly re-mounted but not quickly enough.

"That's the traitor who brought Cleopatra back. Catch him!" exclaimed Achillas. They still had to cross the ford so Apollodorus had a head start. At the next crossing General Achillas and his guards had almost caught up. Apollodorus drove his horse straight into the river which was much deeper than the previous one. The horse lost its footing and fell sideways into the water. This action threw Apollodorus clear which meant that the pursuer's lance which would have killed him only caused a flesh wound and the current swept him down stream.

"Don't bother to follow him" said the general "he is wounded, so the crocodiles will smell the blood and finish him off."

Back in the island palace, Caesar tried to comfort Cleopatra. When at last she calmed down, she said "It's Apollodorus. He has been missing for two days, something terrible has happened."

"Do you think he has got in a drunken fight somewhere because of his jokes and leg pulling? It was only a matter of time before someone took offence."

"No, this is serious. In my dream I saw him on the side of a river in the middle of nowhere, and he was injured. Oh no, I know what he is doing. He has gone back to Askalon across the delta by land."

"Why would he do that?" asked Caesar. "I thought he liked Alexandria."

Cleopatra had regained her composure and realised she must be careful what she told the Roman. "He has gone to collect my Royal Thalamegos."

"Why? There are plenty of ships for him here. I thought you were going to put him in charge of your navy?"

"My friend Olympos, the physician also Charmian and Iras, my handmaids, are there. I have been complaining about there being no one to do my hair and makeup. Apollodorus offered to bring my boat and friends back but I forbade him. Also he wanted to know what the Gabinians were doing."

"The Gabinians have never seen him. He should be able to travel through their camp un-molested" reassured Caesar.

"When was the last time you saw Achillas, commander of Ptolemy's household guard? Apollodorus is head and shoulders above the rest of us also his hair colour and skin tone make him stand out from a crowd along with his stature. The one person, who would not only recognise him but would also like him out of the way, is missing." This last comment galvanised the Roman into action, Caesar remembered all too clearly how the Britannians had taunted his troops about their height. He summonsed

Mark Antony and the rest of his staff officers. Dawn had risen from the bed where she slept with her consort Tithonus bringing light to both immortal gods and mortal men. Zeus flung Strife on to Ptolemy's Gabinian army; the brutal sister of Ares raised her high pitch battle cry filling each man's heart with fighting fury.

"You describe Dawn and Strife as living beings"
"To the ancients they were. Strife or Eris as she was sometimes known was the sister of Ares the god of war she was an entity or demon not a goddess. In cockney rhyming slang 'trouble and strife' means wife. Dawn was the daughter of the Titans, Hyperion and Theia, sister to the Sun and Moon. The sixteenth natural satellite or moon of the planet Saturn also bears her name."

The saline taste of the water confirmed to the shipwright his proximity to the sea. He realised that it was imperative that he reached dry land before he was swept into open water where there would be no protection from the burning heat of the sun. Weakened by the loss of blood Apollodorus had no choice but to allow the current to carry him away from the General to be eventually washed up onto a sand bank where he lapsed into unconsciousness.

"Apollodorus is from Al'bion so he is tough" said Caesar "we have seen how resourceful he is, I am sure he can look after himself." He was interrupted by the staff officers returning with the news that General Achillas was nowhere to be found. Shortly after, another aid came back with the news that Apollodorus had borrowed a horse from the royal mews and been last seen heading east through the 'Gate of the Sun'. "If Achillas is planning an invasion I cannot spare the troops to send out a search party. We must prepare for war."
"Well, if no one will help him, I shall make an offering to 'Sobek' the crocodile god so his people will leave poor 'Pollo unharmed" said Cleopatra as she stormed out of the meeting.
A little later Mark Antony found the Bassilisa in the palace temple. She had made her offering and was crying softly.
"I want to help you, your Highness. Tell me everything about your dream."
"Why? No one believes me that 'Pollo is in danger."
"Does the Jester have Dionysus as his patron?"

"He likes a drink but he is very anti-religion. Why? What relevance are his beliefs?"

"Caesar, privately, is far more of an atheist than Jocus but that doesn't stop him believing himself to be divine. Your Jester's beliefs are terribly important. You know I worship Dionysus; the mysteries of ecstatic transcendence are not to be shared with none believers so I must be careful what I tell you. The way Jocus bewitched the guards to smuggle you into the palace has all the hallmarks of a man highly adept in the rituals of the cult. He may be a druid. Caesar is secretly frightened of the people of Al'bion, particularly the druids."

"I thought it was his sense of humour he didn't like or he was jealous of our friendship, not that he was frightened he could change him into a frog. Why did I say that about changing Caesar into a frog? It's the sort of silly quip 'Pollo would make."

Mark Antony gave Cleopatra a knowing smile. "There is much more to your friend 'the Jester' than meets the eye, the druid apprenticeship is twenty years, their knowledge and wisdom is colossal. The way Apollodorus clowns around and makes silly quips is to disguise a formidable inelegance. That man is all seeing he misses nothing; I believe he has the ability to enter other people's minds. Possibly he is trying to tell you something. Empty your mind and tell me what you see."

Cleopatra had stopped crying and was now concentrating. "Apollodorus said that he left the Tin Island when he was little more than a child, had he been economical with the truth?" she thought, then got up suddenly and marched out of the temple.

"Where are you going, your Highness?"

"I know where he is. If you want to help, meet me at the royal mews between The Basillea and Cape Lochias. I have got to change my clothes."

"You are not planning riding out to rescue him?" said an astounded Mark Antony.

"Yes I am, with or without your help! You did promise to protect me, now is your chance! If you don't I shall tell 'Pollo to turn you into a frog when I find him!"

Mark Antony realised that there was no point arguing with the first lady who had clearly made up her mind, so a short while later they left on horseback through 'The Gate of the Sun' with three of Antony's most trusted centurions.

"Could Cleopatra ride a horse?" asked the actress.

"She was a superb horse woman, one of her many talents, Cleopatra was no airhead perhaps she spoke like one so people wouldn't realise how capable a person she really was. We had a Princess who used the same tactic and sadly also met with an untimely and highly suspicious end. Cleopatra was well educated; spoke several languages, including Egyptian, unlike her predecessors. She had a good knowledge of science, mathematics, astronomy and medicine. Cleopatra was artistic, musical, a good dancer, a superb horse woman and sailor. Additionally she had a sense of humour, with a keen eye for the absurd. All that and good looking, small wonder her enemies hated her!"

"You paint a very different picture to the one I know."

"Most of the stories about her were based on the accounts of Plutarch who visited Rome in the first century of Common Era. His account was derived from the historian Livius who was commissioned by Caesar Augustus and as such was little more than spin! Dio Cassius wrote his History of Rome about one hundred and fifty years after Cleopatra's death and drew heavily from Livius so he is pro Augustus. In other words, Shakespeare's plays 'Julius Caesar' and 'Anthony and Cleopatra' are at best a dramatisation of Plutarch 'Selected Lives', in reality little more than a translation from the original Latin text. What we accept as a true account of the Bassilisa's life is heavily influenced by the records of her enemies and for this and other reasons her character is ambiguous in the bard's play."

"So what you are saying is Caesar Augustus told Livius what to write, Plutarch and Dio Cassius believed this to be an accurate record and Shakespeare translated and dramatised 'Selected Lives'. Are there any surviving copies of Livius, Dio Cassius Roman History and Plutarch Selected Lives?"

"I don't think Livius account survives however The British Library has a copy of Dio Cassius and there is an English translation on the World Wide Web, Plutarch is available in paperback as a sixteenth century translation. Caesar's 'The Civil War' which includes his account of the Alexandrian War and the prequel, 'The Conquest of Gaul' are also pocket book classics."

"I take it that you have copies of all three."

"Naturally."

Cleopatra and her four Roman accomplishes were far better horse riders than Apollodorus, so they made much better progress than he had.

They arrived at the river crossing where he had been attacked by Achillas and found a lone lost horse.

"That looks like a palace horse. Look at the tack" exclaimed Cleopatra excitedly then added in disgust. "He could have chosen a better mount."

They caught the horse and examined it closely.

"If the Jester fell off he may have been taken down stream by the current" replied Mark Antony "but we had better check round here first." The Romans rode off in different directions a short distance but found no trace of Apollodorus. So they returned and all then proceeded down stream and soon found a javelin.

"These markings are Gabinian" said Cleopatra.

The seasoned soldiers recognised the fresh blood so they deduced that if Apollodorus had been attacked and fallen off the horse this may have been the weapon used. Cleopatra was convinced, Mark Antony and the other centurions less so. However, it was the only lead they had and the first lady insisted they follow it.

When Apollodorus regained consciousness he examined the injury to his leg where the javelin had hit him. It hadn't penetrated deeply so the injury was not life threatening. The bleeding had stopped, so he tried to walk. This was a mistake. A stabbing pain shot through his leg and the bleeding started again. The shipwright was accustomed to dealing with injuries so used part of his clothing as a bandage. He had just finished dressing the wound when he became aware he was not alone. A large reptile was slowly approaching him on short stumpy legs.

"Now I know how that pirate with a hook for a hand feels" he said to himself "I really wish I had listened to Thea. If I survive this I had better stop making jokes about being thrown to the crocodiles." Apollodorus slowly and painfully got to his feet and backed away from the reptile.

Cleopatra and her Roman escorts had travelled a little way down stream and were on the point of giving up.

"There is no sign of him down here" said Mark Antony "I think he may have been taken prisoner. We should carry on towards the Gabinians camp and try and intercept General Achillas before he gets there."

"Just a little further" pleaded Cleopatra "round the next bend in the river. There is a mound over there; let's take a look from that vantage point." They spurred their horses on and climbed the river bank. From the hillock they had a good view of the surrounding countryside. "Look! Over there on that sandbank!" Cleopatra had seen Apollodorus then she saw the crocodile and screamed frantically. Without thinking she galloped to where the shipwright was standing. The reptile, on hearing the horse approach, turned to face the danger. Cleopatra's mount, on seeing the crocodile, stopped abruptly throwing the young woman into the path of the beast. She instinctively rolled to counter the inertia of the fall. The soft sand absorbed most of the shock of the impact so only her pride was hurt.

"Don't move" shouted the shipwright. The crocodile looked from Apollodorus to Cleopatra and back to the shipwright with an expression of culinary indecision. Apollodorus backed away slowly holding the reptile's gaze. In the excitement he had forgotten his own injury but was now reminded as his leg gave way and he slumped to the ground. The crocodile was about to attack, but was distracted by Cleopatra's involuntary scream. The reptile turned towards the young woman, its tail lashed out catching Apollodorus injured leg as he was trying to stand and caused a stabbing pain that made him loose consciousness.

Back at the palace on Antirhodos Caesar strode the corridor like a caged animal.

"This is all I need. First that wise cracking shipwright goes missing now The *Bassilisa* and Marcus Antonius have gone looking for him. I really should have stayed in Gaul" he ranted to his lieutenant, Hirtius. "And what the hades are Ptolemy and his advisors up to? I swear I shall slit the throat of that slippery tart of a eunuch of his, what is his name?"

"Pothinus, Dominus."

"Yes, Pothinus, he is up to no good. He is supposed to be Ptolemy's nurse but I think he controls the Gabinian army."

"You have been hurt" exclaimed the first lady "let me have a look."

"It's nothing it is only a scratch" replied the shipwright as he regained consciousness. He looked around and saw Mark Antony and the centurions. The crocodile was in the last throws of death, with a javelin protruding from its mouth; blood was everywhere.

"I don't like to spoil this touching reunion" interrupted Mark Antony "but I really think we should move back onto higher ground. The blood of Sobok there will attract his buddies. Also I want to keep an eye out for the Gabinians. I thought I saw activity on the horizon." He carefully lifted the injured shipwright onto his re-captured horse and helped Cleopatra re mount hers, and then they made their way to the hillock. When they had all dismounted again, Cleopatra examined the shipwright's injury and the Romans surveyed Mount Cusino in the distance.

"The Gabinians must have seen us, there is a detachment heading this way" advised Mark Antony. "We had better get moving, your Highness."

"Pollo's wound is becoming infected, I think he will unable to grip the horse and gallop" she replied. Apollodorus struggled to his feet and saw the detachment moving slowly in their direction. The intricate network of waterways their enemy would have to cross should delay them then he looked out to sea and exclaimed excitedly. "That looks like your Thalamegos on the horizon, your Highness."

"So if we had a boat we could sail out to your Royal Barge and be rescued" replied Mark Antony sarcastically then added thoughtfully. "If we skin the crocodile could you build one of those funny round boats I have seen people use in Al'bion, Apollodorus?"

"There is neither the time nor the need" replied the shipwright. "I never go anywhere without a suitable hide to construct a coracle."

"What are you talking about 'Pollo" asked Cleopatra impatiently.

"Much of Britannia is covered with swamps and marshes, terrain similar to the island, so we build small boats from animal skins stretched over a light wooden framework. Skinning an animal each time you need an instant boat is as impractical as it is smelly so my people always travel with a hide that doubles for a shelter as it rains most of the time there." The shipwright looked around then shook his head sadly. "There is plenty of brushwood and reeds but no willow, the ground is too salty."

Cleopatra paced impatiently biting her bottom lip anxiously while Apollodorus was talking.

"Which in plane speak means?" she prompted.

"To construct the frame I need the type of timber used for an archers bow" he explained. "Are there protection vessels or customs launches stationed at the mouths of the Nile?" he asked.

Cleopatra nodded.

"And will they be undermanned due to all available troops having been transferred to Mount Cusino?"

Cleopatra nodded again then smiled. "Are you suggesting that we indulge in a little piracy Apollodorus?"

The shipwright smiled back at the *Bassilisa*. "Normally I wouldn't dream of taking a boat by force of arms but in light of the circumstances" he replied with an evil grin. "Technically it is your boat as you are *Bassilisa* so it would not be piracy it's commandeering for the good of the state. I think it would be as well to cross over to the other side of the river so the crocodiles will delay our pursuers and then make our way down stream to find what transport the fates have left for us. *Trierarchos* Hook will save the day!" He concluded as he mounted his horse awkwardly.

They had just forded the river and drawn level with the point where the crocodile had attacked when the enemy arrived. The Gabinians were unable to cross over as the bloody carcass had attracted other reptiles and they were forced to make a wide detour. The estuary widened and became a coastline but there were no boats to be commandeered.

"Your Thalamegos does not draw much water, your highness, and you said there are many sand banks. We should be able to ride out through the shallows and try to attract the attention of your sailors" suggested Apollodorus as he shifted himself awkwardly in the saddle, then pointing to lighter coloured water stretching like a giant finger out to sea added. "That looks like our road to freedom. You go on ahead and try to attract their attention; do you have a royal flag or some kind of insignia?"

"They must have seen the detachment from Mount Cusino pursuing us, so hopefully they will realise whose side we are on" replied Antony.

"I will elicit their undivided attention and leave them in no doubt as to our identity" announced Cleopatra fiercely as she galloped into the shallow water. She then unwound her silk veil liberating her golden hair and firm young breasts. "*Olulu! Olulu!*" she shouted as she swung her feet onto the back of her mound and stood up in one smooth movement. "*Olulu! Olulu!*" she cried again and waved her clothing franticly.

"She is quite a girl" commented Antony dryly as they followed at a more sedate pace.

"I think she has attracted the sailor's attention" replied Apollodorus. "Her Thalamegos is changing course."

Soon Cleopatra and the Romans were able to scramble aboard but Apollodorus was not so fortunate, weakened by the loss of blood he lost his footing, a searing pain shot once again through his leg and he slipped back into unconsciousness as the water engulfed him.

Caesar looked out of the palace window at the lighthouse and Hirtius continued, "why not despatch one of our Triremes war ships to Askalon to see what is going on? The surrounding countryside is relatively flat so from the mast head a lookout should be able to see a fair distance"

"It is out of the question, the easterly trade wind has trapped our fleet in the harbour" replied Caesar, the added thoughtfully. "We really need to take control of the lighthouse. From that height we will have a commanding view of both land and sea."

"There is only one way to gain access, sir, via the Heptastadium causeway, which is well guarded by hostile citizens."

Strong slim fingers gripped Apollodorus under the chin and he broke through the surface coughing and spluttering for breath.

"Just relax 'Pollo" said a soft, husky, melodic and utterly captivating female voice "and we will soon have you on board." Cleopatra steered the semi-conscious shipwright into a net that had been lowered into the water then he was hoisted unceremoniously aboard using a hastily rigged block and tackle from the main yard arm.

Olympos was delighted to see Cleopatra and explained "The repairs were completed more quickly than Apollodorus estimated. We heard that you had managed to form an alliance with Caesar, so thought it safe to return to Alexandria. What are you doing coming back this way?" The Bassilisa recounted all that had happened; Olympos listened enthralled and then said "I fear you are not out of danger, your Highness, we are being followed by some hostile war ships and they are gaining on us. We have few fighting men on board."

"Well, you have a few more now" replied Mark Antony fiercely.

Book 5

Night always falls quickly in the Mediterranean so dusk soon became night on the Royal Thalamegos. There was none of the peaceful tranquillity of the previous voyage. The pursuing Trireme warships had been visible on the horizon before nightfall and the wind had dropped so the vessels were being propelled by oars. Triremes had three levels of rowing positions with a man at each oar, and for this reason were described as threes. When cruising, the levels took turns to row, but in combat all three levels were deployed for extra speed and manoeuvrability. The Royal Thalamegos being much smaller only had one level of oars, as its name implied, so the crew could not easily take turns.

Apollodorus had been taken to the small shelter aft where Olympos changed the bandages.

"I don't like the look of him" he confided to Cleopatra when they were out of his hearing.

"He is from Britannia, you shouldn't be prejudiced about his appearance" she replied. "They all have wild reddish hair and blue eyes where he comes from."

"I was talking about the infection in his leg, I have cleaned it up but I think it is going septic and he has lost too much blood already to bleed him or use leaches."

They returned to where Apollodorus was resting, he was now clearly running a temperature and becoming feverish. Cleopatra helped him into a sitting position and the Doctor gave him a drink of water.

"Don't start getting ideas about amputation yet *to fiarokalo*, I may have a better idea" said Apollodorus.

"You were not supposed to hear what I was discussing with Her Royal Highness."

"I didn't, but from the look on your faces and the discomfort, I could make an educated guess. There is a mould that lives on bread and flour that sometimes cures infection in the most dramatic way. I don't know whether it is selective about the infection or difficult to find the right type of mould. Have you ever heard of its use, *to fiarokalo*?"

"No, but I take it you would rather I try it than use surgery, which is out of the question on a boat anyway. What does this mould taste like?"

"Disgusting, that's the third problem, keeping it down."

"So let me get this correct" said Cleopatra "we have to find a particular type of mould that may kill the infection that will probably kill you!"

"No, it won't kill me but it may make me puke all over your nice clean deck. I may behave like a pirate but I would rather not look like one stumping round on a wooden leg." The perspiration was now running off Apollodorus so Cleopatra bathed him with a wet cloth in an attempt to reduce the temperature. She had spoken lightly but felt far from happy when Olympos returned with a small bowl containing some grey green powder.

"You keep this boat too clean, your Highness, there is hardly any mould anywhere, this is all I could find. What shall I mix it with so you can drink it? Wine?"

"No, it doesn't mix with alcohol, use honey if there is any on board."

"Of course there is, I am a royal woman so I am supposed to suckle honey."

"I have often wondered how royals suckles honey" croaked Apollodorus with a weak smile.

Cleopatra looked down towards her breasts and smiled seductively at the shipwright "I may let you try when you are feeling stronger."

"Now that's what I call the way to take medicine."

They gave Apollodorus the mixture of mould and honey; he changed colour from red to green, shuddered violently, then changed back to red but was not sick. A short while later he was soundly asleep in Cleopatra's arms. He woke around midnight so Olympos gave him some more of the mixture and he drifted off to sleep again.

"What do you think?" asked Cleopatra when Olympos had finished changing the dressing.

"That mould is nothing short of miraculous. It has stopped the infection in its tracks and his temperature is coming down. I would not have believed it if I hadn't seen it myself. The sleep I think is self induced by the way. I wonder what sort of miracle he will come up with about the pursuing warships?"

"Olympos, I think you are beginning to like my noble Jester. Antonius was saying that the Druid apprenticeship is two decades and their wisdom formidable."

The doctor nodded thoughtfully. "*Gelotopois*. Is that what you call him?"

"Caesar nicknamed him Jocus which is Latin for jester but I think the Greek equivalent, *Gelotopois*, suits him don't you? I like the way he calls you *to fiarokolo*, Bones."

"I have my doubts about the Alexandrian custom of giving everyone nicknames but I have come to respect Apollodorus. *To fiarokolo* is a better name than Ollie, which was a possibility as he calls Julius Caesar, Jules."

The light house on Pharos was now clearly visible and from its light they could see that the warships were gaining on them.

Mark Antony had spent most of the voyage watching the pursuing fleet from the stern. He periodically moved forward to the bow encouraging the oarsmen on the way. As dawn began to break he joined the first lady and her friends in the cabin. He knew that it was only a matter of time before the Gabinians would be in grappling range so they would soon be fighting for their lives. The sight of the young woman cradling the sleeping shipwright in her arms filled him with jealousy. He dismissed the thought from his mind for he knew that Cleopatra was using Caesar as much as his master was using the first lady, but that was politics. Calpernia was Caesar's fourth wife, but he had had many girlfriends over the years.

"How is the invalid?" he asked, trying to sound casual.

"He will live" replied the doctor "if we escape the Gabinians. How close are they now?"

"They will catch up before we get to Alexandria so we had better prepare for battle."

As the light increased a north westerly breeze sprung up, this slowed the vessels significantly. However, by the time it was fully light they were separated by about two boat lengths.

"Nos dedito - *harasooh* – dedito!" shouted the captain of the leading ship meaning surrender in Latin and Greek.

"Tell them to go and fornicate in their *Mater's* dung" retorted Cleopatra before Mark Antony could reply.

"Where did you learn language like that?" asked the now conscious and astonished Apollodorus.

"Mixing with common soldiers and sailors. Give me a sword someone, I may be cute but I can be deadly too! Let's give those mercenaries a fight to remember."

The high aft superstructure would afford the crew some protected from the first volley of arrows. However, the Gabinians would soon come alongside. The oarsmen were vulnerable on Cleopatra's boat as they sat in the open. On the Triremes the men in the upper rowing position were protected by leather awning, the lower two levels being inside the hull. The marines were on a raised catwalk that ran the length of the ship. Some of the Gabinian Trireme warships were equipped with catapults or giant crossbows as was usual for such craft.

"I don't wish to question everyone's military judgement" commented Apollodorus casually "but I thought the Etesian trade wind had prevented the Egyptian ships from being transferred from Alexandria to Pelusium and there was in any event no where to park them due to the salt pans and sand banks. So who in the name of Seth is chasing us?"

Cleopatra looked at Apollodorus in disbelief then at Antony who looked more carefully at the pursuing triremes.

"Apollodorus is right! Those are not Egyptian ships, they are Roman" cried an ecstatic Mark Antony. He jumped onto the coach roof of the aft cabin so the pursuing warships could see his uniform and he waved frantically. "These must be the remnants of Pompeius' fleet, making their way to surrender to Caesar in Alexandria." As if on queue the following ships raised their oars in unison. "Your Highness, order the crew to raise their oars; those ships were not ordering you to surrender but were offering to surrender to you! Nos deditio not vos deditio."

The wind freshened and backed to the east so the ships were able to deploy their sails. Cleopatra's Thalamegos only carried a single mast and sail. Roman Triremes, as was common with this type of warship, sailed under two square sails, the fore sail known as the boat sail and the larger main or big sail. Some of the ships were larger and had two men to each oar and were described as sixes. The fleet although small would make a welcome addition to that of Caesar's. They had a favourable wind so made a splendid sight in the autumn morning sunshine and were soon in the 'roads', the approaches to the eastern Great Harbour at Alexandria.

The *Trierarchos* (Triremes captains) brought the ships smartly about and ordered the dropping of the sails as they crossed the bar between the breakwaters that stretched out from Pharos and Cape Lochias. Cleopatra's Royal Thalamegos and accompanying Roman war ships then made their way into the inner haven under oars.

"I hope Jules has got breakfast ready for us, I could murder a dish of smoked fish and scrambled eggs" said the shipwright; the adrenalin rush caused by the threat of battle was beginning to wear off along with the medication so the fever was returning.

"He will probably murder us for going off without his permission" replied Mark Antony dryly.

By the time they were safely moored in the Royal Harbour it was mid-day and Apollodorus was again running a high temperature so did not feel Caesar's wrath. He was carried into the palace on Antirhodos, barely conscious. The ships that had surrendered to Cleopatra and Mark Antony more than placated Caesar and the information about the Gabinian movements were invaluable.

"How long will it be before I can talk to the Jester?" he asked Olympos.

"He has shown me a medication that is quite miraculous so you should get some sense out of him by the evening, with luck."

It was late that night before Apollodorus was able to converse coherently.

"Antonius was telling me that you discussed making a boat from animal hide over a wooden frame. I have seen the people of Al'bion use such craft to great effect. Tell me, would it be possible to use this type of craft to mount a rear attack on the Pharos Lighthouse while the main body of infantry cause a diversion by attacking from the Heptastadium Dike?"

"Sounds like a very good idea. How are we doing for crocodiles, your Highness?"

"Last year we were overrun with them. We had to make offerings to Sobok to take his people away."

"I take it from your tone that the prayers were answered and there are no crocodiles?" said the Roman.

"No, none at all" replied Cleopatra sweetly.

"So I have been worrying about being thrown to a reptile that has been conspicuous by its absence all along. Fortunately any hide will do. Alternatively I have seen some very strong cloth made here in Egypt; we may not need to use animal skins. The other problem is springy timber for the framework, there seems to be a chronic shortage of useful wood in Alexandria. What do the Egyptian archers construct their bows from?"

"There will be a stock pile of what you call willow in the armoury, most of our timber in imported from the northern Mediterranean countries" replied the first lady.

During the night Apollodorus' condition deteriorated and he became delirious.

"He was calling out for you, your Highness" explained Olympos who was so concerned he had sent for her, much to Caesar's disquiet. "There must be several types of mould and not all work as Apollodorus suspected."

Cleopatra sat with Apollodorus and bathed him with cold water in an attempt to reduce the temperature. He was clearly having a very vivid dream about the death of the woman he loved.

"I have only ever loved one woman and she is dying in my arms from the venom of the uraeus" whispered the shipwright. "I can hide nothing from you, can I Thea?"

"What I don't understand" said Cleopatra to the doctor "is that he is talking about Cobra's venom, which is how his beloved died and he keeps calling out for me. He is trying to find the reptile in his dream and he calls Thea. What does it mean, Olympos?"

"Perhaps you remind him of this woman. Has he ever told you what she was like?"

"No, he never talks about her, I presume it is too painful for him, except when we were attacked by a Uraeus back in Askalon and I had to stop him from killing the cobra. I have never seen such hatred; the snake was only protecting her young."

Apollodorus continued to mumble and moan then suddenly announced "yes I think that I would, the tragedy is that I held in my hands the means to change the course of history and did not realise……"

"It's right, 'Pollo, I am here, there are no snakes. You have been injured and are running a fever." Cleopatra's soothing voice was like honey and Apollodorus calmed.

By the morning the fever had burned out and the shipwright began to recover. That evening Apollodorus was sitting up in bed when Cleopatra arrived, her handmaids had made a special effort with her hair and makeup. Her naked breasts brushed across his chest as she bent forward and kissed him causing his heart to race.

"I have brought you some figs" she said "they are very good to eat when you have been ill."

"They are supposed to be good for the complexion, as well" replied Apollodorus with a smile. "Seeing you looking a million talents of gold is a tonic in itself." He was trying not to look too obviously at her breasts.

"Didn't you like me in riding clothes then?" she asked with a mischievous grin.

"You could look devastating in sack cloth and ashes and you know it! Does old baldy like the way you dress?"

"I don't think he notices, he is too busy preparing for battle but I know you like to see me like this" she looked down at the tell tail bulge under the bed clothes, then into Apollodorus' eyes. "Come on, try and eat some figs" she put one in his mouth and kissed him again.

"It is true about figs being beneficial," said the actress. "They have a high level of beta-carotene and vitamin C; they are full of antioxidants which help fight the ageing process. Also they are high in calcium which is vital for healthy nails and are excellent for removing toxins."

"With her extensive knowledge of science and medicine it is hardly surprising Cleopatra was keen on eating figs then."

Cleopatra would have liked to ask Apollodorus about his dream but something stopped her. She knew he found her attractive but couldn't understand what held him back. He knew better than anyone that her relationship with Caesar was political. The woman he loved must have died a long time. Surely he had got over it by now. How old was he? He sometimes seemed a similar age to herself and at other times Caesar's age. He had, after all, travelled widely and seen a great deal.

"Do you love Caesar?" he asked.

"You know I am only using him, but he is quite agreeable and I find the power he wields exciting."

"You know he could give you the world if you play your dice right. It is only a matter of time before he becomes master of Rome, then he will be master of most of the world."

"He will never be master of you or your people."

"Rome may well conquer my land but I doubt it will be in his lifetime. I hope Achaean rather than Roman culture prevails in the long term."

"Is that why you are helping me?"

"No, I am here with you because…" he hesitated. "No, it isn't right for me to say it."

"Don't give me that 'tug the fetlock' nonsense. I know you better than that. You believe all people to be equal. Speak your mind, 'Pollo."

The arrival of Caesar prevented any reply. It would be some time before there would be another opportunity and then under very different circumstances.

"I am glad to see you are looking better, Jocus. I thought I would find you here, your Highness." The conversation turned to preparations for the invasion by the Gabinian mercenary army of Ptolemy, so the moment was lost for Cleopatra. She resolved to find another way.

"I am concerned with what Ptolemy may get up to. Have either of you any ideas what to do with him?" asked Caesar.

"Strangle him!" expostulated Cleopatra with feeling.

"Ground him. He is, after all, only a child" said Apollodorus.

"What do you mean" asked Caesar.

"Confine him to barracks; place him under house arrest for his own safety, of course."

Caesar was thoughtful, "Not a bad idea, Jocus. I am going out on a reconnaissance for a day or two, so if you are feeling better look after Her Highness while I am gone." With that he turned and left the room. Cleopatra fussed round Apollodorus making him more comfortable in his bed. She washed his face with a cool cloth. Although his temperature had returned to normal he was still weak, so soon drifted off to sleep.

Around midnight the shipwright awoke and was surprised to find the first lady still with him. His head was resting on her naked breast not the pillow. One of her arms was round his neck and she smiled at him when she realised he was awake and kissed him fully on the lips. He ran his fingers through her golden ringlets and his hand brushed against her other breast. She smiled again at him as he felt her small hand run over his stomach and onto his manhood.

The following morning she was gone. Had it been a dream? Apollodorus could not tell. He was a foreign commoner and she was now Caesar's woman. Caesar was the most powerful man on earth; he could literally give Cleopatra the world. All the Jester could do was patch up her boat and make her laugh.

About mid day in another part of the palace Cleopatra was having a bath attended by Charmain and Iras. The bath was more like a small swimming pool set into the floor of her apartment. Caesar had left early that morning on a reconnaissance of the eastern approaches to the capital.

"Life was unfair! Caesar has a wife in Rome" thought Cleopatra. "I am little more than a concubine." This was perfectly acceptable in her society. A man could have a wife and as many concubines or girlfriends as he liked but it was unacceptable for a woman, not even a royal woman, to do likewise. True, Ptolemy was nominally her consort, but in reality Caesar was, in all but name. He tolerated her friendship with Apollodorus but how would he react if they became lovers?

Her mind went back to the time on 'Mintaka' when Apollodorus had offered to turn the boat out to sea. Was following her destiny really better than following her heart? A prison was still a prison no matter how well appointed; she was still a prisoner of her own destiny. Apollodorus had said that freedom was the most precious gift and how right he was. What would she do now, if he came to her with Caesar away?

Apollodorus was feeling much better and was able to get up. The injury was healing nicely so he dressed and made his way to Cleopatra's apartment. He called out to her at the doorway and Charmain invited him in, smiling sweetly.

"Caesar has gone out on a reconnaissance of the advancing Gabinian army with Hirtius. Her Highness is having a bath."

"I am sorry, I will come back later."

"Don't be so silly, 'Pollo" called Cleopatra "come in. Iras, give him a goblet of wine, and Charmain get him a kline to lie on." The hand maidens showed the surprised shipwright to a couch and gave him a drink. After a short while the *Bassilisa* emerged from the bath like Venus emerging from the sea. Charmain and Iras dried her carefully. When they had finished she stood in front of Apollodorus, naked.

"Don't be shy 'Pollo I know you like looking at me" she said. "You appreciate me far more than Caesar." Her green eyes held the shipwright's blue ones. "I am no more than Caesar's concubine; he already has a wife in Rome. You believe in equality so what is good enough for Caesar is good enough for the rest of us. I know I will never be able to replace the woman you lost to the venom of the Uraeus but she would not wish you to deny you the happiness I long to give you." She sat on the floor in front of him. At that moment she saw a tear run down the shipwright's cheek. Cleopatra bent forward and licked away the salty droplet.

"I know now what you wanted to say to me when Caesar interrupted us yesterday, please don't deny it. I couldn't run away with you in your boat to your paradise so please stay here with me and make Egypt ours. I have no intension of sharing the throne with either my brother or a Roman barbarian."

"Hatshepsus was a female Pharaoh. Why shouldn't you follow her example? I believe you could return Egypt to her former glory but you will need Roman help. I must therefore remain in the background."

"Unfortunately, you are the only one to believe in me so it will be some time before I can dress in the nemes and kilt of the Pharaoh."

Apollodorus ran his fingers through her hair and said "I don't think the head gear would suit you."

"How about the short skirt?" she asked with a grin.

"It would be a lot less revealing than the transparent dresses you usually wear."

"I suppose you would rather I wore animal skins like your friends from the north."

"No, I am quite happy with the skin you are wearing at present."

Cleopatra stood up and ran her hands over her naked body slowly, then sat down again and rested her head on his chest "I am glad you like it" she purred whilst running her hand inside his tunic and looked up at him. "You have a hairy chest. Caesar has his body hair plucked."

Apollodorus looked astounded. "He has the hair plucked out of his chest? Ouch! Now that's what I call a slave to fashion. The thought brings tears to the eyes." They both laughed.

"That's nothing, male worshippers of Iras are castrated" she added rubbing Apollodorus' genitals affectionately.

"That really has put me off religion. Is that why Mardian is a eunuch, Isis is his patron?"

"No, not exactly. He is of the third gender."

"Third gender?"

"Yes, he is homosexual. He loves men. This is the fifth Greek word for love, the one that dare not say its name. Don't you have such people where you come from?"

"Probably, I was too young to know when I left but I have come across such people in my travels. Having your love tackle cut off in the pursuit of religion is a bit drastic, I thought it was done as a punishment, not pleasure."

The two handmaidens brought in food and set it on a low table in front of them. Cleopatra fed Apollodorus from the various exotic dishes, but ate little herself.

"Is it wise to be so intimate in front of Charmain and Iras?" he asked, between mouthfuls of food.

"Don't be silly! They are totally loyal to me and they much prefer you to Caesar" she bent forward and whispered "I think they are as much in love with you as I am."

The bath water had become cold. She had only been dreaming. Her face was flushed and her heart was beating rapidly. She realised that her hand was on her pubis and her legs had lost their strength. It was the first time she had experienced an orgasm. Caesar had not been able to truly satisfy her, there was a knock on the door and he came in.

"Where is the Jester?" demanded Caesar.

"In his room I suppose, I haven't seen him since last night. Why?"

The Roman looked guilty "I need him to get busy with making the coracles. When you have finished your bath perhaps you could find out if he is well enough to get started. I suspect you will have more success motivating him than me."

Cleopatra thought "he suspects that 'Pollo is more than a friend, I must be careful." Caesar turned abruptly and marched out of the apartment leaving her to be dried and dressed by Charmain and Iras.

Apollodorus held the dying woman in his arms. How many times had he re-lived this scene? Where was the serpent? If he could find it they could be together in the afterlife. But suicide was the worse form of sacrilege. Life was the most precious gift and some say that to end it one self would mean spending eternity reliving the last moments over and over again as a punishment. Better that than life without her. At least that way they would be together. Where was the serpent? The only reptile he could see was on the ring he had on his finger. He was mistaken there were two entwined snakes and a bird, three rings in one, on his right hand. He awoke. The bed clothes were tangled round him, and he was drenched in sweat, tears ran down his cheeks.

"Its alright, I am here, 'Pollo, you were dreaming again" Cleopatra was holding him.

"She was dying in my arms but I could not find the snake, so I could be with her in the afterlife. There was a ring that was three rings, two cobras and a bird. A vulture, I think. What does it mean?" he was not fully conscious.

"How long ago was it that you lost her?"

"I don't know. It sometimes seems like yesterday, sometimes an eternity away. A thousand, maybe two thousand years ago" he was now fully awake.

Cleopatra was tempted to say that he was not as old as Caesar, so it could not have been that long ago, but something stopped her. How could he know of the Serpent Ring? Only a hand full of people knew of its existence, a ring that could only be given by the *Bassilisa* on pain of death and only to the one she truly loved and who truly declared his love for her. She knew of only one occasion when it had been given and that was before the Ptolemy's had ruled Egypt.

"You have the ability to talk to the spirits; perhaps you can foretell the future. The gods may be trying to tell you something."

"I hope not. I have spent a life time trying to suppress my psychic abilities. I look on it as a curse not a blessing."

"Why?"

"To be able to see the future carries a terrible responsibility. Should I tell the people concerned and what if I have misinterpreted the vision? Then there is the problem of people wanting you to do it to order, which I can't. That's why most soothsayers are frauds. The visions come when they choose and interpretation is fraught with difficulty. Thanks, but I will stick to building boats, if you don't mind."

"Well, in that case, Caesar asked me to see if you feel well enough to get on with his fleet of coracles?"

"Did you tell him he would have to say 'please' and invite me to dinner?"

"You know that would stick in his throat. You are more likely to be struck by lightning than get him to say 'please'" she laughed. "So will you do it for me?"

"You know I will and thank you."

"For what?"

"I really appreciate your being so understanding and such a good friend by not questioning me about things that I cannot discuss."

She put her arm round him and said "Well, when you are ready I will be there to listen. Tell me something. Do you think I could follow in Hatshepsus' footsteps and return Egypt to her former glory?"

"Yes, I do, but promise me one thing."

"Yes, what?"

He ran his fingers through her golden ringlets "Promise you won't wear the nemes and kilt."

Cleopatra shivered "Let me guess. You prefer the diaphanous dresses I usually wear, rather than a short skirt and headscarf."

"How did you know?" They both laughed. "Do you think you will be well enough to join Caesar and myself at dinner tonight?"

"Yes, I should love to; I will bring some sketches of the coracles for his approval, unless you would like me in my official capacity as *Bassilisa's Gelotopoios*."

"You know I love your jokes. Unfortunately, Caesar hasn't much of a sense of humour, so while he is around stick to being *Bassilisa's* shipwright, I don't want you being turned into lion food" she kissed him lingeringly on the lips then with her hands still behind his neck held his gaze and. added "no more risk taking. You are too precious to me, 'Pollo, Jester. No, I think I will call you Gelotopoios from now on, it suits you."

"This sounds like an ancient story; Aphrodite, Pan and Baccas went in search of a fool, you are the beautiful woman and I the joker."

"And Marcus Antonius is Baccas" said Cleopatra with sudden realisation. "So does that mean that Caesar is the fool we are going to use to protect my final resting place?"

"Caesar is no fool and in the legend the gods were trying to keep secret the location of Aphrodite's final resting place. There are similarities but we have yet to find our fool. Perhaps the god's plan is flawed, not even a fool can be trusted with such a precious secret."

"If a fool could not be trusted, who would you use *Geloto*? How would you protect my secret?" inquired Cleopatra earnestly.

Book 6

Apollodorus arrived for dinner at Cleopatra's apartment and was surprised that he was the only guest of Caesar and Cleopatra. He hesitated at the door thinking, he may have misunderstood the invitation. He was even more puzzled when the Roman greeted him warmly.

"Jocus, I am glad to see you looking better, come in" said Caesar as he offered him a goblet of wine "Her Royal Highness was telling me how you trusted no one when you told her of your plan to smuggle her back to Alexandria, so you will understand why I wanted to see you alone. Both you and I suspect that Pothinus has ordered Ptolemy's Gabinian army back from Mount Cusino and in any event they are on their way here and will arrive in about a week, two if we are lucky. In preparation for the probable conflict I have sent for the ships from Rhodes, Syria and Cilica. There are archers from Crete and cavalry from King Malchus of the Nabateans on their way and I have placed Ptolemy under house arrest for his own protection as you suggested. The legions of Pompeius army in Africa are in my control and will be the first to arrive. How do you see our situation? Speak freely, Jocus."

"I am concerned about three things. Firstly, there are many more Gabinians than Romans; these are disenfranchised troops fully conversant with your military tactics. Secondly, the Egyptian navy has seventy ships, fifty fully equipped following their return from Thessaly and twenty two used to guard Alexandria you have far fewer. Thirdly, whoever controls the lighthouse will have an excellent view of the hostilities. Alexander the Great chose this site for his city because the Achaeans like an offshore island which they can use as a secure base to control a hostile local population. I am glad you have sent for reinforcements and when hostilities start you should attack the lighthouse in the manner you suggested. I have some sketches of a boat to use in the rear attack. With regard to the Egyptian ships, you may have no choice but to torch them."

Cleopatra was horrified at the prospect of setting fire to her navy. Caesar nodded thoughtfully, gave the shipwright a knowing look and added "I had come to much the same conclusion. Where are the Triremes located?"

"Most are in sheds by the docks, west of the Heptastadium Dike, near the Gate of the Moon, some afloat in the western harbour."

"So not all are afloat? That means they will not easily be brought into service."

"Those that are in service have only a skeleton crew aboard; any available sailors are more likely to side with Ptolemy than us. If the coracles are to be built in secret, Cape Lochias would be the best location, away from prying eyes. It would be a good place to launch an attack on the lighthouse. I should like to move my boat 'Mintaka' and the Royal Thalamegos over to the Cape Lochias Royal Harbour."

"That's fine. I was thinking of moving my H.Q. over there as it will be easier to defend than Antirhodos. You will be safer on Lochias, your Highness."

Cleopatra looked unhappy at the prospect and said "I hope you aren't proposing to exclude me just when things are getting interesting."

"Not at all" replied Caesar.

"You can be my assistant shipwright" said Apollodorus "the less people that know what we are building the better. Presumably Charmain and Iras sew. If I am to use cloth to cover the coracles there will be a great deal of sewing to be done and your handmaidens are trustworthy."

Caesar smiled knowingly at Apollodorus as though to say "you are better at pacifying Her Royal Highness than I. Thank you." Both men secretly agreed that it would be the safest place for the first lady when hostilities began. Suddenly Caesar's expression changed. The colour drained from his face and he began to shake. Apollodorus grabbed hold of the Roman as he lost consciousness and lowered him to the ground where he lay shaking.

"What is happening to him?" asked Cleopatra anxiously "he looks as though he is possessed by a devil."

"That is what most people would say. Help me get him on his side and watch out for his arms and legs. Try and speak soothingly to him and calm him." Caesar was shaking vigorously now and breathing with difficulty. Cleopatra tried to calm him. Suddenly he stopped shaking and also stopped breathing.

"Oh Zeus" exclaimed Apollodorus "I was afraid he might do that."

"What's happened?"

"He has swallowed his tongue. Get him on his back and help me get his mouth open." They rolled Caesar on his back and forced his mouth open. Apollodorus put a finger down the Roman's throat "yuck, got it!" he held Caesar's nose and blew into his mouth a few times, as though kissing him.

"I thought you only liked girls, this is hardly the time to get passionate with our Jules" said the astonished Cleopatra. Caesar coughed a couple of times and started breathing again. He was still shaking as he regained consciousness. "You breathed life back into him!"

"Yes, I suppose I did. Help me get him back on his side and find a cushion and wrap to keep him warm. He should be O.K now." The shaking gradually subsided as Caesar regained consciousness although he was confused for some time.

"Should I fetch Olympos?" asked Cleopatra.

"No!" exclaimed the Roman groggily "the less people who know about my condition the better. I owe you my life, Apollodorus. Thank you."

"That's O.K" he replied casually. "When was the last time you had anything to eat?"

"Last night I think, why?"

"Have you had an attack like this before?"

"Yes, but not for about two years."

"What is the matter with him, 'Pollo?"

"Contrary to popular belief he is not possessed by devils or any such nonsense. His condition is caused by abnormal brain activity made worse by irregular sleep and eating patterns. It is more common in children and they usually grow out of it. In adults it can be caused by illness or head injury, but being a soldier the latter is an occupational hazard. We should get him onto a kline in case the servants come in with dinner. I agree with you, Domini, the less people who know about your condition the better."

By the time dinner was served, Caesar's appearance had shown a marked improvement. Apollodorus insisted the Roman had some food but no wine and by the end of the meal he was almost back to normal. Cleopatra excused herself and left the room, Caesar asked in a low voice.

"Why did you save me? If I had died there would have been no one between you and Cleopatra."

"You know how she lays all men under her spell. I admit I am no different. If you were to die I would be trampled to death in the rush and Marcus Antonius would be first in line."

"Don't prevaricate. I have seen how well you two get on together."

"That's as may be, but you know she suffers from the congenital condition of the Cleopatra's - being *Bassilisa* isn't enough, she wants to rule. You can give her the world, what have I to offer? I am but a barbarian from a cold northern country and she is a royal, a goddess. Her Highness needs warriors, I am a man out of my time, and I believe the world would be a much happier place if we all worked together for a common good. I hate fighting and don't enjoy hunting. I can't even kill to eat. I believe in the sanctity of all life. Freemen, slaves and animals, all have a right to live as they chose, so long as they don't interfere with the freedom of others."

Caesar did not reply, but thought "how you underestimate yourself! You can give her something far more precious that I can ever give her."

Apollodorus continued "No one can light up a room quite like Cleopatra Thea Philopater can." At that moment she returned and smiled at him.

"You do say the nicest things, *Gelotopoios*. Don't you agree, Caesar?"

The Roman said nothing but thought "that is exactly what I mean; she will never look at me in the way she looks at you." He was beginning to feel exhausted from the seizure, so excused himself. The shipwright walked with him back to his bedchamber. When Cleopatra was out of earshot, Caesar said softly. "You don't misjudge the seriousness of our situation, unlike her Highness. On the other hand I don't underestimate you. Do not forget that I have done battle with your people, so promise me you will take care of Cleopatra if I get killed. Not that I need to ask, do I?"

When he returned Cleopatra greeted him warmly. "I am glad he has gone to bed I can do something he doesn't approve of."

"What on earth do you have in mind?"

She picked up her seven string lyre and led Apollodorus by the hand out onto the seaward side of the island. There was a full moon and the gentle sea breeze rustled the palm leaves. The light from the lighthouse gave the harbour a warm golden glow. They sat down at the eastern edge of Antirhodos on the temple steps as far from Caesar's chamber as possible. Her low husky voice echoed across the water like a Siren from legends accompanied by the melody of her lyre. When she had finished she said "put your arm round me Gelotopoios and hold me like you did on 'Mintaka'." She looked up into his eyes and saw they were moist, but said nothing.

One of the temple cats started rubbing round their legs, Apollodorus bent down and scratched the animal's head. It was a large, very elegant silver spotted creature. The cat rolled over onto its back so Apollodorus stroked its stomach.

"Do you like cats?" asked Cleopatra.

"Yes, they are very independent. I think they look down on mankind but they seem to like me." The cat was now trying to attack his fist. "Cats love to play fight like this" he continued "it can get a bit painful, though."

Cleopatra laughed as the cat tried to disembowel his fist. "That is supposed to be a sacred cat and you are playing with it as though it's a child."

"That's probably why cats like me because I meet them on their own terms. They are quite rough with each other. This one must be quite young his coat is like moonlight on a rippling sea."

"Well you had better call him *Fangarfoto* as he seems to have adopted you."

"Moonlight, an excellent name, have the Egyptians always kept cats?"

"They first came to live with us two thousand years ago and were used for pest control, each cat needs to kill over a thousand small rodents each year to survive. Being a nocturnal animal they are associated with the moon not least because of the way their eyes dilate and contract mimicking the lunar phases."

Apollodorus nodded and asked "Have you ever swum with Dolphins?"

"No, have you?"

"Yes they love humans. You can ride them like a horse by holding onto their dorsal fin. They have a wonderful sense of humour. I was swimming once off of the coast of Gaul and could see a school of dolphins about a hundred cubits below. Suddenly one swam straight up at me. They can really move when they want to. I was petrified!"

"What happened?" asked the astonished Cleopatra.

"At the last moment it turned away, leaped out of the water, did a somersault and looked at me when it was back in the water making a noise like laughter."

"I have heard the noise they make and seen how they love to follow a boat but I thought they were after food. Do you think animals have a *Ba*?"

"Ba? Another one of your Greek words?" asked the actress.

"The Egyptians called the life force Ka; physical and psychic energy. Ba was the disembodied consciousness and Akh the power to transform. So Ba translates to soul."

"I think all living creatures have a soul and all life is sacred, that is why I don't hunt and would not want to witness the Roman games."

"You eat meat?"

"Yes. I suppose that is a bit hypocritical, but what is the alternative. I don't like to kill but when it comes to survival there is sometimes no choice."

"So you are far from happy about the forthcoming battle, then."

"Yes, people are going to get killed and maimed on both sides. It is so senseless. The people of Egypt could have peace and prosperity under your rule if they would only take the trouble to get to know you and give you the chance. They have listened to Pothinus and his associates who will carry on making the same mistakes as your ancestors. If only people would treat others the way they would like to be treated themselves there would be no war, no famine, and no pestilence" he replied, then added as an afterthought. "Maybe death, also, could be abolished."

Cleopatra hugged and kissed the shipwright "You are such an idealist 'Pollo. I love you, but you will never change the world."

"How long is it since Zeus, the gatherer of clouds, brought civilisation down from Mount Olympos? Several thousand years ago. It may take several thousand years more for mankind to come round to my way of thinking, but eventually it must."

"What if it doesn't?"

"It will destroy itself and the world that we live in."

Cleopatra shuddered and changed the subject "Do you play an instrument?"

"I thought you would never ask" he replied as he produced a set of pipes and started to play. The tune he played was well known to the first lady, so she joined in with her lyre and sang the words in her low husky voice that Apollodorus found so captivating. The sky started to darken as though a cloud was covering the moon but it was a clear night.

"What is happening to the moon, 'Pollo? Are the gods angry? It looks as though a giant beast is covering it."

"There is nothing to fear. The giant is us, or rather the earth, it is coming between the sun and the moon. The moon reflects the sunlight but once a year the earth's orbit round the sun places it in exactly the right position to stop that reflection. When nature gives us a show it does a great job and the tickets are free. See how the shadow is circular? That's the proof that the world is round. You should see the northern lights in the land of the midnight sun. They can only be seen in the winter when there is hardly any daylight, great lights in the sky that dance, another free show."

They sat and watched the lunar eclipse. Soon the only light was from the lighthouse so the water looked like liquid gold. "Do you think it is an omen?" asked Cleopatra "are the gods telling us that we will prevail and bring in a new golden age?"

"I don't know their opinion on the subject and I doubt if they even care but I am going to do everything to bring about a quick victory with the least possible loss of life and then help you rebuild Egypt's prosperity."

"The Roman fight because they enjoy it. Gabinians fight for the money but you fight for what you believe in, don't you, 'Pollo?"

"I am prepared to fight for, and if necessary, die for a better world for all people. A strong Egypt will curb some of the more unpleasant aspects of Roman colonisation, you may even civilise them. Above all I will be fighting for my friend. I would back you up and fight for you even if I thought you were wrong. That's what true *agape* is all about."

The moon reappeared and Apollodorus started playing his pipes again as dawn began to break over the harbour. Cleopatra was reminded of an ancient poem and thought "could Caesar have stumbled on the truth? Could Apollodorus be Mendis, known as Pan to the Romans? 'The Piper at the Gates of Dawn', joker, mischief maker, lover of animals. No, it was impossible. He hated snakes or was it just the uraeus he had a problem with."

"*Gelotopoios*, do you dislike all snakes or is it only the cobra you hate?"

"I find reptiles fascinating but I am terrified of all snakes."

"You should be Jewish. They look on the serpent as the living embodiment of Seth or the devil."

"Not a bad idea, but the men have to cut the end off of their penis, their god must be either very cruel or have a wicked sense of humour" they both laughed.

"Circumcision is an Egyptian custom" replied Cleopatra thoughtfully, "performed as a matter of cleanliness but copied by other people for reasons of religion." She was about to ask Apollodorus a rather personal question but he interrupted her.

"Tell you what, Thea, you are a goddess. I'll worship you."

"I am just a girl."

"Yes and I am just a man" he replied, and this was Alexandria the wine press of love, on the brink of war.

"*I thought 'The Goat of Mendis' was a satanic symbol?*" asked the actress.

"You are suffering from Catholic propaganda and Hollywood's miss-conceptions. Mendis is the Egyptian word for both goat and Pan, Christianity tolerated no other beliefs in the early days, sadly a familiar pattern with young religions. The commandment states 'I am a jealous God; you will worship no other gods but me.' Significantly it does not state that there are no other gods. From the ancients perspective their gods were neither good nor evil, they were above mortal constraints, they had many facets, cruel and kind.. Witchcraft is based on ancient religion both good and evil but the Druids did not write anything down so most of their wisdom is lost."

"Rather like the dark side of the force in 'Star Wars'."

"That is correct, the universe is balanced; for good to exist there has to be evil. For matter to exist there has to be anti-matter. For Christ there has to be an anti-Christ. Today humanity worships worldly goods, our gods are our homes, our jobs and our machines. Knowledge is neither good nor evil; it is the use to which it is put that makes it cruel or kind."

"So is Pan, the Piper at the gate of Dawn known to the Egyptians as Mendis, good or evil?"

By way of an answer I continued with the story.

It was almost daylight when the two friends eventually went their separate ways to bed. The burning question for Cleopatra was did the people of Britannia also practice circumcision or was her friend being less than accurate about his linage. It was nearly mid-day by the time Apollodorus was up again. He made his way to the royal harbour between the mainland and Antirhodos. Cleopatra was organising the crew on her royal Thalamegos when he arrived.

"*Kale emera Kyria mou.*"

"*Kale emera Geloto*" replied Cleopatra returning the traditional Greek greeting.

"How is Caesar this morning?" he asked.

"None the worse for last night and you?"

"All the better for seeing you, your Highness. And you?"

"I really enjoyed our musical interlude last night. It is a pity Romans look down on musicians."

"Romans look down on and disapprove of everything non- Roman, the only thing they really enjoy is killing anything that moves. If you are going to move your boat to the Cape Lochias Royal Harbour perhaps you could give 'Mintaka' a tow as I don't know where the reefs are located."

"Do you think my Trierarchos is up to the job?" she replied with a smile "I didn't think you would trust anyone with your boat. I am sure 'Mintaka' is the only woman you truly love." Cleopatra realised how tactless she had been and quickly added "I am sorry, 'Pollo. I shouldn't have said that, it was very unkind."

"That's perfectly all right. I make jokes all the time so I must accept other people making jokes at my expense, you can't avoid comments that touch on my loss. I know you well enough to know that you are not spiteful. Also you are probably correct, it's the sort of comment she would make. Your Captain is a very competent seaman and you trust him. Why shouldn't I?"

They moved the two boats over to the other more private royal harbour by Cape Lochias that afternoon. It was the first time Apollodorus had seen it and he was delighted. There were no quays and the land ran into the water so boats could easily be dragged up the beach or people could bathe in the sea. There were many multi-coloured exotic birds on the waters edge and palms lined the shore. Behind the trees were the marble and granite palace buildings. The right hand side of the peninsular was cut off from the mainland by the canal and the left protected by the city wall. It was a natural fortress surrounded by water on three sides, away from prying eyes.

"Your ancestors certainly knew how to make themselves safe and comfortable, Thea. This harbour is a sailor's dream. Do you like to swim in the sea?"

"I used to love swimming but I haven't done any for years, it's too much of a security risk."

"Well I am looking forward to a nice refreshing dip after a hard day building Caesar's coracles." They were on 'Mintaka' so they could talk freely. "Have you ever swum naked by moonlight, Thea?"

"That's disgusting!" exclaimed Cleopatra and then continued more thoughtfully, "what would happen if anyone saw us?"

"Since when have you been shy? Anyway the prospect of getting caught is all part of the fun, like or dancing naked under a full moon or making love on the beach by starlight."

Cleopatra felt a growing sense of excitement. "Have you really made love like that?" The Trierarchos had shortened the tow prior to beaching the Royal Thalamegos, so Apollodorus was unable to reply.

"There is a lot of life that you could show me if only the circumstances were different" she thought wistfully "if only I didn't have to give myself to that dirty old Roman. To swim with dolphins, see dancing lights in the sky, frozen rain that falls like cotton wool and to dance naked then make love on the beach by moonlight."

"What were you thinking, your Highness?" asked Apollodorus.

"Now who's being cruel? You must know what was on my mind. Are you trying to make me feel bad about not accepting your suggestion to turn 'Mintaka' out to sea?" The boats had now been hauled up the beach so they stepped ashore and walked a little way from the rowers.

"I am sorry I didn't mean it like that. You made the right decision to follow your destiny and do your duty by your people. It is natural to have your doubts from time to time. I look on you as a friend and am inclined to forget that you are *Bassilisa*."

"You talk to me like a woman, 'Pollo, and I love it. Promise me two things, carry on talking to me like a woman, and …"

"Of course! What was the other thing?"

She touched him lightly on the arm and looked into his eyes, "Take me for a moonlight swim and do it before the Gabinian's invade"

"If you can find an excuse to get away from old baldy how about tonight, as the moon is still full?" They spent the rest of the day moving their personal belongings into their rooms in the adjacent palace overlooking the harbour. Apollodorus then inspected the space allocated for building the coracles. He dined with Olympos then returned to his room where he drifted off to sleep. Around midnight he was awakened by a soft knock on the door, it was the first lady.

"Are you ready for that swim?" she whispered. They sneaked out of the palace and along the beach. Her towel dropped to the ground, Cleopatra was naked. Apollodorus removed his clothes in silence and hand in hand they walked into the water. When they were fully immersed Cleopatra put her arms round Apollodorus' neck and they kissed. "This is the most exciting thing I have ever done."

"Is it more exciting than being carried through a palace full of enemies wrapped in a bed roll?"

"Much!"

"Is it more exciting than rescuing me from the Gabinians?"

"Far more exciting" she was shivering uncontrollably.

"What is left for us to do that is more exciting than this?"

"Make love to me on the beach by moonlight." There was a muffled sound of shouting from the mainland, the Gabinians had arrived.

Apollodorus awoke with a start. There was an urgent tapping on his door and from the mainland were muffled sounds of shouting. The

Gabinians really had arrived. Cleopatra was standing at his door, fully dressed and looking worried.

"We had better not take that swim" she said regretfully "we are under attack so we had better make our way to Caesar's H.Q."

"I promise we will go swimming by moonlight when this is all over, Thea."

Caesar greeted them curtly as they arrived.

"Clearly we moved onto the Cape just in time. Jocus I need those coracles yesterday, how quickly can you get them built?"

"I will get on with them at first light. You can't make the raid with a full moon but they will be ready by the time you have a dark night."

"I can't wait that long! Could you colour them and the marines so they will be difficult to see?"

"We could use black cloth for the boats and dark clothes for the men your Highness, you are the expert on makeup, and could you blacken the men's faces?"

"No problem, 'Pollo."

"Two days to build the boats and one day to train the men in their use. Who is going to lead the attack? Marcus Antonius?"

"No, I have sent him back to Rome as 'Master of Horse' to deputise for me in the Senate. On the way he will send half of my legions here as reinforcements and the rest he will take with him to Rome. Hirtius is leading the frontal attack. I shall lead the marines myself, ten should be enough. You two had better get some sleep as you have work to do tomorrow. We will be perfectly safe tonight, not all the Gabinians have arrived so we can hold then off easily for a few days."

"Alexandria was protected by a double wall" I explained. "There were a number of towers sited between the inner and outer wall at intervals along its length. Each tower could accommodate between four and five hundred soldiers so an army of fifty thousand could be safely be housed between the walls protected from the hostile citizens within and the invaders outside."

Apollodorus was as good as his word and the coracles were built in time. Olympos, Mardian and some Roman engineers helped him construct the framework, while Cleopatra and her handmaids sewed the cloth covering. Caesar surveyed their handy work on the second evening. "You have done well, Jocus. Shall we try one out?"

They took one of the boats to the water and Caesar got into the craft. Apollodorus handed him a paddle. "Being nearly circular, there is a knack in paddling these boats. Don't paddle too hard or you will spin." The boat had started to spin and Caesar looked annoyed. Apollodorus was in the water so held onto the coracle, "Gently does it. One stroke each side." Under his instruction Caesar soon got the hang of paddling the craft, much to the shipwright's relief. Cleopatra insisted on having a go and soon mastered the technique; there was a good deal of laughter in the process of learning.

"Let's launch two more and have a race" suggested Apollodorus.

"This is a serious business" replied Caesar aggressively.

"I know and people learn much faster when they are having fun."

So they launched two more boats "last one to the royal Thalamegos cooks the dinner" added Apollodorus. They all arrived at the barge at about the same time, breathless. Caesar conceded that he had enjoyed the race as the shipwright inspected the boats.

"They stood up to that rough treatment, so they will get you and your marines over to Pharos. We can start training the men tomorrow.

"It was November when the Gabinians under General Achillas attacked the Royal Compound and street fighting ensued. Each side sustained minor losses. The most serious struggle was along the waterfront as either side knew the strategic advantage to be gained by controlling the dockyard at Eunostos and the Egyptian navy."

The next day was spent training the marines in the use of the coracles and by night fall Apollodorus felt that they could manage the short trip to the lighthouse. By the time that Caesar arrived an autumn sea mist had fallen and the shipwright was beginning to have his doubts about the wisdom of the scheme. The eastern side of the bay was full of natural hazards with reefs and rocks just below the surface.

"This mist is a mixed blessing" said Apollodorus "it will help in concealing the attack but we run the risk of the marines becoming disorientated during the crossing."

"I agree, but the bulk of Ptolemy's army is now here. There is fighting in the streets and we have had to fall back to the Palace compound. What do you suggest?"

"I could lead them over there, but I am no warrior so could be a liability in the battle."

"You get us over there and then stay out of the way, but we had better not tell her Highness you are coming."

Unfortunately Cleopatra had just arrived and said. "I think that is a stupid idea. 'Pollo, your leg is far from healed and you were almost in the 'Beautiful West' a few days ago, you mustn't go."

"I agree with both of you" replied Apollodorus "Can you excuse us for a moment, Domini?" he escorted the first lady outside and continued. "This is very much a no-win situation for me, Thea, and I walked right into the trap. Have you noticed how Caesar asks for your suggestions and you end up volunteering for something you would rather not do? If you object to my leading the 'specials' Caesar will think we are more than friends, which will put my life in danger. If I do go there is also a risk but it is better to risk a short water crossing and a few lighthouse technicians who I can see rather than one of Jules' assassins some dark night."

"Do you think he is jealous of you?"

"Put it this way, you raise no objection to him putting his life at risk, if you were him what would you think?"

Cleopatra said nothing but thought "He is right; I do think more of 'Pollo than of Caesar."

Apollodorus answered her thoughts by saying "Caesar can secure your realm for you. I can help win the hearts and minds of your people when the fighting is over. Alexandria is my first real home so it is only right that I should fight for it and for you, Thea."

"All right, 'Pollo, but promise you will be careful. Don't underestimate the risk. There will be more than a few technicians on the island; it is almost a town in its own right, a suburb. Any ships that flounder at the harbour entrance are plundered by the people of Pharos, they are like pirates. It is almost impossible to enter or leave Alexandria by sea without the blessing of the islanders."

"So I will be quite at home there!" replied Apollodorus lightly, then continued more seriously. "We are agreed then that it is imperative that Caesar takes control of Pharos. At heart I am really a coward. All I am going to do is to accompany the marines over to the lighthouse so that they can get on with the bloodshed. Once they are in the building I will make my way back here at ramming speed." They returned inside where Caesar was waiting for them.

"Apollodorus has convinced me that he must attend, so I will hold you personally responsible for his safety."

Caesar said nothing but looked at Apollodorus as though to say "you are well able to look after yourself."

"It sounds like the island of Pharos was the Alexandrian equivalent to the Bronx" quipped the actress.
"The occupation of Pharos was absolutely imperative to Caesar as it was not possible to bring in reinforcements or supplies by sea unless he had control of the harbour entrances."

At about midnight the small flotilla made its way in the lee of the breakwater from the northern tip of Cape Lochias to the Pharos Island. When they were alone Caesar asked Apollodorus.
"How did you talk Cleopatra into letting you come?"
"Simple. I pointed out that if her lover was going to risk his neck for her realm she should let her friends do likewise. Also, Alexandria is my first real home, so I have a right to fight for it."
The night was calm and they made the short passage without mishap arriving on the seaward side of the lighthouse as the mist started to lift. The landing was far from straightforward due to the rocks at the foot of the lighthouse. Most of the coracles were wrecked by the landing but all the men and their weapons were brought ashore.
"So this is the site which overlooks the frog pond" commented Apollodorus with a smile.
"Is that how the locals describe Pharos?" asked Caesar.
"I think they refer to Alexandria as the frog pond because of the thick reed beds in Lake Mareotis to the south of the city. According to the Bassilisa this island is populated by all sorts of thieves, vagabonds and pirates so I think you will be doing everyone a favour by clearing out this rats nest!"
Hirtius led the main attack from the Heptastadium causeway. This kept the men inside the lighthouse occupied so the special marines were able to grapple their way up to the windows un-noticed.
"I had another reason for coming with you domini" confided Apollodorus to Caesar. "Something is going to have to be done with the Egyptian fleet. You have control of the north of the city, your troops are blocking the two main thoroughfares, Canopic and Soma streets by demolishing buildings and building defences. Achillas cannot enter the city by the Gate of the Sun but there are plenty of fishing boats in Lake Mareotis that he could commandeer to transport his troops to the Lake Harbour. The

southern gate of Alexandria is unguarded so from there they will have unfettered access to the Cibotus Harbour and the Egyptian navy."

"Our survival depends on destroying those ships I do not have the resources to capture them! Do you have a plan?"

"I knew you were going to say that" replied Apollodorus smiling ruefully. "Leave it to me, but you can explain things to the Bassilisa, she will be furious."

"What will you do?"

"I can make my way round to the western harbour, over the island and then by sea into the docks. The good thing about a coracle is that it is light enough to be carried. There is only one that is still usable. Fortunately there is plenty of bitumen in the boat sheds to use as fuel to start the fire and I have a fair start on Achillas. I think I am a secret pyromaniac, I love setting things on fire!"

"How about all the thieves, vagabonds and pirates?"

"Don't worry; I will be quite at home they will look on me as a kindred spirit" replied the shipwright with a smile. "With luck they will be far to busy fighting Romans to notice pyromaniac 'Pollo. You can't be everywhere at once, neither can Achillas; I will have the satisfaction of getting even with him over being abandoned to the tender mercies of the crocodiles with a javelin in my thigh!"

Caesar laughed "I like a man who knows how to bear a grudge, I am glad you are on my side!"

"Good luck with taking the lighthouse. With all the coracles wrecked it's a case of 'win or swim'." They saluted each other in the Roman manner.

"Apollodorus one last thing."

"Domini" replied the shipwright.

"My lord in Latin is Dominus, Domini means lord but I preferred your familiarity, it was honest but my familiar name is Gaius." Caesar watched Apollodorus making his way around the coast for a few minuets and muttered under his breath; "You don't fool me with your acting the clown my brave and resourceful Britannian there are far more than triremes over there that you intend to destroy. I can afford to be patient that in the sure and certain knowledge in the fullness of time your secret addenda will be revealed."

Despite his bravado Apollodorus had a long walk along the seaward side of Pharos; the island was three miles in length and the coracle awkward to carry. On the western tip of the island was a temple dedicated to Poseidon and the remains of the prehistoric harbour. It was some time before he was able to re-launch the small boat in Eunostos, the Harbour of Good Return. Apollodorus reasoned that the offshore wind would drive any anchored ship onto the docks if their cables were cut. The shipwright boarded the first Trireme he encountered and made his way to the forecastle at the front of the ship. The forecastle has always been the paint store and traditional dumping ground for assorted equipment and materials for running repairs so Apollodorus was able to find fuel to start a fire. Once the fire was firmly established he re boarded his Coracle and slashed the Trireme's moorings.

General Achillas found the gate of the Sun well guarded by the Roman army so he lead his troops south along the canal that ran alongside the city wall through the eastern cemetery towards the reed beds that lined Lake Mareotis. These dense reed beds were home to another of Alexandria's sub class similar to those on Pharos. On the lake were floating islands of reeds where people made their homes and around the shores were a variety of industries particularly wine making. Passageways had been cut through the reed beds that only the lake's people could traverse without becoming hopelessly lost. These people, long forgotten and neglected by the ruling Macedonians, joined forces with the rebel Gabinian commanded by Achillas and advanced onto the Lake Mareotis harbour and un-guarded southern city gate.

Apollodorus made his way between the Egyptian Triremes setting them on fire and cutting their moorings so they drifted ashore carried by the prevailing wind.
"It's a good thing everyone is busy fighting over by the Gate of the Sun. When the war is over I shall make good this oversight in security and ensure no one else repeats my act of vandalism. My first priority as Sea Lord will be to arrange for the docks and navy to be properly guarded" he said to himself. Having caused chaos in the harbour he paused to observe his handiwork with a feeling of smug self satisfaction. Apollodorus then made his way towards the boat sheds around the Cibotus Harbour where the Heptastadium causeway joined the mainland. Here there was a plentiful supply of pitch so a fire was soon kindled. Unfortunately access to the palace compound was blocked by the fierce fighting along the coastline of the Great Harbour. The only possible way back was along the canal into Eunostos under the bridge at the mainland end of the Heptastadium

causeway and into the Great Harbour; to use the coracle risked being observed but it was a formidable distance to swim.

"I just hope Thea is correct about there being no crocodiles" he muttered under his breath as slipped reluctantly into the canal water clutching a bundle of reeds to aid his buoyancy. The current carried him out into the harbour and he lay in the water pretending to be dead. As soon as he was in the harbour he stealthily kicked his legs to propel himself under the bridge that joined to the Heptastadium causeway to the mainland. Above him was intensive fighting so he passed un-noticed into the Great harbour. The worrying thing for Apollodorus was that his plan had run so smoothly, all too often at the critical moment of success, failure is waiting to strike.

Meanwhile, back on Cape Lochias Cleopatra watched events unfold with her handmaids and the Doctor.

"Look over there!" she exclaimed "the Gabinians are making their way across Lake Mareotis to the harbour south of the city. They are going to try and capture my ships! Oh, Isis" Cleopatra entreated her goddess "why didn't I listen to 'Pollo? If they capture my fleet we will be lost, Olympos. If only 'Pollo was here, he would know what to do."

"It would appear that he or someone has done something already, your Highness. Look over towards the Gate of the Moon!" replied Olympos. Over to the west the sky was lit by a red glow that could only be one thing – fire!

Dawn stretched out her blood red fingers across Alexandria as Caesar returned to Cape Lochias safe in the knowledge that the lighthouse was firmly under Roman control. The fire started by Apollodorus spread to the neighbouring warehouses but was stopped by the canal that encircled the city. Most of the Alexandrian buildings were made of stone with very little wood used in the construction; consequently fire was far less of a risk there compared with other cities of the era. Caesar and Hiritius were back in the palace compound by mid-morning. The casualties had been light and the Romans had effectively drawn a cordon of defence that had cut the city in two. There was, however, no sign of Apollodorus.

Book 7

It was almost daylight by the time Apollodorus came ashore in the sector of Alexandria controlled by Caesar. The houses were still occupied by locals who professed to be sympathetic to the Romans. Tied wet and dirty he made his way to the Basilica at the entrance to Royal palaces on Cape Lochias. Passing the theatre where Caesars legions were billeted the shipwright was confronted by Cleopatra's younger sister Arsinoe and her slave Ganymede. The Egyptian giant faced Apollodorus defiantly with his arms folded across his barrel chest.

"*Kale emera* Arsinoe. Are you taking your pet for a walk?" inquired Apollodorus lightly but their intension was all too obvious. "It is rather early so could it be that you are defecting to the opposition?" Ganymede lunged at Apollodorus who tried to sidestep. Exhaustion slowed his reactions consequently the slave was able to grip the shipwright in a vicelike hold that forced the air from his lungs and threatened to crush his ribs. In desperation Apollodorus brought his knee up sharply into the Egyptians groin. Ganymede responded with a laugh and tossed the shipwright aside as though he was a rag doll. As unconsciousness partially engulfed him the shipwright heard Arsinoe order her slave.

"Leave him. We have no time. The Romans will soon return and General Achillas is waiting for us."

"I am sure Jocus will turn up any time" assured Caesar to a worried Cleopatra.

"You shouldn't have taken him with you, Caesar. He is a boat builder, not a Centurion!" she screamed.

"He is an excellent sailor, very resourceful and fearless except with snakes and you" replied Caesar.

"I know about the snakes, but why is he afraid of me?"

"He offered to set the ships on fire and made a joke about being a secret pyromaniac. I suppose coming from a cold country, he would be an expert in making things burn. He knew you would be furious about the loss of the Navy and insisted that I explain why it was necessary."

"And!" prompted Cleopatra sarcastically.

"You must have seen the invaders making their way through the reed beds into Lake Mareotis and the un-guarded harbour entrance to the south of the metropolis."

Apollodorus forced himself to his feet and staggered after Arsinoe and Ganymede into an opening in the double wall that surrounded the city. With such an efficient infrastructure that afforded accommodation, communication and defence he was at a loss as to why Caesar had billeted his legions in the theatre. This was another item on his 'to do' list; reverse the decades of neglect in the cities forgotten defence infrastructures.

"Incidently, where is your sister, Arsinoe?" Caesar asked by way of changing the subject but he was cut short by the arrival of Apollodorus. The shipwright was filthy and his clothes were wet and torn.
"She went that way" he replied, pointing towards the Jewish Quarter over by the Gate of the Sun. Cleopatra was delighted to see her friend and embraced him warmly.
"Where have you been, 'Pollo?"
"Chasing your kid sister, she has escaped. I ran into her as I sneaked back onto Cape Lochias but she made it to the opposition before I could catch her. Unfortunately the Gabinians are proclaiming her as the true *Bassilisa*. There was nothing I could do, I'm sorry."
"Charmain, Iras, take 'Pollo to my apartment and give him a bath. Mardian fetch some clean clothes for him.
"So did you win or swim?" asked Caesar with a smile. Apollodorus looked both exhausted and surprised and whispered to Cleopatra.
"Our Jules has a sense of humour after all, just goes to show how you shouldn't judge by appearances." When they were back in Cleopatra's apartment she replied.
"What is this about win or swim?"
"The coracles were all destroyed landing on Pharos except the one that I used to get back to the mainland. With no way for the specials to retreat I said it was a case of 'win or swim'. Don't worry I have no wish to go for a moonlight bathe with our Jules." Cleopatra laughed for the first time that day. Apollodorus added "It was an unavoidable disaster having to set fire to the Navy. We couldn't have risked your Triremes falling into the enemies' hands. When this is all over I will help build much bigger and better ships for you, I don't think I have ever seen such an archaeological collection of naval architecture, it is no real loss. By the way that was another example of Jules asking my opinion and I find myself volunteering to do something heroic and dangerous. 'Oh Jocus, there are twenty thousand Gabinians heading for the dockyard in Eunostos. What do you suggest?' says Caesar. 'Don't worry, muggings here will risk his neck and incur the

wroth of the *Bassilisa* by setting fire to her fleet.' I hope you are learning from his example." As he slid gratefully into the bath Cleopatra had a close look at Apollodorus and saw he was covered in bruises.

"Have you been fighting, 'Pollo?"

"I had a bit of a run-in with Arsinoe's minder. I kicked him in the testicles hard enough to stop most men but it didn't have the slightest effect on the brute."

"It wouldn't, he hasn't got any! He is a eunuch."

"Is that why you royals employ eunuchs then? You chop their balls off in case any one attacks them by kicking them there. I thought it was some form of punishment."

"Neither, they are gelded by choice."

"Why?" exclaimed Apollodorus in disbelief.

"It's the third gender, men that are attracted to men."

"So Mardian and Ganymede are homosexual."

"Yes, and they worship Isis the mother goddess."

"So as well as risking a thrashing by the brute Ganymede I may have been violated by him" replied Apollodorus with an exaggerated shudder. "Is that why Pothinus is such a slave to fashion, all the curls, make up and jewellery?"

Cleopatra smiled and nodded understandingly "Don't worry, 'Pollo, you will get used to our customs in time."

"What do you think is going on in the Gabinian camp right now, Thea?"

"I should think Ganymede and Achillas are in an almighty power struggle, which will keep them off of our backs for a few days" replied Cleopatra with a mischievous grin.

"From the look on your face I could have saved myself the trouble of getting into a fight."

"I didn't like to say so but Arsinoe and Ganymede escaping is a good thing. All we have to do now is persuade Jules to let Ptolemy join them and we can sit back and let them fight among themselves until the reinforcements arrive. Divide and conquer." They looked at each other and laughed heartily.

"I never knew politics was so childish, I use a similar type of manipulative logic that I call applied cretinology. What do you call it?"

"Applied cretinology, a cretin is physically deformed with learning difficulties used as entertainers at Roman feasts, from the Latin christianus meaning; although deformed and challenged, human not a beast" replied

Cleopatra thoughtfully. "I think that is an excellent name for the deliberate manipulation of people using their innate stupidity."

They were still laughing when Mardian arrived with some clean clothes. "I had better stay in the bath 'till he has gone" whispered Apollodorus "I don't want to excite the staff."

"How about Charmain and Iras?"

"They are girls, I don't mind them getting excited."

"How about me?" thought the first lady as she handed him a towel. Refreshed and revived by the bath Apollodorus made his way back to Caesar with Cleopatra. There was food and wine ready when they arrived and the Romans were looking pleased with themselves. Cleopatra explained to Caesar that there was likely to be a power struggle between Ganymede and Achillas. In another part of the palace Pothinus had come to the same conclusion. He was, however, pleased that Arsinoe had escaped so sent a message of support and promised to escape with Ptolemy at the earliest opportunity.

Caesar was later to describe the Alexandrians as intelligent and sharp witted due to the way they copied the Romans fortifications. They set up vast workshops throughout the city to manufacture weapons, balusters and towers. The citizens constantly attacked the Roman positions while defending their own. In public assemblies General Achillas announced:

"A few years ago Aulus Gabinius was in Egypt with his army. Pompeius tried to escape from Caesar by coming here. Pompeius is now dead but Caesar has lingered. If we do not drive him from our shores the realm will become a province of the republic. We must act quickly while he is cut off by the seasonal storms and cannot receive reinforcements."

The following day Apollodorus slept late so did not arrive at the command room until mid-day. Caesar had a face like thunder and at his feet was Pothinus begging for mercy.

"Take him away and execute him" ordered Caesar and to Apollodorus he added "I intercepted a message of support from him to Arsinoe promising to escape with Ptolemy as soon as possible. He was one of Pompey's murderers. I always get even! Pompeius was a great rival, not an enemy. That is a concept that people like Pothinus do not understand. Apollodorus, I saw you with a fearsome looking dagger when we attacked Pharos, may I borrow it?"

The shipwright handed him his weapon, amethyst hilt first. Caesar took it and handed it to the guard.

"Use this" he ordered.

"One down, two to go" thought Apollodorus but said nothing. Cleopatra gave him a knowing look as if to say 'I understand why you are so careful not to cross Caesar. I had better not flirt so openly with you when he is around, I don't want you to share the fate of that eunuch.' Apollodorus returned her look and raised an eyebrow signifying he understood and shared her thoughts.

"Julius Caesar didn't hold back when it came to vengeance then?" said the actress.

"He was very ambitious and utterly ruthless but at the same time had a strong sense of fair play. He pardoned more enemies than he executed, ultimately this would lead to his downfall."

During dinner that evening Caesar told the story of how he was taken by pirates as a young man on route to Rhodes.

"The pirates set the ransom far too low at twenty silver talents. I said I was worth twice as much" boasted Caesar. "Demand fifty." It took his men more than a month to raise the money from the surrounding towns. When the ransom had been paid he was released and promised to return and destroy them, which he did, recovering the ransom in the process. The chief pirate had treated him courteously so as a mark of respect Caesar had him strangled before crucifying him. "I always get even!" added the Roman with a sinister smile as he handed Apollodorus the borrowed dagger.

"I don't think there are any bits of Pothinus left on it" he added.

"How much was a talent?" asked the actress.

"A talent was the load of gold or silver a man could reasonably carry, about 26kg. It is difficult to translate into today's money, but it was a substantial sum, about £3,000 in silver or £200,000 gold."

It was clear to Apollodorus that Caesar was getting excited as he strode around the banqueting room. His audience were enjoying his storytelling. He was an excellent orator and the wine flowed freely. It appeared to Apollodorus that Caesar was becoming a little disorientated. Suddenly the shipwright realised what was concerning him and attracted Cleopatra's attention, who came over to where he was reclining.

"What's the matter, 'Pollo?" she inquired, anxiously.

"Get Jules out of here, Thea, and back to your apartment. I think he is going to have another one of his funny turns" he whispered

"How do I get him away? He is enjoying himself."

"Tell him that his oratory has ignited the passionate fire in your loins, which should get him out. I will follow at a discreet distance in case of problems."

The first lady slunk back to Caesar and whispered something into his ear. He looked surprised then smiled and they left a short while later, arm in arm. Apollodorus followed at a distance. As he turned the corner towards Cleopatra's apartment she anxiously called out to him.

"'Pollo, come quickly!"

They were at the apartment doorway. Caesar had a glazed expression on his face and together they helped the shaking Roman into the room and lay him on a couch. Cleopatra spoke soothingly to him. The attack was mild compared to the previous one and Caesar soon recovered his composure.

"How did you know I was going to have another attack, Jocus?"

"You were getting excited as you told the story about the pirates and appeared to become dizzy, although you had drunk very little. I just felt that you were about to have another attack."

"The dizziness seems to be a precursor to the attack. I am grateful that you noticed and got me out in time."

"I think it would be wise in future if you start to feel dizzy to remain seated, even if it is impolite. If you are alright now, I shall take my leave." He made his way back to the banquet but halfway there changed his mind and instead went to the Royal Harbour and stood by the palm trees on the beach. He had been there some time contemplating the stars when he became aware that he was not alone.

"Contemplating which world to go to next *Gelotopoios*?" asked the first lady.

"No this is my home, Thea. How's the boss now?"

"He is sleeping like a baby. I had Olympos mix me a strong sleeping draught for him after the last attack so I was prepared. Tell me some more about these strange places you have visited in the north. How do people get about in the snow, do they use horses?"

"They use sledges pulled by a type of cattle called reindeer. These animals are smaller than horses so it is not possible to ride astride them and their horns are like tree branches." He turned to face her and looked into her eyes.

"What are you thinking?" she asked.

"I was imagining you with a hood edged with white fur... no, a full-length white fur coat and boots. The white fur would set off your blond ringlets and the sledge would have bells that would ring in time with the trotting of the reindeer."

"Wouldn't I be cold?"

"No, because I would have my arm around you."

"Like this?" she put his arm round her and snuggled up to him "that's much better. Are the lights in the sky like the light from Pharos?"

"No, Pharos is a golden light. The Aurora is red and blue like a giant curtain that ripples in the night sky."

"Will you show me some day when the war is over and the Romans have gone home to Italy? And take me swimming with the dolphins?" she asked, and thought to herself "then make love to me on the beach by moonlight." Cleopatra looked up, her emerald green eyes met his, the colour reminded her of the Mediterranean. She added wistfully "we still haven't been swimming by moonlight."

"By the time it is warm enough the war will be over so we will go for that swim next summer."

She looked down again "I don't think so" she added sadly.

"Why?" asked the astonished shipwright. He sensed that Cleopatra was trying to tell him something and was having difficulty. "What is it, Thea?"

"I am pregnant" she said coldly.

"That's wonderful news! Jules will be delighted. He has no son and it's well known that his fourth wife, Calpurnia, is barren."

"It would be wonderful if I was carrying the child of the man I love" she thought, but aloud said "I am Caesar's concubine, not his wife. Unless he acknowledges the child as his heir it will be a *Nothos*, a bastard, like my *Pater*."

"According to the tradition of the Pharaoh's the Lady of Two Lands will be visited by the spirit of the god Amun, who will appear in the guise of a Roman."

"That may placate the people but for me it is as unlikely as Zeus appearing as a shower of gold coins when he seduced Danae the mother of Perseus."

"Cleopatra's pregnancy delighted the Roman. Caesar said that he was descended from the goddess Venus and had come to accept the Egyptian

concept that rulers were also divine. An heir was as important to him as much to carry on the family name as the future embodiment of his divinity."

The next day news arrived that the Rhodian squadron commanded by Euphranar and transport ships carrying the thirty seventh legion, remnants of Pompey's army, were anchored off the African coast, west of Alexandria. They had much needed corn, weapons, missiles and balusters but were prevented from landing at Alexandria by the Etesian trade winds and the men were desperate for fresh water. Caesar took his fleet the short distance along the coast and rendezvous with the Pompeian's at Chersonesus where he despatched small boats ashore to collect water. Some of the seamen allowed their greed for plunder to cloud their good sense. They ventured too far inland and were captured by the Egyptian cavalry commanded by the eunuch Ganymede. These captives were interrogated and their tongue's loosened under torture confessed that Caesar was with the fleet but his troops were still in Alexandria.

Ganymede sensing the possibility of victory dispatched all available ships not destroyed in the fire started by Apollodorus. They confront the Roman fleet as it returned to Alexandria. Due to the late hour, failing light and lack of troops Caesar was reluctant to engage the enemy so withdrew to a safe haven where his ships assumed a defensive formation. Their enemy had the advantage of local knowledge and on seeing a Rhodian ship isolated from the rest of the fleet's right wing seized the opportunity. They attacked with four Egyptian Triremes and several smaller vessels. Caesar countered capturing one Trireme and sinking another. Darkness prevented further action so the remnants of the Egyptian fleet escaped.

The following day Caesar returned triumphantly to Alexandria his warships towing the merchant ships with their desperately needed provisions and equipment. There was a gentle breeze and no further attempt was made by the Egyptians to attack. Caesar had demoralised the Alexandrians and gained their respect for the courage of his troops and the skill of his seamen. The Rhodian squadron and the thirty seventh legion were able to successfully disembark from the eastern harbour, effectively doubling Caesar's army.

"It was now December and they learned that Ganymede had eliminated Achillas. Caesar was pleased as now two of Pompey's murderers were dead. Unfortunately, Ganymede proved to be a capable general."

"I will replace all the ships destroyed by Caesar, old ships will be restored. We control the protection vessels and customs boats stationed at the seven mouths of the Nile, these can be transferred to Alexandria" announced Ganymede to the council. "We are a seafaring nation, we spends our lives on the water. The Romans are landlubbers, they are not true sailors. We can use small boats to harass their shipping. We are a resourceful people our city can provide all that we need."

They stripped timber from the colonnades and roofs of public buildings, restored old and derelict ships and against all expectation accumulated twenty seven Triremes and a number of un-decked smaller ships within a few days. Caesar in addition to his ten original ships had nine Rhodian ships, eight from Pontus, five from Lycia and twelve Asian Triremes. Both sides were full of confidence and ready to fight. The Gabinians won control of the western end of Pharos however Caesar's counter attack secured the whole of the island but not without cost, Euphranor was killed in the battle. The Roman victory meant that the Gabinian fleet in the western harbour, Eunostos, were unable to put to sea.

Caesar's control of Pharos Island and causeway was short-lived. The Heptastadium causeway was in three sections divided by two channels and joined by bridges. This enabled the passage of shipping between the two harbours. The counter attack by the Gabinians left Caesar and his troops stranded in the middle section of the causeway so the Romans had to swim for their lives.

"Your joke about win or swim when we first attacked Pharos is no longer very funny!" Caesar commented as the shipwright helped him aboard one of the rescue ships sent to evacuate the troops. "In the past I have swum for pleasure but this is the first time I have had to swim for my life!"

Caesar had fortified the Great Theatre but the Gabinians contaminated the water supply with sea water.

"I know the Alexandrians are obsessed with hydraulics" he ranted "but how in the name of all that is holy can they contaminate the supply to the theatre but houses around are un-affected?"

Cleopatra smiled sweetly and explained "Alexandria is a City on top of a City. There is a vast network of cisterns under most of the principal buildings. When the Nile floods an underground channel, which runs from west to east, south of the city fills and supplies channels that run north filling the cisterns."

"The whole city must be hollow under the streets and buildings" commented Apollodorus. "I was wondering how water was so plentiful considering it so rarely rains here. Surly the water collected is contaminated with mud and disease?"

"The first three days of the flood are used to flush out the cisterns and once they are full the water is allowed to settle for a few weeks. The Gabinians must have opened the seaward sluices to the cistern under the theatre" continued Cleopatra.

"That is all very interesting" replied Caesar impatiently "but what can be done to replace the water supply for my troops, this could spell disaster!"

"Considering the locals refer to the city as the frog pond the water table can't be too deep why not sink new wells" suggested Apollodorus.

Cleopatra gave him a knowing look as though to say "don't go volunteering to dig them yourself, you know Caesars management technique."

The Roman troops were beginning to panic and started to question why there had not been given orders to evacuate. Caesar addressed the men in the theatre.

"If we dig wells water could be found because every coastal district has veins of fresh water. Even if the Egyptian coast proves to be different from all others we have encountered we need not fear. We have unfettered access to the sea. We can fetch water daily by ship either from the African coast to our left or from the island to our right since the prevailing winds come from one direction or the other never both.

"Flight is not an option; our Roman honour is at stake! Even for those with no regard for their lives! It is taking great effort to hold our positions. If we abandon our fortifications our enemy will slaughter us. They have greater numbers; embarkation by boat will be fraught with difficulty and delay. We would be cut down before we could get to sea and victory would make the Alexandrians even more insolent. Put all ideas of retreat from your minds, concentrate on conquering at all costs! This is more than just Roman honour, it is our very survival! You trusted me in Gaul when the odds were overwhelmingly against us and we prevailed! You trusted me when we marched on Rome with the war cry 'a desperate man knows no fear' and Pompeius is vanquished! Trust me now and I will not fail you!"

Caesar ordered the digging of new wells that would provide his army's needs independently of the cities water supply. To the Roman engineers credit these wells were dug overnight and a disaster was avoided.

"Then what happened?" asked the actress.

"Several days of stalemate were broken by Caesar releasing Ptolemy from house arrest to join Arsinoe. Ganymede was either dismissed or murdered leaving Ptolemy and Arsinoe squabbling as anticipated. By Springtime Caesar learned that further reinforcements had arrived from Syria, Asiun and Arabin under the command of Graeco – Persian named Mithridates."

The weeks had passed into months. In Caesar's command room the news had just been announced. Cleopatra, now obviously pregnant, looked at Apollodorus who smiled back.

"Mithridates will join her Highness' army at Askalon" continued Caesar "then they will take the fortress at Pelusium."

The fortress was taken without much difficulty and the combined armies of Mithridates and Cleopatra marched south along the Pelusiac branch of the Nile. Mithridates then took the two armies North West along the Canopic waterway towards Alexandria. This was to confuse the Gabinian army and to avoid the intricate network of channels in the lower Nile delta. The Gabinian army of Ptolemy and Arsinoe marched south to engage Mithridates' troops on the banks of Lake Mareotis.

Cleopatra looked at Caesar with a mixture of fury and fear. "You can't leave me without protection!" she admonished him.

"Mithridates is outnumbered, Jocus will look after you" said Caesar turning to Apollodorus "do you think you could take care of her Highness and our unborn child while I take my army south to attack the Gabinians? I know how resourceful you are. Why not take her out to sea in your boat?"

"I think that's a crazy idea" replied Apollodorus and thought "here we go again. I am going to find myself volunteering to do something dangerous and heroic".

"You are forgetting" replied Caesar, "I have done battle with the navy of the men from the north." He turned to the *Bassilisa* "the wood they construct their boats from is as hard as iron and ramming them is pointless. 'Mintaka' is faster and more manoeuvrable than anything Ptolemy can use in pursuit."

Cleopatra looked from one man to the other but said nothing. Apollodorus replied. "I know all that, but what kind of signal will it send to the Alexandrians if the First Lady is seen running away?"

"I agree with 'Pollo" said Cleopatra "I shall stay here but with 'Mintaka' ready for sea, just in case."

"So we confidently wave goodbye to the Roman Army as they march off to war as though we have not a care in the world! I suppose it's no sillier than walking boldly through the Palace at midnight with you wrapped in a bed roll."

"Bluffing is the best way to play dice, you of all people knows that" said Caesar with a smile. Apollodorus was far from happy about the plan. Cleopatra looked at him and smiled sweetly, saying.

"You know how you boast about the impossible and miracles?"

"I think it would make more sense to go with the legions" he replied.

"Absolutely not!" exclaimed Caesar. "A battlefield is no place for an expectant mother!"

"Why not have some of your ships put to sea with a skeleton crew as though you are going to meet Mithridates at Pelusium. Dress someone in your purple cloak of office and a short man in one of the Bassilisa's dresses."

Caesar gave Apollodorus a slap on the back and said with a twinkle in his eye. "Good idea! For a shipwright you would make an excellent General. No-one will know Cleopatra's actual whereabouts and we will have far less opposition when we march south."

The next morning Cleopatra and Apollodorus watched secretly from the top of the lighthouse as the Roman fleet put to sea and Caesar marched his army out through the Gate of the Moon and round the eastern banks of Lake Mareotis.

"Why are they going that way?" asked Cleopatra.

"They will engage Ptolemy's army south of the lake. Mithridates will be advancing from the west so your kid brother and sister will be caught between Caesar's army and that of Mithridates. Caesar will have to march at breakneck speed. The Gabinians will be slaughtered and there will be a blood bath."

"If there is no doubt that Caesar will be victorious, why are you so sad, 'Pollo?"

"They may be our enemies but they are someone's sons. They have wives that by the end of the day will be widows and children who will be fatherless, I know the pain they will feel and just wish there was another way."

Cleopatra put her arms round him and held him tightly. "You are such an idealist" she said "you see good in all people, don't you?"

"And so Pharaoh Ptolemy's army was caught in a classic pincer manoeuvre and routed. Panic and slaughter ensued. Ptolemy fled Lake

Mareotis to the Nile in a boat which was overturned during a storm. The Pharaoh was reportedly drowned and Caesar returned to the city triumphant. The Alexandrians gave a typical Greek response and sided with the victor. Caesar, Mithridates and their armies were greeted as heroes."

Back in the palace Cleopatra listened to the news with mixed emotions. Caesar was perplexed by her response.

"According to ancient legend to drown in the waters of the Nile confers instant rebirth and immortality" she explained and held up the Ankh cross she habitually carried.

"No problem, I will have the Lake dredged" replied Caesar. "We will find his body and there will be no doubt or rumours."

"Did they find his body?" asked the actress

"Ptolemy's body was found, dressed in gold armour. His eleven year old brother Ptolemy XIV was crowned Pharaoh."

"What happened to Arsinoe?"

"She was captured and taken to Rome in chains."

"The Ankh cross, what is that?"

"The Ankh cross is a far older symbol than the crucifix. It has a looped top and is the symbol of immortality."

"Akh meant the power to transform. I am beginning to see the origins of Christianity you said were in Egyptian theology"

"Cleopatra's pregnancy was explained to the populace by the Pharaohs' tradition of the spirit of Amun visiting the Lady of Two Lands in the guise of a Roman paralleling the Christian belief that ' the holy spirit visited the Madonna', possibly about the same time in history."

In a quiet moment when Apollodorus and Cleopatra were alone the shipwright commented.

"All three of Pompey's murderers are now dead and Jules must be very pleased with himself. You are the undisputed Lady of Two Lands. Now would be a good time to take old baldy on that grand tour."

"I would rather go for that swim by moonlight."

"Give it a month or two and Caesar will go off on some other war."

"He has got what he came here for, the money Rabirius lent Pater. Caesar inherited that debt and needed the money for his war in Africa. You said his sole motivation was a massive need of money. I have given him what was owed so he will be on his way and no doubt find another royal woman to violate." added the Bassilisa with venom and thought "at least I will be alone with my Jester."

"Caesar stayed in Egypt long enough to ensure that hostilities were ended but did not go on the Grand Tour as many accounts describe."

By June responsibilities in Rome and elsewhere forced Caesar to leave. There was no one sufficiently high ranking and trustworthy to appoint as 'Legate'. A freeman named Rufinus was left in command of three legions as an occupying army to keep the peace or, as one of the troops was to later write:

'so that the power of the monarchs might be stronger, since they had neither the love of their own people (because they remained faithful to Caesar), nor the authority that derived from length of rule, having been established as rulers for only a few days. At the same time, Caesar thought it beneficial to the smooth running and renown of our empire, that Pharaoh and *Bassilisa* should be protected by our troops, as long as they remained faithful to us, but if they were ungrateful, they could be brought back into line by the same troops.' *(Caesar, the Alexandrian War)*

"He might have stayed long enough to see his son born" said Cleopatra bitterly to Apollodorus when they were alone.

"He told me to look after you, which I will and strangely he has conferred me with Roman citizenship. When it is safe he will send word for me to bring you and the baby to Rome. Have you ever been there?"

"Yes, I was there with *Pater* when he was lobbying the Senate to pass his law proclaiming him Pharaoh. I was only ten so I don't really remember anything other than the cold."

"Your baby will soon be born then we can have our swim." He put an arm round the young woman and rubbed her pregnant stomach affectionately. She rested her head on his shoulder. A few days later Cleopatra went into labour.

Book 8

Apollodorus was alone in his boat. The weather was fair and 'Mintaka' flew over the moonlit waves. It was good to relax again after the events of the last year. The war was over and Caesar had left to engage in other conflicts. The shipwright would have a job for life overseeing the rebuilding of Cleopatra's navy. Alexandria would be a comfortable and prosperous home for him.

He became aware that something, no, someone, was approaching. A winged lady dressed in black surrounded with an un-natural brilliance was flying across the waves towards him. She sat next to him in the stern of 'Mintaka'.

"I am Isis" she said "I have come to beg your help for my daughter, only you can save her now."

"Who is she?" he asked.

"The Lady of Two Lands needs you."

The apparition dissolved as a squall hit "Mintaka" Apollodorus was thrown across his boat.

"*Gelotopoios* wake up!" shouted Iras. The handmaid was shaking him vigorously. "Come quickly! Olympos needs your help. The *Bassilisa* is dying."

Cleopatra was in a birthing chair in the last stages of exhaustion.

"What is happening, Bones?" the shipwright demanded as he entered the sanatorium.

"The baby is in trouble, Caesar's first child was still born. His first wife, Cornelia died as a result. I don't know the details but it looks as though history will be repeated. I may be able to cut the baby from its mother but her Highness will not survive."

"Can't you use the drugs the worshippers of Dionysus use to obtain ecstatic transcendence? That way she would feel less pain."

"If I could get them, perhaps, but it's never been tried. Also, what effect would it have on the baby?"

Iras interrupted "You know what to do; My Lord *Gelotopoios*, the Doctor and her Highness may have …."

"No, Iras, we promised" croaked Cleopatra.

"I will not be silenced" replied Iras "I was not part of the pact at Askalon" she sank to her knees and held the shipwrights legs "I beg you, save my Lady and do with me as you wish."

"There is no need for that" he replied as he helped the distraught handmaid to her feet "I know what you are suggesting and I had come to the same conclusion." He turned to the *Bassilisa* "I don't know what effect this will have on our relationship but if you are willing, look into my eyes."

"I trust you with my life, 'Pollo, I am in your hands"

He tenderly lifted her up out of the birthing chair while holding her gaze. Blue eyes filled her whole vision as she drifted into the twilight land where time and space collide and there for the first time she saw snow and the Aurora lights. The lights were as he had described them, a giant curtain of red and blue rippling across the night sky.

"What strange beasts reindeer are? Their horns are like the branches of a tree" she thought then noticed that she was dressed in a long white fur coat. On her head was a white fur hood. She should feel cold but instead she felt a warm security, she was in the arms of the man she truly loved. Was that the sound of bells ringing in time with the reindeer trotting? Then she was naked. The scene had changed and she was swimming with dolphins in the warm blue water of the Mediterranean with her Lord.

"I suggest you make a low incision across the top of her pubis then push the muscles to one side" said Apollodorus softly "I know the usual way to cut out a baby is with a vertical incision over the abdomen but Cleopatra will never forgive us if she has an unsightly scar and can't wear her diaphanous dresses."

"Trust you to think of a thing like that. No one has ever performed an operation like this before and had both mother and baby survive."

"There is a first time for everything, Bones. I don't know why, but I know we will prevail."

"I hope so. Your jokes about being fed to the crocodiles were never very funny at the best of times and I certainly don't want to have to explain to Caesar that we killed the *Bassilisa*. By all that is holy she has a son, look the placenta is coming away naturally!" Iras took charge of the baby as the Doctor cleaned the mother and skilfully stitched up the opening.

"I don't know how long I can keep her Highness asleep, Bones, but when she is awake she will be in a great deal of pain. Have you managed to collect any more of my mould in case of infection?"

"Now the baby is safely delivered I can use narcotics and give her preparations to help with the pain. Your gift was all I believed it could be, my friend" replied the doctor softly.

"Remember our pact. You must tell no one that includes you, Iras!"

"So did Apollodorus and Olympos perform the first caesarean operation?" asked the actress.

"It was believed that the name Caesar was derived from the Latin 'matre caeso' which means cut out of his mother. It actually means hairy. The popular story that Julius Caesar was born by caesarean section is unlikely as the Roman knowledge of surgery was minimal and there is documentary evidence that his mother was alive into his adulthood. In answer to your question, I will claim the fifth amendment on behalf of the Jester and the Doctor."

Cleopatra found herself on a beach with a full moon overhead. Her passion was spent but she felt a warm glow of satisfaction and contentment spreading through her whole being spoilt only by a dull ache in her pubis. She looked into his blue eyes which shone with an eerie light like sapphires.

"It's time to go home, my love" he said softly.

The scene changed again and she was back in the palace birthing room looking down at a prostrate figure of a woman. A man was talking to the woman quietly. There was a younger woman whose skin was as black as ebony holding a baby and talking to a second man. The pain in her abdomen was becoming more intense as she descended into the woman on the bed. It now enveloped her completely and she screamed.

"Lay still, Thea!" shouted Apollodorus. "Get her something for the pain, Bones. We have between us performed a miracle and you have a healthy son."

Cleopatra was vaguely aware that she was being given a drink of bitter herbs. The pain started to ease as unconsciousness enveloped her once again. How long she remained in that twilight zone of neither sleep nor wakefulness she would never know, but gradually the pain eased and her sleep became more natural. She was vaguely aware of being given her baby to suckle. Cleopatra had made it clear that unlike her predecessors she had no wish to use a wet nurse.

"Try and feed him" encouraged Apollodorus "it will be better for both of you and aid your recovery."

After a few days, how long she could not tell, she was able to sit up and take in her surroundings and by the end of the first week began to realise that Apollodorus was very distant. He was a frequent visitor but seemed utterly preoccupied. Her strength gradually returned and halfway through the second week Olympos asked.

"What are you going to call your son?"

"Ptolemy Caesar, of course, but no doubt the Alexandrians will nickname him 'Caesarion', little Caesar" she replied. They were alone so she asked. "Tell me Olympos, 'Pollo is very distant. Is anything the matter?"

"I know what you mean. I don't altogether understand, but I think he paid a high price for what he did for you."

"What do you mean?" she replied in alarm.

"He kept you unconscious long after I had delivered Caesarion. You felt nothing 'till he released your *Ba*, your soul, but during that time I think he felt your pain. I didn't realise it at the time I was too busy. Forces beyond our understanding took over, I am certain that my hands were guided. I cut out your baby in a way that has never been done before; I can hardly remember what I did. If your Apollodorus is Mendis, the Piper at the Gate of Dawn, as Caesar once suggested, they say his greatest gift is that of forgetfulness. We must be patient, just give him time and he may tell us. If not, there are some things mortals are just not meant to know."

"I suppose I will have a massive scar and be unable to have any more children?" she asked.

"That's the amazing thing. I made a small, low, horizontal incision not the usual vertical abdominal cut. *Gelotopoios* insisted on that method, he said you would never forgive us if you couldn't wear diaphanous dresses any more due to an unsightly scar. You are healing nicely and there will be little sign of the operation so there is every chance you will be able to have more children. I suspect your Sea Lords instructions were based on far more serious considerations than mere cosmetics."

Soon Olympos removed the stitches and the first lady was able to get up. She was young and healthy so made a rapid recovery. Apollodorus remained preoccupied and distant for rather longer but Caesarion seemed to have a special relationship with the shipwright and was always more contented when the Jester held him.

"It's as though he knows that 'Pollo saved both our lives" commented Cleopatra to Olympos as they watched the two together in the palace gardens in the autumn sunshine. "Caesar may have sired him, but 'Pollo is his *Pater*" she thought as a warm glow of contentment flooded through her body.

"In due time Ptolemy XV was formally named Ptolemy Theus Philopator Philometor (the father and mother loving god) and it was said that he bore a striking resemblance to Caesar, so all Alexandria called him

Caesarion which means 'Little Caesar' or' Caesar's son' as Cleopatra predicted."

"What was Julius Caesar up to while Cleopatra was having his baby?" asked the actress.

"First he travelled to the Middle East and annihilated King Pharnace of Potus in a battle so short his comment on the victory was the historic quote 'Veni, vidi, vici' (I came, I saw, I conquered). He was elected Pro Consulate a third time, then he dealt with the remnants of Pompey's army in Africa. Mark Antony was appointed Master of Horse, Caesar's deputy with supreme authority that he abused appallingly. Antony returned to Rome with the bulk of the army. Pompey's sons Gnaeus and Sextus, along with Caesar's former second in command during the Gaelic Wars, Titus Labienus, escaped to Spain. Before pursuing them Caesar began extensive reforms to the government and implemented plans to distribute land to the veterans throughout the empire. During the final decisive battle in Spain he was elected Pro Consulate for the fourth time."

In the palace temple on the Eastern tip of Antirhodos Island Cleopatra was giving thanks to Isis, the mother goddess, for her son. As she stood in front of the goddess statue she became aware of an aura of light and the statue seemed to come alive. Cleopatra was filled with fear and wonder.

"I am Isis. Do not be afraid, my daughter."

"I fear not for myself" said the *Bassilisa* "but for my friend, Apollodorus. Did he commit a grievous sin against the gods by saving me and my son?"

"What he did, he did out of true love and he did it on my behest. Take care of him and in time he will be restored. He is your truest friend and greatest ally, such people are rare indeed." The vision dissolved and once again Cleopatra was alone.

The harvest was the best for many years and the people said that once again the gods were smiling on the Upper and Lower Lands of Egypt. Lower taxation resulted in more money being circulated, so by the following spring not only were there buds of new growth on the plants and trees but all could see the buds of a new golden age. By the summer Caesarion was walking and Apollodorus was, on the face of it, back to his usual jovial self.

Cleopatra found the shipwright working on his own boat 'Mintaka' in the Cape Lochias Royal Harbour.

"Are you preparing to leave us?" she asked, half in alarm and half joking.

"No, far from it, Alexandria is my home now. I was feeling that I had been neglecting 'Mintaka' having been so busy re-building your ships and repairing the captured Gabinian fleet. When there is the spare cash I have some ideas for a special Royal Triremes. A seagoing palace for state visits where you could entertain Royalty. What do you think?"

"I think it's a wonderful idea, 'Pollo" she replied wistfully and thought 'Mintaka isn't the only Lady you have been neglecting lately!'

"I had another idea" he said conspiratorially.

"Yes"

"Yes" he teased.

"Well what is?" she asked, stamping her foot impatiently.

"They say that swimming is really good exercise to help a mother get back her figure after a birth, not that there is anything wrong with yours."

"Do they?"

"Yes."

"Go on, I'm listening."

"There is a full moon tonight."

"Really?"

"I have some honey mellowed wine stored in 'Mintaka' and you could bring some figs."

"I could.... 'Pollo."

"Yes."

"I thought you would never ask."

"One other thing, Thea. Bring your lyre."

So that night they walked hand in hand naked through the palm trees into the water lit with a golden aura from the lighthouse. The tranquil silence was only disturbed by the lapping of the sea and the occasional murmur of the wild foul that inhabited the harbour. It was as though all Alexandria held its breath. Although the night was balmy, the young woman shivered uncontrollably with excitement.

"It's not too cold for you?" asked Apollodorus anxiously.

"No, far from it. When you are a royal, no one questions your actions no matter how eccentric! It's so refreshing to do something really naughty!" she replied. "I suppose that is why *Pater* enjoyed getting drunk and disgracing himself in front of the Romans, by playing his flute and dancing."

"Exactly, or your ancestor Ptolemy XII, *Physon*, entertaining the Romans in a diaphanous gown like you usually wear."

"Showing off his body like that is nothing unusual in our culture, 'Pollo. It was the sight of him walking that was so surprising!"

"Did you ever get up in the night when you were a child to raid the food cupboard and have a midnight feast with your brothers and sisters?"

"No, I have never been hungry."

"How about scrumping? Did you ever steal fruit from the kitchen gardens?"

"No, all the wealth of Egypt is owned by the Royal family."

"That's why you Ptolemys don't get on, you have never bonded by doing naughty things together" said Apollodorus with sudden realisation. "I will have to put things right when Caesarion is older and play all sorts of tricks on you with him."

Cleopatra threw her arms round his neck and kissed him passionately "I wish you had been around when I was a child, we would have had so much fun."

"Just because we are grown up doesn't mean there is anything wrong with being a child from time to time and having fun" he replied. In that moment Cleopatra understood what he had meant about taking her away to his fantasy land where no one grows old.

"You couldn't persuade me to take that journey with you. 'Third star on the right and straight on till morning.' You are bringing something of that land to Alexandria."

"Both are magical places and you are a fairy tale royal lady."

After their swim they lay on the beach in each others arms.

"What do you think of my scar, Gelloto?"

"It is hardly noticeable, Thea, but if you are worried you could always have a snake tattooed over it."

Cleopatra laughed. "That's typical of one of your silly remarks" she said.

"Or you could wear a fine chain round your hips, don't be self-conscious the scars we have make us what we are so, there is no need to feel shame about them. What is important is what is inside."

She could think of no reply so kissed him passionately instead. The passion was rising in both of them but more obviously with Apollodorus.

"We mustn't" he said.

"Why? Because of...."

"No, I think she would want me to as much as you do."

"Why then?"

"I don't know how many divine and eternal rules we broke by becoming one mind to save you and Caesarion. How many more would we break if we were to become one body? Also, you may conceive and your body needs more time to recover."

"How much of my pain did you feel, 'Pollo?"

"I honestly can't remember."

They kissed again and then Cleopatra whispered. "There are other ways I can satisfy you without us becoming one body."

"We must not do that either."

"Why ever not? I know you desire me and don't give me that 'commoner and royalty' nonsense." She sounded hurt, so Apollodorus chose his words with care. He knew he could prevaricate no longer but how much could he tell her?

"When you were unconscious during the delivery of Caesarion did you have strange visions? Could you see your own body as though you were in the birthing room observing the birth?"

"Yes. Why?"

"You were in the twilight land between life and death. You call it the Beautiful West and I call it the Astral Plain. We all go there when we sleep but are usually unaware of the experience."

"Is that the ecstatic transcendence that worshipers of Dionysus seek?"

"Probably. I have out-of-body experiences all the time. This gives me the ability to see dimly into the future."

"Is that what was happening to you when you were delirious on my Royal Thalamegos following your leg injury on route to Askalon?" she asked with sudden realisation.

"Yes."

Cleopatra was becoming very frightened. "What have you seen, 'Pollo?"

"It is very difficult to interpret visions so I rarely pass the information on. You are the most desirable woman who has ever lived. Men will tell of your beauty long after they have no use of the gods and the stars have become just another place to make their home. I caused the destruction of the only woman I ever loved. I am so fearful that history will be repeated. If we were to become lovers this may cause your destruction and the end of the Dynasty of the Ptolemys and the Cleopatra's."

"But you are an atheist, you don't believe in the intervention of the gods or destiny."

"That isn't quite true. I said when we first met that I hadn't found a god I could truly worship. Most of the gods people worship don't have the best interests of humanity at heart. At best they look on mankind as a play thing and at worst a resource to be exploited. I believe there is a central order of things, a power that holds all life together. My idea of a god would be one that is our companion and would work with us. *Enthous* god with us, is my idea of what a true god should be. It's relationship with its creation would be *agape*, not amusement."

"That Greek word, enthous, sounds familiar" said the actress.
"Yes, we derive enthusiasm from it, literally 'god with us' or 'possessed by god'." I replied.

Cleopatra thought about what Apollodorus had said for some time, and then she replied, "That *Theus* is you, 'Pollo." They lay in each others arms for a long time saying little and the *Bassilisa* resolved to prove the Jester's vision wrong. She knew that Apollodorus acted for the most noble of reasons and she loved him all the more for it. However, she was used to having her own way so determined to make this no exception.

The actress was sitting close to me so I put my arm round her and continued. "Her resolve would have tragic consequences. Apollodorus had interpreted his vision completely wrongly. This was, after all, Alexandria, the wine press of love. 'Those who emerged were the sick men, the solitaries, the prophets – I mean all who have been deeply wounded in eros.'"

"How could you have caused your lady's destruction? She was killed by an uraeus." asked Cleopatra, then immediately knew she had made a terrible mistake and what Apollodorus answered could so easily apply to her. In a voice that was little more than a whisper and tears in his eyes he replied.
"There is a saying 'beware what you wish for' dreams that come true all too often turn into nightmares. I tried so hard to give her everything she wanted. Her dream did turn into a nightmare. I had been badly injured in battle so I am hazy about the details. She was either murdered or killed herself. As she lay dying in my arms she told me that it was the venom of a cobra that had killed her. By giving her what she wanted I brought about her destruction. I could not find the snake so that I could travel with her to the

afterlife. I pray she had not killed herself as I subsequently learned that suicide is the worst form of sacrilege and would have resulted in an eternity of torment re-living those last moments."

Summer was almost ended when Cleopatra and her brother, Ptolemy, received the invitation to visit Rome. Caesar was now in his fourth term as Pro- Consulate, all Pompey's supporters were eliminated and his murder avenged. It was only a matter of time before he would be made Dictator for perpetuity. Cleopatra, Ptolemy her brother, Caesarion her son and her friends sailed in a recently restored Trireme with two other ships as escort. It was now almost the season of autumn; soon the Mediterranean would be closed to shipping.

"Have you ever been to Rome, *Gelotopoios*?" she asked as the flotilla cleared the breakwater at the Great Harbour entrance.

"No, but I was in Sicily before travelling to Palestine where we met" he replied.

"So that added to the confusion resulting from both Britannia and Sicily being called the Tin Island is why some refer to you as the Sicilian."

"Yes, but I have learned to live with the miss-judgement" he quipped. "When people are ignorant of the facts they invent a story and my origins are my business. I tell those who I choose, the rest can believe what they like."

"To me, 'Pollo, you are an Egyptian-Achaean, a true Alexandrian."

"They say there are as many nations in Alexandria as there are teeth in the mouth of a crocodile" he answered.

"How many is that?" she asked.

"I don't know. The last time I was in a position to count I was a little preoccupied!"

"Next time we need rescuing from one of Sorbek's people I shall tell Marcus Antonius to hold on while you make good that lack of knowledge."

"Did you know the name Caesar means 'hairy'?" commented Apollodorus.

"So that's why he is so sensitive about his receding hairline" replied Cleopatra dismissively and then added more seriously. "Do you think he will formally acknowledge Caesarion as his son?"

"If he truly loves you, certainly he will. Caesar has ambitions of divinity and is Rex in all but name, so he needs an heir and on both counts he must acknowledge him. Do you doubt it?" Cleopatra said nothing just looked sadly at Apollodorus as though to say, Caesar neither loves nor cares for me. If he did he would have stayed in Alexandria long enough to see his son born.

"If he had lingered I may not have been permitted to intervene during the birth" said the shipwright.

Again Cleopatra remained silent but thought "Are our minds still so linked that you can share my thoughts?" This time Apollodorus remained silent but looked at Cleopatra and she knew his answer. "I share your thoughts when you let me, your sorrows and your joys as you share mine." She touched his arm lightly, as anything more intimate in public was not really acceptable, although she longed to hold and be held by him.

"Will you ever forgive me for opening the wound of the loss of your lady?" she whispered.

"How can I forgive when you did no wrong? I should seek your forgiveness for not telling you a long time ago. You have a right to know but when pain is felt that deeply it is hard to talk about it. I would forgive you no matter what you did, agape is unconditional. Caesar has his spies n Alexandria so would have found out if we had become lovers."

"No, he wouldn't. You know exactly who his spies are and had them out of the way when we had our swim."

"How did you guess?" exclaimed the shipwright with an expression of exaggerated innocence.

"I didn't. Charmain and Iras told me how the three of you conspired to get the poor men drunk."

"That's the thing that makes counter-espionage so easy. All spies love a pretty girl, the chance to gamble and a goblet or two of fine wine."

They looked seriously at each other, and then Cleopatra saw the twinkle in his eye. She was first to giggle which Apollodorus found infectious. They laughed 'till their sides ached and the tears ran down their cheeks. When they had recovered their composure she asked, although she knew the answer, "Could you ever be cross with me, 'Pollo?"

"Not for more than a heartbeat and you know it."

Book 9

"What direction will we take from Alexandria?" asked Cleopatra as they headed out to sea.

"Due north 'till we sight land which with luck will be Cilica. If we are too far west we will hit Rhodes which is in the right direction but if we drift east we will hit Cyprus. At night time we will have Polaris, the pole star, to guide us but by day we may drift off course" replied Apollodorus

"Presumably Cilica is Turkey" said the actress.

"Yes that's right; they were making for Turkey a distance of about five hundred miles. The whole journey to Rome was five times that distance, which a sailing yacht today would be able to complete in approximately two weeks with no stop offs. Cleopatra's ships would take at least twice as long as the Triremes could only cruise at four knots. Incidentally, ramming speed, with all three levels of rowers deployed, was about twice that but they couldn't maintain eight knots for long unlike a modern yacht.

Sails couldn't be used as the prevailing wind was against Cleopatra and her courtiers. The Triremes had three levels of oars so the rowers could take turns and good progress was made. Most of the rowing was done at night time and the crew tended to rest during the heat of the day. Cleopatra and Apollodorus spent much of the time at the bows of the Triremes, the only private place on the vessel, as the hundred and seventy rowers faced aft. In front of them was the Great Bear, the constellation later known as the Plough.

"Ursae Majoris was once a handmaid of the maiden goddess Artemis who demanded chastity of her followers" commented Cleopatra. "Callisto was seduced by Zeus and when Artimis discovered this she turned the unfortunate nymph into a bear. Zeus saved Callisto from being hunted to death by setting her image among the stars. The constellation of the Great Bear looks like a giant cooking pan".

"That is a very good description" replied Apollodorus. "The two stars opposite the handle are the pointers to Polaris which is very difficult to see because it is so faint. Polaris is due north so we will use that to direct us across the Mediterranean." Behind them was the constellation of Orion.

Cleopatra explained. "To my people Orion is the Hunter accompanied by his faithful dogs Canis Major and Canis Minor. They hunt the celestial animals Lepus, Taurus and others. Orion was in love with

Merope, one of the seven sisters but Merope spurned his love and his life was tragically ended when he stepped on a scorpion. The gods felt sorry for Orion so put him and his hunting dogs in the sky with all the other celestial animals near him. Scorpius was placed in the opposite side of the sky so Orion would never be hurt again."

"Why didn't Merope return Orion's love?" asked Apollodorus.

Cleopatra thought bitterly. "Probably for the same reason you refuse to return mine. Perhaps my destiny is the same as Orion's." Apollodorus had sensed her thoughts but assumed it was Caesar she was thinking about. He put his arm tenderly round the young woman and said.

"You are not the seventh sister you are the seventh Cleopatra and the most beautiful woman who has ever lived. If Caesar does not acknowledge Caesarion as his heir he deserves to be stung by a scorpion."

To the side of the Great Bear was the constellation of Cassiopeia like a giant letter W. "Cassiopeia was the mother of Andromeda" explained Cleopatra. "Perseus rescued Andromeda from the sea monster Cetus having first killed Medusa."

"Was Cassiopeia the queen of Ethiopia?" asked Apollodorus.

"That's right, her husband was Cepheus."

"Whereabouts in the sky do you want to go when you die?" he asked.

"The Pharaohs go to Orion to spend the afterlife so I suppose that is where I will go. How about you, *Geloto*?"

"Orion sounds nice with all those celestial animals for company, but could you stand having me there poking fun at the gods and telling them where they have gone wrong for all eternity?"

Cleopatra said nothing, but thought "If he wanted to spend the afterlife with her then why not the here and now? What of his first love, his lady who died from the venom of the uraeus, surely he would want to be with her?"

"How big were the ships, the Triremes?" asked the actress.

"The Triremes were over a hundred feet long, thirty five metres or, in the units of the time, seventy cubits. They were long and slender, drawing three feet and four feet freeboard. The basic type with one man at each oar carried one hundred and seventy rowers so dragging the boats out of the water would have presented no problem with that amount of manpower."

"With that many men on board there would have been little room for anything else."

"For that reason they couldn't spend too long at sea so they usually beached the boats at night time, this enabled the crew to purchase food and drink."

"Why did they take the boats out of the water whenever possible?"

"Anti foul wasn't invented and also it was necessary to dry the boats out."

"I am really worried about leaving Alexandria so soon after the civil war. What if there is another uprising while we are away?" asked Cleopatra.

"You have no need to worry for two reasons" replied Apollodorus. "Firstly, the only surviving Ptolemy's are on board this Trireme, apart from Arsinoe who is safely in custody in Rome. Secondly, you have adopted Caesar's command style in which you delegate responsibility and allow ministers to act on their own initiative. They know what is wanted and how they achieve it is largely up to them. If they have a problem they come to you and ask your opinion and rather than telling them what to do you ask for their suggestions. If these are sound you agree with them, if not you suggest alternatives. Undoubtedly these ministers are lining their pockets as they have never had it so good, neither has the crown. You said to me some time ago 'Egypt is a civilised country. Money is a far better motivator than whips.' By the time we get back from Rome there will be plenty of money for your seagoing royal palace or anything else that takes your fancy. Your ministers will have become rich, so the last thing on their mind will be regime change."

"Do you really think so 'Pollo?"

"Yes, I do. You have done a wonderful job of winning the hearts and minds of your people and in less than two years. Now you can afford to enjoy a well earned holiday."

On the eighth day they sighted land. By this time they were running low on food and water for the crew.

"That looks like Rhodes. Your Trierarchos is quite a good seaman, I am impressed" said Apollodorus with a smile.

"More likely he had some good advice, you pointed him in the right direction" replied Cleopatra. "It will be good to go ashore as there is a very manly smell on this ship. When you build me my floating palace you will have to do something about the smell of a hundred and seventy sweaty rowers."

"How about spreading flowers over the deck so the perfume is released as you walk over them or you could have a female crew" replied the shipwright, and then added with a grin. "Why do you think it is that my people don't rely on oars?"

"From what Caesar tells me there is plenty of wind around Britannia, so you don't need to use oars."

"It is a harsher climate and the winds are much stronger" replied Apollodorus, trying to be tactful.

"So what you really mean is that your people are proper mariners and we Mediterranean sailors are children playing boats in the bath by comparison."

"I wouldn't dream of being so harsh."

"Don't prevaricate, 'Pollo. I have had little else to do for the last week other than observe the way you move around this Trireme. I have seen the way you have checked the navigation and all other nautical matters. You have discarded as worthless more than the *Trierarchos* will ever know about seamanship. You made certain we arrived at the right place and my Captain didn't even notice you do it, you were so diplomatic."

Apollodorus looked embarrassed.

"Don't look like that, 'Pollo, it is most reassuring to be in such confident hands" continued Cleopatra. "The *Trierarchos* is grateful for your help and appreciates the way you avoid undermining his authority at all times."

Four centuries earlier Rhodes city, at the northern tip of the island, had replaced the three original capitals Lindos, Cumeirus and Lalysos so the Egyptians had to sail north along the western coast to obtain provisions. Rhodes was a commercial centre for spices, resin, ivory, silver, wine, oil, fish and amber which made it the wealthiest of the Aegean islands. There were no natural harbours but the city, sighted on a bull neck spit of land, had five artificial havens. A bronze statue of Helios had straddled the opening of the principal harbour but this had been toppled by an earth quake. It was said that the sun god was displeased by this sixty cubit *(thirty meters)* high monument so no attempt had been made to restore it. Alexander the Great admired the city which was supposed to have been planned by Hippodamnus, the architect of Alexandria.

The Rhodan fleet, considered to be the finest in the Mediterranean, and the people had successfully resisted the siege by Demetrius three centuries earlier, for which the Collossus monument commemorated but the city would soon be destroyed by the Roman Cassius. A day and night was spent re-provisioning the three ships then the following day a favourable wind enabled the Egyptians to make for the northern coast of Crete under sail. Sailed all day and through the following night they arrive in the middle of the next morning. The mountain range that formed the backbone of the island had been visible from first light while they were still some distance away. This was the largest of the Greek islands, fertile and mountainous like Rhodes and sheltered the inner Cyclades from the forces of the deep water that ravaged the land to the south which dropped away abruptly into the sea.

"I suppose you would have carried on?" said Cleopatra as they landed on the northern coast.

"I like to make the most of a favourable wind" replied Apollodorus "but with so many men on board we had better not push them too hard and risk mutiny. The journey is always more interesting than the arrival so regular stops will keep everyone happy. Now if we were travelling privately, just you, me and 'Mintaka'...."

"Yes, we would stop off in secluded bays for moonlit swims and I could play my Lyre."

"We are carrying a Felucca on deck why don't we sail round that headland this afternoon while the crew are resting. Reconnaissance is an essential part of leadership."

"I suppose there are some figs and honey mellowed wine on board" replied Cleopatra with a knowing smile.

"I thought we may need to sneak off from time to time, that's why I had the small boat put on board."

"Why would we need to sneak off?" teased Cleopatra.

"I can't cuddle the *Bassilisa* with all those sweaty rowers watching and you know how jealous Jules gets."

Cleopatra smiled and thought "It's a pity there are no grounds for jealousy." That afternoon the Felucca was launched and the gentle breeze filled the sail as the two friends cast off.

"We had better remain in sight of the ships in case of pirates" said Apollodorus. "But at least we can have a little privacy for the afternoon."

"I was hoping for a moonlight swim" replied Cleopatra.

"It is very tempting and I can't think of anything I should like more but the closer we get to Rome the more uneasy I feel."

"You were sleeping uneasily last night and muttering things in a language I couldn't understand. Have you had another of your visions 'Pollo or are you concerned that we may bump into the Minotaur?"

"Not exactly. I suppose it is because when I have gone on long voyages before I have only had myself to look after. I am being silly. Three Trireme warships are more than a match for any pirates we may encounter."

Apollodorus noticed that a school of dolphins were following in their wake and hastily changed the subject. "Oh look, we have company!"

They reached the headland without further incident and anchored a little way offshore. After they had eaten some figs and drunk a goblet or two of wine, Cleopatra produced her Lyre and played and sang softly. The soporific effect of the food, drink and music caused Apollodorus to momentarily drop off to sleep. He woke with a start and found Cleopatra looking at him anxiously.

"What did you see, 'Pollo?"

He was momentarily disorientated. "How long was I asleep?" he asked.

"Hardly any time and I understood what you were saying. You said they are stabbing him. 'Pollo, what did you see? I must know!" she pleaded.

"The image was like looking at a reflection in rippled water. I can't make sense of it."

"Are there no incantations or spells you can do so that you can see more clearly, like the Egyptian Sooth Sayers do?"

"They can't accurately predict their next meal! You know that I consider all Sooth Sayers to be frauds."

"Apollodorus!" exclaimed Cleopatra sternly "you are prevaricating again. If you have misinterpreted the vision I will forgive you but if the gods are sending you a warning and you don't share it with your monarch that will be unforgivable!"

The shipwright looked genuinely hurt. Cleopatra had never spoken to him so crossly. Seeing her friend looking sad the *Bassilisa* felt guilty so she put her arms round him and said more softly. "I know there are some things you cannot bring yourself to share with me but this should not be one of them. Tell me what you can see and let's try and work it out together."

"To access the land of dreams I need to be totally relaxed which simply is not possible on this voyage…."

"Apollodorus!"

"No, I am not being evasive. The visions will continue to come so you must sleep near me and note down everything I say. When we are in Rome and we can get some piece and quiet there is a Druid way of looking into the future but it is dangerous. You are my dearest friend and I trust you to drag me back if the ritual goes wrong. One thing is certain; all is not well in Rome. If it were not so important to go there and get Caesar to recognise his son I would be tempted to turn back."

"If you wanted me to sleep with you there was no need to have funny visions" said Cleopatra trying to make light of the situation. "Do you think we will be at a crossroad in our lives in Rome?"

"Not us. Strangely, there is danger but I don't think it is aimed at us. There is a crossroad but not ours. There is evil in the form of a small man." Apollodorus shuddered "I really can't abide small men."

"How about small ladies?" asked Cleopatra with a smile.

"Small ladies are fine. You can't wrap a large lady in a bed roll and smuggle her into a palace at the dead of night. It's a pity you didn't send a spy ahead of us to tell us what to expect in Rome."

Cleopatra looked embarrassed.

"Did you send a spy and not tell me?" he asked. Cleopatra nodded.

"Thea, I love you!"

"You do?" her heart was racing these were the very words she so desperately wanted to hear him say. Words that would change everything, but she knew Apollodorus spoke in jest.

"Yes, you did the right thing and told no one."

"You aren't cross that I didn't tell you?"

"Not in the least, I love a girl with initiative. You know my view on clandestine activities, the less people who know the better. I had no need to know, until now. Where is the rendezvous?"

"Actium." Apollodorus shuddered violently at the mention of the name. "What's so strange about Actium, 'Pollo?"

"I don't know, I have never heard of the place."

"It's at the Gulf of Ambracia, North West Achaea, our last stopover before we cross the Ionian Sea to Italy. It's a natural fortress like Alexandria."

"That's good. It is there that we must find solitude and security so that I can perform the ritual to see what the fates are trying to do to us."

"Do you think you can change what is pre-ordained?"

"I am no play thing of the gods. Also, if it is pre-ordained why warn us? We had better get back to the Triremes before it gets dark."

"Before we go" asked Cleopatra "please hold me tightly."

They embraced and Cleopatra grabbed the back of Apollodorus' hair and kissed him passionately. He did not resist. "If anything happened to Caesar would you....?"

"I may not like Caesar but he is useful and I know how ruthless you Ptolemys can be with rivals." He returned her kisses. "If anything were to happen to Caesar I would be killed in the rush. You may, in that event, for the sake of Egypt, have to take another Roman as consort." He kissed her again. "Your people would never accept a foreign commoner as your consort."

"*Gelotopoios*, as my Sea Lord, you are no commoner and you advocate regular naughtiness....."

"Both are true" he replied.

"As Lady of Two Lands I need some naughtiness from you" strong soft fingers had taken hold of his manhood "I accept that we must not become one body while Caesar is alive." There were more passionate kisses. "If you are no play thing of the gods and believe destiny can be changed then change the visions!"

"It is not safe here but as you are going to have to sleep next to me to monitor my dreams we could make a pleasure out of a necessity." He ran his hand over her breasts. "I am not going to see much of these while we are in Rome, am I?" They kissed again. "We really must get back to the Triremes, how will you explain to the crew us sleeping together?"

"My *Pater* always said 'the good thing about being an absolute monarch is behaving absolutely'. You aren't the only one who knows how ruthless us Ptolemys can be."

"So what you are saying is, if anyone so much as raises an eyebrow...."

"They will be sent on a special mission..."

"Let me guess, Thea. To establish once and for all how many teeth there are in a crocodile's mouth?"

It was almost dark when they got back to the Triremes and Cleopatra's curiosity was getting the better of her but she knew she would have to be careful how she asked.

"My Lord, 'Pollo, there is something I must ask but I am fearful. We have had a lovely afternoon and I don't want to spoil it but..."

Apollodorus pre-empted her question. "Why the change of heart over intimacy?"

"Yes, I am delighted but ..."

"It was something you said that made so much sense. You said 'I know there are some things you cannot bring yourself to share with me but this should not be one of them. Tell me what you can see and let's try and work it out together.' We are both adults and you are by far the most intelligent person I have ever met. We must interpret my visions together. If our relationship is leading us to disaster we know what we must do. You trusted me with your life and that of your son, I must trust you. When you said 'let's work it out together.' it was as though a great burden had been lifted from me."

"How about Caesar?"

"He is fully aware of how close we are, so long as we don't flaunt it and remember he has a wife in Rome so I doubt if he will be making many intimate visits."

"You really don't like him, do you?"

"I respect him as a statesman and a warrior but I would not choose him as a friend despite being given leave to address him as Gauis and conferring me the dubious honour of Rome citizenship. After life and freedom, the next most precious gift is that of children."

"You have never forgiven him for leaving Alexandria before Caesarion's birth; have you, 'Pollo?"

Apollodorus said nothing, he just shook his head and Cleopatra thought. "If Caesar does not publicly acknowledge Caesarion as his heir you will be his *Pater*."

Angrily Apollodorus said "if you were having my child I would not go rushing off to pursue some personal vendetta within days of the birth. It would have taken weeks for him to get to the next theatre of war. A small delay before setting out would have made no difference. I am sorry I have said too much."

"No, you haven't. I have plenty of 'yes' men and I value the way you tell me exactly what you think."

"I find it a great deal easier to deal with an unpleasant truth than a pleasing lie but my outspokenness frequently gets me into trouble" replied Apollodorus.

"You are closer to me than any other living being, 'Pollo, because you tell me what I need to know, not what I want to hear. And if you make so much of a hint of a silly quip about your good looks or charm…!"

Apollodorus smiled broadly "Your Highness, you are getting to know me too well if my jokes are that predictable. But no, I understand fully and I am deeply honoured you feel that way about our friendship."

She touched his arm lightly as they beached the Felucca by the Triremes. "I said when we first met that true agape was a rare gift and you give it to me in abundance" and added in silent thought. "If you now give me eros in equal measure I will have found true love at last."

Over the next few days they rounded the Peleponnese peninsular inside the island of Zacynthus where they stopped over night. They also stopped off at Cephallenia and passed outside Leucas and into the Gulf of

Amracia. The weather was glorious and the islands beautiful. By night they slept in each others arms under the stars. The romance of the journey was intoxicating and Apollodorus had no further visions. The holiday atmosphere evaporated as they entered the Gulf and saw a small Egyptian merchant ship anchored off the Actium peninsular. Apollodorus shuddered as a cold chill enveloped him.

"Whatever is it, 'Pollo?" whispered Cleopatra.

"Has there ever been a major conflict here?" he replied. "It is as though ten thousand tormented souls cried out in agony."

"Actium is of strategic importance so there must have been battles here in the past."

As they came ashore Apollodorus stopped suddenly and said "listen."

"I can't hear anything" replied Cleopatra.

"Precisely! No birds singing, no insects buzzing, no animal calls; nothing. Just silence."

"Stop it, 'Pollo, you are frightening me" cried Cleopatra.

"I am sorry, Thea, but I am frightening myself also! We have found one of the crossroads. We shall pitch out tents here and I must see what is to be seen in the land of dreams."

"No, *Gelotopoios*, it is too dangerous!"

"Ignorance is far more dangerous. We must know what it is that the gods are trying to warn us about, no matter what the risk." He smiled at the frightened young woman and said reassuringly. "If you want to sit on that ornate chair back in Alexandria, I tried it once when no one was looking, it is as ergonomic as a scorpion's nest," jested the shipwright with an exaggerated shudder and continued more seriously. "The choice is yours Thea but risk is all part of the business. The more we know, the less the risk."

"Is there no alternative?"

"There was but you wouldn't let me turn 'Mintaka' out to sea. Anyway, I love living in Alexandria and you wouldn't be without your son, would you?"

"You are right, as usual. What must we do?"

"To perform the ritual I need quiet and security so we must make camp here. We place the marines on a high state of readiness close enough to defend us but not so close that they hear what is going on. We need Olympos and Mardian inside our tent in case I need restraining and Charmain and Iras for you. No one else is sufficiently trustworthy. We really need someone to record what I say as you may not have the opportunity. While the camp is being pitched shall we go and find out what your spy has to report?"

Cleopatra gave the orders to the troops and servants and they made their way to the anchored merchant ship in the Felucca while the camp was prepared. The Captain greeted them courteously and invited them into the cabin.

"Joseph I think you must know Apollodorus, you may speak freely in front of him."

"All Alexandria knows the Jester and his heroic exploits. It is a pleasure to meet you at last, my lord," said the Captain with real warmth. "All is not well in Rome, Madam."

"As you suspected, 'Pollo" interrupted Cleopatra. "Tell us all you know, Captain."

"Caesar has spent little time in Rome. He appointed Marcus Antonius 'Master of Horse,' his deputy in his absence. All major decisions by the Senate have to be ratified by Caesar personally and it takes weeks for the messengers to get decisions back from him to Rome."

"That's a dangerous departure from his usual style of command" said Apollodorus. "I wonder if his disease is making him distrust his subordinates."

"He would have good reason in the case of Lord Antonius" continued the Captain. "The Master of Horse has behaved disgracefully. He travels the countryside in a parody of a royal progress in the company of musicians, dancers and actors. He openly flaunts his mistress, the actress, Cytheris and has extravagant banquets with his low born entourage."

Apollodorus burst out laughing "sounds as though our M.A is having a great time. Jules will be furious when he gets back."

"That's only half of it" continued the captain. When Antonius is in Rome he struts around the city stripped to the waist wielding a broad sword and taking on all comers."

"Sounds like Mark Antony was something of a lager lout" the actress quipped.

"Falernian lout" I corrected.

"So, for Caesar, to put things in a modern context, it was rather like the president of my country having a vice president behaving like a hooligan. Then the lady prime minister of your country, if you still had a lady prime minister, turning up with their illegitimate son and demanding alimony."

"Add to that financial melt down and a homosexual lover demanding to be made heir apparent and you would have the situation accurately summed up."

"Small wonder they re-wrote history."

"You once had a president whose sexual indiscretions became legendary after his assignation."

"He was a democrat and Caesar a republican but I take your point, nothing much changes."

"That's right; the only change is the name over the doors and the size of the bricks thrown. They used catapults and rocks, today its intercontinental ballistic missiles."

"So it is unacceptable in Rome for men as well as women to proudly display their chests?" asked Cleopatra.

"Where I come from the men wrap their legs in the manner of the elderly" added Apollodorus.

"In a cold country that is understandable" replied Cleopatra. "But I can't understand why the Romans are so ashamed of their bodies. What else can you tell me, Captain?"

"The citizens are crippled by debt and the Senate has been powerless to do anything about it. Senator Dolabella proposed to cancel all debts but Senator Trebellius vetoed that idea with Antonius, military support."

"Very wisely" interrupted Cleopatra. "It would have caused financial anarchy. Your feelings about Rome served you well, 'Pollo, Caesar's realm must be on the brink of another civil war."

"I agree, your Highness" continued the captain. "When Caesar returns he will have to stage massive public games to placate the citizens. That is his usual way to make the people forget their troubles. Antonius accused Senator Dolabella of seducing his wife Antonia. Dolabella incited civil disobedience and Antonius formally divorced the poor woman. Caesar had to intervene by replacing the Master of Horse with Lepidus and he took Dolabella with him on the Africa campaign. Antonius has acquired Pompeius' home, the 'House of Ships'. The front of this house is decorated with bronze beaks and trident rams from defeated ships. One last thing, Caesar collapsed when he landed in Africa. The troops were horrified as they thought it a bad omen. Caesar had a hard time in Africa and was unwell some of the time."

Apollodorus gave Cleopatra a knowing look; both thought that his sickness must be getting worse and his fits more frequent. They returned to the camp in a very sombre mood to find the tents had been pitched as instructed and the *Bassilisa's* trusted friends were waiting for them. As darkness fell, Apollodorus explained what everyone had to do. Onto the ground inside their tent he unrolled a large mat on which was drawn a large five pointed star within a circle. Five candles were placed in the valleys of the stars and in the centre a goblet of freshly drawn water.

"The water acts as a medium" he explained to Cleopatra. "We link hands either side of the bowl and concentrate on the water surface. I will partially loose consciousness to release my Ba. The danger is that my soul will be drawn completely into the medium and I will be unable to return. That's where you all come in. If I am getting to the point of no return you must drag me back."

"How will we know?" asked Cleopatra anxiously.

"Trust your instincts, you will know!" replied Apollodorus.

"What do we do if that happens?" asked Iras.

"Shake me, slap me, shout at me. You may need Olympos and Mardian to restrain me. On the other hand, this could all be a waste of time and I will see nothing."

"I thought you needed the four elements to perform magic?" asked Olympos.

"Yes and no. There is a common misconception about the elements. We have the fire of the candles, the water in the goblet. Air and earth are all around us."

"So what is the misconception?" asked Charmain.

"There are five elements."

"So what is the fifth element?" asked Cleopatra but she knew the answer as she spoke. "Its *agape*, isn't it, 'Pollo? We are all trusted friends and that is how I was saved at my son's birth."

Apollodorus nodded "without *agape* I could not and would not attempt this or any other ritual. *Agape* is the fifth and most powerful of all the elements. We may do great things, but if we are without agape we are nothing!"

The two handmaids knelt down opposite each other at the edge of the tent with Mardian and Olympos adjacent. Cleopatra and Apollodorus knelt in the middle and linked hands either side of the goblet of water. The candles flickered and Apollodorus said softly to Cleopatra "concentrate on the surface of the water. The rest of you link hands to form a circle of protection around us."

As he concentrated on the surface of the water the fog lifted from his mind and he saw a blood stained man dressed in a purple toga lying alone on the steps of a Roman building. He described the scene to his companions. "There are now riots and I see a body on a fire. I am now falling through the sky. There is a massive fleet of war ships, a small man is laughing, men are dying everywhere. I am telling you to escape while you can. The ships collide; there is a massive sound like thunder. I am falling again, there is fire…"

"Come back, 'Pollo, you are going too far" screamed Cleopatra.

"No, there is more. I see horsemen, four hooded horsemen. I can see the serpent, no, there are two and a bird, it must be a vulture going round and round and round…………."

Cleopatra was hysterical; she struck the goblet of water with the palm of her hand just before Apollodorus' face hit it. The candles were sent flying as Olympos and Mardian leaped forward to drag Apollodorus to a sitting position. Although his eyes were open they were unfocused. Cleopatra pushed the two men aside and grabbed the shipwright's shoulders and shook him vigorously.

"Come back, 'Pollo" she screamed, then in desperation she slapped him round the face. She was shaking him and slapping him when the two handmaids recovered their composure sufficiently to physically restrain their mistress.

Apollodorus found himself in a vast cavern lit by an unnatural light of such brilliance that for a few moments he was unable to see. There were the most exotic flowers and trees he had ever seen. The cries of birds and animals mingled to form celestial music. A feeling of tranquil calm enveloped him and the perfume of the flowers filled his nostrils, reminiscent of something he couldn't quite recall. The noise of one particular animal stood out from the others, his two dogs came running though the trees and they greeted him enthusiastically. He walked forward through a glade as though guided my some unseen force his two dogs at his side. Emerging from the trees he found himself by the edge of a lake. The incandescent light from the cavern roof was refracted by the wavelets in a riot of colours.

"That lake is strangely familiar" he said to his dogs.

Then a large man appeared in front of him barring his way. Apollodorus felt the blood drain from his face, all feelings of tranquillity evaporated. The man in front of him had a crocodile head. In one hand were scales and under his arm a book. The book was covered with the hide of a strange hairy beast.

"I am Glutton" boomed the demon.

"I know who you are" replied the shipwright, trying unsuccessfully to sound casual. "Surely I have paid the price?"

"Madam, let Olympos get to him, he is the physician and he will know what to do" said Iras. Olympos put the shipwright into a recovery position and placed his head in the distraught Cleopatra's lap where she cradled him, rocking herself back and forth on her knees and sobbing softly. The doctor was then able to examine Apollodorus.

"Re-light the candles, Mardian, so I can see what I am doing. His eyes are open but he isn't conscious. All his life signs are normal but he isn't there."

"For what you have done there can be no absolution. The world has been plunged into a dark age. Gone is freedom forever and you have destroyed your one true love!"

"I did all I could" protested the shipwright.

At that moment a woman dressed in black surrounded with an incandescent golden aura appeared.

"Have you come to beg for your protégé Isis?" demanded Glutton.

"There was something else you could have done" said the goddess softly.

"What must I do" wailed Apollodorus.

"I cannot tell you but in your heart you know the answer. There can be no victory without sacrifice" she replied "when the time comes you will know what to do and only you can do it!"

"You must do something, Olympos" wailed Cleopatra "I knew it was far too dangerous, I should never have let him do it." They had all been so busy they hadn't noticed the arrival of Caesarion.

"*Mater*, what's happened" asked the child "*Geloto*, stop being silly you are frightening *Mater*!" He bent down to Apollodorus and gently shook him, then in a sing song voice added. "Come back, *Geloto*, don't be silly. Come back, *Geloto*, don't frighten *Mater*." Apollodorus eyes flickered and the child kissed him on the cheek and repeated "Come back, *Geloto*, silly old *Geloto*. Come back, *Geloto*, don't frighten *Mater*." Consciousness gradually returned to Apollodorus and his eyes focused on Caesarion and smiled. One of Cleopatra's tears dropped onto his lips. He licked his lips and looked up at the *Bassilisa* and smiled. Licking his lips again he asked "don't you do honey flavour?" He then sat bolt upright, regretted the move and collapsed back into her lap.

"You managed to get back" whispered Cleopatra with considerable relief.

"Did I? That was clever of me. Where did I go? Come to think of it, where am I now?" Apollodorus looked around in a bemused way. "Don't tell me I am on 'Mintaka' and we were hit by a squall. No, I am in a tent and everyone is looking very anxious. I must be in a tent on 'Mintaka' and we have just been hit by a squall which is why everyone is looking very anxious. No, a tent wouldn't fit in 'Mintaka'. That is, a tent wouldn't fit on my boat 'Mintaka' but it may well fit on the star 'Mintaka'. Am I making any sense to you because I am making no sense to me? I know I must be sober but I can't cope with life sober, give me a drink, someone."

Apollodorus sat up again, looked around and saw Cleopatra. The colour drained from his face and he collapsed sobbing into her arms. She held him tightly saying.

"It's all right, *Gelotopoios*, you are back with us now."

It was some time before Apollodorus regained his composure and they were able to sit round and discuss what he had seen.

"Mardian, can you get us all something to drink?" he asked.

"Is that wise?" asked Olympos.

"That is typical of a doctor, always advocating cabbage water and cold baths. If you had been where I have been you would need a very large stiff drink!"

Mardian re-entered the tent with goblets and flagons of wine which he distributed to everyone. The colour was returning to Apollodorus and he bounced Caesarion on his knee.

"It was the purity of this child that brought me back, do you realise he saved my life?" He then became business like "so what have we got?"

Iras was first to speak. "You said you saw a bloodstained man in a purple toga on some steps."

"That must be Caesar, a warning of an assassination. We know that all is far from well in Rome but the risk of assassination must be with him always" said Apollodorus dismissively. "What next?"

"A massive sea battle" continued Iras.

"I remember that piece and I am certain Actium will be the theatre of war."

"Then you were telling me to escape" interrupted Cleopatra "there was a massive sound like thunder and you saw four hooded horsemen."

"I don't like that part" said Apollodorus gravely. "They are the 'Four Horsemen of the Apocalypse' conquest, war, famine and death. Then everything span out of control all I could see were two cobras and a bird going round in a circle. I have seen that symbol before. Does anyone know what it means?"

The three women looked at each other and Cleopatra shook her head.

Apollodorus looked at Cleopatra in puzzlement. "Now who is being evasive?"

Cleopatra was close to tears "I long to tell you, 'Pollo, but it is one of the most closely guarded secrets of the Pharaohs. All I can say is that it is a symbol of protection and of true love."

"So what we have is an impending dark age precipitated by a massive sea battle here in Actium with an assassination thrown in for good measure. You must turn away from this battle; your Highness that much is clear. The twin Uraeus and Vulture are the symbols of immortality and protection. Added to this is true love, anything else?"

"Don't forget the small man" said Charmain with a shudder.

"Oh yes, we have a small man, rather unpleasant he was" added Apollodorus. "It makes very little sense to me, how about everyone else?" They all shook their heads. "Well I am glad I decided to be a shipwright not a high priest. We may as well get to bed and make an early start for Rome in the morning."

"That's the most sensible thing you have said all evening" replied Cleopatra with a twinkle in her eye. "I will settle Caesarion down for the night and be right back." All of them had failed to realise that it was Caesarion's intervention that had averted the disaster and saved Apollodorus from death. That was the key that would have made sense of the visions.

A short while later Cleopatra snuggled up to Apollodorus. "I thought you would refuse to let me come to bed with you, 'Pollo."

"Our relationship is critical in all this but whether we should or shouldn't, you could flip a coin. Have you any change on you?" asked Apollodorus.

"Royals never carry cash; anyway I am naked so have nowhere to keep money."

"So am I, therefore flipping a coin is out. Anyway, I need a cuddle. This place gives me the creeps so the sooner we get on our way the better."

"You are making very light of things, Geloto, considering how frightening it all was. I thought I had lost you again."

"What would you do if you were hit by a sudden squall in a small boat, everything is out of control and you know that any action you take could make matters much worse?"

"Nothing just let go of all controls, hold on tight and wait and see. When things calmed down and a course of action became apparent then take that action. It's the first rule of seamanship." Apollodorus said nothing just held the young woman very tightly then she understood and held him. He lay for some time holding the sleeping *Bassilisa* in his arms. It was the last part of his vision that he had told no one was the greatest puzzle.

"I abhor hunting but those dogs were mine" he thought "the thick coats of long hair would indicate they were beasts from the cold north not Egypt. What is it that I must do? Isis has warned me that in my heart I know what I must do when the time comes. The sent of the flowers reminded me of something."

He fell into an un-easy sleep and following morning they started the final leg of their journey to Rome.

Book 10

Apollodorus was up early; he slipped quietly out of bed without disturbing Cleopatra who was still asleep. At the entrance of their tent he found Mardian wrapped in a bed roll, the eunuch was awake and greeted him. A chill in the air indicated the imminent onset of winter and the grass was wet with early morning dew.

"Have you been there all night guarding her Royal Highness?" asked Apollodorus.

"I feel as uneasy about this place as you, My Lord" replied Mardian.

"Does it make you jealous, my sleeping with the Bassilisa?"

"It is hardly my place to comment, My Lord"

"I disagree. You are part of her inner circle of close friends and less of the 'My Lord,' call me 'Pollo or *Gelotopois*.'"

"I find you charismatic but I know you are not attracted to my kind" answered the eunuch with a smile.

Apollodorus chuckled "I was referring to her Highness"

"I have served the *Bassilisa* all her life and have never seen her as happy as she is since you have been with her. I would rather she had taken you as her consort than that Roman. I am surprised that he wanted her ..." he hesitated, "intimately."

"Why? Surely all men would find her desirable."

"Not all men."

Apollodorus looked at Mardian quizzically then it occurred to him what the eunuch was trying to say. "Mardian, I think you prevaricate as much as her Highness accuses me of doing. Shall I make it easier for you? Is there a way that people like you can identify ...." Apollodorus hesitated, as he tried to find the right words. "How can I put it? Is there a way that people like you can identify a kindred spirits? If there was it would save, shall we say - a rather violent rejection?"

"There is a code of the eunuch's, a 'brotherhood'. Caesar wears his girdle too low."

Again Apollodorus chuckled. "Perhaps that is the fashion in Rome."

"I cannot be certain but it is generally a sigh of effeminacy. The small man you saw in your vision may be his true lover."

"Is that what you felt while I was out of my body or a conclusion you have subsequently come to?"

"I sensed it very strongly at the time, but I have been telling myself it cannot be so."

"Mardian, my friend, I think you have uncovered a little more of the puzzle. You did well to keep your council, as until we know for certain, I think it is best we keep this between ourselves. No doubt you will be able to find out more in Rome. If Caesar has a male lover in the form of a small and very unpleasant man there may be a rival for the position of 'heir apparent'. I intend to persuade the *Bassilisa* not to pay off the rowers when we arrive in Rome and to keep the Triremes in a discrete state of readiness. As master of her household I would appreciate it if you could be ready to pack up and put to sea at short notice. If there is a rival for the affections of the Pontifax Maximus and anything happens to Jules our lives may depend on making a quick getaway."

"Those are my feelings entirely. I am most relieved by what you suggest, *Gelotopois*."

"Shall we go in search of breakfast, my friend?"

"I couldn't possibly allow you to any such thing, my lord," replied Mardian in horror. "What kind of a signal would it send to the people?"

"They would think I was well capable of looking after myself" answered the shipwright dismissively.

"No Pharaoh would prepare his own meals or do anything for himself, it is unseemly."

"Mardian I am Sea Lord not!"

"With the greatest of respect" interrupted the eunuch. "You sleep with the *Bassilisa*."

"Mardian, I thank you for the compliment but I am little more then the Bassilisa's bed warmer and jester – her male concubine" protested the shipwright.

"I can be tortured into saying whatever you or anyone wishes me to say, my lord *Geloto*, but that will not change my opinion."

Apollodorus nodded thoughtfully and smiled "I think you had better keep those thoughts to yourself, my friend. I believe in freedom for all people, particularly freedom of speech but very few are equally enlightened and share my beliefs."

Mardian gave a discrete bow to indicate his agreement and returned the shipwright's smile. "I will arrange breakfast while you 'crack the whip' over the Triremes crews. Her Highness will soon wake up so I will assure her that you have matters well in hand."

Despite the best efforts of Apollodorus it was mid-day before they set off on the final leg of their journey across the Ionian Sea, a distance almost as far as Alexandria was from Rhodes. This time they had the wind on their side so could deploy the sails in a manner known as a broad reach, the most efficient point of sailing. That evening Cleopatra was with Apollodorus in their favourite position of privacy on the forecastle.

"Do you feel better now we are back at sea, 'Pollo?" she asked.

"I feel better being away from that gulf. I can think straight now and am beginning to make some sense of things."

"Have you come to any conclusions?"

"Not yet, but what we should keep clearly in mind is this; my psychic ability is sometimes referred to as the sixth sense, therefore it only gives one sixth of the picture. Matters are in the melting pot in Rome, which although they are not really our concern, may well affect us. We don't know what we don't know until we know all that there is to be known. When we know all that there is to be known, we will know what to do about it."

"Impeccable logic, as usual, *Gelotopois*! So what do we do in the meantime?"

"How would you feel about keeping on the crew when we arrive in Rome and having the ships in a discrete state of readiness for a hurried departure?"

"I had no intensions of paying off the crew and if it will make you more relaxed…." She gave him a knowing look "I think I will be able to live with the expense. We are about two thirds of the way there so let's enjoy the sun, sea and a little holiday romance."

Three days later they arrived at the 'Straits of Messina', the water that separates Italy from Sicily. The Ionian Islands they had seen on the way were barren and rocky. In the distance they could see the Calabrian Massif where the Appennino Mountains terminate. This mountain range formed the backbone of Italy.

"This is where Caesar had his encounter with pirates! We had better be on our guard" said Apollodorus.

"Don't worry, I have already instructed the Trierarchos on all three ships to place the marines on alert" replied Cleopatra, and then noticed some approaching ships. "They look like Roman Triremes. Perhaps Caesar has sent us an escort."

"It would be impolite for him not to do so but it will put a stop to our intimacy, so I am not pleased to see them."

"It is acceptable for Caesar and Marcus Antonius to flaunt their girl friends openly. Why can't I do likewise with my boyfriend?"

Apollodorus said nothing but thought "A male concubine, that all I am!"

Cleopatra continued "I would love to be able to proudly walk through the streets of Rome holding onto your arm." Then she became deadly serious and added. "I fear that the citizens will look on me as little more then Caesar's whore."

"Thea that is far too harsh!" replied Apollodorus.

"Is it?"

Again Apollodorus remained silent but thought "If you are Caesar's whore, what does that make me?"

From the escort ships they learned that there had been a decisive battle in Spain against the remnants of Pompey's supporters. It had been a close run fight and Caesar was heard to say

"Before I fought for victory, this time I fought for my life."

What the Romans were not able to tell them, far more significantly, was that Caesar had been joined by a distant young relative named Octavian. The eighteen year old youth had risen from his sickbed to be with Caesar, who was deeply moved. They had travelled through Spain together in a carriage and were to become inseparable. Caesar had returned to Rome and Mark Antony was now restored to favour. His marriage to Fulvia the widow of Clodius arranged by Caesar was hoped would bridle his madness and insolence. She was a woman not content to spend her time spinning and housewifery duties but would rule her husband in his office abroad as well as in the home.

"My sort of woman" interjected the actress with a smile.

"It was said that Fulvia taught Antony to be obedient to women and that Cleopatra would exploit this weakness" I replied. "There is an English saying that the road to success is paved with men being pushed by their wives."

"In America we say behind every successful man is a good woman and behind her is a sharp attorney."

A week later the Egyptian ships were on their final approach to Rome and by now winter had arrived. As they turned into the River Tiber Cleopatra explained the origins of Rome to Apollodorus.

"According to legend, Romulus and Remus were twin sons of Rhea Silvain, one of the vestal virgins of the royal house of Alba Longa."

"I suppose it caused something of a kafuffle in the royal household when Rhea announced her pregnancy. Was she dismissed from being a vestal virgin?" asked Apollodorus.

"She claimed to have been raped by the god, Mars."

"Typical story put about by a Roman when he gets a royal lady pregnant. If they can't accept the responsibility of fatherhood they should learn to control their libido" interrupted Apollodorus.

"It was your idea that I seduced Caesar!" exclaimed Cleopatra angrily.

"I am sorry, Thea, my remark was unkind and un-called for. There is so much I want to say to Caesar about the privilege and duty of parenthood, but I can't. As I recall, the following morning you felt dirty and used like a prostitute so I have always imagined that he virtually raped you."

Cleopatra's expression turned instantly from anger to tearfulness "There are times, 'Pollo, when your perception is painfully accurate. It was exactly like that!" In her minds eye she travelled back to her bedroom in the palace on Antirhodos Island and once again felt the sharp pain as Caesar entered her. She remembered how she had bitten back her screams, struggling all the time to remain dignified – the smell of his un-washed body had made her want to retch. Hurriedly dismissing these images Cleopatra added "I have never been able to tell anyone." Then in silence thought "Is that why you refuse to become one body with me? Do you feel that as I have been badly treated by one man you have to redress the balance by the purity of our relationship? Oh 'Pollo, how wrong you are!"

Out loud she continued. "Rhea's uncle ordered the drowning of the twins. To that end the babies were left on the banks of the River Tiber where they were suckled by a wolf and fed by a woodpecker. The woodpecker took them to its home in a sacred fig tree. The boys were rescued by a shepherd who brought them up as robbers but unfortunately Remus was caught by the king of Alma Longa. Romulus rescued him and the two brothers killed the king and restored the rightful monarch. Romulus took possession of the Palatine Hill and founded his principality and Remus built his settlement on the Aventine Hill."

"Then they married and lived happily ever after" interrupted Apollodorus.

"Not exactly. Remus jumped over his brother's wall as an act of defiance and Romulus killed him, thereby setting the tone for future civil wars in Rome."

"So rather than living happily ever after, they have been killing each other ever since."

"In a word, yes" replied Cleopatra.

"Thea, why have we come to this festering cesspit of intrigue and conflict?"

"To get Caesar to face up to his parental responsibilities and negotiate a treaty so Egypt doesn't get annexed by Rome."

"Why don't we cut through all this diplomacy and just build a bigger navy. Tell the Romans to 'go fornicate in their *Mator's* dung' to quote your comment when we thought we were being ordered to surrender by the pursuing Triremes."

"If all else fails and there is another civil war in Rome that is exactly what I propose to do. I thought I may have difficulty persuading my pacifist Naval Constructor, who sees the best in everyone, of the wisdom of such action. Caesar was able to defeat a divided Egypt with our help, but only just. What chance would Rome have against a united Egypt, without Caesar?"

"I think they may be reluctant to put it to the test. If you had suggested the belligerent approach before we left Alexandria I would have been reluctant but I am coming round to your contemptuous viewpoint that the Romans are the vermin of the Mediterranean. Naturally, I would have done as you commanded you being the *Bassilisa*, after all. In view of what we now know you will have my full cooperation in a program of re-armament and whilst in Rome I will do everything I can to find out the size and state of their navy."

"*Gelotopois*, I am delighted you feel this way. I never thought you of all people would become a hawk."

"Freedom is the right to say 'no'. We may well have to say no loudly and firmly to Rome and back it up with force. I look on the belligerent approach as a last option where as Rome has the reverse opinion. Given this unique opportunity to prepare well in advance of any conflict, let's make the best of it."

They were joined by Cleopatra's brother Ptolemy and Caesarion. Apollodorus lifted Caesarion onto his shoulder so he could get a better view of the city they were approaching. Ptolemy stood on tiptoe so Apollodorus transferred Caesarion onto his mother's shoulder and lifted with difficulty the young Pharaoh onto his shoulder.

"You shouldn't touch me" protested Ptolemy.

"It's perfectly alright for Apollodorus to pick you up" replied Cleopatra "he is my dearest friend and is always most respectful and correct in public."

"Tell me what you can see up there, your Highness" asked Apollodorus. "I have never been to Rome. Can you make out the seven hills?" Ptolemy's manner became less formal as the excitement of landing grew. Soon he behaved as any child would have under the circumstances, asking questions and pointing out landmarks. As they entered the anchorage, Apollodorus suggested.

"Your Highness, shall we check that the crew are in place and know what to do when we come alongside?"

"I don't know how to operate a ship."

"You are Pharaoh, of course you know what to do, just look confident and I will whisper instructions. No one will know any difference."

"Can I come too?" asked Caesarion.

"Of course you can! You had better hold my hand in case I slip." Cleopatra smiled as she watched the two boys walked along the catwalk holding the shipwright's hands and giving encouragement to the crew on the way.

"What a fine *Pater* you would make for the two boys" she thought "if only the circumstances were different."

Rome was only thirteen miles inland although the Tiber was navigable for sixty five miles from the sea. The grey and languid river curved round to the right as they approached the docks on the east bank. Cleopatra shivered involuntarily as she was gripped by a sense of foreboding; the atmosphere was cold, damp and acrid. Up until this point she had been optimistic that Caesar would acknowledge his son but now the confrontation was imminent she realised he could refuse. She joined Apollodorus and the two boys on the Poop Deck, the raised aft deck where ships are traditionally controlled; here the shipwright was explaining the correct posture for a commanding officer to the amusement of the *Trierarchos*.

"Stand with your legs apart, that's right and hands behind your back. Shoulders back and look out at the crew. Look at each man in turn to see if he is doing his job properly." Apollodorus explained "then look across at the dock. Is everyone in place as we come alongside? Ah look! There is a guard of honour!"

They had passed the massive warehouse, 'Porticus Aemilia', the emporium or commercial river port that had been built about a century before. The Egyptian ships were directed to a berth in old harbour on the east bank adjacent to the Tiber Island or 'Inter Duos Pontes' meaning between two bridges. The island resembled a Triremes war ship, the bridges from the east and west banks were like oars and the southern downstream tip was built like the Triremes prow. Carved in relief under the prow was the head of Aesculapius, his healing staff entwined with a snake, beside him.

The view across the Tiber was dominated by The Temple of Jupiter on the smallest of the seven hills, the Capitoline. This building was of great strategic importance as a natural fortress. Stretching from Capitoline Hill across the valley to the Palatine Hill was the Forum, which had started life six hundred years previously as a market square. Here were housed most of the public buildings, temples, shops and markets, public speeches were delivered from the Forum Rostra.

The Egyptian ships came to rest and Cleopatra led the two boys to the gangplank followed by her handmaids and friends. They were greeted formally as they came ashore.

"I, Gaius Julius Caesar Dictator of Rome, Pontifex Maximus, Father of the Fatherland welcome you Ptolemy and Cleopatra, Joint Monarchs of Egypt and friends of Rome." Then they were taken to Caesar's villa at Trastavere on the western side of the Tiber. The procession made its way from the docks past the place of execution and for the first time Cleopatra witnessed the gruesome reality of crucifixion. Apollodorus was walking alongside her litter so she was able to whisper to him.

"Did you see the way they put people to death, 'Pollo! They use the sacred symbol of immortality, the Ankh Cross. I can't believe the sacrilege and they purport themselves to be civilised. I think I am going to throw up."

Apollodorus stopped the litter and summonsed the handmaids to attend to their mistress. Charmain and Iras were looking equally unwell. Caesar, on horseback, joined them.

"What is the problem?" he asked.

"I fear her Royal Highness is land sick" explained Apollodorus diplomatically. "This is not uncommon after a long sea journey. No doubt you have encountered the problem in your travels. She will be alright shortly."

It was with some relief they arrived at the villa at Trastavere, one of several owned by Caesar. Under Mardian's supervision the servants busied themselves unpacking Cleopatra's belongings. Ptolemy was far from impressed by their temporary home. Apollodorus smiled at him.

"Not exactly a palace is it, your Highness? I fear the Romans have a lot to learn about entertaining Royalty. Shall we go and have a look at the garden and see if there are any good trees to climb."

"Why should I want to climb a tree?"

"Have you never climbed a tree?" inquired the shipwright incredulously.

"No."

Apollodorus looked sad then smiled and said "you don't know what you have been missing all your life."

"What was Rome like?" asked the actress.

"The Seven hills to the west of the river were irregular ridges or spurs with streams running down the valleys" I replied. "These streams became the tributaries to the Tiber. The city had spread far beyond the original republican city walls and three centuries later a new wall enclosing the expanded city was built. Rome was the largest city at that time with about 200,000 households. There was chronic overcrowding and a constant threat of famine, flood and fire so consequently most of the leading families had built villas in what we would call the suburbs to escape the overcrowding."

"Caesar lodged Cleopatra and her party in the suburbs over the other side of the river away from prying eyes."

"It would appear that he was trying to play down her presence in Rome."

"So there she was stuck in the suburbs, no video shops and the telephone wasn't invented so she couldn't even send for a pizza."

"Pizza was definitely out of the question as surprisingly, considering how essential it is to Italian cuisine today, the tomato was as un-known then as the telephone and the Vesper motor scooter!"

Cleopatra was attracted to the garden by the sound of shrieks of laughter. Apollodorus was hanging upside down from the branch of a tree by his legs.

"You look like a monkey!" she exclaimed.

"They are probably a distant relative of humanity" he replied. "Have you ever wanted to climb a tree?"

"Not until now" she replied. "Can you help me?"

Apollodorus lifted himself to an upright position then swung to the ground and helped the Lady of Two Lands in the childish art of tree climbing.

"Where is Jules?" he asked.

"He has gone home to Calpurnia, his wife. I thought he would be all over me like the pox but he has been so……" she hesitated "so formal. You said he would be on his best behaviour in Rome but it's as though we had only just met!"

"I suppose he has left an army of slaves to spy on us."

"No, surprisingly not, it would have been rather obvious as we have ample domestic slaves with us. There is plenty of food and wine in the villa and he said to let him know if there was anything we wanted. He stayed long enough to be polite and has left us to get on with settling in."

"So is there to be a sumptuous feast in your honour tonight?"

"Once again, surprisingly - no. I am rather relieved as I still feel a little queasy."

"It sounds as though we are being treated like private guests rather than state visitors."

"That is an accurate assessment of the situation, as usual, 'Pollo. Do you have any suggestions?"

"Yes I do. If they are going to be reticent about feasting us there is no reason for you not to entertain the leading Romans in your customary lavish style, as a private person, of course. Egypt does, after all, have a reputation to live up to." At that moment Mardian announced the arrival of the Consulate.

"Domini Antonius" said the *Bassilisa* sweetly "this is a pleasant surprise. Have you ever climbed a tree?"

"Your Highnesses, Apollodorus" he replied with a formal nod, then grinned boyishly "not for a long time."

"We were just discussing feasting" said Apollodorus "perhaps you can advise us about Roman protocols in such matters? Their Royal Highnesses would not want to cause offence by being too lavish. On the other hand Egypt is famous for its banquets."

Cleopatra smiled inwardly and thought "That was a brilliant idea 'Pollo, Antonius of all people takes his quaffing and feasting very seriously, being Roman by birth and Achaean by inclination. Also, if we get things wrong he will be a perfect scapegoat." She caught the shipwright's eye and they exchanged knowing looks and she remembered his comment about counter espionage 'all spies love a pretty girl, fine wine and a chance to gamble'. A pleasant afternoon was spent exploring the garden and climbing trees. Mark Antony shared the Jester's ability to come down to the level of the two children. Cleopatra's brother asked Apollodorus to show him how to whistle with his fingers in the way he had seen him attract the attention of the Triremes crew.

"It's easy" explained Apollodorus. "Place the first two fingers of each hand against the tip of your tongue and blow." Ptolemy and Cleopatra tried and after a short while mastered the technique and were able to make the distinctive ear splitting whistle.

"You will regret teaching them to make that dreadful noise" said Antony with a smile. Strangely, Apollodorus was later to be very glad that he had taught them how to whistle in this manner as it gave Cleopatra a unique method of signalling, that only he and the Consul would recognise. As the sun sank behind the hills and the sky turned red they made their way back to the villa, Cleopatra turned to the Roman.

"Dominus Antonius, you will join us for dinner I hope?"

"I should be delighted" replied the Roman.

"I feel certain Mardian will find some cheese in the mouse trap" quipped Apollodorus. Mardian did rather better than that so after a sumptuous feast the three reclined on couches and Mark Antony asked Apollodorus.

"When you first smuggled her Royal Highness into Antirhodos Island Palace you said you had won the boatyard at Askalon in a game of chance."

"That is correct" replied the shipwright with a smile "why?"

"You said it was a drinking contest, as I recall."

"It was a variation on the game of strategy played on a chequered board but instead of counters, goblets of drink are used. If a piece is taken, the loser has to drink the contents."

"Let me get this correct" interrupted Cleopatra. "The loser drinks the taken piece."

"That's right" replied Apollodorus.

"So the more you lose the more drunken you become" continued Cleopatra. "Surely that means that the loser becomes progressively intoxicated and their game deteriorates."

"That, your Highness is the general idea" said Apollodorus with an evil grin. "Would you like to try?"

"You two men play against each other and I will play the winner."

"I don't think the game works like that" suggested Antony. "I think it would be more appropriate for you to play the loser."

"I agree" replied Apollodorus. "There is one other little detail; the drink has to be drunk in one breath, failure results in a forfeit chosen by the observer."

Mark Antony was the first to have a piece taken. He raised the goblet and smiled at Cleopatra then Apollodorus and said "*Yiasoo*" then downed the drink in one gulp.

Apollodorus lost the second piece "when in Rome do as the Egyptians, siHHaok" he said and swallowed the drink. The two men were evenly matched so both were fairly intoxicated by the time Antony had lost. This gave Cleopatra a strategic advantage but unfortunately she was unable to drink her first lost piece in one gulp.

"Forfeit, forfeit, forfeit" chorused the men.

"Impersonate Caesar" ordered Apollodorus.

Cleopatra stood up and draped a shawl round her like a cloak and recited. "People of Alexandria, the people of Rome are your fiends." Both men dissolved into laughter.

"He said friends, not fiends, your Highness" corrected Apollodorus.

"What I have said I have said!" replied Cleopatra still in the manner of Caesar."

"That's just like him" slurred Antony, pointing unsteadily at the *Bassilisa*.

It was no surprise that Mark Antony lost the second game and had to be helped to bed being in no fit state to go home. Apollodorus miraculously became sober when they were alone.

"Is that what you and my handmaids did to Caesar's last spy when we had our midnight swim?" she asked.

"Something like that. Why, do you fancy a swim?"

"No, it's too cold and the Tiber is filthy. What I fancy is a cuddle. Come to bed with me, 'Pollo, please!"

"I had a feeling you were going to say that. It is very risky."

"All the more fun and risk is part of the business, as you said."

"I will have to return to my bed by dawn, just in case."

The following day they did receive an invitation from Caesar to feast at his principle residence. From Apollodorus' viewpoint all of Rome's nobility were there. Cleopatra was devastatingly charming to everyone. Calpurnia, Caesars fourth wife, was icily polite. Of rather more significance was the fair haired youth with unsmiling blue eyes Caesar introduced to the shipwright.

"Apollodorus, this is my nephew, Octavius. Octavius, this is the man who I told you about. He gave me the idea for modifying the calendar to bring it in line with the seasons."

"The Julian calendar had 365 days, not 360 as previously thought. There was a subsequent one, modified many centuries later, when it was realised that the time for one orbit of the Earth round the Sun was 356.25 days. So now we have a leap year every fourth year. Actually it is 365.2566 days or 365days 6hrs 9mins 34sec, which means God has a sense of humour or is a lousy mathematician."

The actress laughed "That would have amused Apollodorus if he had known."

"Obviously time was not measured in minutes and seconds but he would have been fully aware on two counts; firstly because the Celtic could predict planetary movement as accurately as our present calendar can. Secondly it was once said by Professor Hawkins that man has only memory of his past not of his future. Reincarnation is at the heart of Witchcraft or more correctly Wicca that in turn is descended from the lost knowledge of the Druids. If time does not exist on the Astral Plane then there can be no concept of past or future."

"Do you believe in reincarnation?"

"Proof denies faith, a person is either aware of other lives or they are not."

"Did you call the extra month Jules?"

"The Alexandrian mathematician and astronomer Sosigenes did some calculations for me based on your idea. Last year was increased to four hundred and forty five days to bring everything in line with the seasons and the month of my birth has been renamed July" replied Caesar with a smile.

Turning to the youth Apollodorus asked. "Have you seen active service with your Uncle?"

"I was in Spain but did not see much action as I was unwell" replied Octavian. His skin had a greyish pallor and he looked malnourished. Apollodorus thought the youth didn't look strong enough to wield a sword or tall enough for that matter. A little later he was joined by Mark Antony who was showing no signs of ill effect from the previous night. Caesar and Octavian excused themselves.

"I see you have met Caesar's latest conquest" said the Roman with a grin.

"Octavius? He is Caesar's nephew" replied Apollodorus, with surprise.

"That's what he tells everyone. Actually he is his sister's grandson, but I think he is his bum boy."

"Caesar is a ladies man. His troops sing marching songs about his conquests."

"Well he has become very strange lately and I think he is on the turn."

"If what you say is true, why invite Cleopatra to Rome?"

"He hopes to draw attention away from his relationship with Octavius. If all Rome thinks he is having an affair with the beautiful 'Lady of Two Lands' no one will think he is secretly having a sordid relationship with that youth. With respect, such behaviour may be acceptable in Egypt but in Rome men are expected to be men. I have no proof so don't say anything to the *Bassilisa*. I can't understand him. Cleopatra is the most desirable woman I have ever met. Did you notice the way Octavian's sandals are built up to increase his height?"

Apollodorus was non committal but thought "Antonius has said much the same as Mardian but I will reserve judgement till I have positive irrefutable evidence. You can't crucify a man for tying his girdle too low. Also, Octavius' sex appeal was questionable." He excused himself and went in search of the eunoch.

"Mardian, my friend" he asked "what is your considered opinion of that young man with Caesar?"

"From what perspective, My Lord?"

"From your unique perspective as a man who is attracted to men. Is he attractive?"

"Some people like cabbage water as a drink but most people drink it to make them vomit."

"I take it that he doesn't make you go weak at the knees."

"No, he doesn't!"

"Antonius thinks he is Caesar's latest conquest and apparently they are inseparable."

The eunuch laughed "I said I thought Caesar's true love was a small man but I hardly thought it would be that ……" Mardian hesitated "men that are attracted to men are generally attracted to manly men, some find little boys desirable. That little runt is neither fish nor foul."

Their conversation was cut short by the arrival of two men dressed as Gladiators. There was a buzz of excitement as they circulated, the women nearly swooning and the men becoming business like as money changed hands. Apollodorus found Cleopatra and asked "what is going on?"

"There is to be a contest, the men are placing bets on the outcome" replied the *Bassilisa*.

What followed left both of them profoundly disgusted, neither had attended the Roman Games so this was their first experience of a fight to the death for entertainment. As the servants cleaned up the blood and carried away the loser's body Cleopatra confided to Apollodorus "I can't believe how cheaply they regard human life. I can accept that people get killed in war but to take a human life for entertainment........" she hesitated, lost for words.

"It's barbaric" interrupted Apollodorus. "No wild animal kills for pleasure, only humans do that! I suppose we will have to attend the Games at some time, but I don't relish the prospect."

The weeks that followed were taken up with entertainment and being entertained. Caesar's visits were at best sporadic as he spent most of his time engaged in reforms of the Senate or increasingly grandeurs building programmes.

"Didn't Hitler become obsessed with grandeurs building programmes during the last weeks of the Third Reich?" asked the actress. I nodded and she continued with a smile. "I know, nothing much changes, only the name over the doors."

Spring turned into summer and during the second week in July the Games dedicated to Apollo were staged. These games were to last a full week. Both Cleopatra and Apollodorus were appalled by the gratuitous violence. By the end of the week hundreds of wild animals and gladiators lay dead at the altar of public entertainment. Summer turned to autumn. Ptolemy developed a chill and Cleopatra became increasingly frustrated on two counts. Firstly, with Caesar, who avoided the subject of recognising Caesarion and secondly, with Apollodorus, who was reluctant to be intimate with her. In a quiet moment when they were alone together she confronted him.

"Why do you refuse me, 'Pollo? Do you find me unattractive in Roman clothes?"

"I have said before that you look devastating whatever you wear. If Caesar were to discover our intimacy it would give him the perfect excuse not to recognise Caesarion as his son. I long to hold you in my arms, Thea, but for your son's sake I must not. While there is hope that Caesar will act honourably we must deny ourselves happiness. Anyway, if Jules caught us, in the absence of any crocodiles he would probably have me crucified."

"Impeccable logic, as usual, Gelotopoios. Would you risk crucifixion for me?"

"I would risk anything for you, but I have no right to risk Caesarion's birthright for my own selfish happiness."

"Do you have to be so honourable? I think I am going to cry and I want to be cross with you!" exclaimed the Bassilisa stamping her foot with frustration.

As the weather became colder and autumn turned into winter Ptolemy's chill became progressively worse. The political temperature in Rome on the other hand became hotter.

Book 11

In the New Year of what, today, we know as 44 B.C., Caesar became Pro Consulate for the fifth time, this along with other developments were making Apollodorus increasingly uneasy and when they were alone confided to Cleopatra.

"I don't like the way Jules has taken to wearing those knee high red boots."

"I agree. They are far from practical in the summer and they clash dreadfully with his purple toga, but boots are more practical than sandals in winter time" replied Cleopatra with a smile.

"It isn't the fashion statement or his questionable colour vision that concerns me but the mythological significance. The red boots are symbolic of the Kings of Alba Longa from whom Caesar's clan is supposedly descended. Did you know that a diadem was found on Caesar's statue?"

"He told me about that. His response was 'I am not Rex, I am Caesar'" replied Cleopatra mimicking Caesar's voice and posture.

"Your impersonations of him are too accurate" replied Apollodorus with a chuckle and the continued more seriously. "The Romans are fiercely anti- royalist as you know all too well, added to which Caesar's fits are becoming more frequent I fear that they will soon become public knowledge. Did you know he is planning a war with Parthia? He is now in his mid-fifties and he should be planning his retirement in the country, not going off on yet another bloody conquest."

Cleopatra looked alarmed. "I didn't know about the Parthian campaign. According to legend they can only be defeated by an army led by a king." Then she smiled at her friend. "I can hardly see Caesar retiring to the country and spending his time breeding those cute tail-less rodents the Romans find such an irresistible delicacy."

Apollodorus laughed again. "That is the answer Thea; I will go and have words with him. 'Now listen, Jules, you are getting a bit long in the tooth for all these forced marches. Don't you think it's about time you hung up your sword and shield? Why not get a nice place in the country and breed Guinea pigs?' Have you had any success pinning him down about recognising Caesarion as heir?"

Cleopatra looked sad. "All he says is 'I will do what is necessary and expedient'. I don't think he will ever recognise our child; his visits are at best sporadic. He spends all his time with that ghastly Octavius which is a departure from his usually company of *pyson karaflakias* who favour a good night sleep to plotting and scheming until dawn. What do you think, 'Pollo?"

"*Pyson karaflakias,*" replied the shipwright with a brief smile. "Bald, fat old men generally prefer the status quo whereas the young want to change the world. Remember my vision, the image of a blood stained figure dressed in purple? It can only be Caesar. I have heard rumblings of discontent from the legislature. The Senate will not be well pleased with the prospect of another spell of rule by proxy resulting from Jules going off to war yet again. Young Octavius wears platform soled sandals to increase his height so he must be the small man in my vision. There may, in the not to distant future, be another civil war so I suggest that as soon as the weather improves we go home and leave Rome to her fate. Frankly, we are no nearer getting recognition for your son's linage and the only way to find about Caesar's intensions concerning his heir would be to break into the Vestal Virgins and look at his will."

Cleopatra laughed at the prospect of forcing entry into the Vestal Virgins but continued more seriously. "It would be impolite to just pack up and go home. What reason could I give?"

"Ptolemy is far from well, that chest infection is no better and you have been away from Egypt a year and a half. What more reason do you need?"

Cleopatra did not heed the advice of Apollodorus and by mid-February Caesar was appointed dictator for perpetuity. During the fertility rites of Lupercalin, Antony, in the guise of the clown, publicly offered him a diadem.

"*What was a diadem?*" asked the Actress.
"*A white linen strip worn on the forehead. This was the Hellenic symbol of monarchy.*"
"*Sounds like a sports person's sweat band.*"

"Caesar refused the diadem and Lepidus wept openly," commented Apollodorus to Cleopatra as they discussed events later that day.

"Cassius had a look that only raw meat would satisfy but the crowd were ecstatic" added Cleopatra. It was later recorded on Caesar's instruction. 'At the bidding of the people, Antonius, the consul, offered Caesar, the perpetual dictator, the kingship, which Caesar refused.'

"*Did Caesar intend to make himself King of Rome?*"

"The scholastic jury is still out on that question." I replied.

Caesar's behaviour had become more eccentric. Whilst working on the plans of the Julian Basilica in the portico of the temple of Venus Genetrix he had received a delegation of Senators seated. This was considered most disrespectful to all but Apollodorus who realised it was probably due to another imminent epileptic attack. The temple had been erected to honour Caesar's adopted ancestors. Inside was a statue of the goddess Venus modelled on the body of Cleopatra. This statue caused outrage among the citizens of Rome.

The thunder storms at the beginning of March caused Apollodorus to sleep uneasily. Halfway through the second week he had the vision of the bloodstained figure again. The image of the purple clad bloodstained figure dissolved and was replaced by a lady in black surrounded by a golden aura.

"You are Isis" said Apollodorus "and you have come to tell me to take the Lady of Two Lands back to her realm."

The apparition nodded. "There are times when even the gods can't make mortal men turn back from that folly on which they have set their heart. You may try but I doubt you will succeed."

The shipwright woke up and made his way to the villa kitchen where he found the faithful Mardian preparing breakfast.

"You are up early, My Lord *Geloto*" said the eunuch with a smile.

"*Kale emara* Mardian" replied Apollodorus and asked. "How long will it take to prepare for departure?"

"I have been ready since we arrived but it will take a day to load and provision the ships."

"I believe there will be an attempt on Caesar's life at any time. We must be ready to go as soon as her Highness gives the word."

"There is an important meeting of the Senate tomorrow" replied Mardian "the Ides of March, I believe they call that day."

"If the attack were made in the Senate by Senators they could pass a law legitimising their action. Caesar is so confident in his popularity with the people he has dispensed with his bodyguards. But if there is an assassination plot surely his spies will have warned him?"

Apollodorus made his way to where Cleopatra was sleeping.

"Why, *Gelotopoios*, this is a pleasant surprise" said Cleopatra as he slipped into her room."

"I only wish it were. I have had another vision." Then he told the young woman what he had seen.

"We must do everything we can to prevent what you consider to be inevitable, but Caesar listens to no one these days."

"Marcus Antonius is usually in attendance and if I am nearby the two of us may be able to defend him. You must stay in the villa and prepare to leave at short notice."

"I think you are over reacting Pollo and don't fancy staying in all day."

"Thea, I beg you stay in and make preparations to leave and I will do anything for you in return."

Cleopatra looked at him wide eyed. "Seriously? Anything?"

Apollodorus knew what she wanted. "In spite of all the dangers, if you do as I say I will spend the night in your bed tonight and risk Caesar catching us and crucifying me – assuming he survives."

"How about some payment on account?"

"You know the voyage here was the happiest time I have spent with you. We agreed it was far too dangerous for us to be intimate in Rome. I have longed to be in your arms and hold you in mine."

"Well, hold me now, then do what you can to prevent the disaster you consider inevitable and I will play my part."

Later that morning, suitably disguised, Apollodorus made his way to Caesar's house. Entering the garden from the rear of the villa he heard the sound of passion coming from an outbuilding. One of the voices he recognised as Caesar's. Carefully he peered into the building and another part of the puzzle dropped into place. With a heavy heart he made his way to the house and warned Calpurnia that her husband was in mortal danger. By now he didn't really care if Caesar lived or died. Although the shipwright did not like the dictator he respected his qualities of leadership and recognised that his duty was to try and save him but in all honesty his sympathies were with the assassins. How could he tell Cleopatra what he now knew for certain? She would be devastated and Caesarion would never be acknowledged as Caesar's heir.

Having delivered his warning to Calpurnia in a rather theatrical manner, heavily disguised so that she would not realise the source of the information, he made his way to the 'House of Ships', Mark Antony's home. The servants informed him that their master had left earlier for an unknown destination. Apollodorus spent the rest of the day in a futile search for the consulate. Later that afternoon tired and dejected he returned to Cleopatra's villa. The *Bassilisa* was pleased to see him.

"Apparently there is to be a motion presented in the Senate tomorrow that Caesar is to be known outside Rome as 'Rex'" announced Cleopatra. "So there is no way Caesar could be persuaded not to attend."

"That has as good as signed his death warrant!" exclaimed Apollodorus.

"I feel that you are over reacting *Gelotopoios* but I do think it is very much a compromise between the republican hardliners and Caesar's royal ambitions. If I was him I would decline the honour."

"Is everything ready for a quick getaway if my worst fears are realised and there is a successful assassination attempt?"

"The Triremes will be able to sail in less than half a day on my instructions. Caesar plans to depart for Parthian in two days time so we will leave then in any event. Now forget about all this Roman intrigue. Get out of those ridiculous clothes, have a nice relaxing bath and join me for dinner."

The shipwright thought to himself "now I know where Caesar's heart truly belongs, why should I deny my feelings for Thea any longer?"

Cleopatra and Apollodorus, dressed coincidentally in Egyptian clothes, dined together while Caesar was entertaining Marcus Lepidus, commander of the armed forces, in his villa on the other side of the Tiber.

"How do you hope to die?" asked Lepidus. The two men had been discussing ways of dying. There was a rumble of thunder and the wind burst open the outside door.

Caesar looked straight at Lepidus, his black eyes unblinking "Suddenly" he replied fiercely.

While Cleopatra and Apollodorus slept soundly in each others arms, Caesar, over the other side of the Tiber, was restless. The following morning his wife, Calpurnia, pleaded with him not to go to the Senate. He laughed but to placate her summonsed the diviners. Their predictions were unfavourable.

Consequently, Caesar was so long in coming that the conspirators became fearful he would not attend. It was rumoured that he would remain at home that day, their plot would thus fall through and they themselves would be detected. Decimus Brutus was sent, as one supposed to be his devotees, to ensure his attendance.

"You must attend, there is nothing to fear" he insisted. At this an image of the dictator, which he had set up in the vestibule, fell of its own accord and was smashed to pieces. Caesar made his way to Theatrum Pompeium, the meeting place of the Senate. Curia Hostilia, the traditional venue, had been destroyed by fire five years previously. As soon as he left his home he was accosted by a messenger who gave him a small scroll in which all the details for the forthcoming attack were accurately recorded. However, he did not read it, thinking it contained some indifferent matter of no pressing importance. Then he was confronted by Apollodorus who said.

"We have never exactly been friends but we regard each other with mutual respect. I believe you are walking into a trap……"

Caesar laughed, looked around him and exclaimed "Where are your prophecies now? Do you not see that the day which you feared is come and that I am alive?"

"The day has come, but is not yet past!" replied Apollodorus cynically.

Caesar's eyes met the shipwright's for the first time "Cedere Jocus," he commanded "ego faceri omnes, faceri Romae, faceri Aegypto tibi tuigue dea. Capiut Cleopatra matrimonium atque Caesarion filius."

The arrival of Mark Antony forestalled any further discussion and the two Romans made their way to the Senate. Apollodorus followed at a distance, puzzled by what the dictator had said 'stand aside Gelotopoios, what I do is for all people, for Rome, for Egypt and also for you and your god. Take care of Cleopatra, my wife and my son Caesarion.'

At the entrance to Theatrum Pompeium two Senators detained Antony in conversation. Inside, Senator Cimber pleaded on behalf of his exiled brother but Caesar rejected the plea impatiently. Senator Casca struck the first blow. The unarmed dictator looked down in horror as a circle of blood spread over his purple toga. He glanced across at the assailant as Cassius struck him from the other side. Other Senators crowded round jostling for positions, all had sworn to strike a blow for freedom. Caesar tried to cover his face with his toga as a total of twenty three daggers struck. He fell dying at the base of Pompey's statue, surrounded by the faces of enemies he had pardoned and men he believed to be friends. One Senator in particular caught his eye and he gasped.

"Tu quoque, Brute, fili mi." meaning 'you too, Brutus, my son.' This was the unkindest cut of all. Two Senators, who were not part of the conspiracy moved to Caesar's aid. The rest, several hundred, were frozen in disbelief. By the time Apollodorus arrived it was all over. Brutus called on the Senate to give formal approval to the slaying of, in his opinion, the tyrant. He also wanted Caesar's body thrown into the Tiber, as was normal for common criminals. Panic ensued as the appalled Senators attempted to run for their lives. Gladiators had been placed outside in the Forum to maintain order but were unable to restrain the terrified Senators.

"Caesar has been murdered!" exclaimed Antony to Apollodorus.

"Get away from here!" replied the distraught shipwright "and get rid of your consular insignia, they may intend to murder you and Lepidus. I will try and get Caesar's body back to his home and with luck no one will take any notice of me as a foreigner."

The Senate were in no mood to listen to Brutus and fled in terror from the Forum. The conspirators ran through the streets waving their blooded daggers shouting. "We have struck for liberty!" Others, who had not shared the deed but wanted the glory, joined them as they made their way to the Capitol. The sight of the terrified Senators running through the streets filled the citizens with alarm, rumours were rife. The streets emptied and a hush descended onto Rome. In the empty stillness Apollodorus found himself alone with Caesar, where he had fallen. He was contemplating how to carry the body when he realised he was no longer by himself. A small woman, accompanied by a large man, had arrived.

"Thea, Mardian, what are you doing here?" Cleopatra was disguised as a common woman but Apollodorus recognised her instinctively. She was totally composed but her face was expressionless. "Mardian, take her Highness to the House of Ships, home of Marcus Antonius, send a couple of his slaves and a litter to me and then get back to our ships and head for home. I will deal with Caesar's body and then collect Her Royal Highness and catch up with you. If we are unable to rendezvous at sea wait for us at the 'Straits of Messina' where we met with the Roman escort on the way here."

Cleopatra protested so the shipwright explained. "It will be some time before the Romans get organised, then Caesarion will be in great danger, so will you. If our ships have left by then they will assume you are no longer in Rome. Your son will be safe at sea but you and I have unfinished business. Marcus Antonius will find out the terms of Caesar's will and then help us join our Triremes."

The *Bassilisa* nodded.

"Use the whistle I taught you and the boys. Antonius will know who is at his door which will probably be barricaded if he has any sense. Thea, I tried to stop Caesar attending the Senate but he wouldn't listen. I am sorry."

"I know you did, 'Pollo, don't blame yourself for what has happened. Mardian, do as My Lord has commanded and take me to the 'House of Ships' then put to sea as quickly as possible. 'Pollo will look after me; he will find a way to get us to the 'Straits of Messina'. Caesar always said how resourceful he is."

The Forum remained deserted, three people were seen awkwardly carrying a litter a short while later, and a limp bloodstained arm hung loosely dragging along the ground. Caesar's body was taken to his home and then Apollodorus made his way to the 'House of Ships'. Meanwhile the self-styled liberators had congregated at the Capitol. The Temple of Jupiter on Capitol Hill gave them a commanding view of the city. The conspirators had no coherent plan, so they argued among themselves as to their next move.

Lepidus who had been in the forum as the Senators came running out made his way to Inter Duos Pontes, the Tiber Island, where his legion, the only troops in Rome, were encamped. By the time Apollodorus arrived at the 'House of Ships' Antony had received a message from Lepidus placing his troops at the consul's disposal. The citizens began to drift back to the city centre and a crowd assembled in the forum. All were anxious about what had happened and what was to be done. Dolabella addressed the crowd from the rostrum at the top of the forum in front of Theatrum Pompeium.

"Citizens of Rome, as you know, 'The Father of the Fatherland' has been assassinated. It was his intension to appoint me as consul when he left for Parthia in two days time. I therefore assume that office for the good of all Rome. We have a long tradition of democracy which Caesar sought to undermine by becoming dictator. Democracy is government of the people, by the people, through the people. No one person should be in a position of absolute power. It is said that all power corrupts and absolute power corrupts absolutely. Power had become corrupted by Caesar. Brutus and Cassius say they struck for liberty and history will be their judge."

The crowd listened without much enthusiasm and a contingent of supporters of the conspirators chanted.

"Bring us Brutus, bring us Cassius. Let them speak for themselves!"

A delegation of Senators escorted Brutus and Cassius down from the capitol to the forum. Brutus was first to speak.

"Citizens, I think" he said "that the time has passed for any one man amongst us to have absolute power. Rome was once ruled by kings but monarchy is neither pleasant nor good. You know to what length the pride of power carried Caesar. How can a monarchy fit into a sound system of ethics when it allows one person to do whatever they wish without responsibility or control? Look no further than Egypt. Even the best of us elevated to such a position would be bound to change for the worse; Caesar could no longer see things with the clarity he used to.

"The worst vices of monarchy are envy and pride. Envy because it is a natural human weakness whereas pride because excessive wealth and power lead to the delusion that the monarch was something more than a human. Envy and pride are the two vices that are the root of all weakness, both lead to acts of savage and unnatural violence. Absolute power should preclude envy because a person with everything should desire no more. In fact the reverse is true as we have seen from the way monarchs behave towards their subjects. They are jealous of the best of them for merely being content to live and they take pleasure in the worst. No one is more eager to listen to tale bearers than a tyrant. A despotic leader is the most inconsistent of all people; respect is rewarded with anger because that person has not abased there self before the tyrant. Prostrate yourself and be hated for being humble. The greatest of all evil is that a tyrant can break the structure of ancient tradition and law. The young and beautiful are forced to serve their every pleasure, subjects are put to death without trial!

"Contrast this with the rule of the people. Firstly it has the finest of names to describe it – equality under the law! Secondly the people in power do none of the things a tyrant can do. Under a people's government a magistrate is appointed by ballot and is held responsible for his conduct in office, all questions are subject to open debate. For these reasons our republic was born and with it came democracy, liberation and self determination. These values we hold to be sacrosanct. It is only by the restoration of the republic that we can become truly liberated." The crowd listened in silence to Brutus. Next to speak was Cinna.

"Caesar abused his power in a manner that was criminal. Money was squandered on massive schemes of public work. These buildings were un-necessary. Extravagant games were held……" The crowd heckled. Caesar was popular and many people had benefited from the public buildings. The games were popular finally Cicero spoke.

"No one ought ever to sat anything out of favour or spite but everyone ort to declare what they to believe to be best. We demand that those serving in public office shall do everything from upright motives, and we hold them to account if they make any errors even for their misfortune; however absurd. You should remember this, if nothing else, that so long as we have conducted our government in that way we acquire lands, riches, glory and allies, but ever since we were lead into injuring one another, so far from prospering we have become decidedly worse off.

"Sadly we cannot change the past. Let us rather provide for the future. Great is the task, success is dependent on everyone bearing no malice. Certain people have made mistakes but this is not the time to enquire minutely to convict and punish. This is no time for judgement; we must forgive as we would overlook the misdemeanours of a child. Any of us could find much to blame in Caesar so he could have been justly slain or we could bring numerous charges against those who killed him. Such a course is for men eager to stir up strife. Let us consign what has happened to oblivion as we would a deluge or hailstorm and learn to live in harmony.

"In order that none of you may suspect me of wishing to grant any indulgence to Caesar's slayers to prevent their paying the penalty, in view of the fact I was once a member of the party of Pompeius, I will make one statement to you. I think you are fully convinced that I employ neither friendship nor hostility towards anyone for purely personal reasons, but it was always for your sake and for public freedom and harmony that I hated one side and loved the other. For this reason ignoring all other considerations I make one statement to you. In the interests of public safety I affirm that the others too, should not only be granted immunity for their high-handed illegal acts, but also they should keep the honours, offices and gifts received from Caesar."

Meanwhile at the 'House of Ships' Antony was saying "I shall be next on the list to be murdered. I was Caesar's deputy they will come for me, of this there can be no doubt!"

"You have nothing to fear, Dominus Antonius" replied Cleopatra "Brutus claims tyrannicide. This claim will only hold good if no one else is killed."

"They had originally intended to kill you and Lepidus but from what I overheard that is no longer their intensions" added Apollodorus "Lepidus has deployed his legion to Campus Marius over in the field of Mars. You must order the magistrates to patrol the streets. The conspirators have no coherent plan, they are arguing among themselves as to their next move. Act quickly and take the initiative, Dominus."

"Apollodorus is right" said Cleopatra.

"Very well, I shall send a message to Balbus the city prefect and Consulate Hitius. They are both loyal to Caesar."

As Antony's measures took effect an uneasy quiet descended on the city. All the conspirators except Decimus spent the night on the capitol. The assassins had misjudged Caesar's popularity with the ordinary people of Rome. Disquiet was turning to anger. This anger would soon turn to outright hostility. Mark Antony knew that Rome was on the brink of another civil war.

"Dominus Antonius" urged Cleopatra "you must act decisively to exert your authority."

"I know, but if I remove the conspirators from the capitol by force I may cause revolution. I would dearly love to storm the capitol and kill them but unfortunately they are all from Rome's principal families. The Temple of Jupiter is part of Rome's fortifications so removing the conspirators will be fraught with difficulties."

"An uncomfortable night in the open will do much to cool their ardour for revolution, Dominus" added Apollodorus. "They are already tired. Lack of sleep and an empty stomach renders most men compliant. They don't know if or when you will deploy your troops. Their fear will be your ally. Anger can rarely be rekindled."

"I like your logic, Apollodorus. Do you have a name for it?"

"Yes, he does" interrupted Cleopatra with a thin smile. "He calls it 'applied cretinology', it's the science of letting peoples own innate stupidity do your dirty work."

Lepidus was in favour of using force but Antony and Hirtius favoured restraint. Antony had ultimate responsibility for law and order so reluctantly Lepidus conceded to the majority viewpoint.

The following day, the sixteenth, Antony summonsed the Senate to Temple of Tellus on Esquiline close to the House of Ships in Carinae. Shops and markets were opening so normality was beginning to return. Antony knew that the middle classes and commoners were open to persuasion so he bided his time. The Senate he handled with tact and skill, giving all a fair hearing.

There was a move to repeal all Caesar's dictates but this would remove many Senators from office. Self interest and the proximity of troops prevailed. A decree was passed giving amnesty to the conspirators and also confirmation of all Caesar's acts and measures. Caesar was given divine status and made a god; also there was a vote of thanks to Antony. This was warmly received by the crowd who had assembled outside and they applauded enthusiastically. A message was sent to the conspirators advising them that they had nothing to fear. There was then a public reconciliation at forum. That night Antony feasted Cassius, Brutus and Lepidus.

The next day, the seventeenth, there was a meeting of all Senate including conspirators. Foremost on the agenda was the allocation of Caesar's provinces. The priesthoods of Asia was given to Trebonius,

Bithynia to Cimber, Gaul to Decimus, Crete to Brutus, Africa to Sextus, Macedonia to Antony and Syria to Dolabella who Antony had accused of having an adulterous affair with his wife Antonia.

Antony and Piso, Caesar's father in law, were adamant that Caesar's will should be read in public as was normal for a consulate who had died in office. Antony expected to be the principal heir but he was disappointed. Back at the House of Ships he explained to Cleopatra;

"Octavius is to receive three quarters of the estate unless Calpurnia had a son. He is to be admitted into the clan and henceforth be called Gaius Julius Caesar Octavius. The last quarter is to be inherited by the other grand nephews, Quintus Pedius and Lucius Pinarius Scarpus. Myself and Decimus are secondary heirs and executors. The Garden by Tiber he has left to the people of Rome and 300 sesterces each citizen."

"How much money was 300 sesterces?" asked the actress.
"About one-third of the annual pay of a soldier and half that of a citizen's income."

"What about Caesarion?" asked Cleopatra trying to sound casual.
"I am sorry, your Highness, nothing. Perhaps he meant to change his will but never got round to it with all the....."
Cleopatra cut him short. "There is no need to make excuses, Domini Antonius. Obviously he looked on me in much the same way as all Rome," she hesitated then added venomously "AS HIS WHORE!"

Book 12

News spread of the terms of Caesar's will and the Roman citizen's grief turned to anger. On the day of the funeral the procession entered the Forum on the way to Campus Maritus where the pyre was prepared by the tomb of Caesar's daughter, Julia. Speeches were to be made from the rostrum. Octavian, as principal heir, should have made the main speech but he was supposedly at Apollonia ready to go on the Parthian campaign consequently Antony had to give the speech. In front of the rostrum was a gilded shrine model of the Temple of Venus, containing Caesar's toga, torn and bloodstained, for all to see.

Antony instructed the heralds to recite their personal oaths which all Senators had made to Caesar, including murderers.

"So what did Mark Antony say? asked the actress.
I wrapped a sheet round myself and quoted.
"Friends, Romans, Countrymen, lend me your ears;
I come here to bury Caesar, not to praise him.
The evil that men do live on after them.
The good is oft interred with their bones.
So let it be with Caesar.
The noble Brutus hath told you Caesar was ambitious.
If it were so it was a grievous fault;
And grievously hath Caesar answered for it.
Here, under leave of Brutus and the rest.
For Brutus is an honourable man;
So are they all honourable men.
Come I to speak in Caesar's funeral.
He was my friend, faithful and just to me.
But Brutus says he was ambitious; and Brutus is an honourable man.
But yesterday the word of Caesar might have stood against the world; now lies he there.
And none so poor to do him reverence.
If you have tears, prepare to shed them now.
This was the most unkind cut of all;
For when the noble Caesar saw him stab,
Ingratitude, more strong then traitors arms,
Quiet vanquished him then burst his mighty heart;
And in his mantle muffling up his face,

Even at the base of Pompey's statue,
Which all the while ran blood, great Caesar fell,
O! what a fall was there my countrymen;
Then I, and you and all of us fell down,
While bloody treason flourished over us." I replied.
"Really?"
"No, that was the Bards invention"
"So what did Mark Antony say?"

"If this man had died as a private citizen, a Roman citizen, and I had happened to be in private life, I should not have required many words nor have rehearsed all his achievements, but after making a few remarks about his family, his education, and his character, and perhaps mentioning his services to the state, I should have been satisfied, desiring only not to become wearisome to those who were unrelated to him. But since this man when he perished held the highest position among you and I have received and hold the second, it is requisite that I should deliver a two-fold address, one as the man set down as his heir and the other in my capacity as magistrate, and I must not omit anything that ought to be spoken, but must mention the things which the whole people would have celebrated with one tongue if they could speak with one voice. Now I am well aware that it is difficult successfully to utter your thoughts; for it is no easy task in any case to measure up to so great a theme — indeed, what speech could equal the greatness of his deed? — and you, whose wishes are not easily satisfied because you know the facts as well as I, will prove no lenient judges of my efforts. To be sure, if my words were being addressed to men ignorant of the subject, it would be very easy to win their approval by astounding them with the very magnitude of his achievements; but as the matter stands, because of your familiarity with them it is inevitable that everything that shall be said will be thought less than the reality. Strangers, even if through jealousy they doubt the deeds, yet for that reason deem each statement they hear strong enough; but your minds, because of your good-will, must inevitably prove impossible to satisfy. For you yourselves have profited most by Caesar's virtues, and you demand their praises, not half-heartedly, as if he were unrelated to you, but with deep affection as for your own kinsman. I shall strive, therefore, to meet your wishes to the fullest extent, and I feel sure that you will not judge my good-will by the feebleness of my words, but will supply from my zeal whatever is lacking in that respect."

"Antony gave a detailed description of Caesar's life, lineage and achievements. He listed all that he had done for Rome and finished by saying."

"I need not recount in detail, you loved him as a father and cherished him as a benefactor, you exalted him with such honours as you bestowed on no one else and desired him to be continual head of the city and of the whole domain. You did not quarrel at all about titles, but applied them all to him, feeling that they were inadequate to his merits, and desiring that whatever each of them, in the light of customary usage, lacked of being a complete expression of honour and authority might be supplied by what the rest contributed. Therefore, for the gods he was appointed Pontifex Maximus, for us Consul, for the soldiers Imperator, and for the enemy Dictator. But why do I enumerate these details, when in one phrase you called him Pater Patria, Father of the Fatherland — not to mention the rest of his titles?

"Yet this father, this high priest, this inviolable being, this hero and god, is dead, alas, dead not by the violence of some disease, nor wasted by old age, nor wounded abroad somewhere in some war, nor caught up inexplicably by some supernatural force, but right here within the walls as the result of a plot — the man who had safely led an army into Britannia; ambushed in this city — the man who had enlarged its Forum; murdered in the Senate-house — the man who had reared another such edifice at his own expense; unarmed — the brave warrior; defenceless — the promoter of peace; the judge — beside the court of justice; the magistrate — beside the seat of government; at the hands of the citizens — he whom none of the enemy had been able to kill even when he fell into the sea; at the hands of his comrades — he who had often taken pity on them. Of what avail, O Caesar, was your humanity, of what avail your inviolability, of what avail the laws? Nay, though you enacted many laws that men might not be killed by their personal foes, yet how mercilessly you yourself were slain by your friends! And now, the victim of assassination, you lie dead in the Forum through which you often led the triumph crowned; wounded to death, you have been cast down upon the rostra from which you often addressed the people.

Antony's famous speech ended by him lifting Caesar's toga high in the air. Elsewhere a bloodstained wax effigy with all twenty three stab wounds was raised for all to see.

"Woe for the blood-bespattered locks of grey, alas for the rent robe, which you assumed, it seems, only that you might be slain in it"

From the crowd the ghostly voice of Caesar echoed "Ignoscere homos ille illi parricidium ego?" meaning "Pardon I these men that they should murder me?"

There was a brief debate as to whether to have the cremation there in the Forum. This was cut short by someone setting fire to the pyre. Crowds piled on branches, market stalls, triumphal robes, veterans their weapons, women's jewels and the Jews, who Caesar had favoured, wailed. Some snatched torches from the fire and ran to the houses of conspirators. Cinna, the poet and a friend of Caesar's, was mistaken for Cinna the praetor. The crowd tore him, limb from limb. Senator Bellienus house burned to the ground. With difficulty Antony and the city magistrates managed to prevent the whole city becoming Caesar's pyre.

Cleopatra and Apollodorus disguised as commoners watched in horror, the shipwright turned to the 'Lady of Two Lands' and said.

"I think the time has come for me to take you home, Thea."

She looked up at him and nodded, her green eyes were moist but otherwise she was expressionless.

"I can't believe these people, the way they dishonour their dead and allow them to be devoured by fire. To us fire is a living animal which feeds on whatever it can. When fire has eaten its fill it dies along with its food. Egyptians do not permit our dead to be eaten by any living creature hence we embalm them to prevent worms from feeding on their remains. How can Caesar now make his way to the afterlife? 'Pollo - take me home, please!"

The following morning Antony was undisputedly in control. The conspirators were divided for fear of the mob. Lepidus was made Pontifex Maximus to ensure his continued support. Again Antony handled the Senate with skill and tact. He proposed the abolition of office of dictator to much acclaim. Later in the House of Ships, Antony enquired.

"How do you propose to re join the Egyptian Triremes, Jocus?"

"If the Roman roads are as good as we are led to believe, I propose that we shall ride south and rendezvous with our ships at the 'Straits of Messina'. Can you get us suitable horses and provisions? I doubt you can spare any trusted troops as escort, your need of loyal troops is greater than ours. Two people dressed as commoners travelling alone will attract no interest, an escort, although reassuring, will have the reverse effect."

"I think that is a crazy idea, 'Pollo" replied Cleopatra in horror. "You know what a hopeless rider you are!"

"You have being saying for some time that you must teach me to ride properly and now is your chance" answered Apollodorus, brightly. "The craziest ideas are usually the best. No-one will think you would be mad enough to ride all that way to the south of Italy."

"I must agree with Jocus, your Highness, the alternative would be to use a ship and risk discovery. His plan is audacious but I can think of no viable alternative. It was a stroke of brilliance to send your ships to sea; all Rome thinks you left days ago, so no one will be looking for you."

"Was this your intension all along, 'Pollo, that we should ride south and rendezvous with our ships?"

"I had to think quickly and it was the best I could come up with at the time, there was no better way of achieving your objectives while keeping Ptolemy and Caesarion safe. I will protect you, your Highness, but if I fail you can always throw me to the crocodiles when we get back to Alexandria."

Cleopatra touched his arm lightly. "I know you will look after me, 'Pollo. This isn't the first time I have trusted you with my life and I doubt it will be the last."

Antony provided Cleopatra and Apollodorus with horses and provisions, so the following morning they began the long ride south. Bassilisa and Sea Lord rode in silence for most of the morning, both were deep in thought. By mid-day they were well clear of Rome. Horses and riders needed to rest so they sat is the shade of a tree by a stream.

"What shall we do tonight? Where shall we sleep?" asked Cleopatra.

"I think it's too risky to stay at an inn. How do you feel about sleeping in the open?"

"If we do that we will not have to explain ourselves to publicans and other guests and you can cuddle me to keep us warm. I need solitude. I can't cope with conversation at the moment, 'Pollo. Thank you for leaving me to my silence." Their eyes met.

"I know how you feel, Thea" said Apollodorus with total sincerity.

Cleopatra thought "Yes my love. You, of all people, know exactly how I feel and now I know how it is for you." She then added out loud. "I am sufficiently rested, we must press on."

That night they slept in each others arms but without the passion of previous nights together. Apollodorus held her as he would a frightened child. It was the beginning of springtime, but there was still a chill in the air. The shipwright slept fitfully as only a lone sailor sleeps, on the brink of consciousness, resting but not actually asleep, ready to act if necessary.

The next morning the travellers woke early to the sound of birds singing. Both people were cold and stiff. During the day Cleopatra became a little talkative and started to correct Apollodorus' errors of horsemanship. The countryside they travelled through was spectacularly beautiful and they would have been enchanted by the views under other circumstances. To their left were the Appennino Mountains, their snow capped peaks punctured the clouds. Occasionally they had a glimpse of the sea to their right. The trees were beginning to come into bud and yellow flowers lined the drainage ditches by the road side.

There were few other travellers on the road and the market towns they encountered were little more than villages. As they made their way south few showed them any interest.

"It's as though we are almost invisible" commented Apollodorus on the third day. "Do you think your Isis has cast some protective spell over us?"

"I thought you had cast the spell, 'Pollo. I am grateful to whoever is responsible."

About half way through the journey Cleopatra awoke at that quiet moment prior to dawn, it was as though the birds were taking a deep breath ready for their song that would announce daybreak. The travellers had been sleeping between the large exposed roots of an ancient oak tree. In the half light she could just make out the silhouette of their horses and she looked across at her friend but Apollodorus was not there. Suddenly Cleopatra felt a great presence, an indescribable awe. Her muscles turned to water, she felt no fear just a wonderful sense of peace and happiness. Looking down the roots of the tree had become cloven hoofs. In the utter silence the young woman forced herself to look up. Cleopatra knew she was looking at something mortal eyes were not meant to see. She was *Bassilisa*, Lady of Two Lands, the living embodiment of Isis. This may be death itself ready to strike but she forced herself to look.

There above her she saw curved horns surmounting kindly eyes that looked down on her. His bearded mouth broke into a smile. The trunk of the tree was now become his muscular chest and strong arms were folded across his broad torso. The branches were muscular shaggy limbs. In one hand was his sword, in the other, pipes. In the half light she saw him lift the pipes to his mouth, she looked away momentarily distracted by the murmur of the horses. The birds began their dawn chorus, first a single call of a black bird, answered by its mate. Then a robin joined the song, followed by a song thrush. The woodland became a cacophony of sound as more and more birds joined the symphony, punctuated by the mournful call of a solitary cuckoo, bidding her.

"Forget, forget."

When Cleopatra looked back the tree had become a gnarled, ancient oak and she was once again in the arms of the only man she would ever truly love.

The journey took ten days and by the time they were in sight of the 'Calabrian Massif' and the 'Straits of Messina' Apollodorus, although exhausted through lack of sleep, was a much better horseman. From their vantage point on the high coastal road they could see their Triremes anchored in the bay below. They attracted the attention of the crew by whistling when they arrived at the water's edge and the Felucca was launched to collect them.

On board the Triremes, Olympos greeted them warmly but looked anxious.

"What is it, Olympos?" asked Cleopatra.

"It is Ptolemy, his chill is far worse. We must get him back to Alexandria as quickly as possible. I think it is the damp Italian atmosphere that causes him so much trouble."

"There is a favourable wind" replied Apollodorus. "The crew have had a few days rest, so let's weigh anchor and get on our way." Cleopatra nodded, so the shipwright busied himself cajoling the crew. In no time they were at sea. By nightfall Cleopatra found Apollodorus soundly asleep in the forepeak. Turning to Olympos she said. "I think that is the first time he has slept properly since leaving Rome. We must make sure no one disturbs him."

"So was the way now clear for Apollodorus to pursue his love for Cleopatra?"

"Sadly, no. He felt that by hesitating when Caesar told him to stand aside he shared the guilt of the assassins'. To benefit from the Roman's death would bring dishonour to his love for Cleopatra. She may at some

time discover that he had hesitated and conclude that he did so with an ulterior motive."

"That's ridiculous. From what you have said Caesar deliberately walked into a trap."

"That is correct, his death paved the way for his successor to become Rex or Emperor and Caesar knew this. Also the epilepsy was becoming intolerable for him. Unfortunately, Apollodorus was unsure of how Cleopatra felt about the Roman and he had totally misunderstood what Caesar had said about Cleopatra, his wife and son. Conversely Cleopatra was totally mystified by the shipwright's reticence in declaring his love for her."

During the voyage Cleopatra started to see a different side of her friend. It soon became clear that he was utterly determined to get everyone back to Alexandria as quickly as possible. As Sea Lord he was fully within his rights to take charge and this he now did. Rations were organised so everyone had an equal share of available food and drink, this was to minimise stop-offs. The prevailing winds were in their favour so he made directly for Crete. When there was no wind he took his turn at the oars with the rest of the crew and at other times he was busy with running repairs to both the structure of the ships and the rigging.

This was the Apollodorus who had sailed all the way from the strange lands of the north. Gone were the jokes and in their place the professional seaman. He showed the crew how to rig rain water collection devices to could collect drinking water. Fish were caught to supplement their food stock. As the weather warmed, Ptolemy's chill appeared to ease. In a little over a week they sighted Crete. They were all exhausted and food and water stocks were minimal. As the crew beached the Triremes, Apollodorus relaxed for the first time and Cleopatra was able to get a good look at him. She was aghast.

"Your hands, 'Pollo!" she exclaimed. "Your fingers are bent round like birds feet." He could not straiten them as a result of the rowing. Normally clean shaven he now had a reddish brown beard, which along with his hair was matted with salt. His features were gaunt and he had lost weight. Cleopatra summonsed her handmaids and the doctor. Charmian and Iras cleaned him with fresh water and Olympos applied ointment to his hands. They had to cut his clothes off of him they were so filthy and engrained with salt.

"I know that you have driven the crew to the limit and yourself more so for my sake, 'Pollo" whispered Cleopatra. "We are now well away from Rome and safe. We shall rest here in Crete for a few days."

"Crete has been allocated to Brutus" replied Apollodorus. "He may be on his way here. Brutus was one of the main conspirators, so it will be unsafe to linger."

"No one could have covered that distance as quickly as us. We will be safe for a few days."

"If Brutus left Rome at the same time as we did he could have reached the 'Straits of Messina' by ship quicker than us on horseback. Did any of the crew sight any Roman Triremes while they were waiting for us to join them?"

"I shall make enquiries, I take your point."

"There are a couple of small islands due south of Crete. We could rest there and from the vantage point between them we could see any approaching Roman Triremes and have a head start if we have to make a run for Alexandria."

"My lord, 'Pollo, I think that is an excellent idea and the crew will also be happy" replied Cleopatra with the first smile for some time.

A little later, in private conversation with the doctor, she asked.

"Why is 'Pollo driving himself so hard, Olympos?"

"His sense of urgency is well founded, your Highness. I want to get Ptolemy back to Alexandria as quickly as possible. Additionally, the danger from Rome is very real."

"I know all that and I agree we should get home as quickly, but he is obsessed."

"Apollodorus tried very hard to prevent Caesar's assassination. He had insisted that there would be an attempt on Caesar's life but no one really took him seriously, perhaps he feels guilty in some way. He knows that you have been hurt by the death so he may think that he failed you. His actions may be to atone for his inability to prevent what we now all know was inevitable."

"That is ridiculous!" exclaimed Cleopatra. "The only people who are responsible for Caesar's death are the Senators who stabbed him and, to a great extent, Caesar shared their guilt. Calpurnia told me they were inundated with soothsayers warning of the danger. She begged him not to attend the meeting."

"Really!" replied the doctor. "I find it hard to believe that Caesar did not know of the plot. It is as though he deliberately walked into a trap!"

"I had come to much the same conclusion. I have had plenty of time to think about events while we rode south and on the voyage thus far."

As soon as they had re-provisioned the Triremes they sailed the short distance to the two small islands south of Crete where they were able to rest prior to the final leg of the journey back to Alexandria.

From the vantage point at the top of the lighthouse on Pharos the lookouts were able to see the approaching Triremes some distance away. By the time they arrived in the harbour it looked as though all Alexandria had turned out to welcome them. All available ships had been used to meet Ptolemy and Cleopatra. The escort numbered several hundred vessels.

"How much more proof do you need that you have won the hearts and minds of your people, Thea?" asked Apollodorus. The cheering of the crowds was deafening. "Have a Pharaoh and Bassilisa ever had such a welcome home?"

"Are you pleased to be home, 'Pollo?"

"I am pleased to be home and I am relieved that you are home safely. My only regret is that I failed to prevent Caesar's murder."

"You did all you could. What could one man do against twenty three?"

"I should have found a way to stop him attending the Senate" he whispered. "Will you ever forgive me?"

"How can I forgive you when you did no wrong? True agape is unconditional forgiveness whatever the circumstances. That's what you have always said to me. What ever you may believe you did wrong, I forgive you unreservedly, 'Pollo."

It was near midnight as Apollodorus stood on the north eastern side of Antirhodos. So much had happened since he first stood here three years ago and commented that one of the Sphinxes that guarded the palace temple looked like Cleopatra's *Pater, Auletes*. He was looking up at the night sky at a shooting star when he was disturbed by the rustle of clothing.

"I thought I would find you here, 'Pollo" said Cleopatra "what are you looking at?" she asked.

"That shooting star up there."

"Do you think it could be Caesar taking his place with the gods?"

"It's a nice thought, Thea; does it help you to believe that?"

"I know you find it difficult to discuss, but is it possible to get over the loss of a loved one?"

"No, but in time you learn to live with that loss, you get used to the pain but it never truly goes away. In a perverse way it becomes a sacred companion, on which you can't live with but would not be without. The trouble is, all too often we don't realise how much we love someone until they are gone. Did you really love Caesar?"

"That is a very difficult question" she prevaricated, then changed the subject. "What do you think that star is, 'Pollo?"

"The Jewish tradition says that it will be a sign of the coming of the messiah."

"Are you serious?" asked the actress.
"About this time there was an astronomical phenomenon called the July Comet which could have been the Star of Bethlehem. Its appearance is well documented by Roman historians."

"What do you think it is, 'Pollo?"

"Planet X, the home world of the ancients. It is too far from the sun to derive any heat so there would need to be another source to maintain life. A large planet could provide the heat by virtue of its mass without igniting like the sun which is far larger then any of the planets. Most stars in our galaxy are binary systems so why should ours be any different? This second sun would only be visible on Earth every three or four thousand years. Sumerian mythology tells of an advanced civilisation on the edge of our solar system. These people gave mankind knowledge and perhaps life itself. What we can see could be the Brown Dwarf sun that warms the ancients' home world."

Cleopatra looked him; she hardly understood what he had said, as X meant ten in Roman numerals and unknown in mathematics. There were only five planets known to Egyptian astronomers which along with the Sun and Moon corresponding to the days of a week. The Bassilisa wondered "Is that where you come from Apollodorus?" but dared not ask. She just shivered. The shipwright put his arm round her.

"You are my dearest friend" she said "tell me, you must know the answer. You miss nothing. Why didn't Caesar name Caesarion his successor? I could understand it if he had named Brutus. As a young man Caesar was romantically attached Servilius and she gave birth to Brutus when the relationship was at its most passionate. But why nominate Octavius?"

"I have heard similar whispers that Brutus was Caesar's illegitimate son and some say he acknowledged that paternity as he died" replied Apollodorus evasively. "It beggars belief that Brutus would have conspired to murder his own father but with Romans anything is possible. Brutus was always trying to molest you while we were in Rome." Cleopatra nodded and Apollodorus continued. "With respect to Octavius, I really don't want to answer that question, you have enough pain."

"So you do know the answer, tell me, 'Pollo, I must know" she pleaded.

Apollodorus hesitated. He held Cleopatra tightly and looking into her moist green eyes said in a quiet voice "Caesar and Octavius were lovers." He expected her to cry, but instead she said.

"Come with me" she led him back to her apartment where Charmain and Iras were talking softly. "Can one of you bring my jewellery box please? There is a ring, a very old ring that can only be given by the *Bassilisa* to the one she truly loves and who truly declares his love for her, on pain of death. The line of inheritance, as you know, runs down the female line in Egyptian culture. For this reason the Pharaoh derives his divine status from the *Bassilisa*.

"The union has rarely been founded in love, *eros* certainly, *agape* almost never. For that reason this ring has only once been given and never in Ptolemaic times. I could never bring myself to give the Serpent Ring to Caesar, he was not worthy." In her hand was a ring that was made up of three rings, two uraeus and a vulture, the symbol of protection and immortality. "It would appear that my reticence was well founded, 'Pollo." She then collapsed into his arms and the tears she had held back for so long, flooded.

To be continued

'Proyet'

(A Story of Two Cities)

Book 13

    High above the Nile delta a solitary hawk hovered supported on the thermals that rose from the lush green fertile lands below. The delta was in fact an alluvial plane formed over the millennia by deposits of silt into what had been a huge gulf into the Mediterranean Sea. At the apex of the delta a mighty river divided into two waterways separating the fertile land from the parched desert that bordered it. The brown waterways split like bamboo, bent and coiled round islands to emerge into the blue Mediterranean at a further five points. These intermediary estuaries and sandbanks were devoid of human population where birds and fish congregated in secret. This was the only true homeland of the Egyptians as the Nile divided the ancient brown desert wind carved dunes lands of Asia and Africa.

    In times past the hawk had been the god bird of the Pharaoh's, below was a lone horseman galloping as though his life depended on his speed, the rider had reddish brown hair and his horse was dapple grey. There appeared some distance behind the horseman a second rider on a white horse. Golden hair streamed behind the second riders head. Her clothes were of the finest white silk. She was clearly a woman as the silk clung to her figure in a most erotic manner. Unlike the first rider, who sat astride his horse, she was mounted sideways in the manner of a camel rider. The woman rider easily overtook the man and shortly arrived at the edge of a lake. In the lake was a small boat with a pronounced shear, small cabin amidships and a single mast with neatly furled sail. A small boy was jumping up and down excitedly on board. The woman rider dismounted by sliding to the ground and the boy ran up to her as a large man dressed in a white kilt took charge of the horse which was steaming from its exertion.

    "Thank you, Mardian" she said as she lifted the boy into her arms.

    "You beat *Pater Geloto* again, even with a head start, *Mater*" he exclaimed.

    "Shush you must not call *Gelotopoios; Pater*" scolded Cleopatra "Caesar was your *Pater*."

    "But he is dead now. Why don't you marry *Geloto*? He is much nicer than Caesar."

    "Because I married Ptolemy" she replied.

"But Ptolemy is your brother. Normal people don't marry their brothers, do they? Anyway, he is also dead, so you can marry *Geloto*."

The arrival of the breathless shipwright curtailed any further conversation about his mother's husbands. The boy rushed up to Apollodorus who lifted him effortlessly onto his shoulder as he boarded 'Mintaka'. On the coach roof, the cabin top, were laid exotic foods. In the centre was a basket of figs. Caesar had nicknamed Apollodorus Jocus which means Jester in Latin, *Gelotopoios* was the Greek translation. One of the two handmaids handed the shipwright a goblet of wine.

"Thank you, Charmian. I nearly won that time, Thea!" Only two people were permitted to address Cleopatra as Thea, her late father called her his *Mikro Thea* or little goddess and her closest friend, Apollodorus.

"No, you didn't! I gave you a good head start and still you lost, you may be a great sailor but you will never lead a cavalry charge."

Apollodorus put down his drink and the young Caesarion and tried to catch hold of the first lady who ran laughing to the bow of the boat. He caught her there and attempted to put her over his shoulder but lost his balance. They both fell laughing into the tepid waters of Lake Mareotis, Cleopatra pushed his head under the surface. She took off her riding clothes and threw them to the handmaids.

"Spread them out on the deck to dry in the sun, Iras" she said, then pulled off the shipwright's clothes and threw them to the astonished handmaids. "Don't look so shocked, Charmain. We do this all the time, its so liberating. Come on, Iras, Charmian, get undressed and join us, the water is lovely." The two girls looked at each other. They could not disobey their mistress, but were uncertain about being naked outside and there was a very real risk from the indigenous crocodiles. "Don't be so ….so Roman. You don't mind *Gelotopoios* seeing your charms, do you?"

"Don't force them Thea, the water is warm but laden with silt and far from safe" interjected the shipwright diplomatically.

"How long have you been doing this, Madam?" asked Charmian.

"Since you got Caesar's spy drunk just before we went to Rome. It's much more fun in the Cape Lochias Harbour by moonlight, where you may be caught."

They re-boarded 'Mintaka' and lay on the deck to dry in the summer sunshine. Apollodorus was glad to see the first lady so happy after the trauma of the end of their stay in Rome. They had been back in Alexandria nearly a year, it was the best of times, it was the worst of times, an age of wisdom and an age of foolishness. It was a season of light that would be turned into darkness. Egypt's prosperity continued to grow and Cleopatra's popularity with it. There was something Apollodorus had wanted to ask the Bassilisa for some time and now seemed to be as good a time as any.

"I think it's a great shame you were never able to take Caesar on that grand tour of Egypt" he said cautiously.

"I don't. He would have learned how rich we really are and wouldn't have appreciated the scenery."

"No, but I care nothing for riches but would appreciate the sights" he replied softly.

Cleopatra rolled over onto her stomach and looked into the shipwright blue eyes. "Do you want me to show you Egypt?" she asked excitedly.

"Yes, please!" he replied, then added. "If I am to build a navy to rival that of Rome I need to source large quantities of timber. Additionally, it would be good for the people to see their monarchs. You have a beautiful Royal Thalamegos just rotting in the harbour where it has been since we brought her back from Askalon. What was the point of me patching her up if you don't go anywhere in her."

"Apollodorus!"

"Your Highness?"

"You don't have to make excuses. If you want to see Egypt, I would love to show you her. Mardian!"

"Your Highness?"

"Make the necessary arrangements, if you would be so kind."

"With the greatest pleasure, Madam" beamed the eunuch.

Charmian, Iras and the young Caesarion were beside themselves with excitement at the prospect as they discussed what clothes they would need for themselves and the *Bassilisa*. Cleopatra turned to the shipwright and placing a hand round his neck, took hold of a handful of his hair, so there was no escaping her kisses.

"Thank you, 'Pollo that was a wonderful idea."

The sun was now low in the sky which changed colour from blue to violet so they reluctantly dressed and Apollodorus un-furled the lateen sail. Mardian mounted one of the horses and leading the second made his way back to the city.

"Caesarion, could you help your *Mater* steer while I handle the sail, please?" he asked. The boy excitedly joined his mother in the stern. They sailed west across the northern shore of Lake Mareotis until they arrived at the opening in the city wall that marked the Lake Harbour. A fleet of fishermen were departing for a night's fishing in the fertile lake. They waved and cheered the royal party aboard 'Mintaka'.

Apollodorus dropped the sail as they turned right into the canal then lowered the mast. With a long pole he punted 'Mintaka' along the waterway. They passed through an opening in the city wall then turned left into the other canal that led to the Royal Harbour. By the gate of the Sun where Canopic Street left the city the canal passed back inside the city wall. They continued passed the Theatre and Race Course to their left and emerged into the palace area.

The shipwright re-hoisted the mast and sail so they could tack round the peninsular between Cape Lochias and the Royal Harbour, which they entered by the eastern tip of Antirhodos Island. The sun was setting as they came alongside the island palace. The citizens had cheered and waved all the way through the city. No-one could remember a monarch travelling so freely among the people. There were cries of "*Chairete Kyria mou*" and "*Chairete Gelotopoios*", the traditional Greek greeting 'be happy my lady, be happy Jester' as they passed. It had never before been safe for the Royal family to travel so openly without military escort. The story of how Apollodorus had brought the young *Bassilisa* back to Alexandria in his unusual boat 'Mintaka' was legendary and frequently re-told in the city's taverns with pride and affection. The people of Egypt spent most of their lives on the Nile, so it meant a great deal to them to see the first lady handling a boat as well as they could.

"I sometimes wonder" joked Cleopatra "who is *Bassilisa* me or 'Mintaka'?"

"The people don't make that much noise when you are not aboard, Thea" replied Apollodorus with a smile.

"It goes to show how good for everyone a trip up the Nile will be" added Charmian. When 'Mintaka' was made fast the ladies stepped nimbly ashore, Apollodorus carrying Caesarion, who was nearly asleep.

"There is nothing like fresh air and a boat ride to send a child to sleep" he remarked. "It's a pity Ptolemy is no longer with us as he would have loved to go on a grand tour of Egypt."

Cleopatra's brother had died of tuberculosis the autumn they arrived back in Alexandria.

"I am certain he contracted the lung rot in Rome, yet another reason why we should never have gone there" she replied bitterly.

"Olympos did everything he could to save him but there is no cure for consumption." Apollodorus was concerned that Cleopatra was becoming unhappy again, so suggested. "Why don't we take the girls for a midnight swim after dinner?"

"Definitely not, you have done enough ogling for one day. I saw the way you're phallus was swelling up and taking notice. Second thoughts, I think it's a great idea, you may give up your celibacy." They had arrived at the nursery where Mardian greeted them and took charge of the sleeping child.

"I will see you at dinner" said the shipwright "and we will discuss all our arrangements." They went their separate ways to their respective apartments. Charmian and Iras had a bath ready for the *Bassilisa* as she arrived. They helped her undress and she stepped into the warm perfumed water.

"Tonight we shall all look devastating" she announced "My Lord *Gelotopoios* deserves it. Do you agree?"

"Yes, Madam" chorused the handmaids. "Is it his birthday?" asked Charmian.

"Not exactly. He suggested we take you for a midnight swim in the Cape Lochias Harbour. I think he is losing his resolve. Will you help me show him just what he is missing?"

"With pleasure, Madam" replied Iras.

"Come to think of it, I don't know when his birthday is. We must find out" said Cleopatra, thoughtfully.

A very rare and sudden summer storm made a moonlit swim out of the question but Cleopatra was not a woman to have minor inconveniences, like the weather, deter her. Apollodorus arrived at her private dining room to be confronted by the *Bassilisa* reclining on a couch wearing her favourite jewellery and nothing else. Iras and Charmain were in a similar state of undress. The shipwright had become used to the way Egyptians proudly displayed their bodies in diaphanous apparel but this was something else. He was in excellent spirit so smiled approvingly at each of the beautiful young women in turn. The bridge of Cleopatra's nose was a little higher than what would be considered to be ideal and her ears slightly larger than average, the latter signifying great intelligence. These minor imperfections did not detract from her beauty, if anything they enhanced it. It is said that the eyes are the window to the soul and Cleopatra's were large, green and almost hypnotic. Her face was framed by a profusion of golden trusses which on formal occasions were curled into tight ringlets. Charmain was Egyptian, with luxurious thick dark curly hair and hazel eyes whereas Iras was from

Nubia or modern day Sudan, her skin was as black as ebony and her braided black hair was decorated with beads.

"I hope no one else has been invited to the party"

"No" replied Cleopatra. "This is for you only, My Lord. Come and recline beside me, there is much we have to discuss."

"There is?"

"Yes. For a start, when is your birthday?"

"The Celtic calendar is very different to the Egyptian one and Roman calendar has changed so much recently…."

"My Lord, you do prevaricate so!" replied Cleopatra, her emerald green eyes twinkling.

"I was born in the summer so in the absence of a known birthday I will have an official birthday, the day I met you! My life before then was of no consequence. You could make an official royal proclamation to that effect."

"I like your flattery but your idea would make you twenty years younger than me."

"No problem. We have fixed a day and shall remain vague about the year. Alternatively, but rather presumptuously, you could have an official birthday as well as your actual birthday, on the same date."

"That isn't in the least presumptuous. I was hardly alive before I met you; I think it's a sweet idea."

"It might cause tongues to wag if we had the same official birthday, we would be twins. How about your official birthday being the end of the Alexandrian war when you were restored to the throne? That way you would be younger than me."

"I shall give that some thought" replied Cleopatra her heart was racing. She thought "if we were twins you would be my brother and the tradition of the Ptolemy's and Cleopatra's is to marry their siblings. I shall definitely give that some thought, my love!"

"Charmain, Iras, when will you have your official birthdays?" asked Apollodorus, not wishing to leave the handmaids out of the conversation.

"Is it right that servants should have an official birthday?" replied Iras.

"Don't me silly, Iras" interrupted Cleopatra. "You know *Geloto* is a republican, all people are equal in his eyes. Everyone should have an official birthday, shouldn't they, my Lord?"

"On the face of it, yes, equality and all that. On the other hand" he replied with a grin. "You could make it a special honour, as absolute monarch."

"Behaving absolutely" added Cleopatra.

"Absolutely. The only way for an absolute monarch to behave. For special services of friendship you could confer the privilege of official birthday."

"I like that idea. Apollodorus, Charmain, Iras, for your special services of friendship I confer the privilege and honour of official birthday on a date of your choosing."

"Thank you, madam" chorused the handmaids.

"Thank you, your Highness" said Apollodorus. "May I propose a toast?"

"You may."

"To the honour of official birthday graciously bestowed by our friend Cleopatra Thea Philopator, 'Lady of Two Lands' and the only true *Bassilisa*. The *Bassilisa*!"

"The *Bassilisa*!" repeated the handmaids. They drained their goblets and Cleopatra nodded graciously.

"I suppose I should reply to the toast but you have left me speechless."

Apollodorus kissed her, so the two handmaids followed his example then handed round food and refilled the goblets with wine. After the meal Cleopatra produced her seven stringed lyre and sang in her deep seductive voice that all men, privileged to hear, found so captivating. The handmaids danced an erotic dance, swirling and weaving round each other and Apollodorus. At the end of the dance they bowed and made a discreet exit, leaving the shipwright alone with his *Bassilisa*.

"I think my Lady of Two Lands doth try to seduce me." The Egyptian kilt he was wearing made it impossible to disguise the fact that she was succeeding.

"My Lord *Geloto*, you said that the voyage to Rome was the happiest time in your life and I would do anything to re-kindle those times." She placed the palm of her hand on his chest. "I beg you, why deny yourself any longer?"

"The day before the Ides of March on the way to warn Calpurnia I discovered Caesar and Octavius in each others arms. I was so incensed by what I saw that my sympathies went out to the conspirators. When I tried to stop him from going to the Senate the following day and he ordered me to 'step aside', I was literally pulled in two directions. I hesitated and he was gone and by the time I got to the Forum it was too late. Then when you were so obviously distraught by the murder I knew I had failed you. How can you ever forgive me?"

"In the same way you would forgive me. If it was necessary to forgive you I would have done so a long time ago. Why did you never tell me? Caesar must have known about the plot, I think he wanted to die. If he would rather be in that little runt Octavius' arms than mine, you are right; he was unworthy of my love and deserved to die!"

Apollodorus was greatly mystified by what Cleopatra had said about Caesar wanting to die. It was a concept that had simply not occurred to him. Cleopatra having dispelled any misunderstandings between them to her own complete satisfaction was kissing him passionately to prevent any further argument. By the time Apollodorus had the use of his mouth there was a much more pressing matter to discuss. He was adamant that he would not risk Cleopatra becoming pregnant and reluctantly she conceded on that point, for the time being.

"There is something I must ask" he said.

"Ask away."

"The way you remove all body hair, is it a fashion thing or is it to improve oral sex?"

"All Egyptians remove their body hair as a precaution against lice. Why would removing body hair enhance talking about sex?"

"You have misunderstood what I mean by oral sex, let me demonstrate."

Some time later a supremely contented Cleopatra fully understood, she was satisfied in a way that Caesar had never satisfied her. As they lay in each others arms Cleopatra resolved to make the forthcoming trip up the Nile a journey of a lifetime for Apollodorus. Events over the other side of the Mediterranean were conspiring to shatter her dreams and change the course of history for ever.

Immediately after Caesar's death Calpurnia handed over all his papers and money to Antony. There was no practical way to distinguish between the public and private money. Caesar's papers gave authority to Antony's proposals and edicts and if necessary these papers could be amended! Opinion hardened against the conspirators. They found themselves increasingly isolated and virtual prisoners in their own homes.

The Senate was fearful that control of the provinces and client realms could be lost. Decimus slipped away to Cisalpine Gaul, Brutus and Cassius, with Antony's permission, to Antium. Brutus planned to return and preside over the July Games in honour of Apollo as it was his duty to organise and finance these games. It was rumoured that the Senate would take action against the conspirators. This was reinforced by Antony's steps to maintain law and order and also his reluctance to take action against some of the excesses by the mob against the conspirators. Caesar's veterans feared, with good reason, that they may lose their land settlements following the murder of their commander.

The most important single factor no one considered was Octavian's reaction. The eighteen year old youth discussed his options with his friends and brother officers Marcus Agrippa and Salvidienus Rufus. The commander of their garrison offered support and troops to avenge Caesar. The dilemma facing Octavian was that there had been no precedent for a posthumous adoption into a family. To accept it would place him in a blood feud against most of Rome's leading families. In deference to all advice the youth accepted adoption and returned to the city privately.

Mark Antony was away in Campania when Octavian arrived in Rome. Antony's brother, Tribune Lucius called a meeting of the people to announce the adoption. This prompted the return of Antony that May with a substantial personal bodyguard.

A chance meeting on a yacht delivery gave me the opportunity to tell my story. I had a growing feeling that the elements had conspired to bring us together or were other forces at work? We had met at Queenborough, I a Yacht Delivery Skipper and Naval Architect delivering a yacht by sea, she a famous singer who was looking for a part to play in a new film. I suggested Cleopatra she protested that it had already been done. It had, several times, but no one had played the Cleopatra that I knew, Bassilisa or first lady of two lands not Queen as the concept did not exist. During the telling of my story we had become close friends.

"So was all this going on while Cleopatra and Apollodorus were travelling back to Alexandria from Rome following Caesar's assassination?" asked the actress.

"They would have arrived back a week or so prior to Antony's return to Rome."

Mark Antony made a grave mistake that was to have far-reaching historical ramifications. Octavian made him a courtesy visit and demanded payment of Caesar's fortune. The consulate foolishly didn't take the youth seriously. Mark Antony was a giant of a man in the prime of his life, generous and hedonistic by nature. Octavian Caesar, by contrast, was a small, sickly youth with unsmiling blue eyes and fair hair. He was the grandson of a Thurian freedman who earned a living as a rope maker. His father had gained notoriety for putting down an uprising of slaves and was the first of the clan to become a Senator. An early death would deprive Octavian's father of the post of consul and nobility. The young man's outward appearance and humble origin concealed a formidable intelligence and single minded determination. He was cunning and devious beyond his years. The meeting went badly and set the tone for their future relationship.

Octavian's decision to discharge the obligations to Caesar's veterans undermined Antony's authority, causing him to abandon his public policy of conciliation with the conspirators. By the end of May, Antony decided to remove Decimus from Cisalpine Gaul and to this end he called a meeting of the Senate on the first of June. The Senate ratified the decision to allocate Cisalpine and Transalpine Gaul to Antony for six years. Dolabella's tenure of Syria was similarly extended. Antony gave up Macedonia but retained six of Caesar's best legions earmarked for the Parthian campaign.

The Senate appointed Brutus and Cassius as commissioners of corn supply from the provinces. This was to keep them away from Rome and taken as an insult by both men. The move against Decimus cost Antony some support from moderate Senators. Similarly, Octavian's promises of cash combined with inflammatory speeches about the need to avenge Caesar undermined Anthony's standing with the veterans. The Games dedicated to Apollo were staged during the second week of July. During these Games the appearance of the comet, also seen by Cleopatra and Apollodorus in Alexandria, was taken by the superstitious Romans as a sure sign of Caesar's divine status.

At the end of July, Antony formally accused Brutus and Cassius of deserting their posts. Octavian's activities forced him to take firmer action against the assassins. The conspirators began to drift back to Rome and there were angry exchanges in the Senate. Army officers loyal to Caesar were becoming alarmed by the growing rift between their late commander's deputy and his heir.

There was a public meeting at the beginning of October when Antony was formally accused of having no intensions of punishing Caesars murderers. This he vehemently denied. About the same time, in Alexandria, Cleopatra's brother Ptolemy died of Tuberculosis. Antony was becoming isolated and concerned about his position when his term of office as consul ended. He ordered the four Macedonian legions back to Italy to add to the two Cisalpina legions. With his wife Fulvia he left Rome to join the legions at Brundisium, in southern Italy. This was taken by Octavian as a threat; however, his agents had done a good job of inciting discontent amongst Antony's troops with offers of money. These offers Antony was unable to match so, with considerable encouragement from Fulvia, he had the ring leaders executed. Octavian was outnumbered by Antony forces and unable to block his return to Rome. He boldly attempted to get his Army to Rome first. This would be taken as an illegal act and no amount of money would make his troops confront the popular Mark Antony. Octavian's troops melted away leaving the youth no choice but to escape.

A meeting of the Senate was called to declare Octavian a public enemy. The turning point in both men's lives was the defection of troops returning from the provinces to the wealthier younger man. Antony was left with no choice but to cancel the motion in the Senate and depart for Cisalpina and secure his position. He received a warm welcome in the province where his troops were loyal and made preparations for a siege on Decimus' stronghold, Matina. In the absence of a consul there was a political stalemate in Rome. Hirtius and Pansa were to be inaugurated by the New Year. Into this political vacuum returned Cicero with plans to use the consular legions and Octavian's private army to defeat the weakened Antony, but first the consul would have to be outlawed.

Mark Antony had acted within the law whereas Octavian had not. In order to legitimise his position it was proposed that Octavian be given Imperium as a Propreator despite the Senate having no power to co-opt members and that Caesar's heir was too young to hold office. Following several days of debate Cicero's motions were passed and the allotment of provinces cancelled. A message was sent to Antony ordering him to lift the siege of Mutina and hand back the provinces. This amounted to an ultimatum to which he replied.

"The Assembly of the people of Rome lawfully appointed me to the provinces of Gaul and I will prosecute Decimus for not obeying this law. I will punish him for Caesar's death and him alone as representative of all the murderers so that the Senate which shares the guilt through Cicero's support of Decimus shall be purged of the blood guilt."

By spring time this war of words had developed into a war on the battlefields and Antony gaining the upper hand. Decimus was on the point of surrender when Octavian and his army entered the theatre of war. Octavian's troops under the command of Hiritus harassed Antony's men from the rear forcing him to withdraw to Gaul. Hiritus was killed and Pansa wounded in this engagement leaving no one in command of the consulate forces. This caused panic among Antony's enemies. Decimus was given command of the consulate army and ordered into pursuit however Octavian was unwilling to serve the republic.

Antony marched towards Geneva recruiting reinforcements on the way. This action was illegal as he was no longer consul but he was joined by Lepidus so there combined armies were formidable. Octavian insisted that Caesar's supporters should close ranks. News that Antony and Lepidus had joined forces reached the Senate that summer. The conspirators were fearful that Octavian would join the approaching combined armies. Retribution was now imminent and all hopes of restoration of the republic evaporated. Brutus was invited by the Senate to return to Rome from Macedonia with the legions he controlled. This he was reluctant to do as it would have brought together Antony and Octavian so ignoring Cassius' pleas Brutus left Dyrrachium, north of Apollonia where the troops for the Parthian campaign had been massed.

Republican reinforcements arrived from Africa and promptly defected to Octavian as he marched towards Rome. The combined legions occupied Campus Mortius in the 'Field of Mars' and the young man seized the treasury. He was promptly elected Consul then put Caesar's murderers on trial in their absence. They were found guilty in one day of deliberations. Octavian left Pedius in charge of Rome with instructions to repeal the decree outlawing Antony and Lepidus then marched north with his eleven legions to join forces the two former outlaws and settle accounts with Decimus.

Having made up her mind to make the forthcoming journey up the Nile a memorable one Cleopatra looked across at the sleeping Apollodorus. The night was hot so there were no bedcovers and the light from the lighthouse meant she could see his features clearly. She looked at his muscular torso and down towards his slim hips. Her attention was captured by his erect penis. How easy it would be to slide across him and by the time he awoke they would be one body. There would be no further argument then! No, she would be little more than a rapist no better then Caesar. She snuggled up to him resting her head on his stomach facing his erect member that looked like a Cobra ready to strike.

She took hold of his testicles and massaged them gently, they hardened in her hand and Apollodorus murmured appreciatively in his sleep.

"Perhaps I could satisfy you in much the same way as you satisfied me, my love?" She thought as she kissed the tip of his penis. In her mind's eye she saw the phallic paintings of Dionysus. The shipwright's penis slipped into her mouth. "This way we can become one body without my becoming pregnant" she thought as she shivered with excitement. Apollodorus was now awake and although he was enjoying the First Lady's administrations he also was trying to stop her. This excited her all the more and reinforced her determination.

There is a point when the sense of enjoyment will overtake all other considerations and this point Apollodorus had now reached. Instead of trying to pull Cleopatra away he now held her tightly and his whole body tensed as he became bathed in perspiration. Cleopatra felt two conflicting emotions as her mouth filled. At first she wanted to vomit then she thought

"This is his gift of life, like the lethal venom of the Uraeus." With an effort she swallowed. "He did not stop when I reached my climax. My fluid of love can taste no worse." Their passion spent they lay in each others arms for some time. Apollodorus was first to speak.

"You shouldn't have done that, Thea" he said with a total lack of conviction.

"Why not? You did the same for me. Didn't you enjoy it?"

"It was the most beautiful experience in my life, but for you a man's fluid must be unpleasant?"

"Surely no more so than a woman's?"

Apollodorus could think of no suitable reply so kissed her passionately instead.

"If you are still determined that we may not become one body I said before there are other ways I can satisfy you. I beg you don't deny me that happiness or yourself, My Lord." Apollodorus was again pulled in two directions as it was impossible for him to deny his Thea anything she wanted, but he still harboured a suspicion that their love could bring about their destruction and the end of the Ptolemy's and the Cleopatra's. Having visions was easy for him, interpretation was fraught with difficulty. This was Alexandria, the winepress of love.

The actress had snuggled up to me so it seemed natural that we should kiss. We were becoming close friends now and my visits to her flat to tell my story were frequent.

"Why don't we take my Motor Yacht to Alexandria so you can tell me the rest of your story on location?"

"I think that would be a lovely idea but it could be risky" I replied with a smile.

"The winepress of love?" The actress replied with a mischievous look in her green eyes. "We are both adults."

Book 14

Alexandria; I saw her with the same eyes that an old man looks on his lady, not seeing the crone but looking beneath the wrinkled skin scared by the ravages of time. I could see the beauty that still lived beneath the surface but the fates had been as cruel to me as they had to the city beneath. My children had grown up and departed to various universities never to return. The young wine of Eros had matured into the mellow fruitfulness of Agape when suddenly their mother's silver cord of life was cruelly cut. I had resolved never to love again but Aphrodite was beckoning me along with the city like a spider draws a fly into her web. What would my children think? The actress who sat next to me was their contemporary, not mine! Cabin lights were extinguished as the aircraft began its gentle decent; although it was only eight in the evening by local time, Helios had already arrived at the beautiful west. City lights twinkled to left and right as far as we could see.

I have always made a point of not skippering the delivery by sea of a yacht that I haven't surveyed; no matter how well appointed the vessel may appear to be. International maritime law being a minefield of litigation additionally my business commitments meant that I could ill afford the time that the voyage had taken. Consequently we had flown to Alexandria and would join the actresses' yacht which was already there. We stepped off the aircraft into the barmy Egyptian air, serenaded by the loud shrill droning of cicadas. It took about an hour to drive from Borg El Arab airport to central Alexandria and having previous experience with the black taxies with bright yellow wheel arches, known as 'Bumble Bees', I had insisted that we were met by a limousine.

"It is said that it is easier for a camel to pass through the eye of a needle than for a rich man to enter the Kingdom of Heaven" I explained as the limo sped along the palm tree lined, strait three lane duel carriageway of the desert highway. "Whereas the bumble bee defies the laws of aerodynamics by flying, Alexandrian taxies defy the laws of physics by passing through gaps which would not accommodate an anorexic business card; the afore mentioned narrow gateway in the walled city of ancient Jerusalem would not challenge an Alex cabby for more than a heartbeat."

"Why are there snow ploughs by the roadside?" inquired the actress innocently. I chuckled and then replied.

"I thought the same thing when I first saw them; they are for clearing drifting sand not snow from the roadway."

Cleopatra and Apollodorus had to wait for the Nile flood to subside before commencing their journey as the current was far too strong to be rowed against. The floodwater had converted the whole countryside into a sea.

"It looks like the Archipelago – the Aegean Sea" observed Apollodorus, "with only the towns above the surface like Hellenic Islands."

"Water transport is now the principal way to get around" replied Cleopatra. "Carts and wagons drawn by animals will be redundant for the next few weeks."

The flood marked the beginning of the New Year for the Egyptians and brought with it black fertile silt from Africa. This silt turned the barren desert into a lush fertile paradise. It was miraculous to Cleopatra and her people where the water and its life-giving mud came from. The answer to this question was not found for nearly two thousand years.

"So what was the answer?" asked the actress.

"Lake Victoria and the largest lakes in East Africa feed the White Nile and the Blue Nile, which rises in North Ethiopia, joins the White Nile at Khartoum in the Sudan. Annual flooding is caused by the build up of water in the East African lakes and formed the basis of the earliest calendar. This was based on the moon cycle of twenty eight days, known generally as a common law month."

"The same as a woman's menstrual cycle" interjected the actress.

"A fact not lost on the ancients, there are thirteen such months in a year of 364 days but later they realised that Sirius or the Dog Star in the constellation Canis Major, rose next to the sun every 365 days. The Egyptian year started at the summer solstice on or about 21st June when the Nile flooded and comprised of three seasons which mimic the three phases of the moon; new, full and old or the three ages of a woman; maiden, nymph and crone. The Moon was regarded as female and superior to the male Sun, men you will be pleased to know, were considered the weaker gender only trusted to hunt, fish, gather food, mind animals and fight wars. The earliest monarchs were women who took a male lover for pleasure not procreation, the King was sacrificed at the end of the year mimicking the way a drone dies when it successfully mates with a Queen bee because she absorbs his genitals."

"If the earliest monarchs were female I now understand why it is incorrect to refer to Cleopatra as queen."

I nodded, "The earliest Europeans had no gods only the Great Goddess an immortal omnipotent changeling who became known as Chimaera. This she goat had the head of a lion, body of a goat and serpent's tail, a triad identified with the three season's spring/maiden, summer/nymph and winter/crone. The Great Goddess became known as Mother Earth who in the upper air was the maiden Selene, the nymph Artimis on earth and the crone Hecate in the underworld. Understandably the early Kings became dissatisfied with the prospect of being sacrificed after a year of sexual bliss so a boy was substituted and the King's reign extended. Human sacrifices were replaced by animal victims in the fullness of time, Kings acquired political power and the Sun became the symbol of male fertility."

"It is the responsibility of the Pharaoh to mediate with the gods to provide us with the life giving flood" explained Cleopatra.

"So why did Pothinus blame you for the famine, causing you to be deposed when we first met? Surely it was your brother's fault, not yours?" replied the shipwright with a smile.

"Well, if you had been here, instead of winning a boatyard by having drinking contests in Ashkelon, you could have explained that point to everyone. Then a great deal of bloodshed would have been avoided."

"This is definitely a case of being in the wrong place at the wrong time, your Highness. Shall I have myself thrown to the crocodiles?"

Cleopatra laughed and thought "if anyone is going to eat you, my love, it's me, not some nasty smelly reptile!" Then she picked up her seven stringed Lyre and sang 'The Hymn to the Nile flood'.

They made a sedate progress in the Royal Thalamegos along the Nile. Each side of the river were lush fields of cotton, corn, flax and rice and also an abundance of wildlife. There were ibis, herons and birds of prey, such as falcons and eagles. This was the real Egypt and Apollodorus was captivated by its splendour. The Royal party were accompanied by a large flotilla of assorted craft including an escort of Egyptian and Roman Triremes making a very public statement of military might. Some estimates placed the number of boats in the flotilla as high as three hundred craft.

"I have heard that the harvest requires less labour than any other part of the world" commented Apollodorus. "The farmers have no need to hoe or plough but the flood does all their work for them. They wait for the flood to subside then the seeds are sown, pigs are turned out into the fields and they tread in these seeds."

"How much work do you think is involved in the irrigation?" replied Cleopatra coyly.

"Point taken" acknowledged the shipwright. "If all the crops produced are vested in the crown who feeds the people?"

"I feed them the same as I feed you. No Egyptian has any personal expense; the state provides everyone with bread, goose meat, beef, wine and beer on a daily basis."

"A wonderful system until the flood fails then the monarch is held personally responsible for the resulting famine."

Cleopatra nodded sadly.

"Look, *Mater*!" exclaimed Caesarion excitedly. "There are some hippopotami."

"They are the living embodiment of Seth" explained Cleopatra.

"More like the living embodiment of the mother in law" replied Apollodorus dryly, looking at the doctor.

Olympos spluttered into the sherbet he was drinking. "Are you implying that my wife's *Mater* is fat and aggressive, *Geloto*?"

"Well you are always moaning about her large mouth and saying she has bad breath."

"Does the hippopotamus have bad breath?" asked the actress with a smile.

"Presumably. Seth certainly had a reputation for poor oral hygiene, it was a popular Egyptian profanity. We were sat in the stern of her yacht, under the fly bridge awning sipped ice cold pink champagne and watching the sun set over Quait Bey, all that remains today of the lighthouse on Pharos. Our first day in Alexandria had been spent walking along the vast sweep of the Corniche waterfront, a popular local pastime. We had stopped at the mid point, between the modern library and the law courts, to look out into the Eastern Great Harbour where the remains of Cleopatra's palace lay, four meters beneath the surface of the Mediterranean.

Rickety horse drawn carriages, known as Gharrys driven by ancient Jarveys competed for the custom of the tourists and the dusty road space with the donkey drawn produce carts, trams and automobiles. Hooting automobile horns mingled with Asian pop music and the cries of street vendors offering anything from hashish to cotton. Fish markets rubbed shoulders with fashionable open air cafés where both women and men smoked hookers while drinking sherbet, cola or coffee. Cleopatra's city was slowly rising from the ashes of World War II and in time would she would take her rightful place among the primary holiday destinations. The idyllic climate, nearby golden sandy beeches and plethora of ancient monuments a few hours drive south made this inevitable. The authorities were making progress with the infrastructure but they would have a hard job re-educating the local gregarious population for whom generations of poverty had made begging and thieving a way of life.

As the sky darkened the silence that engulfed us was only disturbed by the rustle of cicadas, murmur of mooring lines and gentle tapping of rigging.

"Wasn't there a film called 'Ice Cold in Alex'?" inquired the actress as she looked across at me and took a sip of her drink.

I laughed and replied "Yes. It was a war film but it was ice cold beer that Sir John Mills was fanaticising about as he made his epic journey across the desert, not champagne."

"I would not want to eat my wife's *Mater*" replied Olympos defensively. "She would be as tough as an infantryman's sandal, hippopotamus is delicious."

"You eat those things?" said Apollodorus incredulously.

"Of course we do" continued Cleopatra. "We refer to them as water cattle and they are a highly prized delicacy, particularly among the common people." She made a mental note to have a hippopotamus culled so Apollodorus could sample the flesh but thought it better not to go into details as the shipwright was a little sensitive about hunting. The annual cull of these spectacular beasts had been a great festival in the past as it combined sport with an opportunity to feed the poor.

"So where does Seth fit in with the divine order?" asked Apollodorus.

"Seth is the symbol of evil and chaos and he was defeated by his brother Horus Ptolemy. The Ptolemys are the living embodiment of Horus, the last immortal to rule Egypt," answered Cleopatra.

"So if one of those brutes takes a dislike to us and attacks, it's your job, Caesarion, to provide protection" said Apollodorus looking doubtfully at the small boy.

"Delegation is the first principle of management, *Geloto*. You will protect us" commanded Caesarion.

Cleopatra and Olympos were helpless with laughter but Apollodorus was astounded. "Where did he learn concepts like that?" he asked.

When Cleopatra recovered her composure she replied "from you, 'Pollo! You are always droning on about management concepts that involve your doing as little as possible and everyone else working like slaves."

"Obviously I am teaching him the finer points of being an absolute monarch" replied the shipwright defensively. "The Pharaoh's job is to command others, not to do things himself. Is that not so, your Highness?"

Young Caesarion nodded vigorously in agreement and they all laughed.

"Absolutely!" said Cleopatra with tears running down her cheeks, "the only way for an absolute monarch." That night they pitched their tents among the palm trees and entertained local dignitaries, lavishly.

Over the other side of the Mediterranean preparations for a crucial summit had been made. The venue was a small island in the river Lavinius by the northern foothills of Apennines near Bononia. Lepidus had organised a meeting between Antony and Octavian who had been in communication by letter for some time. Between them they held all provinces from the Atlantic to the Alps and commanded twenty three legions. Antony had left his diminutive lieutenant Varius, known as Cotyla or half pint, to hold the western front with six legions. Octavian was no longer a revolutionary leader at the head of a private army of mercenaries but a consul controlling the western provinces. Lepidus, although vain and ineffectual, was one of Caesars most trusted lieutenants. He was unable to inspire his troops but had been an excellent 'Master of Horse,' this made him the ideal mediator between Antony and Octavian.

The two rival commanders approached the island from opposite sides of the river, each with five legions and made camp. Lepidus had constructed bridges so the two commanders could cross over the river to the island. Tents were pitched and a dais set up within sight of both armies. The island was searched and Lepidus waved his cloak to indicate that there was no ambush. Each commander then crossed over the river to the island with a small escort and this was the first time for over a year that Caesar's lieutenant and his heir had met.

The historic meeting brought into being the 'Second Triumvirate' and the three men took it upon themselves to restore the Roman state. Logic, self preservation and the mood of the soldiers made agreement between Antony and Octavian necessary. The meeting lasted two days during which time they assumed legislative and executive power and it was decided that Antony and Octavian would take to the battle field and avenge Caesar.

Brutus and Cassius would be removed and control of the east taken. Lepidus would govern Rome and Italy, taking with him three legions, the rest of his army being re-assigned to Antony and Octavian so they would have twenty legions each.

The Egyptians had no formal wedding ceremony and it was generally assumed that a couple presenting themselves together were married. Cleopatra omitted to make this point clear to Apollodorus; consequently he was treated with considerable respect by all whom they met as they travelled along the Nile. In the open countryside they saw elephants and lions and the land was also rich in minerals and precious metals. Cleopatra explained where gypsum, limestone, alabaster, quartzite, granite, iron, copper and tin were to be found. It was all too clear to Apollodorus why the Romans coveted the Egyptians land with such wealth literally under their feet.

"We must do all we can, Thea" he said "to make certain that Rome never takes control of your realm. They would rape the wealth of this beautiful country to fuel their own expansion and give nothing in return."

At the apex of the Nile delta they landed at Giza and as they stood in the shadows of the Great Pyramids Cleopatra asked Apollodorus about the burial customs of his people.

"Roman and Egyptian burial customs represent the extremes" he replied. "In Rome the dead are burnt like rubbish but here we find the largest monuments on earth housing mortal remains. My people's customs come somewhere between these extremes but generally we bury our dead in the ground. If a chieftain is a sailor his body is placed on his boat along with his possessions. The boat is set on fire and pushed out into a lake or similar large body of water."

"Is that what you would like done for you?" asked Olympos.

"He would never forgive us if we set fire to his beloved 'Mintaka'" interrupted Cleopatra.

"That is correct" replied Apollodorus with a smile. "You can place me aboard 'Mintaka' with all that I hold to be precious. Then push us out into Lake Mareotis with a hole bored into the bottom of my boat so she will sink gracefully." Apollodorus became thoughtful and added, "A human life is all too often as a traveller's footstep in the sand, blown away by the desert wind like a candle flame. We can tell what an animal looked like by examining it's bones, likewise with human remains, but we are more than that insomuch as it can be seen what we have done with our lives by viewing our works."

"So you think it is more important to be remembered by what you have achieved than what you looked like?" asked Cleopatra.

"The pictures on the tomb walls or on the mummies are highly stylized, they don't give an accurate representation of what the person was really like. All too often people are remembered for the mistakes they made, not the good they did" said Apollodorus sadly.

Cleopatra hugged him and said "I think we have spent enough time with the dead. You are becoming melancholy; let's get back among the living."

"Good idea, you can introduce me to your pet bull" replied Apollodorus brightly. "I must take the opportunity to thank him for trying to jump ship through the side of your Thalamegos, thereby bringing us together at Askalon. What sort of offering is appropriate?"

The following day they were warmly welcomed by the priests and people of the holy city of Memphis. Memories of the young *Bassilisa* bringing the Apes Bull there a few years before was still foremost in everyone's mind. The high priests generally regarded the Ptolemys as the living embodiment of Seth rather than Horus but no such prejudice was shown to Caesarion.

A week later, having travelled through the 'Valley of the Kings', they arrived firstly at Thebers and then Luxor. The entrance of the temple at Luxor was guarded by two huge statues of Rameses II and flanked by obelisks thirty metres high. The walls of the pylons were decorated with scenes showing the Pharaohs' victories in battle. Further upstream they visited the Karnak temple, the largest house of worship of any deity ever built. This was the home of Amon, the god of Upper Egypt. They then travelled onwards to Hermonthis, where the Apis bull came from and further south they visited the temple of Kom Ombo.

"You may not wish to enter this temple, *Geloto*" said Cleopatra with a smile.

"Why ever not?"

"Kom Ombo is dedicated to Sorbek and bejewelled sacred crocodiles are kept in special pools."

Not only was there an abundance of living reptiles but also there were mummified dead ones. Apollodorus was both horrified and fascinated.

"Much of the building was commissioned by my Pater" explained Cleopatra. "The top of the columns depict open lotus and papyrus flowers, symbols of regeneration."

"With all those crocodiles, I don't suppose they get too many visiting pirates" Apollodorus joked as they re-boarded the Thalamegos.

The journey ended at the Egyptian frontier, the Aswan cataract and here on the beautiful Island of Elephantine in the Temple of Dendera they made their formal offerings to the gods. Cleopatra wore the head dress of Hathor, complete with horns and disk and Caesarion his double crown of Upper and Lower Egypt, embellished with rams horns of Amon. The occasion was marked by a sunken relief depicting the scene being commissioned on the rear outside wall of the sanctuary.

"This is where the greatest of Egypt's wealth is to be found" explained Cleopatra. "We are surrounded by gold mines."

"Gold is an attractive but not very useful metal, highly prized by mankind" said Apollodorus. "The greatest wealth of Egypt is her people and one particular lady with golden hair standing right next to me." He placed an arm round the young woman and she rested her head on his chest.

"Thank you, *Geloto*" she whispered and thought. "You say the loveliest things to me except the thing I long to hear, that you truly love me."

The division of territories between Antony and Octavian confirmed what already existed. The younger man would have the job of ejecting Sextus Pompey from Sicily and Cornificus from Africa. They appointed consuls for the next five years which meant Octavian had to relinquish his final two months in that position. Ventidius and Pedius would serve for the first year then Plancus and Lepidus. The third year Servilius and Lucius Antonius followed by Pollio with Domitius Calvinus. Octavian and Antony would serve in the fifth year.

The armies watched as negotiations were completed. It was they who had brought about the reconciliation between Octavian and Antony so their demands for revenge over the murder of Caesar could not be ignored. The Triumvirs also had to satisfy the troops' hunger for land so they nominated eighteen of the richest cities in the most fertile parts of Italy as providers of resettlement land. The agreement was set down in writing and bound in matrimony. Lepidus' son was already betrothed to Antony's daughter and Octavian was released from his engagement to Sevilia and a marriage arranged to Claudia Antonnii, Antony's step daughter by his wife Fulvia. The terms of the agreement were read out to the waiting troops who received the news enthusiastically. The two armies were then able to get on with the important business of celebration and reunion with comrades on the other side of the river.

The return journey for Cleopatra and Apollodorus was as magical as the outward one. The days were filled with laughter and the nights with passion. They slept in each others arms under the stars and became more inventive with ways of satisfying each other without becoming one body. In Egyptian culture inheritance ran down the female line. This meant, from Cleopatra's view point, that she could chose who would rule jointly with her. The divine status of the Pharaoh came from his *Bassilisa* and Cleopatra could make Apollodorus her Pharaoh if only he would declare his love for her. This he would not do, although the first lady was in no doubt about his true feelings.

As the two Roman armies celebrated, the Triumvirs convened in secret session and uppermost on the agenda was one important question.
"How shall we fund the war?" asked Lepidus. "The cost of maintaining forty three legions on a war footing will be phenomenal."
"The provinces of the impoverished west can only just support six garrisoned legions." replied Antony.
Octavian was next to speak. "We could kill two birds with one stone."
"How so?" asked Lepidus.
"We destroy our enemies then seize their property and assets. The people who murdered my Pater have already been convicted in their absence; they were given a fair trial. Let them pay for their treachery with their lives and property!" exclaimed the young man.
"What kind of precedent would we set if we were to take such action." argued Antony in disbelief.
"My Pater has been made a god; I am therefore the son of that god and above the judgement of mortal men. Caesar was merciful to his enemies and forgave them. 'What avail his humanity?'" said Octavian echoing Antony's words at Caesar's funeral. "They repaid his forgiveness by murdering him. 'What avail the law'? I have no intension of repeating his mistakes and if you have no stomach for justice...."
"Octavius is right" interrupted Lepidus. "Your reluctance to punish the conspirators resulted in our being outlawed. Our property and assets could then have been seized. Cleopatra urged you to act decisively

immediately after the assassination, which you did. We must act decisively now and rid ourselves of the republican vermin once and for all!"

"It is your choice to be 'mercilessly slain by your friends' they would have killed you as well as Caesar if they had had the chance. They tried to deprive you of your property as well as your life and will try again. There is no choice, kill or be killed, sequestrate property or be bankrupted! It in not without precedent, Sulla's proscriptions are an example." continued Octavian.

"You are right" conceded Antony reluctantly. "We will purge our land of the vermin and seize their property."

Then in private the three men sat down to cold bloodedly plan a deliberate campaign of licensed murder and sequestration of the property of their enemies. The Roman world would be engulfed in a reign of terror that would destroy the senatorial hierarchy for ever and sweep away the last vestiges of the old republic. In its place would be a dictatorial empire controlled by one man.

"That sounds like the 'Star Wars' films" said the actress.

"Perhaps that is where the film makers got the idea from?" I replied. "History repeated itself with the French and Russian revolutions, George Orwell parodied the latter with his satire 'Animal Farm' and the former by Charles Dickens in 'A Tale of two Cities'. There was even a Roman equivalent of 'The Scarlet Pimpernel'."

"This is your tale of two cities, Alexandria and Rome, not London and Paris!"

"Plutarch stated that Mark Antony, as senior triumvirate, was held responsible for the 'rein of terror' or prescriptions but Octavian gained most by the destruction of the old republic as he was destined to become Rome's first emperor."

They were almost back in Alexandria when Cleopatra, quite innocently but with devastating consequences, did something most tourists do on holiday, she visited a fortune teller.

"A widow will come from the east and usher in a new golden age that will humble Rome" said the soothsayer.

Cleopatra was devastated as she must be that widow and Caesarion was the rightful heir to Caesar and Rome. Because Caesar had never recognised Caesarion as his son or Cleopatra as anything more than a concubine, she was effectively, unmarried. This meant that the husband whom she was fated to lose was the husband of the future. In her opinion, if she were to take Apollodorus as her consort she would sign his death warrant so the answer was clear, she must take another man. This man would be killed making her a widow, then she would marry the man she really loved and together they would humble Rome. The dilemma was that having given Apollodorus so much encouragement how was she to take another consort without alienating the shipwright and losing him forever.

The actress looked worried, so I explained. "Having visions was the easy part. Apollodorus had always said that interpreting them correctly was fraught with difficulty. The vision did not apply to Cleopatra but to a much lowlier woman from an adjacent land. This woman would come to Alexandria with her baby to escape persecution by one of Rome's client kings. If Cleopatra had discussed the prophecy with Apollodorus he would have argued that she had been married twice to her two late brothers and was therefore twice widowed. Conversely who knows what direction history would have taken if he had been more open with her."

She looked at me unhappily so I put my arm round her. "This is going to end very sadly!" she exclaimed.

"The story was a tragedy of epic proportions, this was 'Alexandria the great wine press of love; those who emerged from it were the sick men, the solitaries, the prophets – I mean all who have been deeply wounded in eros.'"

"Did they emerge?"

I shook my head sadly but said nothing.

Book 15

At about the same time as Cleopatra and Apollodorus arrived back in Alexandria the first execution squads entered Rome, the elderly still remembered Sulla but the Dictator was about to be outdone. Autumn was at an end and the cold chill of winter greeted the Triumvirates when they reached Rome, the city gates were locked to prevent escape. At the end of November the Senate was summonsed to ratify the setting up of the Triumvirate and names were posted on the rostra in the forum of the alleged enemies of the state. Wealthier citizens were in fear of their lives and property, political and personal scores of the Triumvirates were settled. Slaves won their freedom by betraying their masters but many escaped, resulting in a saving to the Triumvirates of head money.

In the House of Ships Mark Antony was entertaining a few friends to dinner when they were interrupted by the arrival of a small contingent of legionnaires.

"What is it?" demanded Antony impatiently.

"Cicero sir" replied the centurion. "He tried to escape by ship but returned due to sea sickness and hid in one of his villas. We brought you his head and hands."

"Show me!" demanded Fulvia.

The centurion placed the head on the table in front of her and she inspected it dispassionately. Then she placed her hand inside the mouth and took hold of the tongue and turned to one of the servants.

"Fetch me pins and a small hammer," she ordered. The servant returned with these items and Fulvia pinned the dead man's tongue to the table.

"That will teach you to make inflammatory speeches about my husband!" she exclaimed. Antony was delighted and rewarded the soldiers with a quarter million denarii.

"After dinner you may place Cicero on display with all the other traitors at the rostra" he ordered. "I have no doubt many more will come and view his severed head than listened to him alive." The guests roared with laughter and applauded enthusiastically.

> "This emulated Sulla's treatment of his victims."
> "Who was the 'Scarlet Pimpernel'?" asked the actress.

"Sextus Pompey fulfilled that role, he had been appointed admiral and although he had been removed from his office by Octavian, he nevertheless held on to his fleet and sailed to Italy. On learning that he had been convicted as one of the assassins, he kept away from the mainland sailing about among the islands, observing activities in Italy and supplying himself with food without resort to crimes. He had not taken part in the murder of Caesar so expected to be pardoned by the Triumvirates. When his name was posted and he knew that the edict of proscription was in force against him so resolved to negociate from a position of strength and made ready for war. Sextus proceeded to build triremes, receive the deserters, win the support of the pirates, and take the exiles under his protection. Soon he grew powerful and became master of the sea off Italy."

Cleopatra and Apollodorus arrived back in Alexandria late in the autumn. As soon as they had settled in, the *Bassilisa* called a meeting of her ministers and found that there had been requests for assistance from both Cassius and Dolabella who were at war in Syria. In private she asked the shipwright his opinion.

"This is not the first request I have received from them" she explained.

"Dolabella is one of the Caesarians whereas Cassius is a leading conspirator and republican. But rather more to the point who is winning?" asked Apollodorus.

"Cassius is in the stronger position but Legislate Allienus has requested permission to take the four Roman legions stationed in Alexandria to reinforce Dolabella."

"Can you refuse permission?"

"Yes but I doubt if he would take any notice. Also, if I agree, I will get rid of what amounts to an army of occupation. The last time help was requested I said we were unable to do anything due to famine and plague caused by the failure of the flood last year, when we were on our way back from Rome."

"What famine and plague?"

"Well, they were too busy having a civil war and murdering Caesar to know any difference."

"You lied to them!"

"Yes, I have no wish to get involved in Roman squabbling, remember what happened when I helped Pompeius."

"I think you should let Allienus take reinforcements to Dolabella as we are in the debt of Antonius so we indirectly owe Dolabella the help. I just hope he can prevail against Cassius, that conflict is far too close for comfort."

"I agree. The other problem is my sister Arsinoe, she has been spreading rumours that our brother Ptolemy XIII has risen from the dead and is with her in Ephesus."

"Ptolemy's body was found, everyone knows that but come to think of it I thought Arsinoe was executed in Rome."

"When she was led through the streets in chains the people were so appalled by the cruelty that Caesar gave her sanctuary in Ephesus."

Apollodorus was flabbergasted. "What kind of ruthless dictator was Caesar?" he exclaimed. "The way he went round pardoning and absolving all his enemies it's not surprising he got himself assassinated. Surely he, of all people, knew that dead enemies don't counter-attack!"

"Pollo, this is my sister you are saying should have been executed!" replied the horrified Cleopatra. "Blood is thicker then water, you know."

"Your sister doesn't have blood running through her veins, only venom. Surely everyone knows the world, no the cosmos, is only large enough for one Cleopatra, any number of Ptolemys, but….."

Cleopatra laughed and hugged the shipwright. "Not even Romans execute women surely you wouldn't really kill my sister would you?"

"No, but I had rather hoped Caesar would have done a better job of keeping her out of harm's way. I am beginning to agree with you that he got himself killed deliberately and has left the rest of us an almighty mess to clear up. There was I looking forward to a nice quiet winter building your seagoing palace and now we are surrounded by squabbling Romans. If they must spend all their time killing each other why can't they do it on their side of the Mediterranean?"

Winter arrived and on the other side of the Mediterranean, Sicily provided a rallying ground for the republicans. From this base Sextus harassed the shipping of the Triumvirates and effectively blocked access to Africa. He attacked harbours, towed away the vessels, and engaged in pillage. These activity supplied him with soldiers and money which gave him the means to seize other teratories. Quintus Cornificius also sent him a considerable force from Africa. Allienus, on Dolabella's instruction, marched north with the four legions from Egypt but was intercepted by Cassius who insisted they joined forces.

"As you know the Egyptian and Roman calendars did not coincide" I explained. "The new year in Egypt was at the time of the Nile flood, about mid summer in our calendar. The beginning or opening was marked by the appearance of Sirius, the Dog Star, Canis Major, 21st June and comprised of three seasons, each of four 30 day months giving 360 days, so the extra five were feast days at the opening of the year or 'the going up of the goddess Sothis.' The three seasons were; Inundation, pronounced Akhet, Emergence pronounced Proyet and Summer pronounced Shomu. It was the beginning of what we know as 42 B.C in Alexandria, effectively the middle of their year."

"All very fascinating I am sure" replied the actress impatiently "but the burning question for me is why do the Alexandrians all think we are from Texas?"

We were sitting in the Nefertiti bar of the Green Plaza Hilton, an art deco hotel in the fashionable West Alex. Pale blue Egyptian pillars supported the roof where the bar and reception area overlooked the square below. The barman hooking the lip of the bottle to the edge of the chilled glasses tilting it so the beer was poured with one hand without frothing the drink or warming the glass by touching it. In the corner was a white baby grand piano played softly by a local musician. We had eaten our evening meal in one of the open air restaurants in the plaza, a fashionable haunt of the well healed locals. To the delight of the actress a number of cats had suddenly appeared as the waiters cleared our dishes. These cats were clearly descendants of the ancient temple felines being spotted rather then tabby.

"I think my Panama hat may have something to do with the racial confusion or it may be because of the oil refinery to our east, oil men are usually Texan" I explained, then as an afterthought asked. Where about in America do you hail from?"

"I am from California" she answered.

"A California Rose" I replied, then in a moment of madness I turned to the pianist. "Do you know the song California Rose?"

The Egyptian shook his head and offered me his wireless microphone. "You sing and I will follow."

I hummed the melody and he soon was able to pick up the tune then I accepted the microphone, a bad move for a bathroom baritone, who would struggle to hit the top notes of a tenor for which the song was written.

"California Rose, I see the light of love upon your face.

*California Rose, I live to share the warmth of your embrace.
Hands that caress me, so soft to the touch.
Lips that possess me, and promise so much.*

*"Near and far away they know about the rose that's in your hair.
Lonely lovers say thay'd give the world if only you would care.
But darling, you're mine, and my love I'll always share,
For ever more my California Rose."*

The pianist played the full song as I took the actresses hand and we danced.

*"Near and far away they know, about the rose that's in your hair.
Lonely lovers say they'd give the world if only you would care.
But darling, you are mine and my love I'll always share,
For ever more my California Rose.*
"California Rose I love you, so." (Livingston and Evans)

"Mr, I have sung the world but that is the first time anyone has serenaded me. Do you mean those lovely words?"
I hesitated then swallowed hard "Yes - I suppose I do."

"The situation in Rome is grim" explained Cleopatra to Apollodorus. "Octavius has joined forces with Lepidus and Antonius to form the 'Second Triumvirate'. They are emulating Sulla proscriptions and have embarked on a systematic campaign of elimination of the Republican families and sequestration of assets. Octavius has shown an entirely new side to his character, that so called 'runt' is so ruthless he has been nicknamed 'Pater Argentarius'."
"Father of a silver bull?" asked Apollodorus.
"Idiot! It means father of silver mine or, literally, father of banking. The revenue of the east is in the hands of Brutus and Cassius, added to which Sextus is threatening their corn supply. This means the Triumvirates have to extract all the money they can from the impoverished western provinces they control."
"Are you planning to assist Marcus Antonius?"
"You said before that we both owe him our lives."
Apollodorus looked sad and resigned "you have a plan?" he asked.

"Sort of," replied Cleopatra. "We will have to give Palestine and Cassius a wide berth so we could sail west along the African coast then North to Achaea and assist Antonius".

"In the winter, across the widest part of the Mediterranean?" replied Apollodorus looking nonplussed. "What about your policy of neutrality in Roman battles?"

"I know. Have we any choice?"

"I just hate the idea of taking sides when there is very little to choose between the belligerents. Also crossing the Mediterranean at the widest point in winter….?"

"No crazier than riding south through Italy un-escorted or carrying me in a bed roll."

"Yes, but I do that sort of thing for a living. Your navy are…."

"Children playing boats in a bath? They have been well equipped and trained by my resident hero. The time has come to put all that to the test."

"You are right, Thea, I wish there was an alternative. I suppose you will have to take another Roman as a consort as well." His look of resignation threatened to tear her apart.

"You said I may well have to but you will still be…"

"Your conc…….."

"No, Pollo!" she flared angrily "Don't say that! If I have to give my body for the sake of Egypt I will only do so with your blessing and on the strict understanding that we remain intimate whenever possible!" Cleopatra burst into tears, something that she had done only once before in front of the shipwright.

"I am so sorry, Thea. I know that our relationship will, for the sake of Egypt, have to remain secret." He put his arms round her and held the young woman tightly.

"When I am in your arms it is by choice but when I was in Caesar's it was by duty. If I have to give myself to another man it will be on the same basis. I know it will be hard on you, so I will send Charmain and Iras to satisfy you in my absence."

"You will do no such thing, if a woman does not give herself to me freely…."

"What makes you thing they would be unwilling?" Cleopatra had recovered her composure but Apollodorus was becoming flustered.

"That is apart from the point….."

"Pollo, is there something you are trying to tell me?" her heart was racing and she thought. "Tell me you love me and to hades with the prophecies." They looked into each others eyes for what seemed an eternity, both people knew that they were at a crossroad in their lives and all Alexandria held its breath.

New Year in Rome was marked by Lepidus and Plancus taking office as consuls and formally deifying Caesar. Octavian had already referred to himself as 'son of god' and lost no time in accusing the self-styled liberators as murderers of a god.

"Did Octavian think he was the Messiah?" asked the actress as we had returned to her yacht.
"Jesus referred to himself as 'son of man'; it was his followers who called him the 'Son of God'. Yours is an interesting observation, it depends on what or who you mean by messiah. According to the dictionary the word is derived from the Hebrew 'massias' meaning anointed one, in Greek christe. The secondary definition is; leader or saviour of group, country or cause" I was floundering; the answer would cause considerable offence to deeply held religious belief. *Deification of Jesus by the 'Holy Roman Empire' came in the third centuries of Common Era; additionally the Latin word christanous had a rather derogatory meaning. "You had better ask a theological historian."*
"I think you are as good at evasive procrastination as your hero. Do you share his reticence in matters of love?"
"Are you trying to seduce me?"
"Another glass of Bolly?"
I responded that the appointment of Pontifex Maximus was generally made on religious rather than political grounds, as distinct from the appointment of his opposite number in the Anglican Church who was appointed by the Prime Minister. She pointed out our geographic location and that we were adults. The ensuing re-arrangement of sleeping accommodation resulted in a long delay in continuing my story.
"We drank a lot of champagne, I mean we indulged in a great deal of un-seasonal quaffing and feasting then ended up in bed together" interrupted the actress.
"I know we have and it is considerably more comfortable than the 'carriage of love' in a clapped out Gharry driven by that decrepit Jarvey but what will the crew say?"

"Nothing, this is crocodile country! I confess to having doubts about taking my lusty lover on such an antiquated contraption when I have a comfortable bed on my yacht. Get on with the story! Alexandria is holding its breath and so am I."

"Yes, but I have got to finish telling you about the goings on in Rome."

The actress started hitting me with a pillow so in defence I had to restrain her, resulting in another passionate delay in the narrative.

"Get on with the boring historical Roman bit and then we can get to the important romantic developments in Alexandria."

Antony and Lepidus by birth and upbringing were of the old ruling class and naturally reticent about the destruction of that order, whereas Octavian had no such scruples and could see the personal advantages in eliminating all opposition. The young man delegated the removing of Sextus from Sicily to his friend and brother officer, Salvidienus Rufus. The strong tidal stream and confused sea in the Straits of Messina proved too challenging for the inexperienced crew and commander and consequently Sextus had no difficulty in repulsing the invasion.

Fortunately for Rufus, Sextus did not press his advantage so the young man was able to retreat to Brundisium on the eastern heel of Italy where Antony and Octavian had concentrated their forces. The failure of the invasion undermined the prestige of the Triumvirs who realised that if Sextus, Brutus and Cassius became allies they would control the northern Ionian Sea and Adriatic Narrows. This caused one of them to send messages requesting help from Egypt.

"You referred to yourself as Caesar's concubine" continued Apollodorus.

"That is all I was!" replied Cleopatra angrily "but I will not allow you to describe your relationship with me in that manner."

"In one of the scrolls of the Hebrew God there is a psalm which reads. 'I would rather be a doorkeeper in the house of the Lord than dwell in the tents of the ungodly.' That is how I feel about my relationship with you, Thea. I would rather be your, you know what, than have all the rest of the beautiful women of the world as my wives. We both know that for Egypt you may well have to take another Roman as your consort. The question is which one, they are all pretty un-promising."

The moment had passed, Alexandria breathed again and Cleopatra felt the conflicting emotions of relief and disappointment flow through her. She bit her lip but to no avail, there was no holding back the tears for either of them. Apollodorus tried to make light of the situation. "If you choose Octavius I will never speak to you again."

"How about Lepidus?" sniffed Cleopatra.

"He is all pomposity and ancient lineage, unable to inspire anyone."

"That leaves Marcus Antonius."

"He is the best of a bad lot and madly in love with you; also he knows how to party so when we want him out of the way it will be easy to get him drunk."

"Will it be too awful for you?"

"It may not come to that and in the meantime let's make the most of what time we have together."

Later that night as they lay in each others arms Cleopatra thought to herself "it as almost as though 'Pollo knew what I had to do and made it easy for me."

"I have a present for you, Thea, and now seems to be a good time to give it to you" said the shipwright softly. He handed her a ring.

"Thank you, 'Pollo" replied the Bassilisa "it's beautiful" she looked at it carefully. "The ring is a contradiction, like you. A dionysiac ring with an amethyst stone?"

"Dionysus is the god of ecstatic transcendence," explained Apollodorus. "We have shared in each others thoughts and our minds have been as one. No other man will have that privilege; no one will know you as I do. Amethyst is the stone of sobriety, to protect you from the evils of drunkenness and bring you happiness." He placed the ring on her finger. "When you look into it you will think of me."

"Amethyst isn't mined in Egypt, where did you get it from?"

"The stone came from a country of the far north. I have had it for a number of years but the ring was made locally. I know the Achaean royalty have always prized Amethyst, so I thought you would like it" replied Apollodorus.

"According to Roman scriptures, Baccas was angry with mortals and vowed that the next one to cross his path would be eaten by tigers. Amethyst was on her way to worship Diana, who, knowing Baccas' vow, turned the young woman into a pillar of quartz to protect her. Baccas repented and poured wine over her, changing her colour" explained Cleopatra.

"I thought it was crocodiles, not tigers."

"You once described Marcus Antonius as Baccas" said Cleopatra with sudden realisation. "Did you know I may have to make him my consort? Is this ring to protect me from him?"

"Where the Amethyst came from it is regarded as your birth stone and is associated with your zodiac sign. The other mythological considerations never crossed my mind. Perhaps some deity foresaw your need for protection and gave it to me so I would give it to you."

"Pollo, if I didn't know you better I would think you were being evasive, but time will tell. None the less it is a lovely present that I will always treasure."

"The Dionysus creed is about enjoyment and living life to the full, not about drunkenness. It is about fertility, so he is the male counterpart of Isis, the goddess of motherhood. The Amethyst is supposed to do all sorts of things apart from protecting against drunkenness and poisoning. It makes the wearer gentle and amiable, which you are anyway" continued Apollodorus as Cleopatra gently took hold of his penis. "It gives power of dreams, healing, peace, love and spiritual upliftment." His manhood was certainly becoming uplifted by her ministrations. "It gives courage to the warrior and shrewdness in commerce." She was rubbing the end of his penis against the opening of her vagina in a vain attempt to become one body. Before he could stop her the young woman suddenly and unexpectedly climaxed, her *Ba* was thrown out of her body and she became momentarily unconscious.

"My daughter" said Isis softly. "Apollodorus will never become one body with you until the final battle is over. You cannot force him but there may be another way."

"Will we prevail against our enemies?" asked Cleopatra.

"Time will tell, my child. But when it is all over, win or lose, then and only then, will you know true love. Remember that to win is to lose and they that lose shall win."

Cassius used his twelve legions to establish control of Syria and the Levant. Dolabella was hopelessly outnumbered having only two legions and was trapped in Laodicea, southern Turkey. Rather than surrender he took his own life. Cassius prepared to march to Egypt and punish Cleopatra for permitting Allienus to reinforce Dolabella.

When Cleopatra regained consciousness she found herself looking into the eyes of a very concerned Apollodorus.

"What happened?" he asked.

"I don't know but it was rather wonderful. Did we....?"

"No, almost, but not quite. I think you found the legendary *gamma* spot that causes a woman so much sexual pleasure the orgasm renders her momentarily unconscious. I thought it to be a myth, but from the look on your face that is obviously not the case. Do you think the ring was responsible?"

"*Geloto*, this is no time for your babbling, just hold me tightly – please!"

The following day Cassius' blockade arrived off of Alexandria, along with news of the defeat of Dolabella. After dismissing the ministers Cleopatra turned to Apollodorus. She looked more worried than he had ever seen her look.

"What is to be done, 'Pollo? Cassius commands twelve legions and they will be here soon."

"Don't worry, Thea, Alexandria is a natural fortress and the route across the Nile delta will be fraught with difficulties as the waterways are still swollen with flood water. It will take some time for his army to get here. We will think of something."

It was spring time before they heard that Brutus had sent Cassius a message proposing a council of war, so the invasion of Egypt was called off and the blockade dispersed.

"I told you we would think of something" said Apollodorus with a smile. "Shall we go and give Antonius and co. some assistance? The ships are fully equipped and ready to go."

"The battle lines are drawn" replied Cleopatra. "Reluctantly, the time has come to take sides."

"Once more into the breach, dear friend, and lets loose the dogs of war" quoted the actress, incorrectly.

"Cry Havoc and let loose the dogs of war, or once more into the breach dear friends, once more," I corrected.

"Have you ever heard the saying 'to win is to lose and they that lose shall win'?" asked Cleopatra.

"I can't say I have. Where is it from?"

"When you gave me my ring and I lost consciousness, I had a vision of Isis."

"That was a warning!" exclaimed Apollodorus. "We can't win by entering the fight but we lose if we don't. I have an idea. If we take a few old Triremes and wreck them off the African coast during a spring storm, identifiable wreckage will be carried across the Mediterranean by the wind and current. If you are ever called to account by the Triumvirates you can say you had the best possible intensions of giving assistance but were driven back by a storm sent by Poseidon. Conversely, if the conspirators call us to account you tell them the truth. This way the fleet remains intact in Alexandria in case Cassius attempts an invasion. Heads we win and tails we don't lose."

"Apollodorus, that is dishonest!" Cleopatra remonstrated.

"No more so than saying the flood had failed causing famine and plague. Why should Egyptian blood be spilt for a Roman cause?"

"Your logic is impeccable, as usual, 'Pollo. I and all Egypt are in your debt."

"Don't thank me, thank Isis, I wish all visions were as easy to interpret. I think I shall form a club, 'The Royal Institution of Applied Cretinologists' with you as royal patron. I will be chairman and founder member and Isis our first member for giving us such a good idea."

"I will instruct Mardian to prepare a sumptuous feast to celebrate the inaugural meeting tonight. Who else can we have as members?"

"Caesarion, for being born in a way not believed to be possible, Iras for persuading me to hypnotise you, making the birth possible and Olympos for performing the operation."

"I approve. How about Charmain? We can't leave her out."

"The criterion for membership is performing a great deed of utter stupidity that achieves a good and useful end. Being carried through a heavily guarded palace in a bed roll to persuade the master of the world to take your side in a dispute would be an example. I believe Charmain will say or do something at some time that will qualify her, so we could give her honorary membership until then."

Cleopatra clapped her hands in delight "I love it!" she exclaimed. "I used to have a club when I was a child. The idea that adults can have a club is wonderful and on such a crazy pretext."

Some months before, Brutus had been urged by Cassius on behalf of the Senate to return to Italy with his legions. He had been unwilling to do so because this would have brought together Antony and Octavian. Consequently Brutus had left Dyrranachium in northern Macedonia.

"Whereabouts was this?" asked the actress.

"The rivals were facing each other at the narrowest point of the Adriatic Sea. Dyrranachium was north of Apollonia in modern day Albania, directly opposite Brundisium on the heel of Italy where Antony and Octavian were camped" I replied. "So withdrawing to the east had been fortuitous for Brutus."

Brutus marched east and following an easy victory over the tribes of Thracian, his troops hailed him as 'Imperator'. He continued onwards to Asia Minor taxing and recruiting on the way until news of the Triumvirate of Antony, Lepidus and Octavian reached him. This prompted the message to Cassius and the two generals met at Smyrna near modern day Izmir, Turkey.

"Between us we control the Roman East from the Adriatic to the Euphrates" boasted Brutus. "I propose we march west and meet the threat from the self styled Triumvirates and restore the republic before Antonius proclaims himself Rex."

"We are not strong enough yet" argued Cassius. "The priority is to consolidate our position here in Asia. We need money, so let's emulate the Triumvirate's prescriptions and settle accounts with the treacherous Rhodians who assisted Dolabella and also the people of Lycia. Then from a position of strength we shall march on Rome."

Cassius defeated the Rhodian navy and launched a seaborne attack on the city while Brutus marched east to Lycia and attacked the principal city Xanthus, modern day Kas in Turkey. The citizens of Rhodes sent messages to Cassius reminding him of their treaty of friendship with Rome and that he had attended their university as a young man. This was to no avail and he executed fifty of the principal citizens and extracted money by fines and taxation from the rest. Meanwhile in Xanthus the citizens preferring death and the burning of their city to surrender, in the manner of their ancestors when facing invasion by Persia, gave Brutus a hollow victory.

"The insane Xanthians rejected my kindness and turned their city into their own funeral pyre" commented Brutus afterwards. The rest of Lycia capitulated and were heavily fined and taxed by the victors.

"Strange idea of kindness" commented the actress.
"Like your president bombing the living daylights out of a Middle Eastern country on the pretext of weapon of mass destruction but in reality

to secure oil supplies. Then wondering why his troops were inundated with suicide bombers."

"Are you suggesting that my country's attempts at liberation and democratisation are no different to the Roman Imperial aggression?"

"Not exactly, but spin is just a politically correct name for lies. They had it then, we have it now. When have politicians listened to the people that elect them? The Babylonians know this and rejected democracy three thousand years ago in favour of dictatorship tempered with assassination. Taxation is a polite name for theft by the state so a minority can do as they wish. In a democracy dissidents are politely ignored, elsewhere they are thrown to the crocodiles."

"Lions" corrected the actress.

"I am just the narrator but, Mr President and Mr Prime Minister, if the cap fits, wear it!"

Brutus and Cassius heard that the Egyptian navy were preparing to reinforce the Triumvirates so stationed a squadron of Triremes commanded by admiral Staius Murcus at Taenarum to cover the sea approaches to Peloponnesus. This was to forestall Cleopatra's attempt to assist Mark Antony.

Book 16

Cleopatra and Apollodorus stood on the poop deck of her new flag ship enjoying the spring sunshine. It was the largest Trireme in the fleet classified as a five, the lower two levels of oars having two rowers per oar.

"I think this was an excellent idea of yours, 'Pollo" said Cleopatra "to combine manoeuvres with subterfuge. The navy can hone their ramming skills on the old Triremes and the wreckage will convince Antonius of our abortive attempts to assist the Triumvirates."

"That's only half of it" replied Apollodorus with an evil grin. "Cassius and Brutus will have learned that we are planning assisting Antonius and co. so will send their navy to cut us off at Peloponnesus, thereby adding to the safety of Alexandria."

"Do you think so?"

"I am absolutely certain, Thea."

Cleopatra gave the shipwright a knowing look and asked; "Have you and my handmaids been up to your old tricks with Roman spies?"

"Charmain now fully qualifies for membership of our club" laughed Apollodorus. "It was her idea and I think it was applied cretinology at its best, don't you?"

"But when they discover the wreckage they will come back and threaten Egypt."

"Hopefully, yes. Suitably weakened by rushing up and down the eastern side of the Mediterranean like 'pullium detruncare', Antonius will take the opportunity and attack. Being a bone headed drunken Roman he will not appreciate the subtlety of our actions so will be furious with us. When he summonses you to his democratic eminence, let him make a fool of himself by ranting and raving, then explain in simple but charming terms how clever you have been."

"Now I understand why you told no one that this was only an exercise, not a real invasion. We will have to keep up the pretence until we are off Cyrenaica. Pullium detruncare, headless chickens, a delightful description of confused Romans, *Geloto*."

"This trip will be useful sea trials to prove this Trireme as a warship then when we get back to Alexandria I shall fit her out as a palace. I thought purple sails and silver bladed oars would look attractive. What do you think, Thea?"

"It sounds sufficiently opulent. What do you propose to do about the smell of sweaty rowers? I suppose you will have a scantily clad nubile crew!"

"When Marcus Antonius calls you to account it would certainly be suitably impressive. I think a female crew on the top level where they can be seen would be an excellent idea. The lower two levels can have male rowers for power and if we burn loads of incense……"

"Poor M.A will not know what hit him" interrupted Cleopatra. "That will be a somewhat more impressive entrance than being wrapped in a bed role and slung over your shoulder. We shall have to nickname my flagship 'Bed Roll II' between ourselves."

Apollodorus laughed, then turning on the pretext of attending to some nautical matter, the smile vanished as he thought "it sounds more like a floating brothel than a palace, but that is all it will be as you will have to use it to seduce a Roman hooligan to maintain Egypt's independence." Cleopatra caught hold of Apollodorus and turned him round to face her, then softly said.

"I know what you are thinking, 'Pollo and you are right. I have no wish to take another Roman as consul and I know how hard it will be for you to see me in another man's arms. What is the alternative? How can I make it easier for you?"

"I am sorry, Thea, I was being selfish, it will be harder for you. I will feel jealous but you will feel violated and dirty. It is I that should find ways to make it easier for you, not you, me."

"Well for a start you can make 'Bed Roll II' the finest floating brothel the world has ever seen and secondly….." she gave Apollodorus her most seductive look.

"No problem with the first" replied Apollodorus "and secondly?"

"You can give me a bath afterwards, not Charmain or Iras!"

Apollodorus returned her seductive look "how about we take a bath together afterwards?" He then became serious "has anyone ever fitted a bath on a Trireme?"

"Could you do that, 'Pollo?" asked Cleopatra excitedly. "It would be so, so decadent."

"Your Highness, if you want a bath on your flag ship, you shall have one. The impossible is my speciality, as you well know!"

Brutus and Cassius stationed a squadron of Triremes under the command of Admiral Murcus at Taenarum to cover the approaches to

Peloponnese in response to the threat posed by the Egyptian Navy and their reinforcement of the Triumvirates forces as predicted by Apollodorus.

"This looks like an excellent location for our manoeuvres, Thea, a bay similar to Alexandria but much smaller. If the old ships could be positioned as though they are forming a blockade the navy can demonstrate how they would break through. Most of the crew can be taken off the blockade Triremes and their weight replaced with sand ballast" explained Apollodorus.

"Whatever you say" replied Cleopatra raising one eyebrow quizzically.

"I want to see what usually happens in this situation as I have the beginnings of an idea for a new design of warship to deal with a blockade. Then hopefully we will not be trapped again as has happened twice in recent years."

There followed several days of Triremes smashing by oar and sail during which time the shipwright produced copious notes and diagrams.

"It looks like a storm brewing over to the west so let's raft up the fleet and tell the *Trierarchos'* that we are going home. There is plenty of wreckage that will be carried across the Mediterranean by wind and currents to convince the Romans that your Navy has sustained storm damage" said Apollodorus.

"Is it wise to take them into our confidence?" asked Cleopatra.

"If any of the captains think it a bad idea they are more than welcome to sail across the Mediterranean to assist Antonius and co."

The meeting with the *Trierarchos'* was a great success, they listened to Apollodorus' explanation of his subterfuge and smiles spread across their faces. When he finished they laughed heartily and congratulated the shipwright warmly, afterwards Cleopatra commented privately.

"That was an interesting management technique; they really appreciated being taken into our confidence."

"We have their backing and their support so they will all do their best to make the scheme work. A bloodless victory is in everyone's best interest."

"So what is the master plan for your secret weapon for blockade breaking, 'Pollo?"

"It was an idea Jules gave me. Do you remember what he said about the warships from Britannia?"

"He said they were built of wood as hard as metal and ramming them was pointless, as I recall."

"So just imagine a Trireme built like 'Mintaka', it would go through a blockade like….."

"A hot sword through butter?"

"Exactly. That gives me an idea for a name for the prototype."

They looked at each other and both said together "Orion's Sword!" Cleopatra continued. "Is there no limitation to your inventive deviousness, My Lord?"

"I think it's a case of us being a great team My Lady" replied Apollodorus with a grin.

Cleopatra returned his smile but thought "yes indeed, a great team, if only you would say what I long to hear, if only you could be my consort. Isis keep your promise and when the last battle is over, then I will know true love."

Admiral Murcus received reports of the Egyptian wreckage and heard rumours of storm damage to Cleopatra's fleet. Acting on his own initiative he sailed for Brundisium to blockade the Adriatic narrows, thereby trapping Mark Antony's forces. The Triumvirate countered by mounting artillery towers on barges but it was only possible for his square rigged transport ships to outrun Murcus' rowed Triremes when the winds came from the west.

Antony requested reinforcements from Octavian who had made little progress against Sextus. Sicily's Scarlet Pimpernel still controlled the Messina Straits so Octavian's squadron were obliged to go the long way round the island's west coast. Eventually the reinforcements arrived so Admiral Murcus abandoned his blockade. The Triumvirate forces crossed to Macedonia without casualty although Brutus and Cassius had sent ships to reinforce Murcus' blockade. These ships arrived too late so Antony and Octavian were able to secure Thessalonica and thereby cut off mainland Greece, meanwhile Sextus remained neutral in the conflict.

On the north east corner of the Mediterranean, Brutus and Cassius reviewed their troops. They had patched up their bitter quarrel when they met at Sardis near Ephesus and concentrated their forces on the Gallipoli peninsular. Antony and Octavian now controlled the only practical route from Asia to Europe therefore Brutus and Cassius had been taken completely by surprise. The local client prince had some five thousand cavalry and infantry, the Romans eighty thousand infantry, eight thousand cavalry and four hundred mounted archers. Each centurion had been advanced seventy five thousand denarii (twelve and a half silver talents or over three hundred years' wages) and each soldier one thousand five hundred denarii (six and a half years. wages). A sense of smug self- satisfaction pervaded the whole camp.

Back in Alexandria, Cleopatra received a report about Roman activities and turning to Apollodorus, whispered. "You were right, 'Pollo, they have been running round like 'pullium detruncare.' The only one with any sense is Sextus who is staying well out of the conflict and keeping a low profile in Sicily."

"That was a stupid move on the part of Brutus and Cassius to advance the troops all that money. Troops with full purses have no stomach for battle. I think I shall put my money on the Triumvirates who have little cash so nothing to lose and everything to fight for, including vengeance of Caesar."

"I agree. How are things progressing with 'Bedroll II'? I think I will need my floating palace in the not too distant future."

"I need you to choose some tiles for the bathroom" replied Apollodorus with a smile. The messengers had been dismissed leaving them alone in the throne room so they could talk freely.

"You managed to fit a bath?"

"You wanted one so I have fitted a bath. It's not very big but I think we will just about squeeze into it. There was a slight problem with the silver oar blades as solid ones were too heavy to lift, so we had to use silver plate."

"I am delighted about the bath but disappointed you are using silver plate on the oars. People will think me such a cheapskate if they find out!"

"We could counter weight the other end of the oars but I am worried about the additional weight so high up in the boat and the loss of initial stability" replied Apollodorus seriously. He then saw the twinkle in Cleopatra's eye and realised she had been joking so they both laughed. "How are the Triumvirates fairing?"

"An advanced guard of eight legions commanded by Norbanus Flaccus and Lucius Decidius Saxa have been despatched along the main west/east road from Dyrranachium to Byzantium, the Via Egnatia. They have been ordered by Antonius to secure Thessalonica and thereby cut off the Hellenic mainland. The Triumvirates have a further twelve legions to transport across the Adriatic Narrows."

"So there are twenty legions under the command of Antonius and Octavius advancing from the west and a similar number approaching from the east, care of Brutus and Cassius" concluded Apollodorus.

"That is correct" continued Cleopatra "my guess is that they will meet at Philippi in late autumn or early winter. The Triumvirates will have supply lines stretched to the limit, forty schoenus about three hundred Roman miles and easily broken by Admiral Murcus whereas the Conspirators will be fighting on home ground with plentiful supplies."

"Can that countryside support so many soldiers?" asked Apollodorus grimly.

Cleopatra shook her head sadly "not for long. Another Roman bloodbath, 'Pollo, I am sorry to say and it could end in stalemate. Have you any idea how fortuitous it was that you found a way of keeping Egypt out of the conflict. Our presence would have forced Sextus to take sides with Brutus and Cassius."

"The whole thing is so senseless, there is more then enough land for everyone around the Mediterranean, warfare profits no one!"

"You know that, 'Pollo, and I know it. A partnership between east and west would bring peace and prosperity for everyone. I had hoped an alliance with Caesar would have brought such a partnership into being. Rome was fearful that Alexandria would become the new power base so I am reviled as a wanton whore who seduced and bewitched their principal citizen."

"If Marcus Antonius emerges victorious do you think an alliance with him could bring about that partnership? Your dream is too precious an idea to be allowed to die with Caesar."

"Antonius is the only one who can see beyond the end of his great fat Roman nose. I think it will be possible to convince him of the benefit of my dream, but not without a price."

"That price would be the happiness of Cleopatra and Apollodorus" said the actress.

"Two people's happiness or the rest of the world" I replied. "Don't forget the prophecy about the widow from the east that would humble Rome and usher in a new golden age. Cleopatra believed that to marry Apollodorus would sign his death warrant."

"So Cleopatra's vision was for an E.U two thousand years before the 'Common Market' was created."

"Her vision was for something far large. The Gallic Wars had settled the differences between the warring tribes of France and Germany in the way that the 'Treaty of Rome' was intended to after World War II. Add to that the then wealthy countries of North Africa and the now oil rich countries of the Middle East. A great deal of knowledge was lost from the library of Alexandria; its re-discovery fuelled my country's industrial revolution one thousand eight hundred years later. If Cleopatra's vision had come to fruition there would have been no Napoleonic wars, Bonaparte incidentally had much the same idea as Cleopatra, no World War I and II. Leonardo da Vinci would have designed the Star Ship Enterprise not a helicopter and Shakespeare would have seen his plays shown on T.V."

"I thought you were anti – European Union."

"I am, in its current manifestation, the E.U is un-democratic and expensive. My country puts in much more than we take out. The referendum was on a false premise it was suppressed that the intension was for a 'United States of Europe' as clearly stated in the original 'Treaty of Rome'. A United States works well in your country and it could work for Europe, if the politicians would only stop lying! You have a written constitution based on equality and freedom of the citizens, I am not a citizen but a subject with an unwritten constitution based on convention. Convention is a polite way of saying 'oh good, we got away with that one so lets carry on doing it'. It is said that my countries Prime Ministers are behaving increasingly more like a President, this is un-true. Our Prime Minister was able to take our country to war without the consent of our two legislative chambers; something your President couldn't do! Cleopatra's dream was for a union more along the lines of the 'Commonwealth of Nation'; the Phoenix that rose from the ashes of my countries empire. The E.U is an extortionately expensive bureaucratic stranglehold that hinders people's lives with senseless rules and regulations, ignored by all member states except my country."

"So what you are saying is that Cleopatra was an outstanding visionary stateswoman thousands of years ahead of her time. She was prepared to sacrifice her own happiness and give her body to bring about her vision of peace and prosperity for all people of the known world."

"I could not have put it better myself. Egypt had a society based on religious and ethnic co-existence and also a theology based on a respect of all life. To them, all living creatures mimicked the divine order; the Romans thought they worshipped animals. Today the two greatest threats to mankind are caused by our lack of respect for our planet and our intolerance of each others beliefs."

Brutus, Cassius and their nineteen legions marched north from the Gallipoli peninsular until they met the Via Egnatia, the main road that connected the west with the east, and then they marched west towards Philippi. Cimber covered their seaward flank which forced the Caesarean legions commanded by Saxa to withdraw. With the assistance of local guides, Brutus and Cassius were able to take their army through dense woodland and outflank the other Caesarean general, Norbanus, east of Philippi. Saxa and Norbanus withdrew down the old Byzantium road under cover of darkness and meanwhile Cimber and his single legion joined Brutus and Cassius.

"We shall stand and fight here" announced Brutus. "There are good sea connections with Neopolis and our island base on Thasos. We have control of the Thracian passes; to the north is an impenetrable rocky barrier and marshes to the south. I will make my camp on the high ground to the north of the main road and you, Cassius, to the south on that hill."

"I agree" replied Cassius "there can be no better place to stand and fight. We must build a stockade and gate across the road, dig ditches and raise walls, the armies of Antonius and Octavius will be cut off from Italy by our fleet. Winter is coming, so from this stronghold we can let the weather defeat our enemies."

In the island palace of Antirhodos that evening Cleopatra was attracted to her son's room by the sound of voices.

"Tell me about Britannia, *Geloto*" said Caesarion. Quietly, the *Bassilisa* slipped un-noticed into the room.

"It is very cold and damp there and most of the land is dense forest" replied the shipwright. Some of the trees are very tall. In fact one tree is so tall it is as high as the lighthouse on Pharos. It is a very special magical tree and few people know of its existence. Only children can climb it."

"Why is that?" asked the boy.

"Because it is so high it reaches the sky and you can travel to strange lands that pass over the top of the highest branches."

"Have you ever been to any of those lands, *Geloto*?"

"No, but I have heard stories from people that have. These stories are of giants that eat small children and fire breathing dragons."

"What is a dragon, *Geloto*?"

"A dragon is a giant lizard with wings that can fly. They terrorise the villages so the people have to make offerings to them of beautiful young maidens" replied Apollodorus looking at Cleopatra with a smile.

"Do the dragons eat the young maidens?" asked Caesarion anxiously.

"No, they lock them away in very tall palaces called castles. Brave knights have to rescue the maidens and slay the dragons to prove themselves worthy of their love."

"Have you ever killed a dragon, *Geloto*?"

"Not yet. I have always felt rather sorry for the dragons because they must be very lonely."

"Why is that?" asked Cleopatra.

"Well, dragons have really bad breath which causes the things they breathe on to catch fire, so no-one wants to be their friends."

"Is dragons breath as bad as Seth's foul breath?" asked Caesarion.

"Much worse" exclaimed Apollodorus. "There was once a dragon who befriended a small boy and they had great fun playing together on the beach. Pirate ships lowered their flags when they saw them."

"What happened?" asked Caesarion.

"It ended very sadly. The boy grew up and ran away to sea but dragons live forever and never grew up so this one is still waiting for his friend to come home."

Caesarion had fallen asleep so Cleopatra led Apollodorus by the hand quietly out of the room.

"If I was held captive in a tall castle, guarded by a fire breathing dragon would you come and rescue me?" she asked.

Apollodorus smiled at the *Bassilisa*, "Do you doubt it?" he replied placing his arm round the young lady as they walked along the corridor together.

"Were you, Apollodorus," thought Cleopatra "that boy who deserted his friendly dragon by ran away to sea."

Octavian, having been taken ill at Dyrranachium, was unable to march east with Antony and their twelve legions. On reaching Thessalonica Antony secured Greece and then continued along the Via Egnatia and joined Saxa and Norbanus with their eight legions at Amphipolis a few days later. The speed of his advance caused surprise and consternation in the camps of Brutus and Cassius a few miles away. Octavian arrived ten days later by litter, being still too weak to drive or ride there.

"Thus the stage was set for the greatest battle between Romans commanded by the four greatest generals of that time."

"Time for another cup of Assam?" asked the actress *"or is the sun over the yard arm yet?"*

"Nice of you to join us, Octavius" said Antony, sarcastically.

"What is the situation?" replied the young man.

"The road is blocked by a stockade and to attack along the Via Egnatia will invite a flanking manoeuvre. Brutus is camped on the hill to the north of the road" Antony gesticulated to their left. "Cassius is camped on the southern hill."

"Can we attack their flank?" asked Octavian.

"They are protected to the north by rocks and mountains, to the south are marshlands. Our engineers have been ordered to construct a causeway over the marshes so we will have to distract the republican army by offering battle each day until we can attack their southern flank" replied Antony pointing to their right.

The Triumvirate legions offered battle to the forces of Brutus and Cassius who had formed up behind their fortifications.

"Liberty under the republic" they cried in a lacklustre manner. Although confident of victory they were impatient to go home.

"Revenge and survival" was the emotive reply, not that the Triumvirates legions needed reminding.

Apollodorus had been right when he commented that well fed troops with full purses had no stomach for battle. The army of Antony and Octavian conversely were short of both supplies and money so had nothing to lose but everything to gain from victory, as well as the inspirational memory of Caesar in the living embodiment of a sickly young man carried in a litter. Daily they offered battle by forming up in front of the fortifications and shouting insults. This successfully diverted attention from the causeway being constructed across the marshland to outflank the Republicans.

Working under cover of darkness the causeway was rapidly constructed and on the night of the twenty second of October the first Triumvirate cohorts passed through the marshland, dug themselves in and prepared to attack Cassius' left flank from the south. The following morning Cassius countered by building a causeway to cut off that by Antony. To the north the troops commanded by Brutus, seeing Antony's exposed left flank, acted on their own initiative, and attacked the Triumvirates armies.

Antony led his legions from the front and over- ran Cassius' camp, forcing his withdrawal. Meanwhile, Brutus struggled to regain control of his army. Octavian's troops gave ground amid heavy hand to hand fighting. Brutus ordered his cavalry to attack the northern flank but they lost contact with the infantry so Octavian's legions struck back at the weak point. Reinforcements countered and drove the Triumvirate forces back in chaos but control was lost again by Brutus as his troops looted Octavian's camp. The young Triumvirate had absented himself from the action due to illness and a premonition, Antony was unaware of the routing. Cassius had been forced to abandon his camp and had retreated north east unknown to Brutus who was returning triumphant with three captured eagles.

"Titinius, go and see if that is friend or foe approaching us" ordered Cassius then echoing the words of Homer added, "Their marching feet has raised a cloud of dust, dense as the mist that the south winds wraps round the mountain tops, I can see no further than a man can heave a rock."

Titinius mounted his horse and galloped off. He was warmly greeted by the approaching troops, an action misinterpreted by the short sighted Cassius.

"All is lost!" exclaimed Cassius "Brutus is defeated!" He handed his dagger to a freeman. "Pindarus, stab me to death, I must not be taken captive!" He was dead by the time Titinius arrived, killed by the dagger he had used against Caesar; the distraught Pindarus fell on his own sword and died alongside his commander. By nightfall all were back in their original positions, Octavian had lost sixteen thousand soldiers and Cassius eight thousand and then the weather broke, heavy rain fell.

The same night in Alexandria Cleopatra lay in the arms of Apollodorus; she ran her fingers slowly over his chest. With her index finger she drew hieroglyphic symbols around his nipples causing them to harden. A gentle breeze ruffled the silk curtains by the open windows and the only sound was the gentle lapping of the sea, coloured golden by the light from the lighthouse on Pharos. Apollodorus looked up into Cleopatra's emerald coloured eyes and ran his fingers through her golden hair. Time stood still as they looked into each others eyes, words would have been meaningless.

He ran his finger slowly down the young ladies spine and she arched her back appreciatively in a feline manner. His finger continued down between her buttocks causing them to tense. She purred with pleasure as she rolled onto her back. Apollodorus responded by drawing hieroglyphic symbols around her nipples, he then ran his finger down between her breasts to her navel and onto her maiden-like hairless pubis.

"I love the feel of your skin, Thea, it is softer than silk" he whispered.

"I love the way you explore my body, it is as though it is the most beautiful and precious thing you have ever seen" replied Cleopatra. He looked into her eyes, smiled and nodded. He then repeated his previous caresses with his lips and tongue and the *Bassilisa* responded in a similar way.

The next day a triumphant Antony marched out with both his and Octavian's armies to offer battle, Octavian being still too ill to command his troops. Brutus rapidly deployed reinforcements and fortified his southern flank, frustrating the manoeuvre that had served Antony so well against Cassius the previous day. Urgently needed supplies and reinforcements from Brundisium had been intercepted by Admirals Murcus and Ahenobarus' fleet of one hundred and fifty warships, so along with the torrential rain, the Caesarean's situation was becoming desperate as their camp turned into a quagmire.

Daily the Caesarean troops jeered and insulted the Republicans behind their strong defences and nightly they huddled cold and hungry in their wet tents. Dissatisfaction was also mounting in Brutus' camp. His troops were frustrated by inactivity and impatient to return to Rome but their way was blocked by the bedraggled Caesareans. Cassius' camp was demoralised by the death of their commander and becoming dejected by the words of their captives. Discipline was collapsing and the troops were becoming unreliable with little stomach for another battle. Mindful of the unrest being caused by the prisoners, Brutus had some executed. All were far from home with autumn turning into winter so in desperation Antony despatched a legion to forage the surrounding countryside. Battle was offered each day to boost morale but there was little hope of provoking Brutus.

"The stalemate continued until the middle of November when Brutus, against his better judgement, was forced to line up for battle. Although it was late in the day, for Antony and Octavian, this development was 'as welcome as a breeze from heaven to a sailor numbed in leg and arm by the toil of smiting the sea-water with their blades of polished pine.' Homers words not mine."

Brutus attacked Octavian's left flank forcing him to retreat but the cavalry charge failed to break the young man's line. Meanwhile, Antony held the centre ground while drawing Brutus' reinforcements by attacking the southern flank. Armies clashed, they slammed their shields together spear scraped against spear, sword against sword. Screams of death mingled with cries of triumph, the struggle rocked the earth. The front weakened as Cassius' soldiers broke and fled, spreading panic and disorder. The ground ran with rivers of blood. Brutus found himself cut off from his camp by Mark Antony at his rear, leaving him no alternative but to retreat into the foothills.

Octavian, ill and exhausted handed over command to Norbanus as they advanced along the main road, while Antony cut off the Neapolis road and harassed the retreating Brutus. A lone general approached Antony and one of his aids exclaimed "is that Brutus coming to surrender?" The fugitive knelt before Antony and looked up at him.

"This is not Brutus!" exclaimed Antony "it is Lucilius. What is the meaning of this subterfuge?"

"All is lost to you, Dominus Antonius, but Brutus will never be taken alive. I have been a true friend to him and will be likewise to you."

Antony helped Lucilus to his feet and they embraced. The next morning the republican army refused to obey the orders to fight and re-take their camp, so Brutus accompanied by his shield bearer and two old friends ran onto a sword held up by one of them and died. Casualties on both sides were equal and the surrendering Republican army was absorbed by that of the Triumvirates. The island base of Thasos and all its supplies were surrendered to Antony by Brutus' stepson Lucius Bibulus and Messala. When the body of Brutus was found, Antony covered it with his own red general's cloak.

"Of all Caesar's murderers Brutus motives had been selfless" remarked Antony. "He really believed what he had done was a splendid and noble deed." Turning to a freeman he continued "here is money, see to it that he has an honourable funeral and send his ashes to Servilia, his mater."

"First cut off his head!" interrupted Octavian callously "and cast it at the foot of Caesar's statue in Rome!"

Some of the republican leaders took their own lives rather than surrender and Octavian showed brutal cynicism in extracting revenge by defiling their bodies. The disgusted prisoners saluted Antony as victor but reviled Octavian as they were led away.

News of the victory by the Triumvirates over the republicans soon reached Alexandria

"Stop looking at my breasts *Geloto* and pay attention" scolded Cleopatra as they dined together in her private dining room.

"They are much more interesting than events at Philippi" replied Apollodorus.

"Look, this is important and if you don't listen I shall put some clothes on!" Cleopatra was reclining on a couch wearing nothing but jewellery as had become her custom when they relaxed alone. She smiled at him and continued. "I know you enjoy looking at me and I love being appreciated so much by you but please try and concentrate. Antonius and Octavius are victorious and they have divided the Roman world between themselves. Octavius is to have Spain, Corsica, Sardinia, Appian and Sicily."

"He will have to evict Sextus first" replied Apollodorus dryly. Cleopatra nodded and continued.

"Antonius will have Macedonia, Achaea, Gaul and the provinces of the East and Cisalpina will become part of Italy. Lepidus will take the two African provinces if he protests loudly enough about Antonius and Octavius dividing all the territories outside Italy between themselves. I have received a report of secret negotiations between Lepidus and Sextus."

"What happens if Octavius and Antonius discover that Lepidus has been negotiating with Sextus?"

"The Triumvirates become two and Octavius will take New Africa and Antonius the old province of Vertus. The situation with Sextus is far more complicated than we previously thought. Prior to the assassination of Caesar, Sextus had been appointed Admiral. When he learned that he had been prescribed he fled to Sicily taking the Roman fleet with him. He believed that in time he would be pardoned as he had no part in the conspiracy. As it became clear that this was not going to be forthcoming he has had to learn to live with the misjudgement. To this end he has been building more Triremes and giving sanctuary to other citizens in a similar position to himself. His strength is growing so in time the Triumvirates will have to negotiate peace with him. Antonius will have to establish authority over the East and reorganise the client states of Asia Minor and the Levant. Octavius, when he recovers from whatever ails him is to return to Italy with the impossible task of demobilising and resettling the army with no money. He is to retain five legions and Antonius six."

All this had been set down in writing, signed and sealed and each was to retain the others original.

"Antonius will honour the agreement and assume incorrectly that Octavius will do likewise" continued Cleopatra.

"So with any luck the little runt will expire on the way back to Rome leaving Antony with his hands full and out of our way for the foreseeable future" added Apollodorus brightly.

"With luck, yes, but I doubt it! Seth always looks after his own people, the way Octavian has treated his captives is barbaric. I hope we never come into conflict with him."

"Would you like it if I were to relax with you wearing nothing but jewellery?" asked the actress, giving me a mischievous grin.

"I certainly wouldn't object and in this heat it's not a bad idea" I replied, then continued with the story. "Octavian was carried back to Brundisium where he became dangerously ill, all Italy held its breath and prayed for his recovery."

Book 17

During the springtime of what we know as 41B.C Antony travelled to Asia with two legions where he was welcomed, by the locals, as the living embodiment of Dionysus. He dreamed of matching the military achievements of Caesar and Pompey so decided to implement his former commander's plan for the invasion of Parthia.

Meanwhile in Alexandria Cleopatra was in conversation with Apollodorus as they inspected the newly fitted out flagship, which was lying in the Cape Lochias Royal Harbour away from prying eyes.

"Antonius has ordered two hundred ships to be built in Asia Minor."

"Can he afford them?" asked the shipwright. Cleopatra shook her head sadly and Apollodorus continued. "So it's only a matter of time before he turns up on your doorstep demanding or begging money."

"His envoy, Quintus Dellius is here insisting on an audience. I shall keep him waiting, naturally, but I have no doubt what he wants. Your timing for the completion of 'Bedroll II' is impeccable 'Pollo. I should appreciate your presence in the throne room tomorrow when I receive Dellius and hear the demands of Antonius. I fear the honeymoon is over for us and once again I shall have to give my money and body to preserve the independence of Egypt." Her look of sad resignation threatened to tear Apollodorus apart and for once he could think of no suitable reply.

The following morning in the throne room, Dellius addressed Cleopatra.

"Dominus Antonius insists you attend him at Tarsus, your Royal Highness."

"How dare he!" flared Cleopatra "does he think I am a common woman who can be ordered thus. I am the 'Lady of Two Lands', *Bassilisa* of all Egypt and 'Living Embodiment of the goddess Isis' worshipped by millions!"

"It is in your best interest, your Highness" continued Dellius. "Dominus Antonius charges you with assisting the conspirators by allowing Legislate Allienus to take his legions to reinforce them."

"Does the mighty Domini Antonius believe that I, a mere woman, could stand in the way of the Roman Army and prevent them from leaving Alexandria if they so wished?"

"I am merely his messenger, your Highness" said Dellius, trying to be diplomatic. "There is also the matter of the reinforcements you sent Cassius."

"As I recall" interjected Apollodorus "Cassius blockaded Alexandria and when the Egyptian Navy were finally able to put to sea we turned left towards Africa, not right to Palestine. Forgive me for being vague on this matter, your Highness, but was our navigation in error or has the mighty Antonius a problem with his sense of direction?"

"Well, if it were our navigation perhaps Domini Antonius could send us an escort, in case we get lost" replied Cleopatra, smiling sweetly at Dellius.

"Our ships would take far too long to get here from their present location, your Highness."

"This presents us with a problem, do you not agree, Apollodorus? We will have to confer with our Admirals; we shall meet again tomorrow and tell you of our decision. Mardian, will you find suitable accommodation for our Roman guests."

"Certainly, Madam," replied the eunuch "where do you suggest?"

"The temple of Kom Ombo would be appropriate, Mardian" answered the *Bassilisa* without a hint of a smile.

"That is rather far away" interjected Apollodorus, trying desperately not to laugh. "I think it would be prudent for him to be accommodated on Antirhodos."

"You do, do you Apollodorus?" asked Cleopatra.

"Very much so, your Highness."

"Very well. Make the necessary arrangements, Mardian, if you would be so kind. Now, if you will excuse us I have much to discuss with my Sea Lord." As soon as they were alone, Apollodorus and Cleopatra collapsed with laughter.

"Why did you want him accommodated on Antirhodos, Geloto? He would have been far more at home with the crocodiles in the temple of Kom Ombo."

"If he is stuck on Antirhodos he can't go snooping around and find all your warships over in the 'Harbour of Good Return'. I certainly don't want him seeing 'Bed Roll II'. I thought you might like to try out the bath I installed in your flagship and the catering arrangements. Afterwards we could have a midnight swim."

"An excellent idea, we never did take my handmaids for a moonlit dip. Do you mind if I invite them to join us?"

"There is a full moon and we are once again up to our gunnels in Romans, all round naughtiness is definitely the order of the moment. By the way, Dellius was lying!"

"Of course he was lying, he is a diplomat."

"I know that but this was something else. They have precious few ships so cannot arrange an escort. Our friend Marcus Antonius needs Egypt far more than you need him. Do your spies know M.A's current whereabouts?"

"Naturally. Why?"

"So we can time your arrival at Tarsus after his. It is a lady's prerogative to be late and this should be no exception.

Later that evening Cleopatra was on board her flagship, taking a bath attended by Charmain and Iras. Apollodorus looked on anxiously.

"As I recall, you were supposed to join me in the bath, Geloto" commented Cleopatra.

"Do you think I would fit? It looks smaller with you in it than I thought."

"Charmain, do you think My Sea Lord is prevaricating again?" asked Cleopatra.

"I think he is shy, Madam. What do you think, Iras?" replied Charmain grinning wickedly.

"I think you could be right, Charmain. He doesn't mind looking at our charms but all this talk about equality goes out of the window when he has to get undressed" replied Iras.

"Charmain, Iras, you are right! You know what you must do" ordered Cleopatra.

Suddenly Apollodorus found himself being undressed by the handmaids and propelled into the bath amid much giggling. It was a tight fit but not uncomfortable for the two people. Charmain and Iras poured scented water over them then massaged their shoulders.

"Why do you think Antonius has made those wild accusations against me?" asked Cleopatra. He must know that Legislate Allienus was acting on Dolabella's orders when Cassius intercepted him and that we were on our way to reinforce the Triumvirates."

"I should think he was fully aware on both counts, Thea, but attack is the best form of defence. Rome must be monstrously short of cash so the only one who can finance a Parthian campaign is you. This being the case, I would suggest the price of your assistance should be…."

"The return of Egypt's former territories!" interrupted Cleopatra.

"Exactly!"

"Do you think he would pay such a high price?"

"After much protesting on his part. He will throw all sorts of tantrums like a spoilt child but the first bunch of accusations is the equivalent of lying on his back and screaming."

"So the next step will be holding his breath till he goes purple" continued Cleopatra, getting into the spirit of the analogy.

"Exactly. He will say something along the lines of 'I want my war with the Parthia and I will have my war. If not I shall scream and scream till I vomit'. I told you he will have a tantrum but just keep cool and when he calms down tell him how clever we have been in making Cassius run around….."

"Like pullium detruncare'. Do you ever take Romans seriously, Geloto? First you describe them as headless chickens then as spoilt brats……"

"Well, lets face it, that's what they are, Thea. They need you to mother them and keep them in order, you never know you may even persuade them to grow up and stop fighting."

Cleopatra stood up and wrapping a towel round her like a toga, said, mimicking Caesar.

"Now be a good boy, Marcus Antonius, stop having tantrums and that nice 'Lady of Two Lands' may lend you the money to buy some new boats."

They all laughed and Apollodorus added "I wonder if he has heard the expression 'beware Macedonian Achaeans bearing gifts'. He is going to pay dearly for his Triremes."

The handmaids dried Cleopatra and Apollodorus carefully and massaged them with scented oils. The Trireme had been equipped with a miniature royal apartment in the raised aft cabin where they reclined on couches there for their evening meal.

"I will not be able to entertain many people on board" commented Cleopatra.

Apollodorus smiled and replied. "The forward end of the cabin can be opened fully onto the deck, and then with an awning rigged you can use the whole length of the vessel as a banqueting hall. Extra furniture will have to be carried by the support vessels. This area can be used as a throne room as well as for private entertaining; also you have a bedroom and bathroom behind the aft bulkhead."

"*Geloto*, you have thought of everything. I am delighted! I can do everything on Bedroll II that can be done on Antirhodos."

"Not quite, there wasn't room for a temple and I would advise against the transport of bulls."

Cleopatra laughed and kissed the shipwright passionately. "It is unwise to go swimming immediately after a meal" she said picking up her Lyre. "So I shall sing for you and Charmain and Iras will dance." Sensing what Apollodorus was thinking she add "these performances are for you and you alone, My Lord. I will entertain you as a woman but Romans as Bassilisa."

Octavian eventually recovered from his illness and returned to Rome. Lepidus was able to convince him that he had not conspired with Sextus, so the two African provinces were allotted to him. Sale of the defeated republican's property did not yield enough money to pay off the soldiers who showed their dissatisfaction by being insubordinate. Civil disorder and mutiny became widespread throughout Italy.

Cleopatra dived off her flag ship and entered the water almost without sound, surfacing next to Apollodorus.

"That was a superb dive" he congratulated her. "A dolphin could have done no better." The two handmaids joined them in the water and they swam towards the beach. In the shallows they embraced as they waited for Charmain and Iras to catch up. Below the surface of the water Cleopatra rubbed her pubis against Apollodorus causing his penis to become erect. The two handmaids embraced him when they arrived, the administrations of the three beautiful women caused Apollodorus to loose his balance amid much laughter.

"I know what you are trying to tell me, Thea…."

Cleopatra put her finger to his lips "I have not ordered them, their affection is genuine, *Geloto*. They will do for you whatever you want."

"What I want, we both know I can't have. Not until…."

"The last battle is over" interrupted Cleopatra.

Apollodorus nodded, "however in the mean time I think we should have fun whenever possible and I would not want Charmain and Iras to think they were unattractive. Equally I have no wish to make you feel as jealous as I shall be in the not too distant future."

"You have a compromise, my Lord?" asked Cleopatra with a quizzical smile.

"I do, my Lady. Kissing, cuddling, baths and massages are acceptable, but not intimacy. Have you ever played kiss-chase?"

"No, but knowing your idea of fun and games, you do the chasing and whichever girl is caught has to kiss you." There followed a great deal of splashing, giggling and kissing. Despite what Apollodorus had said about intimacy each lady when caught kissed him passionately whilst rubbing themselves against him seductively, encouraged by the other two. The three young women were uniquely beautiful; Iras had the most athletic figure almost boyish. Her breasts were small and her nipples as hard as ebony, the timber that her skin tones resembled. Charmain and Cleopatra had slightly fuller figures and luxurious long curly hair the handmaid dark brown and the Bassilisa was golden blond. Charmain was olive sinned where as Cleopatra had the fairest complexion of the three.

Eventually Apollodorus lay exhausted on the beach under one of the many palm trees and commented breathlessly.

"I think there was a game within a game seeing how big you could make my erection."

Cleopatra lay next to him and taking hold of his penis said. "Well you are a big boy, don't you agree, girls?" Charmain and Iras examined him closely. "Don't be shy *Geloto*, you like looking at our charms, we like looking at yours. You are much bigger than the Romans, do you think that's the reason why they are always fighting, to make up for having small" she hesitated "charms?"

"I had wondered" replied Apollodorus seriously. "You know what they say about big noses and small charms."

"Are all the men from Britannia so well equipped?" inquired Charmain.

"I can't say I ever made a great study of the subject. I never thought I was unusual."

"It's just like the phallic puppets of Dionysus" added Iras thoughtfully as she ran her index finger over the head of his penis.

"Kissing is permitted" said Charmain. Both handmaids then proceeded to kiss his manhood. Cleopatra was whispering into his ear as the whole world swirled and spun out of control, time and space becoming a maelstrom that collided at a point in the distant future. How far forward he could not tell as time does not exist in the astral plain.

The Greeks of Asia Minor believed that Dionysus had many faces, cruel and kind, mean and generous. Mark Antony was hailed as the new Dionysus as he travelled with his entourage of musicians, actors and dancers; he also had many faces and those facets he now showed. Some said that he was the new Pompey and Octavian the new Caesar. The city states that had suffered at the hands of Brutus and Cassius were rewarded; Lycians and Tarsus were exempted taxation. Rhodes and Athens repossessed their islands and the Temple of Artemis at Ephesus had its rights of sanctuary confirmed. The client kings of Asia Minor had little choice in supporting the republican cause, so Antony did not depose them. A delegation from Judea petitioned for the removal of Governor Herod but he answered the accusation of cruelty in person. This so impressed Antony that he dismissed the charges.

"Was that the King Herod that killed all the baby boys in the nativity story?" asked the Actress.
"He was yet to me made king but you are correct, he was known as 'Herod the Cruel' for a good and obvious reason and we shall be hearing more about him later."

Apollodorus was vaguely aware of being helped back to the Trireme and having the sand and salt washed off by the handmaids.
"I think we found your gamma spot" whispered Cleopatra.
"Do men have one?" asked Apollodorus.
"You are the one who is always going on about equality; I am surprised you doubt it." By the time they had finished drying him and he was sitting up in bed with Cleopatra, full consciousness had returned. Charmain and Iras were sitting on the end of the bed massaging his feet while Cleopatra ran her fingers through his hair. All three ladies looked supremely pleased with themselves.
"You all look like cats that have stolen the cream" he commented.
"Why should a sacred cat need to steal anything?" asked Cleopatra with an expression of complete innocence on her face. "They have all they could possibly desire."
"Where I come from cats aren't sacred, it's an expression" he snuggled up to the *Bassilisa*. "I will explain some other time." As he drifted off to sleep Cleopatra gave the handmaids a knowing look as though to say.
"I know exactly what the expression means, rather more literally than you intended, my Lord."

The following morning in the throne room, once again Quintus Dellius attended Cleopatra.
"Have you arrived at a decision, your Highness?" he asked.

"You slept well, I trust and has Mardian fed you and your staff?" inquired Cleopatra sweetly.

"I have no complaints about the domestic arrangements; there are more important matters…"

"I disagree; I would not wish Rome to think I could not entertain their principal citizens properly. Do you not agree, Apollodorus?"

"Undoubtedly, your Highness" replied the shipwright. "I think we should arrange a sumptuous feast in honour of our guest tonight. Egypt does have a reputation to live up to."

"That is an excellent idea, Apollodorus! Mardian, make the necessary arrangements." Cleopatra then turned to the Roman. "I have arranged for you to be shown the sights of Alexandria today. You would never forgive yourself if, having come all this way, you didn't see Alexander the Great's tomb. Tomorrow I thought a trip up the Nile, so you can see the Pyramids…."

"Your Highness, I really must protest. I must return to Dominus Antonius as soon as possible, with your reply" interrupted Dellius. "I am here as an envoy not a tourist. If I could have your answer then I will be on my way. There is a favourable wind."

Cleopatra looked genuinely hurt. "Oh, very well, if you insist. Tell your Domini Antonius I will only answer his accusations on Egyptian soil. However if he wishes to discuss the continued friendship between our countries, I will be delighted to accept his kind invitation" she hesitated dramatically and looked at the Roman coldly "as soon as the necessary security arrangements can be made."

"How long will that take?"

"Not long. I also should like to make use of a favourable wind" replied Apollodorus, with a smile.

"You had better cancel the arrangements for the feast, Mardian" added Cleopatra sadly.

Later that day from the seaward north eastern tip of the Island of Antirhodos Cleopatra and Apollodorus watched the Roman Trireme clear the harbour breakwater.

"You will have to send one of the support ships in advance to purchase fresh food and masses of flowers" explained Apollodorus, then added. "Have you seen this trick before?" he dropped a large pearl into the goblet of wine he was carrying.

"The pearl has dissolved!" exclaimed Cleopatra. Apollodorus drained his goblet and smiled.

"That is so decadent and extravagant, *Geloto*!"

"Hold out your hand." Cleopatra obliged and Apollodorus emptied the remains of the goblet into her hand including the pearl. "Just an illusion, but rather impressive, don't you agree?"

"Another moonlit swim tonight?" asked Cleopatra. Apollodorus looked unsure. "My Lord, I know what you are thinking. In my culture noblemen have wives and concubines. The *Bassilisa* is the Pharaoh's principal wife. My handmaids are my slaves, to do with as I wish…"

"Slavery is wrong, no one human should own another" protested Apollodorus. Cleopatra placed her index finger across his lips.

"There was a Pharaoh, a long time ago who thought as you do. He tried to abolish slavery, but it was the slaves who protested loudest. Unlike the Romans we treat our slaves well and provide for all their needs. I am as much a slave to my people as they are to me. But it is I that will have to be the whore to preserve Egyptian independence and you that will have the pain of having to watch me being violated. Would you deny me being able to imagine your sexual enjoyment when I shut my eyes as that Roman uses me?"

Apollodorus shook his head in resignation as Cleopatra continued. "What Charmain and Iras did last night they did willingly, they are your handmaids as much as they are mine. You were the one who started confiding and scheming with them, getting Roman spies drunk, etc. Iras offered herself to you unconditionally in exchange for your saving my life and that of my son. A debt of honour is forever."

"Yes but…" protested Apollodorus. Once again Cleopatra silenced him by placing her finger over his lips.

"You honoured my handmaids by asking me to give them official birthdays and making them members of your club."

Apollodorus put his arms around the young woman and said "Is there any point arguing with you, Thea?"

"No, none whatsoever, particularly when your logic is flawed and I have made up my mind. Remember, I am an absolute monarch who behaves absolutely. You spoil me by building me a beautiful boat so why shouldn't I reciprocate by giving myself to you or offering you an attractive woman if I am unavailable."

"You paid for your flagship. I just designed and supervised the construction."

"That's apart from the point," replied Cleopatra firmly, "it's the thought that counts!" they had arrived back at Cleopatra's apartment.

"Will you take your bath here or on the Trireme, madam?" asked Charmain.

"The Trireme is swarming with workers preparing for the voyage to Tarsus" replied Apollodorus. "So we will have to spend our evening here" he turned to Cleopatra and winked. "If that is your wish, your Highness?"

"Absolutely!" replied the *Bassilisa* smiling broadly and returning his wink. "I am glad that we have arrived at an understanding, my Lord."

"Did a Pharaoh really try to abolish slavery?" asked the actress "and were there protests?"

"The prosperity of the world was built on slavery. We still have it today, and our attitude towards our slaves is unchanged. Their slaves were made of flesh and blood, ours are metal and plastic. The motor car is the largest single purchase after a home most of us make and if we have any sense we spend a good deal time and money looking after our machines. The way most employers treat their employees would horrify the ancient Egyptian slave owners. Slaves were extremely valuable and well treated in the main so the last thing they wanted was freedom. A bad master, from their view point, was better than no master."

"So they looked on their slaves in much the same way as we look on our cars, yachts or private jet."

"So, while your handmaids…"

"Our handmaids" corrected Cleopatra.

"While our handmaids" continued Apollodorus "make preparations for our evening, I will go and tell Caesarion a bedtime story."

"I had better come with you, in case he is frightened by your tales of monsters and strange lands."

"I think you like my stories as much as he does."

"Yes I do!" answered Cleopatra, blushing.

"How did the world begin?" asked young Caesarion.

"That is a very good question" replied Apollodorus thoughtfully. "Some say that in the beginning the Goddess of All Things, rose naked from Chaos but there was nothing for her to stand on so she divided the sea from the sky and she danced alone on the waves. Her dance caused the winds of the north and the south, the east and west. As she spun around she caught hold of the north wind and rubbed it in her hands. The wind became the great serpent Ophion. Eurnome, that is the name of the goddess, danced more wildly to warm herself and this excited Ophion who coiled himself around her and they became one body. Eurnome changed into a dove and laid the Universal Egg, Ophion coiled himself around the egg seven times until it hatched. The egg split into two and out tumbled the moon, sun, planets and the earth with all living things. Eurynome and Ophion then made their home on Mount Olympus."

"Did they live happily ever after?" asked Caesarion.

"Not exactly, they argued about who was the creator and in a fit of temper Eurynome stamped on the snakes head, kicked out his teeth and banished him to the underworld for good measure!"

"Is that why the Uraeus has the markings on its hood?"

"Possibly, but the people of India say that those markings were caused when Krishna fought with Kaliya who was poisoning the river Yamuna with his foul breath. Having subdued the reptile Lord Krishna danced on its many hoods and it was his lotus feet that caused the distinctive markings. In some versions of the creation story Ophion was a peacock."

The young boy had dropped off to sleep during the story so Cleopatra and Apollodorus returned to her apartment where the bath was ready for them. They undressed, then settled into the warm perfumed water, Charmain and Iras poured more water over them.

"Any chance of a goblet of wine?" asked Apollodorus. "Sharing a bath like this has given me an idea for the theme of your arrival. You shall be 'The Star of the Sea', to make the point about Egyptian maritime superiority. The way Sextus has defied all attempts to evict him from Sicily must have made Antonius realise that whoever rules the waves, rules the world."

"So what you are suggesting is that I arrive in Tarsus like a female Poseidon attended by mermaids and sea nymphs."

"A few pretty boys for good measure just in case M.A swings both ways like Jules."

"I shall recline in the aft cabin like Venus, being fanned by two cupids."

"Multicoloured ostrich feathered fans?" inquired Apollodorus.

"The only way to be cooled" conceded Cleopatra with a smile.

"You could have a necklace made from gold coins" suggested Iras getting into the spirit of mythological symbolism. "I am sure Antonius will be familiar with the story of Zeus turning himself into a shower of gold coins when he seduced…."

"Yes, I know the story, Iras" interrupted Cleopatra "but it has always lacked a certain ring of truth for me."

"Better use Roman gold coins with Caesar's image on them to remind him of his place" added Apollodorus. "Incidentally, I am having the aft cabin of 'Bed Roll II' sides sheathed with gold leaf."

Charmain bent forward as she massaged the shipwright's shoulders and her naked breasts brushed against the back of his neck. "Should Iras and I dress as mermaids, my Lord" she whispered.

"Could you make a long clinging green skirt that looks like a fish tail?" he asked. Iras had also started to massage his torso, Cleopatra not wishing to be left out attended to the lower part of Apollodorus.

"I would rather we were making all these plans and preparations for you, 'Pollo" she thought wistfully.

"Marcus Antonius will be seeing a parody of you, a Roman fantasy of the exotic east. I see the real Cleopatra, without make up, jewels or clothes...."

"Don't you like me dressed up then, *Geloto*?" asked Cleopatra.

Apollodorus hugged the *Bassilisa* and said. "You know I like you dressed up, and wearing make-up, also the way I am seeing you now. The point I was trying to make" he hesitated then saw the twinkle in Cleopatra's eye. "You know what I mean; you are just putting on the insecure act to get me flustered."

"What my Lord *Geloto* is saying, Madam" interjected Iras coming to the shipwrights rescue, "is where women are concerned men like Caesar and Antonius, to use a culinary analogy, favour their cheese green with mould and crawling in maggots, whereas Lord *Geloto* favours a freshly pressed curd."

"*Geloto* will give you anything and do whatever you wish without you making any elaborate displays" added Charmain.

"I know that" replied Cleopatra becoming flustered, "it's just that I would rather..."

"You would rather be making these plans for me than our Roman friend" interrupted Apollodorus. "I know that as well as Charmain and Iras..." he held the *Bassilisa* tightly and kissed her passionately forestalling any further discussion.

"Cleopatra's arrival in Tarsus was an historic event by all accounts" said the actress.
"The bard described it beautifully but he was no mariner;
'The barge she sat in, like a burnish'd throne,
Burn'd on the water: the poop was beaten gold;

Purple the sails, and so perfumed that
The winds were love sick with them; the oars were silver
Which to the tune of flutes kept stroke, and made
The water, which they beat, to follow faster,
As amorous of their strokes. For her own person,
It beggared all description: she did lie
In her pavilion (cloth of gold of tissue),
O'er-picturing that Venus, where we see
The fancy outwork nature: on each side her
Stood pretty dimpled boys, like smiling Cupids,
With divers-coloured fans, whose wind did seem
To glow the delicate cheeks which they did cool,
And what they undid, did.
Her gentlewomen, like the Nereides,
So many mermaids tended her I'the eyes.
And made their bends adorning: at the helm
A seeming mermaid steers; the silken tackle
Swell with touches of the flower-soft hands,
That yarely frame the office. From the barge
A strange invisible perfume hit the sense
Of the adjacent wharfs. The city cast
Her people out upon her; and Antony,
Enthron'd I' the market-place, did sit alone,
Whistling the air; which but for vacancy,
Had gone to gaze on Cleopatra too,
And made a gap in nature'.

What the bard described was a Thalamegos" I replied. " There was no 'Recreational Craft Directive' or legislation prescribing clearly defined areas of operation of marine vehicles but it is unlikely that Cleopatra with her formidable navy would have crossed the Mediterranean in a river boat, a distance of five hundred miles."

"Could she have hugged the coastline?" asked the actress.

"That is what some scholars have suggested, the outward journey would have been along the Syrian coast taking advantage of the currents that circle Cyprus anti clockwise and the north westerly Sirocco wind. The return journey along the coast would have been against the wind and current so they would have left Tarsus and rounded the west coast of Cyprus taking advantage of the current but the wind would have been against them. Wind over tide is the most uncomfortable way to sail. The description of events by

Dio Cassius were rather more clinical than Shakespeare; 'During this same period, following the battle at Philippi, Mark Antony came to the mainland of Asia, where he levied contributions upon the cities and sold the positions of authority; some of the districts he visited in person and to others he sent agents. Meanwhile he fell in love with Cleopatra, whom he had seen in Cilicia, and thereafter gave not a thought to honour but became the Egyptian woman's slave and devoted his time to his passion for her.'"

"So what really happened?"

The massive evaporation of water in the eastern basin of the Mediterranean distorts the anti clockwise currents that circle Cyprus and these currents carried the Egyptian ships along the Syrian coast. The offshore wind, the Sirocco, was also in their favour and they made good progress as they were on a broad reach all the way to Cyprus which they passed to their port or left hand side. In the channels between the island and mainland the current flow increased causing outfalls and broken water off the headland, giving the Egyptian fleet a bumpy ride. They rounded the north western peninsular that pointed out from the island like a gnarled finger and approached mainland Turkey or Cilicia as it was known in those days. Tall mountains along the coastline plunged straight into the sea affording deep water anchorages close to the shore, inland the countryside was dense woodland.

"So this is where we get most of the wood for our shipbuilding" commented Apollodorus as the mainland emerged through the early morning mist.

"To the north west are pine forests" explained Cleopatra, "elsewhere there are chestnut, oak, walnut and hazel."

Each side of the Anatolian plateau two mountain chains ran the length of the country. A considerable mass of sediment had been washed down these mountain ranges over the millennia and this had built up a flat alluvial plain similar to the Nile Delta. The river Seyhan ran through this plain to emerge into the sea through an area of coastal swampland and inland was a sea of olive groves.

"This is the Cilician Gate" continued Cleopatra "Tarsus, the largest Cilician city, is twenty miles up the river Cydnus on the eastern side. Apparently the climate is pretty unhealthy. Alexander the Great nearly died from an infection resulting from his bathing in the river."

"I thought it was the river Seyhan. Is Cydnus the ancient name?" inquired the actress.

"The Seyhan was the river that had been responsible for the build up of silt in that area making the Anatolian plateau. Apparently the 'Cilician Gate' was further inland than Tarsus on this river. The city of Tarsus was located on the second river, the Cydnus, and that was the river Cleopatra sailed up."

"In that case it's a good thing I installed a bath" replied Apollodorus, then gesticulating towards an anchored merchant ship continued. "That looks like our advanced support ship over there; I hope Mardian has been able to purchase masses of fresh flowers. How many ships do you plan having in attendance when we sail up the river?"

"I think an escort of six Triremes will be sufficient. The rest of the fleet can anchor in the mouth of the river and join us a few at a time. We don't want to look like an invasion force, just a discreet show of strength, Geloto."

"Good idea, Thea, Antonius will undoubtedly know the war ships are here without being intimidated unduly."

"I hope he will be a little bit intimidated, one should always negotiate from a position of strength!"

Apollodorus looked across at the fleet of over a hundred Triremes and various support ships then he smiled at Cleopatra. "You are undoubtedly 'The Lady of All', all seeing, all powerful, Bassilisa of the known world and 'The Star of the Sea'. We must prepare your ship for the most spectacular entrance ever made in history."

"Given the resources anyone can make an entrance. You and I are becoming experts" replied Cleopatra. "But making a spectacular exit takes brilliance, no … genius!" Apollodorus said nothing but felt as though venomous fangs had pierced his heart.

Book 18

Mark Antony travelled from Ephesus to arrive at Tarsus during the late summer; this city was the Roman administrative centre for that area and therefore the centre of tax gathering. It had been conquered by Alexander the Great three centuries before, Julius Caesar had been a visitor and Octavian had studied at the university under the philosopher Athendorus. Despite the unhealthy climate the university and library rivalled those of Alexandria. The town was uninspiring with narrow torturous streets, mud huts and small markets. In gratitude for the support given to the Triumvirates during the civil war Antony had made Tarsus a free city.

Word of the arrival of the *Bassilisa* from Egypt spread rapidly and the streets emptied as the inhabitants rushed to the river bank to watch the spectacle unfold. Antony and his retinue of officers were relaxing in one of the market squares.

"What is going on?" demanded the overlord as the square became deserted.

"The Egyptian fleet was sighted offshore early this morning, Dominus" replied one of the officers.

"So Cleopatra has obeyed my summons" replied Antony with a smile of self satisfaction.

Four Triremes sailing two abreast preceded Cleopatra's flag ship and two similarly brought up the rear. The flag ship's heavy functional sails used on the voyage to Tarsus had been replaced by those of purple cotton. The upper level of rowers and deck hands had been replaced by a specially trained bare breasted female crew dressed in short white kilts, their oiled skin glistened in the sunshine. The oar blades were silver and timing was being kept by an orchestra of flutes, rather than the usual solitary Alutus. Trails of flowers ran the length of the ship and up the rigging. Thuribles of incense swung in harmony with the vessel, perfuming the air.

Cleopatra reclined in the open fronted aft cabin which had been sheathed in gold leaf was fanned by two naked boys using multi coloured ostrich feathered fans. Charmain and Iras dressed as mermaids, were in attendance. Cleopatra was dressed in a diaphanous gown made from cloth of gold and on her head was the vulture headdress of the Egyptian monarchs. The wings of the headdress partly covered and contrasted with her golden hair which was curled in tight ringlets. Her eyes were heavily made up in the traditional Egyptian style and her nipples coloured red with henna.

"I don't think there can be a pretty girl aged between sixteen and twenty five left in Alexandria" commented Apollodorus.

"Are you enjoying the spectacle, Geloto?" asked Cleopatra.

"The ship is a picture, the crew are the most erotic sight I have ever seen and our handmaids gorgeous, but all are as nothing against you, your Highness, you are every cubit the goddess."

"Would you have liked it if I had these preparations for you, 'Pollo?"

"If Domini Antonius does not appreciate the effort, I certainly do, Thea!"

"That's good, because in my mind I have done what I would like to do for you" thought Cleopatra. "The picture would have been complete if you were standing beside me dressed in the nemes and kilt with your arms folded proudly across your chest, flail in one hand and crook in the other. That Roman may become my consort but he will never dress as Pharaoh." Had Cleopatra's dream been made a reality the future for mankind would have been totally different. Not only were they at a major crossroad in their lives, but so was all humanity.

As they approached the city the river banks were becoming lined with cheering crowds, the river widened into a lake and Cleopatra's flagship glided to a halt at the city quay. The attendant Triremes and support ships stationed in an offensive / defensive formation anchored in deep water. There was a hastily formed Roman guard of honour led by Quintus Dellius waiting on land for them. Cleopatra remained in the poop deck cabin being fanned serenely and Apollodorus moved forward to amidships so that he could address the Romans.

"Dominus Antonius extends his welcome" announced Dellius from the quayside. "He regrets he is unable to be here personally but requires that her Royal Highness attends him at dinner tonight."

"That will be unacceptable" replied Apollodorus "it was made totally clear in her message to Domini Antonius that the Bassilisa would only answer to his accusations on Egyptian soil. This Trireme is technically Egyptian soil so by sailing to Tarsus her Highness has more than...." he hesitated "more than compromised. If Domini Antonius wishes an audience with our Lady of Two Lands he should attend her on this ship, unless of course he has dismissed his allegations."

Dellius looked as though he was about to spontaneously combust and was about to board the Trireme when he remembered naval etiquette.

"Permission to come aboard?"

"Denied!" exclaimed Apollodorus as he signalled to the attending warships. "We have come in peace but prepared for any eventuality. Please advise Domini Antonius that he is invited to feast with her Royal Highness but if he has no appetite for Egyptian hospitality, regrettably we will sail in the morning. Good day, Domini Dellius." With that he turned abruptly and returned to the poop deck as the Trireme cast off and anchored with the other Egyptian ships.

"You enjoyed that little showdown, didn't you, *Geloto*?" commented Cleopatra as he rejoined her.

"It was most satisfying and with the whole of Tarsus come to look at you, Marcus Antonius must be sitting all alone in a seedy tavern feeling like Nero non amicis."

Cleopatra laughed "Nero no mates? I think the expression is sine amicis Antonius, without friends Antonius."

During the day further Egyptian Triremes, by prior arrangement, joined them in the lake. By late afternoon, when a messenger arrived by small boat with Antony's acceptance of Cleopatra's invitation, there was a formidable fleet anchored off Tarsus.

When Antony arrived, Cleopatra's ship had once again come alongside. An awning had been rigged; the sides were tapestries of gold and silver and above were nets filled with roses. The deck was thick with petals which released their perfume as the Romans walked on them. The scent of flowers mingled with the purple smoke of incense as Apollodorus greeted him.

"Have you come for a return match with the drinking game, Domini Antonius?" inquired Apollodorus with a smile. Mark Antony's attempts at formality evaporated and he smiled broadly as the two men embraced.

"It is good to see you again, Jocus, you rascal!" exclaimed Antony.

"It is good to see you, Marcus and under much happier circumstances than the last time. Come, we must not keep her Royal Highness waiting." He led the Roman to the aft cabin where Cleopatra was reclining. "There is a great deal of catching up to be done, my friend, and don't give me any of that 'answering to charges' dung. You knew perfectly well our situation and that we were helping you as much as we could, all be it discreetly. Cassius had blockaded Alexandria and was looking for an excuse to invade."

"Domini Antonius, may I welcome you aboard, please recline next to me" said Cleopatra sweetly "and let us exchange tales of courage and bravery. I understand that you fought well and prevailed against overwhelming odds at Philippi. Caesars murderers are now vanquished."

While she was speaking, dinner was served. The gold dishes and goblets were decorated with precious stones, laden with sumptuous food and exotic wine. Mark Antony and his officers gave themselves fully to the banquet, whereas Apollodorus and Cleopatra ate and drank sparingly. The shipwright told how they had ridden south through Italy to join their ships in the Messina Straits and Antony told of the battle of Philippi. After the meal they were entertained by music and dancing. Cleopatra was her most enchanting and Antony was captivated. Later that evening when the Romans had departed Apollodorus stood alone on the fore deck of the flagship contemplating the stars. The rustle of clothes that disturbed him he expected to be the Bassilisa, but to his disappointment, it was Charmain and Iras.

"My Lord, the climate here is unhealthy" said Charmain softly, as both handmaids took hold of his arms and led him below. "Come back to your cabin and we will take care of you."

"I would appreciate your company, ladies, but please nothing more. The Bassilisa has invited Domini Antonius to winter in Alexandria."

"What will you do, *Geloto*?" asked Iras.

"I may use the opportunity to return to Britannia. With the Romans in Alexandria, her Highness will not need my protection."

"You are not planning to leave us?" asked Charmain, aghast.

"No, Egypt is my home now but I need to purchase the stronger timber available from Northern Europe to build a special ship. I fear we are being dragged into another Roman conflict and an idea I have for a new type of weapon will be needed. I have not definitely decided, so please say nothing to your mistress."

"We will keep our council" replied Iras "on the condition that you swear you will come back to us." They were now back in the shipwright's cabin sitting on his bed, so he put an arm round each of the handmaids and continued. "I never really had either a family or a home before. Do you honestly think I would be parted from you any longer than necessary?"

Charmain placed her hand on his naked chest. "Your heart must really ache now, so I would not trust you not to run away, My Lord."

Iras was running her hand slowly up his leg and added. "Like it or not we are staying with you tonight and every night that Domini Antonius is with our mistress."

"Are those her orders" replied Apollodorus looking doubtfully at his bed.

"We have been dismissed for the night" said Charmain with an expression of wide eyed innocence "our time is our own but her Highness did say you may prefer Mardian's company."

Apollodorus chuckled. "That sounds more like a threat than a suggestion."

"Lay down, My Lord, and we will massage you with aromatic oils" suggested Iras. Under the administrations of the handmaids Apollodorus drifted of into a deep sleep and he found himself in a familiar place where once again he held the dying woman in his arms. Isis was there also pointing accusingly at him.

"Where are the snakes?" he demanded.

"There are none" replied Isis "this is all you're doing!" The goddess's accusing voice became slow and distorted as the scene dissolved in a kaleidoscope of colour, spinning round and round. All that he could make out were two Cobras and a Vulture. For some time he drifted in and out of consciousness and was vaguely aware of an intense heat, someone was bathing him with a damp cloth; another held him as he vomited. Eventually full consciousness returned but he was so weak he could hardly move. From the motion of the ship he knew that they were at sea, Cleopatra was looking down at him.

"What happened?" he croaked "and where am I?" As his eyes focused he could see the signs of dried tears on the *Bassilisa's* cheeks. He tried to sit up.

"Lay still, 'Pollo. You picked up an infection from the water you drank at the feast," replied Cleopatra softly. "I have agreed to back Antonius in his Parthian campaign, so Egypt's independence is secured. We are on our way back to Alexandria; I thought it better to get you away from that accursed place."

"I know I promised it the other way but is there any chance of you giving me a bath, Thea? This bedding smells like a camel's stable."

Cleopatra smiled weakly and turned up her nose "I think I can arrange that for you."

The *Bassilisa* and her hand maids assisted Apollodorus as he staggered to the bathroom.

"You are still too weak. Give yourself more time" suggested Cleopatra.

"I am master of my own body and it will do as it is told!" croaked Apollodorus weakly. "The infection needs to be washed away and I should try to get up on deck where the fresh air will aid my recovery. My bedding must be burned along with the clothes I was wearing, to prevent the infection spreading."

"That is sound advice" added Olympos, who had arrived in the bathroom. Apollodorus settled into the water and the doctor handed him a goblet. "Try and drink this, *Geloto*." The shipwright tasted the concoction and started to retch.

"What is it with you medics that they don't feel they are doing any good unless their treatment is either painful or tastes disgusting?"

"It's chicken soup, not medicine" replied the doctor defensively. "You must be on the mend as you are being rude."

"Sorry, Bones, but I never could abide chicken soup. The irony of the situation is that I drank water so I would have a clear head for the negotiations. You managed admirably without me, Thea, I am proud of you." Olympos excused himself so Apollodorus continued "why don't you join me in the bath? I would not want you to think I didn't keep my promises."

When Cleopatra was in the water with him he carefully washed her tear stained cheeks and pubis without saying anything. Afterwards being too weak to make it on deck, Mardian was summonsed and the powerful eunuch carried him to Cleopatra's bed where he slept soundly in her arms for the rest of that day and the following night. He awoke in the early hours the next morning. Cleopatra was already awake.

"Does it worry you that I am a whore, 'Pollo?" she asked.

"Thea, if you are a whore I am your pimp" replied Apollodorus "and not a very good one. You should dismiss me, a prostitute is supposed to be paid for her services not the other way round."

"Does it matter to you that I have been with another man?"

"Our relationship is on a far higher plain than the physical one; although we have not been one body our minds have been linked. Fidelity is a matter of choice, a privilege not a right. What choice is there for you? Caesar as good as raped you; Antonius doubtlessly has done little better. To preserve Egyptian freedom you have had to allow yourself to be violated and given financial support to a cause that is of neither concern nor interest to your people. The thing that frustrates me is a nagging doubt that we have taken the wrong direction but I can't for the life of me see an alternative. We will just have to make the best of it. Fortunately, the way Antonius quaffs and feasts I doubt he will often be in a position to make any intimate demands of you. Also, unlike Caesar, he is a very likable person."

"That has given me an idea. When he comes to Alexandria unseasonal quaffing and feasting will be the order of the day I shall entertain him most lavishly, that way he will rarely be capable of having me."

Apollodorus turned on his side and grinned broadly at the Bassilisa. "Cleopatra Thea Philopater, if you were not already its royal patron that sort of thinking would definitely qualify for lifetime membership of 'The Royal Institution of Applied Cretinologists'."

Cleopatra grinned back and thought. "That is only the half of it, my love. If you knew the rest of my scheme you would say that I qualify for eternal membership."

"So did Antony and Cleopatra become lovers at Tarsus?" asked the actress.

"It is a grave error to assume they shared our values" I replied. "This was no meeting of lovers, a concept alien to that world."

"So no one fell in love in those days?"

"Of course they did, but at that level of society marriage was a way of cementing alliances and usually arranged by people other then the couple concerned. Love existed in extra marital relationships; lovers, mistresses and concubines. Strangely, for that period, the Ptolemys were a fastidious lot having mistresses was acceptable but they didn't maintain harems like the ancient Pharaohs."

"So they practiced incest to maintain the purity of their lineage?" inquired the actress.

"That is the widely held view but like the suicide story it is in conflict with medical knowledge."

"How so?"

"The lineage of the Ptolemys and the Cleopatras is well documented for seven generations over three centuries yet there are no records of any birth defects or abnormalities which one would expect if they had indulged in any incestuous relationships. The Romans would have delighted in drawing attention to any such genetic defects. What I think is far more likely is, to put it in a modern context: The heir to the throne in my country is married to a divorced Roman Catholic and it is contrary to the 'Act of Succession' for her to become queen. An earlier Prince of Wales had to abdicate for this reason. So when the present monarch dies the constitution will have to be changed as his royal highness is unlikely to follow in the footsteps of his predecessor. A simpler solution would be for his sister to become queen, as has been suggested in some quarters, and his mistress remains only his wife."

The actress nodded in understanding, then asked "and the suicide story?

"It is generally accepted that Cleopatra chose to be bitten by an asp because death would be painless and not disfigure her, neither is true and she would have known this. When we return to London I will take you to the Regents Park Zoo so you can see for yourself the graphic photographs in the reptile house showing the results of a cobra bite. But we digress, Mark Antony was an opportunist who liked his women intelligent and ambitious, this was his weakness as he didn't consider what Cleopatra wanted until it was too late. Roman propaganda depicted her as a promiscuous drunkard who seduced and lead astray their heroic Dictator and Triumviri. She was actually held in far higher esteem than any of her predecessors by the indigenous Egyptians. The propaganda was designed to cast doubt on Caesarion's paternity as he was Caesar's rightful heir, not Octavian."

"And Antony was the original rat pack bad boy" interrupted the actress.

"Your sort of man" I replied giving her a knowing smile. "It is generally accepted that Mark Antony could not decide between his Roman wife and Cleopatra, this is why the story has captivated people for two millennia. The Bassilisa also faced a similar dilemma in choosing between a man who could give her territories and one whose gift was priceless. Only Cleopatra knows whether the relationship with Mark Antony was consummated at Tarsus, if ever!" The actress looked at me and raised an eyebrow quizzically.

Octavian had already returned to Rome at the beginning of that year and at first observed the terms of the Philippi agreement. Antony's wife, Fulvia, was a moderating influence on his ambitions. Rufus and six legions were despatched to depose Gaius Carrina from Spain but the main problem for Octavian was that he only had sufficient resources to re-settle forty thousand time-expired soldiers. Meanwhile, in Sicily, Sextus was reinforced by a squadron of ships commanded by Admiral Murcus and together their blockade disrupted Rome's corn supply.

Provision of land on the scale promised by the Triumvirates required extensive expropriation and the soldiers had insisted that no relative or dead comrades were to be dispossessed. Boredom turned to frustration, which in turn led to insubordination, widespread violence and mutiny. Bands of heavily armed soldiers terrorised the countryside, looting and seizing property.

The voyage back to Alexandria was around the western coast of Cyprus where the prevailing currents carried the fleet across the Mediterranean. The winds, although light, were against them so the crew had to row all the way, consequently the return journey was longer than the outward voyage. Apollodorus was soon able to relax on deck and recovered rapidly.

"Did Antonius agree to your demands in exchange for your support, Thea?" asked the shipwright.

"He has agreed to preserve Egypt's independence; the support I have promised is minimal, so when he comes to Alexandria in the winter he will need much more money, this is when I shall press for the return of territories."

Apollodorus was a little nonplussed at this. He would have insisted on knowing exactly what Antony wanted and in turn would have made Egypt's price clear. The conflict they had so skilfully avoided was in danger of being replaced by a far worse one, so that they would be unable to avoid becoming embroiled. This was in the future. The 'Four Horsemen of the Apocalypse' could yet be released and the ship 'Orion's Sword' would have to be built. Summer turned to autumn, Cleopatra and Apollodorus made the most of their remaining period alone together in Alexandria. Both were mindful that it was only a matter of time before Antony would arrive to spent winter there. Egyptian prosperity continued to grow resulting in word spreading to the neighbouring countries and a trickle of refugees started to come from Judea to escape from the cruelty of the Roman Governor, Herod. There was plenty of work available for these people, particularly in the dockyard at Eunostos, the western 'Harbour of Good Return,' where the naval ships were being built and carpenters were in great demand.

It was approaching the time that the Mediterranean would be closed to shipping so Cleopatra knew the arrival of Mark Antony was imminent.

"Charmain, Iras, tonight may be the last opportunity for me to entertain Lord *Geloto* intimately" explained Cleopatra.

"So you want to prepare for a special moonlit swim in the Cape Lochias Royal Harbour?" replied Charmain.

"Are we invited, madam?" asked Iras enthusiastically.

"The horse of the mind, as Plato termed it; that is so hard to rein in most men, must be unleashed in Apollodorus. I mean to un-rein his lust of concupiscence" continued Cleopatra

"You intend to exercise his horse madam?" asked Charmain with a quizzical smile.

"Your Lord *Geloto* is enthusiastic for the gustus, madam" interjected Iras "but reticent when it comes to the centa proper."

"Your Latin is greatly improved Iras" replied Cleopatra with a giggle, and then continuing with the handmaids culinary analogy "with your help not only will he partake of the centa proper but also the secundae. We must send my Lord wild with desire as we did before travelling to Tarsus. The time is ripe for me and this may be our last opportunity, Domini Antonius is on his way to Alexandria and will arrive here shortly."

"Between us we will release the ira in Lord *Geloto*, madam!" exclaimed Iras.

"I have no wish to anger him…."

"Ira in my language means stallion, madam"

Cleopatra looked at the handmaid as though seeing her for the first time. "So is your name the feminine of stallion with the same undertone of eros?" Iras remained silent but looked down, her dark tone skin made it impossible for the Bassilisa to tell if she was blushing, Cleopatra smiled knowingly and thought "Ira also means the watcher in Hebrew."

Later that day as Cleopatra and Apollodorus finished settling Caesarion for the night, Cleopatra announced.

"You have been working far too hard lately, so tonight I have prepared a special programme of relaxation and pampering for you on my flagship."

"Is there a full moon?" asked Apollodorus.

"No, it is a new moon, *akhet* has ended, and we are now in the season of *proyet*. The cities cisterns have been flushed and re filled with the Nile flood, a time to celebrate fertility and new life."

"I thought that was after shomu during the opening of the year?" replied the shipwright with a smile. "However, as absolute monarch if you decree that we shall celebrate such matters tonight, far be it from me to argue." He knew that winter was imminent and realised that Antony was on his way to Alexandria so this would probably be their last night alone together. This being the case, he would graciously accept what the Bassilisa had planned as he had made his own decision regarding the future. This was going to hurt her deeply.

On instructions from Antony, Arsinoe was dragged from her sanctuary in the temple of Artemis at Ephesus and executed. Plancuus was allocated the province of Asia and Saxa received Syria. Parthians assaulted Romans legions, their leaders Labienus and Pacorus, son of King Orodes who was ally of Brutus and Cassius. Labienus lived with barbarians after defeat at Philippi and on hearing that Mark Antony was travelling to Alexandria persuaded the Parthian King to attack the Romans.

    News of the approach of Antony to Alexandria arrived the next morning and Cleopatra rode out along the Canopic Way to meet his entourage. She was accompanied by a division of her household guard so Apollodorus explained that his presence would be unwise and unnecessary. Antony was dressed in Greek civilian clothing rather than Roman uniform and unlike Caesar before, this did much to endear him to the populous. Caesar's apparel and military insignia had incensed the people of Alexandria eight years earlier.
    When Cleopatra arrived back at her apartment she knew something was very wrong. Charmain and Iras were in tears then she realised what had looked different as she had crossed over from the mainland to Antirhodos, 'Mintaka' was missing from her berth. There was a small papyrus scroll on her bed, she picked it up trembling.
    "My dearest, Thea,
    For the sake of Egypt you must do what must be done. For my sanity I cannot stand by and watch. With the Romans here your safety is assured however I fear we will be dragged into another Roman conflict. Antonius, I sense, is destined always to be outdone by Octavius and it is imperative therefore that I travel north to my homeland to purchase the timber to build 'Orion's Sword'. We may be all that stands in the way of Octavius who I believe will plunge the world into a dark age of slavery and cruelty. If we fail then freedom will be lost forever. No doubt the growing unrest will demand Antonius' presence in Rome by spring time. The Nile will not flood before I return to fulfil my promise, please pass on my premonition to Lord Antonius but be vague as to the origin.
    Agape – Geloto

    I was greeted by a distraught actress in the main saloon of her motor yacht; she was surrounded by the morning's English newspapers.
    "Whatever is the matter?" I asked.

"Look" she handed me one of their tabloids. The front page was devoted to a story of the sexual intercessions of her husband, a well known professional footballer. "You no longer live with him" I commented.

"That's apart from the point" she wailed. "How could he?"

"He is a famous footballer; they all behave like that, anyway we are no better......."

"With us it's different!" she replied. I have difficulty following women's logic so thought it better not to say anything further.

"I will have to go back to London to sort things out" she continued.

"Would it be prudent for us to take separate flights? We don't want to add to the scandal."

"Nonsense!" she exclaimed. "You are not married or anything."

I was even more perplexed by her logic but said nothing. Then she asked me the question I had been dreading. "Have you ever been married before?"

"A long time ago."

"What happened? Was she unfaithful?"

"I have a funny attitude towards fidelity. I look on it as a privilege not a right. Being a mariner, you know how it is with sailors, a girl in every port. There is a Greek saying 'a thousand miles from home isn't adultery, I was no angel."

"So you drifted apart and have regretted it ever since?"

"No, nothing like that."

"Tell me what happened!" her own problems were now forgotten. She took hold of me and looked into my eyes so I tried to look away. "My husband has been found in bed with two under age hookers and you didn't bat an eyelid. What can be so terrible that you can't tell me? Did she find out you were gay or something?" Whatever it is I don't care, my feelings for you will be just the same."

"No, it was nothing like that; I am a very ordinary heterosexual man with fairly normal sexual tastes. It was another life and I don't want to discuss it."

"Neither do I, just tell me what happened. I will pass no judgement, I am no angel either."

I hesitated, then in a quiet voice, almost a whisper replied; "She was murdered." The actress tried to say something but I stopped her. "It was a long time ago and I have learned to live with the loss," I lied as neither was true the vision of her last days were as yesterday and would haunt me for the rest of my life, memories too precious and too terrible to share. "I know you *feel you should say all sorts of conciliatory things but I would rather you didn't. You probably have lots of questions but please don't ask and yes, you are a lot like her."*

"It makes my problems seem trivial by comparison. I shouldn't have asked, I am sorry."

"You had a right to know and I am sorry I could not bring myself to tell you before. It was only a matter of time before it came out. Does it make any difference to us?"

She shook her head and held me tightly. We said little on the flight back to London until we had cleared customs.

"You realise the paparazzi will be out in force" she said.

"Just hold my arm, smile sweetly at them and say 'no comment' to all their questions."

"You don't mind being photographed with me?"

"Why ever not? We are both adults, there is nothing pervy about our relationship and I certainly will not let you 'run the gauntlet' by yourself. It will give them something to write about. Who is the latest man in your life? Once more into the breach dear friend and let loose the dogs of journalism!"

"Don't you care?"

"On the contrary, I am looking forward to being a celebratory; Andy Warhol said everyone is famous for fifteen seconds. Here comes my big quarter of a minute, I am proud to be associated with you."

"And I with you. I should have married a sailor not a footballer. Come on, let's do it!"

I put my arm round her, the automatic doors swung open and we emerged into the arrival hall and an army of speechless journalists. Later in her flat overlooking the Thames, she confided "Applied Cretinology really works; they didn't know what to say. The way you posed for them, 'would you like us cheek to cheek? How about us kissing? Yes, I am old enough to be her father'. You told them the truth and they didn't believe a word of it, they thought you were winding them up!"

"The thing that worries me is that your old man may believe me and come round to punch me on the nose."

"If he does no doubt you will duck, smile sweetly, then pick him up and throw him out the window."

"No, I wouldn't. I would invite him in to discuss things in a civilised manner, tell him he was a pervert then throw him out the window, in the absence of any crocodiles."

The actress laughed "shall I put the kettle on? A nice cup of Assam then you can continue telling me your story. There is one thing that bothers me about your applied cretinology, cretin is deprived from the Latin christianus which means 'although deformed and challenged, human not a beast'. It sounds remarkably like Christian."

"I know and it is a frightening thought. Christ in Greek means anointed one, the original Roman name for Christians was a derogatory term. Saint Paul describes himself as being repulsive in appearance as someone whose birth was abnormal. The Romans used cretins, small people challenged in wisdom and stature, as entertainers. Early Christians were put to death as entertainment in the arenas."

Book 19

Cleopatra stabbed and slashed Antony's clothes with her dagger and screamed his name. Again and again she cut into them and finally sank exhausted and sobbing to the floor.

"Where are you now, 'Pollo, when I need you most!"

"Right here" replied the shipwright. She turned and, unable to believe her eyes, saw him standing in the doorway which opened onto the seaward side of Antirhodos. Looking at the weapon he casually inquired "is that a dagger in your hand? I thought you would be pleased to see me?"

She looked incredulously at the knife and dropped it as though it were red hot. "Where have you been all this time, 'Pollo? When did you get back?"

"Just now and I have been getting the wood to build 'Orion's Sword' as I promised." He picked the young lady up in his arms and carried her to the handmaid's room. "Charmain, Iras!" he called "Your mistress needs a bath. Come out from wherever you are hiding and get busy!"

"*Gelotopoios*" they cried in unison and all three ladies smothered him in kisses as Mardian appeared to investigate the commotion.

"My Lord, *Geloto*!" exclaimed the eunuch "I am so pleased to see you." Then in deference to the shipwright insistence that he was not a kindred spirit, kissed him as passionately as the ladies. A large silver spotted cat had appeared and was rubbing it's self affectionately around the shipwright's legs.

"And I am pleased to be home, my friend. Can you warp 'Mintaka' into the inner harbour and arrange something for me to eat and drink. Anything other than wild boar, I have had enough of that particular delicacy over the last eight lunar cycles to last a life time and have come a long way to give Her Royal Highness a bath, as I promised."

"As I recall," interrupted Cleopatra, "we were to have a bath together, *Geloto*!"

"Shhh, not in front of the servants, Thea"

"Put me down, I want to have a good look at you" said Cleopatra as she wrinkled her nose. "I think your need of a bath is far greater than mine."

Looking down at her abdomen Apollodorus commented; "I see our friend Antonius is consistent with the Roman practice of running away when you are expecting…."

"Please don't say it, *Geloto*" interrupted Cleopatra. "It is nothing like that and I don't want to spoil this joyous time. The important thing is you are home for the birth."

They were now in the bath so Apollodorus was able to examine her properly, Fangarfoto, the silver spotted cat, was sat on the edge of the bath purring loudly. "When are they due" inquired the shipwright.

"How do you know I am carrying twins? Not even Olympos would be able to tell that!"

"I sensed their presence as I passed through the 'Pillars of Heracles', the entrance to Mediterranean, a few weeks ago. It was as though they were calling me home."

Cleopatra threw her arms round his neck and held him tightly so he could not see the tears of joy running down her cheeks.

"Thea, why were you stabbing at those clothes when I arrived?" asked Apollodorus softly.

"That Nothos Antonius has returned to Rome because of a major breach in the Philippi agreement. There has been some sort of reconciliation between him and Octavius ratified in the betrothal of Antony to Octavia, the sister of Octavius."

"I thought Antonius was married to Fulvia."

"She died recently; I wouldn't be surprised if her demise was at the hands of Antonius, he was very cross about something. To add to his problems the Parthians have invaded Syria."

"Octavius has been involved in a war with Perusia and there has been conflict between the Triumvirates and the Consulate in Rome, M.A's brother is one of the consulates. I really don't understand those Romans, their homeland is a mess and they can't hold onto the territories they already have but they still try to take over more. In Britannia we celebrate a home coming by lighting beacons.... "

"So you are suggesting" interrupted Cleopatra "that we mark yours by burning everything Roman we can lay our hands on!"

Apollodorus smiled and nodded. There are times when words are unnecessary between people who know each other well. "Nothing like that?" thought Apollodorus. "Antonius has behaved even more despicably than Caesar", it would be three years before they would see Lord Antony again.

The timber for the construction of 'Orion's Sword' arrived by merchant ships a few days after Apollodorus. The shipwright's excitement was completely lost on Cleopatra.

"You are like a child with a new toy" said the *Bassilisa* incredulously as he supervised the unloading. "It's just a load of tree trunks!"

"Timber is for me as precious stones are for you, Thea" he replied. "Wood is a living breathing thing, to be turned into a living breathing ship. From these tree trunks I shall create our own fire breathing dragon."

"I know you consider yourself to be a genius in these matters but how are you going to make a Trireme breath fire?"

"Shall I let you into a secret, Thea?" replied Apollodorus conspiratorially.

"Yes, please do!"

"I haven't the faintest idea, but I am working on it!"

Cleopatra laughed. "It's good to have you home again, *Geloto*. Some all round silliness is just what I need."

"I am looking forward to some all round naughtiness after...." he hesitated, "after Dot and Dash are born."

"I don't know about naughtiness. You are still not forgiven for running away without saying goodbye or asking my permission" replied the Bassilisa with mocking seriousness. "As for the twins, surely you mean Ptolemy and Cleopatra?"

"Don't worry I will never run away again, being apart from you was more painful than seeing you with Domini Antonius."

"Do you mean that, 'Pollo?" demanded Cleopatra. The shipwright nodded, so she put her arms around him and whispered seductively "In that case you are forgiven" then she drew away and in a voice that mimicked Caesar, paraphrasing Homer, continued "But 'if I catch you playing the fool like that, let my head be parted from my shoulders and Ptolemy Caesar be called no son of mine, if I don't lay my hands on you and strip you of your clothes, cloak, tunic, all that hides your nakedness, and then thrash you ignominiously and throw you off Antirhodos to go and blubber by the ships' in the Cibolus Harbour dockyard at Eunostos!"

Apollodorus laughed till his sides ached and the tears ran down his cheeks. Eventually he was able to continue "The twins may be Ptolemy and Ptolemy."

"Or Cleopatra and Cleopatra. There hasn't been an Alexander for some time" said Cleopatra thoughtfully.

"I like the name Alexander, it has a ring of greatness about it" replied Apollodorus.

"My ancestor had fiery red hair and blue eyes like you my love" thought Cleopatra, then announced. "In that case if one of them is a boy I shall name him Alexander, especially for you, *Geloto*."

While Apollodorus sailed north and Antony wintered in Alexandria, events in Rome were causing alarm in the Senate. Publius Servilius and Mark Antony's brother Lucius became consuls for the year. Antony's brother and wife Fulvia both recognised the long term threat posed by Octavian. It was highly inconvenient to them that the young man had survived his illness. Chiefly of concern to them was the way he favoured his own soldiers in his re-settlement program. Lucius was a champion of old republican ideals and in reality it was he and his brother's wife, Fulvia, who were consuls. Octavian was married to Claudia, Antony's daughter by Fulvia, but this alliance was destined to collapse. Fulvia had no respect for Lepidus due to his laziness and managed state affairs on behalf of her husband with such efficiency and dedication that in time neither Senate nor the people transacted business against her wishes.

Octavian knew that he could not take direct action against the popular Mark Antony so as a prelude to the inevitable breach dissolved the alliance of marriage and sent Claudia Antonnii back to her mother Julia. He stated, on oath, that she was still a virgin and that he could not endure the temper of his mother in law. This gave the appearance that he was at odds with the Anton women rather than his co Triumvirate and would not be the only occasion that the cowardly Octavian would attack Antony in this manner.

Fulvia, while in Brundisium, incited discontent prompting her son in law, Octavian, to send cavalry there on the pretext of countering the activities of Sextus. Lucius took this as a personal threat and enlisted his brother's veterans as a substantial body guard. Some Senators were fearful that the turn of events was heading towards another civil war but following a meeting at Teanum, reconciliation was reached whereby Lucius would disband his body guard and Salvidienus Rufus would be given safe passage through Cisalpina to Spain. In return, Octavian promised equal share in the re-settlement for Antony's soldiers and that the Triumvirates would not interfere with the Consuls prerogatives. Relationships continued to deteriorate as Octavian consolidated his hold on the colonies. Lucius was gaining widespread support from republican sympathisers and Fulvia, concerned as to the long term ambitions of Octavian, sort to contain or eliminate him.

"What a crazy way to run a country" commented the actress.

"Don't be too scathing. Your country's Senatorial system of government is based on that of Rome. America owes a great debt to Cicero and his ideas of parliamentary democracy."

"That's the guy who had his tongue nailed to the table by Fulvia" interjected the actress with a shudder.

"Did Antonius know what was going on in Rome and the threat posed by Octavius?" asked Apollodorus.

"He received a number of dispatches from Fulvia and a deputation of veterans" replied Cleopatra.

"So if she was doing her best to look after the Roman interests of Antonius why was there a rift between them? Was she jealous of you?"

Cleopatra shook her head "Roman ethics and values are very different to yours, *Geloto*. Antonius knew nothing of the Perusian war and little about civil unrest in Rome, so it is reasonable that Fulvia was equally ignorant of his activities. The invasion of Syria by the Parthians prompted his premature departure from Alexandria. I had only just discovered that I was pregnant."

On the way to Syria, Antony could see that all was lost so continued to Cyprus where he was met by Fulvia and Julia, his mother in law. The two women had fled with the children and supporters from Octavian. Julia and Claudia Antonnii, Octavian's former wife, had travelled to Sicily where they were treated with great kindness by Sextus Pompey. Among their company were Tiberius Claudius Nero and his wife Livia. Nero's wife Livia was destined to become the wife of Octavian. Julia brought with her proposals of friendship from Sextus, this was not an isolated offer of an alliance. Antony refused to believe allegations about Octavian's breach of the Philippi agreement. In the absence of Lucius to substantiate the claim, he considered that his wife and brother had breached the agreement, thereby compromising his position with Octavian. This caused a bitter rift between Antony and Fulvia that was destined never to be healed. They sailed on towards Rome but Fulvia was taken ill and was left at Sicyon. On the way from Athens, Antony received a report that Octavian had taken control of the Gaul army following the sudden suspicious death of the commanding officer, Calenus. This was the first real evidence Antony saw of the threat posed by Octavian and that he had misjudged his spouse and sibling.

"Matters came to a head, this summer, when the rival forces met at Brundisium. Octavius had locked the city gates, denying access to Antonius" continued Cleopatra. "He could have easily finished off the little runt once and for all."

"But Antonius being Antonius and always seeing the best in everyone" interrupted Apollodorus "agreed to talks."

"That is correct. Incidentally, he didn't see the best in everyone" continued Cleopatra sadly. "He had Arsinoe dragged from her sanctuary in the temple of Artemis and executed."

"I am sorry, Thea. I was going to suggest that I travel to Ephesus and try and broker reconciliation between the two of you."

"Thank you, 'Pollo, it was a kind thought. You of all people could have tamed my sister. Octavius and Antonius agreed that Lepidus should retain the provinces of Africa and they have divided the rest of the territories with Octavius taking control of the west and Antonius the east. Italy is to be common ground."

"If Antonius had pressed his advantage he would have ended up with everything and all the Roman world would have rejoiced."

"I know, but it was not to be. During the negotiations Antonius learned that Fulvia had died so Octavius offered his sister Octavia in matrimony to bond their agreement and Antonius accepted."

"Poor Fulvia had assessed the situation correctly and acted in the best interest of Antonius but she died un-reconciled with her husband who immediately accepted his enemy's sister in matrimony, turning his back on you and your unborn children. The man is beneath contempt and we are back to square ena" replied Apollodorus, venomously.

A few days later Cleopatra and Apollodorus were relaxing together in the *Bassilisa's* private apartment in the palace on Antirhodos.

"Tell me something 'Pollo, do you find me unattractive when I am pregnant?"

"You have been keeping yourself covered up since I returned from the north," he replied the shipwright defensively "so I assumed that you didn't like being looked at in your present condition" Apollodorus looked into Cleopatra's green eyes and realised there was much more to her question than leg pull or mere vanity. He joined her on her couch and put his arms around her. "What is it, Thea?" A solitary tear ran down her cheek.

"By all accounts Octavia is young, vivacious, highly intelligent and popular with her people" she sobbed.

"You are all those things and more" replied Apollodorus.

"She is younger than me and I am reviled as a whore in Rome!"

"What does it matter what Rome thinks of you? That city state is a mess. Egypt is peaceful and prosperous and you are loved and worshipped by your people."

She was about to ask if Apollodorus loved her, but a sudden sharp pain made her flinch. Apollodorus placed his hand on her stomach and smiled.

"I think your time has arrived, I shall send for Olympos. Charmain, Iras!" he called. "I think her Highness has started labour!"

Some time later all matters of state were forgotten as Cleopatra held the twins for the first time. The miracle of new life does much to dispel doubt and depression for all of us. The birth had been straightforward and Cleopatra was surrounded by her closest friends.

"You have a boy and a girl" announced Olympos "what will you name them?"

"Alexander and Cleopatra" whispered the *Bassilisa* as she smiled up at Apollodorus, who was holding her tightly. Exhausted by the delivery she rested her head on his chest and drifted into a peaceful sleep. Charmain and Iras took charge of the twins and Apollodorus carried the sleeping Bassilisa to her bedroom and carefully laid her on her bed. She woke briefly and said

"Stay with me, 'Pollo. I want to sleep in your arms, like we used to."

Ours is the era foretold in prophecy:
Born of Time, a great new cycle of centuries
Begins, Justice returns to earth, the Golden Age
Returns, and first-born comes down from heaven above,
Look kindly, chase Lucina, upon this infant birth,
For win him hearts of iron cease, and hearts of gold
Inherit the whole earth – yes, Apollo reigns now.
And it's while you are consul – you, Pollio – that this glorious
Age shall dawn, the march of it's great month begin.
You at our head, mankind shall be freed from its age-long fears,
All stains of our past wickedness being cleansed away.
This child shall enter into the life of the gods, behold them
Walking with antique heroes, and himself seen by them,
And rule a world made peaceful by his father's virtuous acts.

…Come soon, dear child of the gods, Jupiter's great viceroy!
Come soon – the time is near – to begin your life illustrious!
Look how the round and ponderous globe bows to salute you,
The lands, the stretching leagues of sea, the unplumbed sky!
Look how the whole creation exults in the age to come!.....
…Begin, dear babe, and smile at your mother to show you know her
This is the tenth month now, and she is sick of waiting.
Begin, dear babe. The boy who does not smile at his mother
Will never deserve to sup with a god or sleep with a goddess.

(Translated C. Day Lewis)

"For two thousand years scholars have argued about the identity of the baby."

"I thought it was pretty obvious" replied the actress.

Following the invasion of Syria by the Parthians, the trickle of refugees from Judea and Palestine intensified.

"We have a rather distinguished visitor" announced Cleopatra a few weeks later. "Herod, the Viceroy of Marcus Antonius from Judea, has come here seeking sanctuary from the invading Parthians."

"The refugees that I have employed in the dockyards refer to him as 'Herod the Cruel' and a delegation petitioned Domini Antonius for his removal" replied Apollodorus, dryly.

"He, like the Ptolemys, is a foreign ruler, Idumaean – Arab, I believe, so it is not surprising his people wanted him deposed" explained Cleopatra defensively. "I understand he is devilishly good looking and utterly charming."

"In that case we had better get rid of him as quickly as possible; it's bad enough sharing you with a Roman."

"Apollodorus, I do believe you are jealous" exclaimed Cleopatra gleefully.

"Very!" replied the shipwright with a laugh. "Also I have a really bad feeling about him according to some of the stories I have heard, I think he is every bit as cruel and ruthless as the worst of your ancestors," then he added with a sinister smirk. "How about we give him a job in the dockyard, his own people will know what to do with him?"

"Certainly not! However, I am inclined to agree with your feelings about him, 'Pollo. I propose to entertain Herod in the appropriate Egyptian manner then pack him off on the next available ship to Rome and let Marcus Antonius deal with him. He is his protégé, after all."

"So is my presence required in the throne room when you formally meet him?"

"Your presence is always appreciated, but no wise cracks about accommodating him with the crocodiles in the temple of 'Kom Ombo'. He will be lodged over in the Cape Lochias palace."

Apollodorus had to concede that Herod was indeed very handsome and charming. "Does he make you go all weak at the knees, Mardian?" he whispered to the eunuch.

"He certainly does, my Lord. I shall enjoy serving him tonight!"

"I hope you mean food and drink only, my friend."

"Alas, yes. He is not what you would so eloquently refer to as a 'kindred spirit'."

Apollodorus bit the inside of his mouth to suppress a chuckle as Cleopatra looked at him sternly.

"If you two don't behave" she hissed "you will be spending the next month sleeping in the temple of Kom Ombo."

Later that day as Apollodorus and Cleopatra were playing with Caesarion, the shipwright made a suggestion.

"If we were to place a Trireme at Herod's disposal and provide escorts we could take the opportunity to find out what is going on in Rome."

"My thinking entirely, but don't think you are going!" exclaimed Cleopatra. "There is a certain Arimathean merchant shipping captain of our mutual acquaintance who is skilled in these matters and could accompany them in command of a support ship."

Alexandria had a large number of Jews living over by the Gate of the Sun to the east of the city and there were a number of Palestinian carpenters employed in the Cibolus Harbour dockyard, so the presence of Herod began to cause unrest. Both his father and grandfather had been governors of the province and they had done nothing to endear themselves to the indigenous population.

"Why don't we form an alliance with the Parthian?" asked Apollodorus. "They have been able to stand up to the might of Rome."

"Because they were conquered by Alexander the Great and Egypt was once part of their empire!" explained Cleopatra.

"But that was three hundred years ago, surely they would have got over it by now?"

"I doubt it, but carry on, I am listening."

"When we first met, you said that you had gone to Palestine because your grandfather had assisted the Palestinians when the Judeans invaded. This means that Herod is not a natural friend of Egypt. We could be the Parthian's ally against Rome, as Caesarion is Caesar's rightful heir not Octavius."

"I take your point entirely and this would bring about an alliance between east and west and hit Rome while it is weak. There is one snag. The Parthians would not negotiate with a woman and my excuse for a consort is a Roman, currently unavailable and unlikely to cooperate with your scheme."

"Why ever would they not negotiate with a woman?" asked Apollodorus incredulously.

Cleopatra laughed "You have been living in Egypt too long and have become accustom to the way we do things the other way round to the rest of the world. Men carry water and do weaving whereas women can become artisans and trades people."

"Yes and men crouch to urinate whereas women do it standing up, not that I have seen any evidence to the latter!" replied Apollodorus sceptically then continued more seriously. "I agree it is unusual for women to involve themselves in politics in either Achaean or Roman society but not un-heard of Fulvia being a case in point."

"In and around Babylon once a year all the women of marriageable age are gathered in one place and an auction is held. The prettiest are offered first and the wealthy noble men bid for them as wives. As the sale progresses the girls offered become less attractive so the poor and working men who have no use for good looks are able to acquire wives at a lower price. The ugliest or deformed are the last to be offered and generally the auctioneer pays for these women to be taken as wives."

"That's horrible!"

"That is only part of it. Elsewhere, once a year the wives have to offer themselves to the goddess of love. They go to the temple and stay there until a man pays to have intercourse with them. Price is irrelevant but the coins become sacred. Once they have been used they are free to leave having made their offering to the goddess. The ugliest women can find themselves trapped in the temple for several years. In other parts of the country fathers send their daughters to work in brothels to earn the money to pay for their dowry."

Apollodorus held up his hands in submission "Alright Thea I take your point! The Parthians do not hold women in high esteem."

"I am sorry but I don't believe any of that about Egyptians doing things the other way round or the way the Babylonians treated their women!"
"In 'The Histories' by Herodotus, one of the classics written about five hundred years before common era you will find detailed accounts of such things. Herodotus was a sort of roving reporter the Alan Whicker of antiquity, if you are familiar with British television," I replied.

A day later Apollodorus was at the Cibolus Harbour dockyard in Eunostos where the Triremes were being built. His attention was caught by a small Hebrew boy who looked vaguely familiar. The boy was slightly younger than Cleopatra's eight year old son, Caesarion.
"I have seen you before?" he asked "in the library. You are always asking the scholars lots of difficult questions."
The child nodded and replied "You are Lord Apollodorus."
"That's right, but most people call me *Geloto*."
"Would it be right for me to call you by your nickname, my Lord?"
"Over on the palace, probably not, but in the dockyard we are rather less formal."
"Do you believe all people are equal?" asked the boy.
"Yes, I do, but not many people agree with me. What do you think?"
"I agree with you, Lord *Geloto*. The world would be a far happier place if everyone thought as you and I do."
"Well, you carry on believing that but be careful who you say it to or you may get yourself crucified" replied Apollodorus, with a smile.
"They say you are a man of peace. How do you reconcile that with the warships you are building?"
The shipwright was taken aback by the child's perceptiveness "I hope to persuade our enemies that it is not a good idea to invade Egypt but I fear we will yet again be drawn into one of Rome's conflicts and the ships I built for defence will be used to attack" replied Apollodorus sadly, then in an attempt to change the subject asked; "Are you from Judea?"
"Yes, I came from Bethlehem as a baby to escape Herod's cruelty."
"Many of your countrymen have come to Alexandria for that reason. I shouldn't say this but you could safely go home now, Herod has been

expelled by the Parthians. He is on his way to Rome trying to enlist help in recovering Judea. I take it your *Pater* is working for me in the dockyard." The boy hesitated. "What is the Hebrew name? Abba, father." The boy nodded and Apollodorus continued. "Do you know which ship he is working on?" The child indicated a Trireme that was being fitted out afloat. "Let's go and have a chat with him." He picked the boy up on his shoulder and waded through the water. It was only a short distance but the child became heavier as he approached the vessel. When he placed him on board he quipped breathlessly. "What have you in your pockets, sonny? Ships ballast?" They found the boy's father and Apollodorus explained to him that Herod was deposed.

"The Romans may help him re-capture Judea" replied the carpenter.

"I doubt they have the resources, but if you were to go north of Judea or to southern Syria you would be safe. Your son is a fine young man. The way he discusses things with the scholars in the library shows a maturity beyond his years. Your return to your homeland will be Alexandria's loss!"

"Thank you, Lord Apollodorus. I am surprised and gratified you have noticed him."

"A good *Trierarchos* knows everything that goes on and everyone in the Triremes he commands, their strengths and their weaknesses, where they live and how much money they owe. I should be grateful if you keep that information I have given you to yourself. My need for craftsmen is great, but I sense that your country's need for your son is greater than my need of his *pater*."

"If you are saying what I think..." said the actress.

"St. Luke's account in the bible, states that at the time of Caesar Augustus and when Quirinius was governor of Syria, all the world was to be taxed. Caesar Augustus was Octavian and the Romans were extracting taxes like it was going out of fashion to fund their wars. Quirinius is the Latin adjective for Romulus, Quirites means Roman Citizen, so we have a translation error. It is a hotly debated scholastic issue, the time of the birth of Jesus, but don't forget the July Comet, a well documented astronomical phenomenon. According to Luke, Herod only killed the boys in and around Bethlehem; the invasion of the Parthians during 40B.C. would have given the holy family a window of opportunity to return to Nazareth which was on the edge of Herod's territory. Herod died 4 A.D, some time after the birth of Christ which is generally taken as about 30 B.C. Christian era is taken as

starting at the commencement of Christ's ministry, aged about thirty, not his birth."

"So you are arguing with scholastic opinion by about ten years. Why was Mark Antony not mentioned in biblical texts?"

"Following Antony's death, Octavian commissioned Titus Livius to write the 'History of Rome' from the perspective of the victor not the vanquished, this account no longer exists but both Dio Cassius and Plutarch drew heavily from it. The Bible as we know it was written for Roman consumption and incidentally some of the best stories were left out. The Church of Rome would have been mindful of what they believed to be a true historic account. Caesar Augustus, nee Octavian, was in power firstly as Triumvir from 43 B.C, then Emperor until his death in 14 A.D."

"So you are saying that Roman spin influenced the accounts in the gospels?"

"Pontius Pilate was shown in a good light. I have always thought that his involvement in what amounted to the conviction of a minor criminal would have been more than his life was worth unless of course Jesus or Joseph of Arimathea were rich men."

Autumn turned into winter and in Rome the mood of euphoria following the marriage of Antony to Octavia, faded. It had been widely believed that the reconciliation between Antony and Octavian, ratified in the marriage to Octavia, would usher in a new golden age of peace and prosperity. Sextus intensified his attacks on the mainland from his naval basis on Sardinia. Admiral Menodorus had re-captured these bases from Octavian who had controlled them briefly. Mark Antony had been unable to broker an agreement between Sextus and Octavian but the young Triumviri had no navy to challenge Menodorus. Antony did have the naval resources but these were commanded by Admiral Bibulius, a veteran of Gnaeus Pompey, father of Sextus.

The invasion of Syria by the Parthian halted revenue from the east and corn prices rose sharply causing rioting in the city. Another civil war was looking imminent which prompted demonstrations at the Plebeian Games during November where spectators saluted the statue of Neptune, Pompey's patron. Public opinion was forcing reconciliation between Octavian and Sextus and a summit was arranged at Port Misenum near Puteoli. The degree of mutual distrust was clearly evident from the bizarre security arrangements whereby two platforms were erected on piles driven into the seabed near the shore. These platforms were far enough apart to prevent negotiators attacking each other but close enough that they could hear what was said.

Sextus Pompey arrived, resplendent in his blue admiral's cloak aboard his sumptuously fitted out 'Six' (a Trireme with two men on each oar). Antony and Octavian, dressed in red general's cloaks, were only prepared to end the exile, whereas Sextus was demanding he should replace Lepidus as Triumviri.

"They must have been pretty uncomfortable perched on oversized bird tables in the middle of winter with wind and spray adding to their discomfort" suggested the actress.

"You are probably correct. The negotiations didn't last long and the whole encounter has a slightly comical atmosphere."

No agreement having been reached, the three men withdrew and the senior lieutenants continued haggling. Their wives and mothers were insistent that an agreement was reached so there was a further meeting aboard a ship stationed alongside the wharf. Pressure from the troops once again forced conciliation, Sextus receiving Corsica from Octavian and Peleponnese from Antony. He retained Sicily, Sardinia and the smaller islands. In return for the payment of all Sicilian taxes and the lifting of the blockade enabling corn supplies to be resumed, one quarter of the prescribed properties would be returned, all refugees pardoned and seventy million sesterces reimbursed from the Pompey estate. Sextus would have the right to be nominated consulate. This agreement was set down in writing and a copy lodged with the Vestal Virgins.

"Was it bound in matrimony?"

I laughed "You are getting into the Roman way of thinking. Macellus, Octavian's two year old son who was also Mark Antony's step son, was betrothed to the infant daughter of Sextus."

"And the troops got on with the serious business of renewing of acquaintances with old comrades amid much un-seasonal quaffing and feasting."

"Yes. Everyone got riotously drunk."

On board Sextus' Trireme, where he entertained Antony and Octavian, the former outlaw commented; "It is ironic that I am feasting you in my home, the carina of my ship, the keel, whereas your home, Dominus Antonius, 'The House of Ships,' is in the Carinae district of Rome."

The triumvirates laughed, food as wine flowed freely and Mendorus whispered to Sextus; "If we were to slip the moorings, Antonius and Octavius would be at your mercy. You would be able to avenge both your brother and father then become master of the world."

"It is a pity you didn't do so without asking" replied Sextus with a sinister smirk.

"So now the Triumvirates are four" explained Cleopatra "there has been reconciliation with Sextus Pompeius."

"This should be interesting," replied Apollodorus when Cleopatra had finished reading to him the report of the events at Port Misenum. "Antonius believes Rome can be run by a committee whereas Lepidus has no opinion on anything, Octavius has burning ambitions to be sole ruler and Sextus is something of a loose ballista. With the extra territories allocated to him, the heir of Pompeius will be in a far better position to blockade the corn supplies, which mean Octavius, will be looking for an excuse for his removal."

"So you think the peace will be short lived in Rome?"

"Not only that, but I think Marcus Antonius would be well advised to get rid of Octavius before the sickly little man learns how to be a general. He is a far greater threat to all of us than the Parthians. I am beginning to think Jules saw much more in that little runt than a pretty face and tight buttocks."

"You don't think Octavius will honour the agreement at Misenum?" asked Cleopatra.

"Octavius honours agreements only when it suits him or when he has to, Philippi being a case in point. If filius Pompeius was a proper pirate like me instead of a lovable rogue he would have slipped his cables when the Triumvirates were on board his Trireme and avenged his family."

"Would you have done that, 'Pollo?" exclaimed Cleopatra aghast "it would have broken all the sacred laws of hospitality!"

"I most certainly would have done so! 'All is fair in love and war', that is the modus operandi of Octavius; he seeks to be sole master of the Roman world. Everyone else thinks they are playing a nice cosy game of dice amongst friends with a few sesterces at stake. That little runt has ruthlessly swept aside the senatorial hierarchy of Rome for ever and the last vestiges of the old republic are long gone. What he lacks in experience, he makes up for with single minded determination and, unlike the other Triumvirates, has age on his side."

Cleopatra looked worried, "So, what do you suggest, 'Pollo?"

"The next time we see Marcus Antonius I shall not drink any water or go running off to northern Europe. We must press for the return of Egyptian territories, particularly those rich in shipbuilding materials as natural resources. Sadly, you will have to insist on him acknowledging the birthright of your children by marriage and I will have to explain to him in the simplest terms possible that Octavius will eliminate each Triumviri in turn, and then the next on his list will be Egypt."

"The last time you were this adamant was when Caesar was about to be assassinated! This time I will not argue with your wise council, my Lord. It would appear your prophecy that Antonius is destined to be always outdone by Octavius could be horrifically accurate, I hope he heeds the warning I gave him when he returned to Rome" replied Cleopatra sombrely. "Incidentally, Salvidienus Rufus was executed by Octavian when he learnt that his friend and brother officer had offered to defect to Antonius during their confrontation at Brundisium."

"Who has taken over his command of the army in Gaul?"

"The other acolyte of Octavius, Marcus Agrippa."

Book 20

Herod made the hazardous winter sea crossing but the ship loaned to him by Cleopatra was severely damaged. However, he was able to obtain a replacement in Rhodes and the following spring the *Bassilisa* received reports from Italy.

"Herod has been well received by the Roman aristocracy" she explained to Apollodorus. "Antonius has been pressing the Senate to proclaim him Rex of Judea. By making him king, not high priest, they hope this will make him acceptable to the populace.

"I don't understand why Herod would be acceptable as a secular ruler if he was unacceptable as religious head of state, dung by any other name smells as rank" commented Apollodorus.

Hope was fading in Rome that the marriage of Antony to Octavia would bring to an end a decade of civil war and famine. Although the Senate had passed a law proclaiming Herod 'Rex of Judea' he had been left to him to make something of his new title. Mark Antony gave command of eleven legions and most of the ten thousand cavalry retained after Philippi to Ventidius, a field promoted soldier and veteran of Julius Caesar's. Southern Illyrian tribes continued to raid Macedonia and Pollio was assigned seven legions from Macedonia and four from Epirus to contain them. He secured the Thracian passes, thereby removing the threat to the Via Egnatia, the only road from west to east. That spring Ventidius crossed to Asia and begun the recovery of the Roman East. Mobile forces commanded by Quintus Poppaedium Silo advanced through Lydia and the Parthian commander, Labienus, was taken by surprise and withdrew eastwards. The retreat halted at the Taurus Mountains, west of Tarsus, where Labienus awaited reinforcements from Parthia and Ventidus and Silo joined forces and waited for reinforcement from Rome.

Later that spring Apollodorus and Caesarion were night fishing from 'Mintaka' on Lake Mareotis. They were exploring, by lamplight, one of the many dense reed beds that surround the lake. Bubbles of gas came to the surface as they punted their way through the vegetation. Suddenly a sheet of flame flashed across the surface of the water from their lamp. It happened so quickly that they had no time to be frightened.

"Whatever happened, *Geloto*?" asked Caesarion.

"I think our lamp ignited the gas that bubbles up from the mud at the bottom of the lake. Let's try and do it again" replied Apollodorus. He prodded the bottom of the lake near their lamp and the gas ignited as it came to the surface. "We may have failed to catch any fish, but this gives me an idea about how to achieve something I have been working on for some time."

"What is that?" asked the boy.

"I have been working on an idea for a secret weapon. I want to turn a Trireme into a fire breathing dragon."

Caesarion laughed "You can't make a ship breathe fire" he exclaimed.

"Just because it has never been done before, doesn't mean it's impossible" replied Apollodorus defensively. "If we could fill the ship with that gas then blow it out through a hole in the bows the effect would be devastating."

"So all you have to do is collect enough gas to fill a Trireme and hope it doesn't poison the crew. Surely it would be far easier to use flour? Fire in a mill or bakery is devastating."

Apollodorus looked at the boy in disbelief, "Ptolemy Caesar you are a genius. I will ask your Mater to have a medal especially made to present to you, proclaiming your brilliance."

Despite Apollodorus' best efforts, accidents in the dockyard were a part of life, the combination of inflammable materials used and the physical size and weight of the marine structures had always made shipbuilding a hazards profession. As the shipwright approached the latest scene, a sense of foreboding enveloped him. The Trireme lay on its side where it had fallen and it was some time before the workers were able to lift it back into position and replace the broken timbers that shored up the vessel. It was only then that Apollodorus made the grim discovery that sickened him. The dead worker he recognised immediately.

"If only he had gone back to Judea when I told him" he said to the charge hand. "Give me his address and I will go and tell his widow myself."

A little later in the Jewish quarter the carpenter's wife took the news without showing any emotion, she hardly looked old enough to have a child the age of her son.

"Why did you not return to your country when I suggested?" he asked.

"My husband told me what you said but our son was receiving such a good education here in Alexandria" she replied.

"What will you now do?"

"I should like to return to Judea but the Parthians are retreating so it will be dangerous to travel through Palestine."

"I could arrange for you to be taken on one of our merchant ships on it's way to collect timber from Tarsus, you could be landed in the Roman sector to the north, where you will be safe." There was one particular merchant ship Apollodorus had in mind whose Captain was both skilled and trusted by the shipwright and Cleopatra in clandestine activities.

"Why would you do that for me, my Lord? I am not ungrateful but…"

"Your son is a fine young man, I feel helping you is the right thing to do."

"Do you worship the Hebrew living God?"

"I worship no gods but I am fascinated by your holy scrolls and respect your people's beliefs. The Captain of the ship I will assign to take you home does, however, worship your God and is one of your fellow countrymen. He knows the Judean coastline well and will care for you as he would his own family."

The young woman smiled weakly "In that case I will accept your generous offer, Lord Apollodorus. The people say you are a good man and I now know this to be true."

The shipwright handed her a bag of money and said "I hope this will help you through your difficult time."

The woman protested at his generosity.

"It is the wages your husband is owed" he lied. "You are entitled to this money."

Apollodorus slowly walked back along Canopic Way passed through the 'Gate of the Sun'. The main highway was very wide but in common with the cities of the time it was not permitted to drive chariots within the confines of the city wall. To his left was the Park of Pan and in the shadow of the statue of the god to which the park was dedicated basked a pair of cobras. No Egyptian would harm the sacred Uraus and the common people brought the reptile's bowls of milk which they had learned to lap from like cats. The shipwright looked at the serpents coldly and giving them a wide berth decided to sit for a while to contemplate what the Hebrew woman had said.

"Joseph was a good man. In my culture when an unmarried woman becomes pregnant she is stoned to death."

"That is so senseless" replied Apollodorus "The gift of children is the most sacred thing a person can receive."

"That is exactly what Joseph said. Children are a gift from God, so he married me to save me from my fate and has been a good father. You and he are very much alike."

"What do you mean?"

"Forgive me for saying so, my Lord, but you are abba to the Roman's children. The *Bassilisa* is fortunate to have you at her side quietly accepting that which you cannot change. Your love of Cleopatra must be very great."

There were tears in the shipwright's eyes as the young woman softly touched his arm and said "Just let it be, My Lord, let it be."

It was almost nightfall when eventually Apollodorus made his way past the Theatre and Race Course and then into the palace compound. The young Hebrew woman's words of wisdom still were ringing in his ears.

'When I find myself in times of trouble
Mother Mary comes to me
Speaking words of wisdom, let it be.
And in my hour of darkness
She is standing right in front of me
Speaking words of wisdom, let it be.
Let it be, let it be.
Whisper words of wisdom, let it be.

And when the broken hearted people
Living in the world agree,
There will be an answer, let it be.
For though they may be parted there is
Still a chance that they will see
There will be an answer, let it be.
Let it be, let it be. Yeah
There will be an answer, let it be.

And when the night is cloudy,
There is still a light that shines on me,

*Shine on until tomorrow, let it be.
I wake up to the sound of music
Mother Mary comes to me
Speaking words of wisdom, let it be.
Let it be, let it be.
There will be an answer, let it be.
Let it be, let it be,
Whisper words of wisdom, let it be'*

(Lennon/McCartney, words based on the Magnificat, the Song of Mary.)

Labienus, commander of the Parthian army was out-manoeuvred and out-witted by Ventidius forcing him to give up much of Asia Minor without a fight. Pressure from the feudal Barons forced Orodes and Pacorus, the other Parthian commanders and Labienus to discard the highly efficient and greatly feared mounted archers in favour of heavily armoured Knights. These Knights refused to re-group with Labienus but charged the Roman positions on the slopes of Mount Taurus.

"Ventidius must have thought he had won the equivalent of the Roman lottery when he saw the Cataphracts (Parthian Knights) attempt to charge up the hill" I explained. *"The Roman slingers used lead shot which penetrated their armour so a retreat was soon turned into a rout. Labienus fled to Cyprus and was subsequently executed as a traitor. On the slopes of Taurus and at the Amanic Gates, Ventidius inflicted the first two of three crushing defeats by the Romans on the Parthians; the third would not be until the following year."*

From the bank of Lake Mareotis at the end of a small wooden jetty Apollodorus and Caesarion piled brushwood around a copper barrel. A pipe led back from the top of the barrel along the jetty to a granite block and a short tube pointed in the opposite direction out across the lake. The shipwright lit the brushwood then they hurried back to rock, crouched behind it and pumped furiously on the bellows attached to the other end of the tube. Construction of the device had been relatively straight forward in a city whose populous, as Caesar had previously commented, were obsessed with hydraulics.

"The bellows pressurise the barrel and forces the heated liquid in a fine jet across the lake" explained Apollodorus as he counted down in Greek. "*Pente, teoora, tria, dna, ena*." The spray of liquid ignited and a jet of flame sprayed across the water. "Behold one fire breathing dragon!"

Just as he finished speaking there was a blinding flash and a massive noise like thunder. When the smoke cleared nothing was left of the equipment or jetty. Man and boy looked at each other in disbelief. Caesarion was first to speak.

"That wasn't exactly what you had in mind, was it, *Geloto*?"

Apollodorus raised an eyebrow. "Not even a blast from the round horn of Seth's rump could cause that much damage!"

Among the charred remains of the jetty were a number of fish floating on their sides, stunned by the explosion.

"The device works but needs some fine tuning additionally it may be difficult to find crew mad enough to operate it," continued Apollodorus thoughtfully. "But, on the bright side, we have discovered a novel way of fishing!"

"That's much better than Domini Antonius' method," replied Caesarion with a smile. "When we took him fishing he cheated by arranging for a diver to attach fish to his line. He thought we didn't know, so the following day Ma did the same thing but used salted fish, to show she knew he had cheated. What is the connection with a bakery fire and this device from hadies?"

"Flour in a sack in not particularly inflammable but in a defused mist the individual particles ignite easily. Hot air expands enhancing the fire like a volcano where hot liquid under high pressure is suddenly released into the atmosphere. My device is a volcano on its side, equally as dangerous and unpredictable!"

About the same time as Cleopatra's twins celebrated their first birthday, Octavia gave birth to Antony's daughter, Antonia, then later that summer the Triumvir took his family to Athens where they lived in domestic bliss for the next two years. They attended lectures and religious ceremonies together and became greatly loved by the Athenians. Octavia was a devoted mother to Antony's children by his former wives as well as to their daughter, Antonia.

"What is the latest news about Herod?" inquired Apollodorus.

"He has been able to raise an army against Antigonus, the Parthian's puppet king" explained Cleopatra as they relaxed together in the bath one evening. "Antigonus is popular with the locals whereas Herod is neither of the old priestly dynasty or a Hasmonaean. Antonius is reluctant to help until Herod's betrothal to Mariamme becomes marriage."

"Why would his marital status make any difference?"

"Because Mariamme is of suitable birth" replied the Bassilisa giving Apollodorus a long suffering look. "Incidentally, Antonius has married again" she continued.

"Why?" asked Apollodorus in disbelief. "Didn't Octavia come up to his expectations? Or is he addicted to wedding banquets?"

Cleopatra laughed "No. He and Octavia are still together. Antonius insists on being addressed as Dionysus so the Athenians thought it would be a nice idea if he were betrothed to Pallas Athena of the bright eyes, daughter of Zeus. Antonius being Antonius always ready to exploit a financial opportunity accepted. He was able to extract a dowry of one million drachmae from the citizens but also, rather more to the point, saw it as an excellent excuse for some highly un-seasonal quaffing and feasting."

"I hope that doesn't give your Chancellor of the Exchequer ideas" commented the actress dryly.

I laughed and replied "From the size of his girth he is well acquainted with the un-seasonal quaffing and feasting, regarding fund raising it was certainly more stylish than lining the 'Queen's Highway' with speed cameras."

"I thought Antonius considered himself to be the living embodiment of Hercules, I just can't keep up with these Roman's delusions of deity" interjected Apollodorus cynically.

Cleopatra laughed and then continued "Herod appealed to Ventidius for assistance but this would have provoked a civil war in Judea. The citadel at Jerusalem is well fortified so they would need siege artillery which the Roman could not spare. Therefore Ventidius gave Herod money instead."

"So what are Herod's chances of becoming 'King of the Jews' in reality as well as name?" asked the shipwright.

"I would think non-existent without Roman assistance according to legend that title is reserved for a descendent of their heroic King David and will be born in Bethlehem."

Apollodorus shivered involuntarily so Cleopatra cuddled him and added "The water is getting cold we had better get out of the bath, I don't want you catching any nasty diseases! Enough of world politics let us eat, drink and talk of lighter matters." The handmaids dried them and oiled their skin, so the shipwright's body heat was soon restored and he thought no more of the Judean dynasty. The Romans were out of the way and otherwise occupied so for the next two summers Cleopatra and Apollodorus were able to live in idyllic bliss.

Caesarion learnt much from the shipwright; in the dockyard man management as well as practical skills and in the lake and harbours of Alexandria, seamanship. His mother taught him to ride a horse and Mardian showed him how to cook. The twins were weaned and, encouraged by their half brother, walking before they were a year old. The palaces were their playground and the corridors echoed to the sound of children's laughter. Unlike their mother's childhood they didn't live in fear of assassination.

"It is good that they will not grow up looking on each other as rivals for the crown" commented Cleopatra.

"Having a loving *Mater* will teach them to love each other but remember they are Ptolemys so they will inherit your burning desire to rule" replied Apollodorus cautiously.

"We had better make sure there are sufficient realms for all of them, the return of Egypt's former territories should stop any sibling arguments. If we could secure Caesarion's birthright, he could rule Rome and Alexander would have Egypt."

"It is a lovely dream, Thea. The word would then be peaceful and prosperous and all humanity would rejoice."

They were on the western end of Antirhodos sitting on the temple steps between the two Sphinxes that guarded the entrance, watching Sirius rise, the time longest day, to us mid summer's night and for Cleopatra and Apollodorus the beginning of a new year in Egypt. In the distance was a faint roar that heralded the arrival of the life giving flood that would turn the parched desert once again into a lush green paradise. The next five days would be devoted to feasting and celebrations as last year's sediment was flushed out of the cities cisterns, these would then be re-filled and the muddy water allowed to settle.

"The 'going up of the goddess Sothis' means the cycle of life has begun again, *Geloto*" commented Cleopatra.

"Will you sing for me the 'Hymn to the Nile flood'?" asked Apollodorus. Her low husky voice echoed across the harbour like a Siren of mythology as the *Bassilisa* accompanied herself on her lyre and the shipwright listened in captivated silence. The cisterns were filled and the days began to shorten as the nights lengthened. On the other side of the Mediterranean the leaves turned from green to many shades of gold and red.

Autumn saw relations between Octavian and Sextus deteriorate as the treaty of Misenum had placed the son of Pompey in a far stronger position to interrupt the corn supplies to Rome. By the end of the first season, Inundation, Cleopatra received news of events in Rome.

"Octavius has fallen in love" announced the Bassilisa incredulously.

"You are kidding!" exclaimed Apollodorus. "He isn't capable of that or any other emotion; you will tell me next that he has been seen smiling."

"Don't be silly, *Geloto*, he never learned the sequence of muscle movements to do that! He has cut the matrimonial ties with the Pompeii dynasty by divorcing Scribonia, no doubt as a prelude to eliminating Sextus and on the day she gave birth to their daughter Julia. Don't say it, Pollo, 'typical Roman behaviour', I know" she continued to read from the scroll. "He fell in love with Livia, wife of Tiberius Nero who has been forced to divorce her, and then the poor man had to give her away in the marriage ceremony as her pater killed himself after the battle of Philippi."

"Marriage into the ancient Claudine dynasty should give the little runt the respectability he craves" commented Apollodorus dryly. "Matrimony in Rome appears to be a dreadfully complex business."

"Why do you think we don't have a formal marriage ceremony and the associated legal ramifications?"

Apollodorus was thoughtful, then he added "I was wondering why in all the time I have lived in Alexandria I had never been invited to a wedding."

Livia was pregnant with her second child at the time of her marriage to Octavius but it was not until February of 38 B.C that she gave birth. By now it was the third season in the Egyptian calendar.

"Octavius gave Livia's son to Nero shortly after the birth" explained Cleopatra. "Unfortunately, Nero died a month later so the little runt is a father of three children within three months of marriage, Julia by Scribonia and Livia's two sons by Nero. He has been the butt of many jokes as a consequence."

"Amusingly, in the words of Dio Cassius;" I added "'Now the populace gossiped a great deal about this and said, among other things, The luck having three children in three months; and this saying has passed into a proverb.'"

"Is that why three is regarded as a lucky number?"

"Very possibly! The Romans had a bit of a thing about the number three, their dining grrangements were in multipuls of that number. The couches they reclined on were called triclinium as three were arranged around a square table with the fourth side open for serving. The dining room was also called the triclinium."

"So if the Bible we know today was written for Roman consumption and they had this thing about the number three, does that explain why there is the emphasis on the trinity?"

"I don't know but Sir Isac Newton would probably agree with you, he did a great deal of research into that issue and looked on the concept of the trinity as a heracy. He also looked on the church of Rome as the Anti-Christ but that was a long time ago so your church has learned to live with the missjudgement."

I was back on the dangerious ground that I had inadvertently strayed into when we first became lovers on board her yacht in the bay at Alexandria and the actress had asked if Octavian looked on himself as the messiah. Hurredly I changed the subject. "Newton is sometimes called the last sourcerer so he probably tripped over gravity whilst looking for the philosopher's stone! The apple story is apocriphal, probably invented by the scientist himself."

"Has this taken his mind off warfare?" asked Apollodorus.

"Apparently not. He has transferred troops from Gaul to southern Italy and a newly built fleet of Triremes from Ravenna. Agrippa is occupied with the warring tribes of Germany and Bogud similarly in Spain."

"Octavian was fearful that Sextus would form an alliance with Lepidus or Antony and that the son of Pompey would make a pre-emptive attack" I explained.

"Sounds like the kind of paranoia that brought about the 'Cold War' between America and the Soviet Union not so long ago" commented the actress.

"The leaders looked on each other with un-justified mutual suspicion and spent a fortune on armament while the populous starved, then as now." I replied.

"Was Sextus a threat?"

"Not really, certainly his Admirals made a nuisance of themselves raiding coastal towns and harassing merchant shipping but Sextus was doing his best to keep a low profile and trying to stay out of trouble."

"Admiral Mendorus offered to defect to Octavius bringing with him Corsica and Sardinia, a fleet of Triremes and three legions" explained Cleopatra.

"Why? Wasn't Sextus paying him enough?" replied Apollodorus dryly.

"Possibly, but more likely he was fearful that he may have shared the fate of his brother officer, Murcus, who was summonsed to Sicily by Sextus on suspicion of plotting against him."

"Who, no doubt, chopped his head off first and then questioned him afterwards, knowing Roman paranoia. The absence of any response from Admiral Detruncare convinced Sextus of his guilt."

Cleopatra laughed "Something like that" she replied. They were relaxing together in bed.

"Would you cut my head off if you thought I was going to defect to the little runt?" asked Apollodorus.

"No, but I might cut off something else" replied the Bassilisa as she took hold of his manhood and rested her head on his chest.

"In that case my loyalty is assured, your Highness. I have no wish to join Mardian's rather exclusive club!"

"I have no doubt about your allegiance, my Lord." They kissed passionately to reinforce the point.

On the other side of the Mediterranean the Roman year came to an end. Octavian cast around for an excuse to go to war against Sextus, it was the un-paid taxes due from Sextus' territories were the rather trivial pretext he eventually claimed and to this end he requested a summit at Brundisium with his co Triumvirates. Mark Antony arrived on the appointed day to find the city gates locked against him, so he returned to Athens furious that his plans to invade Parthian had been delayed again by a meeting that Octavian had requested, and then failed to attend.

Apollodorus was in his room in the palace studying some scrolls when the twins came in, followed by Caesarion.

"I was telling Alexander and Cleopatra that your chair is a very special magical one" explained Caesarion "but they don't believe me."

"Do you think it wise to tell them the secret?" exclaimed Apollodorus in horror. "Can they be trusted?"

"Of course we can" chorused the twins "we are royal!"

"Well, very occasionally the chair sprouts wings" explained Apollodorus. Then it will take you to all sorts of magical lands." It was at this point that Cleopatra and the two handmaids crept in so the shipwright entertained his audience with stories of strange and magical places then finished with something more traditional.

"Back in the mists of time Hera ordered Titanus to seize Dionysus, newborn son of Zeus who was then torn to pieces and boiled in a caldron."

"Why?" exclaimed the young Cleopatra in horror.

"Because he was an ugly baby" replied the shipwright as if it was the most natural thing in the world for a disappointed parent to do. "He was horned and crowned with serpents. Pomegranates sprouted from the soil where his blood was spilt. The child was rescued by Rhea his grandmother who brought him back to life" he continued reassuringly. "Hermes temporarily transformed him into a ram. The infant was cared for by nymphs who cosseted him and fed him honey. Dionysus grew up into an effeminate man and was driven mad due to the overindulgence of hallucinogenic substances."

"The ancient gods were partial to the odd spliff then?" inquired the actress incredulously.

"Very much so" I replied. "Anything that could not be eaten, drunk, screwed, smoked or snorted was considered useless to the Olympians. The intoxicants Ambrosia and Nectar, wine or ivy ale, were brewed by the ancients to wash down far stronger drugs, magic mushrooms, marijuana and possibly opiates. This gave them erotic energy, remarkable strength and prophetic sight."

"That is all very fascinating but what has it to do with your story?" asked the actress impatiently.

"It has a great deal of significance in the understanding of the mind set and way of life of Mark Antony."

"So did M.A, in his self appointed capacity as the living embodiment of Dionysus, like a toke?"

"There are indeed accounts of Roman worshipers of Dionysus sitting around pungent bonfires and becoming intoxicated without consuming wine or ale.

"Dionysus wondered the world with his tutor Silenus and a wild army of Satyres and Maenads. He was armed with an ivy twined staff tipped with a pine cone. The young god and his companions sailed to Egypt bring with them the grape vine and were received hospitably. An alliance with the Amazon ruler of Pharos was formed and together they marched against Titaus to restore Ammon to the throne. Encouraged by this early military success Dionysus travelled east to India conquering, teaching the art of viniculture, giving law and building cities. Eventually he returned to Europe where Rhea purified him of the many murders and atrocities committed during his madness."

The twins had fallen asleep sitting on the shipwrights lap so as Charmain and Iras put them to bed Cleopatra commented "I never really know which of your stories are about real countries and which are fictitious."

"That's what makes a good story; the audience should never be able to distinguish fact from fantasy."

"Perhaps one day you will tell my story."

Apollodorus considered this for a little while then replied "That would be a daunting prospect. Would I do your story justice? I would be terrified of not pleasing you."

At first Cleopatra could think of no suitable reply then she announced. "The Romans will tell the story that will suit their propaganda. I am relying on you to give the world the truth."

"Do you think I am up to the task, Thea?"

"I can think of no one better."

"Well, I won't tell everything. Some things are too precious and too private to be shared with the world." As they embraced, Ventidius received reports that Pacorus was preparing for a counter offensive.

"Roman history records that it was the ninth of June 38B.C. that the attack took place" I explained.

"The end of the Egyptian year and halfway through the Roman calendar" added the actress.

"Once again the Cataphracts lead the assault and those that were not killed by the armour piercing slingers presumably died of coronaries as a result of charging up a hill in full armour. Suffice to say the Parthians

were once again annihilated, the commander, Pacorus, was killed and their control of eastern Syria collapsed."

"You would have thought they would have learned from their earlier mistake."

"Ventidius was of exactly the same opinion, so set about recruiting his own mounted archers for which the area was renowned."

"Marius Antonius has been hailed as Imperator for a third time" announced Cleopatra.

"Will he be able to get a helmet big enough?" replied Apollodorus. Cleopatra looked puzzled so he continued. "When someone is proud my people describe them as being big headed."

"Like the Egyptian expression 'breaking wind higher than their....' " Cleopatra stopped speaking abruptly and coloured deep red.

"Higher than their own fundamental orifice?" suggested the shipwright helpfully. They both laughed.

"I would rather he addressed the problem of Octavius before it's too late" continued Cleopatra.

"Hopefully he will now feel that Roman honour is satisfied with the recovery of their former territories and will not be tempted to pursue the Parthians across the Euphrates and into their homeland."

"That is exactly what he is planning. Antonius will not be content until the Parthians have been humbled in their homeland and the lost eagles of Crassus and Saxa recovered."

"All the Parthians will have to do is continue to retreat and draw Antonius deep into their country, then when his supply lines are stretched to the limit, attack! If they burn the land as they retreat there will be nothing for the Romans to forage and the result will be the biggest bloodbath in history."

Cleopatra looked at Apollodorus as though she was seeing him for the first time. "Is that what happened to Caesar when he invaded your country?"

"More or less, the one weakness in the Roman method of aggression is the way they rely on what they plunder from the countries they conquer to satisfy and motivate their armies. If there is nothing to plunder there will be unable to pay or feed the troops, and then the whole system will collapse, result – chaos and mutiny."

In less than a decade Cleopatra would attempt to use this strategy to defeat the enemy but would her love of one man be used to bring about her downfall? Would her courage fail her at the critical moment? Perhaps her fate was already sealed and only by losing could she ultimately win and then find the true love she craved.

That autumn Octavian attempted to invade Sicily and just before the Mediterranean was closed to shipping Cleopatra received the news.

"I have received a report from Rome" announced the *Bassilisa* "perhaps you had better read it, 'Pollo, as you understand naval strategy better than I do." They were in her day room, a combined office and saloon where she could study state papers in comfort as well as entertain. On the walls were a number of beautifully drawn, ornate maps. Apollodorus had been standing by the doors overlooking the lighthouse and he moved to the map of Italy as Cleopatra handed him the scroll.

"It would appear that the little runt has finally plucked up the courage to attack Sextus" said Apollodorus, and then continued to read from the scroll. "Octavius had a fleet of 370 war ships in two squadrons. Admiral Calvisius was in command of the first, stationed here on the Etrurian Coast" he indicated on the map near Rome. "Admiral Lucius Corificius at Brundisium" he pointed to the heel of Italy "in command of the second squadron. The plan was for the two squadrons to meet at Caladria, which makes no sense!

"Calvisius sailed slowly south hugging the coastline, probably due to an inexperienced crew. Octavius boarded at Tarentun" he pointed to the instep of Italy "east from Brundisium, and then they sailed through the Messina Straits to join Calvisius. Sextus' fleet of 40 ships let them pass then attacked their rear. Octavius was forced to shelter near Cape Scylla. How daft! Any heavy weather would whip up the outfalls round the headland and make for a very confused sea. Sextus attacked them at anchor and Cornificius tried to counter but was no match for the experienced Pompeian captains and crew. The light failed so Sextus withdrew.

"The next day half the fleet was scattered along the coast wrecked or burning but the following day the wind freshened – surprise, surprise - and Sextus returned to Messina as the weather deteriorated. The wind veered south west and the southerly gale increased to a storm over night. By dawn nature had finished what Sextus started, the crew, including Octavius, only survived by swimming ashore."

"I told you Seth looks after his own!" added Cleopatra.

While Octavian and Sextus were locked in battle, Veritidius marched north to punish Antiochus for harbouring Parthian stragglers and matters came to a head at Samosata, the capital city on the banks of the upper Euphrates. Caesar had planned to cross the Euphrates at Commagene, east of Tarsus, in the first phase of his Parthian campaign so control of Samosata was vital if Antony was to implement his late commander's plan. The gates of the city were closed and Antiochus attempted to bribe Veritidius with a sum of one thousand talents.

"The Roman commander left all political decisions to Marcus Antonius" explained Cleopatra.

"So General Veritidius allocated the thousand talents to his retirement fund, being a contemporary of the late Jules and in his sixties, and then sent M.A a message asking what to do" replied Apollodorus.

"Who responded with the comment 'am I surrounded by idiots? Or do I have to do everything myself?' He hastily travelled to Samosata, prompting the remnants of the Parthian invasion force to surrender without a fight."

"This means that his helmet size is now at crisis point."

Cleopatra laughed and added "And the altitude of his personal biological gaseous emissions is doubtlessly celestial."

"Have you heard the expression 'pride comes before a fall', Thea?"

"It is funny you should say that but Mardian's heart throb, Herod, made the hazardous journey over land to beg for assistance from Antonius against Antigonus."

"What is his marital status now?"

"Betrothed but not yet married. However, Antonius placed two legions at his disposal under the command of Sosius, Ventidius having returned to Rome."

"Did M.A object to Ventidius pocketing the thousand talents?"

"Nothing of the sort. Antonius is generous to a fault and not over-scrupulous himself with other people's money. It was what you joked about earlier. Ventidius had fulfilled all that Antonius required of him and has returned home to a well earned retirement"

"Breading Guinea Pigs in southern Italy?" asked Apollodorus with a chuckle. "Admiral Mendorus defected back to Sextus disgusted by the incompetence of the navy of Octavius. The son of Pompeius refrained from cutting his head off and welcomed him back into the fold. These Romans have a somewhat perverse idea of loyalty."

"If you were Sextus, would you have beheaded him, 'Pollo?"

"Probably not, but I would certainly have 'stripped him of all that covered his nakedness and thrashed him ignominiously' as you would undoubtedly have done."

"Perhaps he is 'blubbering by the ships' somewhere on the coast of Sicily at this very moment" replied Cleopatra with a twinkle in her eye and they both laughed.

Book 21

In the new Roman year, 37 B.C, Agrippa took up his post as Consulate. He had returned from Gaul the previous autumn having subjugated a rebellion Aquitania and founded a colony that was to become Cologne. Agrippa had the distinction of being the first Roman after Caesar to bridge the Rhine. In order to save Octavian's blushes he declined the honour of a triumph and was rewarded with the unenviable task of building and training a navy to defeat Sextus. Meanwhile, Antony sailed from Piraeus with his wife, children and fleet of three hundred warships.

At Brundisium he was not permit to enter the haven with his fleet and once again the city gates were locked so Antony continued onwards to arrive at Taraentium in the late spring for a meeting with Octavian. Octavia was by now heavily pregnant with their second child but in deference to her personal comfort and the superstitions of the sailors she was determined to avert an open breach between the Triumvirates. When they arrived at Tarentium Octavian refused to meet with Antony but did receive his sister.

"I was the happiest woman alive" entreated Octavia when she was alone with he brother. "For all people looked up to me, as I am the sister of one Imperator and the wife of the other. If the worst should happen, the gods forbid it, and my brother and husband go to war. As at Troy in the Iliad it is uncertain which of you the gods have assigned to be the victor and who will be vanquished. For me, like Helen, which ever side prevails, I will know no happiness."

Cleopatra related events in southern Italy to Apollodorus who commented "Was Octavius consistent with his normal practice of failing to attend without giving any apology or explanation?"

"That is correct" she replied "First Antonius stopped off at Brundisium where the gates were locked against him. He continued on to Traentium and was similarly rebuffed."

"So presumably he is now on his way back to Achaea grinding his teeth in rage. Do you thing it is beginning to sink in that an alliance with Octavius on equal terms is impossible?"

"No. Octavia managed to persuade Antonius to stay at Taraentium to avoid an open breach between her brother and husband but when Octavius eventually arrived he was adamant that he needed no assistance from Domini Antonius and refused to meet with him."

"I suppose the presence of his latest acolyte, Agrippa, in Rome has given the little runt the confidence to decline support from Antonius. Why in the name of all that is holy doesn't he form an alliance with Sextus and rid the world of that little vermin?"

"Because Octavia prevailed on both of them to hold talks and another reconciliation was staged" replied Cleopatra continuing to read from the scroll.

"By Seth's foul breath, I don't believe it! Why?"

"Because Antonius wanted to exchange some ships that he didn't need for Legions he does require" replied Cleopatra. "Antonius has lent Octavius one hundred and twenty ships in exchange for a promise of four legions and you and I know that Octavius' promises are like pita bread, all air and no substance. Antonius has reluctantly consented to a re-match with Sextus although he will not be involved, Lepidus however will give military assistance. Rather more importantly, the Triumvirate has run for five years so it was necessary to renew the agreement for a further period."

"Was the agreement bound in matrimony?" asked the actress.

"Of course, Antony's eldest son was betrothed to Octavian's infant daughter, Julia" I replied.

"Then everyone got riotously drunk!"

Sosius and his legions marched south with Herod to laid siege on Jerusalem. They had to wait five months for the necessary reinforcements to successfully breach the city's defences during which time Herod married Mariamme. In Egypt the Nile flooded ushering in a new year, the sixteenth of Cleopatra's reign and that August Jerusalem surrendered so Herod was at last King of the Jews, in fact, as well as name. Antony returned east and in preparation for the invasion of Parthia set up his headquarters in Antioch. He left his family in Rome and sailed for Athens. As he watched the Italian coastline disappear in the autumn mist for what was to be the last time he remembered what Cleopatra had said a soothsayer had prophesied.

"You are destined to always be outdone by Octavius" was the shipwright's warning.

"If co-operation with Octavius is impossible" he thought "surely the world is big enough for both of us."

That November in Rome Ventidius enjoyed his richly deserved triumph but died a few years later to be honoured with a state funeral. In Alexandria, Cleopatra received advanced secret warning that Fonteius Capito was on his way from Antioch with a summons from Mark Antony so she and her handmaids made preparations for a very special night of intimacy with Apollodorus. The Mediterranean would soon be closed to shipping so they would have to depart for Antioch at short notice and be unable to return to Alexandria for several months.

    As soon as Apollodorus entered Cleopatra's private apartment he knew from the way she and the handmaids were dressed, or rather the lack of clothing that events in Alexandria were about to change. The sight of the three beautiful ladies wearing nothing but jewellery sent a flood of conflicting emotions through his very being. He felt excitement as his libido rose along with sadness as he thought Mark Antony must be on his way to their paradise island. Cleopatra approached him slowly like a temple cat advanced on its prey. She was flanked by Charmain on her right and Iras to her left. The precious metal and stones of their jewellery contrasted beautifully with their individual skin tones and hair colouring. With such beauty clothing would have been an irrelevance.
    Cleopatra was first to kiss him, her soft hands slithered around his neck and she took hold of a handful of his hair so there was no escape as her hungry lips found his. Charmain and Iras put their arms around him and pressed their naked bodies against him. He ran his hands down each of their backs to their buttocks as they nibbled his ears and kissed his neck. When at last he had the use of his mouth again he said softly.
    "I take it that we have unwelcome but necessary visitors on their way to us."
    Cleopatra nodded sadly and the shipwright continued "If what you have in mind for tonight you are each giving freely I will gladly accept but if what you are doing is to stop me from running away again…." He shook his head, his blue eyes were moist, the words he desperately wanted to use he could not. To say what he so desperately wanted to say and what Thea so desperately wanted to hear he could not say for fear that the course of history would be changed forever. He was right. If he had declared his love for her history would have been changed. What the Jester had totally misunderstood was that history would be changed for the better!
    "I will stand my ground and be by your side for the final battle, win or lose" he whispered and they both thought "Then, at last, we will know true love."

High above on Mount Olympos Isis looked down on them sadly and said to herself; "Yes, win or lose, then my children you will know true love. To win is to lose and they that lose shall win."

Antioch; in the words of Libanius 'if a man had the idea of travelling all over the earth, not to see how cities looked, but to learn their ways, our city would fulfil his purpose and save him his journeying. If he sits in our market place he will sample every city, there will be so many people from each place with whom he can talk… the city loves the virtues of those whom have come to it exactly as it does the virtues of its children, imitating the Athenians in this also.'

"The climate made it a favourite vacation spot for the Romans and others wishing to escape the extreme heat and dampness of other parts of the Mediterranean region" I explained. "Like Tarsus, Antioch was to feature prominently in the later books of the biblical New Testament."

The attention of the Paparazzi had made the actress' London flat intolerable so we were in my small weatherboard fisherman's cottage on the east coast of Essex. The young woman was curled up in one of the two elm rocking chair and I was sat at my mahogany desk, a replica of the one designed by Captain Davenport. The fire was crackling and hissing in the 'pot belly stove' and the curtains were tightly drawn against the winter chill. Outside the easterly wind whistled but we were snug and warm drinking Assam tea and eating hot buttered crumpets. I swung around on the buttoned leather ' swing and tilt' captain's chair to face the actresses who smiled at me like a contented cat that had found the warmest most comfortable seat in the house.

"The press will never find their way across the causeway which floods at high tide" I commented reassuringly.

"How can a house with no central heating be so cosy and warm when there is snow outside?" she asked.

"The stronger the easterly wind blows the colder it is outside and the more the fire draws. There is nothing like the heat of a real fire" I replied.

"We are like Sextus, keeping a low profile, but this is West Mersey not Sicily!"

Located in northern Syria on the east coast of the Mediterranean bordering present day Turkey and lying just eighteen miles inland the City of Antioch was close enough for easy communications by sea but far enough from the coast for safety from invasion. The voyage along the Syrian coast had passed without mishap or incident despite the lateness of the season and as they sailed up the River Asi, known today as the Orontes, Cleopatra commented.

"You are unlikely to suffer any ill effect from drinking the water here, *Geloto*. Alexander the Great described it as being sweeter than his own mother's milk! This is where Apollo fell in love with Daphne and tried to violate her. Mother Earth turned her into a yew tree to save her from the god's amorous desires. These elegant trees are now prolific in the orchid fields of Antioch."

Cleopatra's flag ship and attending support vessels had entered the River Asi from the Mediterranean Sea south west of Antioch. They approached from the south so the walled city was to their right, the river dividing to flow each side of a substantial island to their left where the Palace and Hippodrome were sited. The city was located on the eastern bank of the river Asi which after the two waterways merged north of the Palace Island and continued north for a short distance, curved around to the east then south forming an un-navigable corridor between Asia Minor and Egypt. The streets of Antioch were laid out in a grid formation similar to Alexandria with the main highway from Daphne, in the south, running north, north east to Beroea.

"Antioch was founded by Seleukos, one of Alexander the Great's generals" explained Cleopatra. "This was the capital city of the Seleucid kings until the Romans occupied it when I was five years old. It is one of the finest cities after Alexandria; there is an abundance of fresh food and water. The locals take their hunting very seriously, so there is some good sport available, not that you will be interested, *Geloto*."

"I will not indulge myself in that particular activity while we are here but it does explain why Antonius has made it his headquarters" replied Apollodorus. "The Seleucid kings must have been avid charioteers to have built a Hippodrome on the Royal Island." They were coming alongside the palace wharf so further discussion about the delights of Antioch was curtailed. Mark Antony was there in person to greet them, after three years absence Apollodorus expected this to be a tense reunion, he thought he knew every aspect of the Bassilisa but he was about to discover that his Thea was every cubit a Ptolemy, so also was Mark Antony, to his cost. As they came alongside the shipwright was about to move forward from the gilded pavilion aft cabin where Cleopatra sat on her throne.

"Stay where you are, *Kyrios mou*," commanded the *Bassilisa*. "Admiral, you will escort the Romans aboard." Cleopatra was dressed in the state robes of cloth of gold and Vulture headdress. Apollodorus looked at her with a puzzled expression; she rarely addressed him as my Lord and never in public.

"There was a time when you told me to do your bidding without question" she whispered.

"Now you want me to reciprocate and trust you as you trusted me?" he replied. Cleopatra nodded imperceptibly, so the shipwright gave a small bow to indicate his compliance.

Mark Antony strode confidently aboard and made his way aft smiling broadly. He had a very good and noble appearance; his beard was well grown, his forehead large, and his nose aquiline, giving him altogether a bold, masculine look that reminded people of the face of Hercules in paintings and sculptures. As was his custom whenever he had to appear before large numbers, Mark Antony wore his tunic girt low about the hips, a broadsword on his side, and over all a large coarse mantle. Cleopatra eyed him coldly, Apollodorus looked everywhere except at Mardian, mindful of the eunuch's opinion of men who tied their girdle too low, and this was definitely not a time to get a fit of the giggles.

"Welcome to Antioch..." Antony started to say but Cleopatra cut him short with a look that would turn milk sour.

"Domini Antonius, you are well aware that you are on Egyptian territory and it is protocol to kneel in the presence of royalty or has the length of time since our last meeting affected your memory?" expostulated the Lady of Two Lands in formal Latin.

"I WILL NOT KNEEL BEFORE YOU!" replied Antony with a mixture of fury and disbelief.

"Caesar did" replied Cleopatra quietly. "Do you consider yourself greater than him?"

Antony's broad grin was replaced with an expression like a camel chewing a scorpion. It is well known in Diplomatic circles that in tense situations whoever speaks first loses. Cleopatra was expressionless. Her green eyes were piercing and she sat bolt upright, like a Cobra ready to strike. In the silence the centurions shuffled uncomfortably. Antony looked around at the people assembled and then across the river at the formidable fleet of Egyptian ships. It has been said in hindsight that with a legion posted in Judea he could have helped himself to whatever he wanted from Egypt but this would have presented enormous logistical problems and Mark

Antony knew from first hand experience that Alexandria was well fortified. He was also mindful that Cleopatra had had plenty of time and money to prepare for just this sort of eventuality.

He then looked across at Apollodorus, the man who his late commander had nicknamed Jocus meaning 'Jester' in Latin or *Gelotopoios* in Greek, and his mind went back to their first meeting. This man had single-handedly smuggled the *Bassilisa* in a small boat past an army of twenty thousand Gabinians. Then he remembered how the Lady of Two Lands had been prepared to ride across the Nile delta alone to rescue Apollodorus and how jealous he had felt when she cradled the unconscious shipwright in her arms as they sailed back to Alexandria. The Jester had recovered Caesar's body from the Forum after the assassination while he, Antony, was fearfully barricading himself in his home. Then Apollodorus had safely taken Cleopatra back to her ships in the Messina Straits of southern Italy, un-escorted and on horseback a distance of five hundred miles. In short, he was confronted by the two people whom he admired as much as he admired Caesar, two people he wanted on his side not as his enemy. Very slowly he knelt and indicated to his escort to do the same.

"I will send a member of my household to inspect the arrangements you have made for me" continued Cleopatra, softly "and will grant you an audience aboard my flag ship tomorrow morning, provided you are appropriately dressed. We will then discuss whether I shall be staying here in Antioch and I will hear your proposals. It has been a long journey and I need to rest. You may go!"

"May I see my children?" asked Antony.

"Your children? What do you mean your children?" replied Cleopatra with venom. "Were you present at the birth? No! Where you there to teach them to walk? NO! Have you told them bed time stories? NO YOU HAVE NOT! *Kyrios* the Apollodorus has done all those things and more; he is their *Pater*, not you. All Rome looks on me as a whore, you have treated me like one! Now you have grown bored with your enemy's sister you have the audacity to summons me to your presence like some common woman.

"You expect me to fund your pathetic wars and satisfy your carnal desires. While Rome has indulged its favourite pastime of civil unrest, Egypt has been peaceful, prosperous and has grown strong. You consider that your noble linage, sprung from Anton son of Hercules, should be transmitted as widely as possible. Be mindful, Domini Antonius, the day is not far off dawning when I will mete out justice on Capitol Hill to you and all Rome. Be gone and think on all these things then return tomorrow morning having given serious consideration to how you have wronged me and what you propose to do to make amends!"

As the Romans departed Cleopatra turned to Apollodorus. "You will escort me to my chamber, I am quite exhausted." When they were alone in her cabin the shipwright was still speechless as he looked at her. Cleopatra was first to speak "*Geloto*, hold me." The shipwright put his arms around her and found himself face to face with the Vulture but the atmosphere was still far too tense for him to laugh. She looked up at him and realising the discomfort that the headdress was causing, a snigger became a giggle and then they both dissolved into laughter until their sides ached.

"My people use the same word for being exhausted, euthanasia of an old or injured horse and the surgical deprivation of a creature's masculinity, which pretty well sums up Domini Antonius demeanour" commented Apollodorus, thoughtfully.

"I confess he did look as though he had just undergone the initiation rites into, what you eloquently refer to as, Mardian's rather exclusive club."

Their eyes met and Cleopatra raised one eyebrow quizzically, the shipwright responded by mirroring her expression and asked "Surely you would have been far more comfortable sleeping ashore, Thea?"

"Probably, but after a confrontation like that I need to sleep in your arms - and don't give me any of that dung about the risk!"

"With you in that sort of mood I wouldn't dare to argue!" replied Apollodorus with real feeling.

"Are you going to tell me I said far too much and how dangerous it was and…."

"Thea, you said all the things I have wanted to say and a lot more besides. To Hades with the risk, it's about time someone told the Romans a few painful truths" cut in Apollodorus then added "Please take that retched bird off of your head. Every time I try to kiss you I get a filthy look from the Vulture as though it wants to peck my eyes out." In one smooth movement Cleopatra took hold of the headdress and threw it aside then grabbed a handful of hair from the back of the shipwright's neck and they kissed passionately.

Apollodorus gradually became aware that Cleopatra had climbed up him and her legs were wrapped around his waist, somehow she had lost her clothes and soft hands were removing his kilt. There were more hands than Cleopatra could possess. Ebony hands were taking hold of his manhood and massaging it gently. Cleopatra's hands were around his neck holding him tightly; she was whispering something into his ear as Charmain guided him back onto the bed.

"Relax, my love" Cleopatra whispered as she straddled him and started to rock back and forth. "The final battle is over and we are now one body" she reassured him. Time and space collided and once again Apollodorus found himself on the beach at Cape Lochias, overhead was a full moon. The warm gentle breeze rustled the palm leaves and wild foul murmured in the background. Cleopatra moved up and down, the muscles of her vagina gripped his throbbing penis. Simultaneously they both arched their backs and cried out as orgasms racked their bodies. He held Cleopatra tightly and she nibbled his ears and neck as they lay, for some time, exhausted and bathed in perspiration.

Dawn was about to rise from the bed where she slept with her consort Tithonus as consciousness returned to the shipwright. He had been asleep in Cleopatra's arms in the middle of her large bed aboard the flag ship. Was last night a dream or had it really happened? Cleopatra pressed his head to her breast and he kissed her nipple which hardened in his mouth. When he next awoke he was alone and bright sunlight was streaming through the portholes, outside the birds were singing. The door to the cabin opened and Cleopatra came in followed by Charmain and Iras. All three looked supremely pleased with themselves as they arranged his favourite breakfast of smoked fish and scrambled eggs. The *Bassilisa* sat him up resting his head between her breasts as Charmain held the bowl of food and Iras fed him as though he were an invalid.

"Did I die during the night and is this paradise?" thought Apollodorus as he enjoyed the attention of the three beautiful women.

Throughout the Roman world ominous signs were reported; there was a massive bloody battle of dolphins off the African coast near the city of Aspis. A white bird carrying a laurel stem was dropped by an eagle into Livia's lap. Octavian's wife cared for the bird and planted the stem which took root. This was taken as a sign that Livia was destined to hold Octavian's power in her lap and dominate him in all matters.

Meanwhile Agrippa was fully occupied in Italy building new fleet for Octavian. Both men were in their mid twenties but unlike his commanding officer, Agrippa was a man although born to be first was content in being second to Octavian. He was descended from a provincial family with no naval tradition Agrippa had a formidable task changing the mind set of the Romans that the Pompey dynasty with their Greek Admirals ruled the waves. The young man had distinguished himself in Gaul and Germany, and like Octavian showed wisdom and cunning beyond his years.

The two men decided to build larger, heavier and stronger ships than those of Sextus. What they sacrificed in manoeuvrability was compensated for by the equipment they could carry and the additional marines. These ships were strong enough to withstand the trident rams, carried fighting towers and boarding bridges. To compensate for the inferior speed and manoeuvrability the harpex was developed. This was a specially adapted catapult that fired a grapnel. The problem of obtaining crew for these ships was resolved by giving twenty thousand slaves their freedom in exchange for their manning the rowing benches.

The Italian coastline had few natural harbours and Agrippa needed a secure base out of reach from Sextus, the location chosen was the 'Hell Mouth' mid way between Rome and the Messina Straits. A canal was cut from the Bay of Baiae and the Lucrien Lagoon then to the dark crater, Lake Avernus known to the Romans as the gateway to the underworld. The resulting wide inland waterway was an ideal base for shipbuilding and crew training and it was named Portus Julius. Mountain springs were naturally heated by the volcanic activity of the surrounding mountains. Steam was conducted through pipes into the people's homes to be used in their vapour baths.

From his forward base, two hundred miles from Sicily, on the Island of Aenaria off Cape Mesenum Sextus was able to attack the newly built ships as they emerged from the 'Hell Mouth'. To counter this, Agrippa ordered his engineers to cut a canal from Lake Avernus across the Misenum peninsular into the sea at Cumae. They drove a tunnel one thousand eight hundred cubits *(nine hundred metres or three thousand feet)* under the foothills of Mounte Corillo. While this work was being completed a statue of Ulysses, in the vicinity, was seen to be covered in moisture as though it was sweating.

"I thought it was only traditional for the Captain to tour his ship prior to a battle" said the ten year old Caesarion to Apollodorus as he fell into step with the shipwright as they walked slowly around Cleapatra's flag ship.

"This time it is a battle of words but I fear we will be involved in a battle of blood in the not too distant future" replied Apollodorus sadly.

"I thought Domini Antonius was our friend"

"He is, but even the best of friends quarrel at times."

"You and Ma have never argued."

"Marcus Antonius is not a man you could dislike" interjected Apollodorus hastily changing the subject. "Unfortunately he is picking a fight that he is unlikely to win when he has a far more serious threat that if he acted now he could destroy."

"What do you mean, *Geloto*?"

"The Parthians, according to legend, can only be defeated by an army led by a king. Egypt is being forced to support a cause that is of little concern to us and we are likely to make many more enemies than friends. Meanwhile, Octavius is preparing for another war against Sextus and from what I have heard he has learned from his mistakes and this time will win. The war against the Parthian will weaken Antonius while Octavius grows strong."

"So will Domini Antonius be coming back to Alexandria with us?"

"Not yet, he will be leading his army into battle. If he survives then no doubt we will have to entertain him again. Why?"

"He was such a show off last time. His club, 'The Inimitable Livers' had the most extravagant banquets. The palace kitchens had to prepare several dinners at intervals so one would be ready whenever Domini Antonius decided to eat and the rest was thrown away. Then there was the drunken fighting." The boy shuddered. "Promise you will not go away this time, Geloto."

"I have no intension of going away again."

"Will Ma take Domini Antonius as her consort?"

"She will have to, unfortunately."

"Then that Roman will be my Pater. Geloto I don't want him telling me what to do" the boy burst into tears so the shipwright bent down and put his arm round him. "Why can't you be Ma's consort? You don't order me around or get drunk!"

It was some time before the shipwright could think of a suitable reply. "Your mater is Bassilisa; I am an ordinary man in a foreign country and no warrior. Antonius can give her all the territories she desires and help to defend them from her enemies. You are Caesar's heir, and Rome belongs to you, with the help of Marcus Antonius we may be able to secure your birth-right. Also he is Alexander and Cleopatra's *Pater*."

"No he isn't, you are! I heard Ma say so!" exclaimed Caesarion tearfully.

"By Seths foul breath, what have I got myself into?" thought Apollodorus as he inhaled deeply, then aloud replied. "Your *Mater* didn't mean that I was literally their *Pater* but that I had acted as father in the absence of Domini Antonius. You know where babies come from and how they get there?"

The boy nodded so Apollodorus continued "Your brother and sister are the fruit of the loins of Antonius, as you are Caesar's. Surely you understand that?"

The boy nodded and in a manner that was frighteningly like that of Caesar. "I understand fully, *Kyrios* the *Geloto*, and what I have said I have said."

"Well, if Antonius survives the Parthians and comes to Alexandria while he is having meetings of 'The Inimitable Livers' I will be having meetings of my club of which you are a member."

Caesarion smiled again "What is your club called?"

"The Applied Cretinologists" announced the shipwright proudly "to be a member you have to do great deeds of utter stupidity that achieve a good and worthwhile end but above all in an amusing way that makes people laugh so no Romans are aloud to be members."

"Why is that?"

"Because Romans do stupid things that make people sad, like going to war so they can pay their troops. If they didn't go to war in the first place they wouldn't owe the troops any money so the troops wouldn't be troops they would be farmers and the citizens of Rome wouldn't be hungry."

"I like your logic, *Geloto*."

"I call it applied cretinology. I would far rather make people laugh than go to war so I would be a hopeless general. That is why your Mater needs men like Caesar and Antonius. Egypt is prosperous because we have managed to avoid any conflict for the whole of your lifetime."

"What have I done to be a member of your club?"

"The manner of your birth, which no one believes possible, is your qualification."

Mark Antony returned later that morning resplendent in his best uniform and Cleopatra received him in the pavilion but this time the front of the aft cabin of the flagship was closed, affording some privacy. The Bassilisa eyed him coldly as Mardian escorted the Roman inside. It is said that anger can never be re-kindled but the 'Lady of Two Lands' was obviously the exception to this rule.

"You slept well, your Highness?" inquired Antony, sheepishly.

"I am suitably rested but my displeasure is un-diminished" replied Cleopatra in the manner of a school mistress addressing an insubordinate pupil. "The last time you summonsed me to your presence and insisted that I, *Bassilisa* of all Egypt, the living embodiment of Isis and Lady of Two Lands should answer to your charges as though I were a common criminal. I explained how I had been acting discretely in your best interests. Had I not done so I would now probably have been discussing Egyptian support for Rome with Brutus and that pretender to the Julian dynasty would be no more!"

"What do you mean?"

"It was *Kyrios* the Apollodorus and my own wise council that helped you regain control of Rome after the assassination. Was it not *Kyrios mou* Apollodorus who recovered the body of Caesar? You are fully aware that Ptolemy Caesar is the rightful heir of Gaius Julius Caesar, not Octavius! Have you fulfilled your promise to force the Senate to acknowledge my son's birthright?" Antony shook his head sadly. "Also, you were fully aware that I was on your side against the conspirators and would have acted in your best interests at all times. If that were not so, what basis could we possibly have for any sort of alliance?"

Antony nodded then made what was probably one of the worst mistakes of his life by asking "On what basis would you form an alliance with me now, your Highness?"

"You will acknowledge Alexander and Cleopatra as your rightful heirs and return Egypt's former territories." Antony looked at her in disbelief as she continued. "If this is unpalatable to you, consider the alternatives."

"Which are?"

"For you none, for Egypt an alliance with Sextus Pompeius or the Parthians" replied Cleopatra and then smiled for the first time at him. "I have not met Sextus but I did meet his late *Pater* and found him most agreeable."

Antony looked across at Apollodorus who was standing by Cleopatra's side and again his mind went back to the scene on her Thalamegos as they were being pursued by what they had believed were enemy Trireme and the unconscious shipwright lay in the *Bassilisa's* arms. In public they were like brother and sister. What was their relationship? Were they in reality secret lovers? Why then had Apollodorus disappeared while he, Antony, wintered in Alexandria?" He became vaguely aware that Cleopatra was speaking to him again.

"Perhaps the hour is too early for you to make such a difficult decision? Did you have a heavy night last night in your worship of Dionysus, Dominus? I think it best we adjourn this meeting until the afternoon, do you not agree, *Kyrios* the Apollodorus?"

"There is a great deal for Domini Antonius to consider and perhaps he will need to confer with the other Triumvirates. Would you like me to begin preparations for our return to Alexandria as we have only a short time before the weather deteriorates….."

"I do not need to consult with anyone, I am Tyranni Orienus, Overlord of the East!" interrupted Antony angrily.

"I had not forgotten that you are master of half the Roman world" replied Cleopatra emphatically, and then continued sweetly "Caesar, of course, was master of all of it." Mark Antony's expression was like a camel chewing a porcupine garnished with scorpions and it was some time before he could reply.

"I met young Sextus Pompeius while I was living in Sicily" interjected Apollodorus "I considered him quite promising, he is the only Roman sailor of any consequence and defeated the fleet of Domini Octavius, some three hundred ships, with only forty Triremes. Would you like me to arrange a meeting your Highness?"

"I had quite forgotten that people used to refer to you as the Sicilian before we called you the *Gelotopoios, Kyrios mou*" replied Cleopatra with a look of wide eyed innocence that Apollodorus knew signified his friend was fully aware that he was lying about knowing Sextus. "You look unwell, Domini Antonius. Mardian fetch come cabbage water for his Lordship. I understand it to be most beneficial in cases of over indulgence" continued the first lady sweetly as she examined the Dyonistic amethyst ring Apollodorus had given her.

"Your Highness we had promised the children….."

"Thank you, *Kyrios* the Apollodorus, it had quite slipped my mind and it is so important to keep promises to the little ones, don't you agree, Domini Antonius. Children are far less forgiving than adults with respect to broken promises. You must excuse us, shall we say same time tomorrow?" she handed Antony a small scroll and continued; "These are my requirements, will a day be sufficient time for you to consider how best to implement them? You may leave!"

Mark Antony looked from Cleopatra to Apollodorus then back to the Bassilisa and nodded. He then turned abruptly and left muttering "Same time tomorrow."

"If he files that with the Vestal Virgins they will renounce their vows of chastity and take to the wine skins" commented Apollodorus dryly after a suitable time. They looked at each other and dissolved into laughter.

"So was the agreement lodged with the Vestal Virgins?" asked the actress. I nodded. "And ratified in matrimony?"
"That was the way of things in those days. Cleopatra didn't get all she demanded and Apollodorus would have the unenviable task of 'giving away' his Thea to Antony under the ancient rite of the Ptolemys."
The actress looked at me in horror then burst into tears.

Book 22

"There is something I want you to do for me without question, 'Pollo" announced the *Bassilisa* as she dined alone with Apollodorus. The shipwright could always gauge Cleopatra's mood by the way she addressed him. If she called him Apollodorus she was cross but 'Pollo meant she was serious and Geloto, fun loving. "We agreed that I would have to take Antonius as my consort so I want you to give me away in the ancient rite of the Ptolemys."

"What ancient rite?"

Cleopatra placed a finger over his lips "Without question" she ordered.

"I thought there was no such...."

Again Cleopatra cut in "Without question!"

"The Romans had weddings but no such ceremony existed in Egyptian culture. I think I am beginning to understand" said the actress with sudden realisation.

"She sought to fool the Romans, the gods and she even fooled us. It is generally accepted that she never married Caesar and it is a hotly debated issue if she ever married Mark Antony. The Romans knew of the prophecy of the despotic widow from the east who would humble Rome and usher in a new golden age, which is why they feared Cleopatra as much as they feared Hannibal before her."

"You beast!" exclaimed the actress as she started hitting me with a cushion. *"You made me cry for nothing!"*

"In return for you giving me away under the ancient rite of the Ptolemy's" continued Cleopatra "it is customary for me to give you something in return or, more to the point, some one."

Apollodorus protested but Cleopatra continued. "I will give you Charmain and Iras to be your concubines because in that way Antonius' suspicions about us will be allayed. Also it is the best way for me to make sure you don't go running off again. Before you ask if there is an alternative you always say how imaginative I can be with jewellery" she looked knowingly in the direction of his manhood.

"You wouldn't" protested Apollodorus looking anxiously in the same direction.

309

"I would!" replied the *Bassilisa* with a sinister grin. "Would you like to examine the artefact?" she continued sweetly.

"No thanks! I will take your word for it. Thea you have marked the sixteenth year of your reign by becoming very forceful and domineering."

"Yes, I suppose I have" replied Cleopatra innocently "Do you find it attractive?"

"Why do you ask questions that you know the answer to all too well? You are not an insecure little girl, you are *Bassilisa*."

"No, it is not insecurity, I just like hearing nice things about myself, that is no sin" replied Cleopatra with a smile, then she became serious. "You are always saying that in a world where you can lose you need to be able to win sometimes. The Romans refer to me as a wanton drunken whore; would you deny me the right to hear some nice things about myself from time to time to redress the balance?"

Apollodorus shook his head "The Romans don't know you as I do."

"No one knows me as you do, *Kyrios mou*" replied the Lady of Two Lands as their eyes met and the formality of her address caused the shipwright to shiver involuntarily. In common with latter day royalty, Cleopatra held the view that there were only two classes, royalty and others. As a consequence, from the lowest slave to the highest peer all were addressed in the same manner, by their name. To be addressed as *Kyrios*, the Greek for Lord with its spiritual undertone and subtle difference to the Latin Domini, marked a significant development in their relationship. One of Cleopatra's titles was 'lady of two lands' in Greek being '*Kyria dna Tohas*' so the implication was of equality. "That's settled then. I marry M.A who will get himself killed fighting the Parthians if we can't persuade him to get rid of Octavius" continued Cleopatra brightly. "If he defeats the Parthians his position with Octavius will be unassailable. If he loses, we tell Octavius that we knew he would but had no choice in supporting his futile quest."

"There are two things I am unhappy about. Firstly, I am not willing to enter into any formal arrangements with our handmaids, Charmain and Iras. They are lovely girls and I am very fond of them. If you think it will allay M.A's suspicions about us and you would feel happier with them keeping me company in bed in your absence, fine. I have told you and Caesarion that I will stay at your side, come what may! And further, if we are parted in some future battle while there is life in my body I will find a way of getting back to you. As you know I worship no gods so there is nothing I can swear by…"

Cleopatra put her index finger to his lips and then hugged him and added "Enough said, *Kyrios mou*. I believe and trust you, but secondly?"

"Secondly, there is the nightmare scenario. If Antonius is defeated but not killed in the war with the Parthians he will be considerably weakened, Octavius may then seize the opportunity to eliminate him."

"Antonius is far more popular than Octavius in Rome; the little runt wouldn't dare to go to war against him."

"I agree, but Octavius is devious, cunning, highly intelligent and learning fast, so much so that if his hand had been bitten off by a crocodile like the pirate in my story he would qualify as my nemesis. The thought processes of Octavius are strikingly similar to my own, he is preparing for another round with Sextus and has learned from his mistakes so will probably be victorious this time. From this position of strength he could attack a weakened Marcus Antonius by declaring war against you!"

Cleopatra felt her flesh crawl as realisation was beginning to dawn on both of them. "Is that the vision you had at Actium?" she asked.

Apollodorus nodded sadly "It could well be. If you are unable to persuade Antonius not to go to war with the Parthians, we must do all we can to secure and strengthen Egypt against Octavius."

"But Antony was stubborn and would not listen to reason" I explained. *"He was determined to invade the Parthian in deference to all other considerations and history was to be his judge."*

"Then two thousand years later my President and your Prime Minister did exactly the same thing" replied the Actress.

"And history, which has a nasty habit of repeating itself, will pass judgement on them also!"

"Kyrios and Kyria sound familiar?"

"For a good catholic like you I should hope so, 'Kirie eleison, Christe eleison, Kirie eleison. Lord have mercy, Christ have mercy, Lord have mercy. In Modern Greek Kyrios and Kyria correspond to Sir and Madam or Mr and Mrs but the spelling may be slightly different, domini or domina, depending on gender, implied master as opposed to servius or slave. The Disciples of Christ, according to the Greek gospels, addressed him as Despota, from which we get despot, as in despotic regime, and it implies tyrant or master of all. Cleopatra's method of address of both men was highly significant in its subtlety."

"So, my Lord," announced the actress. *"I shall call you Kyrios mou and you can call me Kyria mou if I am to be your Lady."*

Antony arrived on board Cleopatra's flag ship and was shown to the pavilion aft cabin.

"I will return Western Cilicia to you" he announced, "which should please Apollodorus, as it is the traditional Ptolemaic source of shipbuilding timber."

The shipwright bowed graciously and smiled.

"Cyprus?" asked Cleopatra.

"I confirm Caesar's order that Cyprus is returned to Egypt, also Chalchis and the non Jewish Decapolis, as a punishment for their support of the Parthian" continued Antony with an evil grin.

"How about Judea?" asked Cleopatra impatiently "and the seaports to the river Eleutheris?"

"I cannot give you Judea as the Senate has given that to Herod. However, he will surrender Jopin to you. Coele Syria and the seaports to the old Ptolemaic frontier at the Eleutheris are yours but Gaza is to remain with Judea to give Herod an outlet to the sea. Tyre and Sidon will continue to be free."

Cleopatra looked disappointed so Antony continued with a smile. "I know how you covet the prolific cropping date palms and balsam groves at Jerico."

"Mine?"

"Yours!"

"The bitumen deposit at the southern end of the Dead Sea?" enquired the shipwright, who had a vested interest. Bitumen was a caulking material in shipbuilding and was also a valuable insecticide.

"Malchus of Nabataei will hand over those deposits and a strip of land from the head of the Sinus Aelanites" replied Antony.

"The twins, Cleopatra and Alexander?" inquired the *Bassilisa*.

"They will be given the additional names Selene and Helios."

"So Alexander will be linked with the sun and maybe he will fulfil the ancient prophecy so long awaited by the people of both the east and the west" thought Cleopatra.

"May I now see the twins?" inquired Antony anxiously.

"You may but give them time; they are unlikely to accept you at first. The love of children has to be earned, Domini Antonius, it cannot be bought with territories"

Apollodorus excused himself while Mardian was sent to fetch the twins. Cleopatra gave him a knowing look as though to say "Domini

Antonius will have a hard job competing with your bed time stories." Later that evening they entertained Antony for dinner aboard the flag ship, the atmosphere was still tense. The pavilion aft cabin had been arranged in the traditional Roman manner with three couches each side of a square table but in deference to tradition Cleopatra reclined in the central triclinium flanked by the two men. As the 'Lady of Two Lands' described herself 'a rose between two thorns'. Charmain and Iras had served them from platters of gold encrusted with precious stones.

"Apollodorus has severe reservations about your proposals for your Parthian campaign and so do I" announced Cleopatra. "Perhaps you could explain, 'Pollo?"

"In short, Marcus, both Her Royal Highness and I consider Octavius a far greater threat to you than the Parthians. Time and time again he has broken agreements. He has accused you of duplicity when he is guilty of double dealing."

"I have been coming to a similar conclusion but the world is big enough for both of us. He has Rome and the west, I have the east. The Parthian invasion will expand my territory and strengthen my position. Octavius is planning another campaign against Sextus so with luck the son of Pompeius will finish him off this time" replied Antony.

"I am no gambler" explained Apollodorus cautiously "to gamble one has to be prepared to accept the consequence of losing."

"What 'Pollo is trying to say" interjected Cleopatra "is, have you considered the ramifications for all of us if you are vanquished?"

"Don't be ridiculous!" exclaimed Antony angrily.

"You are going into totally uncharted territory" continued Apollodorus. "My little country was able to push the mighty Caesar back into the sea, TWICE! Parthia is far bigger! If you fail and Egypt has supported you, where does that leave us in the eyes of Octavius? Surely you can see that his ambition is to be sole ruler of the Roman world. He will pick off each of us one at a time, first Sextus Pompeius, then Lepidus, then Marcus Antonius and finally Egypt. He is learning from his mistake as the latest preparations for invading Sicily bear testimony to. It would be far better for all of us for you to form an alliance with Sextus and get rid of Octavius. I don't think I need to remind you that Pompeius treated Fulvia, Julia and the children with great kindness when they fled from Rome to Sicily. The prescription of Sextus was totally unjust as he had no part in Caesar's murder."

Antony looked at Cleopatra who added "The last time 'Pollo was this adamant was when Caesar was about to be assassinated and in hindsight he had assessed the situation accurately. Together we could rid the world of Octavius then all Rome would be yours! You could take over Caesar's mantle and be Rex."

"I am much more than that already. I am a maker of kings" replied Antony scornfully. "Rome's greatness is in her giving of Realms rather than their annexation. I can contain Octavius, he is no threat!"

"Didn't the German establishment say that about the fledgling Nazi Party in the early twentieth century?" asked the actress.
I nodded.

"With the greatest of respect, Domini Antonius" replied Apollodorus calmly "the only way to contain Octavius would be for someone to enter his mind and pull his strings from within."

Cleopatra was about to ask if it was possible but a stern look from the shipwright made her refrain and diplomatically suggest "I think we have discussed political strategies enough for one day, let us not forget this is a reunion of old friends and talk of less weightier matters."

The two men conceded and the rest of the evening passed light heartedly and it was agreed that the Egyptian visitors would transfer to the palace accommodation the next day. After Antony had departed and Cleopatra was relaxing in the shipwright's arms the *Bassilisa* was able to ask.

"Is it possible to enter the mind of another person in the manner you suggested?"

"Possible, but inadvisable, as it would break every sacred rule and risk eternal damnation" replied Apollodorus. "When I briefly entered the minds of the guards to smuggle you into the palace to meet with Caesar I committed a grievous sin."

"But you did so for a good and honourable reason" argued Cleopatra.

"I know and just hope you will be there to present that mitigation when I come before whatever judgement awaits me!"

"Do you doubt it?"

"No" replied Apollodorus with a smile "I am relying on it!"

Cleopatra put her arms around his neck and her legs around his waist so there was no escaping her kisses "Octavius isn't your nemesis, he is your antithesis. He is motivated by selfish greed but you, Kirios mou, are motivated by what is best for everyone!"

Under Mardian's watchful eye the next morning Cleopatra's court was transferred to the palace.

"I think it may be as well if I stay aboard 'Bedroll II'. You know how badly I sleep ashore" suggested Apollodorus.

"You have no difficulty sleeping on Antirhodos!" replied Cleopatra in astonishment.

"You know that and so do I. However, Antonius does not! The children may need to sneak away for some non Roman quality time" explained Apollodorus with a smile.

"The *Bassilisa* may also…"

The shipwright placed his index finger over her lips and they embraced. "The arrangement should satisfy all our needs and avoid any tense situations. We will be stuck here for several weeks so it will be difficult for all of us. Presumably you will wish to entertain some of the local dignitaries on Egyptian soil and Mardian will appreciate my assistance."

"You don't need to convince me, I think it an excellent idea!"

"I know, but we do need to convince that muscle bound Hercules look-alike excuse for a consort of yours!"

"Domini Torus Maximus will believe whatever I tell him with respect to you, *Kyrios mou*" replied Cleopatra fiercely.

"*Kyria* the *Thea mou*, you must stop being so forceful, you know it makes me go all weak at the knees."

Cleopatra put her arms around his neck and kissed him softly then added "I like two things, making you weak at the knees and you calling me 'my Lady Goddess'. Domini Antonius will never make me feel as special as you do, *Kyrious* the *Theos mou*."

"How are the children taking to Antonius?" asked Apollodorus "I had a rather tearful session with Caesarion yesterday."

"I told him to give them time" replied Cleopatra evasively. "He has lost the ability to come down to their level like he did with Caesarion and my brother Ptolemy when we were in Rome."

"The way in which these Romans change when they get into their fifth decade! Do you think senility kicks in earlier than it does for the rest of us?"

"Marcus Antonius is only forty seven, but I take your point, 'Pollo" replied Cleopatra thoughtfully. "He has become impervious to reason and stubborn in his objectives, perhaps the way he drinks has affected his thought processes. You and he are a similar age but you think and act like you are my age" then she stopped abruptly and added. "I am sorry, 'Pollo, I didn't mean to offend you."

"No offence taken, Thea. Actually I am older than Antonius; my people enjoy a much greater longevity than the Romans, so in terms of percentage of lifespan I am his junior." He smiled at her broadly.

"When you smile like that you shed at least two decades. I never look on you as being older then me, 'Pollo."

"There is a rather rude saying" replied the shipwright with a twinkle in his eye.

"A man is as old as the woman he feels?" suggested Cleopatra coyly raising one eyebrow. "Unless, of course, if the man is a Roman. By the way, your presence is required at the feast Marcus Antonius is giving in my honour tonight. If it goes the way most Roman banquets degenerate, I expect you to give Charmain and Iras plenty of attention. This will save them being molested by drunken Centurions, allay the suspicions of Antonius with respect to us and more importantly, keep you young for me!" Apollodorus nodded but looked non-plussed. "What is the problem, 'Pollo? You did promise."

"I promised Caesarion that when there was a meeting of 'The Inimitable Livers' I would hold a meeting of the 'Applied Cretinologists'. He was rather upset by the behaviour of the Romans while in Alexandria."

Cleopatra hugged him then replied "That was sweet of you, 'Pollo. After tonight we will have to arrange things so you can keep that promise, but it may be difficult."

"The impossible we do right away…."

"Miracles take us a little time" interjected Cleopatra.

Cleopatra, who was dressed as Isis in long black clinging gown, and Apollodorus in a toga made their way to the palace. The shipwright had been granted by Caesar the privilege of Roman citizenship and its associated apparel. Apollodorus had expressed his doubts regarding the colour of the Bassilisa's dress as in his culture black was associated with death.

"The reverse is true in Egypt as the Nile flood brings with it black fertile mud and new life" responded Cleopatra. "You don't like my dress because you can't look at my breasts."

"A woman without breasts is like a ship without sails," replied the shipwright with a chuckle. "I can't look at Charmain and Iras' charms either."

They arrived at the palace at the eighth hour, in modern time's four o'clock in the afternoon and were greeted warmly, in the street, by Mark Antony. The traditional arrangement for dining was for nine people to recline on three couches or triclinium around a square table. The fourth side of the table was left open to facilitate serving, the dining room was also known as the triclinum. The Romans considered the optimum number for a dinner party to be nine however larger banquets were generally held in an open air hall or garden. Cleopatra's entourage of courtiers was extensive, as was Mark Antony's so consequently the banquet was set up in the palace gardens.

Mark Antony, as host, reclined at the locus summus, in the left hand couch at the top adjacent to Cleopatra who was to the left of the central couch, the meduis ismus, being the place of honour. The Bassilisa was flanked by her children, so Apollodorus reclined with Charmain and Iras at the meduis or right hand couch opposite Antony. A Roman dinner or Cena was in three phases; gustus, cena proper and secundae. There were seven courses, hors d'oeuvres, three entrees, two roasts and, finally, fruit.

Charmain offered Apollodorus a large platter of assorted cooked rodents. The shipwright looked at them doubtfully.

"I had forgotten just how disgusting a Roman banquet was! If this is the appetizer....."

"Don't be squeamish, *Geloto*" replied Charmain "you have lapine in Britannia, the only difference being they are much larger."

"Come on, *Geloto*, you eat meat" encouraged Iras.

"I know, but I have a problem when the dish still resembles the beast and particularly when it looks up at you from the platter with accusing eyes." He started pointing to the various carcases. Is that mouse? That is Guinea Pig and this is a rat! Do the Romans think I am *Bastet Theos* or one of the temple cats?"

"Well, there is one sacred cat that always makes a great fuss of you, *Geloto*" continued Iras "*Fengarafoto* look on you as one of his own people."

Charmain stroked the shipwright under his chin with her index finger. "Shut your eyes and have a nice crunchy dormouse. Just be thankful it isn't a snake."

"With the way my luck is running that will probably be one of the centa proper courses. This is dreadful. I can't even look at your charms to take my mind off of this ghastly ordeal! Why do Romans feel the need to drink cabbage water to make them vomit? I want to throw up just looking at the dishes!"

Caesarion had joined them and asked "Is it true that the Romans feed their horses with the babies of their enemies?"

Apollodorus laughed "No that is just a nasty rumour they put about after Britannia drove Caesar back into the sea." He fixed the boy with a fierce look. "My people feed our horses with Romans and our babies with our enemies horses!"

"Well, if you were fed on horse as a baby, why are you having so much difficulty with one small mouse?" asked Charmain with a wicked smile. "I think you should have dressed as a Britannic warrior, you look ridiculers in that bed sheet."

Apollodorus laughed, then nearly choked "I doubt if our prudish guests would have approved. You know how the Romans keep themselves covered up!"

"Why? How do your people dress for battle?"

"It's more a case of un-dress. A lot of purple body paint and a fierce expression is the usual uniform" replied the shipwright.

"Your people go into battle naked?" asked Iras with an enormous smile and Apollodorus nodded. "If I had known that I would have come with you when you travelled back to your homeland!"

"So would I!" added Charmain, enthusiastically.

"Now we know how your people drove Caesar back into the sea, it wasn't your superior armaments or battle strategy, it was the sight of all those well built warriors charging at them with their manly charms..." added Iras.

"Swinging?" suggested Charmain helpfully.

"I was going to say threatening" continued Iras.

"I really don't think we should be having this kind of conversation in front of Caesarion. He is only eleven" interrupted Apollodorus.

"Nonsense! He is nearly a man" replied Charmain. "You aren't embarrassed, your Highness?" The boy shook his head.

"I like hearing about your land, *Geloto*. Will you take me there some time?"

"Are you enjoying yourselves?" asked Cleopatra who had joined them.

"The food is questionable but the conversation has been enlightening" replied Apollodorus.

"Did you know that *Geloto's* people go into battle naked and their bodies are coloured with purple war paint, Madam?" asked Charmain.

"You never told me, *Kyrios mou!*" replied Cleopatra in astonishment. "So that was what all the laughter was about."

"The funny part was Charmain's suggestion that I should have dressed as a Britannic Warrior not a Roman citizen." Cleopatra looked at each of the handmaids in turn, then at Apollodorus her green eyes twinkling.

"Well, if you ever lead us into battle I shall expect you to be appropriately undressed, *Kyrios mou*" she added with a chuckle. In less than five years Cleopatra would remember this light-hearted exchange with considerable sadness. As the meal progressed food and wine flowed freely. Toasts were proposed on the slightest pretext and the guests were expected to drain their goblet in one breath. Music and dancing was provided by professional entertainers. Comical dwarfs, known as cretins, had been hired to make everyone laugh and the sillier they were the more the Romans liked them. As the evening progressed and the guests became increasingly intoxicated, fistfights broke out, so Apollodorus decided it was time for Cleopatra's children to leave.

"Thank you for rescuing me, *Geloto*" said Caesarion. "Domini Antonius was trying to make me drink wine; he said it would make a man of me."

"It is manlier to say no to the things we don't want to do and takes greater courage. If you don't enjoy wine, don't drink it! Look at the effect it had on the Romans, they were drinking to get drunk not to enjoy the fruit of the vine. The way they treat those dwarfs is appalling, christianus means deformed and challenged but none the less human, not a beast. Just because their gods have seen fit to dim the light of their wisdom is no excuse to use them as figures of fun." They departed as the gladiators arrived. "We could not have timed our departure better" added Apollodorus. "Charmain and Iras, you can look after the children but it will be impolite for me not to return to the banquet." Turning to the children he asked "Would you prefer to sleep on the flag ship tonight rather than in the palace? With all those drunken Centurions rampaging around you will sleep better afloat."

"You have rescued us" commented Charmain "but how can you rescue her Royal Highness."

"I can't. The best I can do is stay with the *Bassilisa* giving moral support and try to resist the temptation to punch M.A as he gropes and drunkenly molests her."

By the time Apollodorus returned to the feast, Antony was unable to stand.

"You must help me put his Lordship to bed" whispered Cleopatra as he arrived.

"He will be incapable of any intimately demands tonight" replied the shipwright as he dragged the Roman to his feet.

"That was the general idea!" replied the Bassilisa.

Apollodorus looked at Cleopatra in surprise and nearly dropped the semi-conscious Antony. "Did you get him drunk deliberately, Thea?"

"We agreed that was what I would do when we pretended to send Antonius reinforcements before the battle of Philippi five years ago."

"I had quite forgotten you had said that you would entertain our friend most lavishly so he would be rarely capable of having you!" Between them they partly dragged and partly carried Mark Antony to his chamber and dumped him unceremoniously onto the bed. "So are you coming back to Bed Roll II with me?"

"I should love to but I must stay with Antonius tonight. Don't worry, *Kyrios mou*, I will be perfectly safe. You go back to Charmain and Iras."

"If it is your intention to keep Antonius in a semi-permanent state of inebriation while you are with him it would save a great deal of trouble if you had Olympos mix a supplement to add to his goblet...." Cleopatra coloured red. Apollodorus looked at her incredulously and continued. "You didn't?" Cleopatra looked down and nodded. "You did!" Apollodorus laughed. "Thea you are a demon not a goddess." He put his arms around her and they kissed passionately.

"As I recall you once said that you love a girl with initiative" replied Cleopatra defensively. "You had better get back to Charmain and Iras or I shall have to put a supplement in your goblet. It is imperative that we keep up the subterfuge, Kyrios mou."

"*Kali nichti, mikro daimouas*. Good night my little demon" replied Apollodorus and reluctantly made his way back to the flag ship thinking "I wonder if you have been spiking my drink, Thea. There are some strange gaps in my memory as though things are not quite as they appear." The sight of the beautiful naked handmaids as he came aboard dispelled thoughts of intrigue.

"Welcome back to Egypt, *Kyrios mou*" said Charmain seductively.

"A goblet of honey mellowed wine, *Geloto*?" inquired Iras innocently as she handed him the drink "to take away the taste of rodent."

He accepted the drink and thought "whatever you are up to, my little demon, as an absolute monarch there is nothing I can do to resist so if it is inevitable I may as well lie back and enjoy myself." He looked at Iras then to Charmain and said "*Yeia soo*!" then drained the goblet in one breath.

Antigonus the Parthian puppet king deposed by Herod was held captive in Antioch and his presence had become a rallying point for all disaffected Jews. Antony, mindful of the risk of civil unrest had the unfortunate man bound to a cross, flogged and then executed. This was a punishment no other monarch had suffered at the hands of the Romans.

"It has set a terrible precedent, the execution of royalty. First it was my sister Arsinoe, now Antigonus" confided Cleopatra to Apollodorus when they were alone, "who will be next? The manner by which the Romans perform capital punishment, on the sacred Ankh Cross of immortality, beggars belief."

"I shouldn't have thought the theological considerations were uppermost in poor Antigonus' mind as his flesh was ripped from his back by the lash followed by his limbs being slowly torn from their sockets as he hung dying."

"Do you have to be so graphic in your descriptions, 'Pollo" replied Cleopatra with a shudder.

"I am sorry, Thea. I was just thinking that that would be the fate awaiting us if we fail."

Cleopatra was thoughtful then announced; "*Kyrios mou*! I want you to make me a promise" she held both his arms and looked up into his blue eyes. "If your nightmare scenario vision becomes a reality," she hesitated and swallowed hard then continued. "In the event of the unthinkable and Egypt being vanquished, you must kill me then Charmain, Iras and finally yourself, thereby depriving the Romans their macabre satisfaction."

"I don't know if I could bring myself to harm you or our handmaids but if it would save you from crucifixion" he hesitated. "To end one's own life is the ultimate sacrilege, the punishment for which would be to spend eternity re-living all the events leading to the decision to commit suicide." Then he thought "if I were to do your bidding, who would take care of the children or would I have to kill them also?"

Cleopatra interrupted his thought. "You must act quickly and unexpectedly. Give me no warning!"

From the depths of Hadies a Hippopotamus wallowed in a pool of molten lava and through the fumes of sulphur could be heard the anguished cries of countless tormented souls. Seth watched, his eyes glowing red and a smile of satisfaction crossed his huge mouth.

"In making that promise your fate is sealed my noble Jester and so is that of your Goddess. You feasted on the flesh and blood of my people but soon, soon you and also all the people of your miserable world will be mine to devour, the gods will abandon Alexandria then the Ptolemy's and the Cleopatra's will be no more and with their passing none will mediate with their gods for the continued prosperity of Egypt!"

Elsewhere in a vast cavern where the sun sets to begin its night time subterranean journey, Gluton was impassive as he made his meticulous entries into his hairy hide covered book.

Book 23

Apollodorus awoke with a start. The cabin was in near darkness and what little light there was came from the moonlight that filtered through the portholes.

"What is it, my Lord?" inquired Iras softly. She placed her hand gently on his chest. "I think you were having a bad dream but I could not understand what you were saying. Did you know you talked in your sleep?"

"Can you help me light the lamps, please, Iras" replied the shipwright. Charmain was also now awake.

"It is all right, Charmain, Lord *Geloto* was having a bad dream" reassured Iras. It was clear that both handmaids were very concerned but it was not their place to question Apollodorus.

"You will not ask so I will tell you anyway. Have you ever had a dream that is so realistic that you wake up uncertain what is reality, the dream or being awake?"

The handmaids looked puzzled.

"I have a recurring dream that I am in some sort of cavern filled with smoke, people are screaming in the background and there are pools of molten larva. Strange creatures are accusing me of wrong doing and it is as though I am on trial but I don't know what crimes I have committed."

"It sounds awful!" interrupted Charmain.

"It sounds like Hades!" added Iras.

"It feels as though that nightmare is real, but this" he gesticulated around him, "all this is almost unreal. I sometimes feel as though I have been here before or that I am living a dream, someone else's dream. Do either of you go to places that you know you have never been to but they are strangely familiar?" He put his arms around the handmaids. "I am sorry I am frightening you, ladies, it was just a bad dream, let's get back to sleep." He lay back and the two handmaids snuggled up to him.

"That Autumn Apollodorus handed over to Antony a large sum of money by way of a dowry as was the custom of matrimony"

"What happened if the bride's family were poor?" asked the actress.

"If the family could not afford a dowry the girl remained un-married or could become the concubine of a rich man with the means to support an extended family. For this reason Charmain and Iras could become concubines to Apollodorus but not marry as they had no family to pay the large sum of a dowry. The Romans viewed marriage to a foreigner as in-

valid in law so Antony's marriage to Cleopatra would have caused no disquiet and would have been regarded as a convenient means of extracting the funds for the Parthian campaign."

"So is that why it is questionable as to whether the marriage of Cleopatra to Antony ever took place?"

"From the Roman perspective it did not happen and in the absence of a tabloid press publicising the politicians every indiscretion the citizens would have neither known nor cared. The money Cleopatra gave Caesar was by repayment of her father's debt so from her perspective she was his concubine not his wife. Any money she gave Antony would have been regarded as a dowry so she would have considered herself married to him."

"Is that why there is a general reluctance among men to let a girl pay her way even today?"

"That is a very interesting point, you could be correct. In the Anglican Church traditional language marriage ceremony, the bride gets all the groom's worldly goods but has to obey him. In the modern version, however, the word 'obey' is omitted and the possessions are shared."

The Roman year came to an end and Mark Antony invited Aristobulus, Herod's brother-in-law, to Antioch.

"He says the man is too young to make the perilous journey" ranted Antony as he read the reply.

"I should think that he is afraid the youth will share the fate of Antigonus" replied Cleopatra coldly.

"Antigonus was executed at the behest of Herod, why should I harm his brother-in-law?"

"In that case he probably wants to keep an eye on him himself, Herod's realm is far from secure" added Apollodorus.

"You would have been far better off giving Judea to me; under Egyptian rule the country would be peaceful and prosperous. Herod will have to instigate a massive fortification program so there will be little spare cash to pay taxes and tributes to Rome!"

"How many times do I have to tell you" shouted Antony angrily "the Senate has made Herod Rex of Judea there is nothing I can do about it!"

"Yes there is" replied Cleopatra equally angrily "give up this futile quest against the Parthian! Rid the world of Octavius and be Imperator of all Rome! Then you can do as you wish!"

Apollodorus had positioned himself between Antony and Cleopatra, fearful that they were going to come to blows. The powerful Roman picked up the shipwright and threw him aside; the impact against the wall rendered him momentarily unconscious.

"How dare you manhandle my *Kyrios* the Apollodorus like that!" screamed Cleopatra as she slapped Antony around the face. The Roman was about to retaliate but was stopped by the shipwright flying across the room like a tiger. Antony felt his life slipping away as Apollodorus held him in a vicelike strangle hold. Despite Antony's superior strength there was no escape, the man on top of him had an expression of utter ruthlessness.

"Apollodorus let him go!" pleaded Cleopatra.

Three centurions burst into the room and dragged Apollodorus of the barely conscious Antony. Two soldiers held the shipwright while the third drew his sword. Cleopatra screamed. Apollodorus twisted around, the two centurions were sent flying in opposite directions then he took hold of the third soldier's sword arm and in one smooth movement disarmed the unfortunate man hurling him through the window. Apollodorus turned again towards Antony who was struggling back onto his feet, the shipwrights eyes were not their usual blue they had changed to steely grey. Cleopatra had only once seen him look like this, when they were confronted by an Egyptian Cobra at Askalon. Further centurions arrived but it was the *Bassilisa* who did what the soldiers were unable to do.

"Apollodorus don't do it, Antonius is our friend!" she whispered.

The centurions held him and he made no attempt to escape, Mark Antony faced him.

"For that I could have you flogged and crucified" he tried to sound angry but it came out as a croak.

"With the might of your troops you may succeed, but one to one, never! Remember this Domini Antonius while you are fearful of one small bum boy I am prepared to take on the entire military might of your army to protect the one I...." He hesitated "to protect the *Bassilisa* and her unborn child."

The two men faced each other unblinking for what seemed an eternity but it was probably only a heartbeat, Antony was next to speak, turning towards Cleopatra. "Is this true?" he demanded.

The *Bassilisa* nodded and thought "True on both counts but how did you know I was pregnant, I have only just discovered that myself."

He faced the shipwright and whispered "Forgive me."

Apollodorus smiled for the first time and nodded. "We both got a little hot under the toga."

"Release him men, say nothing of these events" ordered Antony "you are dismissed."

When they were alone again Apollodorus added "I think we should both apologise to her Royal Highness for behaving like hooligans. Antonius I am sorry I nearly killed you."

"I deserved it! Apollodorus you are the most peaceful man I have ever known but when angered…" he hesitated then added with real feeling. "Jocus, if you ever get bored with building ships you can always have a job teaching my men to fight unarmed like that! I doubt I had enough centurions to hold you down."

Cleopatra stepped forward and placed a small hand around each mans upper arm. She could feel that Antony was relaxed but Apollodorus muscles were as hard as iron. "Will you two boys shake hands and make up please?" Gradually Apollodorus relaxed and the two men embraced.

Some time later Cleopatra boarded her flag ship and found the shipwright sitting in the forecastle repairing some rigging.

"I thought I would find you here 'Pollo. What are you doing?"

"Splicing rope is very therapeutic; it helps me to calm down. Is M.A at the wine skins boasting to his troops how he was about to overcome me when they intervened?"

She sat next to him, took hold of his arm and rested her head on his strong shoulder. "*Kyrios* the Apollodorus *mou, Geloto* why are you such a man of mystery?"

"There is no mystery I am just a rather short tempered shipwright."

"You would have killed the whole of the army of Antonius for me; you fought in a manner I have never seen, it was almost like dancing. Where did you learn such skills?"

"Thea, I honestly don't know! I was momentarily back in a strange land far away. A land like no other where the people have yellow skin and slanted eyes."

"You are not telling the children stories now!" protested Cleopatra.

"It is no story. I was there a long time ago, maybe in another life time. There are paintings of ferocious dragons on the walls and the people eat lots of rice."

"Now I know you are telling stories…"

"I have these strange visions…"

"Charmain and Iras said you had been having nightmares."

"They shouldn't have told you" there were tears in his eyes.

"What is it, 'Pollo?" entreated the Bassilisa.

"I have done something terribly wrong!"

"What is it?"

"I don't know! I am being punished but I don't know what for. Thea! Can you ever forgive me?"

"Of course I forgive you for whatever you think you have done wrong!" She held him tightly and thought "What is it that troubles you my love? What torments are you enduring that prevent you from saying what I so long to hear?"

In a vast deep cavern far below Lake Serbonis, the lagoon east of the Nile delta, something began to stir, its top half was human but below its waist in the place of legs were vicious vipers. The Typhon had been born at the dawn of time, this vile creature had been sired by Ge, whose anger was the greatest following the defeat of the giants. Born of Tartaros in Cilicia the creature was taller than the highest mountain and its arms could reach from east to west. The arms were covered with hundreds of dragon heads and its body with wings. Fire flashing eyes were topped by filthy long hair. The Typhon had attacked the heavens by hurling flaming rocks forcing the god's flight to Egypt where they transformed themselves into animals. Zeus became a ram; Apollo a crow; Dionysus a goat; Hera a white cow; Artemis a cat; Aphroditi a fish; Ares a boar and Hermes an Ibis.

Athena alone stood her ground taunting her father with cowardice, Zeus known to the Romans as Jupiter, being the senior and most powerful of all the gods was the only one with the strength to stand against this new menace. Having resumed his true form he countered the attack with thunderbolts and chased the creature across Syria; they met in hand to hand combat over Mount Casion where Zeus was seriously injured. The gather of clouds retreated to Mount Olympus. When Zeus had recovered he harnessed winged horses to his chariot and once again pursued the Typhon. At Mount Nysa the Fates tricked the Typhon into tasting the ephemeral fruits so Zeus was able to vanquish the creature at Mount Haimos in Thrace. It is said that the power of evil can never be truly vanquished; only contained, to await an opportunity and re-emerge from its prison when the time is ripe.

While Antony prepared for the invasion of the Parthian, Octavian and Agrippa built ships and trained their crews for the final conflict with Sextus Pompey. The huge civil engineering works were completed in a very short space of time which was testimony to Octavian's determination and the skill of his engineers. The remains of Portus Juius and the tunnel under Mount Corillo would still be visible two thousand years later.

Armenia was invaded by Roman troops under the command of Legiti Canidius, the defeated King Artavasdes transferred his allegiance from Parthia to Rome so was permitted to retain his throne and the invading army wintered there in preparation for the Parthian invasion. Orodes the Parthian king died of old age. His eldest son Parorus had been killed when the Romans, under the command of Ventidius, defeated the occupying Parthian forces. Phraortes, Orodes youngest son, became king and being fearful of rivals for the crown murdered his brother's children prompting many of the noblemen to flee the country. One of these nobles was Monaeses who arrived in Antioch. Although the hour was still early Antony had been drinking for some time and was being entertained by actors and dancers when Fonteius Capito announced that Monaeses was requesting an audience.

"Let him wait" replied Antony angrily.

"With respect, Dominus Antonius" replied Capito. "I understand that this man is of some consequence in Parthia and his fortune is comparable to that of Themistoces and the Persian kings."

Antony's attitude changed abruptly "You had better show him in so we can find out what he has to offer."

"Domini Antonius" began Monaeses in broken Latin. "King Orodes has died, his youngest son Phraortes is now king."

"I am fully aware of that" replied Antony impatiently.

"What you may not know, Dominus, is that Phraortes' hold on the western marshlands is tenuous. These marshes form a key defence of Parthia."

While Antony was occupied, Cleopatra seized the opportunity to slip away to her flag ship. Her handmaids had secretly delivered a message from Apollodorus that he wished to see her in a matter of some urgency. The shipwright had been preoccupied for several days spending much of his time on maintenance of the ships or lonely walks. She knew from experience that he was best left alone when he was in that frame of mind so was delighted to receive the message. Her excitement increased as she boarded the trireme and Apollodorus instructed the handmaids to ensure they were not disturbed. When they were below deck and had kissed passionately the shipwright said.

"I need to talk to you as much as I need to hold you in my arms, Thea."

"Charmain and Iras said you have been rather preoccupied for some time. Have you now resolved that which has been troubling you, Kyrios mou?"

"Some things are beginning to fall into place. I now have a rather unlikely theory which at first I dismissed."

"I had better keep my clothes on in that case" replied Cleopatra looking disappointedly at her friend.

"We may not have much time" replied Apollodorus as his hands caressed the back of her neck and her dress slid to the ground as if by magic. "So we had better talk intimately."

"How did you do that, *Geloto*?" asked Cleopatra between kisses.

Apollodorus gave her a wicked smile. "It isn't just ships that I design. I thought your Roman wardrobe also needed the attention of my genius."

"So what else has your fertile imagination been applying itself to?"

Apollodorus picked up the naked *Bassilisa* and carried her into the bedroom so they could recline in comfort. They took turns to kiss each others' bodies and with their physical passion partly satisfied were able to discuss more serious matters.

"I have really missed you, Thea, but I must tell you what I have reasoned then we can satisfy each other." Reluctantly, Cleopatra conceded so the shipwright continued. "Do you remember how we suspected that Antonius may have been responsible for the death of his wife, Fulvia?" Cleopatra nodded as she took hold of the shipwright's penis and caressed it gently. "From what I have learned Fulvia was, in reality, consul. If she was as powerful as I am lead to believe, she was the brains behind the brawn of the Anton brothers. Jules arranged the marriage of Antonius to Fulvia as a means to control his wild behaviour, very wisely in my opinion. Fulvia and Octavius were bitter enemies, she realised the threat posed by the little runt and was trying to contain or eliminate him."

"So what you are saying is Octavius sought to neutralise Antonius by eliminating Fulvia" replied Cleopatra with sudden realisation. Apollodorus nodded then kissed her nipples. Although Cleopatra was enjoying his administrations she grabbed a handful of his hair from the back of his head and gently pulled him up so she could make eye contact. "If Octavius realised that Antonius could be manipulated via an intelligent woman he could manipulate him through his sister."

Apollodorus nodded again and said "Precisely!"

"What was that Gallic expression that means treading in dung?"

"So far you are in clear water, Thea; you have reluctantly done the bidding of Antonius. You made it clear from the outset that you had no wish to be involved in the Parthian campaign by negotiating a ridiculously high cost for Egyptian support. If M.A was stupid enough to pay that high price it is hardly your problem. The future of Octavius is far from certain as is that of Antonius."

"That's a relief; you can carry on kissing me."

"With pleasure, but how could Octavius have killed Fulvia without it looking like murder?"

"Snakes can be milked of their venom. With something as poisonous as the Uraeus, a tiny drop in her food would be undetectable until it was too late. Her death would be dismissed as common food poisoning."

"Surely her food is tasted by her servants for precisely that reason?"

"It would take a while for the venom to be absorbed into the bloodstream. If the taster didn't go into convulsions immediately it would be assumed the food was safe to eat."

"Sextus and Octavius are evenly matched so there is a fifty, fifty chance that the problem of the little runt will go away but somehow I doubt it. With respect to Antonius his battle plan with the Parthian is…." He hesitated lost for the right words so Cleopatra obliged with a colourful metaphor.

"His battle plan is as the rags the Romans use to wrap their private parts" she interrupted as she massaged his testicles as well as his penis so there was no doubt about the meaning.

Apollodorus laughed. "So that is why they have so much difficulty in the latrine. I can't understand why they call their manhood private, they can't control their libido yet they regard the equipment of intimacy with such shame. Yes his battle plan is linteus lumbus. Last autumn he should have advanced to Zeugma, where the Euphrates is nearest the Mediterranean and mustered the troops. They will be exhausted by the march and could have rested during the winter then made their attack in the spring."

"How far is it to Zeugma?" asked Cleopatra.

"Eight thousand furlongs, about a thousand Roman miles!"

"One hundred and thirty schoenus! By Seth's foul breath, the troops will arrive at Zeugma feeling like a eunuch who has just been initiated into the brotherhood! So what are the chances of Antonius being victorious?"

"Non-existent, which with the even chances of Octavian failing against Sextus means the possibility of Egypt being dragged into a conflict between the Triumvirates is diminishing. I would add a word of caution. If

Octavius has been manipulating M.A via Octavia, your coming back on the scene will have scuppered his plans. He may well consider you to be a very unwelcome influence on his co-Triumvirate."

"But I have failed miserably to influence Antonius."

"I know that and we may have to explain this to Octavius in simplistic terms at some stage in the future. However, overall our situation looks considerably brighter and my nightmare scenario is now highly unlikely."

"That is a cause for celebration" exclaimed Cleopatra.

"I have had more of my fill of un-seasonal quaffing and feasting over the past few weeks, thank you" replied Apollodorus with a smile.

"Perhaps I can invite you to quaff from a chalice that no one else is allowed to sup from" replied the *Bassilisa* as she rolled over onto her back. In one smooth movement she ran a hand down her side then slowly opened her legs. She gently stroked her inner upper right thigh seductively as she smiled at the shipwright.

"I will give due consideration to all you have said" replied Antony. "In the mean time you will stay as my guest here in Antioch." Turning to an aid he continued "make the necessary arrangements and accommodate Domini Monaeses here in the palace."

"Do you trust him?" enquired Capito when the Parthian had departed.

"I have no need to place any trust in that man. However, he will prove to be useful. The defection of so many noblemen undoubtedly will cause Rex Phraotes much anxiety so he will make overtures of conciliation to Monaeses and bribe him into returning. I will give Domini Monaeses three cities of little consequence and send a message with him offering friendship in exchange for the return of the lost eagles and prisoners. The invasion will continue as planned."

"Antony was now in a position to negotiate terms for the return of the prisoners and military insignia, Roman honour would have been satisfied."

"I take it that he remained as stubborn as ever and in the words of your hero failed to see beyond the end of his big, fat, Roman nose" replied the actress.

"Sadly like Pompey and Caesar before him he ignored the long term advantages of securing the eastern frontier in favour of fame and glory."

The tip of Apollodorus' tongue probed Cleopatra until he found her most sensitive spot. In her mind she travelled forward in time to a special place among the palm trees that lined the beach of the Cape Lochias royal harbour.

On deck of the Royal Trireme the two handmaids gave each other knowing looks as they heard the muffled cries of pleasure from their mistress.

"If the Gustus is that enjoyable" commented Charmain. "I wonder if we will ever know such ecstasy."

"Our *Kyrios* only has eyes for the *Bassilisa* and is still uncomfortable with some of our more intimate customs and pleasures" replied Iras sadly.

"Perhaps when the final battle is over we may all find true happiness" added Charmain thoughtfully.

Helios began his decent to the Beautiful West and aboard the flag ship Apollodorus was playing with Caesarion and the twins. Cleopatra and the two handmaids were with them. It is said that truth comes out of the mouths of babies and small children and Cleopatra's daughter Selene asked a question that was on all of their minds.

"*Geloto*, what is true happiness? Where can it be found?"

"That is a really good question" replied the shipwright thoughtfully. "Once upon a time there was a Pharaoh who believed himself to be the happiest man alive so he went in search of a wise man to get proof of his belief."

"If he believed he was that man why did he need proof?" asked Caesarion.

"That is a very good question" continued Apollodorus. "The wise man realised that the Pharaoh wanted proof of his belief but refused to flatter him so answered 'An Athenian named Tellas, he had fine sons, wealth and a glorious death. He died in battle and his enemy honoured his bravery by giving him a public funeral where he fell.' The Pharaoh was disappointed so asked 'who was the second happiest man?'

"The wise man replied. 'There were two young men from Argos, Cleobus and Biton. During the festival of Hera it was important that the mother of the two men should be driven to the temple. They could not find suitable animals to pull the cart so being young and strong pulled the cart themselves. At the temple the townsfolk congratulated them on their strength and told the mother how lucky she was. The mother prayed to Hera to give her sons the greatest blessing.' After the feast the young men fell asleep never to awake again. Great statues were erected in their memory. The Pharaoh did not like the answer so asked. 'So what of my happiness?'

"The wise man answered 'The gods are envious of human prosperity and delight in troubling us. Time passes and the seasons come and go no one day is like another. The rich are better able to cope with adversity than the poor, consequently the poor avoid trouble. If we are lucky we have many blessings; freedom, health good looks and fine children. A person thus blessed if he dies as he has lived deserves to be called happy, until then he is not happy only lucky.' What the wise man was saying was that while we live we strive for more and no matter how many blessings we have we are never content. Blessings are not only given they can be taken away from us. While we live we have glimpses of happiness but cannot be judged truly happy until we are dead. Happiness is diametrically opposite to pleasure and they are all too often mutually exclusive."

"That is ridicules, pleasure and happiness are one and the same" retorted Cleopatra.

"Most people would agree with you, Thea, and they deceive themselves. The transitory pleasure of quaffing and feasting is followed by the discomfort of a hangover and in the long term the misery of obesity."

Antony's army advanced alongside the Euphrates following the river's great sweep north east to Carana and he ordered Canidius to move his forces from their winter headquarters near Artaxata to meet him at Carana by the middle of June. In the southern foothills of Caucasus the Albanians and Iberians made raids on the field army of Canidius but they were not a viable threat and offered little resistance. Meanwhile, in Rome, Octavia, the sister of Octavian, gave birth to her second daughter sired by her husband Mark Antony.

At the same time in the Parthian throne room Lord Monaeses was warmly greeted by the monarch.

"What news of the Roman infidel and his Egyptian whore, my friend?" asked King Phraortes.

"On the one hand, Lord Antonius has promised me the Parthian throne, your Highness and as a down payment given me lands in eastern Syria including the cities of Larissa, Arethusa and Hierapolis" replied Monaeses.

"And on the other?" prompted the king, smiling wickedly.

"On the other he sends messages of friendship and says that you and he can be good friends living in peace and harmony if only you return the Roman Eagles and prisoners captured in the war with Marcus Crassus."

Both men laughed and the king replied "In the meantime his forces continue to muster at Carana. And Cleopatra?"

"Cleopatra is making her way to Judea to take possession of territories given to her by Lord Antonius. King Herod will not be well pleased by the generosity of his patron so with luck will find a way to eliminate the harlot, then the throne of Egypt will once again be vacant and you will be able to restore the lands to Parthia taken by that Macedonian infidel Alexander."

Admiral Menas, who had defected to Octavian only to change allegiance back to Sextus, arrived off Mylae in the aftermath of the storm to find Octavian's fleet in chaos. Sextus regarded Menas with suspicion and had neither given him a command or permitted him to engage the forces of Lepidus on Sicily. Once again Menas defected to Octavian who welcomed his expertise but like Sextus did not extend him any trust. With the assistance of Menas, Agrippa's fleet was repaired and then made its way south to join the ships loaned by Antony at Lipara. Octavian returned to Italy to supervise the transportation of infantry to Sicily. The fleet of Sextus anchored off Messana to counter Octavian and the Pompeian Admiral Demochares anchored his fleet off Mylae to counter Agrippa's ships.

"Once more into the breach, dear friend!" quoted the actress.
"Cry havoc and let loose the dogs of war!" I replied.
"Time for another cup of Assam? Yes, I know, is the Pope a Catholic?"

Off the coast of Sicily, at Mylae, the fleets of Agrippa and Demochares tested each other's strength but were reluctant to risk a full scale engagement.

"The Pompeian squadron commanded by Demochares are in home water and have no need to risk an engagement, they know it is only a matter of time before the weather will fight their battle for them" said Menas.

"I don't know how many ships they have, we may be outnumbered. Do you know the size of the fleet?" replied Agrippa.

Menas shook his head, and then added with ill concealed sarcasm "Why not go and look, Dominus? You could take a small contingent of your best triremes as a reconnaissance to arrive at the haven around dusk when they will be off their guard."

"An excellent idea, Menas. You can show us the way, but be warned; at the first sign of treachery and I will kill you myself!" exclaimed Agrippa.

Book 24

It would be said in hindsight that Mark Antony was no Caesar and this now manifested itself in his lack of attention to detail and preference for hedonistic, over practical, pursuits. In order to hasten his advance on Carana, he had left behind his slow moving support vehicles and the artillery equipment they carried. This included three hundred auxiliary carts, engines of battery and, critically, a fifty cubit long battering ram (*twenty five metres*). The equipment and its associated manpower of twenty thousand men were in the command of Legiti Oppius Statianus and their ally King Polemon of Pontus with instructions to follow the main army.

King Artavasdes of Armenia advised Antony to attack his namesake King Artavasdes of the Mede. The Median king had gone to the assistance of the other Median monarch King Phraortes but the whole region approaching the Euphrates, contrary to expectations, was well guarded. Consequently, Antony laid siege on the Median principal city of Phraata and royal residence. The city wall was strong and well protected so the citizens and royal family were in little danger from such a poorly equipped enemy. There were no trees large enough in Asia to replace the battering ram left behind, so realising the Roman's tactical blunder, King Phraortes and his ally King Artavasdes countered by attacking Legiti Statianus. The Parthian cavalry destroyed the Roman auxiliary carts, burnt the equipment and killed many of the troops. Those men not killed, including King Polemon, were taken into captivity. This prompted King Artabazus of Armenia to return to his country with his army thereby abandoning the Romans to their fate. The Parthian army were then able to attack Antony's army at Phraata.

On the deck of Octavian's flag ship Agrippa looked at his opponent's fleet anchored in the haven at Mylae in disbelief. He turned to Menas and commented contemptuously; "If that is the sum total of ships Pompeius has at his disposal, small wonder they are skulking in sheltered water fearful of the military might that confronts them." He then ordered "Set a course back to our fleet! We attack at first light."

The Pompeian Admiral Democharas on his flag ship observed Agrippa's retreating fleet and came to a similar conclusion. "Octavius has so few ships! They are large but move so slowly." Turning to his aid, he added "Send a message to Domini Pompeius. Our enemy has few ships; we will sail tomorrow morning to attack Lipara."

As the fleets converged, both sides were horrified that they had grossly underestimated the size of their opponents. Agrippa's fleet had the advantage of the physical size of their ships and the amount of men and equipment they carried. Conversely the Pompeian's had manoeuvrability, speed and expertise on their side so the opponents were evenly matched.

The sea battle raged all day with neither side gaining the upper hand and the Pompeian's soon realised the futility of ramming their opponents. They found themselves assaulted by missiles from the fighting towers when they came close to Agrippa's ships. Each side inflicted as much damage as they sustained but when they came into close contact, Agrippa's marines were able to cross over to the Pompeian ships. The Pompeian sailors realising they were overwhelmed countered by jumping overboard. They were all lightly equipped good swimmers and so had no difficulty joining other ships in their fleet.

As the sun descended into *Dat*, 'The Beautiful West', to begin it's night time subterranean journey back to the east, Agrippa's fleet were at last victorious.

"Give chase, Dominus!" urged Menas as the remnants of the Pompeian fleet retreated.

"Our ships are too slow and we have no knowledge of the shoals and sandbanks that abound this coastline. There will be another day."

Octavian, realising that Sextus was no longer at Messana seized the opportunity to transfer his army to Sicily and embarked from Tauromenium in the ships loaned by Antony. He was un-molested by the Pompeian fleet during the voyage and arrived safely to made camp on the island. Sextus hurriedly returned and attacked Octavian's forces at sea and despatched infantry under the command of General Cornificus to confront the invaders. The Triumvirate did not engage the infantry on land but sailed against the inferior sized fleet of his enemy. Once again the greater maritime expertise of the Pompeian's prevailed and Octavian's fleet was vanquished. The survivors, including Octavian, fled to the mainland leaving his army isolated on Sicily.

The next day a small fair haired dejected young man stood on the mainland beach surveying the Sicilian coastline in the distance.

"I am secure, but my army is cut off" thought Octavian. Then a fish leaped out of the water and landed at his feet which reminded him of the words of a soothsayer some months previously.

"My lord" the Sage had said, "you will make the sea your slave but not without sacrifice." The Triumviri's confidence was restored and he sent an urgent message to Agrippa ordering him to assist his besieged troops on Sicily.

The Fates did not favour Antony as he besieged Phraata, food was in short supply as all the available victuals had been plundered from the immediate vicinity. Men sent out to forage further a field were an easy target for the Parthians so Roman casualties mounted.

"If we lay still and do nothing the men's hearts will fail" announced Antony to his staff officers as they met in his tent. "I will lead ten legions, three cohorts and all available cavalry on what will appear to be a foraging expedition. This, the gods willing, will draw the Barbarians into battle."

Each legion should have comprised of six thousand men divided into ten cohorts but, as was invariably the case, these legions were under manned. After a day's march the enemy was sighted in the distance. "Truss up the tents and fardels. We will give the appearance that we are preparing to return to our camp" ordered Antony. "Then sound the signal to make ready for battle!"

The Roman army turned to confront their opponents who had adopted a crescent or half moon formation. Antony's cavalry charged and in silence the foot soldiers followed a wall bulked together, shields interlocking. Their helmet crests brushing as they tossed their heads, shoulder to shoulder, tightly packed brandishing their pikes, in a fearsome display of military discipline. This was a single minded fighting force facing straight ahead with no man breaking rank. Romans primed for combat! As soon as they came within an arrow's shot the Parthians scattered and the legions gave chase with a great shout and rattling of armour. For six miles they pursued their quarry, killing eighty and taking thirty prisoners. Antony considered himself to be the victor but in reality he had sustained similar number of losses to those he had inflicted. The Parthian mounted archers were using a well practiced tactic of turning around in their saddles and firing arrows at their pursuers, a strategy not comprehended by the Roman legions.

The Romans continued with their return journey having found nothing of value in the countryside. As they made their way back to the camp the next day their enemy attacked at intervals in increasing numbers from all sides. During Antony's absence, the men within the city walls of Phraata seized the opportunity to attack the Roman earthworks and drive the remaining legions back into the countryside. On his arrival at the siege encampment Antony lost no time in calling a meeting of his Legiti, the legion commanders. From them he learned the grim truth of how the Phraata's had made frequent sallies and driven the remaining Roman troops from their positions.

"Supplies are at crisis point" announced Antony after they had recaptured their encampment; his face was black with anger. "Desperate situations demand desperate measures, so if we cannot increase our food supply we will have to decrease the numbers of mouths to feed. Our army must be reduced by a tenth. Lots will be cast to decide who will live and who will be sacrificed and those who remain will be fed on barley as we have no wheat."

There were cries of protest from the Legiti to which Antony replied; "The forage expedition has been a disaster, those left behind fought no better than children. Divide the army into ten legions by casting lots, the tenth legion will be put to death. Any of you that are unhappy with my decision are welcome to join the condemned legion!"

The actress looked at me in disbelief "Surely it would have made sense for him to negotiate a truce and withdraw back into Roman territory?"

"For any normal General, yes but Antony was as stubborn as a mule, had a highly inflated opinion of his own capabilities and added to which he was a heavy drinker. This incident is possibly the origin of the expression 'decimation'."

The Legiti departed from Antony's tent in silence leaving him alone with his manservant.

"Eros, old friend, I want you to make me a promise and swear a solemn oath."

"What is it you would have me do, Dominus?" replied Eros.

"If I am vanquished in this or any future campaign you are to kill me" replied Antony sadly.

"Dominus, I cannot harm you, I beg you please do not speak of such things."

Antony rounded on his servant, gripped him by the shoulders, shook the man and insisted. "You will promise, Eros, swear it by your gods and all you hold sacred!"

"I have served you all your life Dominus Antonius and have never refused to obey your orders" replied Eros with a heavy heart.

On the coast of Sicily the situation for Cornificus and the army of Octavian he commanded was little better than that of Antony. It was only a matter of time before starvation would compel retreat or surrender. Their enemy were reluctant to give battle but harassed the invaders with frequent hit and run attacks. Cornificus ordered the burning of the remnants of his fleet beached behind the entrenchments and the army advanced towards Mylae.

The Sicilian cavalry and light armoured troops made lightning raids on the invading army only to retire to a safe distance before Cornificus could retaliate. The Roman legions were unable to pursue their retreating attackers due to the weight of the equipment they carried; consequently the Sicilian defenders were able to inflict many injuries whilst sustaining minimal casualties. There were many rivers, streams and swamps that hampered Cornificus as he slowly made his way across the island. For three torturous days his army advanced towards Mylae while the defenders, who had been reinforced by Sextus and his heavily armed troops, rained them with missiles at every step.

Agrippa had sailed back to Lipara but on learning that Sextus had withdrawn to Messina crossed back to Sicily and occupied Mylae. From this stronghold he was able to reinforce Cornificus and send supplies to the beleaguered troops. This action prompted Sextus to hastily withdraw abandoning some of his army's supplies and equipment which were seized by the impoverished invaders. The two combined armies confronted each other near Artemisium, neither side wishing to make the first move but the stalemate was punctuated by the cavalry on both sides indulging in sporadic skirmishes.

On the western coast of Sicily Lepidus had safely disembarked his formidable army and was immediately confronted by troops commanded by Demochares, Lilybaeum and Gallus. In hindsight it would be debatable if Lepidus intended to draw troops away from Maylae or to leave Octavian to an uncertain fate but seeing that there was no advantage to be gained by remaining on the coast he made his way across country to reinforce his co Triumvirate. On arrival at Maylae Octavian treated Lepidus as a subordinate, not an equal, which prompted the older man to enter into secret communications with Sextus.

"How in God's name did such a bunch of disloyal back-biting hooligans manage to subjugate all of Europe and beyond?" asked the actress in disbelief.

"It does beggar the question" I replied. "The Roman army was probably the world's first paid professional army and relied on their commanding officer's ability to pay them."

"So the soldier's loyalty was to the highest bidder, what of events in Alexandria?"

"While Apollodorus built his secret weapon 'Orion's Sword' Cleopatra gave birth to her fourth child, a boy."

"You have a healthy son, your Highness" announced her friend and physician, Olympus proudly.

"What will you name him?" asked Apollodorus. "Ptolemy Antonius?"

The exhausted *Bassilisa* looked up at Apollodorus from the birthing chair "No" she replied softly. "I will name him Ptolemy Philodelphus."

The shipwright was puzzled by Cleopatra's choice of name as he carried her back to her bed. He was not always forthcoming with explanations and Cleopatra left him to his silence in the knowledge that he would offer an explanation when he was ready; it was only fair that he should extend her the same courtesy. Time would tell why she had named her son after her ancestor Ptolemy II.

"So why did she name him Philodelphus?" asked the actress.

"It is a mystery. Philos, as you know, means love of family and, Delphi was the most important religious sanctuary dedicated to Apollo. The oracle at Delphi was the principal source of advice for the ancients. Delphinius is the constellation of the dolphin. Dolphins, according to mythology, were the messengers of Poseidon and Zeus changed himself into a dolphin so he could seduce a sea nymph" I replied.

"Delphic is the adjective meaning to be deliberately obscure" interjected the actress. I said nothing, just raised one eyebrow quizzically.

Wherever Antony looked he saw, mounted on a black horse, Famine. The rider held a pair of scales in one hand.

"A modius of wheat for a week's wages" taunted the apparition. "Three modius of barley for a week's wages, and do not damage the oil and the wine!" it sneered.

King Phraotes, who had returned to Praaspa, faced a similar dilemma; both men knew if the siege lasted all winter men would begin to desert in ever increasing numbers.

"Lord Monaeses, you will instruct our troops" ordered King Pharaotes. "Whenever they encounter foraging Romans they are no longer to harass them. Let the infidels carry away their forage, our men are to try and befriend them."

"By your command, your Highness, but forgive me. Why?"

"Antonius has made overtures of friendship whilst secretly preparing for war."

Monaeses smiled as cognition dawned "Two can play at that game, your Highness."

"Precisely!" replied the king with a sinister smile.

Thereafter, when Parthian encountered Roman, they gradually obtained the trust of their enemy and commiserated as to their plight. The Parthians explained how the Roman's misfortune was as a consequence of the stubbornness of the Imperator and that their king, Phraortes, desired only peace.

These overtures were brought to the attention of Antony who, thinking the Parthians were losing their resolve sent the king a message. Pharates received the Roman delegation with ill concealed contempt; he was seated on a golden throne, his archers bow in his hand.

"Dominus Antonius would be prepared to withdraw his army and end all hostilities in exchange for the return of the Roman ensigns and prisoners taken from Dominus Crassius" explained the envoy.

The king sighed in a long suffering manner "You may inform your master that I have heard his overtures before" he replied whilst twanging the string of his war bow. "In the past your Imperator made offers of friendship while making clandestine preparations to invade my lands. What was that colourful metaphor, Monaeses?"

"Forked tongue, your Highness?"

"Quite right, my lord! Domini Antonius speaks with the forked tongue of the dreaded serpent of Hades. Since Sarah, the wife of Abraham cast out her slave girl Hagor and her son Ishmael we have lived in this wilderness. Until we were invaded by the Lydians we dressed in leather. So rough is this country we ate as much as we had, not as much as we wanted, unlike the peoples of the Mediterranean. We drank no wine only water. We did not have any good things not even figs for dessert. You have lived but a short time as we have always lived! The living God took pity on Hagor and gave her water to drink and a war bow to her son Ishmael, like that of the archer god Apollo." The King twanged his bowstring again to emphasise the point, then continued. "The living God has fulfilled his promise and made us a great nation. You will inform your Imperator that if he withdraws his aggressive army of invasion peacefully from our sacred lands he will be in no danger but the prisoners and precious Roman Eagles I will retain as surety of good faith!"

"It was now late September and winter came early in this country. The Romans were short of supplies and had no winter clothing so Antony had no choice but to retreat but pride prevented him from giving the order personally and Aenoborbus was delegated that un-enviable task."

Octavian suspected that Lepidus was in secret communications with Sextus but dared not risk an open confrontation; conversely he could not reveal all his plans which would inflame the already tense situation. The younger Triumvirate realised that the longer he delayed an encounter with Sextus the greater the risk of defection. Agrippa was given the order to confront the inferior Sicilian fleet and several days of stand off ended in Sextus reluctantly giving the order for his ships to engage those of Agrippa.

Standards were raised, trumpets sounded and the sea water was smote with blades of polished pine. Ships smashed into ships, screams of death once again mingled with cries of triumph, the ocean boiled and turned red. As the sea battle raged those on land watched in silence. When it eventually became clear that Agrippa would be the victor the land forces of Sextus retreated to Messana with those of Lepidus in hot pursuit. The Pompeian fleet was routed, ships were set ablaze or driven onto the sandbanks and wrecked, and few escaped. Demochares was on the point of capture so in order to avoid humiliation took his own life. His brother officer, Apollophanes, whose ship was un-damaged, defected to Octavian. Sextus Pompey seeing that his situation was unassailable packed his fastest trireme with most of his valuable possessions, money and escaped in the dead of night with his daughter.

Lepidus attacked Messana setting fire to the houses and pillaging from the citizens. Octavian also advanced on the city prompting Lepidus to take up a defensive position on high ground in the nearby countryside. From this position of strength he sent envoys to Octavian demanding Sicily by right of conquest as he was the first to land troops on the island. He also accused the Triumvirate of withholding tactical information. Octavian ignored these accusations and the delegation tried to persuade the troops to defect to Lepidus. Angry scenes developed and some of the delegated were killed.

Octavian sent for reinforcements and laid siege on the camp of Lepidus. The older Triumvirate was unpopular with his troops and consequently men defected in ever increasing numbers to Octavian. In a short space of time Lepidus lost all authority and was taken captive.

"For your treachery I could have you flogged and crucified" announced Octavian when Lepidus was brought trembling before him. "But in victory I can afford to be magnanimous. You will live but no more as Imperator; you are relieved of your command and priesthoods!"

Although Lepidus had escaped with his life and retained the position of Pontifex Maximus he would be unable to live in Italy without a substantial bodyguard. Octavian punished the Senatorial and Equestrian classes of Sextus but the rank and file were absorbed into his legions. The Sicilian cities that surrendered were pardoned but those who resisted were punished.

Antony withdrew from Praaspa leaving his engines of siege in place, just as he would have had he been in friendly territory, and made camp a little way off to await ratification of the truce. The Parthians and Medians seized the opportunity to destroy the mounds and siege equipment then attacked the Roman encampment inflicting heavy casualties.

"I will not negotiate with those deceitful barbarians" ranted Antony to his officers. "We will make our way back to Armenia and settle accounts with King Artavasdes."

"The road will be impassable" protested one of the officers. "The barbarians will have blocked our retreat."

"Then we will find another road!" replied Antony angrily.

"Dominus there is a soldier who is from the Mardian he has local knowledge and offered to be our guide."

"Bring him to me."

The Mardian was summonsed, he had proved himself in the battle for the support wagons and engines of battery none the less Mark Antony was sceptical.

"There is a way through woodland and the mountains" explained the Mardian.

"How do I know if you can be trusted, what pledge can you give me?" asked Antony.

"May I suggest that you bind me hand and foot till we get to Armenia?"

The route took the Romans through unknown territory and for the first three days they were un-molested by their enemy so the soldiers were permitted to march in disorder. On the fourth day their guide became concerned.

"Look at the waterways Dominus Antonius, the dams have been broken recently" he said. "This must have been done by the enemy to slow our progress we must prepare to be attacked."

"Call the men to battle order" ordered Antony, "archers and slingers to the rear!"

In Sicily the victorious Roman army began to press for land settlement and their discharge from service, the troops demand for reward was becoming insatiable. Octavian, being secure in the knowledge that he had no enemy confronting him, at first ignored these representations. When discipline began to break down the young Triumvirate gave orders for the legions to be assembled.

"It is only natural that you should seek reward for your heroic fighting and loyal service to the fatherland" announced Octavian. "That which begun when Caesar drove Pompeius from Rome has not ended with the son of Caesar driving the son of Pompeius from Sicily. The son may emulate his Pater and flee south to form an alliance with our enemy, this is not the end it may well, the gods willing, be the beginning of the end. I desire nothing more than to give you your discharge but the peace we have won is far from secure, I must be cautious. Some of you will be able to return to your families. The worthiest will be first to demobilise and receive their land settlement and I solemnly promise not to recall any veterans no matter how desperate the need." The army listened in silence as Octavian continued; the implications of what their imperator was saying were all to clear.

"Those who served at Mutina will be first and those with more than ten years service." The rank and file were inspired with hope; centurions were promised enrolment to the Senates of their native cities. Agrippa was awarded the unique decoration of a gold crown adorned with Trireme beaks. This crown was to be worn on the triumphal occasions were the Legiti customarily wore their laurel crowns.

On the eastern end of Antirhodos at the base of the letter *tau* Cleopatra and Apollodorus sat on the steps between the two sphinxes that guarded the palace temple. The *Bassilisa* had fully recovered from giving birth to Ptolemy and proudly displayed her figure in a diaphanous white gown. It was the first day of Emergence, and music wafted across the moonlit water of the Royal Harbour from the theatre on the mainland.

"About the twenty first day of October within a few days of Halloween for us" I explained.

"Olympian goddess – above my heart – song and I – to hear the voice of – of girls singing a beautiful song – will scatter sweet sleep – for my eyelids and lead me to go to the contest where I will surely toss my golden hair – delicate feet – with limb loosened desire, and more melting than sleep and death she gazes towards – nor is she sweet in vain." This music was from an unseen passing company, the clear voices and ravishing harmony of an invisible choir.

Lights from the buildings in the distance twinkled mimicking the stars above, it was still warm but the oppressive heat of Inundation was now over.

"For she herself is conspicuous, as if one set among the herds a strong horse with thundering hooves, a champion from dreams in caves" the distant female voices sang to each other accompanied by the amorous harmonies of cicadas. Cleopatra stood up and started to sway in time to the music, slowly caressing herself with the multicoloured ostrich feather fan she was carrying.

"Don't you see? The mount is a Venetic: but the hair of my cousin Hagesichora blooms like pure gold;" continued the invisible choir. The Bassilisa's bare breasts were full as she was still nursing her baby so she supported them gently with her hands and fan in an erotic manner. Seeing that the passion was rising in Apollodorus encouraged her to dance more provocatively.

"Where I come from men and women dance together" he commented softly.

"You can dance?" replied Cleopatra ambivalently. Her father had danced when drunk but it was not an acceptable form of behaviour for a high ranking nobleman in her culture, actors and dancers were of a low order. Apollodorus rarely drank to excess; it was the atmosphere of the moment that intoxicated him not the fruit of the vine.

"And her silvery face – why need I tell you clearly? There is Hagesichora herself; while the nearest rival beauty to Agido will run as a Colaxian horse behind an Ibenian."

The shipwright stood up and took Cleopatra's right hand in his left, placed her left hand on his shoulder so her fan draped down over his back.

"For the Pleiades rise up like Sothis to challenge us as we hear the cloak to Orthria through the ambrosial night."

He held her tightly around the waist so her breasts pressed against his chest causing the young woman to shiver with excitement.

"A vertical expression of a horizontal desire" he explained as they swayed in time to the sound of flutes and voices. Cleopatra was surprised that his sense of rhythm and timing matched her own.

"There is no abundance of purple sufficient to protect us, nor our speckled serpent bracelet of solid gold, nor our Lydian cap, adornment for tender eyed girls, nor Nanno,s hair nor Areta who looks like a goddess, nor Thylacis and Cleesithera – no,it is Hagesichora who exhausts me with love."

To these sound of flutes and voices they began their mystic dance. Very slowly in step and gesture over the limestone paving, in and out of the garnet pillars, through marble statues they pirouetted. Treading softly like the temple cats, her diaphanous white dress swirling; he leaped with the agility of Mendis, the Egyptian name for Pan. As they learned each others steps their movements becoming more adventurous and they danced more swiftly whirling leaping till the sand and clothing became a whirlwind. The powerful shipwrights lifted the diminutive Bassilisa with ease and swing her around as though she were a child causing shrieks of laughter. Gradually their wild dancing slowed to a seductive sway. Cleopatra transferred her hands around Apollodorus' neck and they kissed passionately. Exhausted they collapsed onto the limestone paving; the *Bassilisa* fanned herself serenely with her multi-coloured fan of ostrich feathers. The silence that descended across Alexandria was only broken by the shrill droning of a solitary cicada.

"Universal Pan, knit with the graces and the hours in dance, led on the eternal spring" quoted the actress from Milton's; 'Paradise Lost'.

On the other side of the Mediterranean Sextus was defeated and Antony in full retreat, for Cleopatra and Apollodorus their fortunes were about to fail, all hope would be gone and a lifetime of desire turned to smoke. With Octavian victorious and Antony vanquished but not dead the shipwright's nightmare scenario was now inevitable, the Four Horsemen of the Apocalypse were released. In less than six years the gods would abandon Alexandria. The *Bassilisa* and her loved ones would wonder if it had all been a dream or had their senses had deceived them, the last dark rapture from the mystic throng past deceiving, all useless hopes to be shed with pride and resignation. The gods would say farewell, farewell to Alexandria and for Cleopatra and Apollodorus there would be no escape from what the Fates on Mount Olympus had ordained.

To be continued

Shomu

(The Last Pharaoh)

Book 25

'Only a fool chooses war instead of peace – in peace sons bury fathers but in war fathers bury their sons.'

Apollodorus stirred restlessly as he slept in his bedroom on the seaward side of the palace on the royal island of Antirhodos. The refreshing sea breeze ruffled and fluttered the silk curtains causing the light from the Pharos Lighthouse to dance across the walls in intricate golden patterns. Cleopatra rolled over; her golden hair cascaded around her naked shoulders as she put her arm tenderly around the shipwright then whispered soothingly into his ear.

"What troubles you my love. Will you share your vision with me my lord?" She knew from past experience that Apollodorus had the ability to see dimly into the future but was reticent in sharing his premonitions as, in his words, interpretation was fraught with difficulties. As deep sleep engulfed him he saw a nightmare vision of columns marching in undress across sparse vegetation and a thorny coast. He saw men driven to extremities with sharpened vision of death which inhabits every warrior's soul. Weapons followed in carts, baggage animals dieing for lack of fodder and men for lack of water. They dare not to pause at the poisoned spring wells, wild asses were loitering exasperatingly out of bowshot maddening them with the promise of meat never to be secured and an ever present stench of unwashed bodies. By contrast the enemy were of breath taking elegance; cavalry in white armour, infantry in purple cloaked with embroidered tunics and narrow silk trousers. Chains of precious metal adorned their necks and bracelets on their arms. The adversaries defiantly farting like goats at the Romans.

Antony's men were case hardened veterans, motivated by promises of gold and land not passion or the protection of their homeland, parched by the desert sun and rendered voiceless by dust. Their brave plumed helmets too hot to wear at midday. Now the Romans were camped in hills, fingers and noses lost by frostbite, squeaking, munching noise of footsteps in the snow, feet frozen to their sandals which had in summer sweat dried the leather underfoot until it was as hard as marble. Their summer uniforms tattered rags in a territory where their enemy wore fox skins on their heads and long hide tunics which covered their legs.

A chance meeting on a yacht delivery gave me the opportunity to tell my story. Had the elements conspired to bring us together or were other forces at work? We had met at Queenborough; myself a Yacht Delivery Skipper and Naval Architect delivering a yacht by sea, she was a famous American singer now an actress looking for a part to play in a new film. I had suggested Cleopatra; she protested that it had already been done. It had, several times, but no one had played the Cleopatra that I knew – Cleopatra Thea Philopater, seventh of her line, Bassilisa or first lady of two lands, not Queen, as the concept did not exist. During the telling of my story at her London Docklands flat then on location in Alexandria we had become close friends, and then fallen in love.

I had explained how Cleopatra had met Apollodorus, history recorded him as a Sicilian carpet merchant but I knew him as a Britannian shipwright, both countries in those times were known as the Tin Island. They met at Askalon on the Palestinian coast, the Gaza Strip, and had conspired to use Roman military might to regain control of Egypt from her younger brother and his Regents. Following the Alexandrian war Julius Caesar had sired Cleopatra's firstborn son but failed to acknowledge his birthright before being assassinated on 'the Ides of March'. The republic had collapsed, civil war and a reign of terror followed but now Rome was ruled by a Triumvirate of three men; Mark Antony, Mark Aemilius Lepidus and Caesar Octavian, the adopted son of Gaius Julius Caesar. Antony in an attempt to equal the reputation of Julius Caesar had implemented his late commander's plan to invade Parthia and Media, the Persian empire or Iran and Iraqi of today. It would be said in hindsight that Mark Antony was no Caesar and this now manifested itself in his lack of attention to detail and preference for hedonistic, over practical, pursuits. It had been prophesied a long time ago that these lands could only be conquered by an army led by a King. The invasion was a disaster; many Roman lives were lost resulting in a humiliating retreat for Mark Antony.

Octavian, in the mean time, once again attempted to expel Sextus Pompey, assisted by Lepidus, from Sicily. The island was captured and the son of Pompey the Great was vanquished. A bitter quarrel ensued between Octavian and Lepidus over the spoils of war resulted in the older Triumvirate being deprived of his command and honours. There was now only one man who stood in the way of Octavian's burning ambitions to be sole ruler of the Empire. Mark Antony and his beleaguered army was also all that could prevent Cleopatra's realm from becoming a province of Rome. The close relationship between the Bassilisa and her Sea Lord Apollodorus had become mimicked by my relationship with the actress; ours had been consummated whereas Apollodorus had been more reticent in his, or so he believed.

The Parthians had scorched the earth as Apollodorus had predicted and began attacking the Romans from all sides in an attempt to break the ranks. Antony countered by ordering the Gaul cavalry to charge but the enemy scattered. Passage was blocked by trenches and palisades, water was contaminated and pastures destroyed. On the fifth day of the retreat Flavius Gallus believing that he saw a chance to hit the enemy hard enough to force them to call off their pursuit requested a contingent of light armed troops and cavalry to confront the Parthian skirmishers. The invaders were dieing of malnutrition; those who tried to desert were shot down by the enemies mounted archers. Everywhere Antony looked he saw an apparition of a pale horse, Death was the riders name and Hades followed close behind. In desperation he granted the young officer's request.

Gallus pursued the enemy too far rearwards prompting Antony to dispatch Legiti Titius with orders to return. These orders were ignored, Titius returned without Gallus who continued in his quest determined to make a name for himself. His inexperience proved to be his un-doing as too late he realised that he had been drawn into a trap and was surrounded. Instead of withdrawing so as to draw the enemy archers into range of his slingers he stood his ground. The enemy came down like a squall of brawling gale-winds. Initial attempts to send reinforcements failed; finally Anthony personally led the third legion to rescue them. Three thousand men were killed including Flavius Gallus and five thousand were wounded.

That night Antony past from tent to tent trying to comfort the sick and dieing, one blood stained soldier weakly took his hand.

"Imperator pray go and be dressed, do not trouble yourself on our account" gasped the infantryman. "You are our Emperor and our captain, your life is more important than mine." The injured man coughed twice a trickle of blood oozed down from the corner of his mouth, and then darkness filled his vision. In silence Antony lowered him and gently closed the man's eyelids as the sturdy soul trudged down to the 'House of Death'.

Encouraged by their victory the Parthians in increasing numbers kept to the field all night depriving the Romans of any repose. By morning they were confronted by nearly forty thousand enemy horsemen. There was no choice, they would have to stand and fight, retreat was not an option.

"Eros, fetch my black cloak" ordered Antony. "I need to emphasise the graveness of our situation."

"I must urge you to re-consider Dominus. The men need to have their spirits raised, dress in your blood red general's cloak" replied Eros.

Desperate situations can bring out the best in people; somehow Antony was able to call on a deeply hidden reserve of strength to lift and inspire his troops. He relented to his manservant and gave a rousing speech.

"There are no adequate words of praise to describe how you have fought the enemy; you have repeatedly driven them back. No general could wish for finer soldiers, I count myself privileged to be your commander. Yet again we are confronted by many thousands of barbarian horsemen. But we shall prevail! Father Jove has shown me how! We will form up into a square, the baggage carts and injured in the centre surrounded by the lightly armoured troops. These shall be surrounded by the cavalry and around the perimeter our heavily armoured troops will interlock their shields."

The heavily armoured troops carried an oblong, curved shield; by interlocking them around the perimeter the side of the army was protected. The rest of the troops carried a flat circular shield which they held above protecting them from airborne enemy missiles. The formation Antony had invented resembled a giant tortoise and became known as the 'Testudo'. He ended his speech by lifted his hands to heaven and the men joined his prayers to the god Jupiter, known as Zeus to the Greeks and Egyptians.

"Father Jove, gather of clouds," he prayed. "I would willingly exchange all my former victories if you should now send some bitter adversity to alight on me alone and give victory to my army!"

This provoked cries offering to take lots of decimation or any other punishment from the rank and file. The warrior spirit was re-kindled and the Parthians were confronted by well disciplined resolute troops. The front ranks of the Testudo dropped to one knee to form the lower part of the shield. This action was misinterpreted by the Parthians who pressed home their attack only to be thrown back at close quarters by Roman spears and swords.

A sombre atmosphere greeted Apollodorus as he entered the throne room a few weeks later where Cleopatra was receiving a Roman delegation. The shipwright had received his summons from the *Bassilisa* and had made his way hurriedly, by boat, from the dockyard in the Cibotus Harbour where he was supervising the re-building of the Egyptian navy.

"There is grave news from Armenia, Antonius has been forced to retreat from Parthia" announced Cleopatra.

"Where is he now?" inquired Apollodorus, his face was as expressionless as that of the *Bassilisa* to disguise the sensation they both felt in their bowls.

"He is at the port of Leuka; the Parthian campaign has been a disaster and the casualties are high. Antioius has requested food winter clothing and money from us" explained Cleopatra.

"The troops will be cold, starved, sick and dieing; we must help" replied Apollodorus. He then turned to the Roman messengers. "What news of Sicily?"

"Sextus Pompeius is vanquished, Dominus" replied the Roman courier.

"I wonder if he will emulate his late Pater and come here to raise another army" pondered the shipwright ruefully but his train of thought was interrupted by Cleopatra's anguished questions.

"How can we get supplies to Antonius? The Mediterranean is closed to shipping; the land route will be fraught with danger, added to which the Syrians may seize the opportunity to revolt as soon as they learn of the Roman's predicament."

"They were not the only people with a predicament" I announced.

"I suppose you are now going to be delphinius" replied the actress whilst giving me a knowing look, like Cleopatra she had green eyes and golden hair.

I took a deep breath "History is a temporal land of ifs, buts and maybes."

"I am sitting comfortably, so tell me your pro quos and addenda."

"According to Plutarch, Mark Antony left the bulk of his army in the snow covered fields of Armenia and made his way south to a small fishing port known as Blancbourg which was supposed to be located between Berytus and Sidon on the Syrian coastline. The enforced idleness after weeks of living on the edge resulted in him indulging his favourite pastime."

"Quaffing and feasting during an in-appropriate time of the year?"

"Exactly! Also Plutarch goes on to say that he pined for the love of Cleopatra left the banquets early to peer mournfully out to sea for signs of the approaching Egyptian fleet. Dio Cassius says much the same."

"So if the two earliest surviving accounts agree, what is the problem?"

"Nose bag time for the Romans was the eighth hour, four in the afternoon for us. Given that a Roman dinner comprised seven courses and wine was not generally served until the end along with the fruit."

"Quaffing would have been a no no if he left early."

I nodded "Rather more to the point what time does the sun set around the Mediterranean coastline in winter?" The actress smiled at me in cognition so I continued. "Mark Antony was looking out to sea in the pitch black for a fleet of ships that were undertaking an impossible journey against the prevailing trade wind. Granted the lead ship of any flotilla carried lights but the really serious ambiguity....." I hesitated.

"Don't be reticent, Kyrios mou, stick to what you are good at. You have already said, for totally plausible and logical reasons, that mankind got Christ's birthday wrong!" replied the actress, her method of address Kyrios mou being Greek for my lord, Dominus is the equivalent in Latin.

"The problem is Blancbourg, a French name meaning white village, Luka as some accounts call the port."

"A rose by another name would smell as sweet."

"Very aptly put for more than the obvious reason Kyria mou," I replied addressing her as my lady. Our method of addressing each other was the same as used by Apollodorus and Cleopatra. "The location of Blancbourg, the white village, otherwise known as Luca Combe is no where near Sidon."

"Wherever it was the wind would have been against the Egyptian fleet" suggested the actress helpfully.

"The direction of the wind is irrelevant."

"It is?"

"Yes!"

"Like Alice I like to believe six impossible things before breakfast. Go on then!"

"The exact location of the white village is uncertain but it is thought to be near the modern day village of Khuraybah, Luca Combe isn't on the Mediterranean coastline it's on the Sinus Arabicus known to us as the Red Sea!"

"Oh shit!"

"The profanity of the time would have more likely been a colourful metaphor with respect to Seth's haemorrhoids."

"Does the hippopotamus suffer from piles? OK so history got it wrong again. What really happened?"

"Before I go on let me show you Plutarch's description of events." I took my copy of 'Selected Lives' from the book shelves and read the relevant passages. We were in my small weather board fisherman's cottage at West Mersey, an island off the east coast of Essex. The attention of the Paparazzi following our premature return from Alexandria, due to the publication of the sexual in desecrations of her estranged husband, had made life in the Actress's London Docklands flat intolerable.

"It sounds like a desert crossing" commented the actress when I finished. "The river of 'cold clear water that was salty and venomous causing terrible ache' would be an apt description of the 'Dead Sea'.

"That was my reaction when I first read the account, Luca Combe had something that Antony needed desperately, it was on the ancient Incense Route. Incense being a valuable commodity heavily taxed by the Romans. Luca Combe was where that tax was collected. Plutarch and Dio Cassius are vague as to where M.A got the money from to pay his army. Both imply it came from his private resources and those of his friends and that Cleopatra claimed the credit without providing the cash. A classical if, but and maybe."

"A cover up?"

I nodded "Up until now the amount of time Antony and Cleopatra had spent together was minimal, all that was about to change but intriguingly, in an era before birth control, Cleopatra had no further children."

"Perhaps she was too old."
"She was in her early thirties and in her prime" I replied.

"How can we get supplies to Antonius? The Mediterranean is closed to shipping; the land route will take far too long and will be fraught with danger, added to which the Syrians may seize the opportunity to revolt as soon as they learn of the Roman's predicament."

"Herod managed to cross the Mediterranean in the middle of winter" answered the shipwright thoughtfully, his mind was racing.

"The ship fell apart by the time he arrived at Cyprus" replied Cleopatra desperately.

Apollodorus gave Cleopatra a knowing look to remind her that the ship she had loaned Herod was intended to do just that. Herod the Cruel, as he was known by his subjects, had fled to Alexandria following the invasion of the Parthians. Aloud the Sea Lord explained;

"You do have a ship in your navy that can make such a crossing your Highness."

"Orion's Sword is ready for service?" asked Cleopatra incredulously and Apollodorus nodded. "But what of the Etesian Trade Winds?" she continued. "No ship can proceed against them."

"Do you remember the sign I had in my office at Askalon when we first met?" replied Apollodorus whilst giving Cleopatra a fierce look.

She nodded her understanding remembering that Apollodorus boasted to do the impossible immediately but miracles took him a little time and then turning to the Romans announced "We will exceed to your masters, Domini Antonius, request with all speed. Mardian make our guests comfortable, give them whatever they desire, they have endured a great deal of hardship."

When the Romans had departed and the *Bassilisa* was alone with her Sea lord, Apollodorus started to explain "We must not take the Roman messengers back with us. The less people that know we have build warships that do not rely on oarsmen….." He was cut short by Cleopatra bursting into tears.

"Your nightmare scenario is now inevitable, Pollo!" she wailed.

"I know, but that is only the half of it. By deploying our secret weapons prematurely I have sealed my people's fate."

Cleopatra stopped crying abruptly "What have we done?"

"When the Romans learn the secret of Orion's Sword they will have an overwhelming reason to invade Britannia, to harvest the forests of the finest shipbuilding oak in existence. They will pillage the natural resources and our warriors, already coveted as much as they are feared, will satisfy the bloodlust of the Senate and People in the Amphitheatres of Rome."

"In that case we must leave Antonius and his legions to that which the fates have decreed."

Apollodorus held Cleopatra tightly and looked into her moist green eyes, in his mind he saw again the nightmare vision he had seen a few weeks previously. "We cannot leave them, Thea," continued Apollodorus, addressing the *Bassilisa* by her familiar name which he alone was privileged to use; her late father had called her *Micro Thea*, his little goddess. "Men are dying - Antonius is our friend and, rather more to the point, he is all that stands between our Egypt and Octavius. We will just have to come up with some sort of a miracle! Antonius' survival is now inextricably linked with our own!"

"So how can we get supplies to Antonius?"

"Do you know where he is?" inquired the shipwright casually.

"Leuka, which presumably is somewhere on the Syrian coastline, I can't say I have ever heard of the place. Why?"

"Where do you get your frankincense from?"

"From the Nabataens – why?"

"And how does it arrive in Alexandria?"

"It is brought overland from the Sinus Arabicus – by the warts on Seth's anus. Apollodorus, what has this got to do with Anton's starving army? Stop being delphic and get to the point!"

"How does the frankincense get to the Sinus Arabicus? By boat. Where do the boats land?"

"Myos Hormus and Leuce Combe, of course" retorted the *Bassilisa*, her face was flushed with anger and she was about to hit Apollodorus with the ceremonial flail she carried but stopped abruptly. "I am sorry, Pollo." They looked at each other and nodded, Cleopatra addressed the shipwright by the short form of his name when she was serious but when fun loving as *Geloto* the abbreviation of *Gelotopois* his Greek nickname meaning Jester. Julius Caesar had been the first to call him Jocus being the Latin for clown; Alexandrians loved these endearments so the Greek equivalent name had stuck. "The impossible has now become a miracle."

"Actually no, Thea, it's a great deal easier" replied Apollodorus smiling broadly.

"Granted we can travel overland to the Sinus Arabicus through Egyptian territory but how do we get across the Sinai? It's impassable!"

"The children of Israel managed it!"

"Yes, but it took them forty years, we haven't got forty days!"

"True. In that case we had better sail around in a boat."

"You are annoying me again Apollodorus. There are no Egyptian ships in the Sinus Arabicus and if you say anything about that canal you want me to have dug I really will hit you with this flail!"

Apollodorus took hold of Cleopatra and gave her his most charming smile so she was torn between a desire to kiss him or bring her knee sharply up into his groin. "You do have some ships there, Thea."

"What!"

"I thought it would be prudent to provide you with an escape route in case of my nightmare scenario ever becoming a reality and in the process kill two birds with the same stone."

Cleopatra's mood changed abruptly from frustration to distress. "That scenario is now looking like a distinct possibility" she wailed.

"I know; that is why we will have to do everything we can to drag M.A out of the dung he has got himself into and unfortunately it involves deploying one of my secret weapons prematurely. There are three ships stationed at the north eastern end of the Sinus Arabicus. They are not very big vessels but they are proper sea boats unlike the Mediterranean flat bottom rowing tubs. These were the prototypes for the much larger 'Orion's Sword' and have been built in secret well away from prying eyes using the oak I imported from my homeland, Britannia."

"How did you get the ships there without anyone, including your monarch, knowing" asked Cleopatra in a progressively stern tone. "The operation to drag them across land must have been monumental!"

"Archimedes boasted that given a place to stand and a long enough lever he could move the Earth. For a people whose ancestors built the pyramids supervised by a descendent of the builders of Stonehenge nothing could have been simpler" replied Apollodorus dismissively. Cleopatra looked at him severely so he continued more seriously. "As you know, there is a waterway that branches off the Pelusic branch of the Nile which, although no longer strictly navigable, particularly for V bottomed sea boats which draw much more water than the traditional flat bottomed Mediterranean vessels. I was able to use the Heroopolis watercourse through the 'Bitter Lake' which is passable after the flood. Adapting a Roman idea; the bare hulls were built in the Cibotus dock yard then towed through the Heroopolis/Bitter Lake waterway to Arsinoe Cleopatris. All the fitting out parts were cut in your dock yard then taken by cart overland and assembled on site by trusted workmen."

Cleopatra forgot royal protocol and leaped at the astonished shipwright wrapping her arms and legs around him. "*Geloto*, you are a genius!" she exclaimed, smothering him with her golden hair and moist kisses.

On the same day that hostilities ended in Sicily a lone soldier in Rome was seen behaving very oddly. Some said he was in Dionysus, the polite description for being intoxicated, others that he was possessed by gods or evil spirits. The man did many strange things before finally making his way to the temple on Capitol Hill where he laid his sword at the feet of the statue of Jupiter.

"Father Jove, gatherer of clouds" he prayed, "I have no further use of this weapon. I beg you that no more shall Roman take up arms against Roman."

Several days later Octavian stood on the rostrum in the forum and addressed the Senate and People of Rome in accordance with ancient custom. His oratorios were in sharp contrast to the speech delivered eight years earlier from the same spot by Mark Antony at Caesar's funeral.

"The war against the son of Pompeius is over!" announced the diminutive fair haired young man smiling imperceptibly as he looked across the assembled crowds with his unblinking blue eyes. The buildings around the market place shook to the sound of thunderous applause.

"Hail Caesar! Hail Caesar! Pater Patria!" cried the crowd.

"Marcus Antonius has also prevailed against the Parthian barbarians" continued the Imperator somewhat inaccurately. "To celebrate the dawning of a new golden age of peace and harmony and also in the spirit of reconciliation, all edits of prescription are henceforth cancelled."

There were more applause and chants of father of the fatherland, son of god. "Hail Caesar! Hail Caesar! Pater Patria! Filius Deus!"

"Certain taxes are to be abolished and debts to the fatherland arising from the civil war are cancelled with immediate effect" continued Octavian. It was unlikely that there were any surviving prescribed citizens of consequence and the debts to the state would have been impossible to collect but these facts were not considered in the euphoric atmosphere.

"The Senate has offered me the exalted post once held by my Pater, that of Pontifex Maximus, but it is unlawful to take an office from a man that still lives. I must therefore decline the high priesthood of Lepidus. This Imperator, this filius deus is not above the law!"

A house was presented to Octavian at public expense as the property he had previously purchased on the Palatine Hill had been consecrated to Apollo, the archer god, after the building was struck by a thunderbolt.

Sextus Pompey having packed his fastest trireme with most of his valuable possessions and money then announced to the remnants of his fleet that he intended to cross the Mediterranean.

"Extinguish the ship lights as soon as we are in clear water to thwart any attempt by friend or foe to follow" he ordered. "From Messana we will follow the coast around Italy and thence to Achaea."

Some time later Sextus arrived at the Greek island of Caphallenia, together with other ships from his fleet that had by chance run before a storm. The defeated Legiti discarded his general's uniform prior to addressing the assembled sailors and marines.

"While we remain together we can render no lasting aid to each other and increase the risk of detection. If we scatter, our chances of escape will be greatly enhanced."

The majority heeded his advice and departed in various directions, those that remained crossed with him to Asia. On arrival at Lesbos, Sextus learned of Mark Antony's abortive campaign against the Parthians and that Octavian was in conflict with Lepidus, so he decided to winter in Asia. The Lesbians, out of regard for his father Pompey the Great, welcomed Sextus enthusiastically.

Cleopatra's ships had sailed south along the Gulf of Suez, with the western desert to their right and the Sinai to the left. They arrived at the Nabataean port of Leuce Combe in the first month of the Roman New Year, the thirty fifth before Common Era. As they made their final approach Apollodorus had stationed a man on the foredeck who was dropping a weighted line over the side and calling out numbers.

"This is an entrance to challenge the best of sailors" explained the Sea Lord to Cleopatra between giving instructions to the men on the steerboard and to the following vessels. These orders were punctuated with many profanities and colourful metaphors in a variety of languages as they picked their way through the hazardous roads. "There are many razor sharp reefs and the profusion of wreckage bears testimony to how easily the coral will cut through the hull of less cautious mariners but fortunately the water is crystal clear."

Cleopatra took the opportunity to explain the origin of coral to Apollodorus. "Perseus, after rescuing Andromida from the sea monster, did not want to harm Medusa's snake covered head, so he laid the Gorgon on a bed of leaves and covered her with seaweed. The fresh fronds absorbed the force from the head and hardened under Medusa's touch. Sea-nymphs tested this miracle with additional sea weed with the same result and tossed the plants seeds into the breakers. Coral still has this property and is flexible until it comes into contact with the air; shoots under water are turned into rock on the ocean's surface. Perseus then built three altars of turf to the three gods, Mercury, Minerva and Jupiter, so shall we name these three ships by the gods Achean names Hermes, Athena and Zeus."

"By your command, your Highness" replied Apollodorus with a smile and a bow.

Book 26

Mark Antony was at the quay side as they arrived and in deference to military dignity and maritime protocol leaped aboard before the ships were made fast. He ran aft to the poop deck and embraced Cleopatra and Apollodorus warmly and then burst into tears.

"Get him below!" ordered Apollodorus sternly. "He must not be seen making such an emotional display."

It took some time to secure the ships so when Apollodorus eventually entered the cramped cabin Antony had partially recovered his composure.

"I have lost twenty thousand footmen and four thousand cavalry" he sobbed. "They were, in the main, not killed by the enemy, they died from disease and starvation"

Apollodorus placed a reassuring hand on his shoulder, "Take it easy old man, you are safe now." The shipwright poured him a goblet of honey mellowed wine, a heady mixture of Mead and Retsina, and added reassuringly "Get your chest across this."

"It has taken twenty seven days to retreat during which time we overcame the Parthians in eighteen separate battles. We had neither the strength nor equipment to settle accounts with that Nothos the Rex of Armenia" continued Antony implying that the King of Armenia was illegitimate.

"It will take time to re-equip your army and restore the men's health" added Cleopatra. "Why not return with us to Alexandria where in comfort you can take stock and decide what best to do next. When you and your army have recovered your fighting spirit – then you can settle accounts with the Rex of Armenia."

"Where is your army now?" asked Apollodorus. "The fort here could not possibly accommodate such a large number of men."

"The bulk of my forces are wintering in Armenia" replied Antony.

"So how did you get here and, rather more to the point, how are we to get the supplies to your troops in Armenia?"

"I travelled south over land with a small contingent of troops along the Asi and Jordan valleys. Then from the 'Dead Sea' via Petra and Aealana on the northern tip of the Sinus Aelanites and along the coast to the Sinus Arabicus."

Apollodorus nodded thoughtfully realising that the route was through territory friendly to Rome and would serve as a reminder to those who may be tempted to defect to the opposition that Mark Antony was very much alive and in control. Over the next few weeks there would be a great deal of Roman traffic through Herod's realm along the 'Via Nova Traiana' highway. Killing two birds with the same stone was not a modus operandi unique to the shipwright.

The fortress at Leuce Combe was cramped and uncomfortable and privacy was impossible so consequently the atmosphere was becoming tense. For the last eight years apart from a few days at Tarsus, six months while the shipwright returned to his homeland and the winter in Antioch, Cleopatra and Apollodorus had lived together in secret, almost as man and wife on their island paradise. On the way to Leuce Combe she had made it totally clear that if she could not sleep in her Sea Lord's arms she was not going to sleep with Antony.

A little later Cleopatra joined Apollodorus, by prior arrangement, aboard one of the Egyptian ships and was aghast to see that he was preparing the vessels for the return voyage.

"I hope you are not planning on running away again Apollodorus!" She put her arms around him and softly added "I know it is hard on you when we are with Antonius" there were tears in her eyes as she spoke.

"Nothing of the sort. I would like to take Hermes, Athena and Zeus back to their secret base in Egypt before anyone has chance to have a close look at their design and construction" replied Apollodorus and then added thoughtfully. "I am concerned that the Senate will be furious when they find out that Antonius has helped himself to the Roman tax revenue"

"I agree, so it would probably be advisable for him to say that I provided the cash, which, the gods willing and on your principal of the second bird killed with the original stone, may enhance my standing in Rome."

The shipwright nodded in agreement "I suggest that you go with Antonius as far as Laodicea, south of Antioch and wait there for me. All the to-ing and fro-ing of Romans hordes through his territory should remind Herod, our cruel Idumaean – Arab, Hasmonaean pretender, which side his pita bread has humus on. By the time I get to Alexandria the weather will have improved so I can bring further supplies using conventional shipping along the Mediterranean coastline and hopefully endear ourselves further to the Senate and People of Rome."

While Cleopatra and Antony made their way north over land to Laodicea and Apollodorus sailed east to Egypt, the *Bassilisa* was able to take the opportunity to advise the Imperator of events in Judea.

"Herod placed Aristobulus, his wife Mariamme's brother and her Mater Alexandria under house arrest" she explained. "They tried to escape, rather ingeniously, in coffins but the attempt was thwarted and Aristobulus drowned under rather suspicious circumstances. Alexandria wrote secretly to me appealing for help."

"What would you have me do?" replied Antony impatiently.

"I refrained from taking any action as you had made your position perfectly clear with respect to Judea. All I ask is that you order Herod to attend you at Laodicea to give his version of events in the same way you have, in the past, summonsed me to account for any suspected wrong doing" replied Cleopatra with a look of wide eyed innocence. "Unless, of course, you consider Herod more trustworthy than myself or hold him in greater regard. Perhaps he will bring with him supplies for your army, as a token of his esteem."

Antony gave Cleopatra a long suffering look and nodded, indicating that he would reluctantly consent to her wishes. Herod, known by his subjects as 'Herod the Cruel' for good and obvious reason, in due course, arrived in Laodicea. The Rex of Judea gave a reasonable explanation that did not altogether convince Antony of his innocence so, as a punishment, the Imperator give Gaza to Cleopatra.

News of the humiliating retreat of the Romans from Parthia reached the Island of Lesbos. In anticipation of a change in his fortune the son of Pompey resumed the attire of a general, rallied sympathizers and made preparations to occupy the mainland land opposite. Sextus believed Antony to be dead and was optimistic that he could succeed him as Triumvirate.

Gaius Fornius was appointed as governor of Asia succeeding Plancus who had been given the priesthood of Syria. Reports that Sextus was recruiting an army caused a dilemma for Fornius who had neither instructions nor adequate resources to confront the fugitive. Consequently, the son of Pompey was observed but not challenged. Believing that Antony had perished, Sextus made what was to be a fatal error by sending an embassy to the Parthian King proposing an alliance.

"I have heard that relations between Pharaotes and Artavasdes are far from harmonious and a state of war now exists between them" announced

Antony. The news that Parthia was in conflict with Media had clearly given him new purpose. "Also, I have received a dispatch from Octavia; she proposes to sail to Athens with supplies and reinforcements including the seventy ships I loaned her brother."

"I thought you said you loaned him one hundred and twenty triremes?" replied Cleopatra.

"I did!" replied Antony crossly. "That is all that survived the conquest of Sicily. Octavius is sending the minimal amount of support; the assistance is an insult."

To Cleopatra it was clear that Octavian was using his sister as a pawn and that Antony's treatment of her could be used as propaganda. Of greater concern was the length of time it was taking Apollodorus to bring the supplies from Egypt.

"What is taking him so long?" she demanded of her handmaids when they were alone. "I should have sent you with him to make sure that he doesn't go running off to Britannia again."

"He gave you his word, Madam" assured Charmain.

"Yes, he said that being parted from you was more painful than seeing you with Antonius" added Iras. This remark brought memories flooding back to Cleopatra of how Apollodorus had suddenly appeared at the doorway when she was stabbing Antony's clothes, having learned of his marriage to Octavia. Now Octavia was on her way to Athens with ships, reinforcements and supplies, threatening Cleopatra's position once again. Tears welled up in her eyes just as Antony entered the chamber. She turned away quickly in the hope that the Roman would not see her crying.

"What is the matter?" he demanded.

Cleopatra had to think quickly, she could not admit to the real reason for her unhappiness. "How long will it be before Octavia arrives here?"

"I don't know. Why?"

"She is your lawful spouse whereas I am little more than your amica, your *erthmeni*! I am content to be your solace and comfort but it is not right that I should live under the same roof....."

"I am not that inconsiderate, I have sent Niger with a message for Octavia to wait for me at Athens."

"So is it your intention to make Athens your headquarters?" replied Cleopatra. Her sadness had been replaced by alarm.

"I have made no decision as yet, there is much for me to consider" replied Antony sharply. "I have sided Gaza to you depriving Herod of his only outlet to the sea, don't press me further!" He turned abruptly and marched out of the room. Charmain and Iras looked at each other in stunned silence while Cleopatra cried softly.

In the days that followed Cleopatra refused to eat and was tearful each time Antony saw her although she did her best to conceal her unhappiness from him.

"Eros old friend" he confided to his elderly valet. "I face a dilemma; Octavia or Cleopatra, Rome or Egypt."

The servant smiled broadly "To have the choice between the two most beautiful women in the world, a dilemma most men would die for! On the one hand the domestic virtues of the sister of the other Imperator or alternatively the wit and intelligence of the charismatic Lady of Two Lands."

"I wish to the gods it were that simple. The choice is between two incompatible roles, to jointly rule Rome as Triumvirate or to be co- founder of a new dynasty here in the East."

"Why choose before the choice is forced onto you? May I suggest that you tell your wife that you have to go to go to Araxis?"

Antony smiled "Naturally it is far too dangerous for Octavia to come to Syria so should send the ships, reinforcements and provisions but she must return to Rome."

"If Apollodorus were to have sailed south through Sinus Arabicus where would have gone to?" asked Cleopatra.

"It is believed to be possible to sail around Africa and into the Great Ocean and north to Britannia but the seas are so violently stormy that no ship could survive" replied Olympus.

"Alexander the Great travelled overland beyond Media and Parthia to India" suggested Charmain. "Perhaps the land of his dreams where people with yellow skins live is no fantasy. We know he travelled far before we met him and it is impossible to tell fact from fiction in his stories. He knew of the way to Leuce Combe…."

"Stop it!" shouted Iras. "*Kyrios* the Apollodorus gave us his word that he would not run away ever again and I believe him. Forgive me, madam, I have spoken out of turn."

"What is your view, Mardian?" asked Cleopatra, ignoring the handmaid's outburst.

The eunuch took a deep breath before replying. "I concur with Iras, madam, when *Kyrios* the Apollodorus returned to his birthplace he did so for a specific reason. He left a letter explaining his reasons and did exactly what he said he would do. You should all, with respect your Highness, be ashamed of yourselves for doubting him."

Meanwhile Antony greeted his friend Niger who had returned from Athens.
"Imperator Octavius is preparing for a campaign against Illyria and Domina, your wife Octavia is in excellent health, Dominus" he prevaricated. "She totally understands that it is unsafe for her to continue east so she will await your instructions in Athens. You are indeed a lucky man to have the love of such an understanding spouse."
"It is my wish that she should return to Rome but send the reinforcements, ships and supplies to Laodicea which should put a stop to the *Bassilisa's* blubbering" replied Antony harshly. "Eros, where is Cleopatra now?"
"She spends most of her time at a vantage point looking out for her fleet; which I think has been sighted on the horizon."
"It would appear that you were right, Eros. The way forward is now clear. The army will soon be re-equipped then we can go to Alexandria and enjoy some Egyptian luxurious hospitality whilst awaiting a proposal for an alliance from one of the Asian belligerents."

Cleopatra was overjoyed by the arrival of Apollodorus and the news that Antony had ordered Octavia back to Rome.
"What took you so long, 'Pollo" scolded the *Bassilisa* as she greeted him aboard her flag ship.
The shipwright looked genuinely hurt "I returned as quickly as I could. I hope you didn't think…"
"No, of course not!" replied Cleopatra but her green eyes were moist so the shipwright knew that she was being economical with the truth.
"Well if you did doubt it I shall just have to learn to live with the misjudgement" he replied grinning broadly. This good humoured remark proved too much for the *Bassilisa* and the tears she had been struggling to hold back were in danger of flooding.
"You must not cry, Thea" whispered Apollodorus. "The Romans must not know of our relationship. It is only natural you should have worried that I may have not returned; it is the first time we have been apart since Antonius wintered in Alexandria. I became so frustrated by the slow progress of the fleet; the crew had to physically restrain me from jumping

overboard and pushing 'Bedroll II'! Shall we inspect the cargo? This may give us the opportunity to embrace."

Cleopatra laughed for the first time in several weeks and as they passed from ship to ship she was able, between surreptitious cuddles, to update Apollodorus about events.

"So if Octavius is planning a campaign against Dalmatia" observed the shipwright "also Parthia and Media are at variance...."

"The gods could be giving us a second chance!" interrupted the Bassilisa.

"They could indeed! Octavius may yet be killed in battle against Dalmatia, a far more formidable opponent than Filius Pompeius."

Cleopatra smiled inwardly and thought: "Also Antonius may yet be killed in battle against Media or Parthia."

"Over the next few weeks Antony's army re equipped and re clothed with the stores brought by Cleopatra and Apollodorus. With so many troops to remunerate, the money they were able to raise enabled Antony to pay each man the equivalent of half a year's salary."

"Surely that would not have been a derisory amount?" asked the actress.

"By anyone else's standards, no, but Mark Antony had a reputation for generosity. The Roman troops had been forced to abandon booty and personal positions in retreat, so they were expecting to be compensated handsomely.

The ships sent by Octavia arrived by late spring and the provisions and reinforcements were then dispatched overland to the Roman army in Armenia. With no further need to linger in Syria, Antony returned to Alexandria with Cleopatra and Apollodorus aboard the Egyptian flag ship, re-named Antonia.

"You realise it is dreadfully unlucky to change the name of a ship" complained her designer.

"If I believed you to be superstitious, *Kyrios mou*, I may have been concerned" replied the *Bassilisa*.

"You know me too well, *Kyria mou*. Superstition has nothing to do with it, I am jealous!" replied Apollodorus fiercely.

"Well don't be. She will always be 'Bedroll II' between us and if it keeps the Tyranni Orienus quiet, along with a supplement in his goblet courtesy of my physician...."

Octavia arrived back in Rome by early summer and was met at the quay side by her brother. "So he was prepared to accept the reinforcements but not his wife. I insist that you do not return to 'The House of Ships'. If he prefers the Egyptian harlot to the most beautiful woman in all Rome..."

"My duty is to my husband and his children," replied Octavia decisively. "It is not the place for a wife to question her husband's motives, Antonius had his reasons for telling me to return home and I trust him and will continue to maintain his household. Please do not plunge the fatherland into another civil war on my account. He thinks nothing of Cleopatra but is using her to finance his military campaign."

"If that is the case why did he plunder the treasury at Leuce Combe? That woman has ambitions to rule the world and she caused the death of my Pater by persuading him to be declared Rex by the Senate. You know the prophecy as well as anyone, you know of the despotic widow from the east."

"The *Bassilisa* has never meddled in affairs of the fatherland; it is more than eight years since she left Rome and has remained in Egypt except when Antonius summonsed her to Tarsus and Antioch. Her Royal Highness sent humanitarian aid to my husband's starving troops, something you were reluctant to do! During the Parthian retreat bread had sold for its equivalent weight in silver. Warm clothing was far more valuable than money. I don't know how Cleopatra was able to get to her provisions to the legions so quickly but all Rome should rejoice that she did. Caesar never acknowledged Cleopatra's son as his heir, he named you! She has been but only a few weeks with my husband, mostly before our marriage and slightly longer with your adopted Pater during the Alexandrian war. It is inconceivable that such a beautiful woman, as passionate as we are led to believe the *Bassilisa* to be, has had no lover in all this time."

"Antonius is her lover, she bore him three children!"

"That is only a rumour; she has spent a decade in the company of her Sicilian Sea Lord, they are virtually inseparable. It is far more likely that the man they call 'the Jester' is the Pater of her children! How little you understand women, Fratus. You have met Apollodorus, the giant who acts the fool but in reality is all knowing, he looks like a deus with eyes like sapphires and wild copper coloured hair. Caesar fearfully described Apollodorus as the living embodiment of Pan, that's why he called him Jocus! Never forget, Fratus, were it not for Apollodorus and Cleopatra the body of your adopted Pater would have been cast into the Tiber, like a common criminal!"

In the throne room on Antirhodos, Antony received envoys from Sextus Pompey.

"Dominus Pompeius stresses the threat to all of us posed by Domini Octavius" explained the delegate.

"I have been stressing this for some time" interrupted Cleopatra. Antony gave her a long suffering look but said nothing so the messenger continued.

"Additionally, Dominus Pompeius would respectfully remind you of the kindness he showed to Julia and other members of your family when they fled to Sicily to escape persecution." At that moment other Roman troops burst in.

"Imperator, please forgive us for interrupting but we have vital news for you. Our army has intercepted envoys sent by Sextus Pompeius to King Pharaotes proposing an alliance. He has crossed over from Lesbos to the Asian mainland and is recruiting an army."

Antony's attitude changed abruptly. "By the gods, so help me, I will kill that….that…." he ranted.

"Son of a camel drivers whore" suggested Cleopatra sweetly. "What was that colourful Britannic metaphor, *Geloto*?"

"It never rains but it pours," replied Apollodorus ruefully. Up until that point Antony had been giving the Pompeian delegates a sympathetic hearing. "King Pharaotes must be fearful for his realm and his life if he has sent overtures of friendship to Sextus."

"Titius, take the squadron of ships returned from Octavius and pursue that, that son of a camel drivers whore!" ordered Antony.

"With respect, Domini Antonius" interjected Apollodorus diplomatically. "The man who ended the Pompeian dynasty by killing the last in that honoured line will be reviled throughout the Roman world. An alliance with Sextus has always been in your best interest as experienced mariners are hard to come by."

Antony hesitated then announced "Very well. If Sextus submits, you treat him as a friend, Titius!" He caught Cleopatra's eye and added good humouredly, remembering the *Bassilisa's* impersonation of Caesar "not as a fiend." The Sicilian envoys breathed an audible sigh of relief.

"Dellius, you will take an invitation to Artevasdes of Armenia to attend me here in Alexandria" continued Antony.

Cleopatra and Apollodorus exchanged knowing looks as it was more likely for the Nile to freeze over than the Armenian monarch to voluntarily come to Alexandria. The river would soon flood, turning the dusty countryside into an archipelago and render animal drawn carts temporally obsolete. Confirmation of conflict between Phraates and Artevasdes of Media had encouraged Antony to plan another offensive.

Sextus arrived at Nicomedia and in order to emphasise to the troops that there could be no turning back, burned the remains of his fleet. From here he marched west to Lampsacus of the Helliespont and tricked the city guards into opening the gates. The three Sicilian legions failed to take Cyzicus in Mysia in a battle with Furnius who had been reinforced by Amyntas of Galatin. At this point Marcus Titius arrived with several legions and the fleet of seventy two triremes to join forces with Furnius against the fugitive.

The Nile flood subsided and fertile black mud from Africa once again made the desert bloom and the oppressive heat of Inundation gave way to the mellow fruitfulness of Emergence. An envoy from King Artevasdes of Media arrived in Alexandria to propose an alliance and as a token of good faith he brought with him Polemon. The client king of Lycaonia and Armenia Minor had been taken prisoner during the attack on the baggage convoy as it followed Antony's troops the previous year. This alliance would give reinforcements and a secure base for a renewed attack on Parthia. Not surprisingly the Median's namesake from Armenia declined Antony's invitation fearing a coup while he travelled to Egypt.

"Was the alliance with Artevasdes of Media bound in matrimony?"
"Naturally, that was the way, baby Ptolemy was betrothed to the Median king's daughter" I replied.

"I have come to the conclusion that co-operation with Octavius is futile to the point of being dangerous" announced Antony to Cleopatra and Apollodorus who listened in stunned silence. "It is my hope that I can safely continue with expansion of my eastern territories if I leave Octavius to do likewise in the west. I am however concerned that he has a formidable navy following the defeat of Sextus."
"Presumably it is pointless trying to persuade you into making a pre-emptive strike against Octavius in preference to a renewed offensive against Parthia" replied Cleopatra.

"I have considered such an action but dismissed it for two reasons. Firstly, I do not wish to be the instigator of further bloodshed between Romans."

Apollodorus nodded "Secondly?" he prompted.

"I concur with your philosophy, Jocus, that whoever rules the waves rules the world. How long would it take to build a fleet that would surpass that of Octavius?"

"Such an action will precipitate an arms race with Octavius already in the lead."

"Apollodorus don't prevaricate" interrupted Cleopatra sternly. "How long would it take to build the ships so that the combined numbers of mine and those of Antonius would be greater than that of Octavius?"

"Given that we have vastly better reserves and infrastructure than Rome" replied the shipwright hesitantly, "if Octavius has his attention diverted away from Egypt for three years I can give you a Navy to vanquish him."

"The Dalmatian Islands and coastal mainland of what is known to a 'baby boomer' like myself as Yugoslavia had been the Roman province of Illyricum for several centuries but the area to the north where this land connected to Italy had never been controlled by Rome. The local tribesmen had been troublesome for years and the Adriatic islands were infested with pirates. This thorn in the side of the Republic, Octavian started to address while Antony was re equipping his army."

The tribesmen fought desperately in the densely forested mountains of Illium in an attempt to repel the two pronged Roman offensive. Octavian secured Croatia while his fleet, commanded by Admiral Menodorus, cleared the Lapudes pirates from the islands and coastal planes. These pirates made their last stand at the capital city of Metulum. Octavia and Agrippa rallied the Roman troops and led the final assault.

Octavian then marched along the side of the river Kupa to link up with troops advancing along the river Save. During a thirty day siege on the town of Siscia, Admiral Menodorus was killed. Final victory enabled the Romans to re establish the colony of Pola and also to create Enona and Tergeste.

Sextus Pompey, realising that his cause was a lost one offered to surrender to Furnius and Amyntus. Three of his senior officers had defected to Titius taking with them Libo, the father in law of Sextus and the two surviving murderers of Caesar, Turullius and Cassius of Parma. Titus refused to negotiate until all troops and equipment had been surrendered. Sextus retaliated with a failed attempt to set fire to his adversary's ships; he was pursued inland, surrounded and taken captive by Amyntus.

"What happened next is confused" I explained. "Some accounts have it that Antony sent instructions for the execution of Sextus. These instructions were regretted and a second message was sent instructing that the life of Pompey was to be spared. Unfortunately the second letter arrived before the first."
"So nothing has changed in two thousand years with respect to the postal service" interjected the actress.

That autumn a messenger arrived at the Roman encampment in Dalmatia and was taken to Octavian's tent.

"Hail Caesar! Sextus Pompeius is dead" he announced breathlessly.

"Excellent!" exclaimed Octavian. "How did he die?"

"Troops of the Fatherland led by General Amyntus pursued and surrounded him. Amyntus handed the traitor over to Legiti Titius who ordered the execution."

Octavian smiled imperceptibly "We will hold games to celebrate at the earliest opportunity!"

"I beg you reconsider, Dominus" interjected Agrippa. "The dynasty of Pompeius is well respected and popular in Rome. It would be most unwise to be recorded in the glorious history of the Fatherland as the Imperator who ended their noble line. May I respectfully suggest that you contrast your own lenient treatment of Lepidus against the high handed way in which Antonius has dealt with Sextus Pompeius?"

"I take your point" replied Octavian thoughtfully. "Blame for the demise of one of the Fatherland's oldest families along with the disquiet caused by the way he has treated my beloved sister will do much to undermine his position and social standing in Rome. Little by little his popularity is being chipped away."

"The way Octavia has lovingly kept house for him and cared for his children has done Domini Antonius a great hurt. Soon the Senate will beg you to go to war against him – then the Filius Deus will fulfil the destiny set in motion by Domini Deus Caesar. Rome will be ruled in peace and prosperity! You will be our Emperor and god!"

"It is Titus, in fact, who holds the dubious distinction of being the Roman who ended the Pompeian dynasty. During the winter, Fufius Geminus defended the recently captured Siscia against a local uprising then, the following spring, the whole of Octavian's army advanced inland while Antony departed from Alexandria to settle accounts with King Artavisdes of Armenia. Cleopatra and Apollodorus travelled with the Roman forces as far as Euphrates then they sailed back towards Egypt stopping off at Apamen, Damascus, Coele Syria and finally Judea."

"So have you planned a spectacular entrance for me when we meet Herod?"

"Well, you could arrive naked on the back of an elephant, your nipples coloured purple and an Amethyst stone in your navel, like the *Bassilisa* of Sheba."

"Those sorts of displays are reserved for you, *Kyrios mou*" replied Cleopatra thoughtfully "and it was Jezebel, not Sheba!" The Lady of Two Lands smiled to herself as she imagined the coronation procession of her Pharaoh. The ceremony would take place at the ancient city of Memphis at the apex of the Nile delta and would combine all the elements of their two cultures. She would arrive, standing on the back of a huge elephant and he by Trireme, in the same manner as her arrival at Tarsus. Her body would be coloured pale purple and nipples several shades darker. There would be a large Amethyst stone in her naval and precious stones attached to her ears and nipples, linked with fine gold chains. Her pubis could be covered with a thong of precious stones and on her head the Vulture headdress with its winged cape of cloth of gold. People would tell of the spectacle for thousands of years. The wedding of Cleopatra Thea Philopator to and the coronation of her consort Pharaoh Ptolemy Neos Mendis, the new Pan, affectionately known as Gelotopoios. This would be the new Hellenistic dynasty that would usher in a golden age of peace and prosperity so long awaited by all the people of the Mediterranean and beyond.

"How about on horseback at the head of your cavalry, full gallop and dressed in the robes of the desert people?" interrupted Apollodorus.

Cleopatra's emerald eyes twinkled; "I like the sound of that, theatrical and a show of military strength. The hills that surround Jerusalem are teaming with bandits so we would combine security with spectacle. How far is the city from the coast?"

"About three hundred furlongs."

"Three hundred stades, five schoenus, an easy day's ride."

"Ordinarily, yes, but Jerusalem is nearly fifteen hundred cubits above sea level. The ground drops away steeply on all sides except to the north."

"So that is why Herod and his Roman allies had so much difficulty capturing the city."

The shipwright nodded "I think the best approach would be to land at Askalon which is your territory and has an established a garrison. Then we could travel overland and approach Jerusalem from the north along the Damascus road."

"Incidentally, the Jews look on Jerusalem as the naval of the earth, their city is the centre of their affections."

"So do Jewish women decorate their navels with precious stones like Egyptian women do?"

"I doubt it; they look on their bodies with even more shame than the Romans" replied Cleopatra with a chuckle. "*Kyrios mou*, you are going to enjoy this state visit even less than the last and 'Bedroll II' will be far too far away for us to sneak away to for some quality Egyptian time."

"What is Jewish food like?" asked Apollodorus.

"Much of what the Romans consider a delicacy the Jews regard as unclean" replied the *Bassilisa* with a smile.

"No more crunchy dormice!" interjected Iras.

"That's a relief!" replied Apollodorus. "I suppose there are many fine buildings to look at."

"The principal building is the temple which Herod is massively extending in an attempt to endear himself to the populous" continued Cleopatra. "The rest, tortured narrow streets and cramped housing, much like Tarsus."

"So 'navel of the earth' is an apt description among people who do not bathe as frequently as the Egyptians, full of muck and fluff and not a precious stone" replied Apollodorus with a grimace. "It sounds as though the city is an unholy alliance between a building site and a latrine!"

Book 27

Jerusalem; a busy cosmopolitan city of thirty thousand people set on high ground between the Hinnom and Kidron Valleys, Cleopatra could not have chosen a worse time to visit Herod. The feast of the Passover attracted pilgrims from the whole of Judea and beyond, increasing the cities population to about two hundred thousand. These pilgrims were housed in tents in the surrounding countryside and in the nearby villages. Cleopatra at the head of her cavalry made slow progress through the crowds. This was fortunate from the viewpoint of Apollodorus as, in the manner of the Spartan female nobility; the *Bassilisa* was mounted sideways like Helen of Troy.

"That is a very elegant way for a lady to ride" commented the shipwright. "But I think the tack needs some re-designing to give you full control."

"Nonsense!" exclaimed Cleopatra. "I can control a horse which ever way I sit or stand on it."

"The way you perform acrobatics on a galloping horse will get you injured one of these days, Thea" scolded Apollodorus light-heartedly.

"You perform miracles of seamanship, Geloto, and I perform the equestrian impossible! If you had your way every horse would be fitted with a steer board."

"Now there is a thought! I could re-design the equestrian control systems when we get back to Alexandria."

Cleopatra chuckled in her deep musical way. The Egyptians were receiving a very mixed reception from the crowds that lined the road, some cheered enthusiastically whilst others booed and there were also cries of 'Hosanna', the Hebrew word meaning 'save us'.

"To the Palestinians I am an ally" she explained "but to the Judeans an enemy, not least because of the assistance given by my grandfather. They also despise me for my links with Antonius who inflicted Herod on them, added to which our timing is tactless as they are about to celebrate their feast of the Passover."

"Was that when the tribes of Israel escaped from Egyptian slavery?" Cleopatra nodded and Apollodorus continued "I have read the account in the scrolls of the Hebrew God but find that story hard to believe. You said a Pharaoh once tried to abolish slavery but it was the slaves who protested loudest. Why would the Jews wish to escape and surely there would be other evidence of such a mass exodus of people? I have never found any records in the library of such an event recorded by the Egyptian historians."

Cleopatra laughed again "No Pharaoh would allow any evidence of such a public humiliation to survive. It was a long time ago, so we have learned to live with the miss-judgement. First sign of trouble in their homeland and we are over run with Jewish refugees, as you have seen for yourself."

"That reminds me, the last time I saw Herod he was an impoverished refugee. I think I will have the greatest difficulty keeping a straight face addressing him as your Highness."

"You will do no such thing, *Kyrios mou*, you will address him by his name and you will address me as Cleopatra!" The shipwright looked puzzled so the Bassilisa explained. "You addressed Antonius by his name and only as Domini when you were trying to strangle him; Herod is Rex of Judea because the Senate gave him that title. He is a pretender not a real monarch!"

"What if he takes my lead and addresses you as Cleopatra?"

"He will be reminded in no uncertain terms that he has not been given permission to be familiar!"

Apollodorus nodded thoughtfully, mindful that Cleopatra owed her position to Roman interventions but considered it unwise to remind her of these facts. He then looked around and asked, by way of diplomatically changing the subject "Are there any other natural resources other than olives?"

"That is the problem for this country, there are few natural raw materials and Jerusalem isn't located on any trade routes."

"So what do the locals do with themselves? How do they earn a living?"

"The aristocratic upper classes are divided into four factions; Sadducees, Pharisees, Essnes and Zealots. Their total preoccupation is in religious observance so they have little time for anything else. Most of the populous are from the poor rural communities, peasants and artisans, who have little time for strict obedience of the Torah as they are too busy trying to scratch a living from this impoverished land."

"Sadducees were basically a political party comprising high priest families, land owners and the wealthy aristocracy. They claimed to be descendants of Zadok, chief priest to both King David and Solomon."

"They must have been fearful that under Roman rule they would share the fate of the Senatorial hierarchy and be prescribed?" suggested the actress.

I nodded "The Pharisees were the forerunners of the Rabbis, lawyers and teachers of the Torah. They were very anti Roman - Essnes and Zealots were the fundamentalists. John the Baptist is thought to be one of their numbers. They were also a political party campaigning for autonomy of the lands of Israel, again anti Roman."

"So the people of Judea were being squeezed between three major powers, Rome from the northwest, Parthia from the east and Egypt from the southeast."

"Cleopatra controlled the coastal towns from Pelusium to the River Eleutherus due west of Cyprus. The division of territories by Mark Antony laid the foundations for the conflict that still exists today. Tyre and Sidon were given freedom and became part of Lebanon. Judea was effectively land locked since Gaza, to the south of Palestine, had been allocated to Cleopatra as a punishment to Herod, depriving him of his only access to the sea."

"Salted fish from the Sea of Galilee is greatly prised in Rome" continued Cleopatra. "The Seleucid Kings tried to re vitalise the economy and encourage trade but made the classic error of inflicting Achaean values and religion onto the populous."

They now came in sight of the city and the crowds had been cleared away from the road.

"*Olulu! Olulu!*" shouted Cleopatra. This was the triumphal cry in honour of Athena which ordered the Egyptian cavalry to charge.

"*Olulu! Olulu!*" responded the cavalry as leafy branches were spread over the road in that country's traditional manner for greeting visiting royalty. To their right was Golgotha, the place of execution aptly nicknamed 'the skull' and to the west of the walled city was Herod's Royal palace. The Egyptian Royal party were escorted to the newly completed Antonia fortress, named after Herod's patron, and located on the north east corner of the temple. It would be in this fortress that Paul the apostle was destined to be imprisoned.

King David's city was to the south of the temple and Royal Palace, but the original wall had been pulled down about a hundred and fifty years earlier by the Seleucid King, Antiochus, in response to a revolt and replaced with an armed citadel overlooking Mount Zion. Antiochus went on to desecrate the temple, forbidding Jewish Law and religious observance.

"You will join me for the Passover meal?" inquired Herod.

"We should be delighted, provided it will cause no offence or embarrassment" replied Cleopatra sweetly.

Herod smiled broadly "I was concerned about causing you offence by asking. It is after all a celebration of the children of Israel's escape from Egypt."

"Think nothing of it Herod, it was a long time ago before the Ptolemy's and Cleopatra's ruled Egypt. We allow all people to come and go freely, to worship their gods without persecution and to share in our prosperity."

That evening they joined Herod and his courtiers in the banqueting hall, a large but gloomy room near the top of the Antonia fortress.

"This is my wife, Mariamme" announced Herod indicating to a young woman reclining next to him.

"Pleased to meet you" replied Cleopatra. "Herod you have already met *Kyrios* the Apollodorus, my Sea Lord."

Servants removed the diner's sandals, washed their feet and then brought in food which lacked the gruesome variety of a Roman feast or the opulence and colour of an Egyptian banquet.

"During the Passover week only Matzos is permissible" explained Cleopatra to the dubious Apollodorus. "That is unleavened bread."

"That is almost correct, your Highness" interrupted Herod. "Chametz is the Hebrew word for leavened bread. The 'Seder' family meal is eaten on the first two nights of the Passover."

On the table in front of each guest were three Matzos placed within the folds of a napkin.

"You must only eat two of these Matzos" whispered Cleopatra to Apollodorus while their host's attention was diverted. "The third, 'the Afkomen', is spirited away and hidden when you are distracted. Later we play hunt the Afkomen."

"That sounds like fun. Shall I challenge our host to a game of 'Dyonistic Draughts' afterwards or do we rampage the town playing 'Persecute the Peasant'? Herod has something of a reputation for cruelty to live up to, after all." The shipwright helped himself to an off-white paste in the mistaken belief it was puréed chick pees, from the expression on his face this obviously was not the case.

"You look just like Antonius did when I presented my demands at Antioch" observed Cleopatra who was having the greatest difficulty remaining dignified as her friend's face turned purple and his eyes watered profusely. She gesticulated to the master of revelries who was scooping wine with a long spoon from an amphora *(a twenty six litre jar)* and filtering it with a sieve. "Here have a goblet of wine. That was 'Maror' the bitter herbs that symbolise slavery."

When Apollodorus recovered, he replied "We have something similar in Britannia, a root vegetable called Horseradish. I thought it was humus. Is there anything else on the table that bites back that I should know about?"

"Zeroah is the traditional roasted lamb" replied Herod, who had returned to the table and indicating to the platter of shank bone, "which symbolizes the paschal sacrificial offering. Beitzah, roasted egg, is the symbol of eternal life similar to the Egyptian Locus flower and Karpas is parsley and celery which represent hope and redemption, served with a bowl of salted water."

"To represent tears shed?" suggested Apollodorus.

"That is correct" replied their host "and Charmoses is a mixture of apple, nuts, wine and cinnamon to remind us of the mortar used by the Jews in the construction of buildings. Tell me, Apollodorus, have your people ever been persecuted?"

"Caesar tried to twice without success. The distance between Gaul and Britannia at the closest point is only twenty five Roman miles or three and a third schoenus. With such a lot of water from the north being forced through a small gap, a Mediterranean ship is utterly unsuitable for the crossing."

"I thought you came from Sicily" interrupted Herod incredulously.

"Most people do, both Sicily and Britannia are known as the Tin Island. Until recently the Tin Island in the Great Ocean beyond the Pillars of Heracles was believed to be a myth. People are suspicious of Britannians as they think we feed our babies on our enemy's horses or some such nonsense, so I am happy to let them believe me to be a Sicilian."

"So what happened when Caesar invaded Britannia?"

"The first attempt ended in disaster when his fleet of flat bottomed, shallow draught ships floundered in a storm. The following year with a newly constructed fleet of ships with deep draught and V bottoms he was able to make the crossing. His army made it as far as our principal river but the swamp lands to the north east proved impenetrable so he was forced to retreat. Britannia is bitterly cold most of the time and it hardly stops raining so Roman clothing was as unsuitable as the design of their ships."

"In view of the way your people humiliated him, how were your relations with Caesar or did he believe you to be Sicilian?"

"He guessed correctly where I came from and regarded me as useful but I think we looked on each other with mutual secret loathing."

"You do exaggerate, *Kyrios* the Apollodorus" exclaimed Cleopatra. "You and Caesar were the best of friends; it was just that he was frightened of you."

"Why was Caesar frightened of your Sea Lord?" asked Herod.

"He was frightened of all the Britannian high priests, the druids; you know how superstitious the Romans can be. Caesar thought Apollodorus could turn him into some sort of disgusting reptile, ridiculous really." Cleopatra gave the shipwright a stern look as though to say "don't say it! He managed to be a disgusting reptile without any Britannic assistance."

"The principal river Apollodorus referred to was named the Thames by a later colony of Romans who established London. The mash lands being Dagenham Marshes which extended north to what is now Essex."

Later, when Cleopatra was alone with Apollodorus, the shipwright confided "I don't like the way Herod was cross examining me about my background and origin."

"You are secretive about your origin with everyone except Caesarion and the twins!" replied Cleopatra with a smile.

"I know I am inclined to be sensitive about being regarded as a barbarian from a cold, wet, northern country but it was as though Herod was assessing me as a warrior weighs up his enemy. He certainly has an eye for the ladies."

"So have you, *Geloto!*"

"Yes, but I hope I don't look at you, Iras and Charmain as he was."

"I know what you mean; you look at us appreciatively as though we are special whereas Herod looks as though he is mentally fornicating with us."

Apollodorus put his arms around Cleopatra and whispered "You are special; you are the most beautiful woman in the world."

"Talking of matters intimate and pleasurable I suppose you are going to say it is too dangerous and if Herod found out about us he would go blubbering to M.A."

"Discretion would, on balance, be prudent." Cleopatra looked disappointed but Apollodorus continued "you go to your room and have Charmain and Iras with you as though they are attending in the normal way. Then change clothes with Charmain and come to my room with Iras leaving

Mardian guarding Charmain in your room. Unless of course you would rather have a good nights sleep in this cold, damp, fortress."

"An excellent idea but what if Herod's spies are watching. Who is going to get them drunk?"

"The problem with information obtained clandestinely is it can be rarely be used. You are supposed to be Herod's friend. How could he admit to spying on you?"

"It would appear that as usual, *Kyrios mou*, you have thought of everything" replied Cleopatra with a seductive smile. Unfortunately, this was one occasion when Apollodorus hadn't. The walls of this recently constructed fortress did have ears and Herod would use the information he was able to obtain against them.

The following day they visited the temple but were only permitted into the southern 'Court of Gentiles'.

"According to Jewish tradition the third temple would be built by the Messiah, consequently the temple that was under construction is referred to as the second temple" I explained. "Herod's temple was to replace the one built by Zerubbabel which replaced the original built by King Solomon and destroyed by the Babylonian King Nebuchadezzar. Although Zerubbabel's temple stood for over five hundred years its existence is politely ignored. The construction site by any standards then or two thousand years later was monumental. A mound sixty four cubits high (thirty two metres) covering an area five hundred and seventy six thousand square cubits (one hundred and forty four square metres or twelve football pitches) was held in place by four huge retaining walls of interlocking stone. The temple of Zerubbable was incorporated into the construction wherever possible. Although the project was not completed for another thirteen years, in less than a century all that would remain would be the mound to stand empty as a humiliating reminder to the citizens of Jerusalem of Christian supremacy. At the end of the seventh century of Common Era an Islamic temple was built by the invader Caliph Omar.

"I wonder how they determine who is a genuine Jew and permit them beyond this point" inquired Apollodorus. "It isn't as if they can establish it by examining everyone's manhood."

Cleopatra giggled then mimicking Herod replied "Get your phallus out. Yes, you have been circumcised, you can enter."

Apollodorus laughed "In view of the fact that the custom of circumcision was copied from Egypt, it would be a far from conclusive form of identification."

Cleopatra took hold of the shipwrights arm and looked up at him coyly "Where did your people learn the custom from?"

"They haven't. My people's knowledge of surgery is non existent."

"That's what I thought. So how is it that you....?" Cleopatra indicated towards his groin with her eyes and the handmaids moved closer.

"Yes, come on *Geloto*" asked Iras. "We all are dying to know."

"Don't be shy, *Kyrios mou*" added Charmain. "This has got to be one of your best stories."

The shipwright coloured and indicated to their bodyguards, Cleopatra instructed the troops to give them more space.

"You know how it is that people do the silliest things when in Dionysus" began Apollodorus in a low, conspiratorial voice. Cleopatra and the handmaids nodded sympathetically. "When I first arrived in Askalon I had no money, or at least nothing recognisable as cash, so to supplement my income in the boatyard I capitalised on the local's enthusiasm for gambling and my ability to drink most people under the table. In the game of Dyonistic draughts my forfeit was to be circumcised."

"Did it hurt?" inquired Cleopatra trying desperately hard not to laugh.

"Very much! I lost consciousness and when I came around the surgeon had my penis in his mouth; to add insult to injury!"

"That is normal" interrupted Cleopatra with difficulty. "They take a mouthful of wine and" she hesitated. "It's to ease the pain and prevent infection."

"Well it didn't do a very good job" replied Apollodorus indignantly. "I was in agony for weeks. The upshot of all that was; I lost my foreskin and gained a boatyard." The last remark proved too much and Cleopatra dissolved into peals of laughter joined by the handmaids.

"So is that why you were in such a bad mood when we first met?" asked the *Bassilisa* when she had recovered. The shipwright nodded.

"That really was one of your best stories" added Charmain as she wiped away her tears. In the distance was a rumble of thunder and the sky was darkening.

"I think we had better get back to the fortress, it looks like there is a storm brewing" commented Apollodorus. Cleopatra nodded and they made their way back. The rumbling continued for some time but the storm did not break until later that evening.

"Do you mind getting wet, Thea?" asked the shipwright conspiratorially as they made their way back to their rooms after the evening meal. Cleopatra shook her head and held his arm tightly.

"What do you have in mind, *Geloto*?"

"We could go up onto the roof and watch the storm, one of nature's free shows." He took hold of the young woman's hand and they excitedly ran up the stairs onto the flat roof. From here they had a commanding view of the city and the surrounding countryside. All around them flashes of sheet lightning rippled from cloud to cloud lighting up the night sky with eerie blue phosphorescence that threw the landscape and buildings into sharp relief. Suddenly the sky cracked over to the east as a bolt of lightning snaked to earth followed by a deafening bang that shook the building. Cleopatra screamed involuntarily and held onto the shipwright with both arms. Apollodorus responded by lifting the young woman up so she could grip his waist with her legs. She flung her arms around his neck and they kissed passionately.

"This is madness!" exclaimed Cleopatra excitedly. Their eyes met, lit by the un-natural radiance of the lightning.

"Yes it is!" replied Apollodorus fiercely, his blue eyes were wild with excitement and months of pent up sexual frustration. The storm slowly circled around them in a symphony of insane flashes and crashes. They were at the epicentre of a wild maelstrom. "We must be one with the storm!" he shouted. To their south another bolt of lightning tore the sky asunder followed a heartbeat later by an explosion that took their breath away. Cleopatra responded by devouring Apollodorus with kisses.

The flashes of lightning illuminated the city as brightly as day and the crashes of thunder rocked the foundations of the hills that surrounded Jerusalem, the inhabitants cowered in their beds. All were filled with fear except two lone foreigners at the top of the highest building in the centre of the storm. The rain had soaked their clothes and Cleopatra's makeup ran in psychedelic rivulets down her face, her golden ringlets liberated by the water.

"Thea I want you so badly!" exclaimed Apollodorus.

"Then have me! I am yours!" she screamed. "Our final battle is over!"

The lightning became fire and the thunder artillery. Metal chariots powered from within, not drawn by animals ploughed up the desert. Metal dragons circled around the sky spitting deadly fire at each other, claps of thunder became pyrotechnic explosions. Mighty ships locked in a deadly embrace. Tall buildings collapsed, people screamed in agony. Long thin metal birds with stubby wings screamed as they propelled themselves with their wake of fire up the Persian Gulf and ripped apart the lands that once were the Garden of Eden. The final battle was not over, it had just begun!

Cold cruel eyes watched from a hiding place in the corner of the roof as Cleopatra and Apollodorus passionately embraced and the storm raged all around them. From the highest cloud a massive charge of energy accumulated till it could be contained no more. Like a titanic dragon it launched itself at the city as travelling faster than sound it ripped through the atmosphere, ionising every molecule as it passed. Rain drops were turned to plasma. The lightning bolt fragmented across the sky zigzagging insanely, one bolt plunged to Earth at Golgotha. The main body of energy travelled south west towards Egypt, it screamed towards Lake Sebonis, the lagoon east of the Canopic branch of the Nile. The lightning impacted on the lake's surface, the release of energy vaporising the water with a mighty bang that was heard from Africa to the Gaza Strip.

Back on the roof of the citadel in Jerusalem Cleopatra gripped Apollodorus tightly with her arms and legs as he moved her up and down in time with the lightning bolts that ricocheted around the night sky. The storm reached its climax, they screamed as orgasms racked their bodies. Cleopatra ripped the shipwright's flimsy, sodden clothes and her sharp nails lacerated his broad shoulders. Blood mingled with rain and Cleopatra's tears; ecstasy obliterated agony, the powerful Britannian's legs which quivered under the strain of remaining standing.

A column of high energy vapour rose from the surface of Lake Sebonis like giant vipers and fanned out in the upper atmosphere rolling out in a mushroom cloud that captured the energy of the lightning. Gradually the mushroom cloud took on human form and transformed into a creature taller than the highest mountain; its arms could reach from east to west. The arms were covered with hundreds of dragon heads and its body with wings. Fire flashing eyes were topped by filthy long hair. The Typhon was weak and could not sustain its ghostly form for long but it would soon be nourished by the ephemeral food of mankind's jealousy, mistrust, religious intolerance and persecution.

"I never knew a thunder storm could be so erotic" confessed the actress as she carefully bathed the scratches on my back. "I am sorry I got

carried away and have made rather a mess of you. Wasn't it rather dangerous, we may have been struck by lightning at a critical moment?"

"The risk made it all the more exciting" I replied "like the possibility of being seen, you can just imagine the tabloid headlines. 'Shock horror! Charred remains of famous singer/actress and her middle aged, maritime lover found on isolated Essex Island." I was lying on my stomach white the actress tended the injuries; the tattered soaking remains of our clothes were strewn around the floor and the stereo played softly.

> *'Imagine there's no heaven,*
> *It's easy if you try,*
> *No hell below us,*
> *Above us only sky,*
> *Imagine all the people*
> *living for today...*
>
> *Imagine there's no countries,*
> *It isn't hard to do,*
> *Nothing to kill or die for,*
> *No religion too,*
> *Imagine all the people*
> *living life in peace...*
>
> *Imagine no possessions,*
> *I wonder if you can,*
> *No need for greed or hunger,*
> *A brotherhood of man,*
> *Imagine all the people*
> *Sharing all the world...*
>
> *You may say I'm a dreamer,*
> *but I'm not the only one,*
> *I hope some day you'll join us,*
> *And the world will live as one.'*
>
> *(John Lennon)*

Cleopatra helped the bemused shipwright back down the stairs and into his room. Assisted by the handmaids she removed the sodden remains of his clothing and with her lips and tongue tenderly soothed the injuries she had inadvertently inflicted on him during her moments of highest passion.

Herod received Cleopatra, Apollodorus and her courtiers in the throne room of his palace, the Praetorian as it was later known. The Rex of Judea was flanked by his wife Marriamme and other courtiers.

"Dominus Antonius has ordered me to surrender the date palms and balsam groves at Jericho to you, Cleopatra" announced the king of Judea.

"I have not given you leave to be familiar, that honour is given to *Kyrios* the Apollodorus and Domini Antonius alone" flared Cleopatra angrily. "I hardly need to remind you that Judea was once a Ptolemaic province so I think you should consider yourself fortunate that you do not have to surrender your entire realm to me."

"I apologise, your Highness" replied Herod with a total lack of sincerity. "I assumed that as your, er, friend? I thought that as Lord Apollodorus addressed you by name…."

Cleopatra cut him short and fixed him with her emerald green eyes "Herod, you were made Rex by the Roman Senate but I am *Bassilisa* by birth and ancient lineage! Out of regard for Domini Antonius I am prepared to accept that you are a ruler of territory that by right is mine. However, I will never acknowledge you as an equal!"

"I thought the Senate had passed a similar law proclaiming Cleopatra's father Pharaoh" commented the actress.

"No doubt a similar thought crossed the minds of both Herod and Apollodorus but neither had the courage to voice the Judean or Egyptian equivalent of pot, kettle and black."

"King Malchus of Nabataea has been ordered to hand over the bitumen deposits at the southern end of the Dead Sea and adjoining lands" continued Cleopatra. "I was going to lease them back to him as a good will gesture and was considering a similar arrangement with respect to Jericho and yourself."

"If I may be so bold, your Highness" interjected Herod. "Perhaps it would be helpful if I were to collect the rent from Malchus on your behalf?"

This was exactly what Cleopatra had in mind as she was well aware that there was an old score Herod wished to settle with King Malchus, she smiled inwardly then nodded. "That will be most helpful, Herod, in which case I will lease the groves at Jericho to you." Cleopatra's green eyes were unblinking, Herod felt like the prey of a cobra unable to move in the knowledge that its demise is both imminent and certain. "But cheat me and rest assured I will take what is rightfully mine by force of arms!"

Apollodorus remained silent but his mind raced ahead as he realised that Cleopatra's act of friendship could so easily turn into the perfect excuse to invade and Mark Antony would have no grounds for objection. Herod also realised he had walked into a trap that had so skilfully been sprung and resolved retribution at the earliest opportunity.

The Passover was now over and the pilgrims began returning to their villages. A few days later Apollodorus saw a boy in the temple discussing theology with the elders. From the eloquence of the boy's arguments the shipwright knew who the child was before he was close enough to recognise his features. They greeted each other warmly.

"Where is your Ma?" inquired Apollodorus anxiously. "Most of the country people have left Jerusalem."

The boy was dismissive "She will know that I am about my Abba's business."

"Naturally" replied Apollodorus, sceptically, then diplomatically continued; "I should like to see her again so perhaps you can show me where you are staying?" The boy lead Apollodorus to the camp but all that remained was rubbish, the people had departed that morning.

"You go back to the temple and continue with your discussions I will ride north and escort your Ma back to the city. Is the Arimathean with her?" The boy nodded. The shipwright hastily collected his mount from the mews.

Herod watched as Apollodorus passed through the Damascus gate, smiled and turned to his aid said; "Our opportunity has arisen sooner than we could have hoped. Cleopatra's brave warlord from the fabled 'Tin Island' in the 'Great Ocean' beyond the 'Pillars of Heracles' was most unwise to travel un-escorted in all his finery through the bandit country of the northern hills. Make it look good! I shall prepare to comfort the *Bassilisa* in her sad loss."

Apollodorus made sporadic progress. It was necessary for him to slow down as each group of travellers, from his stand point, all looked exactly the same. He was relying on his own distinctive appearance to be recognised by the people he was seeking but conversely his features made him an easy target for those who wanted him eliminated.

Book 28

Cleopatra felt no disquiet when Apollodorus did not join her for the evening meal, she respected the way he sometimes needed solitude. Charmain and Iras helped her to prepare for bed and disguise her as the handmaid so she could slip un-noticed into the shipwright's room. The way Jewish women kept their heads covered made it easy to conceal her distinctive golden trusses by observing local custom. Accompanied by Iras she made her way down the corridor and entered the shipwright's un-lit chamber. In the half light she assumed the bulge under the bed covers meant Apollodorus was already in bed so slipped in beside him. Too late she realised in horror these were not the strong arms of her Sea Lord that held her tightly. She tried to scream but the vice like grip on her throat rendered her mute.

Apollodorus made slow progress north, each group of Pilgrims he encountered had to he carefully scrutinised. The further he travelled the greater the gaps became between parties and the countryside became more baron rocky and inhospitably, he was exposed but there was ample cover by the roadside for bandits and robbers. The shipwright stopped under a palm tree to contemplate his next move, he reasoned that he had travelled as far as the pilgrims could have gone in the time available. His anxious deliberations were rudely interrupted by a man dropping from the tree above. Apollodorus was taken completely by surprise, other men miraculously appeared and they systematically kicked and beat him then left him unconscious by the side of the road.

When consciousness returned the shipwright was vaguely aware of pilgrims passing but none stopped to give assistance, his clothes and possessions had been taken and the horse had bolted. In the heat of the sun he lapsed in and out of consciousness. Apollodorus found himself in a vast cavern lit by an unnatural light of such brilliance that for a few moments he was unable to see. There were the most exotic flowers and trees he had ever seen. The cries of birds and animals mingled to form celestial music. A feeling of tranquil calm enveloped him and the perfume of the flowers filled his nostrils, reminiscent of the flowers on the deck of Cleopatra's flag ship at Tarsus. The noise of one particular animal stood out from the others, his two dogs came running though the trees and they greeted him enthusiastically. He walked forward through a glade as though guided by some unseen force his two dogs at his side. Emerging from the trees he found himself by the edge of a lake. The incandescent light from the cavern roof was refracted by the wavelets in a riot of colours.

"That lake is strangely familiar" he said to his dogs. He became aware that something, no, someone, was approaching. A winged lady dressed in black surrounded with an un-natural brilliance was floating across the waves towards him.

"Your time has not yet come" said Isis "and my daughter is once again in grave danger."

"I am not doing too well myself" replied Apollodorus, gesticulating towards his blood stained body that was covered by flies beside the road to Damascus.

"Fear not *Kyrios* the Apollodorus, help is at hand from the very people you were seeking."

"*Kyrios* the Apollodorus, *Kyrios* the Apollodorus, *Gelotopoios* wake up! It is Lord Apollodorus he has been attacked come quickly Joseph!"

The shipwright was vaguely aware of a young Hebrew woman who was trying to lift him into a sitting position. Water was being forced into his parched mouth and a course blanket rapped around his naked body.

"Joseph you found me" croaked Apollodorus.

"What in Gods name were you doing coming out this way unescorted?" replied the Arimathean. "You could have been killed!"

"I was looking for you, I found young Joe in the temple and took him back to your camp but you had already departed."

"Is he safe?" asked the young woman anxiously. "We thought he was with his friends and had only just realised he was missing…."

"I told him to stay with the temple elders" replied Apollodorus as they cleaned up as best as possible and helped him onto their donkey then made their way slowly back to Jerusalem. As darkness fell Apollodorus became more and more concerned about Cleopatra.

"We must hurry I sense grave danger!"

"Dressed as a common man no one will think you worth robbing again my Lord" replied the Arimathean reassuringly.

"It is not for my self that I am fearful and your boy is in safe hands, it is the *Bassilisa*. That Idumean pretender has been lusting after her all the time we have been in Jerusalem. Herod has been ordered by Antonius to hand over some territory to Egypt so relationships are strained to put things mildly."

"Do you think he could have been behind the attack on you my Lord?" inquired the young woman.

"I think it unlikely, I rode out on the spur of the moment, no one knew where I was going but Herod will undoubtedly be aware that I have gone missing and may take advantage of my absence."

"Her Royal Highness has plenty of bodyguards; surely she does not rely on you for her security" added the Arimathean.

Apollodorus said nothing, he just looked worried.

"What is it my Lord? I trusted you with my life and that of my son..."

Apollodorus hesitated but it was the Arimathean who spoke next. "You and the *Bassilisa* are very close, could it be that she will come to your room disguised as a handmaid?" He hesitated as Apollodorus nodded imperceptivity as the colour drained from his face. "If Herod also knows.... We must hurry!"

Cleopatra tried to scream but the vice like grip on her throat rendered her mute. She lay still for a moment as she tried to remember what the shipwright had taught her.

"All forces in the universe go in circles" Apollodorus had said. "You will not be as strong as your assailant or as heavy. Use his weight and re direct his force."

Cleopatra gripped Herod's wrists and turned them in opposite directions in the way Apollodorus had shown her. His grip was broken so she rolled out of the bed and made a dash for the door but not quickly enough Herod was on her again. Instinctively she was about to bring her knee up into his groin but once again she heard the shipwright's soft voice in her head.

"A kick in the manhood is painful but it causes a surge in the victim's life force which will give him super human strength, aim for the heart, eyes or nose."

Cleopatra was held in a bear hug, unable to use her arms.

"Always show your enemy respect" Apollodorus had said. "Bow to them!"

Herod had lifted Cleopatra off the ground and her face was level with his, so she nodded. A very satisfying crunch was heard as her forehead connected with his nose which spurted blood. She was free again so she tried to open the door but it was jammed.

"I will make you pay for that, you Egyptian Whore!"

"Macedonian Whore" corrected Apollodorus "and you cannot afford her prices."

The two men faced each other from opposite sides of the room. A bronze dagger appeared in Herod's hand and Cleopatra found her voice and screamed. Herod slashed at Apollodorus who was moving awkwardly, the two men circled each other. Herod slashed again and Apollodorus dropped to the ground behind his bed. When he reappeared he had a sword in one hand and a dagger in the other. Both Cleopatra and Herod were momentarily transfixed by the beauty of the weapons. The dagger Cleopatra had seen before, it was the one Caesar had borrowed to execute the treacherous eunuch Pothinus.

"Catch!" shouted Apollodorus. A flash of rotating silver flew across the room and imbedded itself in the wooden door next to the *Bassilisa*. Cleopatra pulled the dagger out of the door. She looked across at the shipwright who was now gripping the black leather hilt of his sword with both hands and she knew from the look in her friend's eyes that Herod's fate was now decided.

The first blow from the sword, which was much longer and narrower than a gladius, the Roman broad sword, cut through the dagger blade in Herod's hand as though the knife was made of butter. The Rex of Judea looked down at his useless weapon in horror then across at the shipwright whose pose was not the usual one for a swordsman. From the way Apollodorus was standing Herod realised that his head was in imminent danger of being parted from his body with the same ease as his dagger blade had been parted from its hilt. Grey eyes bore into Herod's brown ones; Apollodorus had a look of utter ruthless hatred and time stood still for all of them.

Cleopatra's mind raced. Apollodorus must have climbed in through the window, attracted by her screams. If he killed Herod there would be an uprising by the Jews and she did not have sufficient troops in the city to re-establish order. The citizens may well accept her rule but the actions of Apollodorus would place Egypt in direct conflict with Rome. Once again she heard her Sea Lord's voice in her head.

"Don't worry, Thea, I may be short tempered but I am not stupid, help is at hand."

The door opened and Mardian burst in brandishing an Egyptian sword, he was followed by Olympus, the two handmaids and a number of Cleopatra's household guard. At that moment Apollodorus struck, his sword swung through a graceful arc at frightful speed. Cleopatra screamed in horror.

"Apollodorus! Nooo doooon't do it!"

The shipwright's sword halted a hairs breadth from the terrified Herod's jugular vein and slowly the point traced around the petrified man's neck caressing his skin. The white line slowly turned red as blood oozed from the scratch. Cleopatra was astounded at the skill and control, she had never seen such swordsmanship; Apollodorus turned to face the *Bassilisa* and saluted her with his blade.

"Now is not the time Cleopatra but when you can legally occupy this land I shall take great pleasure in making a centre piece for your dinner table of this pretender's head."

"And I will take great pleasure in watching you do it, Apollodorus" replied Cleopatra in a similar blood thirsty tone. She then turned to Herod, smiled and continued. "The cut to your throat inflicted by *Kyrios mou* should serve as a reminder to you as to just how ruthless us Ptolemy's can be!" The smile vanished. "Now get out! Mardian, we will leave in the morning, make the arrangements."

The eunuch bowed and followed Herod out. Olympus and the handmaids were about to leave but Apollodorus said "Bones, one moment please, I think I need your services." The sword fell from his hand as he collapsed into Cleopatra's arms.

"Mardian come back quickly!" ordered Cleopatra. The powerful eunuch took in the situation at a glance and lifted the semiconscious shipwright onto his bed. Olympos tried to remove the rough Hebrew clothes the shipwright was wearing but they were stuck to his flesh by the blood that had oozed from his injuries.

"Charmain, Iras fetch water to bathe him" ordered the doctor.

"Geloto, what happened to you?" wailed Cleopatra.

"I was riding out on the road to Damascus when robbers attacked me, they stole my clothes and horse then left me for dead by the roadside. Fortunately an Arimathean of our mutual acquaintance found me and brought me back to the city on his donkey."

"Where is Joseph now?" demanded Cleopatra.

"I told him to make himself scarce once you were safe and only intervene if necessary. The less people like Herod know about our friend the better. His passing was fortuitous for me."

Apollodorus was badly bruised but no bones were broken. However, it took some time for Olympus to remove the blood stained clothes and clean his injuries.

"I now know why my people go into battle naked, clothing causes more problems to an injured warrior than it solves" commented the shipwright.

Meanwhile Cleopatra took the opportunity to examine her friend's sword and dagger. The weapons were made of a metal that looked like silver but were clearly much harder. The blades were beautifully engraved with snake like dragons that intertwined with meaningless hieroglyphics and the Amethyst pommels were decorated with stars that represented the constellation of Orion. The balance of each blade was perfect and the craftsmanship exquisite. The *Bassilisa* turned to Apollodorus.

"These blades could not have been forged on Earth by mortal hands, they are beautiful" she lifted the sword to the 'on guard' position. "I thought 'Orion's Sword' was a ship under construction back in Alexandria but she is here in my hands."

"There is nothing beautiful about those weapons, they are no more than instruments of death" replied Apollodorus bitterly "and I can assure you they were forged on Earth by mortal yellow hands in a strange country a very long way away."

"Do the craftsmen have slanted eyes by any chance?"

The shipwright nodded "Yes and they eat lots of rice and raw fish with seaweed. Their civilisation is far older than even the Egyptians; the people are very peaceful but have the capacity for incredible cruelty. Those are the weapons of their knights, noble men that are both warrior and magistrate who administer justice wherever and whenever they see fit without recourse to discussion or deliberation. Capital punishment is administered to the common people on the slightest pretext without hesitation."

"You learned their ways but rejected their customs?"

Apollodorus nodded. "They combine great knowledge with questionable wisdom and a religion with no gods; please question me no further, the information is far too dangerous to share even with my closest friends."

Olympus had finished tending to the shipwright's injuries so made a discrete exit and indicated to the handmaids to do the same.

"*Kyrios mou*, if it were anyone else I would be very angry and order you not to go un-escorted" there were tears in Cleopatra's eyes. Apollodorus placed his arms around her.

"I know, Thea, it was the height of stupidity on my part, this is a hostile land, and your enemies could so easily attack you by taking me hostage. I will consider the beating I received from those bandits the flogging I deserve to receive from you for my lack of forethought and consideration." Their eyes met, Apollodorus was smiling but Cleopatra was not.

"Those were no ordinary bandits, 'Pollo, they were under instruction from Herod. He knows exactly how important you are to me and was totally confident you were not coming back."

Apollodorus tried to protest but deep down he knew Cleopatra was right. "In that case I wish I had cut his head off!"

Cleopatra smiled for the first time. "I nearly let you!" she exclaimed. "When we get back to Alexandria you must show me how to use 'Orion's Sword' properly."

"So you can cut off my head if I behave like an idiot again?"

"No, purely for defence but if I catch you acting the fool again I may use your sword to cut off something else!" replied Cleopatra fiercely as she slipped into the bed beside him. She held the shipwright's head to her breasts and he was soon sleeping soundly. Cleopatra sat for a long time; the tears flowed freely down her cheeks as she pondered the day's events in her heart.

"What other secrets are there that you cannot bring yourself to share with me, my love? Who are you? What is your real name? Where did you really come from? What is your secret agenda? Did you not hear me when I referred to us as Ptolemy's?" Eventually a deep sleep engulfed the *Bassilisa* and she found herself in a vast cavern lit by an unnatural light of such brilliance that for a few moments she was blinded. Her vision cleared; there were the most exotic flowers and trees she had ever seen. The cries of birds and animals mingled to form celestial music. A feeling of tranquil calm enveloped her and the perfume of the flowers filled her nostrils, reminiscent of the flowers on the deck of the flag ship at Tarsus.

She was sailing 'Mintaka' across Lake Mareotis, Charmain and Iras were with her. As they approached the bank she could see her true love making his way to the waters edge accompanied by his two dogs, the strangest and most beautiful creatures she had ever seen. Her curiosity regarding his dogs was eclipsed by the joy that at last she would be one body with him; their final battle was now over. Then the strength vanished from her limbs; an apparition with a crocodile head barred his way. Glutton turned to Cleopatra.

"You are no better!" exclaimed the demon. "You have your guilty secrets also; they are all recorded in this book!"

King Artavasdes of Armenia withdrew to Artaxta hotly pursued by Antony's army. The Romans laid siege and ordered the monarch to surrender his city and treasury and the king's wife and two youngest sons were taken into captivity. Octavian, who had sent a secret message encouraging resistance, alleged that Artavasdes was taken prisoner by Antony under a flag of truce. The eldest son, Artaxes was eventually defeated and fled to Parthia but his parents and siblings were transported to Alexandria, Armenia was now a Roman province.

In the Royal palace on Antirhodos Cleopatra lay in the arms of her Sea Lord. Unusually they were in his room and Moonlight, the large silver spotted cat, who had adopted the shipwright when he first came to Alexandria, watched them with an expression of regal distain.

"Apollodorus" she said and the shipwright's heart sank as he thought "This means trouble if I am being addressed by my full name."

"Apollodorus"

"Cleopatra" replied the shipwright in the same tone.

"Apollodorus, *Kyrios mou*, I have been wondering. You possess three Amethyst stones - one you gave to me, one is the pommel of your sword and one on the dagger. Large stones like that usually have names so is one Alnitak, one Alnilam and one Mintaka, by any chance?"

"They could be or there again they could be called Rigel, Bellatrix and Saiph."

Cleopatra rolled over on top of Apollodorus so she could face him. "What of Betelgeuse?"

"The largest brightest star in the constellation of Orion" teased Apollodorus. "If such a stone existed it would be so large what could it be used for?"

"I could decorate my navel with it."

Apollodorus carefully rolled Cleopatra onto her back and thoughtfully examined her abdomen through the flimsy fabric of her dress and shook his head. "No, if such a stone existed it wouldn't fit."

Cleopatra tried desperately to conceal her excitement. "There is such a stone, isn't there?"

"There may be, perhaps I had better look in my desk." The shipwright got up and went over to his desk followed by the cat but he stopped mid way and turned to Cleopatra. "If Betelgeuse does exist and you wish to see how the stone would look on you we shall have to wait till Antonius returns to his Roman wife. You don't like me seeing you naked whilst we cannot enjoy an intimate relationship, following events in Jerusalem."

Cleopatra bit her lip and gave Apollodorus her most appealing look.

"It's no good looking like that!" he said as he folded his arms across his broad chest to emphasize the point. "The stone, if it existed, would have to be examined against your skin tones, we could have no confusion with clothing. Get un-dressed lie on your back and shut your eyes" he ordered.

Reluctantly Cleopatra obliged. She felt something large and cold placed on her abdomen. "You may now open you eyes, your Highness."

The stone was more magnificent than she could have imagined. It was the deepest purple and larger than the other three stones and her breath was taken away by its beauty. So much so that she forgot her nakedness.

"Is there a jeweller in all Egypt with the skill to cut, polish and set such a stone?" asked Apollodorus softly. "I have been too frightened to enquire, which is why I haven't given it to you before."

There were tears in Cleopatra's eyes "Apollodorus, I couldn't accept it."

"Yes you can! It is a magnificent Amethyst to adorn the most beautiful woman of all time. Is there a craftsman who can do justice to you and the stone?"

Cleopatra was speechless; she nodded and kissed her Sea Lord passionately, her passion was tinged with sadness. They both knew that Antony would soon return from Armenia and that conflict with Octavian was unavoidable, they would lose whatever the outcome. If Antony prevailed their secret relationship would be ended and if Octavian was victorious they would all be destroyed.

The Nile flood had long since subsided leaving its fertile life-giving black mud, seeds had been planted and the feathery date palms liberated from the weight of fruit when the Roman fleet arrived back at Alexandria. By prior arrangement Antony landed in the western harbour, Eunostos, so the troops could disembark by the Cibotus dock yard and make their triumphal entry through the Moon Gate. From the perspective of Apollodorus it looked as though every royal from around the Mediterranean had descended on Alexandria to witness the spectacle. Envoys from client states carrying gold crowns preceded legions whose shields were adorned with Antony and Cleopatra's insignia. Following the troops were floats laden with treasure and war materials captured from Armenia, then the prisoners of war with Antony bringing up the rear in a chariot pulled by four white horses. The Imperator had discarded his Roman uniform and blood red general's cloak in favour of the regalia of his patron Dionysus. He was dressed in a golden kilt with a panther pelt singlet, on his head a wreath of ivy and on his feet, buskins, which were thick soled knee high laced leather boots. Eros, the manservant, controlled the horses while Antony stood next to him waving to the crowds with his right hand and in his left holding the sacred thyrusus of Baccas, a staff tipped with a solid gold pine cone.

The procession made its way slowly along 'Canoptic Way;' the principal thoroughfare of Alexandria which was straight and very wide. At the tomb of the city's founder, 'Alexander the Great', the procession turned left into the 'Street of the Soma' which led directly towards Antirhodus Island. Halfway along the street, the procession turned right, passed the race course and mainland palace complex, theatre and gymnasium. The route was lined with cheering crowds many of whom had climbed the palm trees at the edge of the roads. Finally the procession turned south to arrive at the park dedicated to Pan.

Cleopatra was dressed in the manner of her patron, Isis, in a translucent flowing black gown and her cloak was of cloth of gold encrusted with jewels. Her head was adorned with the crown of Hera, two golden curved horns around a deep red orb. Apollodorus stood to her right and slightly behind, as befitting her principal courtier. He was dressed as Pan with suede breaches and black leather ankle boots so his lower half looked like a goat and the pelt of a lynx was draped over his broad shoulder. Two small horns protruded through his curly auburn hair. In his right hand was the fearsome 'Orion's Sword' held a few degrees off vertical in the offensive/defensive position. The thin, curved bladed was polished like silver and engraved with fearsome dragons. His dagger was sheathed on his left hip so only the black leather hilt and amethyst pommel were visible.

The shipwright had been a little reticent when Cleopatra suggested he dressed in the regalia of Mendis.

"Perhaps because Pan spends all his time chasing nymphs through the forest" suggested Charmain.

"That is just like our lord, *Geloto*" replied Cleopatra with a smile.

"But Pan never catches the object of his desire because he is ugly" added Iras defensively.

"Not necessarily" interjected Apollodorus raising one eyebrow quizzically. "The advantage of being immortal gives 'the Piper at the Gates of Dawn' all the time in the world to learn to live with such misjudgements. I will dress in the manner suggested on two conditions" he continued light heartedly. "Firstly I need reassurance that you consider me like Pan in temperament, not because you think I am ugly."

Cleopatra nodded and smiled reassuringly.

"Secondly, Charmain and Iras can dress as forest nymphs."

"So you have something to chase?" suggested the *Bassilisa* with a chuckle.

Antony had to climb two hundred steps to reach the *Bassilisa* who was seated on a raised silver dais on a golden throne under a vast circular golden dome. The dome was supported by a double ring of columns and this vast amphitheatre was on an artificial hill shaped like a pine cone. Also on the silver dais were Cleopatra's children, Caesarion sitting on another gold throne beneath his mother and clad in a purple toga and slightly lower were the other three children. Alexander was dressed in a long gown and tall pointed hat of the kings of Media and his twin sister, Cleopatra Selene, was dressed in a white translucent flowing gown of Grecian style, whereas their infant brother, Ptolemy Delphinius, wore the apparel of Alexander the Great and the ancient Macedonian royalty.

As Antony arrived at the silver dais Cleopatra stood up and Apollodorus muttered under his breath;

"As jolly Bacchus, god of pleasure
Charmed the wide world with drink and dances
And all his thousand airy fancies."

The *Bassilisa* gave a stern look to silence her friend but in her head she heard his voice continuing;

"In peace purple robe, in war panther skin and Ivy diadem;
the fruit of the vine wrecks more men than oceans."

Cleopatra knelt down on her right knee, stretched out her arms so the jewel encrusted cloth of gold cloak opened out like wings, the precious stones being arranged to give the appearance of feathers.

"Your Highness, you are the *Bassilisa* of many Pharaohs" announced the Imperator. "You are Reginae, Rexii and your son Ptolemy

Caesar is the only legitimate son of Gaius Julius Caesar, Fillius Deius, King of Kings, Rexus Rexii!"

There was thunderous applause from the citizens as Cleopatra stood up. She then resumed her seat on the gold throne and indicated that Antony sit on the adjacent one. King Artavasdes of Armenia and his family were brought before them shackled with gold chains, Apollodorus was appalled.

"You will kneel before The Imperator and the Queen of Kings" shouted one of the guards.

"I will never abase myself before you, Cleopatra" retorted Artavasdes, defiantly. The guard struck him in the stomach with the shaft of his spear but in spite of the pain the deposed king refused to bow down.

"Your Highness" whispered Apollodorus. "Never humiliate your opponents when they are vanquished because they will do far worse to you if you ever fall."

Cleopatra nodded imperceptibly. "Enough!" she shouted. "Egypt is a civilized country where all people are treated with respect, whatever their station in life. Artavasdes, if you cannot show me any respect then you cannot expect me to reciprocate courteously. You may be my prisoners but I was prepared to treat you as my guests." The *Bassilisa* turned to the Captain of the Guard. "Take them away!" she ordered.

Antony then announced the distribution of provinces "I give you Cyprus, for in very truth you are my wife and your son, Ptolemy Caesar is Deius Caesar's son. To Ptolemy Delphinius I give Syria and the entire region west of the Euphrates as far as Hellespont; to Cleopatra Selene the Cyrenaica in Libya and her twin brother Alexander Helios, Armenia and the rest of the countries to the east of the Euphrates as far as India."

During the cacophony of cheers and clapping Apollodorus whispered to Cleopatra;

"That should stop any sibling quarrels!"

Antony then feasted all the citizens of Alexandria but the shipwright took the earliest opportunity to slip away from the banquet to his own room on Antirhodos. Some time later his was disturbed by the door opening on the seaward side of his chamber. Cleopatra stood there, framed by the doorway, softly lit by the lighthouse on Pharos and dressed as he had last seen her in the crown of Hera and cloak of Isis. The *Bassilisa* dropped onto her right knee in front of him and spread her arms as she had done for Antony. However she had discarded the black chiffon dress and was naked except for a gold chain attached to her navel. On this chain were seven amethyst stones, cut from the huge stone recently given to her by

Apollodorus, four large representing Betelgeuse, Bellatrix, Saiph and Regal, the shoulders and legs of Orion and the three smaller stones Alnitak, Alnitam and Mintaka his belt which adorned her navel. Her oiled skin glistened in the golden light cast by the lighthouse across the bay. Their moist eyes met as the 'Lady of Two Lands whispered;

"For Antonius I am *Bassilisa*, for Egypt Isis, for the children *Mater* but for you I am the woman." Apollodorus looked around anxiously and was about to speak but Cleopatra pre-empted his objection.

"Dionysus has given himself to the oblivion brought on through over-indulgence. You and I both know that the fruit of the vine will be his downfall whereas Pan deliberately fails to catch the nymphs and patiently awaits his goddess. We must grasp what opportunities are left to us, *Kyrios mou*."

Book 29

Octavian was in Dalmatia recovering from a battle injury when he heard rumours of the triumphal procession in Alexandria. These 'Donations' formulated a long term settlement of the east by establishing a heredity hierarchy and no claims were made beyond the dividing line agreed three years previously by the Triumvirates at Tarentium. Antony's procession was considered to be sacrilegious and prompted the younger Triumvirate to hastily return to Rome. The year was coming to an end, the thirty fourth before Common Era, so Domitius and Sosius were designated to take office as consuls in the New Year. They had met in an anti chamber off the Senate debating hall to read the dispatches from Antony and were joined by Octavian.

"Hail! Caesar"

"Senators" replied Octavian. "What news from the East?"

"Imperator Antonius seeks ratification by the Senate for his allotment of territories" replied Domitius. "Ptolemy Caesar has been allocated Syria and all land west of the river Euphrates as far as Hellespont. Alexander Helios, Armenia and all land to the east of the Euphrates as far as India."

"These countries are not in his possession" exclaimed Octavian in disbelief.

"He has also allotted Cyrenaica in Libya to Cleopatra Selene" continued Domitius.

"The Senate must be informed, Antonius must have taken leave of his senses, he gives what is not his to give, his actions amount to treason!"

"Caesar, with respect I beg to differ, the Senate must not be informed" interjected Sosius. "Cleopatra's children are very young; Ptolemy is thirteen and the twins six so it is an empty gesture to his Egyptian mistress in return for the support given for his Parthian campaign."

"I concur with Consul Sosius" added Domitius. "Given time Antonius will tire of his Egyptian whore and make her country a Roman province.

"In that case you cannot disclose his victory in Armenia" announced Octavian decisively.

"He goes on to say that the time has come to end the office of Triumvirate and return power to the Senate and People of Rome"

"He does, does he? I very much doubt if he has the slightest intension of doing any such thing. Antonius is trying to manipulate the people against me to compel me to lay down my armaments, and then he will attack!"

Octavian stayed in Rome until the New Year, thirty three before Common Era; when he was due to serve as consulate.

"Members of the Senate" he announced. "I must decline the post in favour of Volcius Tullus and returned to Illyricum. Of great concern to me is the conduct of my once honourable friend Marcus Antonius who is bringing into disrepute his position as Triumvirate. No one can deny that he has achieved great things for the Fatherland and our eastern frontier is now secure, the barbarians will no longer be able to invade Syria. This security will bring with it great opportunities for trade and commerce. But success does not justify the blasphemy of holding a Triumph in a city other than Rome. His relationship with the Egyptian Bassilisa is at the root of his madness, so drowned is he with the love of her that he claims Cleopatra's eldest son is the only legitimate heir of the god Caesar. I am Caesar's heir. I am Filius Deu, I am the only son of the god!"

"Hail Caesar! Filius Deu! Pater Patria" shouted the Senators in response with some encouragement from Octavian's troops.

"This was the first time that Octavian had publicly criticized Antony, who should have been satisfied with the security and opportunities the conquest of Armenia and the unexpected alliance with the Media had given. From this position of strength he could have negotiated for the return of the Eagles and prisoners but, alas, yet again he favoured fame and glory also a burning ambition to emulate Julius Caesar" I explained. *"The following spring Antony, once again, travelled to Araxes to make a renewed offensive against Parthia."*

"I should think Cleopatra and Apollodorus were delighted" suggested the actress.

"It would be a mixed blessing" I replied. *"This would be the last time they would be alone together."*

"So time was running out for them" commented the actress sadly. *I nodded; it was running out for us also, a psychic had warned me some time ago that this type of relationship could only last a year. More to the point time was running out literally for me, the symptoms the medics had warned were beginning to emerge and this was a precursor to what was inevitable. I had so much still to pass on. My train of thought was interrupted by a question from the actress.*

"I found a book on your shelves 'Apollodorus the Library of Greek Mythology' is that Cleopatra's shipwright?

"Apollodorus was a relatively common name, like John Smith today. No one knows who the author of 'The Library' was, but some say it was written by the famous writer 'Apollodorus of Athens' who was born about two hundred years before Common Era. Socrates had a sidekick named Apollodorus but he was from an earlier time. The style of the Greek in 'The Library' is however from Cleopatra's era."

"I also found two photographs of sheep dogs."

"They are the Rough Coated Collies I owned in the past, the sable one like Lassie was the first then when he died I had a Blue Merle, he looked more like a wolf than a dog. They were lovely animals, beautiful and highly intelligent; I would love to have another dog and a cat but I am no longer able to give a pet a proper home." The time had come to return to the actresses London flat as she was finding out too much too quickly.

"We have a rather distinguished visitor" explained Cleopatra. "King Artavasdes of Media has sent his daughter, Iotape, to Alexandria as she is betrothed to Alexander Helios."

"Alexander is only seven, he is a child, there is plenty of time for him to become involved with women" replied Apollodorus aghast. "I think I had better have words with him, anyway there are no formal matrimonial arrangements in Egypt."

Cleopatra laughed "It is a political arrangement to ensure that the Medians keep to the terms of the treaty."

"So she is a hostage!"

"No, she isn't. As in Egypt the Median realm is vested in the female line so the presence of the girl gives a personal and material security."

"Has she come here of her own free will?"

"Not exactly…"

"So she is a hostage. Where I come from people marry out of choice. Does Alexander want to spend the rest of his life with a girl he has never met, who probably can't speak the same language? By marrying this girl he gets to be Rex or Pharaoh of Media, whatever the royal designation, but surrenders his fundamental freedom to choose his own consort?"

"That is the way the system has always been here and in the east. In order to become a king a young man has to marry the daughter of a king because the son of a monarch does not inherit the realm."

"So, if I were to marry you, not that you would have me, I would become Pharaoh" replied Apollodorus brightly.

Cleopatra turned away hurriedly and made a fuss of the shipwright's cat so that Apollodorus would not see her tears, she had to think quickly.

"I have intercepted a letter from Antonius to Octavius which I found rather upsetting" she handed him the manuscript. "This is a copy."

Apollodorus studied the document intently. "What does ineo mean?"

"It is a rather vulgar colloquial sexual expression" replied Cleopatra.

"Uxor mea est. She is my wife."

"Is she my wife?" corrected Cleopatra.

Apollodorus nodded, he had become very serious "I think I have the sense of it. 'Why the sudden change' Antonius is asking, 'because I shag the Bassilisa, she is not my wife. I have been shagging her for nine years. Do you only shag Drusilla? Fuck off if by the time you read this you haven't shagged Terulla and Terentilla, Rufillia, Salvia Titisensia and the rest. What does it matter where you get your erection/satisfaction?' Thea, I am so sorry, Antonius looks on you as his stabbing block!" The shipwright picked up the tearful *Bassilisa* in his arms as though she were a child and held her tightly. "I thought Antonius loved you, I don't know what to say.

"Don't say anything, just hold me. I agree with everything you were saying about arranged marriages but this is the world where we live and I must abide by its rules."

"That letter to Octavian still survives and gives a rare insight into the humanity and mind set of Antony" I added. "It is generally taken that my people are unique in that they use the word for the act of love making as a profanity but Antony's letter contradicts this assumption. Also there is considerable scholastic argument about the translation of the phrase uxor mea est...."

"Clearly he thought nothing of Cleopatra, contrary to both historic and popular perception" interjected the actress.

I nodded, "I told you that the encounter at Tarsus was no meeting of lovers! The Triumvirates went on to exchange letters which became progressively angrier; Antony complained that he had not received any benefit from the conquest of Sicily."

"He had not shared any of his conquered territories with Octavian so what basis had he for complaint?"

Again I nodded in agreement, "Octavian replied in much the same vein. Antony was critical about the way Lepidus had been deposed to which Octavian replied that Triumvirate power had been grossly abused by their former colleague."

"The Latin equivalent of 'pot, kettle and black' would have been an appropriate response" interjected the actress with a smile.

I laughed and continued, *"Antony then bitched on about the old chestnut of land settlements for his veterans, to which Octavian reposted that he was welcome to half of Sicily in exchange for half of Armenia."*

"Rightly so! Antony had plenty of conquered territory to satisfy his obligations to the troops."

"Octavian concurred with that viewpoint and then Antony bemoaned the lack of reinforcements sent following his humiliating retreat from Parthia which elicited the reply that round two had been successful."

"Presumably at this stage, to use one of your colourful English metaphors, Antony threw all his toys out of his pram and marched on Rome."

I laughed. *"Not yet, it was Apollodorus who would spit out his dummy. The Consulates designate for the New Year, Senators Domitius and Sosius had begun to hyperventilate and sent an anxious despatch to Antony warning him that Octavian was preparing for war and urged him to take action before it was too late."*

"Was Octavian in a position to attack Antony?"

"Not really. Octavian had neither the financial nor military resources; taxes would have to be raised and he was mindful that it was unlikely Italy would unite in another civil war. Antony believed that military success in Parthia, the annexation of Armenia and an alliance with Media would swing the balance of power in his favour. Despite these considerations he decided that the danger from the west was too pressing to ignore and that reluctantly Parthia would have to wait, but age was not on his side, as Mark Antony was now in his fifties."

"So Antony decided enough was enough and abandoned being Domini nice guy."

"Indeed. The living embodiment of Dionysus metamorphosed into the living embodiment of Hercules. Legiti Canidiuss was instructed to bring the army on the long march back to the Mediterranean and the fleet was to muster in western Asia Minor, headquarters being established in Ephesus. Client Kings from Syria to the Mareotic Lake and from Aemenia to Illyria were ordered to send men and war materials. The stage was now set for

what would be the final conflict and an Armada assembled, the like of which would not be seen again for two thousand years."

The first day of Emergence brought with it no happiness for Cleopatra and Apollodorus; they would not dance by moonlight to the music of a distant unseen choir as they had in the past.

"We are to take the fleet to Ephesus" announced Cleopatra as they surveyed the Egyptian navy in the Cibotus Harbour. They were aboard the Royal Thalamegos, the river boat with one bank of oars and an ornate cabin aft similar to the vessel used by the *Bassilisa* when they first met at Askalon. "Antonius has at last decided that the threat posed by Octavius can no longer be ignored."

"I told him we needed three years to prepare for this conflict" exclaimed the exasperated shipwright. "We recommended action before Octavius became strong and Antonius prevaricated. The little runt stole the advantage in the arms race so we urged caution until we could redress the balance of power. I also said he should divert the attention of Octavius well away from Egypt. So what does the drunken fathead do..."

"Yes, I know, *Kyrios mou*" interrupted Cleopatra soothingly. "How many warships have we ready for service?" They had passed between rows of anchored triremes and were making their way towards the bridge at the mainland end of the Heptastadion Causeway which linked the Island of Pharos to the mainland of Alexandria.

"Not enough! Do we have the crew trained to operate them in combat? No! Do we have transport ships for the army? I doubt it! Can you please explain to that son of a – to Domini Antonius that ships don't grow on trees, they are made out of trees. The trees have to be cut down, sawn into planks, and allowed to season, all of which takes time."

"When you first came to Alexandria there was a fleet of seventy ships which you described as an 'archaeological collection of Naval Architecture' and to underline your contempt you proceeded to set them on fire. In fifteen years you have tripled the size of the navy with larger modern warships. This is an incredible achievement, *Kyrios mou*. If we delay another year, could you double the size of the fleet? I very much doubt it. Antonius, we know, has a fleet of seventy ships which were returned by Octavius in addition to his existing navy. He has ships under construction and other allies as well as Egypt so there could be as many as four or five hundred. Has a fleet as large as that ever been assembled before?"

"Octavius probably has a fleet of that size crewed by combat hardened watermen and unlike our headstrong impetuous Antonius, his planning will be meticulous! He will have been waiting and hoping that Domini Antonius would be stupid enough to make the first move which will give him all the justification with the Senate he needs."

"We have both known for a long time that this conflict was inevitable. Will we be any stronger if we delay?"

Apollodorus shook his head in sad recognition. They had now passed from Eunostos, the Harbour of Good Return, into the Great Harbour and were rowing sedately towards the Royal Harbour and the Palace on Antirhodos. The pavilion aft cabin of the Thalamegos gave them a measure of privacy from the rowers who sat in the open. "Thea, let me embrace you." They held each other for some time then the shipwright continued. "There is no alternative, so we had better get on with the preparation before the winds become unfavourable."

Cleopatra and Apollodorus arrived in Syria a few weeks later with two hundred warships and almost as many support vessels commandeered from the Egyptian merchant fleet. Here they were joined by Mark Antony and together sailed onwards to Ephesus, a city with an origin shrouded in myth and legend, its name being derived from a pre Greek word *Apasas*, meaning bee. This thriving metropolis had been a popular stop over for mariners since the late Bronze Age due to the abundant fresh water springs on the beach. The temple of Artemis, or Diana as she was known to the Romans, at Ephesus was one of the seven wonders of the ancient world. Artemis, the daughter of Leto, was an archer like her twin brother Apollo. She had three forms, in the sky Selene, the moon goddess associated with fertility although she had asked Zeus her father, when only three years old, to grant her eternal virginity. On earth she was Artimis goddess of the wilderness, wild animals and hunting and Hecate in the under world associated with deeds of darkness and evil magic.

The maiden goddess was very protective of her purity and demanded no less from her companions. Some say that Orion attempted to rape Artemis who conjured up a scorpion which fatally stung him and his dog Sirius. One of Artemis' nymphs, Callisto, was seduced by Zeus and gave birth to Arcas, the result of this infidelity being that the goddess turned the nymph into the Great Bear, known to us as the constellation of the Plough, the signpost for the north. Artemis was very possessive and showed no mercy to those who disobeyed her. Arsinoe, Cleopatra's sister, had a few years earlier, been dragged from the sanctuary of the temple at Ephesus and executed. In less than two years the perpetrator and benefactor of this sacrilege would feel the retribution of the goddess and pay the ultimate price.

"The symbol of the goddess Artemis was the honey bee, hence the name Ephesus is derived from the ancient word 'apasas', similar to the Latin word apis but nothing like meliooa in Greek."
"So did she sting like a bee?" enquired the actress.
"The bee's sting is barbed so the insect is unable to withdraw it from her human victim, her vengeance results in her death. Artemis' Roman namesake, a princess of our own time as you know, died in tragic and highly suspicious circumstances. At risk of sounding superstitious, I would not want to be the perpetrator of any wrong doing in that respect, if there is any substance in the abundant conspiracy theories" I replied solemnly.

"Unlike neighbouring settlements, Ephesus had survived the Hellenistic Dark Age un-changed until King Kroisus, the 'Golden Monarch of Lydia'; re located the city further inland. He was succeeded as ruler by the Persian King Cyrus and during the Persian occupation the citizens did not join the 'Ionian Rebellion' so Ephesus was saved from destruction" explained Cleopatra as the Egyptian fleet neared landfall. "The city was finally liberated by my ancestor, Alexander the Great, who re located the metropolis at its present site further down stream of the River Kaystros."

From the quayside Cleopatra, Apollodorus and Antony were escorted through the basilica where commerce and business was being transacted. Behind this bustling concourse was a courtyard surrounded by a covered walkway, the roof being supported on ornate pillars. They made their way around the portico to the northern side and into the ceremonial hall to be formally welcomed. In the centre of the building was a square pit where the sacred fire burned and at the far end was an altar where offerings and sacrifices to the gods were made.

"Seeing an open fire like this makes me feel like I am back in Britannia" commented Apollodorus irreverently ribbing his hands together near the flame. It was now late autumn so the weather was cold and damp.

"This is the sacred flame" hissed Cleopatra. "It is never extinguished and is the heart of Ephesus."

After the speeches of welcome they gave thanks to the gods and made their offerings then they were escorted to the terraced houses opposite the temple. These houses known as the 'houses of the rich' were on the slopes of Mount Bulbul. The plain exterior was in sharp contrast to the ornate mosaics and frescoes inside. The rooms had no windows and were illuminated from the hallway in the centre of the houses.

"It's a bit gloomy" commented Apollodorus. "I think I shall sleep aboard ."

"You will do no such thing" retorted Cleopatra crossly. "These are the most prestigious homes in Ephesus; it would be the height of bad manners not to accept the citizen's hospitality. And don't give me that dung about not being able to sleep on land!"

Had they been alone the shipwright would have protested that Cleopatra was not going to trust him out of her sight or suggest that she may wish to sneak off for some quality Egyptian time.

"Yes, on both counts, and I am not taking any chances in either respect" added Cleopatra knowing full well what he was thinking. "We are now in a state of war and I want my Sea Lord at my side at all times. Is that clear, Apollodorus?"

"Crystal clear, your Highness" replied Apollodorus, grinning like a recalcitrant school boy who had been caught in the act of some minor misdemeanour.

"Iras, you will escort *Kyrios mou* to his room and assist in his unpacking. Charmain, you will assist me."

"Yes, madam" replied the handmaids in unison.

A little later Apollodorus and Iras were joined by Charmain who handed the shipwright a note.

"The fates may soon part us, what time we have left together will be precious. For that reason I want you with me whenever possible. I know it is difficult for you, so the handmaids will attend to your every desire while I am unable to. *Agape* Thea."

"It will not be a committee of celestial vestal virgins that will tear us apart, it will be those fornicating Romans" muttered Apollodorus ruefully as he cautiously burned Cleopatra's note.

Legiti Canidius arrived shortly after the Egyptian fleet and it was now November. It had taken two months for the Roman army to march back from Araxes. Herod arrived by sea about the same time, his troops followed by land.

"I refuse to have that pretender involved in this campaign" shouted Cleopatra.

"Why ever not?" replied Antony

"He is a lying treacherous..."

"Son of an Idumaean camel driver's whore" interjected Apollodorus helpfully "who tried to rape her Royal Highness and have me murdered while we were his guests. I am not normally a vindictive man but in his case I am prepared to make an exception!"

Antony looked dumfound at Cleopatra and then at Apollodorus. He was used to the *Bassilisa's* outbursts but he knew from past experience that it took a great deal to annoy her Sea Lord.

"Send him away, Antonius or I will return to Alexandria with my ships and the war chest" ordered Cleopatra. "He could make himself useful as King Malchus of Nabataen has defaulted on two of the annual payments of rent for the Bitumen deposits, and Herod was supposed to collect this money."

Some time later with Cleopatra and Apollodorus well out of the way Antony received Herod and explained that he was unable to accept his assistance.

"I have no choice. Her Royal Highness has provided a substantial fleet and twenty thousand talents towards the war chest."

"Domini Antonius, with the greatest respect, man to man, are you that besotted with her?" replied Herod. Antony shook his head imperceptibly. "Use your imagination, Dominus. Get rid of her, arrange an accident then make Egypt a Roman province. With Egyptian wealth and Roman military you would be master of the world!"

Meanwhile on the poop deck of 'Orion's Sword' Apollodorus grasped the black leather hilt of his sword of the same name as the ship. The long slender blade curved behind his neck and the sunlight made the amethyst pommel glow. Cleopatra was some distance away on the other side of the ship; she had a large apple in her hand. Without warning she tossed the fruit into the air. The intricately engraved blade flashed as Apollodorus sped across the deck and an instant later two halves of the apple landed.

"Herod's head?" inquired Cleopatra sweetly.

"Or Antonius'. I am not fussy" replied the shipwright.

"I have sent instructions to General Athenion in Coele Syria to ensure that there is no satisfactory outcome for Herod against Malchus." From the corner of his eye Apollodorus saw Iras throw another apple into the air, the shipwright lunged and skewered the fruit on the point of his sword. Turning, he offered the impaled apple to Cleopatra and looked mischievously into her eyes. Cleopatra accepted the fruit and took a bite while holding his gauze.

"You seem to have recovered your normal humorous outlook on life, *Kyrios mou*. Why the change of heart?"

"Being philosophical about events thus far the best that can happen is that Antonius and Octavius will end up killing each other which would be a great relief to the rest of us" replied Apollodorus.

"And the worst case scenario?" prompted Cleopatra.

"The worst that can happen is that we get killed, which wouldn't be that bad. It's not as though we haven't done it before."

"What in the name of the gods do you mean, Apollodorus!" exclaimed Cleopatra.

"The people who made this sword have a religion without any gods, they believe that we spend a relatively short time here on Earth but when we die we go to a place of rest. When our spirit has recuperated we are re-born, how we live this life will determine what sort of life we have next time around but normally we are unaware of previous lives." Cleopatra and the two handmaids had sat down at the feet of the shipwright and were listening intently, so he continued.

"Have you noticed how some of the gods are very similar, although they have different names and come from different times and countries? Perhaps they are not gods' at all but merely higher forms of live that retain the memory of previous incarnations and continue with their individual quests and addenda through several lifetimes with new bodies and different identities. Here in Ephesus it is totally accepted that Artemis, Cynthia, Phoebe, Selene and Hecate of the underworld are one and the same. She is also Diana to the Romans, as Dionysus is Baccas."

"So what you are saying is that I could be more than the living embodiment of Isis, I could be the goddess?" suggested Cleopatra.

"Well, to me, Thea," replied Apollodorus, with a smile. "You are Isis, the perfect mother for your children and to your people."

Cleopatra put her arms around her Sea Lord and with tears in her eyes said; "Thank you, 'Pollo, you make up for all the horrible things my enemies say about me." In silence she continued "just say what I long to hear you say, then in deference to the prophesies I will send my ships and treasury back to Alexandria where I will place the 'Serpent Ring' on your finger. You will be my Pharaoh and these squabbling barbarians can be victims of their own fate."

"Could Cleopatra have turned her back on Mark Antony and left him there to face Octavian alone?" inquired the actress.

"Very easily. None of the other allies wanted her to be involved and by abandoning this futile quest she would have deprived Octavian of his only excuse for going to war against the ever popular Mark Antony. Cleopatra would have lost the territories given by Antony, but she was no fool, she knew they were empty gestures of good will. The Bassilisa had learned from the bitter experience of giving military assistance to Pompey the Great and incurring the displeasure of Caesar. For fifteen years she had kept out of any conflict and Egypt had prospered as a result, a fact not lost on her people. If Cleopatra had wanted to increase her territory she had the means to do so by force of arms while Rome degenerated into anarchy."

Book 30

"People of Rome you have been robbed of your democracy" began Domitius, at his inaugural speech as consul. "But we have not yet become a monarchy as Antonius and Octavius still control affairs on an equal footing, having divided by lot most of the functions of government between themselves. It is my belief that the restoration of the Republic is still possible through Antonius. I do not advocate revolutionary measures having experienced many such disasters. What is your opinion, consul Sosius?"

"Lepidus is removed from office and Sextus Pompeius has perished, their territories are possessed by Octavius. But has the adopted son of Caesar shared these spoils of war with Antonius? I think not! Our eastern frontier has been secured by Antonius, the Armenian king is held captive and Parthia is quiet. Why then does Octavius collect funds? This grandchild of a rope maker, some call him Thurian, is not of noble birth but his intentions are all too clear. He is following in the footsteps of his adopted Pater and seeks to become sole ruler of Rome, so we must act before it is too late! Measures must be implemented. I propose a motion of censure on Octavius, the so called adopted son of Caesar." There were howls of protest from a number of senators.

"Consul Sosius, I must protest" interrupted the horrified Tribune Balbus. "What you propose will plunge Rome into another civil war! I veto the proposition!"

"Hear hear" shouted some of the Senate.

Mark Antony had amassed a total allied army comprised of twenty five thousand infantry, twelve thousand cavalry, five hundred warships and three hundred transports. Some of the triremes were newly built in Asia Minor where Turtullius gained notoriety by felling sacred trees on the Island of Cos for ship building timber. The allied navy was organised into eight squadrons and deployed to various Greek islands. In the city of Ephesus Cleopatra stood alone before the alter of Artemis and entreated the goddess.

"What offence have I caused the gods that I am tortured by loving a man whose actions leave me in no doubt of the feelings he refuses to articulate. I am forced to take as consort a man who says he loves me yet uses me as his whore; a man that has plunged my realm into conflict for a foreign cause."

"If you are in no doubt about the feelings of the man you love, why do you need them to be spoken?" replied a soft feminine voice in Cleopatra's head. "Why do you not ask him if he loves you? Is pride your only obstacle? Are you fearful that he may not feel as you believe he does?"

"You know that I cannot give that which I so long to give him, unless or until he declares his true feelings freely, on pain of death."

"Envy can be a powerful ally, my child" replied Artemis.

Octavian suspected that there would be rumblings of discontent in the Senate and had wisely absented himself from Rome. In this way he did not have to answer to the criticism but could await reports and act having given considerations to all the possibilities. In due course he did return to Rome with a substantial bodyguard which surrounded the Theatrum Pompeium while he took his chair of state with well armed friends who made no attempt to conceal their daggers.

"Senators and People of Rome" began the young Triumvirate. "I am shamefully criticized and people who should know better have stirred up all Rome against me. This action amounts to treason! It is true, firstly, that I did spoil Sextus Pompeius and did not give Antonius part of Sicily. Secondly, I have returned the warships loaned by Antonius to prosecute that war. And, thirdly, I deposed our companion Triumvirate Lepidus because he shamefully abused his power. Antonius has retained that which he won by right of conquest yet he condemns me for doing the same. Furthermore, he has amassed a substantial force of arms against the fatherland at the behest of his Egyptian mistress."

Having defended his own actions and castigated Antony and his supporters, Octavian named the date of the next meeting when he would place before the Senate further evidence of Antony's wrong doing. Faced with what amounted to an armed coupe and in fear of their lives, Consuls Domitius and Sosius fled the country to join Antony before the next meeting, accompanied by nearly four hundred Senators.

"Your Highness, I think you should return to Alexandria" explained Antony. "You will be much safer there as I have stationed four legions in Cyrenaica commended by Lucius Pinarius Scarpus to protect Egypt against any attack from the African provinces."

"My place as monarch is at the head of my army. I cannot order my people to endure the suffering of war if I am not prepared to suffer with them" replied Cleopatra defiantly.

"It is a measure of the distrust felt by many of the people of Rome that a third of the Senate have been prepared to place their family, property and careers at risk and leave Italy to join forces with me. But some will argue that they will not fight Rome on your behalf."

"That is a rather perverse view" retorted Cleopatra angrily. "You summonsed me to assist in your fight against Octavius. It is Egypt that will be fighting the republican cause! What do you think, *Kyrios* the Apollodorus?"

"I think, with respect, that Her Royal Highness having invested the entire armed forces of Egypt and most of her treasury into your campaign has every right to stay and ensure that her country's resources are spent appropriately. Others have argued that if the *Bassilisa* were to return to Alexandria there would be every chance that the Egyptian forces would lose their stomach for battle and begin to desert in ever increasing numbers. I agree with this viewpoint" replied the shipwright. He then turned to the *Bassilisa* and added "Cleopatra you can no more afford to take that risk than Antonius. The influx of so many disaffected Romans will be a mixed blessing. They will be old men wishing to press their own agenda, not young men eager to obey and fight for a single cause."

At the first meeting of the exiled Senate in Ephesus it became all too clear that the misgivings voiced by Apollodorus were justified. Consul Domitius insisted that Cleopatra be sent back to Egypt.

"I disagree! We should not forget that Cleopatra has provided more than half the war ships, most of the auxiliaries and a substantial amount of money. The Egyptian warriors will lose heart if their Regina is sent home and they will probably return with her" replied Candius echoing the words of Apollodorus. "If the *Bassilisa* was a man, we would not be having this discussion. She is inferior to no one in either wisdom or judgement. Egypt has been wisely governed for some considerable time and has prospered under her stewardship. Were this not the case she would not have been able to provide the generous funding of our war chest. Cleopatra has learned to manage great affairs so will be a major asset to our cause."

"How much has she paid you to be her spokesman?" Titius retorted angrily.

"It is well known that you were her courtier in Alexandria" added Plancus.

Elsewhere Cleopatra and Apollodorus were having a similar discussion in the central courtyard of their temporary home.

"It is really an argument of ideology" explained Apollodorus. "The Romans passionately believe in democracy until it bites them in the buttocks."

Cleopatra giggled musically "What on earth do you mean, *Geloto*?"

"Democracy is supposedly government of the people, through the people by the people from which they hope to get consensus but it results in mediocrity and populist policies. Unfortunately not everyone in Rome has the vote so what they end up with is government of the rich over the poor, they call them plebs, through the military."

"I thought you believed in democracy?"

"In an ideal world I would but, as we both know, unfortunately that isn't the world we live in. I believe in equality and as far as possible I treat everyone as an equal; equality and democracy go hand in hand. In reality people are far from equal in both education and financial status, mobs are a feckless lot often ignorant, frequently irresponsible and sometimes violent. Consequently within a democracy malpractices are inevitable, corruption leads to unholy alliances as the politicians responsible conspire in mutual support until one person emerges as the people's champion."

"As happened with Caesar" interrupted Cleopatra.

"Indeed. Caesar broke up the cliques, won the admiration of the mob and found himself with absolute power as frequently happens in these situations."

"And then got stabbed to death by his opponents" suggested the *Bassilisa*.

"This resulted in an Oligarchy of three men competing for distinction in public service which led to violent personal feuds as each competed to be supreme. We have witnessed an all too familiar pattern with this form of government in Rome. Personal feuds have inevitably led to civil war and bloodshed. A democracy lacks the consistency of a monarchy, the disadvantage is that monarchs are just as prone to human weakness as the rest of us so most abuse their power appallingly. A good monarchy is far more preferable to a bad democracy. In your case you have acted autocratically in everyone's best interest and Egypt has been peaceful and prosperous. There is no better form of government than one good ruler but unfortunately good monarchs are rare. Great monarchs like you come every thousand or so years with the rest being at best awful and some downright evil. Antonius has been enjoying the advantages of being an absolute ruler for several years, he is now going to have to come to terms with all the disadvantages of consensus decision making."

"So what is the answer?" asked Cleopatra.

"In the macro or the micro sense?" prompted Apollodorus.

"Both!" she replied.

"You have read Plato's 'The Republic'. What did you think?"

"I was horrified."

"I had much the same reaction but the Spartans thought it a good idea and almost made it work at considerable human cost. With the exception of the golden haired monarch sat next to me, the world is not run by well meaning logical minded people acting in every one's best interest. It is run by mean minded vindictive individuals whose only motivation is self interest and the gods are no better, which is why I worship none of them."

"So, what is the answer?"

Apollodorus thoughtfully picked up a goblet "To a pessimist this goblet is half empty and to an optimist it is half full." The shipwright paused and Cleopatra nodded. "An opportunist sees it as a means of quenching his, or her, thirst." He drained the goblet in a breath and smiled. "Or of making glad the heart. As you know, I have a healthy respect for the fact that I am an idiot and I extend the same courtesy to everyone I meet."

"I thought you considered yourself to be a genius?" protested Cleopatra.

"I do but there is a fine line that divides brilliance and insanity" replied Apollodorus with a chuckle. "On the odd occasion that I am confronted by someone sensible I look on it as a bonus. In short I make the best of things.

"So?"

"Egypt is much closer to a democracy and has far greater equality than Rome because you are prepared to listen to your subjects and try to act in the best interest of the populous. Rome takes all giving very little in return and what it does give is available only to a very small minority. We have a stark choice; destroy Octavius before he destroys us. It is very tempting to accept that our presence is unwelcome and return to Alexandria, but if we do Antonius will patch up his differences with Caesar's bum boy."

"And then?" prompted Cleopatra.

"And then some dark night as M.A, in a state of Dionysus, staggers back from some un-seasonal quaffing and feasting in a less than fashionable part of Rome to his enemy's beloved sister...."

"Twenty three stabs later and goodbye cruel world" interjected Cleopatra.

Apollodorus nodded "Yes, and about the same number of days later the fair haired grandson of a rope maker will be knocking at the 'Gate of the Sun' demanding satisfaction for the way Antonius declared the truth about Caesar's rightful heir."

"I suppose if we are going to die anyway it is better to die fighting, Pollo."

"A war is only lost when one side gives in Thea! We have a unique opportunity to rid the world of a great evil, an opportunity, for the sake of all humanity, we must seize with both hands." Apollodorus took hold of the *Bassilisa's* hands and their eyes met. "We don't give in do we, so if the men with big noses and small private parts tell you to go home you tell them...."

"Where to go and fornicate" interrupted Cleopatra forcefully.

"That's my Thea! Roman knows that you are one of the finest rulers in history which is why Octavius accuses you of every kind of evil and depraved human practice. They will continue with their campaign of hatred of you long after you are no more. All too often the good people do is interned with their mortal remains but their evil lives on after them. The world we live in sadly reveres mediocrity and despises brilliance; Rome will destroy us unless we subjugate them! The gods have given us a chalice which we have little choice but to drink from, no matter how unpalatable the content!"

"Speaking of unpalatable subjects" replied Cleopatra hesitantly. "I have located my sister Arsinoe's grave.

"I was rather hoping you would" answered the shipwright "I have an idea for a memorial clearly identifiable to an Alexandrian but pretty well meaningless to the rest of the world. I assume you would like to be discrete." Cleopatra nodded so Apollodorus unrolled a drawing of a monument which represented the three sections of the Pharos lighthouse reduced in height.

"That is beautiful Pollo, it is recognisable as Pharos but you have changed the proportions so it will not be overly ostentatious, her final resting place will remain secret to all except those who knew her."

"That was the general idea, Domini Antonius believes that he did you a great favour by executing your sister so I suggest you commission the work to be done after we have left and cause no offence."

Cleopatra nodded and thought "Hopefully this will plicate Artimis and she will forgive the sacrilege in her temple." It would be two thousand years before anyone would identify the grave but it would remain a mystery who had been responsible for the memorial which by then had all but been destroyed.

'Orion's Sword' was on the final approach to the Island of Samos, Cleopatra and the handmaids reclining on an impromptu tryclinium of sail bags. The *Bassilisa's* golden hair glistened in the spring sunshine and her green eyes sparkled as she watched Apollodorus steer the ship with the effortless automation gained through years of experience.

"Rhoecus, Theodorus and Herodotus; some of the Earths greatest thinkers have contemplated on this island" mused the shipwright.

"And Pythagoras" added Cleopatra.

"Oh yes, we must not forget dear old Pythagoras of Samos."

"The square of the hypotenuse of a right angle triangle is equal to the sum of the square of the other two sides" quoted Cleopatra dreamily.

"There was no limit to Pye's genius. Where would modern architecture be without his theorem? Come to think, of it how did your predecessors manage to build the pyramids without that knowledge?"

"The ancient Egyptians knew about the three, four, five right angle triangle" answered Cleopatra defensively.

"Yes, of course three, four and five" replied the shipwright thoughtfully. "Pythagoras believed all things could be reduced to numbers."

"He established a school of Philosophy and Religion at Croton which attracted many followers" added Cleopatra. "New members were expected to remain silent for the first five years and listen to older members, after that initiation period they were free to express their beliefs."

"I wouldn't have been any good as I can't keep my mouth shut for more than five heart beats" replied Apollodorus grinning broadly.

"Pythagoras was deeply religious; he ate no meat, drank no wine and wore no woollen clothing. He would not poke a fire with iron or handle beans" continued Cleopatra solemnly.

"With all those prohibitions I suppose the only way to keep warm during the winter in his commune was by carrying out fiendishly difficult mathematical calculations. Presumably they refrained from all intimate relationships and had cold baths for good measure. I suppose I could, if necessary, become a vegetarian and wine I could live without with difficulty. However, given the choice I would dress in cotton in preference to wool any day. I threw the last of my beans overboard when I brought you back to Alexandria from Askalon, but I am sorry. Thea, I wouldn't give up poking a fire with an iron bar for anyone."

Cleopatra chuckled in her deep musical way that Apollodorus found so irresistible. "Its interesting that the probationary period was five years" continued the shipwright thoughtfully. "I wonder if he knew of the divine constant." They could now see clearly the highly indented coastline and profusion of sand and shingle coves and in the distance were two magnificent mountain ranges. The short sea crossing from Ephesus had given Apollodorus and Cleopatra a much needed opportunity to relax and also the minimal crew required to operate Orion's Sword afforded a semblance of blessed privacy. The city of Samos, their ultimate destination, was at the end of a long horseshoe bay at the mouth of the river Imvrasos.

"Herodotus described the island first among all cities" explained Cleopatra. "It was founded by King Ancaeus a contemporary of Jason on the Arganatic expedition. He built the first temple to the goddess Hera, the island's protector."

"I always felt rather sorry for Hera, having to put up with all the indiscretions of her husband Zeus, the way he was always changing himself into showers of coins or other unlikely objects so he could satisfy his carnal desires on unsuspecting nymphs." Cleopatra looked at Apollodorus in disbelief. "I suppose as a god you are going to say he was above moral consideration?" he continued.

"Given the opportunity all men spread their lineage as widely as possible and those with the means have extensive harems of wives and concubines so why should a god be any different?" asked the bewildered Cleopatra.

Apollodorus looked at the *Bassilisa* as though he was seeing her for the first time. "Surely you wouldn't want to be one of several wives."

"Why not? *Bassilisa* means principal wife of the Pharaoh. *Pater* had a number of concubines." Cleopatra had to think carefully, part of the mystery of Apollodorus was beginning to make sense; she would have to phrase her next question very carefully. "No species mate for life" she thought and then she realised that was not true, the swan being one of a few exceptions along with the uraus. There was no way she could ask why the ethics of the Egyptians were so alien to him, as the consequences of a truthful answer were incalculable, and hopefully patience would bring its reward.

The magnificent Polycratean wall that surrounded and protected the city was clearly visible. Built during the rein of the tyrant Polykrates by the engineer Efplinon using four thousand slaves, this wall had thirty five towers and twelve gates along its twelve thousand cubit (*six kilometres*) length.

Two breakwaters divided the natural harbour which was protected by an artificial mole nearly two thousand cubits *(two kilometres)* in length. Apollodorus ordered the lowering of the sails as they entered the outer harbour and he brought Orion's Sword skilfully alongside the wide quay. Cleopatra was used to the way he berthed Mintaka under sail but to perform the same manoeuvre in the much larger warship without deploying oars, as all other Trierarchos did, was impressive.

"The Samian fleet had travelled extensively bringing wealth and knowledge to this ancient city so the sailors considered themselves among the finest in the Mediterranean, now you have arrived, *Geloto*, to show them how a real mariner handles his ship."

"Thank you, Thea, I know you like to make an impressive entrance but I did have the crew ready with the oars in case things went wrong."

"This will be the war to end wars" announced Antony to the assembled Senators and allied commanders at Samos. "Octavius accuses me of all kinds of vices, natural and un-natural. This grandson of a rope maker, at Philippi abandoned his camp and hid in the marshes. This son of a baker, at Naulochus lay prostrate with fear in the carina of his ship while Agrippa prevailed against the enemy. This moneychanger seeks to be master of Rome while committing blasphemy against his patron at the 'Feast of the Divine Twelve' whilst playing the part of Apollo. His friends act as slave dealers providing him with the wives and daughters of the nobility for his sexual gratification."

Cleopatra and Apollodorus were listening at the back of the assembly as women were not welcome in the Roman Senate.

"Octavius suffers from poor health and lacks experience" protested the shipwright softly. "The best of sailors suffer from seasickness occasionally which is probably why he handed over command to Agrippa at Naulochus."

"Whose side are you on, Pollo?" whispered Cleopatra indignantly.

"Yours, of course, Thea, but it is a grave error to under estimate the enemy."

"Octavius was only adopted by Caesar because he submitted to his sexual advances" continued Antony. There were howls of protest from the assembly.

"You know that is the truth, Pollo. Tell them what you told me that you saw with your own eyes" entreated Cleopatra.

"It is far safer to do the bidding of Antonius without becoming embroiled in the character assassination, Thea. Any insults I may wish to make to Octavius I will deliver personally when I confront him. The little runt may be un-healthy, un-lucky and at times inept as a commander but that does not make him a coward. Antonius has his fair share of shortcomings and failures but his gravest error would be to believe his own propaganda.

Antony concluded his speech by announcing "I give you my solemn oath soldier to soldiers, warrior to warriors, I will admit no truce in this war and I swear that I will relinquish my office as Triumvirate within two months of victory and restore to the Senate and People of Rome all authority. Long live the Republic!"

The gods had blessed Samos with a dramatic coastline. Abundant fresh water springs irrigated the island's two mountain ranges and encircling gently rolling hills.

"I think the Hebrew's Garden of Eden must look like this island" commented Apollodorus as he and Cleopatra strolled along the long, wide, marble paved road lined flanked by two thousand statues that linked the city to the temple of Hera.

"I agree. Samos looks as though it has been deliberately planted and tended by some unseen celestial hand" replied Cleopatra. "This island was enormously wealthy in ancient times but also the theatre of bitter conflict. The final battle between Achaeans and the Persians which ended Persian domination of the Mediterranean took place here nearly five hundred years ago."

"It is all wrong, Thea, preparing for war on such a beautiful Island. Rome is in uproar because Octavius has imposed a twenty five percent income tax and a wealth tax of twelve and a half percent on property valued at more than two hundred thousand sesterces. There have been riots and civil disorder so the military have had to become collectors of this revenue. What evil are we about to unleash?"

"I seem to recall your country hanging out all the flags when base rate income tax was reduced to twenty five percent not so long ago" commented the actress. *"How much was two hundred thousand sesterces?"*

"It was equivalent to the amount the average citizen earned in one third of a millennia. To put it another way; a modulus of wheat (six kilograms) cost six sesterces or a measure (twenty six litres) of the best quality wine, one sestertius, so anyone owning more than two hundred

metric tonnes of grain or ten million bottles of vintage wine was liable for wealth tax. Inflation did not become a problem until Common Era."

Cleopatra, Apollodorus and the handmaids had arrived at the temple, a magnificent building supported by one hundred and thirty four columns that rivalled the Parthenon in its splendour.

"I do not think there is much preparation for war going on as all Antonius does is trade insults with Octavius. The little runt says that Hercules was bewitched by Omphale the *Bassilisa* of Lydia and Dionysus is a cannibal" said Cleopatra and then added defensively. "The story of how the young god was rescued from the Titans caldron is well known."

Apollodorus laughed "Antonius took great delight in pointing out that Apollo is known as the destroyer and Octavius is illiterate, apparently his hand writing is illegible and his command of Koine, the Achaean tongue, non existent."

The days that followed lengthened and became warmer as the theatres of Samos echoed to the sounds of music and dancing. Allied Kings arrived with ships and fighting men with each monarch in competition to give the most generous gifts for sacrifice.

"Having enjoyed all these sumptuous feasts at the beginning of the war what more can Antonius do to celebrate victory?" commented Apollodorus dryly. "When we eventually confront Octavius we will all be too bloated to fight."

"Don't be so cynical, *Kyrios* the *Geloto*. All this is good for moral" replied Iras.

"That's as may be, but what concerns me is the waste of time."

"Nonsense!" protested Charmain. "You rarely go to the feasts and usually leave early when her Royal Highness insists on you attending."

"It may have escaped the notice of the living embodiment of Dionysus but we have a chronic shortage of men qualified to operate our ships and most of the Roman triremes have been thrown together. Planking fits where it touches and they are so ornate they are more like floating brothels than warships. When I designed 'Bedroll II' or 'Antonia' as she is now known, I was in no doubt she was intended for ceremony not conflict. There is much more to preparing for war than making sacrifices to the gods which is all Antonius and his generals do. Men need to be trained and ships made serviceable! I am a sailor not a priest but my understanding from those who believe such things is that Zeus, otherwise known to the Romans as Jupiter, does not take sides in the conflicts of mortals!"

"I knew it was a mistake leaving his cat at Alexandria" said Charmain to Iras understandingly. "Stroking *Fangarfoto* is the only thing that calms him down when he is in this frame of mind."

"As you are well aware, ladies, *Fangarfoto* refuses to go anywhere near water or aboard anything that remotely resembles a marine vehicle."

"Well, you could always stroke us" offered Iras, coyly, "as both your cat and our Lady of two Lands are unavailable."

Apollodorus looked crossly at the two handmaids and was about to reprimand them but changed his mind and put his arms around them instead.

"Iras, Charmain, I don't think you appreciate the seriousness of our situation. This war is far from the foregone conclusion Domini Antonius considers it to be. There is much more at stake than the independence of Egypt as the destiny of humanity will be decided by the outcome of this conflict. Her Royal Highness has risked everything on a commander who doesn't exactly have an unblemished record of victory and whose idea of preparation for battle is to get riotously drunk. I don't want to see my Thea dragged through the streets of Rome in chains as the highlight of Octavius, adopted son of Caesar's, triumphal procession."

Iras placed her ebony coloured hand on the shipwright's chest and her moist, dark eyes looked into his. "You will never let that happen to her or us, *Kyrios mou*."

Apollodorus smiled weakly "I am deeply touched by your confidence, Iras but I am no miracle worker."

"Yes, you are" protested Charmain. "I saw the sign in your office at Askalon proclaiming the fact. You will take care of everything *Geloto*."

Book 31

Athens, the city described as the cradle of western civilisation was named after the goddess Athena, patron of wisdom, law, art, culture and learning; a woman of many facets like Cleopatra. The immortal daughter of Zeus was the brave protector of heroes in battle, her mother's child; just and compassionate. Unlike other gods she acknowledged her mistakes as when new to this world she misjudged her own strength and accidentally killed her dearest friend, the mortal maiden, Pallas. In her memory she placed her name before her own and became Pallas Athena. She was the favourite child of Zeus, a virgin goddess, but unlike Artemis, Athena was compassionate to both men and women.

"The city started life as a small fortified enclave about two thousand years ago," explained Cleopatra as they approached Piraeus. "The goddess of wisdom argued with the sea god as to who should give the settlement a name. It was decided that whoever gave the inhabitants the most useful gift should name the city. Athena, the goddess of wisdom, created the olive tree and Poseidon gave the horse. An olive branch is the symbol of peace whereas the horse is the symbol of war. Peace is preferable to war so Athens was named after Athena."

"There's a lesson to be learned there" replied Apollodorus. They had crossed the Aegean Sea from Samos in Cleopatra's flagship Antonia and were approaching the Greek mainland from the south east. Having passed the two seaboard harbours, Mikro Limano and Zea on their right hand side, they rounded the headland and passed between the two breakwaters into the principal harbour of Piraeus. Athens was forty stades *(five miles or eight kilometres)* from the sea and linked to these three harbours by a fortified corridor known as the long walls. In the distance Cleopatra and Apollodorus could see the natural citadel of shear limestone standing nearly two hundred cubits (ninety metres) above the surrounding habitation.

The Acropolis was the heart of Athens and housed the temples of Athena and Poseidon. In the pre democratic past this natural fortress had been the home of the Tyrannical rulers of the city state. The three ports had been protected by bastions higher than those around the Acropolis but these were destroyed by the Roman Dictator, Sulla, half a century earlier. From the deck of 'Antonia' Apollodorus surveyed the remnants of the cities defences in dismay. They could in time be re-built but time was not on their side. Hundreds of derelict ship sheds lined the harbours; each shed could shelter two triremes. On the seaboard side of the peninsular near the harbour of Zea were the remains of a huge arsenal that had in the past stored ships rigging, equipment and weapons. Sulla had been thorough in his destruction of the Greek naval power and this magnificent maritime city was in decline.

"Why has Antonius brought us here?" demanded Apollodorus. "The defences are in ruins!"

"We have arrived in time for the festival of the 'Great Dionysia', the *Ago.*"

"Which is? prompted Apollodorus dubiously.

"A contest of playwrights with political overtones, it is a time also for the collection of tributes."

"Well I am glad that the living embodiment of Dionysus will be here in person for his festival. It is re-assuring that Antonius does not let the insignificant business of inter continental warfare and battle for control of the Roman world interfere with his social calendar" replied Apollodorus sarcastically.

"I get the distinct impression that my consort is descending in the esteem of my Sea Lord. Is that so, *Kyrios mou*?"

"Your intuition has served you well in that respect, your Highness. I am of the increasing opinion that Antonius is about as much use as an ostrich feather fan as a weapon of defence against a herd of hungry crocodiles."

"Shoal" corrected Cleopatra. "Shoal of fish, herd of cattle and flock of birds."

"Well, if you are going to be critical about my grammar, how about as much use as a liquorice phallus to a rampant god!"

"That was a delightful double innuendo, the sweet, liquorice sounds the same as liquorish meaning fondness of liquor an apt description of Mark Antony and a cause of impotence in men" interjected the actress with a chuckle.

"Unfortunately not, the Greek word is giukurrhiza" I replied *reluctantly.*

Cleopatra was uncertain of the welcome she was about to receive and felt overshadowed by the memory of Octavia who the Athenians had taken to their hearts and still regarded as Antony's wife. She gently touched the shipwright's arm, their eyes met and, although they said nothing, they sensed each others feelings of foreboding and sadness. Antony was on the forecastle excitedly supervising the docking arrangements and it was clear to

Apollodorus that their future was in the hands of a man who saw the world around him as it used to be not as it was now.

"I hope you have a contingency plan, *Kyrios mou*" said Cleopatra softly.

"I take it that you were having the same thoughts that I was" replied the shipwright.

The *Bassilisa* nodded. "I want you to plan for all eventualities, something that Domini Antonius is reluctant to do" Cleopatra hesitated, and then added. "You already have, haven't you? Specially designed ships stationed conveniently at our south eastern frontier in the Sinus Arabicus and 'Orion's Sword' tucked away in some Achaean backwater. You are the antithesis of Octavius, *Kyrios mou*. You must know how to draw him into battle on our terms."

Apollodorus nodded but said nothing, he knew what to do, he always had known. His plan was ugly, deceitful and dangerous; he doubted they would have the courage to implement it. 'Orion's Sword' with an accompanying merchant vessel commanded by the Arimathean carrying a lethal cargo of bitumen, quicklime resin, naphtha and sulphur were on the way to a remote natural harbour and fortress. They had visited this place fourteen years earlier where Apollodorus had seen the destiny he had tried so hard to change. Joseph would ask no questions as bitumen was used by boat builders as a calking material, resin a preservative and sulphur for refining metal. Isis had said there could be no victory without sacrifice but how much more of a sacrifice could he make than that of not following his heart and telling his Thea what she so desperately wanted to be told?

The bringing home of Dionysus had been celebrated each spring by the Athenians since the time of Pisistratos and represented five days of frustration and annoyance for Apollodorus. Under any other circumstances he would have enjoyed the sceptical and drama. On the first day there was a huge parade of citizens and visitors. Hundreds of cows and bulls were led along the streets to the temple for sacrifice. Each person held up an enormous phallus as springtime and Dionysus were synonymous with fertility. On the second day the bearers each carried a talent of silver, these tributes were lined up and part of the money would be used for the support of the children of those killed in battle. This festival was a show of unity for all Athenians.

During the five days of plays there were four tragedies, a satire and five comedies performed by over a thousand men and boys. At times the audiences were rowdy and threw food at the performers consequently women were not encouraged to attend. The *Bassilisa*, however, was not a woman to let mere human convention interfere with her zest for life and threw missiles at the performers with the best of them.

Despite her misgivings the citizens of Athens welcomed Cleopatra as a head of state and as a friend. There had been close ties between Alexandria and Athens for some time as these were the two foremost centres of art and culture. That summer a statue of the *Bassilisa* was erected among those of the gods in the Acropolis, an honour not given lightly.

"Do you propose to sit here and wait for Octavius to attack or are you going to invade Italy?" demanded Cleopatra angrily.

"If I may be so bold" interjected Apollodorus diplomatically.

"Be my guest Jocus" replied Antony in the full knowledge that the shipwright was the only one able to pacify Cleopatra when she was in this mood.

"The fleet is being deployed to blockade the sea lanes around Achaea from Crete in the south to Corfu in the north."

"I know that Apollodorus" replied Cleopatra sarcastically.

"There are no safe havens further north than Corfu, the Adriatic narrows are treacherous and our ships do not have the sea keeping ability to operate offshore in winter time. It is now autumn; given time we may be able to take control of the island off Brundisium but that did not prevent Caesar and Antonius from ferrying troops across sixteen years ago or Antonius six years later for the Philippi campaign. If we had acted earlier when Sextus Pompeius was in control of Sicily we could have formed an alliance with him and mounted an invasion from there. Our only option now is to disrupt the food supply to Rome and force Octavius to engage us here in Achaea. I would always choose to fight my enemy in my world not his."

"Very succinctly put Jocus, do you now see the problem amica?"

Cleopatra ignored the endearment from Antony and asked. "How do you suggest we draw Octavius into battle on our terms Pollo?"

"Octavius is as cool as the highest snow capped mountain, only angry men make mistakes!"

"I am fully aware of that fact Jocus" flared Antony "and have spent the best part of a year trading insults. Nothing gets under his skin!"

"There is one thing Octavius holds precious" replied Apollodorus looking sadly at Cleopatra, "his sister! Octavius has been trying to persuade Octavia to leave your home for several years. Beware of what you wish for; dreams that come true all too often turn out to be a mixed blessing."

Cleopatra felt her flesh crawl as Apollodorus concluded with what he knew secretly neither of them wanted. "Make Octavius' dream his nightmare, divorce Octavia and tell him that our 'Lady of Two Lands' is your wife!"

Octavia stood erect and dignified in the atrium of the 'House of Ships,' Antony's home in the Carina district of Rome. She read the document handed to her by one of the three large, intimidating men who confronted her.

"We are instructed to escort you from the premises forthwith Domina" explained the largest of the men.

"You come armed and at night times, like thieves, to turn a defenceless woman and her children out onto the streets?"

"Please don't make it any more difficult Domina, we are only obeying orders. Our weapons are so we can give you safe conduct to the house of your Pater, Gaius Octavius."

"May I have some time to explain to the children and pack a few belongings?" The bailiffs nodded so Octavia turned and gave instructions to the servants. She had anticipated this event for some time and now that it had happened she felt a perverse sense of relief.

The following morning Octavia sobbed in the arms of her father "Fratus has been trying for four years to persuade me to leave the 'House of Ships' but I have steadfastly refused saying that I am Dominus Antonius lawful wife. I promised to keep his home, care for his children and protect his interests for as long as he wanted me to. This, the gods willing, I have done to the best of my ability."

"All Rome knows that you have done this diligently, my daughter, but sadly Domini Antonius actions will plunge all of us once more into civil war."

Octavia had taken with her the two daughters sired by Antony also her son and two daughters from her previous marriages. Antony's son, Marcus and half brother by Fulvia were already with their father in Athens. Antony's divorce resulted in Plancus, the governor of Syria and Titius, who had ordered the execution of Sextus, refusal to fight Rome on behalf of Cleopatra. The defection of his two principal deputies was a great loss particularly as they were privy to many of his plans and intimate secrets. Plancus had a reputation for duplicity and deceit, Velleius described him as 'diseased with treachery and venal to all men in all things'. He had a talent for picking winners and ensured himself a warm welcome from Octavian by the information he brought to Rome.

"So gentlemen what news do you bring from the decadent east" inquired Octavian with the air of a hungry lion surveying a group of condemned criminals in the Roman circus.

"Antonius has amassed a great fleet of war ships and divided them into eight squadrons stationed at various Achean Islands" replied Plancus.

"He has formed a Senate of the defectors and refers to his headquarters as 'The Palace' also he dresses in the regalia of his patron Dionysus" added Titius. "I believe it is his intension to make Egypt his home and wishes to be interred there."

Geminius, a supporter of Antony, arrived from Rome in Athens that summer and urged Antony not to allow himself to be deprived of office and declared a public enemy by Octavian. The *Bassilisa* suspected that the visitor was acting on behalf of Octavia and matters came to ahead at the tryclinium that evening.

"Where are Plancus and Titius?" inquired Cleopatra.

"They have returned to Rome" slurred Antony.

"They are no loss to our cause, Plancus was the most obsequious of flatterers, and he played the part of the sea god Glancus at one of the feast. Titius ignored your specific orders to the contrary and had Sextus Pompeius executed." Cleopatra turned to face the visitor, fixing him with her unblinking green eyes and enquired. "Geminius what exactly is the nature of your business here in Athens?"

"I would prefer to discuss this when we are all sober" replied Geminius. Then turning to Antony added "but drunk or sober I can at least say, to you Dominus Antonius, that it would be better for all of us if you sent Cleopatra back to Egypt."

Antony attempted to rise and would have struck the man had Apollodorus not placed a strong restraining hand on his shoulder. This he did in the full and certain knowledge that his 'Lady of Two Lands' was well capable of fighting her own verbal battles.

"Domini Antonius may well be drunk, Geminius, but you are deceitful, however tomorrow as certain that Helios will rise in the firmament he will be sober" replied Cleopatra coldly. "You do well to tell the truth before you are compelled by torture."

"So Antonius wishes to be buried in Egypt" replied Octavian. "Have you seen his last will and testimony, as his closest associates you must have been witnesses to the document."

"That is a question we are honour bound not to answer Dominus Octavius" answered Plancius. The young Triumvirate looked anger but Titius offered a solution.

"My colleague has said too much already but, undoubtedly, you could establish the content of the document, in this state of emergency the Vestal Virgins could hardly stand in your way and we will not contradict whatever you may discover."

Octavian nodded "I think we understand each other perfectly gentlemen. I will not declare war on the noble Antonius, the Senate must beg, no demand retribution and I will reluctantly concede to their wishes."

In the 'Theatrum Pompeium' Octavian took his place in the seat of state and surveyed the assembled Senators impassively, his pale blue eyes were un-smiling. Silence descended so he began his address.

"Some of you say that Antonius bas been bewitched by the love of the *Bassilisa* of Egypt. Others argue that he is still loyal to the fatherland and that Antonius loves Rome. We all know and love Marcus Antonius. He was once described as the right arm of the Deus Caesar. Antonius the brave warrior! Antonius the generous! Antonius the clown! Yes my friends we all know and love Marcus Antonius and we have forgiven him a great deal. And Antonius loves Rome!

"It was believed that his marriage to Fulvia would curb his insolence and wild behaviour. The Deus Caesar, my Pater, gave him a second chance because Antonius loves Rome and the fatherland loves Antonius! Sadly, in their wisdom, the gods took Fulvia from us and Antonius, who loves Rome, fell under the influence of Cleopatra and the Lady of Two Lands is ambitious!

"Matters came to a head when the armies of the fatherland confronted those of Antonius at Brundisium but Roman would not fight Roman so war was avoided. A truce was signed and ratified in the matrimony of Antonius to my own dear sister. We all prayed to the gods that the love of Octavia would make Antonius see the error of his ways and for a time he did, because Antonius loves Rome!

"It is common knowledge that Cleopatra of Egypt is ambitious and boasts that one day she will melt out justice in the 'Temple of Jupiter' on the 'Capotiline Hill'. Her ambition is grievous and grievously must she pay for it! But you say Antonius loves Rome more than he loves the 'Despot of the East'. A woman who surrounds herself by soothsayers and fortune tellers, people the like of whom will mislead the citizens of the fatherland no more as they have been expelled by Dominus Agrippa. Cleopatra who chooses her lovers in the manner of a man and keeps the company of eunuchs, men who enjoy practising un-natural acts of fornication upon each other. Yet they say that Antonius loves Rome more than he loves the company of actors, dancers and other undesirables. Antonius, who loves Rome, but dresses in the manner of an eastern monarch not as a General of the fatherland, he is Tyranni Orienus, the overlord of the east, yet he addresses Cleopatra as Regina and as amica. But still they say Antonius loves Rome!

"So Senators and People of Rome what is the truth? How much does Antonius love the fatherland?" Octavian reached inside his toga and produced a small scroll. "This is the last will and testimony of the man of whom it is said Antonius loves Rome!"

"So what was in Antony's will that caused so much offence" inquired the actress impatiently. "From the expression on your face pro quos and addenda.

The actual reason for my expression was the discomfort in my abdomen that was a precursor to the inevitable exasperated by the sickly motion of the actresses stretched limousine as it threaded its way along roads in East London not designed for such a vehicle. We were on our way back to her flat overlooking the Thames.

"Only Octavian's side of the story survives as it would be several generations before Mark Antony's clansmen would rule Rome. By then it was too late to give his side of the conflict."

"Had you been around at the time you would not have believed Octavian if he said it was daylight outside unless you poked your head out through his tent flaps and looked."

I smiled in agreement "To be fair I would have extended Mark Antony the same courtesy."

There were murmurs of protest as a citizen's last will was private until his death.

"Read here how Antonius who loves Rome declares that the son of the Egyptian harlot is the rightful heir of the Deus Caesar! Read how he loves Rome so much that he wishes to be interned not in the fatherland but in his beloved Egypt!"

The Senate unanimously voted for war against Egypt and dressed in their military cloaks made their way to the 'Temple of Bellona' in the 'Field of Mars' to perform rites preliminary to war. Antony was deprived of consulship and all authority but not made an enemy of the state as it was hoped he would repent.

Men of fighting age were assembled, money and equipment was collected on a scale not previously seen. The two commanders arranged their forces like Grand Masters in the opening stages of a Chess match. There were various ominous signs of great significance to the superstitious Romans, for instance an ape caused chaos in the temple of Ceres during a service. An owl flew into the temple of Concord and then into most of the other principle places of worship in Rome. The chariot of Jupiter was demolished in the Circus and Mount Aetna erupted causing widespread damage. Then a shooting star was sighted over the sea around Greece where Antony had transferred his headquarters.

"Was Octavian a Chess player/" inquired the Actress.

"Apparently it was his passion, the game would not have been exactly the same as it is today but he was an avid and expert player. The origin of Chess is shrouded in mystery along with Draughts and Backgammon. Chess, as we know the game, has its origin in sixth century Common Era India, draughts and backgammon were from ancient Egypt much earlier than Ptolemaic times, known as Alquerque and Senet respectively. Octavian probably played Senet which was closer in concept to Chess than Backgammon of today."

"And Mark Antony?"

I shook my head. "He spent all his spare time down the pub, Pool and Snooker hadn't been invented otherwise he would have been an expert."

"And you Kyrios mou?"

"Being a good Snooker player is regarded as a sign of a miss spent youth, mine was spent in the pursuit of wisdom and learning. I consider myself unlucky at cards but I am a reasonable Chess player."

Antony sent a recognisance squadron of triremes towards Italy which arrived at Corfu by autumn. Octavian's fleet were lying off the Ceraunian Mountains and it was suspected that Octavian was present so Antony's ships withdrew. This action prompted Octavian to send a letter to Antony suggesting that he withdrew a day's horse ride from the sea so his forces could be landed safely. Alternatively Octavian would withdraw a similar distance so Antony could land on mainland Italy, neither side to engage the other for five days.

"Who will be our arbitrator if the compact is transgressed in any way" responded Antony sarcastically.

Antony had now moved his army to winter quarters each side of the Gulf of Corinth and his own headquarters to Patras, Bogud held the fortified harbour of Methone. Half the fleet were deployed among the islands covering the south west coast of Greece the rest of the warships including 'Orion's Sword' were anchored or beached inside Akri Point on the peninsulas of Actium.

"I find it unbelievable that Mark Antony was so stupid and lodge such damming information with the Vestal Virgins. He played right into Octavian's hands and totally justify his enemy's actions" observed the actress.

"You are not the first to ask that question Kyria mou. Such precise provisions which exactly substantiated Octavian's allegations were so opportune, in my view; the document must have been a fake. If there had been a will lodged with the Vestal Virgins it would have been an earlier one as Antony had been absent from Rome for several years. This document would have named his sons Marcus and Iullus as heirs. Provision to be interned in Egypt would have been un-necessary if he were victorious and irrelevant in defeat. The Roman citizens were fearful that the seat of power would be transferred to Alexandria, Octavian played on that fear. Personally I think Antony's greatest love was for Athens and he would have chosen to be interned there, not Alexandria."

As consul designate for the New Year, thirty one before Common Era, Antony was declared un-fit for office and stripped of all Roman titles by Octavian. He then compelled the Senate, army and all leading citizens throughout Italy to swear an oath of loyalty. Maecenes was left in charge of Rome to guard against a military coup and the entire Senate were ordered to accompany the army to Brundisium. There was only one decentre, a man born out of his time, of great courage and integrity.

"My service to Antonius is too great, his kindness to me too well known; I shall stand aside from your dispute and be the victors prize" replied Velleius when Octavian canvassed his support.

At Brundisium in southern Italy Octavian mustered sixteen legions, comprising of eighty thousand battle hardened heavy infantry and twelve thousand cavalry. At the Gulf of Corinth Antony had nineteen legions of which only sixty thousand of the infantry were Italian, battle weary after the

Parthian campaign and anxious to return home. The two belligerents were evenly matched in cavalry numbers and realising the strategic advantage Octavian's larger ships had overwhelmed the fleet of Sextus and the newly constructed allied ships matched those of their opponent in size.

"There is a commonly held misconception that the allied ships were heavier than Octavian's but this is untrue. Each fleet comprised of Biremes, open boats with two levels of oars and fully decked Triremes with three levels of rowers. Ships of the line were fives and sixes, the former with two men at the lower two levels of oars and the latter having two men at all rowing positions. The longitudinal number of oars did not vary so all ships were of similar lengths, governed by engineering knowledge and the materials available at that time. Sixty cubits or one hundred feet on the waterline was the upper limit of their knowledge of longitudinal strength, height and width did increase with the number of rowers."

"Could they have more than two men per oar?" inquired the actress.

"In theory, yes. The problem is that the inboard sweep of the oar became unwieldy so a third and subsequent rower had to run backwards and forwards as well as leap up like a jack in a box. Taller ships with more than three levels of oars resulted in an inefficient angle of the blade to the water. Ships larger then sixes had been built but the design concept was discarded as inefficient. The six was the battle ship of the era, the five a destroyer and the three would have been a frigate" I replied.

"So what were the Biremes?"

"They were the Cutters and Schooners."

"A Thalamegos on that basis was the Admirals Barge" added the actress gelling into the spirit of the analogy.

"Good lord no! An Admiral was not that important only royalty and occasionally Sea Lords, as a special treat, travelled around in a Thalamegos. Antony had the advantage in overall number of warships but nearly half his fleet were deployed around the coastline to protect his supply route."

Book 32

"Dominus Agrippa I want you at the earliest opportunity to mount an amphibious attack on Methone similar to that on the Aeolian Islands which unlocked Sicily for us five years ago" announced Octavian.

"Such an undertaking would involve an extended sea crossing out of sight of land to avoid the Anton patrols," replied Agrippa.

"Can it be done?"

"Neptune willing, I believe it is possible."

"How many ships will you require?"

"Three squadrons should be enough. I take it that this is part of a wider strategy."

"Your action will cause panic in the Anton camp, all his troops are in winter quarters throughout the Peleponnese and half his fleet are at the Gulf of Ambracian. While Antonius is distracted by your action I will transfer our army and the rest of the fleet across the Adriatic Narrows as expected by our enemy. If I were Antonius I would evict you from Methone and protect my supply route."

Agrippa smiled broadly. "But Antonius is not Caesar and will gamble all on a quick decisive battle."

"Exactly!" replied Octavian. "I will march south and make a half hearted attack to ensure that our enemy concentrates all his forces in one place. He will then make every effort to draw me into battle which I will decline while you fortify Methone. Access to the Gulf by land is almost impossible, which means that Antonius will be trapped. As the temperature rises vermin will multiply and spread disease. You will harass the enemy's supply shipping causing famine, death will follow and his supporters will melt away. We shall be victorious, the gods willing, without pitching Roman against Roman."

Early that spring Agrippa sailed from Tarentum, on the south coast of Italy. The Roman squadrons crossed the two thousand four hundred stades *(three hundred miles)* of open water, successfully avoiding Antony's patrols and attacked Methone in the southern Peleponnese near Sparta. This original thinking had added a new dimension in Roman naval warfare, Methone was captured and Antony's friend, Bogud was slain. The allied legions were still in their winter quarters scattered around the Peleponnese so Agrippa's action prompted Antony to hastily concentrate his forces in one location as anticipated by Octavian.

Apollodorus had a growing sense of foreboding as they entered the Ambracian Gulf from the straits of Preveza. On the left were Cape Paliosarama and half a mile away to the right, the Actium peninsular. The Egyptian fleet passed between the headlands and into about two hundred and fifty square miles of easily defended sheltered water. Access by land was over mountain tracks to the west and on the southern shore were flat marshland which would become infested with mosquitoes and snakes in the summer.

"What are you thinking *Kyrios mou*?" enquired Cleopatra softly.

"As a drinking companion one could wish for none better than Marcus Antonius but as a war lord" Apollodorus hesitated. "This haven could become a trap!"

"What danger if Octavian stays at Toryne?" answered Cleopatra with a smile. Apollodorus laughed at the double meaning, Octavian had crossed over from Italy to Toryne a secluded bay off Epirus, and the name also meant a ladle. "I don't think that the little runt will sit by the fireside *scrumming* the pot for long your Highness" he replied. "Fortifying the port of Methone will make it the ideal base to harass our supply ships. Sparta and Psamathos are nearby and the Roman governors Lachares and Atratinus I fear are likely to defect to Octavius depriving our ships of an important stopover."

Octavian's army, escorted by one hundred and thirty war ships, had landed on the narrow coastal strip below the Acroceraunian Mountains at Port Panormus. This prompted Antony's withdrawal from Corfu. Finding the island un-defended enabled Octavian's fleet to take the inland channel and capture Toryne and Glycys Limen, the Freshwater Harbour at the mouth of the river Archeron.

"Toryne and Glycys Limen today are the Greek towns of Parga and Fanari near the Albanian boarder" I explained.

On arrival at Actium Cleopatra and Apollodorus learned that a squadron of Octavian's ships had mounted an attack but were successfully repulsed by the hastily constructed artillery on the headlands each side of the Preveza Straits. Octavian was camped forty stades *(five miles)* north at Mikhilitzi an eight stades *(one mile)* wide sandy strip of land between the Gulf of Gomaros and the Mazoma Lagoon at the north east corner of the Ambracia Gulf. From this low range of hills he had a commanding view of Antony's seaward approaches but the high ground on the isthmus in the centre of the Preveza peninsular obscured Actium and the Gulf. This phallic shaped peninsular divided unto two, one formed the northern headland of Cape Paliosarama the other pointed south east into the Gulf of Ambracia. Akri Point extended north from the Actium peninsular between these two headlands. It had taken a week for the first of Antony's reinforcements to arrive and another three would pass before the operation would be competed and the fleet brought into combat condition.

"Surely the ships would be ready for battle on arrival?"
I shook my head. "The war ships doubled as troop transports, men were squeezed in like sardines." The actress looked at me blankly; I was inclined to forget that we were born of two nations divided by a common language. "At English expression tinned, sorry canned, fish tightly packed. The ships had a compliment of two to three hundred rowers and twenty to thirty marines, depending on the size of the vessel so there would be eighty to a hundred extra troops on board. These extra men and their equipment would have to be unloaded also the mast, spars and sails were generally left ashore when the ships went into combat."
"The Peveza Peninsular?" asked the actress.
"From the air looks like the side view of the male genitals with the Akri point pointing at the junction between the scrotum and the penis.

During this vulnerable time Octavian mounted another attack by sea, Antony responded by ordering the rowers to dress in armour and impersonate his missing troops. This attack was successfully repulsed by moving allied ships from the Gulf of Ambracia into Preveza Bay. It had been a wise choice to locate the camp site on high ground but the beach head was a mile away and could only be used in good weather. Octavian's engineers constructed a jetty, the remains of which would still be visible two thousand years later. Parallel defensive walls were also constructed from the jetty to the camp at Mikhalitzi. Antony would be reluctant to undertake an uphill frontal attack so Octavian could decide whether or not to accept battle.

"Did you manage to persuade our leader to re-take Methone?" inquired Apollodorus when Cleopatra returned from the council of war.
"No" she replied curtly. "He has ordered King Rhoemetalces of the Thrace and Deiotrarus of Paphlagonia to take their cavalry around the eastern side of the gulf and deny Octavius access to fresh water from the river Louros."

"That is a distance of about eight hundred stades through difficult terrain, swamps to their left and mountains on the right. I do not envy them their assignment."

The cavalry were able to complete the one hundred mile ride but were engaged by Octavian's cavalry commanded by Taurus and Titius who forced them to withdraw west of the river. This prompted the two monarchs to defected taking their cavalry with them. Octavian eyed the kings suspiciously when they were brought before him.

"Domini Antonius has no clear plan and his control of his forces is breaking down" Rhoemetalces started to explain but was cut short by the Roman.

"Your Royal Highnesses the fruits of treachery are welcome but I do not like the perpetrators!" Octavian then sent troops east to challenge Antony's hold on Thrace while Agrippa captured the naval base on the Island of Leucas.

The news of the capture of the base and subsequently the whole of Leucas had a demoralising effect on Antony.

"A man who was able to connect Lake Avernus and the Lucrine Lagoon to the sea then tunnel through the Misenum Peninsular is quite capable of dredging a channel through the mudflats between the north east corner of Leucas and the mainland. His ships will then be able to pass through and challenge us from the south" he confided to Cleopatra.

Agrippa consolidated his position on Leucas then defeated Nasidius and captured Patras his squadron were able to penetrate the Gulf as far as the ruined city of Corinth.

"Our supply ships will have to take a much longer passage outside the islands of Zacynthus and Caphallenia" commented Apollodorus when Cleopatra informed him of the capture of the winter headquarters. "Agrippa is using sea power to dictate the course of the land campaign in the way we should have done."

"I agree" replied Cleopatra sadly. "He is loosing control of Achaea and we will soon be trapped."

"Thea, I hate to say it - we are trapped!"

"What is to be done?" inquired Cleopatra tearfully.

"I am no general and if I offer Antonius any advice he will remind me of that fact very clearly."

"So do you propose to sit back and let Antonius get us killed!" flared the *Bassilisa* her sorrow replaced by anger.

"Nothing of the sort, Thea. My view is that we should retreat and draw Octavius deep into our territory as the Parthians did to Antonius."

"Destroying all useful resources as we withdraw as the Britannians did to Caesar then attack when the Roman supply lines are stretched to the limit" added Cleopatra thoughtfully. "My consort will never agree to such a strategy."

"I know, that is why we will have to give him 'enough rope to hang himself'. We are going to have a very uncomfortable summer but unless by some miracle M.A can draw the little runt into battle and vanquish him, there is no alternative. Domini Antonius will only be prepared to listen to my plan when he is absolutely desperate!"

"But if we are trapped here how can we break out and withdraw to Egypt."

"By deploying 'Orion's Sword' she was built for exactly this eventuality Thea" replied the shipwright and in deploying his secret weapon he knew that he would never see Alexandria again. As Isis had said 'there could be no victory without sacrifice.'

The arrival of the hot Mediterranean summer brought with it from the stony wastelands of Scythia, Hunger where the demon plucked with her nails at the scant herbage. Her grey hair was tangled, eyes hollow and complexion pallid. The demon's skin was so hard and fleshless that her entrails were clearly visible. Sunken bones protruded under her sagging loins, her belly was an empty space and her pendulous breasts appeared to be strung on her ribcage. The demon arrived at night time and as Antony's the two hundred thousand men slept. Twining her arms around them she poured herself deep inside each man dispersing starvation through their veins. Her consort, Famine mounted on his black horse, watched impassively.

The stagnant marshlands became polluted with human and animal excrement causing the mosquitoes and snakes to multiply. Malaria and dysentery swept through the camp. Moral and discipline were increasingly difficult to maintain. Many nobles and aspiring leaders advocated different courses of action at first in secret then as time passed openly. Senators began to regret their hasty action and longed to return to the comfort of their homes in Rome.

"The page boys in Octavius' service are able to enjoy the finest Falernian while we must make do with rough Achaean wine" grumbled Dellius.

"I am suppressed he can tell the difference" whispered Apollodorus to Cleopatra. "Romans consider themselves to be famous drinkers yet they mix so much water with their wine."

"From the perspective of our Roman friends you are a Bibba! Are you unique or do all your countrymen refuse to add water to their wine?" asked Cleopatra?"

"Wine can't swim!" replied the shipwright with a smile. "I drink either water or wine not both together, water I look on with some suspicion and after my experience in Tarsus do you blame me!"

"On that first voyage aboard 'Mintaka' you gave me a heady mix of Mead and Retsina. You said fresh water was far too precious a commodity on a boat to waste on quaffing."

"Water carries disease, alcohol does not. Look at how our men are becoming infected. Water is only safe to drink after it has been boiled."

"I think Jocas has a very valid point" interrupted Antony. "My friend Ahenobarbus has become seriously ill and has been rowed secretly over to Octavius. I will be magnanimous and tell everyone he wants to be with his amicas in Rome but it is unlikely he will live long enough to see her or his family again. I will send his belongings and servants after him."

Cleopatra looked at Antony in disbelief. "The man is a traitor" she exclaimed.

"Ahenobarbus is a republican autocrat and he is dieing" replied Antony firmly.

Cleopatra turned to Apollodorus who added "It is the decent thing to do, at a higher level." He then gave her a very sinister look and concluded "Or alternatively it's one less body to cremate and fewer less non combatant mouths to feed."

Ahenobarbus died a few days later and Apollodorus became increasingly worried about the condition of the ships.

"The rowers numbers are becoming seriously depleted by illness and death" he confided to Cleopatra.

"Antonius says that while there are able bodied men in Achaea there will be no shortage of men for our ships" replied the Bassilisa.

"I am well aware of his opinion but the reality is that with no opportunity to exercise in open water the fleet is loosing battle fitness. As for training novice rowers, there is no chance."

"Antonius is under great pressure from his allies to send me back to Egypt because I am always pressing for a battle at sea."

"I know Thea; Romans are reluctant to get their feet wet to the point of being superstitious. They don't understand that 'salum er carinae pignora vitae', salt, sea and ships shall be the means of salvation. I am beginning to think that if they really don't want you here we might just as well go home and leave them to whatever the fates have decided."

"Are you serious Pollo?"

"If I could think of a way of getting ourselves and our people safely away, it is a very tempting prospect. The action could not make matters any worse and it would call Octavius bluff in declaring war on you as a means of attacking Antonius."

"If Antonius is unable to comprehend the merits of your scorched earth withdrawal strategy why don't we implementing one of your devious 'killing two birds with one stone' schemes? Perhaps the time has come to use some of your 'applied cretinology' and force the issue."

"I know what you are saying Thea, 'applied cretinology' is supposed to be funny, this will be deadly serious, but I confess that I have been thinking along these lines for some time."

"You had better formulate your plan quickly as there are swallows nesting in my flag ship."

"How cute!" replied Apollodorus. "Do you wish to return to Alexandria before the chicks are hatched and save the parents having to fly south in the autumn?"

"There is nothing cute or funny about those birds nesting, it is a bad omen!" retorted Cleopatra angrily.

"What a load of superstitious dung, Thea!" exclaimed Apollodorus in disbelief. "The only conclusion to be drawn from such an event is that swallows have good taste in choosing a nesting site on a trireme built by me!"

"You do not believe such things are warning signs from the gods?"

"No I don't and neither do you. The gods hardly need to tell us what is blindingly obvious. The rank and file of Roman military care nothing about ideology; it will make not a scrap of difference to the plebs if they are ruled by Octavius of Antonius. There only concern is to be on the winning side and secure their land settlement. Your consort has timed his attack appallingly. He delayed when he should have attacked and his opponent has grown strong but instead of waiting until our resources were overwhelming he has charged in like a rampant bull in a field of oestrus cows. Antony is relying on his popularity and reputation to hold together the diverse fighting force and he is surrounded by senile aristocrats with no military experience, empty heads and big mouths. You and I are the only people with any idea how to salvage this desperate situation but his Senate are so blinded by arrogance, envy and prejudice that they want to send you back to Egypt!"

"You have always maintained that if I were not here Antonius would patch up his differences with Octavius who would then arrange an assassination and annex Egypt."

"That was last year and the situation is changing."

Cleopatra gave Apollodorus a knowing look "You do have a diabolical plan don't you *Kyrios mou*!"

"Diabolical is my second name" he replied with an evil grin. "What would you do if you were confined with two mad dogs; either of them were capable of killing you."

"I would set them against each other and while they were so occupied" Cleopatra hesitated but Apollodorus finished her sentence.

"While they were otherwise occupied you would take the opportunity to slip quietly away. If one of the dogs survived the conflict it would be unlikely to have the strength to pursue you. Conversely any attack by a weakened assailant against you would be easily repulsed."

"Apollodorus I am ashamed of you, have you no conscience?" replied the *Bassilisa* whilst trying not to laugh.

"Yes Cleopatra I do, however. In the first instance Octavius used you as an excuse to attack Antonius; an honourable man declares war on his enemy, unambiguously. Secondly we did everything possible to persuade M.A to act before it was too late and he refused. Thirdly I did not ask Rome to interfere in our lives, they chose to! Fourthly I treat honourable people honourably and sensible people with good sense. I like Antonius but he does have the capacity, at times, to behave like one of the poor unfortunate dwarfs Romans so enjoy making fun of at their feasts."

Cleopatra threw her arms around Apollodorus and kissed him passionately. "If we survive *Kyrios mou* and get safely back to Alexandria I shall have a statue of you erected with the inscription manipulate a manipulator at your peril."

Apollodorus smiled and enjoyed Cleopatra's embrace but in his heart he knew that his flippancy was to hide his severe reservations. The plan was extremely hazardous and very much a desperate action of last resort. Caesar had once said 'Desperate men know no fear.' The time to implement his plan was when he ceased to be frightened by it.

"*The long hot Greek summer had exactly the effect that Octavian anticipated and in an attempt to deter further desertions Antony ordered the execution of Senator Quintus Postumius and Prince Iamblichus of Emesa who were suspected of treachery. Consulars Candius, Sosius and Poplicola were all that remained of the Senate in exile.*"

"*Presumably that restored Antony to his autocratic role*" commented the actress.

"*There were certainly less people to argue strategy, Dellius and Amyntas were sent to raise reinforcements from Macedonia and Thrace.*"

"Antonius is following Dellius and Amyntas north with the rest of the army" announced Cleopatra as she boarded Orion's Sword. "Sosius has been ordered to attempt to break out of the gulf under cover of the early morning sea mist. If he is successful the rest of the fleet is to follow and we will rendezvous with the army."

"Really" replied Apollodorus, with a total lack of interest. "I assume the intension is that we sail north also and attempt to cut Octavius off from Italy." The shipwright suddenly staggered to the stern of his ship and was violently sick. "Sorry about that your Highness, I seem to have a touch of Actium abdomen." He tried to focus his eyes on Cleopatra but both images of the *Bassilisa* were blurred. The shipwright was vaguely aware that the *Bassilisa* and the handmaids were helping him below. "It is better if I stay on deck in the fresh air" he protested before passing out.

Throughout the heat of the day Apollodorus lapsed in and out of consciousness as Cleopatra, Charmain and Iras attempted to reduce his temperature with damp cloths. Evening brought with it blessed relief from the heat and a semblance of coherence from the shipwright.

"We must transfer you to the flag ship" said Cleopatra.

"I shouldn't trouble yourselves" he protested weakly.

"Don't say such things Pollo; you are coming with us when we break out!"

"I didn't mean it like that" he replied with an attempt to laugh which sounded more like a croak. "The attempted break out will fail."

"How do you know" demanded Cleopatra but Apollodorus had fallen into a deep sleep. Under cover of darkness the comatose shipwright was transferred aboard Cleopatra's ship but when he opened his eyes he was no longer aboard any of the Egyptian triremes.

The soft sunlight was streaming through the gaps in the bamboo blinds. On the walls were exquisite hangings depicting ferocious dragons and beautiful flowers. Through the open door Apollodorus could see small maple bushes with elegant leaves of red, green and silver. There was a cool gentle breeze and in the background the chuckle of running water. His head rested in the lap of a heavily made up young woman but he knew that under the white face paint her complexion was pale yellow.

An ancient man with skin like parchment entered the room and knelt down beside him. The geisha helped the shipwright into a sitting position and offered a bowl of hot green liquid that partly revive him.

"It has been a long time Sensei" muttered Apollodorus.

"I have been watching over you my apprentice."

"And you disapprove?"

"You must live your life the way you see fit. Do you love her?"

"How could anyone not fall under her spell" the shipwright prevaricated.

The old man smiled knowingly at Apollodorus "You have not changed" he replied. "Still refusing to acknowledge your true feelings, remember I know you better than you know yourself."

"So why ask that which you know so well, master?"

"Why are you so afraid to admit to loving her, I can understand that you may not want to tell an old man but why deprive her of her only true happiness?"

"Because I will change the future, you taught me that we are pebbles washed up on a beach for but a short time to return to the ocean when we have completed our allotted time and learned our lessons. Nothing can change that."

"Your actions have already changed that which was ordained, you were my most promising pupil and as a foreigner, the elders thought me insane teaching the 'White Ghost' our secrets."

"They will remain secret!"

"Yet you plan to use one of our most dangerous weapons, you plan to unleash a power that in the hands of such violent and war like people will be devastating."

"Do not concern yourself master, your peoples secrets will die with me!"

The old man's kindly expression was replaced with alarm. "You know the consequence of that course of action!"

"I may be killed trying to save the one I love; this war was lost before it even started. I have always known that I was fighting for a lost cause but to continue to fight against overwhelming odds is totally different to the way Romans deliberately take their own life as a means of escape from the humiliation of defeat." Apollodorus laid back and closed his eyes again.

"Who is Sensei? asked a deep musical voice softly. The shipwright opened his eyes again and realised he was aboard the Egyptian flag ship and his head was resting in Cleopatra's lap.

"It is a what rather than a who" he replied. "Sensei is like the Hebrew word Rabbi, it means teacher and master." The shipwright tried to sit up but Cleopatra restrained him gently.

"Stay where you are *Kyrios mou*, none of us are going anywhere, it was as you predicted. Sosius attempted to break out under cover of the morning mist and encountered a squadron of triremes under the command of Taius Rufus at anchor in the Preveza Straits."

"I shouldn't have thought that would have been too much of a problem."

"Our ships were getting the best of the encounter until Agrippa arrived with the rest of Octavius' fleet."

"There must be a spy in our midst."

"Possibly, but I think it more likely that Agrippa was cruising offshore and was in the right place at the right time from Octavius' perspective."

"For a little runt he is incredibly lucky Thea."

"As I have said before Seth looks after his own people, the enemy pursued our squadron back into the gulf and we have sent word for Antonius to return as quickly as possible. Agrippa has withdrawn but I understand that there has been some sort of engagement east of the river Louros, Amyntas has gone over to Octavius taking with him his two thousand cavalry. I think it likely that Antonius will be prepared to listen to the plan of my devious Sea Lord. You must recover from the sickness quickly *Kyrios mou*, you are all that is between the world and the evil that is Octavius."

"You described me as the antithesis of Octavius, he and I are astute manipulators. He is the strategist and has in Agrippa a capable general, born to be first but content to implement his master's orders. In times passed Agamemnon had a reluctant Achilles. What have I got?"

"You have me" replied Cleopatra softly.

"Will you do exactly what I tell you to do without question, whatever happens?"

The *Bassilisa* nodded. "Do you want me to swear it?"

"As you know I worship no gods, your word is good enough for me but it is imperative that you trust me and when we break out whatever happens do not turn back or look back. Come what may you must return to Egypt and I will join you in Alexandria as soon as is humanly possible."

"So what is your plan?"

"Get over this Actium abdomen, have a good nights sleep, in your arms if M.A is out of the way. Any objections Thea."

"None what so ever *Geloto*!"

Book 33

On his return Antony withdrew most of the allied army from the northern shore to the already overcrowded Actium peninsular leaving only his most loyal legions to defend Peveza. This was to prevent any further desertions. He did not call a council of war until the eighth Roman month and by then the allies had been trapped in the Gulf of Ambracia for three months. There was little relief from the burning heat, dust and all pervading stench. Supplies were critically low due to Agrippa's blockade and disease was widespread. At the council of war were Antony's remaining generals; Canidius, Dellius and Sosius also admirals; Poplicola, Insteius and their enemies namesake, Octavius. Cleopatra had insisted that Apollodorus attended with her.

"Regina, Dominus" began Antony. "We are all agreed that it will be disastrous to remain defensively here at Actium but Octavius has repeatedly refused to be drawn into battle. This leaves us with two alternatives; either retreat over the mountains and join the 'Via Egnatia' to Thrace and Hellespoint. The fleet would have to be burnt to prevent our enemy capturing it." Cleopatra looked horrified but said nothing so Antony continued. "Or we break out by force with the fleet placing a third of the army aboard white the rest withdraw over land."

Canidius was next to speak. "To split up the army is folly; our legions have no experience of fighting aboard ships. Agrippa had specially trained soldiers which defeated Sextus Pompeius."

"I conquer with Senator Canidius" added Dellius.

"*Kyrios* the Apollodorus you are being remarkably quiet, what is your opinion?" asked Antony.

"Your Royal Highness, gentlemen, I confess to being somewhat prejudice in this matter" began the shipwright, "having as you know spent a considerable amount of time building the Egyptian navy. But what you do not know is that my people drove Caesar back into the sea on two separate occasions, I do of course speak of your deius Caesar not pretender to the clan who refuses to be drawn into battle."

"When did Sicily vanquish Caesar?" interjected Dellius scornfully.

"Sicily is not the tin island of my birth; Caesar retreated because Britannia rules the waves! Agrippa has adopted some of the maritime tactics of my people and controlled the land war as a consequence. Octavius does not fight by your rules any more than the Median did." Apollodorus caught Antony's eye and the Roman nodded in agreement. "To put things succinctly generals and admirals Octavius and Agrippa are dirty fighters, they will not be drawn into battle for as long as Octavius has a hole in his anus." Apollodorus looked at Cleopatra who was stifling a giggle, both were thinking "that particular orifice was put to good use by his adopted *Pater* and resulted in his exulted status."

Then he continued. "If we retreat Octavius will follow, our supply lines become shorter as his lengthen. We become stronger as he weakens, but if we destroy the fleet it will take two or three years to build a replacement. This means that it would be two or three years before we could counter attack. It is a long march back to Egypt and we will be attacked all the way by Agrippa at sea and Octavius on the land. Our enemy on land can choose to enter into battle or not, at sea there is no option."

"That has given me an idea" interrupted Antony.

"I rather hoped it would" muttered Apollodorus under his breath as he gave Cleopatra a knowing look.

"What we shall do is put our fittest soldiers on our largest and most seaworthy ships and burn the rest. Then make an all out attack on Agrippa's fleet, if all goes well we may be able to make the battle decisive if it is balanced I will give the signal to withdraw east. The Egyptian fleet will be responsible for the war chest so will remain well away from the battle; all ships are to carry sailing gear so we can outrun Agrippa if necessary. What do you think Apollodorus?"

"In principal an excellent strategy which needs detail planning" replied the shipwright. "Your Royal Highness, do you agree?"

Cleopatra nodded; she was accustomed to her Sea Lord's tactics and principal of, as he said, 'killing two birds with the same stone'. This was a classic *Gelotopoios* 'heads we win tails we don't loose' provided nothing were to go wrong strategy. But with Mark Antony in command going wrong was a possibility which they were acutely aware could happen. The *Bassilisa* was not going to agree to anything until she had heard all of her Sea Lord's secret contingency plans.

"Due to the anti cyclonic conditions in that part of the Mediterranean the weather pattern has hardly changed for millennia. There is a good offshore breeze in the morning, ideal to clear the northern headlands of Leucas. This wind dies away in the forenoon as the temperature rises. It is calm in the middle of the day then a westerly onshore wind develops in the afternoon. This wind veers north-west and freshens

towards evening. Ships of the time could not sail closer than ninety degrees into the wind."

"*Which means in plane English?" inquired the actress patiently.*

"*Sailing from Actium in a southerly direction was only possible first thing in the morning or later in the afternoon."*

"*Presumably Mark Antony was aware of the metrological considerations."*

"The worrying aspect of his plan is that Antony will not take his *Trierarchos* into his confidence so they will not looking for a signal to withdraw" explained Apollodorus when he was alone with Cleopatra.

"I would think he is working on a need to know basis to guard against any deserters giving Octavius details. It is vital to appear that we are preparing for battle not a retreat" replied Cleopatra.

"The *Trierarchos* are neither willing nor able to desert; there is more of a risk of that with his warlords who know how desperate our situation is."

"So what are your contingency plans *Kyrios mou*?"

"As you know most of the Roman fleet will be stationed in a line across the straits with a reserve squadron behind. The Egyptian fleet will be the last ships to depart; I will take up a position to your north in 'Orion's Sword'. My preference would have been to depart at first light when the winds are most favourable and our enemy would be half asleep but that is irrelevant. As soon as the wind freshens and backs north east Antonius should give the signal to break off the engagement and run but Antonius is at heart a gambler and will probably linger, hopeful of a decisive outcome. In the ensuing confusion you must make your move. 'Orion's Sword' can sail closer to the wind, is faster and more manoeuvrable than any of the ships in either fleet so my role will be as hunter killer to clear away any opposition and ensure you to escape There is unlikely to be a decisive outcome to the battle which could result in the 'two mad dogs scenario'. If Antonius withdraws his fleet when we do, we could all live to fight another day. A wise general knows when to withdraw and has the courage to do so! It is vitally important that you make your break as soon as the wind is favourable, having done so you must keep going whatever happens. No looking back like Lots wife in the Hebrew scrolls or Orpheus when he tried to bring his bride Eurydice back from Hades. Do not concern yourself with either Antonius or my actions, no heroics or rescue missions. I will make my own way back to Alexandria as will Antonius, if he survives."

A centurion approached Octavian. "Imperator I have observed that Domini Antonius is in the habit of walking along the high ground that runs through the sea from his encampment to the anchorage. Would it amuse you if I were to abduct him in the midst of his solitary contemplations?"

Octavian smiled weakly. "It would amuse me greatly, take what men you require and lay in ambush."

Antony burnt un-seaworthy ships and most of the Egyptian fleet except Cleopatra's flag ship, Orion's Sword and squadron of triremes to transport war chest. A pool of smoke hung over the Actium peninsular like an autumn mist but the departure was delayed for four days due to onshore storm and breaking sea. From the poop deck of 'Orion's Sword' Apollodorus and Iras watched the destruction by fire of the ships that had taken so long to build.

"Does it pain you *Kyrios mou* to see all your work going up in smoke?" asked the handmaiden as she took hold of the shipwrights arm. "All those beautiful ships."

"There is nothing beautiful about weapons of destruction; in fact it gives me a certain amount of perverse pleasure. I would rejoice in the sight of all such armaments being destroyed."

"You are such an idealist *Geloto*."

"That is what Cleopatra used to say" Apollodorus hesitated for a moment then continued. "When you asked me to save her life and enable Olympos to cut Caesarion from the *Bassilisa* you offered yourself to me unconditionally."

Iras smiled seductively. "I live in hope that one day you will call in the debt."

"That day has arrived but I am sorry it is your mind I want not your body." The handmaid looked puzzled and disappointed. "The time has come for you to honour that pledge and save the life, once again, of your mistress. I need to give you a message for her and implant instructions as a contingency then make you forget. If the message needs to be delivered and my instructions are required you will remember."

"You want to enter my mind *Kyrios mou*."

"If you are agreeable - yes."

"Do you not trust me with your secret?"

"Iras I trust you and hold you and Charmain in the highest regard after the *Bassilisa* and for that reason I am not prepared to burden you or place you in a position of divided loyalty. For all our sakes you must do exactly as I tell you but it is human nature to question. Will you do that for me - please?"

Iras remembered what she had overheard Olympus say after the birth of Cleopatra's firstborn.

"Tell me Olympos," Cleopatra had asked. "Pollo is very distant. Is anything the matter?"

"I know what you mean. I don't altogether understand, but I think he paid a high price for what he did for you" the doctor had replied.

"What do you mean?" asked Cleopatra in alarm.

"He kept you unconscious long after I had delivered Caesarion. You felt nothing 'till he released your *Ba*, your soul, but during that time I think he felt your pain. I didn't realise it at the time I was too busy. Forces beyond our understanding took over but I am sure my hands were guided. I cut out your baby in a way that has never been done before; I can hardly remember what I did. If your Apollodorus is Mendis, the Piper at the Gate of Dawn, as Caesar once suggested, they say his greatest gift is that of forgetfulness. We must be patient, just give him time and he may tell us. If not, there are some things mortals are just not meant to know."

Iras made her decision. "I am yours *Geloto*, do with me as you wish" she said.

"Look into my eyes and submit to my will" began Apollodorus softly. When he had finished speaking he handed her his sword, dagger and a small scroll with instruction to place them safely and secretly aboard the Egyptian flag ship. "Now Iras you will forget, forget, FORGET!"

On the fifth day Octavian emerged from his tent, it was the morning of the second day of the ninth month, a day destined to be a turning point in the history of Rome. The attempt to abduct Antony had not been successful as the wrong man had been captured but this was compensated for by Dellius, one of Antony's principal generals, defecting the previous night bringing with him details of the allies plan. The sun was shining and the sea calm, a man with a donkey was passing.

"Who are you?" demanded Octavian.

"My name is Eutychus and my ass is called Nicom" was the reply.

The omens for Octavian could not be better. The peasant's name meant fortune and the donkey's conqueror.

"Warriors of the free world" announced Antony "Citizens and allies we are the finest of many nations brought together for a single common cause – freedom and equality. Victory in battle generally favours the better equipped, but what use are weapons in the hands of those who know not how to use them and are poorly led. You have seen our magnificent ships – we are experts in all forms of combat. You could prevail with the poorest leadership – our enemy does not have the diversity of armaments – their leader is young and in experienced – never cited in an important battle. At Philippi when we were on the same side Octavius was forced to abandon his position and retreat while I was victorious.

"I have been a soldier all my life and am in my prime – hampered neither by the rashness of youth or the slackness of old age. I would be victorious with the poorest of soldiers but the gods have blessed me with the finest. Together we have known good fortune and adversity – this means we are able to avoid the twin evils of despair and excessive pride. Our funds are plentiful – those of our enemy are scant – money raised by forced contribution - the people of Rome are in open revolt. Octavius cannot continue to rob the citizens – we have aggrieved no one – our resources are from our accumulations and will aid us all collectively.

"Do not imagine that our enemy are better seamen because Agrippa vanquished Sextus Pompeius. What part is Sicily of the whole empire compared with ours? Sextus had far fewer ships than Octavius yet the Sicilians prevailed against him twice. We have many more ships than Sextus and are far better equipped. Time and again we have offered Octavius battle on land and he has refused. At sea the only place to hide is on an islet where they will be easily subdued, if only by hunger. Ours is the strongest navy ever assembled and we will prevail!

"We are fighting for a great reward but if we are careless we will suffer grievously. All the followers of Sextus were mercilessly executed as were many of the followers of Lepidus. My friend and colleague Lepidus had co-operated with Octavius but he was shamefully deprived of his command although guilty of no wrong doing. Will Octavius be magnanimous in victory? In times passed he committed every conceivable outrage. At Philippi I ordered the ashes of the noble Brutus to be sent to Servilius, his Mater – Octavius insisted on defiling the body by beheading it prior to cremation.

"I was once the colleague of Octavius and shared with him in the management of public affairs. But now I am a private citizen – deprived of my command – disenfranchised and no longer consul! This was not by the action of the Senate and People but by one man – a friend and table companion – a kinsman. Octavius pretends not to regard me as an enemy and has declared war on my friends and allies. We recognise his desire to reign as sovereign and I have declared on oath that I will relinquish all authority as Triumvirate within weeks of victory and hand back power to the Senate and People of Rome. Let us earnestly strive, warriors to prevail now, and gain happiness for all time!"

On the other side of the Gulf of Ambricia Octavius addressed his army.

"Soldiers of the fatherland I have learned from others and confirmed by personal experience that in war fortune favours the righteous. Romans are masters of the world and it would be un-worthy of our forefathers to be subjugated by a foreigner and a woman. Egyptians who are slaves to a woman not a man – they worship reptiles and animals as gods and who embalm their bodies to give a semblance of immortality! It is an insult that Roman soldiers act as Cleopatra's bodyguard. Knights and Senators of the fatherland fawn to her like eunuchs. Who would not weep to hear and see Antonius, twice Consul, often Imperator, Triumvirate, abandoned his ancestral habits in favour of alien and barbaric customs. He pays homage to a wench as though she is Isis, calling her children Helios and Selene also himself Osiris and Dionysus. Antonius gave Cleopatra territories and islands as though he is master over all the earth and sea. All this would beggar belief and be reasonable cause to pass all bounds of rage.

"I was devoted to Antonius – I gave him my own dear sister in matrimony – granted him legions. I was unwilling to wage war merely because he insulted Octavia and neglected their children, preferring the Egyptian woman. For this reason I did not declare war on Antonius but on Cleopatra, a foreigner and an enemy by virtue of her conduct. Later I hoped that as a citizen of the Fatherland, Antonius could be brought to reason – if not voluntarily – reluctantly, to change his course as a result of the decrees passed against his Egyptian amica. He is heedless or mad, bewitched by that accursed woman and impervious to our generosity. In view of this it is our duty to fight him together with Cleopatra and repel them!

"Do not call him Antonius, he is Serapis (the Ptolemaic lord of the underworld) – look not on him as a Roman but as an Egyptian, he is no longer Consul or Imperator only Gymnasiarchs. These names are of his own choosing he has cast aside his auspicious titles of his own free will. Do not fear him because of his reputation; I have already defeated him at Matina. It is impossible for one who leads the life of royal luxury – coddled like a woman – to think manly thoughts. Look no further than his disastrous retreat from Praaspa – so many sturdy Roman souls hurling down into Hades! Antonius is past his prime – he is no longer physically fit but worn out by un-natural lusts. If he were pious to our gods why has he waged war on them and the Fatherland? If he is faithful to his allies why has he imprisoned the Rex of Armenia?

"I have heard it said that the wealth of Antonius and his allies is greater than that of Rome. Why then are so many of their troops defecting to us? His legions are not prepared to risk life and happiness by fighting their own countrymen. The riches of the enemy of the Fatherland are yours for the taking but there can be no greater prize than to maintain the renown of our forefathers. We must preserve out tradition and reek vengeance against those who are in revolt against Rome!

"You prevailed against Sextus Pompeius and won Sicily also against Antonius to win Mutina. Now you will show no less zeal against Cleopatra who has designs on your property, equally against her consort who has distributed to her children our territories. Indeed there is no need to speak further when we have already shown our superiority not only off Leucas but here the other day. Be encouraged not by my words but by your own deeds and put an end to this war!

"It is in the nature of all men when faced with failure in the first contact to be disheartened by what is to come. We are superior and I have received reports that the Egyptians are already in despair and endeavouring to make good their escape. Antonius has placed aboard his ships the best and most valuable of their positions. Do not spare those who insult the Fatherland and seek to subjugate all mankind. Let us conquer them and take away their treasure. Dominus Agrippa, you have command our ships and Tarius Rufus you command our legions. Warriors of the Fatherland allow no woman to be equal to a man!"

It took several hours to embark all ships from the Actium peninsular and station them in the Preveza Straits. The two headlands were only four hundred cubits *(two hundred metres)* apart. To the north by the sand bar and shoals at Pandokrator Popliccola was in command of the right squadron, Antony was with him. The middle squadron was commanded by Octavius and Insteius and to the south near the Cape Skilla shoals Sosius commanded the left squadron. Behind this line were a reserve squadron and the remnants of the Egyptian fleet. Agrippa's line was parallel eight stadies offshore coincidently the same distance which separated the two opposing armies on high ground each side of the Peveza Straits.

Antony had resigned himself to having to fight his way out but Agrippa did not to close for battle so the two fleets faced each other without moving for some time. Tension and frustration mounted until mid day when Sosius squadron advanced on their own initiative to confront the squadron commanded by Marcus Lurius.

"Back off back off!" ordered Octavian from his Thalamegos. "Back water and draw the enemy squadron away from the protection of Cape Skilla."

Antony responded by ordered his right squadron to keep pace with left so his line formed a crescent formation stretching and weakening the central squadron. The two fleets met at northern end of the line and heavy fighting ensued. The opening salvoes were from the ship's ballistae and archers rained down arrows from the protection of the fighting towers. Agrippa's ships did not attempt to ram but came alongside individual trireme and boarded from each side using boarding bridges. Helmsmen fought with steering gear in attempt to smash opponent's oars whilst protecting their own gear. Catapults fired grappling lines which were desperately cut away wherever possible, if not boarding bridges smashed onto deck and Agrippa's marines swarmed across like starving locusts.

The Egyptian squadron and transports were motionless in calm sea; the battle hung in the balance. Then wind backed.

"Hoist the sails!" ordered Cleopatra. "As soon as we are clear of Cape Skilla set a course south, south west!" From the poop deck the *Bassilisa* saw Orion's Sword accelerate towards the nearest of Octavian's ships. It looked as though Apollodorus was going to ram the ship but at the last moment a jet of fire belched out from tube in stem controlled by figure in purple war paint on foredeck. The effect was devastating on the enemy ship as the freshening wind fanned flames.

"So my love you have succeeded in building your fire breathing dragon. Why did you not tell me? With several of those weapons we could easily conquer the world." Cleopatra then remembered what Apollodorus had said about looking back. "He must feel a great sense of shame creating such a devastating weapon. Do not reproach yourself *Kyrios mou* you are doing your part and I will do mine."

The Egyptians turned south when they were clear of Cape Skilla, but despite the shipwright's warning Cleopatra continued to watch 'Orion's Sword's destruction of the nearest of Octavian's ships by fire.

"We are clear why does he not follow us?" she demanded of the handmaids, Iras looked at her blankly and said nothing.

"That fire ship must be captured!" ordered Lurius. "It is only dangerous from the front. All available ships are to get alongside!"

The forepeak of 'Orion's Sword' had been lined with copper sheathing to prevent the planking from burning. A large copper barrel surrounded by brushwood filled this space from keel to deck, behind this was a solid bulkhead reinforced with iron straps. This was to protect the men in the carina who operated the bellows which pressurised the fuel in the copper barrel that in turn was heated by the brushwood fire. There were holes in the bottom of the bulkhead to supply air for combustion. For Apollodorus on the foredeck there was no protection as he ignited the hot liquid as it sprayed out through the tube in the stem. He had taken the precaution of removing all his body hair as this and clothing would easily ignite.

Apart from the two bellows men and Apollodorus the rest of the crew were sighted aft as far from the flame throwing equipment as possible. When Lurius' ships were alongside the shipwright ordered the bellows men aft. This was the pre arranged signal for the crew to abandon ship over the stern. He would then open the sluice that would drain the hot liquid from the barrel into the brushwood fire setting off a chain reaction through the ship. Greek fire would not be rediscovered for another five hundred years and his sacrifice, he hoped, would give Cleopatra a fighting chance against the overwhelming odds.

The *Bassilisa* could see that Agrippa's right squadron was now making a concerted effort to capture 'Orion's Sword. Her bowls turned to water as she realised the horrible truth. By deploying the secret weapon escape was impossible for Apollodorus; his ship was surrounded by the enemy. The Egyptian crew were desperately running aft and jumping into the sea. The purple figure on the forecastle saluted her with his flaming torch; he was making no attempt to escape. Suddenly there was a blinding flash followed by massive sound of thunder, the sea boiled and the earth shook. When eventually the smoke cleared where 'Orion's Sword' had been only burning timber remained. None of the nearby enemy ships were in position to give chase.

"Apollodorus!" screamed Cleopatra as she attempted to jump overboard. "Apollodorus - Nooooo!" Charmain grabbed hold of her mistress and tried to restrain her; Iras lost her blank expression, became focused and helped control the distraught *Bassilisa*.

"Madam, last night *Kyrios* the Apollodorus entered my mind and implanted a message for you" shouted Iras as she wrestled with the insane monarch. "Please listen" she begged. "*Kyrios* the Apollodorus said; 'I have kept secret what you have just witnessed because the weapon is unstable and impossible to control safely. My action will ensure your safety and my sacrifice will be bare testimony to what I know you have longed to hear me say. Our handmaid has details of an escape route from the Sinus Arabicus, east around India and beyond the reaches of Rome, the last of my contingencies. If I survive I will find a way to follow you.' I have a scroll from him and entrusted me with his sword and dagger, madam."

When Iras finished speaking Cleopatra remembered the light hearted exchange with her Sea Lord during Antony's feast at Antioch.

"Did you know that *Geloto's* people go into battle naked and their bodies are coloured with purple war paint, Madam?" Charmain had asked.

"You never told me, *Kyrios mou*!" Cleopatra had replied in astonishment. "So that was what all the laughter was about."

"The funny part was Charmain's suggestion that I should have dressed as a Britannic Warrior."

"Well, if you ever lead us into battle I shall expect you to be appropriately undressed, *Kyrios mou*" she had added with a chuckle. The last picture the *Bassilisa* would have of Apollodorus, in her mind, was the naked figure covered in purple war paint bravely saluting her from the bows of his ship. Cleopatra collapsed sobbing onto the deck of her flag ship; she was still there with the two handmaids vainly trying to be of comfort when Mark Antony came aboard. The Roman took in the scene, nodded in understanding and then made his way to the forecastle a broken man to find solace in drunken oblivion.

"So Antony did not abandon his army and chase after Cleopatra as most accounts state. It was all part of a pre arranged plan which went horribly wrong."

"That is correct, Antony's signal to withdraw was miss-understood or ignored because he failed to take his captains into his confidence. It was utterly imperative that Cleopatra escaped as she had the war chest. Money wins more wars than bravery and poor communications reek disaster on the best of schemes" I replied.

"What became of Apollodorus, did he survive?"

Book 34

Dark water engulfed the shipwright cooling his burns but the salt stung his lacerations as though he was being dragged through briars; unconsciousness engulfed him as he sank into a realm shrouded in mist and cloud.

"It is easy to go down to the underworld" explained a disembodied voice. "The black doors of Hades are open day and night but to retrace your steps and escape to the upper air and sunlight is a task few have succeeded."

"To sail twice upon the pools of Styx I must seek the golden bough hidden in a dark tree" thought the shipwright. "The golden leaves are sacred to the master of the underworld."

An old man was standing at the bank of a vast quagmire of boiling whirlpools; his ragged grey beard was surmounted by eyes like burning embers, a foul cloak hung from a knot on his shoulder. Apollodorus had arrived at the deep pools of Cocytus and swamps of Styx.

"As all the rivers on earth flow into the sea," announced the ferryman, "so Hades admits every soul that arrives, never too small for its new population, never crowded."

A cold shiver ran through the very bones of Apollodorus and the shipwright sank to the ground pouring out prayers from the depth of his heart.

Casualties at Actium had been remarkably light, had Agrippa succeeded in driving the allies onto the lee shore the entire fleet would have been destroyed, however Antony and Cleopatra had escaped with over one hundred ships. In the final count less than forty triremes had been lost, indicating that fighting had been half hearted. The land army, including ten thousand cavalry was intact on the Actium peninsular and they withdraw across the mountains.

Three days later the Egyptian fleet arrived at Taenarum near Sparta and Methone, Antony had spent the voyage alone and intoxicated in the forecastle of Cleopatra's flag ship. News that Canidius had successfully withdrawn the army improved Antony's spirits and he sent a message confirming orders that they should march to Asia Minor. Cleopatra insisted on waited at Taenarum for survivors of the conflict. Apollodorus was not among the tattered remnants of the allied forces that arrived so reluctantly, after a few days, the *Bassilisa* ordered her fleet to sail directly across the Mediterranean, south to the African coast.

Octavian intercepted Antony's army and offered terms for surrender, overtures he was not in a position to honour but the troops were anxious to return home consequently the army disintegrated. Six legions anticipated duplicity and insisted on being incorporated into the victors army, retaining their officers and eagles. Canidius, out of loyalty to Antony, refused to surrender and he made his way to Alexandria.

Apollodorus opened his eyes and for a moment he was unable to see, when his vision cleared he realised that he had been washed up on the reed lined banks of a lake that was strangely familiar. He was in a vast cavern lit by an unnatural light. The incandescent light from the cavern roof was refracted by the wavelets in a riot of colours. There were the most exotic flowers and trees he had ever seen. The cries of birds and animals mingled to form celestial music. A feeling of tranquil calm enveloped him and the perfume of the flowers filled his nostrils, reminiscent of the flowers on the deck of Cleopatra's flag ship at Tarsus. The noise of one particular animal stood out from the others, his two dogs came running though the trees and they greeted him enthusiastically licking his wounds. A large man appeared in front of him and Apollodorus felt the blood drain from his face, all feelings of tranquillity evaporated. The man had the head of a crocodile, in one hand were scales and under his arm was a book. The book was covered with the hide of a strange hairy beast.
"I am Glutton" boomed the demon.
"I know who you are" replied the shipwright, trying unsuccessfully to sound casual. "Surely I have paid the price for my sacrilege by re-living those times over and over again?"
Glutton did not answer instead he drew a sword from his hip, the shipwright's own weapon. The demon used 'Orion's Sword' to dig a trench then poured liberations to the dead. First milk and honey mellowed wine, water and finally sprinkled the mixture with barley all the while chanting to the dead. Glutton took a black ram and a heifer then, using the shipwright's dagger, slit their throats over the trench, the victim's dark blood flowed.
All around the Mediterranean coastline from Alexandria to Rome including Actium and Philippi the ghosts of the dead came flocking, brides and un-wed youths, old men and maidens, girls who had suffered, their tender hearts scared by sorrow and grief. Great armies killed in battle, stabbed by sword and spear, warriors wrapped in bloody armour. The multitude swarmed around the trench filling the air with unearthly cries. Terror gripped the shipwright!

The Egyptian fleet arrived at Paraetonium the natural harbour where Apollodorus a decade earlier had practiced techniques for breaking a blockade. This wreckage had been carried across the Mediterranean and convinced the Romans that the Egyptian fleet had been damaged in a storm, subterfuge that had enabled Cleopatra to remain neutral in the civil war. The fleet was divided Antony remained with half the ships while Cleopatra sailed on to Alexandria to arrived three days later to confront a choice; fight, negotiate with Octavian or flight.

Apollodorus sank deeper into the abyss and he found himself in a dank cavern never blessed by the warmth of sunlight or refreshed by a sea breeze. The eyes of Helios could never flash his rays through the dark and bring light to the people of this domain. This filthy place of black corruption was numbingly cold and for a moment the shipwright thought he was back in his birthplace. He had arrived at the threshold of a foul abode, the door swung open and inside was an evil apparition, she was consuming the flesh of vipers to feed her natural venom. The shipwright looked away in disgust as the spirit rose from the frozen ground, dropping her half eaten snakes and lethargically ambled towards him.

She looked at Apollodorus and groaned her face was pallid, eyes squinting and teeth decayed. The body of this apparition was totally shrivelled, nipples green with gall and poison dripped from her tongue. The shipwright smiled nervously as he sensed bile in his throat.

"The only thing that makes me smile is watching pain" explained the demon. "I am denied sleep by endless torments and loath the sight of human success."

Apollodorus could see that she was wasting away, gnawing herself as she devoured her victims.

"Your torture is also self-inflicted" she announced. "Wherever I go I trample the flowering meadows, grass withers and the tallest trees are lopped. My foul breath pollutes countries, cities and family homes."

"Who ever you are I can see you must be very hard to love" the shipwright quipped.

"I am Envy!"

Apollodorus nodded in understanding. "You believe that I coveted Antonius but I can assure you that you could not be more wrong! The Roman gave that which was not his to give, the earth belongs to all men, to all beasts of the field, all birds of the air and all fish of the sea. Mankind are only stewards of the creation, they do not own it! They deceive themselves when they believe they have dominion over all other life. Cleopatra lay with Antonius and with Caesar in order to preserve the freedom of her realm, when she was in my arms it was through choice and of her own free will! You have poisoned Octavius, you will try to poison all humanity but you will never ever poison me or the woman I love!"

News of Octavian's victory at Actium spread rapidly, without an army Antony posed no threat so Agrippa had not pursued him to Africa instead he travelled to Athens with Octavian. The Romans received reports that Antony's authority in Asia Minor was collapsing and the client monarchs were declaring for the victors.

After several weeks Antony arrived in Alexandria to find Cleopatra preparing to move treasure and supplies to the port of Arsinoe Cleopatris on the Sinus Arabicus.

"I have a small fleet of ships there" she explained "and details of an escape route far beyond the reaches of Octavius"

"Such action is unnecessary amica I will defend you" replied Antony.

"With what, an Ostrich feather fan?" retorted Cleopatra angrily. "All that remains of your army is Canidius. Your legions and cavalry have surrendered to Octavius!"

Apollodorus walked slowly along a long wide marble paved roadway flanked by two thousand statues. He knew that ahead was the end was the temple of Hera and behind him the city of Samos.

"Mortal, you defiled your body with sinful eating!"

Apollodorus turned in the direction of the voice and found he was facing a statue of a kindly old man with a full beard and luxurious silver hair. The shipwright was transfixed as the statue became a living being.

"You ridiculed my teachings yet in your heart you know my wisdom to be sound" continued Pythagoras. "You would have benefited from five years of silence as my disciple and learned much. There are crops to sustain you, the fruit forces down the branches under its weight, grapes swell on the vines, scented herbs and vegetables that fire can soften; milk's sweet flow cannot fails you, nor honey fragrant with thyme. The earth supplies her riches and nourishing food in lavish abundance; she offers you feasts that demand no bloodshed.

"Only the beasts whose natural instincts are savage and untamed, angry lions, tigers, or bears and wolves delight in the taste of blood. What a heinous crime is committed when the guts disappear inside a fellow creature's intestines, when greedy bodies grow fat on the flesh of the carcases they have eaten, and one living thing depends for its life on the death of its neighbour! What have the oxen done, those totally guileless creatures, those simple, innocuous beasts that were born to a life of labour? How could a man have the heart to remove the yoke of the plough from his faithful worker and almost at once to make him a victim, wielding his axe on the toil-worn neck, whose strength allowed him to break and renew the soil each year that had yield a harvest? Mark my words, when you cram your mouth with the members of slaughtered oxen, remember you were eating your own farm workers"

"The gods demand blood sacrifices, and for this and other reasons I worship none of them. How do you reconcile your deeply held religious views with your respect with the sanctity of all life?"

"You of all people know that not all religions have gods and I believe that no loving creator would delight in the shedding of blood, life as you have frequently said is our most precious gift."

"I agree with all that you have said" replied the shipwright. "We are men born out of our time; you chose to live apart from the world whereas I have lived in the world but tried not to be part of its evils. I hope to have influenced humanity to strive towards a more peaceful coexistence based on a respect of all living creatures and religious tolerance. I have been reluctantly forced to shed blood in order to protect a society that, in the main, thinks as you and I do. You imply hypocrisy and I concede that I have eaten meat whilst taking no part in the killing of the creatures that have sustained me but you share in my guilt. Your knowledge and wisdom has been used to create devastating weapons of mass destruction and will continue to do so."

The old man nodded and smiled at the shipwright in a kindly and understanding manner. "So why then do you judge yourself so severely?" Pythagoreans then handed the shipwright a small bouquet of golden foliage. "I think you will find this useful, *Chairete Kyrios o Apollodorus*."

From Athens Octavian continued on to the island of Samos where he established his winter headquarters, Antony's officers were brought before him and many were executed. Sosius was pardoned leading to speculation that his attack on Agrippa's right flank had been restrained and his premature surrender pivotal in Antony's defeat. Agrippa returned to Rome to deputise for Octavian in the same way that Antony had done for Caesar during the Alexandrian war sixteen years earlier.

King Malchus of Nabataen extracted revenge for the loss of his bitumen deposits to Cleopatra by destroying her ships in the Gulf of Suez, escape was now impossible. In an attempt to rescue Antony from the depths of depression the Bassilisa held a lavish ceremony for the coming of age of her sixteen year old son Caesarion and Antony's son Antyllus who was two years younger.

The Furies blocked Apollodorus way, firmly extending their arms coiled round in knots of vipers, the adders responded by hissing and spitting. The two daughters of night were sitting at the great iron gates of hell. One of the sisters wrenched two of the snakes from her hair and flung them at the shipwright with lethal aim. He smelt their noxious breath; the deadly effect was felt in the mind they did not inflict physical wounds.

Here also were the spirits of Sorrow, Panic and Fear also the wild faced demon of Madness but most incongruous of all amongst all the demons was a strikingly good looking dark haired man with a neatly trimmed beard and dressed in a twentieth century business suit.

"Lord Apollodorus, this is pleasant but not altogether unexpected surprise" said the man as he brushed an imaginary speck of dust from his immaculate trouser leg. "I suppose I am not exactly what you were expecting. Is this more like it?"

The man turned into an enormous hippopotamus wallowing in a pool of molten larva. Red eyes bored into the shipwrights causing him to shudder.

"We meet face to face at last Seth you have been in my nightmares for some time" replied Apollodorus calmly.

"I have been following your progress with interest, your pathetic attempts to change what was ordained and that which is to come. You have failed the woman you love the Ptolemy's and Cleopatra's will be no more. This is the dawn of a new era."

"Nothing lasts forever" replied the shipwright. "You must be sinful pride but this is not the start of a new world order, merely another sandbank in the shifting stream of eternity. There is still life in my body, while there is life there is hope. Your disciple is a victim of envy and pride; his empire will crumble and be destroyed as will yours. If I am guilty on any wrong doing I accept my punishment, if not stand aside and let me pass!"

Satan returned to his original form as he accepted the golden bough from the shipwright and gesticulated to the Furies to open the gates. "It is far better to be master of hell than a servant in paradise; you have made your choice. Now quit this loathsome place and take yourself back to your home in the healthier air of the heavens."

Apollodorus passed through and Satan whispered "until the next time *Gelotopoios*. What need my punishment when you are doing such a good job yourself, until the next time *Gelotopoios*, and for all eternity!"

Herod entered dressed in his royal robes and carrying the crown of Judea which he offered to Octavian. The Roman looked at the King coldly with his unsmiling blue eyes.

"Now that your patron is vanquished I suppose you wish to transfer your allegiance to me. What do you think you have to offer that I could possibly want?" Octavian inquired, sarcastically.

"Information Imperator" replied Herod nervously.

"I know the whereabouts of Antonius; he is in the arms of his Egyptian whore. Nothing else concerns me."

"You believe as all Rome believes that Antonius is bewitched by Cleopatra and that she is in love with him."

Octavian nodded then brushed away his fair hair from his eyes and studied the King more intently.

"The former may well be true" continued Herod "but the latter is far from the case. Cleopatra has a highly astute consort and that is where her heart truly lies."

"The Sicilian, Apollodorus!" exclaimed Octavian. "My Pater spoke highly of that man and greatly admired him."

"You are correct in all but one thing; he is no Sicilian. The tin island of his birth is Britannia and he boasts that his people drove the Deius Gaius Julius Caesar back into the sea, twice! I am surprised he never told you. Control Apollodorus and you control Cleopatra. Destroy the Jester and you destroy Cleopatra! But be warned he is your nemesis not Antonius; underestimate the Britannian at your peril!" The king indicated the scar that ran around his neck. Octavian realising that he was probably facing the only man able to rule the Jews and keep the country loyal to Rome and so he placed the crown on Herod's head.

Strong slim fingers gripped Apollodorus under the chin and he broke through the moonlit surface coughing and spluttering for breath.

"Just relax 'Pollo" said a soft, husky, melodic and utterly captivating female voice "and we will soon have you ashore."

When he next opened his eyes and his vision cleared he realised that he had been washed up on a reed bed. The shipwright staggered through the blood red shallows forcing his way through dense patches of reeds. He collapsed exhausted on the muddy flanks starred by sheets of radiant anemones growing through the plasticized mud of the shore of what looked more like Lake Mareotis than the Gulf of Ambricia. The shipwright rolled over onto his stomach and tried to lift himself up. In the distance across the lemon-mauve surface of the lake he could see the grim outline of concrete industrial units where fine marble buildings and granite pillars had once stood. Looking down onto his hands he saw a ring on his finger, not one ring but three, two serpents were entwined with a bird, the eyes were made of emeralds. He then looked up and found himself looking into much larger green eyes but these were not precious stones, they were real! On the creature's hood were two lotus footprints. The cobra reared up and her forked tongue flicked as she tasted the balmy night air.

"I am your greatest fear and your salvation" hissed the reptile in a soft, husky, melodic and utterly captivating female voice as it struck. The narrator was gripped with a sluggish inertia, his joints stiffened as a creeping chill invaded his body. Over head was a rhythmical throbbing noise, a bright white light and swirling dust. Strong arms lifted him onto a stretcher then the lights of Alexandria fell away as the air ambulance rose into the night sky. Bright lights were flashing passed, a tube was being attached to his arm and people were speaking reassuringly in a language he did not understand, then the dark once more engulfed his vision.

Cleopatra stood in Apollodorus' room, it was smaller then she remembered, but like hers, was on the seaward side of Antirhodos, overlooking the lighthouse. She was reluctant to disturb anything as she still hoped against hope that he was not lost and would sometime return, although nearly a year had passed since Actium. Charmain and Iras were with her but remained silent. There was a large silver spotted cat on the bed the handmaids stroked the animal which responded with a mournful cry. Cleopatra sat down at the desk where she found the shipwright's ledgers. Here were all the financial transactions of the rebuilding of the Egyptian Navy meticulously recorded. It took some time to read through them but gradually it dawned on her something she had never known before. She turned to the handmaids and said.

"He never used his position as Sea Lord to accumulate any wealth for himself. I thought by giving him that position he would have become rich but all he took for himself was the same wages he paid the shipyard hands. Did you know he had no money?"

"He always said you provided him with all he needed, madam" replied Iras.

Cleopatra became distraught and hurried between each cupboard and investigated all the storage places. She found drawing instruments and scrolls, various items of marine equipment and some charts but nothing of value.

"Apart from the clothes he stood up in he had nothing and I gave him most of them. He always maintained he was too busy to worry about what to wear. Iras, Charmain" she wailed "he had absolutely nothing of value." Then she looked at the Dyonystic ring he had given her "the Amethyst stones were the only treasure he possessed and he gave them to me. We have his boat 'Mintaka', his weapons but not his body, we cannot bury him and he had nothing of value to place in his boat for the journey to the afterlife."

"I don't understand, madam" interrupted Charmain.

"When we were visiting the Pyramids I asked him about the burial customs of his people. He asked to be placed aboard 'Mintaka' with all his possessions and pushed out into Lake Mareotis. A hole was to be bored into the bottom of his boat so she would sink gracefully. We have neither him nor any possessions………" She sank to the floor and her body was racked with sobbing. The handmaids ran forward and put their arms round their mistress to try and comfort her. Iras was first to speak.

"He didn't say possessions he said 'all that I hold precious' that was you, madam. Nothing else mattered to him only you."

Octavian strode the catwalk of his Triremes in deep contemplation; he was interrupted by one of his aids.

"There is a message from one of our ships; they think they have a rower you will be interested to see."

"Have they found Antonius?" he asked sarcastically.

"No Dominus they think they have the Jester, Apollodorus. You have met him before so they hope you can positively identify him."

Octavian's attitude changed abruptly. "Bring him to me and do not harm him that man is worth his weight in gold. If that is truly Jocus we have the bait I need."

A little later the dishevelled shipwright faced Octavian, he was gaunt having lost weight and prolonged exposure to the sun had bleached his auburn hair to a colour not dissimilar to the Romans.

"We meet again Domini Octavius" quipped Apollodorus. "This is the point when I say 'I suppose you think I am going to talk' and you reply with a sinister laugh. 'No *Kyrios* the Apollodorus I think you are going to die!' Can you arrange a crucifixion at sea or are you carrying some crocodiles in the bilges? No - Lions perhaps?"

"So you truly are Jocus, you are worth far more to me alive than dead" said Octavian eyeing the shipwright carefully. Turning to the guards he ordered "clean him up, give him fresh clothes" then he turned back to Apollodorus. "If you give me your word not to try and escape you will be treated as my guest...."

"What makes you think I want to abscond? You are going where I wish to be, I have no other means of getting to Alexandria given the choice between rowing or being your guest, I accept your hospitality graciously" replied Apollodorus with a bow and smile.

"If what you say is true" went on Cleopatra "and he wanted to be interned with me, which meant he looked on me as his *Guvaika*."

"He was not alone in that view madam" replied Charmain. "All Egypt prayed that you would make him your consort, not Antonius. Forgive me I have spoken out of turn."

"No, you have spoken the truth Charmain I will not punish you. It was my dearest wish that we should become one but a soothsayer many years ago said I would be widowed so I took Antonius as consort to save Apollodorus' life. It seems he was destined to die anyway so I denied our happiness for no good purpose."

Amongst the papyrus and drawings they found a scroll which Apollodorus had been reading.

"It is from the Hebrew God, madam" said Iras.

"Let me see it" replied Cleopatra. "Everything is meaningless" she read aloud. "The words of the teacher, son of David, king of Jerusalem. What does man gain from all his labour at which he toils under the sun? Generations come and generations go, but the earth remains forever. The sun rises and the sun sets and hurries back to where it rises. The wind blows to the south and turns to the north; round and round it goes, ever returning on its course. All streams flow into the sea, yet the sea is never full. To the place the streams come from, they return again. All things are wearisome, more then one can say. The eye never has enough of seeing, nor the ear its fill of hearing. What has been will be again, what has been done will be done again; there is nothing new under the sun. Is there anything of which one can say, 'Look? This is something new?' It was here already, long ago; it was here before our time. There is no remembrance of men of old, and even those who are yet to come will not be remembered by those who follow."

She skipped over the next few passages but her eye was caught by part that had been underlined. "Toil is meaningless. So I hate life, because the work that is done under the sun was grievous unto me. All of it is meaningless, a chasing after the wind. I hate all things I have toiled under the sun because I must leave them to the one who comes after me. And who knows whether he will be a wise man or a fool? Yet he will have control over all the work into which I have poured my efforts and skill under the sun. This too is meaningless. So my heart began to despair over all my toilsome labour under the sun. For a man may do his work with wisdom, knowledge and skill, and then he must leave all he owns to someone who has not worked for it. This too is meaningless and a great misfortune."

Cleopatra then remembered what Apollodorus had said when they visited the Great Pyramids at Giza.

"A human life is all too often as a traveller's footstep in the sand, blown away by the desert wind like a candle flame. We can tell what an animal looked like by examining its bones, likewise with human remains, but we are more than that insomuch as it can be seen what we have done with our lives by viewing our works." She began to understand then once again the tears flooded. When the shipwright declared that he worshiped no gods he meant that he did not worship the one god held in greater esteem than all others by all people; he did not worship money! The Bassilisa remembered how at Antioch Apollodorus had told the story of the wealthy Pharaoh who believed he was the happiest man alive. The wise man in the story had said that the gods are envious of human prosperity and delight in troubling us.

"Blessings are not only given they can be taken away from us" he had explained. "Happiness is diametrically opposite to pleasure and they are all too often mutually exclusive."

"That is ridicules, pleasure and happiness are one and the same" Cleopatra had retorted.

"Most people would agree with you, Thea, and they deceive themselves. The transitory pleasure of quaffing and feasting is followed by the discomfort of a hangover and in the long term the misery of obesity" Apollodorus had replied.

In choosing the short term pleasure of territories, power and wealth Cleopatra had denied herself the long term happiness of true love. It was some time before she regained her composure; rolling up the scroll determinedly the Bassilisa turned to her handmaids.

"The time has come for Domini Antonius to know the truth! I suppose he is sulking in his Timonium, I will force my fingers down this throat and purge the wine from his system. My Lord, 'Pollo gave his life to give us a chance, your sacrifice will not be in vain, my love!"

Octavian landed at the eastern frontier of Egypt where his legions were massing in preparation for an attack on the fortress of Pelusium. The commander, Seleucus, was under secret instructions from Cleopatra to give only token resistance so the fortress was quickly secured and the Roman army, commanded by Gallus, advanced across the Nile Delta towards the Hippodrome to arrive there at the end of July.

The Timonium, a small pavilion, had been constructed on reclaimed land on an outcrop from Poseidium and was directly opposite the palace temple at the base of the letter tau that formed Antirhodos Island. Between the Timonium and Antirhodos was the seaward entrance of the Royal Harbour, Antony had made this his home here for some time where he lived as a recluse. Access to the Timonium was by a jetty from Poseidium so Cleopatra had made her way there via the mainland. The smell of stale wine, urine and human faeces made her retch; Antony was huddled in the seaward corner clutching a goblet.

"You Nothos!" she exclaimed as she dragged him to his feet and hurled him across the pavilion. "You feeble excuse of humanity!" and kicked him in the stomach. "You said you loved me, you don't know the meaning of the word!" Her next kick sent the Roman across the other side where he hit the wall with so much force the flimsy structure threatened to collapse. "Do you know how much money Apollodorus took for himself from the funds I gave him for building the Navy?"

Antony looked at Cleopatra and shook his head.

"Nothing!" screamed Cleopatra as she kicked him again. This kick emptied his stomach. When he had finished vomiting Cleopatra grabbed him by the girdle and collar then hurled him at the opposite wall with so much force his head passed right through so he could see the sea. She dragged him back inside and the bemused Roman asked.

"What has the money for shipbuilding got to do with love?"

"I will tell you, you pathetic son of a camel driver's whore! Every last denarii I gave him was spent on ships that we gave to you! He never joined our feasting because he hadn't the means to entertain us. Those ships you threw away without so much as a fight! Apollodorus burnt himself to a cinder to give us a chance!" She kicked him again but the Roman lifted a hand in submission.

"He lay down his life for us" he whispered "and he gave me the woman he loved more dearly than his own life. I know that now, I have always suspected that there was far more to your relationship than mere friendship." Cleopatra nodded and Antony continued "He didn't give up when he knew that my forces had no stomach for battle; he went down fighting against overwhelming odds. When I saw your face as I came aboard your flag ship I knew the truth. What is the military situation?"

"Pelusium has fallen and the legions of Octavius are making their way across the Nile Delta" explained Cleopatra calmly. "I have loaded all the treasures I can in my Mausoleum with firewood, pitch and oil around the base. When Octavius arrives I will be locked and barricaded in there with Charmain and Iras, we will turn my Mausoleum into our funeral pyre! Octavius will have neither me nor the treasury! I will send Caesarion to Upper Egypt with his tutor, Rhodon, they will, the gods willing, take a ship East from one of the Sinus Arabicus ports."

"Help me get cleaned up, I will take charge of the army and go down fighting. I owe that much to you and the memory of the man you really love, to say sorry sounds pathetic but I am both. I am sorry and I am pathetic."

Cleopatra smiled at him "I accept your apology, come Dominus and I will help you ready yourself for this our final battle." She then remembered the words of Isis a decade or so before.

"My daughter, Apollodorus will never become one body with you until the final battle is over. Do not try to force him."

"Will we prevail against our enemies?" Cleopatra had asked.

"Time will tell, my child. But when it is all over, win or lose, then and only then, will you know true love. Remember that to win is to lose and they that lose shall win.

Book 35

Antony rode out east at the head of the cavalry and confronted an advanced guard from Octavian, who were soon routed and pursued back towards the camp at the Hippodrome. From a discrete distance he had leaflets shot by his archers at his opponent's camp promising six thousand sesterces (*six years wages*) to any defectors, he also challenged Octavian to single combat.

"Six thousand sesterces! Does he think you would be so cheaply bought?" Octavian read aloud the messages to his troops. "Single combat!" He laughed, scornfully. "Can he think of no better way to die?"

Meanwhile in the royal mews near Cape Lochas Cleopatra helped Caesarion, disguised in the robes of a desert nomad, saddle his horse.

"I think you had better take these" announced the Bassilisa as she handed her seventeen year old son the shipwright's sword and dagger.

"Ma I cannot accept them" he replied, tearfully. "They belong to – to *Pater Geloto*."

"*Kyrios* the Apollodorus gave them to me for safe keeping on the day that his ship 'Orion's Sword' was destroyed. His sacrifice enabled the Egyptian fleet to escape from Actium; everything our Sea Lord did was done for a good reason - he trusted my judgement implicitly. I have felt for some time he would have presented these weapons to you at your coming of age - I know he has secretly instructed you in their use. Amethyst has always been greatly prized by Achaean royalty and has been of great significance to Pollo and myself because of the protection these stones give. As you know, the pommels are amethysts engraved with the constellation of Orion where the Pharaohs...." Cleopatra was unable to continue as grief racked her body. The young man held his mother tightly and replied.

"I know what you are trying to say, Ma, and accept these weapons as symbols of love and protection of my true parents." Ptolemy Caesar placed the dagger carefully in his belt and mounted the horse. In a wide sweep he brought the junction of the blade with the hilt to his lips then sheathed the sword. Cleopatra looked with pride at her son, now a fully grown man and saw in him the image of both his sire and the only man she truly loved. He looked back at the lonely diminutive figure dwarfed by the splendid marble palace buildings and granite pillars; both mother and son knew in their hearts they would never see each other again. Caesarion turned his horse and instructed his small entourage to follow; they galloped off towards the 'Gate of the Moon' and an uncertain future.

Some time later Antony returned to the city triumphant and introduced one of his soldiers to Cleopatra.

"This man distinguished himself if battle today" he said. Cleopatra presented the man with a gold helmet and breastplate, that evening he defected to Octavian.

"The Inimitable Livers Club is henceforth to be known as the Inseparables in Death," announced Antony at dinner. "I have given orders for battle at sea and by land" then turning to his servant he ordered. "More wine Eros! Only the Fates can tell if it will be I or Octavius you will serve tomorrow, my friend."

"I serve you and you alone, Dominus Antonius" replied Eros. Some of the guests wept at these words.

"I have no wish to involve you in the fighting, victory is impossible I only seek an honourable death for myself on the battlefield" continued Antony. An air of impending doom descended over Alexandria and about midnight an invisible choir was heard singing. It was said that Dionysius was leaving, fulfilling the ancient legend that the gods would abandon the doomed city.

> *'When suddenly at darkest midnight heard,*
> *The invisible company passing, the clear voices,*
> *Ravishing music of invisible choir –*
> *Your fortunes having failed you now,*
> *Hopes gone aground, a lifetime of desires*
> *Turned into smoke. Ah! Do not agonize*
> *At what is past deceiving*
> *But like a man long since prepared*
> *With courage say your last good-byes*
> *To Alexandria as she is leaving.*
> *Do not be tricked and never say*
> *It was all a dream or that your ears misled,*
> *Leave cowards their entreaties and complaints,*
> *Let all such useless hopes be shed,*
> *And like a man long since prepared,*
> *Deliberately, with pride, with resignation*
> *Befitting you and worthy of such a city*

Turn to open the window and look down
To drink past all deceiving
Your last dark rapture from the mystic throng
And say farewell, farewell to Alexandria leaving.'
('The God Abandons Antony' C. P. Cavafy)"

On the first day of the eighth month, subsequently re-named August by Octavian in his honour, thirty years before Common Era, the Egyptian fleet sailed from the Great Harbour of Alexandria. Antony and his legions watched aghast as the oars came up in unison as a sign of surrender. The invading fleet responded by raising their oars as a signal of acceptance. Then the two armies met on the high ground outside the city but Antony's troops fought half- heartedly, most surrendered or deserted so their dejected commander returned to the city.

"Octavius denied my request to live as a private citizen in Athens, now he has denied me an honourable death in battle" announced Antony when he arrived back at the palace then demanded "were is Cleopatra now?"

"She and her handmaids are in her mausoleum" replies Eros, his servant, as he helped remove the armour.

"She intends to turn the mausoleum into her funeral pyre and deprive Octavius of the treasure she has accumulated there. Cleopatra, I am ashamed I have shown no less courage than you. Eros, my faithful servant, the time has come for you to honour the oath you have made to me."

Sadly his servant drew his sword and pointed it at Antony. They looked at each other. Eros lunged but suddenly turned his weapon and fell forward onto the point and died instantly. Antony cried out;

"That was well done Eros; you have shown me what I must do even if you had not the heart to do it!" Turning his sword on himself he fell forward but the blade was deflected away from his heart by the breast bone to enter his stomach. As the digestive acids seeped into his chest cavity Antony knew that his death would be slow and agonising.

"You must be feeling very pleased with yourself" said Apollodorus. "The forces of Antonius are giving only token resistance; soon the wealth of Egypt will be yours to plunder."

"Cleopatra has barricaded herself and the Egyptian treasury in her mausoleum and is threatening to turn it into her funeral pyre" replied Octavian. "I have sent Proculeius to negotiate terms of surrender with her."

"She has learned some bad habits from me," chuckled Apollodorus to disguise his real feelings. As his muscles and bowls turned to water he thought in horror; "Thea believes fire to be a living creature which devours with an insatiable appetite. Surely she cannot allow her body and her spirit to be consumed by any animal! In her despair she is prepared to sacrifice her Ba, she will never enter the afterlife and Egypt will have no monarch to mediate with their gods and secure the countries continued prosperity. I cannot let her spend eternity re living these final moments. She must be stopped whatever the cost! No realm however beautiful is worth such a high price, no treasure however valuable is worth eternal damnation." Aloud he continued "The *Bassilisa* has become a pyromaniac like me. No doubt her response to Proculeius will be 'go fornicate in your *Mater's* dung'. Presumably you consider yourself too important to carry out the negotiations yourself or are you afraid she may seduce you?"

At the mausoleum Cleopatra and her handmaids struggled with the ropes to haul Antony, mortally wounded, in a sling up to a window. Their faces were contorted as they strained at the limit of their strength. The Roman held out his arms to them as he swung helplessly below and the crowd shouted encouragement.

"That is what she did to Caesar" replied Octavian.
"You flatter yourself!" exclaimed Apollodorus. "Caesar raped her; he took the most precious gift a woman can give! She gave it to preserve the freedom and independence for her country. He repaid her by leaving Egypt two days before his son was born, he didn't have the decency to acknowledge him as his heir."
"I am Caesars heir, I am the son of god!" cried Octavian.
"Caesar non deu, tu non filius dues. Caesar was no god and you are no son of god! Neither you nor he knows what it is to be a god. To be a god is to hear every cry for help from every troubled soul and be unable to respond to all of them. To be blamed for every human ill and have your name used as a profanity and have your good advice corrupted for the convenience of mortal rulers they persecute or exploit their subjects. You believe that being a god is to be above mere mortal constraints but I tell you this; that to be a god demands a far higher standard of integrity, morality and truthfulness than that of mortals. To humanity any evil no matter how horrendous is justified when it is done in the name of a deity. To be a god is to look at humanity and struggle against an overwhelming desire to turn

away in disgust - that is what it is to be a god! Tu non pater patria, tu pater argentarius. Why don't you give Antonius clemency in exchange for him persuading Cleopatra to surrender her treasury so you can pay your troops?"

Finally Antony was high enough to slide through the window.
"Try to remain calm" he gasped. "Have you any wine, I don't think I could face the afterlife without a stiff drink." He smiled weakly "I beg you Cleopatra, look to your own safety."
"Why have you done dreadful thing?" wailed Cleopatra.
"Apollodorus sacrificed himself to give us a chance, Octavius wants me dead, and nothing less will satisfy him. This way you will have a second chance, he has no fight with you, only me. The time has come to return you to the man who you truly love, the only one worthy to be your consort. He gave you to me with a dowry of cash I am giving you back with a dowry of my life. When you see the Jester again, and I truly believe you will, please tell him that my only regret is that I ignored his good council at Antioch. Do not grieve for me, I am honoured that I have been more fortunate than most men. I am content to die a Roman, vanquished by another Roman, whatever I have given, that I still have. I will be judged to be a happy man."

"Marcus Antonius is dead" said Octavian softly.
"Is that how you say it?" replied Apollodorus in a voice that started as little more than a whisper but became progressively louder as he continued. "Marcus Antonius is dead? The soup is hot - the soup is cold? Marcus Antonius lives - Marcus Antonius is dead! When Caesar was presented with the severed head of Pompeius he wept at the death of a great rival he did not rejoice at the demise of an enemy. You announce the death of your greatest rival as though you are discussing a mundane matter of domestic arrangement. One of the greatest men whoever lived is dead; you must proclaim it from the highest point at the top of your voice. Marcus Antonius is dead! The world must know that Marcus Antonius is dead!"
"Yes Marcus Antonius is dead but Caesar lives!"
"You are no Caesar, neither was Antonius!" shouted Apollodorus scornfully as he held Octavian's expressionless gaze. "Antonius was Caesar's right arm whereas you were nothing more than his phallus quaffing bum boy and a travesty of creation!"
Octavian's face was crimson with anger as he struck Apollodorus, the shipwright turned and once again held the younger mans gaze, blood ran down from the corner of his mouth. "The brave Imperator has summonsed

up the courage to strike a bound man whose only crime is in speaking the truth. It is gratifying to have succeeded where Antonius failed, he will enter the afterlife content in the knowledge that it is possible to provoke an emotional response by insulting you" he continued softly. "You want me to persuade Cleopatra to surrender." Octavian, unable to move as the shipwrights grey eyes bore into the depth of his very being, nodded as Apollodorus continued. "The Roman way would be to have me flogged outside her mausoleum; my screams would bring her out. Please do not insult my intelligence by saying that you will spare her children if I do your bidding because I know that your word counts as nothing. But I will do as you wish, not because I am fearful of the lash, so I can give Cleopatra the one thing she desires above all else. She longs for more than anything else in the world, the one thing she will give her lands and treasury for, to spend her last few moments with the man she truly loves and to hear me say 'I love you with all my being, I have always loved you and only you.' She never loved Caesar or Antonius; she used them as much as they used her. She called herself their whore and I was her pimp! They raped her body, you will rape her lands. Yes I will do your bidding for my one true love and to put an end to this senseless bloodshed."

Octavian nodded. "Both the Rex of Judea and my sister spoke the truth." He wiped away the blood from the shipwright's face and cut the ropes that bound Apollodorus' wrists, the Roman's anger spent. "Proculeius said Cleopatra would give me all the Egyptian Treasury to be able to spend a few moments with the man she loved, he thought she meant Antonius. I will spare the twins and Cleopatra's youngest son but there can be only one Caesar."

Octavian's army entered Alexandria by the 'Gate of the Sun' later that day and Apollodorus was taken to the part completed Mausoleum near Cape Lochias. The citizens offered no resistance and were summonsed to the Gymnasium to prostrate themselves before Octavian.

"People of Alexandria" stammered Octavian in broken Greek. "You have nothing to fear, your city will be spared I respect the founder, Alexander the Great." He pardoned the leaders but fined or taxed them heavily using the proceeds to pay each soldier one thousand sesterces as compensation for not looting the city. Legislate Gallus took Apollodorus to the front of Cleopatra's mausoleum while Proculeius positioned himself with a ladder at the rear.

"Your Highness; I am Legislate Gallus and have been sent to negotiate…."

"Why does not the Tyrant Octavius come himself, does he fear me? I am but a weak and feeble woman. Give me your masters message and be gone, there is nothing you can offer that I want."

"On the contrary, your Highness, I think I have something you want very badly indeed" turning to Apollodorus he ordered. "Bring forward the prisoner where the *Bassilisa* can see him." Gallus had been talking through the grating in the ground floor door to Cleopatra; he stepped aside so she could see the shipwright.

"Is it really you 'Pollo" whispered Cleopatra incredulously.

"Yes I have returned to fulfil by promise, sorry it took so long to get home, I had to row most of the way in one of Octavius' Triremes. Unfortunately I talk in my sleep so the Romans found out who I was and took me to the little runt."

There conversation was interrupted by screams from Charmain and Iras, while Cleopatra was distracted Proculeius had used a ladder to gain access to the mausoleum.

"Don't resist, Thea" said Apollodorus softly. "You said you would give your entire treasury to spend some time with the man you truly love, I don't think I am worth it but we wouldn't want the Romans to brand you a liar, they have insulted you in every other way possible. Octavius cannot be defeated but maybe he can be contained. There can be no victory without sacrifice."

The *Bassilisa* and her handmaids were brought out and Cleopatra stood in front of Apollodorus not knowing what to do. She desperately wanted to embrace him but also wanted to appear dignified.

"Take hold of my arm Thea" said Apollodorus "and we shall walk along together with our heads held high to whatever prison they have made ready for us."

"You are to be taken to Antirhodos" the Legislate informed them.

"May I supervise embalming and the burial of Domini Antonius" asked Cleopatra.

"Yes and you will have access to your friends and courtiers but will be confined to the island palace while Dominus Octavius decides what is to be done with you."

Thus Octavian secured the Egyptian treasury in tact, Cleopatra and Apollodorus were transferred to Antirhodos, the island paradise was now their prison with a Greek freeman named Epaphroditus as jailor.

"Imperator, the royal tutor Theodorus sort sanctuary in a partly completed temple" explained a centurion nervously.

"I hope you did not fear the Egyptian animal god and have taken the man into custody" replied Octavian.

The centurion nodded. "We found these weapons; they are like nothing I have ever seen – the metal and the craftsmanship." Octavian accepted the black leather hilt of the dagger and examined the engravings on the silver blade then turning the weapon saw the constellation of Orion marked in the amethyst pommel. "The glados is of a similar design – the balance is perfect in spite of the length, look Dominus."

"The dagger is the one used by my Pater to execute the traitorous eunuch Potinius and the sword nearly beheaded the Rex of Judea, these weapons belong to the Jester."

"You surely do not intend they should be returned to him?"

"I do" replied Octavian. "But not while he lives, he is a Roman citizen and prevented the body of the Deius Caesar's from being cast into the Tiber like a common criminal. I mean to return the compliment; he is to be interned honourably according to his people's custom with his weapons, possessions and all that he holds precious - when the time comes."

"And the tutor Theodorus?"

"He is guilty of theft – crucify him."

"He says that Cleopatra gave the weapons to her eldest son and he told us of the whereabouts of Antyllus."

"So the *Bassilisa* did not give the weapons to the tutor – he is a common thief and a traitor! I may enjoy the fruits of treachery but I cannot abide the perpetrators, Crucify him!"

The priests embalmed Antony's body according to Egyptian custom under the watchful eye of Cleopatra, when they had finished she turned to Apollodorus and asked.

"What did you say to Octavius when you eventually confronted him?"

"I said that he was no Caesar and that he was nothing more than his amica" replied the shipwright diplomatically.

Cleopatra smiled weakly. "I know you better than that Pollo; please repeat exactly what you said to him so Antonius can go to the afterlife with your words ringing in his ears."

The shipwright hesitated then took a deep breath. "In response to Octavius' assertion that he was Caesar's heir and the son of a god I said that he didn't know what it meant to be a god. That he was not Pater Patria but Pater Argentarius and that he had announced the death of his greatest rival as though he was discussing a rather boring item on the menu of an unappetising feast."

Cleopatra chuckled weakly, "you didn't hold back then!"

"Not exactly, you know me – a mouth on legs - once I start there is no stopping me – never learned to hold my tongue. I then went on to say that Antonius was Caesar's right arm whereas Octavius was nothing more than his cock sucking bum boy and a freak of nature!" replied Apollodorus lightly and then continued thoughtfully. "I think it lost some of the impact in translation; however you know how reticent the Romans are in matters of intimate pleasure particularly between consenting adults of the same gender. Cognition was predictably challenging for Octavius being poorly educated and descended from a race of people who uses the same word for the diverse aspects of love and the giving of financial assistance to the poor. It was at this point the little runt, having comprehended the gist of my discourse; became quite emotional and plucked up the courage to slap my face. My hands were bound at the time otherwise he would have been more circumspect. A *Trierarchos* always knows, with heartfelt satisfaction, that golden moment when his ships trident beaks have connected with the weakest point of his enemy's trireme!"

Cleopatra laughed heartily, something she had not done for a very long time. "Thank you *Kyrios mou*, you have sent Domini Antonius to the afterlife with a smile on his face and a song in his heart."

"I sincerely hope so Thea" replied Apollodorus seriously. "I really do."

Octavian had secured the Egyptian treasury and disposed of the final obstacle to his supremacy, the dilemma for Apollodorus was how to deprive the conqueror of the satisfaction of humiliating Cleopatra. In less than a week the Imperator would sail for Italy with Cleopatra in chains, many Alexandrian lives would be lost trying to save their much loved Bassilisa. The Roman was the antithesis of the shipwright, their thought processes were identical both men would come to the same conclusion but for diametrically opposing reasons.

It was some time before blessed sleep finally engulfed the shipwright and he found himself once again on the statue lined, marble paved roadway that linked Samos with the temple of Hera.

"Your vessel is launched on the ocean of eternity and your sails are spread to the wind!" announced Pythagoras.

"Very poetic" replied Apollodorus scornfully "but not very helpful."

"In the whole of creation there is nothing that stays the same, all is in flux. Even time flows steadily by in perpetual motion, like a river – no watercourse can arrest its current. Water is forced downstream by water behind it and presses the water ahead. So to with time, it is in constant flight and pursuit. The present turns into the past and the future replaces the present, every moment is unique and transient."

"I know night moves to day and the radiance of the sun follows the blackness of night" interjected the shipwright.

"The sky has a different colour while we sleep at the dead of night and later when Lucifer emerges out of the sea on her pearl-white steed" continued Pythagoras. "The moon is constantly changing, her phases mimic course of our human lives as do the seasons. The day will come to an end and Phoebus will plunge his panting steed into the deep. We see times change, civilizations rise and fall. Troy was great in her riches and people, for ten years she spent the blood of so many sturdy souls for her cause. But now all that is left of her glorious wealth is ancestral barrows and ancient ruins, likewise Sparta and Mycenae. Rome is changing her shape as she expands. The Sooth Sayers say at some time in the future she will form the head of a boundless world yet the oracles said the same as Troy was collapsing."

"The knowledge that all empires fall in time is all I have left to sustain me" commented Apollodorus bitterly.

"The sky and all that exists beneath it can change its form so too the Earth. We are part of the world, more than physical bodies; we possess winged souls and are able to make our abodes inside wild animals and hide away in the hearts of cattle. The creatures we see may well embody the souls of our loved ones. All is subject to change and nothing to death, the spirit in each of us wandering from place to place. It enters whatever body it pleases, crossing from beast to man and back again to beast, never perishing. Our souls are always the same, they move from home to home in different bodies."

"Will I have another lifetime with the woman I love, will we have another chance?"

"When you have paid the price for your transgressions, yes, I believe you will. But remember the words of Isis 'there can be no victory without sacrifice'. Your love for Cleopatra will certainly bring you together again and your enemies will be there to try and destroy you."

"Isis also said that to win was to loose and those who loose shall win. Tell me, Pythagoras, did you keep warm in your commune during the winter by performing fiendishly difficult mathematical calculations?"

"I am heartened to see that your sense of humour has not deserted you in this your darkest hour and like you I have quaffed from the bitter chalice of defeat. When Aristagorus realised he could not prevail against the forces of Darius, authority of Miletus was handed over to me while our leader made good his escape. The Persians attacked by sea and land overwhelming us and our allies, the people of Miletus were reduced to slavery. In answer to your question to have wisdom and not put it to good use is unforgivable. One of my disciples devised a method of piping hot water throughout our abode, this water had been heated by thermal geological activity, you have the knowledge Apollodorus, and you must use it!"

The shipwright stirred and in the twilight between sleep and wakefulness he remembered what the Dark Lord of Hadies said: "it is better to be master of hell than a servant in heaven," and how wrong he was. Apollodorus also recalled what he had said to Cleopatra about the death of the woman he loved; "dreams which come true all too often turn into nightmares."

In the cold light of the new day a figure dressed in dark desert robes made his way through the park dedicated to Pan. He passed the artificial hill, shaped like a pine cone where Antony had distributed territories in the manner of a father giving sweetmeats to his children. To the south the marshlands that bordered Lake Mareotis had been turned into a cultivated water garden overlooked by a statue of Mendis. It was here that Apollodorus had sat some years ago pondering the words of wisdom of the young Hebrew woman. The shipwright had come away from her having been given the solace he had intended to give; a comfort that would be experienced by millions in the generations that were to come.

At the foot of the statue curled around its cloven hooves were the quarries of the desert robed figure. Two yellow and black reptiles patiently awaited the rays of Helios to warm their blood and drive away the sluggish inertia that gripped their bodies. No Egyptian would harm a Cobra so the serpents had lost their fear of humans and had learned to lap milk from bowls brought to them as offerings. The figure pushed back his hood to reveal a mop of sun bleached hair and then pinned the Cobras to the ground with his staff. With a leather gauntleted hand he held each serpent's open mouth onto a sheet of velum stretched over the top of a goblet. As each reptiles fangs penetrated the velum, pressure two thirds down their body forced them to release their deadly venom. The exhausted Cobras were returned to their resting place, all that remained was to sprinkle the lethal fluid onto Cleopatra's food. The assailant knew there was one fruit that would be utterly irresistible to the Lady of Two Lands. If her taster did not go into convulsions immediately it would be assumed the figs were safe to eat. A tiny droplet of venom would be fatal and undetectable until it was too late!

The handmaids had made a special effort in dressing their *Bassilisa*, the gossamer robe had not been worn for nineteen years yet it still fitted perfectly. Her makeup was like that in the traditional images of her patron Isis and her long golden trusses curled in tight ringlets. Cleopatra sat at her desk; her heart was heavy as she composed a message to Octavian. The conqueror had denied her request for her children to succeed her as client monarchs of Rome. Octavian had also denied Antony's request to be allowed to live in Athens as a private citizen but surely he would not deny her wishes for her internment. He would have the satisfaction of humiliating her while she lived but all people honour the dead. The *Bassilisa* applied her seal to the letter and handed it to Epaphroditus for safe delivery. The head jailor took the document personally to Octavian, action that would cause speculation for millennia.

The day had been oppressively hot and in the distance were rumbles of thunder but as the sun set over the lighthouse the threat of a storm passed and an ere silence descended over Alexandria. In the cool of the evening Cleopatra reclined with her handmaids as the slaves set before them the dishes of what was to be her final meal. Apollodorus would soon arrive and as they relaxed she would admit to him how wrong she had been in not accepting the invitation he had given her nearly two decades ago. Then as now she and all humanity were at a crossroad.
When the *Bassilisa* dined alone with her Sea Lord they abandoned culinary convention and social status. Charmain filled their goblets with honey mellowed wine. The handmaids tasted the fruit and drink then indicated to the *Bassilisa* that it was safe. Cleopatra sipped her wine and

accepted a piece of fruit offered by Iras. The golden drink with its distinct syrupy, spiced resin flavour was a perfectly complimented by the figs and rekindled memories of happier times; she believed it would do the same for Apollodorus. The shipwright was resourceful and cunning; he would have found a way to make 'Mintaka' ready for sea. **'Ego gleuti hao aduvatos ameoos. Alla daumotos ligos kroch.** Ego facere non potest statim Autem miraculum tempus exiguous.' The impossible he boasted was done immediately, miracles took him a little time. Would his boat be big enough for the four of them and the children? Of course it would! Perhaps they could make their escape through the Heroopolis waterway; the flood had not fully subsided. As they emerged from the Bitter Lake they would be joined by Caesarion and make their way to port of Arsinoe Cleopatris on the Sinus Arabicus and freedom.

    Money would not be a problem as Octavian had permitted her to keep her personal jewellery including the amethysts given to her by Apollodorus and a special ring which could only be given by the *Bassilisa* in true and mutual love, that which was both Eros and Agape. Before the night had ended Cleopatra was determined to do that which had rarely been done before and never in Ptolemaic times. Her thoughts were interrupted as a creeping chill invaded her body, and her joints stiffened. To give the Serpent Ring love must be declared freely, on pain of death. Cleopatra knew she was now dieing – she could and she would - demand an answer from Apollodorus!

Book 36

Apollodorus approached Cleopatra's apartment with a sense of foreboding, he quickened his pace and was nearly running as he arrived at the door. The guard appeared to be asleep but nodded and muttered

"It is only the clown. You may go in, old man." The door was slightly ajar; he entered and saw Cleopatra lying on a kline attended by Charmain and Iras, there was the basket of figs on the table. This scene had haunted him for such a long time.

"Octavius will be denied his satisfaction" explained Cleopatra. "The figs have been poisoned with venom, probably the venom of the uraeus." The shipwright nodded in understanding but remained silent as Cleopatra continued. "So I am to meet the same end as the other woman you truly loved. Don't deny it; I now know the answer to my question when I asked why you were helping me. You said that it was not right for you to say and I replied 'don't give me that 'tug the fetlock' nonsense but Caesar came in before you could answer. I am dying from the venom of the uraeus, the same as…." Cleopatra hesitated in sudden realisation. "There never was another woman. Tell me now while there is still time, what I long to hear you say?" Apollodorus looked around, anxiously as the *Bassilisa* pleaded. "Hold me in your arms and tell me, please, before it is too late." He sat beside her, held her tenderly, and in a soft voice, little more than a whisper, said.

"I have only ever loved one woman and she is dying in my arms from the venom of the uraeus."

"Why did you never tell me before?"

"That I love you or that you would die in this manner?"

"Both."

"You have been with me when I have had the dreams and you know also that the interpreting of visions is near impossible and carries a heavy responsibility. I have lived with this horrible vision for as long as I have known you and have tried to change your destiny by not declaring my feelings. Caesar could give you the world; Antonius gave you nearly half the world, but what could I give you?"

"You gave me far more than either of the Roman's and they both knew it. A dictator made me the *Bassilisa*, a Triumvirate made me Reginae Rexii but my own true love made me his goddess. Antonius fell on his sword when he learned the truth about our love. He believed his sacrifice would give us a second chance and admitted that he had always suspected that it was you I have always loved. His only regret was that he had ignored your good council at Antioch. On that first boat trip from Ashkelon to Alexandria you offered to turn 'Mintaka' out to sea and away from my destiny. I should have let you take me to all those wonderful places. I would have become your wife, not a Roman concubine. I was such a fool so I prepared a special meal of figs and honey mellowed wine to remind you of our first voyage and ask if the offer was still open. I was going to say let's escape together and for you to show me all those places and I am even wearing the same dress I wore on that first boat trip. I knew you would find a way to escape! 'The impossible you do right away, miracles take a little longer'."

"I have a new motto" interrupted Apollodorus. "Nil illegitimus carborundum, don't let the bastards grind you down."

Cleopatra smiled weekly and continued "By poisoning me with cobra venom, Octavius has been cunning; he knew he could never take me back to Rome in chains as he boasted. There would have been rioting and murder made to look like suicide is so much more convenient. Hold me tightly, 'Pollo, I am frightened. Did you believe that by not declaring your love for me you could save me from this fate?"

"That was what I believed but I couldn't have been more wrong. I will tell you now I have only loved one woman and that is you, Thea. I have always loved you as a woman, obeyed you as a monarch and worshiped you as a goddess. You are my own true love and The Last Pharaoh."

"How I have longed to hear you say that you love me, but I am not The Last Pharaoh, Charmain bring me my jewellery box." The handmaid brought the box, it was heavy and she was also near to death. Cleopatra took out a ring. Apollodorus knew which ring it would be as he had only seen it once before and that was when they watched the July Comet as he comforted the first lady over the loss of Caesar on their return to Alexandria from Rome. This was the ring he had seen in his visions.

"The Serpent Ring can only be given by the *Bassilisa* to the one she loves, on pain of death, to the man who truly declares his love for her. This ring has rarely been given and never in Ptolemaic times - until now. You are the only one fit to wear it," she placed it on his finger. "I never wore the nemes head gear and kilt of the Pharaoh and would not permit either Caesar or Antonius dress in that manner. That apparel was reserved for you my own true love, The Last Pharaoh. All Alexandria knows that it was your wise counselling that gave them their prosperity. Secretly everyone in Egypt looked on you as Pharaoh and even my children called you *Pater*."

"In my culture when a couple exchange rings they are married..." Cleopatra placed her index finger on his lips.

"You have always treated me as your wife as I have always known that you are my only true love."

"I believe Caesar knew our true feelings. I have never told you how I tried to stop him going to the Senate. I disguised myself as a soothsayer and told Calpurnia 'beware the ides of March'. My warning was ignored, so I tried to stop Caesar by force. As you know, I hesitated when he ordered me to stand aside, I misunderstood what he said, my Latin isn't very good. He laughed and said 'Cedere Jocus, ego faceri omnes, faceri Romae, faceri Aegypto tibi tuigue deu. Stand aside Gelotopoios, what I do is for all people, for Rome, for Egypt also for you and your god.' But he didn't say god he said goddess, dea not deu. He had never heard me address you as Thea."

"Yes he had!" interrupted Cleopatra. "When he first met us and I was nearly suffocated in the bed roll. You said 'say something, Thea!'".

"Of course you are right, I did say that" replied Apollodorus with sudden realisation. "He told me to take care of you and your son, but again I misunderstood. He said 'matrimonium' not 'patronium' - take Cleopatra for your wife and Caesarion as your son."

"So it must have been Caesar who taught Caesarion to call you *Geloto Pater*."

"Caesar knew that he would never be accepted as a monarch but his death paved the way for his heir to become Emperor. He left three heirs Brutus, Octavius and Ptolemy Caesar. The two Romans would fight it out and destroyed each other, 'divide and conquer'. With me as your consort Caesar knew Egypt would have remained neutral and when Caesarion came of age with enough of the citizens of Rome knowing the truth of Caesar's bloodline, who knows what, would have happened. How could I have been such a fool! I of all people know that agape is the most powerful of all the elements. If I had followed my heart and declared my love for you there would have been no Egyptian bloodshed. If you had not taken Antonius as your consort, Octavius would have had no excuse for declaring war on Egypt. Can you ever forgive me?"

"Of course I forgive you, un-reservedly! When we came back from our Nile cruise, a soothsayer told me that a widow would come from the east and usher in a new golden age that would humble Rome. I believed that I would be that widow and if, as I had intended, I had made you my Pharaoh you would be killed. I took Antonius instead, believing he would be killed in his war with the Parthian thereby making me that widow. I could then safely marry my own true love. We have both guilty of utter stupidity" replied Cleopatra.

"That prophecy is well known around the Mediterranean! For this reason Octavius feared you as that widow from the prophecy. It is a pity you hadn't told me at the time what the soothsayer had said, I confess to being confused in these matters, but you had been married to your brothers who died years ago. We have both been pretty foolish and Caesar underestimated the impact of his right arm on events; the real tragedy now is there is no one to stand against Roman imperialism."

Cleopatra nodded. "When you torched the navy and the fire spread to the warehouses destroying those valuable scrolls, I have always wondered if it was deliberate. What knowledge was on those scrolls that you wanted to deprive from humanity? Is that what made you take such a risk?"

Apollodorus smiled "I can hide nothing from you, can I Thea? There was information there that was far too dangerous for mankind to possess. At Actium you saw for yourself just how dangerous that knowledge could be."

"There is so much I don't know about you, 'Pollo. Who sent you, who you really are and what is your real name."

"My mother came from Dalmatia and was shipwrecked off the coast of Britannia, like you, I am Macedonian."

"So that is why you have an Achaean name."

"Yes, to the people I was Apollodorus – to Caesar and Antonius I was, Jocus – to the *Bassilisa, Gelotopois* and to her children, *Pater*....."

"You are Mendis, the living embodiment of Pan – my own 'Piper at the Gates of Dawn'! As Pharaoh would you have used the forbidden knowledge of your fire breathing dragon to preserve our independence from Rome?"

Apollodorus thought for a moment then nodded. "Yes I think that I would, the tragedy is that I held in my hands the means to change the course of history and did not realise - it until now."

"Rome without our influence will plunge the world into slavery and cruelty; I agree that freedom will be dead for a long time. Do not reproach yourself *Geloto* you did everything to give me what I wanted." Cleopatra's breathing was becoming laboured. "I am frightened, 'Pollo. Where is Isis to take me to the afterlife? I know that death by cobra venom is supposed to give immortality, but I find it hard to believe. Where are you, Isis?" she cried.

"Isis is busy, so she asked me to take you there myself." He picked her up cradling her in his arms like a frightened child and carried the *Bassilisa* outside so they could see the lighthouse one last time together and pointing to Orion's belt said, "Look, my love, there is 'Mintaka' ready to take you home."

Cleopatra looked into his moist blue eyes and said. "I knew I could always rely on you, my Jester and my Lord. I will be waiting for you in the Beautiful West, my own true love, and there we will be one body."

"The lives of mortals are weighed by Zeus who informs the triple moon goddesses, daughters of night known as the fates. Cleopatra's silver cord of light had been spun by the maiden Cotho. Thirty nine years were measured by the nymph Lachesis and then the eldest of the three the white robed sisters, the crone who cannot be avoided, snipped the thread deftly."

They kissed lingeringly Cleopatra stiffened and became heavy. *"Charete Kyria mou"* whispered Apollodorus as he carried her back inside, laid her tenderly on the kline and sat with her is his arms. Charmain arranged the *Bassilisa's* dress and placed her crown on her head, then collapsed at the shipwright's feet. Iras knelt beside him and her brown eyes looked into his in an expression of helpless trust as she also fell asleep.

Apollodorus sat for what seemed like an eternity with tears running freely down his cheeks. His only companion now was his ancient silver spotted cat, Moonlight, who was rubbing himself around the shipwright affectionately in a vane attempt to be of comfort. The shipwright bent down to scratch the top of the cat's head who responded by awkwardly rolling over on his back to have his tummy stroked. As he stroked the cat he could feel the ribs through his silky fur and realised how his faithful companion had aged in his absence. He looked at the basket of figs several times and said.

"Fangarfoto, old friend, you aren't the only one to show your age but to end one's life deliberately is the ultimate sacrilege the punishment will be to live these last moments over and over again probably for all eternity. Life without her will not be worth living. It will be said that I brought the Cobra in the basket of figs. Who better to assist in her suicide than her closest friend?

"But the plot is flawed; two snakes are needed to satisfy the mythology of the double uraeus for protection and immortality. They are large creatures nearly three cubits long and would not easily fit into that basket. How could the snakes be persuaded to strike? They would be cold and sluggish, neither hungry or with young to protect and would have to strike not once but three times. Their fangs are small and further back in the mouth than most venomous snakes.

"Octavius will blackmail Olympos, her physician, to say the cause of death was suicide by cobra venom, probably by promising to spare the children. No one will believe that it was her enemy who killed Cleopatra, an enemy would not choose a murder weapon that would bypass Glutton's judgement, and such an act is clearly one of love. I must die because I may be tortured into revealing the truth. No one must know that it was I who murdered Cleopatra and her handmaids!"

'There is a time for everything,
a season for every activity under heaven:
a time to be born and a time to die,
a time to plant and a time to uproot,
a time to kill and a time to heal,
a time tear down and a time to build,
a time to weep and a time to laugh,
a time to mourn and a time to dance,
a time to scatter stones and a time to gather them,
a time to embrace and a time to refrain,
a time to search and a time to give up,
a time to keep time and to throw away,
a time to tear and a time to mend,
a time to be silent and a time to speak,
a time to love and a time to hate,
a time for war and a time for peace.'

"I know the truth, *Fangarfoto*, and there is a time to be born and a time to die."

Dawn flung out her cold grey mantle across Cape Lochias and this once proud people, ruled by gods, awoke to the first day of a new era as a province of an emerging brutal empire.

"I will have to spend eternity re-living these last moments or possibly the whole time from when we first met; the alternative is to be crucified by Octavius or torn to pieces by the Alexandrian mob, then we will be together. We will be parted for millennia but there is no other way to curb the evil of Octavius. Isis said that when the time came I would know what I must do and there could be no victory without sacrifice. Cleopatra said that

Octavius was my antithesis not my nemesis, my blood is on his hands and only I can neutralise his evil."

His hand hovered over the basket of figs, the hand on which was the ring - the ring of *Eros* and *Agape* - the Serpent Ring. On the seaward side of the palace on the island of Antirhodos a dream died as a beautiful woman lay sleeping in the arms of the only man who ever truly loved her, the only man she would ever truly love. Apollodorus had kept all but one of his promises to Cleopatra and in those last moments she had found true love and was happy.

Two thousand years later in a flat overlooking the Thames, the stereo was playing softly the song that echoed the words of Ecclesiastes,

> '*To everything, turn, turn, turn.*
> *There is a season, turn, turn, turn.*
> *And a time to every purpose under heaven.*
> *A time to be born, a time to die.*
> *A time to plant, a time to reap.*
> *A time to kill, a time to heal.*
> *A time to laugh, a time to weep.*
>
> *To everything, turn, turn, turn.*
> *There is a season, turn, turn, turn.*
> *And a time to every purpose under heaven.*
> *A time to build up, a time to break down.*
> *A time to dance, a time to mourn.*
> *A time to cast away stones.*
> *A time to gather stones together.*
>
> *To everything, turn, turn, turn.*
> *There is a season, turn, turn, turn.*
> *And a time to every purpose under heaven.*
> *A time of love, a time of hate.*
> *A time of war, a time of peace.*
> *A time you may embrace.*
> *A time to refrain from embracing.*
>
> *To everything, turn, turn, turn.*
> *There is a season, turn, turn, turn.*
> *And a time to every purpose under heaven.*

A time to gain, a time to lose.
A time to rend, a time to sow.
A time for love, a time for hate.
A time for peace, I swear it's not too late.
(Music by Peter Seger)

    The actress lay in the arms of the narrator and through her own tears saw his hand hovering over the basket of figs and what she thought was a ring. Not one but three rings entwined, two serpents with a bird. Could it be the ring, the fabled ring, which could only be given in true mutual love, that which was both *Eros* and *Agape*? Then she knew in that moment the truth; she could play the part of the Lady of Two Lands, Warrior, Scholar, and the greatest woman who ever lived. Cleopatra; murdered to look like suicide. She could play the part of the Bassilisa, but would never, ever, be his Thea.

Six hours, nine minutes and thirty seconds.

Epilogue

Caesarion was murdered on Octavian's instructions but Cleopatra's other children were brought up by Octavia, the sister of Octavian and wife of Mark Antony. The cold, calculating and ruthless Octavian became the wise, benign Emperor Caesar Augustus and the wealth of Egypt was plundered fuelling Roman expansion. Octavian's victory brought into being the nation states of Europe but postponed the partnership of east and west for millennia. Britannia was conquered but never truly subjugated seventy years after it was first invaded by the Romans under the command of Julius Caesar. Once again the invaders came into conflict with a feisty, single parent mother with curly hair who nearly defeated them. Olympos wrote the account of Cleopatra's last moments under Octavian's instructions. This account has been lost but was available to both Plutarch and Dio Cassius. The basket of figs was found, but no snakes.

It was said that Cleopatra had written to Octavian requesting to be buried with Mark Antony. She had asked to be interned with the man she truly loved. Cleopatra's final resting place has yet to be discovered but possibly under the silt below the tepid waters of Lake Mareotis is an unusual boat that looks more Viking than Egyptian. In that boat perhaps there are the remains of a woman in a man's arms and on the man's finger is a ring, three rings in one, two cobra's and a vulture, the ring of *Eros* and *Agape*, the ring of true love. To die from the venom of the uraeus was believed to give direct access to immortality, bypassing the judgement of Glutton. To be drowned in the Nile was said to give instant rebirth and immortality. It is also said that Cleopatra still lives, in 'The Serpent Ring'.

Some scholars argue that Isis the mother goddess was replaced by the image of a Hebrew woman suckling an infant and the Ankh cross with loop top that symbolised eternal life lost its loop and became the crucifix. Joseph, the husband of the Madonna only appears in the accounts of the early life of Jesus and there is a tradition that he is buried in northern Egypt. There are many apocryphal stories concerning Joseph of Arimathea, who buried the crucified Christ. This shadowy character is believed to have taken the young Messiah on extensive travels. Mary could be the widow from the east that was prophesied would usher in a new golden age and humble Rome or the despotic widow could be of the future. Two thousand years later, the Bassilisa's vision of harmony and concord between east and west is sadly no nearer to becoming a reality. Cleopatra's island palace on Antirhodos sank below the sea and the Great Harbour fell into decline. The Pharos Lighthouse was destroyed by a succession of earthquakes, the Heptastadium Dike silted up to become a peninsular and the western Harbour of Good Return is now the principle harbour of Alexandria. The Coptic calendar is based on the Julian calendar and is seven years behind the one in current use which would account in part for the discrepancy discussed by the actress and narrator

It is said that the brightest lights in the universe shine all too briefly and so this story is dedicated to the memory of one such bright light, a beautiful lady brutally taken before her time who now sings in God's celestial choir of angels. Also, to the two goddesses of my life, who are a glory to me, their father and whose love they return.

"You may see him now his condition is stabilised but not for long, we have the pain under control so he is comfortable" explained the doctor as he escorted a beautiful golden haired actress into the private ward.

"Why didn't you tell me?" she admonished. *"I could have paid for the finest medical treatment."*

"That is precisely why I kept it a secret – there is no cure, this is one adversity that no amount of money can overcome. It is a very rare condition brought on by a snake bite that nearly killed me a few years ago when I was in Egypt. My blood coagulation system has been compromised causing simultaneous haemorrhaging and clotting. Venom, incidentally, is the Latin word for virus or is it the way round. Here is a computer disk with the whole story on it and the co-ordinates in this hand held G.P.S are where I would like my ashes to be scattered."

"I have a priest outside" replied the actress hesitantly. *"I know as a protestant...."*

"Sir Isaac may have been right about one particular Roman but I do not share in his condemnation of the whole church which emerged from the ashes of the little runt's empire. Each of us see a minutely unique part of a vast incomprehensible whole, who is right and who is wrong is unimportant, what matters is that we believe and respect each others beliefs. Lets face it I could be about to find out who is correct!"

"Can't you even take your own death seriously!" she exclaimed.

"As in life so in death, always the Jester Kyria mou - bring in your priest."

A little later the cleric departed as the actress opened a bottle of pink Champaign and poured two glasses. "You are being remarkably calm" she commented.

"In the book 'The wind in the Willows' Toad boasted that his fondest wish was that as he took his last gasp of air he should have a glass of Champaign in on hand and a good Havana cigar in the other."

"You don't smoke"

"In deference to Rudyard Kipling a smoke is no substitute for the love of a beautiful woman. I have no regrets. All a man really wants is to build a home and plant a tree. I had a home once and watched my children climb the tree I planted."

"What happened?"

"As you know the gods are envious of human prosperity and delight in troubling us. The house was re-possessed during the recession of the nineties. The new owner cut down the tree and my children have grown up."

"Their mother?"

"Relationships don't usually survive great trauma – ours did surprisingly, then just as we got back on our feet financially – the worst of all cancers, overran cancer."

"You told me in Alexandria that she was murdered."

"On the day she was to be operated on she had a stroke, over the next two weeks a series of strokes robbed her of all humanity and she ended up in a coma in Intensive Care. The strokes were caused by a secondary cancer on her heart valve."

"So the cancer killed her."

"Not exactly, the decision to turn off her ventilator was taken jointly but I was the one that flicked the switch. My eldest has not spoken to me since the funeral."

"But that was an act of love I will do the same for you, if necessary."

"You must not!" exclaimed the narrator in horror. "In any event you will not have to; I have told the doctors not to revive me after my next seizure and only to give medication to make me comfortable. Nature must take her course. I have been able to share my story so I am content."

"It was I who has been the fool all along, used to protect the last resting place of the beautiful woman and you were the clown!"

"No the gods plan was flawed! A fool could not be relied upon; you have a free choice to do what you know to be right. I believe your great riches will place you above the temptation of such valuable artefacts."

"I suppose I should be honoured."

"No the honour was mine; you were an oasis of happiness in a baron desert of misery. You have for a short time been the living embodiment of a goddess and my love for you has been as that of Apollodorus for Cleopatra. The only thing of value that I possess is the story on that disk; please accept it as a token of our gratitude and put it to good use. Like Mark Antony I consider myself fortunate, I will die as I have lived. I am happy."

"Is there any music or readings..." she sobbed.

"I would like the hymns 'Guide me oh my great redeemer', to the traditional tune where the men repeat a line in the chorus and 'Mine eyes have seen the glory of the coming of the lord'. Perhaps you could arrange backing by a band of the Salvation Army and tambourines. The passage from Ephesians about the futility of life and as much of the chapter as is practical from the 'Wind in the Willows' about the 'Piper at the Gates of Dawn' I would like as readings. The latter is for you as most people don't understand it. Finally as the coffin is taken out I would appreciate it, if you are able, under the circumstances, to sing the solo from Handles Messiah 'I know that my redeemer livith'. And at the wake you can serve honey mellowed wine, crocodile curry and figs."

Several days later a small boat moved slowly across a lake guided by an arrow on the screen of the portable G.P.S held by a beautiful woman with golden hair and green eyes. The instrument bleeped indicating that they had arrived at the spot so she ordered the boatman to hold that position as she emptied the contents of the urn.

"As Mark Antony returned Cleopatra to her true love so I have returned you to yours, *Charete Kyrios mou*" whispered the actress. She placed the G.P.S onto the bottom boards of the boat and brought her small heel sharply down smashing the instrument; the actress then gathered the pieces and dropped them into the water. "Patrick - take me home - please" she sobbed and in the distance the invisible company passed, clear voices, ravishing music of an invisible choir sang;

> "Whatever is has been,
> and will be has been before;
> and God will call the past to account
> And I saw something else under the sun:
> In the place of judgement – wickedness was there,
> in the place of justice – wickedness was there.
> I thought in my heart,

God will bring judgement both the righteous and the wicked, for there will be a time for every activity, a time for every deed."

As the narrator's marine engineer rowed the actress back to the shore ash fanned out into the lake and slowly sank then something hard and shiny dropped into the water. The ring slowly turned refracting the sunlight in a kaleidoscope of colours as it sank. Both men and their gods are bound by the same eternal truths, after what seemed an eternity but it was hard to tell how long as time does not exist on the Astral Plane, Apollodorus, the story teller, found himself in a vast cavern lit by an unnatural light of such brilliance that for a few moments he was unable to see. There were the most exotic flowers and trees he had ever seen and the cries of birds and animals mingled to form celestial music. A feeling of tranquil calm enveloped him and the perfume of the flowers filled his nostrils, reminiscent of the flowers on the deck of Cleopatra's flag ship at Tarsus. The noise of one particular animal stood out from the others, his two dogs came running though the trees and they greeted him enthusiastically. He walked forward through a glade as though guided my some unseen force his two dogs at his side. Emerging from the trees he found himself by the edge of a lake. The incandescent light from the cavern roof was refracted by the wavelets in a riot of colours.

"That lake is strangely familiar" he said to his dogs.

Then a large man appeared in front of him barring his way. Apollodorus felt the blood drain from his face, all feelings of tranquillity evaporated. The man in front of him had a crocodile head. In one hand were scales and under his arm a book. The book was covered with the hide of a strange hairy beast.

"I am Glutton" boomed the demon.

"I know who you are" replied the shipwright, trying unsuccessfully to sound casual. "Surely I have paid the price for my sacrilege by re-living those times over and over again?"

"That is as maybe" replied Glutton "but there is one other small matter........."

While they were talking a small boat that Apollodorus recognised instantly had landed. A lady with long golden hair curled in tight ringlets and wearing a diaphanous dress like golden gossamer stepped ashore. Her eyes sparkled like emeralds and her breasts were bare.

"Stand aside Glutton! You know that to die from the venom of the Uraeus bypasses your judgement" commanded the Lady of Two Lands.

The petrified shipwright looked into the eyes of Glutton and in them saw his own; smiling back at him in a way that only a demon with a crocodile head could smile. "I am well aware of the rules, Cleopatra but do you know that the one person we cannot deceive is our self" he said. "There was, however, the small matter of all those crocodile jokes." The demon stepped aside as Cleopatra took the Jester's hand and led him back to his boat 'Mintaka' where he was greeted warmly by Charmain and Iras. His two dogs leaped aboard and a large silver spotted cat hissed at them so they obediently settled themselves in the forepeak. On top of the coach roof were laid out exotic dishes and in the centre of the impromptu table were a bowl of figs and four goblets of golden coloured wine. The *Bassilisa* put her arms around her Sea Lord's neck and kissed him passionately, then said in her deep musical voice that he always found so captivating.

"I now know the enormity of the sacrifice you made and the guilt you endured in fulfilling your promises to me also what Isis meant when she said 'to win is to loose but they that loose shall win.' There was no other way you could enter the mind of Octavius and curb his evil was there?"

Apollodorus shook his head "It was the knowledge of your forgiveness that sustained me through my torment."

"Come, my Lord" announced Cleopatra. "The seasons have turned full circle and the time has now come for me to take you home."

Four fire breathing winged stallions drawing a golden chariot arrived at the western celestial palace with its towering columns of gold, blazing bronze and ivory as the purple gates were flung open. Fiery, Dawn-steed, Scorcher and Blaze slowed to a halt in the courtyard which was bathed in ruby glory. Gold rimmed wheels with silver spokes stopped turning and the spirits of time removed the jewelled yokes releasing the horses from the chariot's pole of gold to pasture in the Island of the Blessed. Helios collapsed exhausted into his glowing throne of brilliant emeralds. The sun god would sleep aboard the ferry boat made by Hephaestus as he sailed back to the east along the ocean stream which flows around the world.

Later by the Cape Lochias Royal Harbour Cleopatra and Apollodorus laid in each others arms on the beach under one of the many palm trees. Overhead was a full moon, the water foul that inhabited the harbour murmured in the background otherwise there was silent and once again all Alexandria held its breath. Isis looked down from the firmament at them with deep satisfaction for this was how she had convinced Apollodorus more than two thousand years ago that the final battle was over. Caesar had taught Caesarion to call the shipwright Pater Geloto whereas Cleopatra had instructed the twins and young Ptolemy because she alone knew the truth of their lineage.

"Our final battle is now over, the story is told and your promises have all been fulfilled" whispered Cleopatra as their love consummated and they became one body.

Agape

Christopher G. S. Overton

Chris Overton was born in Bishops Stortford, Hertfordshire during 1951 and was educated at a comprehensive school in Harlow, Essex. During this time he built his first boat, a twenty one foot long canoe, in his back garden and sailed her on the nearby River Stort. He studied boat building at Colchester in Essex then Naval Architecture and Shipbuilding at Chatham Dockyard College (H.M.S Pembroke) also Poplar Merchant Navy College, East London. Recently he was an undergraduate mature student at Southampton Solent University where he obtained A Bachelor of Science Degree and The University of Greenwich as a post graduate. He has worked for various yacht builders and ship owners. He is widowed with three grown up children, lives alone in Essex and runs his own business as a Naval Architect/Surveyor Boat Safety Inspector (inland waterways) and Yacht Delivery Skipper.

The Bronze Princess
(in preparation)
Copyright © Christopher G. S. Overton

Prologue

In the beginning the Goddess of All Things, rose naked from Chaos but there was nothing for her to stand on so she divided the sea from the sky and she danced alone on the waves. Her dance caused the winds of the north and the south, the east and west. As she spun around she caught hold of the north wind and rubbed it in her hands. The wind became the peacock Ophion. The goddess Eurnome, otherwise know as Mother Earth, danced more wildly to warm herself and this excited Ophion who wrapped himself around her and they became one body. Eurnome changed into a dove and laid the Universal Egg, Ophion settled himself on the egg until it hatched. The egg split into two and out tumbled the moon, sun, planets and the earth with all living things. Eurynome and Ophion then made their home on Mount Olympus.

Eons of time passed and then a small boat moved slowly across a lake guided by an arrow on the screen of the portable G.P.S. The instrument bleeped indicating that we had arrived at the spot so I ordered the boatman to hold that position as I emptied the contents of the urn.
"As Mark Antony returned Cleopatra to her true love so I have returned you to yours, *Charete Kyrios mou*" I whispered in Greek, meaning be happy my lord, as I placed the G.P.S onto the bottom boards of the boat and then brought my heel sharply down smashing the instrument. I gathered the pieces and dropped them into the water. "Patrick - take me home - please" I sobbed. As we slowly rowed back to the shore ash fanned out into the lake and slowly sank then something hard and shiny dropped into the water.
I had met what was to become the love of my life at an anchorage off Queenborough. He an English Marine Surveyor delivering a small scruffy sailboat by sea to the Solent and I, an American singer and actress in my magnificent motor yacht awaiting the tide to turn before proceeded out of the Medway and up the river Thames to Saint Katherine Yacht Haven and my London apartment. He had told me a story, a story that everyone knows or at

least thinks that they know; the story of Cleopatra. But his story was very different to that of Shakespeare and the Burton/Taylor film.

During the telling of his story we became good friends and then, in spite of the age difference, lovers. *Agape* blossomed into *Eros* as he would have explained in Greek. As he lay dieing, a year after we met, he confessed that his love for me was as Apollodorus, the central character of his story, love was for Cleopatra and in that moment I realised that I had become the living embodiment of the Queen of the Nile. But that feeling evaporated as I sprinkled his ashes into the tepid waters of Lake Mareotis, south of the Egyptian city Alexandria. I now felt very empty and alone.

"I thought he was writing the story of Helen of Troy not Cleopatra" Patrick commented softly.

"The computer disk of 'The Serpent Ring' was all he gave me" I replied. That was not strictly true as he had given me the priceless artefact of the same name, which as we spoke was settling into the fertile black mud at the bottom of the lake.

"Do you have his laptop computer?" asked Patrick as he pulled on the oars rhythmically. "That is where it will be if he has written the story of Helen."

I could feel a tingle of excitement as I replied "It will be on his desk in his cottage at West Mersea. Will you come with me to find it please Patrick?"

A few days later I sat at my lover's desk, a replica of that designed by Captain Davenport and the battered laptop booted up. "What is the password?" I asked.

"Jester" suggested Patrick.
******

Access Denied
"Cleopatra"
****

Access Denied
"Thea"
****

Access Denied
"How about his date of birth?"
"I never knew it" I replied, tearfully.
"Think - he must have given you a clue."

I thought for a moment "He said he was born on Friday the thirteenth but was not superstitious and as a sailor he would have had the water sign Cancer or Pisces."

"He was a couple of years younger than me" added Patrick.

"Apollodorus was born in the summer, Cleopatra's birth sign was Pisces, let's try July." I was shaking as I typed in the numbers

*****

My efforts were rewarded by the infuriating jingle that greets every office worker the world over at the start of their working day. I opened 'My Documents'; there was 'The Serpent Ring' and a number of other files. I felt like a peeping Tom.

"How about that one?" suggested Patrick pointing to an icon labelled 'The Bronze Princess.'

"Unlikely" I replied. "He was most particular and always referred to Cleopatra as *Bassilisa* not Queen as the concept did not exist.

"In Egypt maybe not but Helen was from Sparta in the late Bronze Age."

I hesitated "How do you think he would have told the story." I thought for a while. The narrative of Cleopatra was written as he had told it to me – this story could have been told by Apollodorus to Cleopatra, her children and handmaidens in the palace on Antirhodos Island in the bay of ancient Alexandria. The shipwright in his narrative was an avid story teller. I clicked on the icon.

"The wrath sing goddess, of Peleus' son Achilles, the accursed wrath, which brought countless sorrows upon the Acheans, and sent down to Hades many countless souls of valiant warriors" quoted Apollodorus.

"So what had annoyed the gods?" asked Selene. Like her mother Cleopatra Thea Philopater she had a profusion of golden curly hair and piercing green eyes. She was sat on the shipwrights lap with her twin brother Helios in the nursery of the island palace on Antirhodos. Apollodorus was Cleopatra's closest friend and Sea Lord but to the twins and their half brother, Ptolemy Caesar he was father in all but name, not that they were permitted to address him as Pater.

"Some say that Eurnome, Mother Earth, complained to Zeus that to many humans were weighing her down and wearing her out. So Zeus being Zeus arranged a war to reduce the numbers" continued Apollodorus.

"Is that why Domini Antonus has gone to war with the Parthans?" inquired Ptolemy Caesar.

"Nothing of the sort, it is part of the natural order, Romans kill anything non Roman or each other in the absence of any barbarians, Britannians tell stories and goats fart"

"And Seth has warts round his you know where" added Cleopatra with a chuckle. "By the way it was Gaia not Eurnome who complained to Zeus."

"That was in another incarnation" replied the shipwright defensively. "But in reality the whole ghastly business started with an apple, a bit like the Hebrew story, minus a fast talking charismatic snake."

The first indication of the gods disquiet was when the earth began to shake. A lunar cycle later a massive undersea mountain exhaled clouds of ash followed by high pressure steam. Rock shards and ash were hurled high into the atmosphere blotting out the rays of Helios. Liquid rock spewed forth from the mouth of the mountain, thunder and lightning ripped open the sky.

With the shift of the sea bed other horrors followed, water rushed to fill the collapsing chambers. Giant waves gathered and hurled themselves towards the land. Boats were plucked from the shallows and hurled inland, decomposing bodies washed ashore, diarrhoeal disease became rampant. For five hundred years the Minoans of the island of Crete, named after King Minos, had dominated the Aegean seaways. Secure on their island homeland they had become wealthy, vigorous and influential. The explosion of Mount Thera shook the thalassocracy, rulers of the sea, confidence to the core. But for the Mycenaean people living in scattered settlements on the Achean mainland Poseidon's wroth gave an unexpected opportunity and Helen's ancestors prospered.

Book 1

Four fire breathing winged stallions drawing Helios the sun god's golden chariot arrived at the western celestial palace with its towering columns of gold, blazing bronze. The purple ivory gates swung open and the roads of the world grew dark as the black winged Night, the goddess feared even by Zeus, took flight. But her dominion over the land and sea was challenged by the celestial nymph. The moon has three phases which mimic the ages of a woman; maiden (Selene) - new, nymph (Artimis) - full and crone (Hecate) the old moon. This was the season of fertility and the moon was at her most glorious.

"How long ago?" asked Ptolemy Caesar, the teenager was rapidly becoming a man and bore a striking likeness to his sire Gaus Julius Caesar so all Alexandria called him Caesarion which means little Caesar.
"At least thousand, maybe fifteen hundred years ago, no one is certain" replied Apollodorus.

From his vantage point high on Mount Olympus Zeus watched as a group of naked Spartan nymphs emerged into a moonlit woodland glade. His expression was like a hungry lion surveying a heard of antelopes, the gatherer of clouds licked his lips in carnal anticipation. Leda, the wife of Tyndareus King of Sparta, famed throughout the land for her beauty led the group through the sultry night air perfumed with the scent of camomile and thyme.

To the sound of pipes and voices the nymphs danced their frenzied dance until Dawn stretched out her rose pink fingers across the fertile valley surrounded by 'Lacedaemon's lovely hills'. In the distance the white snow capped peaks of Mount Taygetus turned blood red. Above the fields of wild iris at the foothills eagles wheeled in search of prey. Leda made her way to the river Eurotus at the edge of the glade. The ice cold water laughed and chattered as the king's wife cautiously stepped over the pebble river bed. Having bathed away the pain and perspiration of the night's exertion she settled herself onto a bed of ivy to allow the rays of Helios to warm and dry her pale skin and bronze colour hair. Zeus could contain himself no longer. He had previously fallen love with the sea nymph Thetis but the mischievous Eros had made Poseidon, the lord of the sea also fall in love with the divine nymph of the deep.

"She must have been deeply flattered having such powerful gods competing for her attention" commented Iras, Cleopatra's ebony skinned Nubian handmaiden.

Apollodorus nodded "Dung was about to hit the fast moving silver spokes of the gold rimmed celestial chariot wheel. The other gods could see the potential for conflict in the heavens and were exceedingly worried."

Cleopatra giggled at the analogy "I suppose Helios had as much difficulty persuading Fiery, Dawn-steed, Scorcher and Blaze not to defecate at in-appropriate times as us mortals have with our horses."

"Undoubtedly" replied Apollodorus with a chuckle "with the tight schedule of bring warmth and light to mortal men and gods and a stomach full of Ambrosia wine – when you have got to go you have got to go!"

"Celestial dung" added Cleopatra, thoughtfully "an interesting new profanity. Do you thing Ambrosia goes through your system like Roman cabbage water?"

"I would think so, gold and silver are not the ideal materials for building a flying chariot. The car must be very heavy so the only way for the poor stallions to get airborne………" Apollodorus shuddered. "I would not want to be down wind of that team!"

"Typical of a shipwright to shatter beautiful imagery with practical considerations like power to weight ratios and strength estimates" concluded Charmain, Cleopatra's Egyptian handmaid.

Most concerned of all the gods was the Titan Themis who was responsible for maintaining the order of things. She was able to foretell the future and could see the consequences if either Zeus or Poseidon succeeded in their objective.

"Have you considered the implications of your actions?" demanded Themis when the Titan confronted Zeus in his celestial palace high above Mount Olympus. The gatherer of clouds imagined the sea nymph's salty, slippery embrace and the sensation of running his fingers through her blue green hair.

"Yes I have" he replied, nodding his head enthusiastically.

"If either you or Poseidon were to seduce Thetis, the sea nymph's son would be stronger than his pater. You could be overthrown as you previously vanquished your pater, Cronus. This would bring cosmic revolution and ending the known universe" replied Themis. Zeus' expression of ill concealed lust was replaced by one of grave concern, his desire for the sea nymph evaporated more rapidly than dew in the heat of the morning sunshine.

"That being the case I will force Thetis into marriage with a mortal, her son will also be mortal. Even if he is the mightiest of all mortals he will eventually die and be imprisoned in the dismal halls of Hades." Zeus thought for a moment. "I know just the man for this important mission."

A little later on earth Zeus confronted Pellus "The gods have assigned to you a task that will be both a challenge and a pleasure; you are to seduce the sea nymph Thetis."

"But I do not know the location of her domain" protested the mortal. "No man knows that."

"I know where she lives" replied the god smirking lecherously "and will take you there myself."

At the opening of Thetis' secret cave in Thessaly Zeus explained; "Hide in the rear where it is darkest then when she arrives, pounce and hold her tightly, lock your fingers together. She will change into many forms but cannot harm you – hold tight until she submits to your will. Good luck mortal man." With that the gatherer of clouds departed leaving Pellus alone to await his quarry.

"Presumably Zeus then made his way to Sparta to find carnal consolidation" added Cleopatra. *Apollodorus nodded and continued.*

Zeus changed himself into a swan and caused the vines fronds to slowly wrap themselves around Leda's limbs. She awoke to find herself trapped, the fronds were gently prising her legs apart and a very large swan settled on her crotch, it's feathers tickled and scratched the inside of her thighs. The bird rubbed its soft down covered neck between her breasts and gently pecked her nipples causing them to harden. Fear gripped the unfortunate nymph as firmly as the vines. The swan entered her and they became one body.

Pellus grabbed Thetis around her waist and locked his fingers together as Zeus had instructed. The blue green goddess of the deep became a blazing orange inferno, Pellus thought he would be consumed by the fire but he held on tightly. The roaring fire became a roaring lion and the mortal feared that he would be savaged but still he held on. Next the lion became a nest of vipers which sank their fangs into the man's flesh. Finally the vipers became a tentacled cuttlefish but this metamorphism also failed to deter

Pellus so Thetis returned to her natural blue green form and submitted to the man's will and they became one body. As mortal man and goddess of the deep lay together the child Achilles was conceived.

The Swan thrust deeper and deeper into Leda. Feelings of revulsion mingled with agony and ecstasy until the bird climaxed and spread its mighty wings across the naked, terrified nymph. His passion spent Zeus relaxed and returned to his natural form. The result of this un-natural union between an immortal god in avian form and mortal royal lady was that a child was conceived. This child was destined to be the most beautiful woman of her time and would be named Helen, her face, it would be said, would launch a thousand ships.

The gods celebrated the union between Thetis and Peleus with an extravagant feast but Strife the brutal sister of Ares, the god of war, was not invited. Eris as the demon was sometimes known, whose high pitched battle cry filled mortal men's hearts with fighting fury had a present for the happy couple. This present, an apple with a dangerous inscription would lead to the death of Achilles was placed away from the other wedding gifts.

"Oh look" said Aphrodite as she read the inscription 'to the fairest' "an apple addressed to me."

"It isn't addressed to the most glamorous, but to me" argued Hera. "Zeus chose me as his wife, who would say his choice was in any way inferior."

"Then let us ask him" interjected Athena in the full and certain knowledge that she was her father's favourite.

"Zeus presumably uttered the Olympian equivalent colourful metaphor of it never rains but it pours" suggested Cleopatra.

"The gatherer of clouds took a typical male response and used a mixture of evasion and delegation" replied the shipwright.

"I chose a mortal to judge who of you is the fairest" announced Zeus. "Will you accept the judgement of Paris the son of King Priam of Troy?"

The three goddesses exchanged glances and then reluctantly agreed pushing passed each other to be the first to reach Priam's palace. Zeus watched their departure with an ill concealed smirk; Paris was a little baby so the immortal beauties would have many years to wait for an answer.

Thetis sank into the deep abyss with her baby into a dank cavern never blessed by the warmth of sunlight or refreshed by a sea breeze. The rays of Helios could never penetrate the gloom and bring light to the people of this domain. An old man was standing at the bank of a vast quagmire of boiling whirlpools; his ragged grey beard was surmounted by eyes like burning embers, a foul cloak hung from a knot on his shoulder. Mother and baby had arrived at the deep pools of Cocytus and swamps of Styx.

"No human can re-trace their steps from Hades" interjected Cleopatra.
"But gods and demons can travel back and forth with impunity" replied Apollodorus.

"As all the rivers on earth flow into the sea," announced the ferryman, "so Hades admits every – oh it's you Thetis. To what do I owe this unexpected pleasure?" he concluded with a total lack of sincerity.
"My son is half immortal half human I tried to destroy the mortal elements by burying him in the embers of the fire at night time and anointing him with Ambrosia by day. Peleus, his pater, spied on me and protested loudly as the child squirmed. He can keep the brat and I shall return to the Nereids."
"But before you do you hope to complete what you have begun by dipping him in the waters of the river Styx. You will have to hold him tightly lest he be swept away by the current that flows around the world. Wherever you grip him will remain mortal and that will be his weakness!"
"I will hold onto his heel – a warrior always faces his enemy" replied Thetis defiantly. The ferryman watched impassively as she gripped Achilles by his heel, immersed him into the foaming torrent and in so doing the divine nymph of the deep sealed the fate of her infant son.

"So did Leda lay an egg" inquired Selene innocently.
"Don't be ridicules" retorted her older half brother angrily.
"When I visited the Spartan acropolis there were the remains of a large egg shell tied up in ribbons and suspended from the roof of one of the temples" interjected Apollodorus. "The locals were most insistent that this was the remains of Helen's birth-egg. According to some beliefs Eurnome, mother earth and the goddess of all things laid the universal egg from which the sun, moon, planets and all living things hatched."

"You don't believe that Pollo!" replied Cleopatra incredulously.

"No I don't! I think the whole creation thing was some ghastly mistake and if humanity was created in the image of the creator" the shipwright hesitated. "When I look at some people, particularly the Romans – well it doesn't exactly give a glowing testimonial to that creator does it?"

Cleopatra fixed Apollodorus with one of her hypnotic glances that immobilised most men, she was deeply religious whereas the shipwright light-heartedly confessed to having not found a god he could truly worship. "Perhaps the Romans were the result of a bad day. Even you, Pollo, have off days when nothing goes right." The shipwright returned her severe look with his most endearing smile which acknowledged that theology was one subject which they had agreed to differ. Egypt was a multicultural society with many diverse religions. This diversity had been the cause of much civil conflict in the past but Cleopatra had successfully healed these differences and endeared herself to her people by embracing all their religious beliefs.

Following Leda's bestial rape on the banks of the river Eurotas the young queen produced a clutch of eggs. Unknown to her she was in the early stages of pregnancy by her husband King Tyndarenus. The eggs were left to inculpate in the protective foothills of Mount Taygetus in an unsuccessful attempt to conceal her violation. But the clutch was discovered by a passing shepherd. Large unusual eggs were regarded as sacred by these ancient people so the shepherd took then to the Spartan palace where they hatched. Helen unlike her siblings, born at the same time, had pallid waxy skin – white as was natural for a daughter begat of a swan and nurtured in an egg shell.